Yar

#36847

P9-CLR-809

WRIT
IN
BLOOD

By Chelsea Quinn Yarbro from Tom Doherty Associates

WRIT IN BLOOD

A NOVEL OF SAINT-GERMAIN

Chelsea Quinn Yarbro

TOR®

A TOM DOHERTY ASSOCIATES BOOK

WRIT IN BLOOD

This book is printed on acid-free paper.

A Tor Book
Published by Tom Doherty Associates, Inc.
175 Fifth Avenue
New York, NY 10010

Tor Books on the World Wide Web:
http://www.tor.com

Tor® is a registered trademark of Tom Doherty Associates, Inc.

Library of Congress Cataloging-in-Publication Data

Yarbro, Chelsea Quinn.
    Writ in blood / Chelsea Quinn Yarbo—1st ed.
        p.   cm.
    "A Tom Doherty Associates book."
    ISBN 0-312-86318-7
    1. Saint-Germain, comte de, d.   1784—Fiction.   2. Russia—History—
    Nicholas II, 1894-1917—Fiction.   3. Vampires—Fiction.   I. Title.
    PS3575.A7W75   1997
    813'.54—dc21   97-161
                            86847   CIP

First Edition: August 1997

Printed in the United States of America

0   9   8   7   6   5   4   3   2   1

for

Elizabeth Miller
Dennis Miller
and
Daniel Richler

Canadians in Transylvania

Author's Notes

From the end of the nineteeth century into the first decade of the twentieth, the three most powerful nations in Europe were ruled first by an uncle and two nephews: Edward VII of Britain, Czar Nicholas II of Russia, and Kaiser Wilhelm II of Prussia and Germany, then by three cousins when George V succeeded Edward VII. Through their mother/grandmother, Queen Victoria, the bonds of family were used—with varying degrees of success—to supersede the ambitions of military and political power brokers alike, providing the appearance if not the reality of continued cordial relations among those powers. This did not mean that there was always accord—no family can make such a claim, and when the family in question controls nations, the problems inherent in these relationships are even more fraught with difficulties.

Because of this and because of an escalation of social changes brought about by emerging technology, the peace and prosperity of the time were more fragile than they looked, and the diplomatic balance was more precarious. The Ottoman Empire was crumbling, and many of the European powers were waiting to rush into the vacuum its collapse would create. During the two years in which this novel takes place (1910–1912) there was a brief opportunity to secure a negotiated peace without resorting to armed aggression in Eastern Europe and the soon-to-be-former-Ottoman territories; the possibility of war, at first unthinkable, became increasingly likely as the chances for peace slipped away. Hapsburg (Austro-Hungarian) interests were the most crucial ones in Eastern Europe at the time, although there were Russian involvements as well. Instability in the Balkans had reached a level that made negotiations unlikely to achieve any lasting peace, and given the complex state of treaties and ethnic stresses in Europe, the concern that the Balkans would provide a flashpoint for trouble proved to be all too real; as the starting-place of World War I, the ongoing conflicts in the Balkans spilled across Europe through a bewildering maze of treaties and alliances that caught up the Continent and then the world. Ironically, the Balkans continue to be a center of ethnic hostility to this day,

as though neither World War—nor any of the earlier centuries of conflict—had resolved anything in that troubled region.

Although most of the major technological and scientific developments were still European, the widening of the world stage had eroded
the preeminence of Europe in global affairs. America and Asia were
gaining a prominence that had not been apparent a generation earlier;
the expansion of the New World was starting to have an impact on the
Old, both in terms of immigration and in terms of innovation.

As is usually the case in many of these novels, there are a number of
actual persons appearing as characters: Czar Nikolai/Nicholas Alexandreivich Romanov and his family: Czarina Alexandra Feodorovna,
Grand Duchesses Olga, Tatiana, Marie, and Anastasia, and Czareivich
Alexei; further references are made to several other relatives, household members, government officials, and court figures, including Grigori Efimovich Rasputin-Novyhk, the charismatic priest whose presence exercised so much influence on the Russian royal family; Edward
VII and George V, Kings of England, with passing reference to such figures of the day as Prime Minister Herbert Henry Asquith; President
of the Board of Trade, Winston Churchill; theatrical luminaries mentioned in passing include Sir Henry Irving; his manager, Bram Stoker,
author of *Dracula*; Sarah Bernhardt and her leading man, Jean Mounet-
Sully; divas Mary Garden and Nellie Melba; among the Germans and
Austrians Alois, Graff Lexa von Aehrenthal; Helmuth von Moltke;
Theobald von Bethmann-Hollweg; the late Otto von Bismarck; auto-
motive designer Wilhelm Maybach, and his daughter Mercedes for
whom his automobile was named; Austro-Hungarian Emperor Franz
Josef; his heir, Franz Ferdinand and his morganatic wife, Sophie
Chotek; and the German Kaiser Wilhelm II contribute to the historic-
ity of the story. Of all historical figures in this novel, however, no one
has more impact than Sidney Reilly, the British (and possibly Russian)
spy, whose many identities and aliases (including, as well as the name
Oertel Morgenstern used in this story, Mister Constantine, Nicholas
Steinberg, Mister Massino, Senor Pedro, Comrade Relinsky, and Karl
Hahn) rival Saint-Germain's. For the sake of the story, I have assumed
that he continued as an agent of the British, under the control of "C"—
Sir Mansfield Cumming, head of British Secret Service—during the
time he had supposedly resigned; it is certainly as possible that he did
as that he did not. What the truth may have been is anyone's guess, for
a more perplexing, contradictory figure would be hard to find, making
him well-nigh irresistible for this novel.

Of necessity, I have simplified—as complex as the story is, it is simplified—much of the political and diplomatic skulduggery of the time, limiting myself largely to the blood relatives ruling major nations, as well as the most prominent members of their respective governments. I have dealt only in passing with the French, the Italians, the Ottoman Empire, the Swedes and Danes, Africa, India, the Americas, and China; the sprawl of including so much tangential information in what is a story about families was beyond the scope of the tale, and the characters in it. I have done all that I can in preserving the personalities of the historical figures appearing in the book as accurately as accounts of them and my research will permit, with one exception: I have occasionally put them in places at times they were not actually there. For these lapses, I plead exigencies of story rather than deliberate misrepresentation.

All automobiles and other technological advances mentioned in the story actually existed in 1910–1912; for roads and similar references, I have used maps and travel guides of the period: some of the streets identified no longer exist or have new names, and a fair number of the buildings referred to do not appear now as they did at the time depicted in this book, due, in many instances, to the massive destruction wrought in World War II. Tourist references and magazines of the period supplied most data in terms of railroads, geographic features, and road conditions as well as schedules and travel times.

In the first decade of the twentieth century social unrest was rampant; many old notions of nations, laws, and government were changing, often through violent public demonstrations. For the first time mass communication and its step-child fame played a significant role in governmental politics. The status of the working classes, including child labor, was being altered, as was the position of women. If some of the issues discussed by characters in this story seem anachronistic, too modern in tone, I encourage you to read journals of the day, as I did, to see how many of the social debates affecting the end of this century began.

Thanks are due to (as always) Dave Nee for an exhaustive research bibliography; to Robert Eighteen-Bisang of Transylvania Press for the crucial information regarding the publishing and performance history of *Dracula*; to Alicia Rosen for her expertise on early twentieth-century jargon, slang, and journalistic style; to Patrick McCarthy for records of military preparedness and materiel of the period; to H. V. Martin for access to his grandfather's and great-grandfather's journals; to Jonathan Stimmer for the loan of his great-grandparent's address in Berlin; to Sandhya Whaley for the information on Sidney Reilly; to my father,

Clarence Erickson, for loan of the *Kalevala,* and help with my rusty Finnish; and to Dale Midkiff, whose insightful remarks threw light on a perplexing aspect of Rupert's character. Any foot in my mouth is mine and not theirs.

Thanks are also due to the First World Dracula Congress, and Nicolae Paduraru of the Transylvania Society of Dracula, whose brainchild it was, for having me as their novelist-guest in 1995; to Lindig Harris for the newsletter; to my agent, Donald Mass, for his energetic efforts on Saint-Germain's behalf; to my attorney, Robin Dubner, for continuing her vigilance; to Maureen Kelly and Megan Kincaid, who answered a good number of questions for me, as well as to Holly Dodgeson, Stephanie Moss, and Jerry White, all five of whom read the manuscript for clarity; and to Thomas Adams, who read it for historical accuracy; to my editor, Greg Cox; and to Tom Doherty and Tor Books for continuing to give life—if that is the word I want—to Ragoczy Saint-Germain.

Berkeley, California
March 1996

PART I

SIDNEY REILLY

Text of a letter from Sidney Reilly to "C", sent in code using Key 43, from St. Petersburg, Russia, to London by diplomatic courier, delivered 7 January 1910.

To answer your inquiries of 9 December last, I have met Franchot Ragoczy but once, and that was at a gala for the ballet, where all we exchanged was half a dozen pleasantries on the evening's performance. My investigations, and they have not been aggressive in order to ensure confidentiality, so far have not revealed much about the man that would be useful to you. He is not Russian and apparently has no Russian relatives—this in spite of his obvious wealth. His erudition is of legendary proportions. His titles, of which he claims several, have not successfully been disputed by anyone at court: attempts to discredit him have been made but none have prevailed. He lives stylishly and elegantly but there is no talk of debauchery, not even from those who might be expected to make such claims. If he has a mistress or lover of either sex, I have not been able to discover who it is. He has a large house here in St. Petersburg and another in Moscow; he owns several factories and is said to provide a free education to the children of his workers. He has endowed two hospitals that I know of, and it is possible there are others. I am told he owns an impressive collection of paintings and original manuscripts, some rumored to date back four and five hundred years. He has given generous sums to artists of all stripes and is said to be a creditable musician himself. Whatever the truth of that may be, I have learned he does possess a fine collection of instruments and an enormous library which occupies most of a large room adjoining his study. They say he maintains a private laboratory in his house, but no one I have spoken to has ever seen it, and therefore I tend to discount its existence as another of those tales that cling to foreigners in Russia.

Why the Czar should wish to employ him in his dealings with his uncle, King Edward is not clear to me, or even if he is going to be employed in any fashion whatsoever, which I take leave to doubt until I have more reliable confirmation. The relationship of Edward and Nicholas is sufficiently close that it is outwardly absurd to think any intermediary is required. You say your information is reliable, but you must allow me my reservations about it; things in Russia are never so clearly defined as things in England. There are rumors, of course, but rumors are common at court, and it would not be sensible to believe all one hears. Currently there has been a suggestion that Ragoczy is a spy for Franz Josef. Of course, Ragoczy has said nothing about such dealings, either with the Emperor or the Czar, which is to be expected no matter what commission he may be offered, or what his intentions might be in regard to that supposed commission. The trouble at the heart of it is, of course, that Nicholas seems to like him. He has achieved a degree of acceptance from Nicholas that is not shared by his ministers, most of whom consider Ragoczy an interloper and a meddler. A few fear he may be in the employ of other governments with the purpose of harming Russia; these men exhibit the most extreme of Russian fear and hatred of foreigners and their opinions are generally discounted for that reason. Although I have yet to ascertain who has employed them, I have discovered that there are three other men who are also assigned to watch Ragoczy. I can, of course, learn to whom these men have allegiance, but that may bring my own efforts into scrutiny. I will not pursue the matter unless you instruct me to do so.

For the most part the man Ragoczy is a mystery. If you do not object, I will try to gather more information about him and report my findings to you, particularly any information in regard to his possible mission in London.

Sidney Reilly (Capt.)

1

This wing of the house overlooked the Nevsky Prospekt, although at this time of night the heavy silken draperies were drawn across the windows blocking out the storm that swathed Saint Petersburg in snow; the two rooms were lit by gaslights, their soft glow imparting the illusion of warmth to the upper floor where Franchot Ragoczy received this guest. He had chosen the study instead of his library for this meeting: the study was cozier and far more private than the library behind it. It was also less than a third the size of the library with its twelve thousand volumes as well as a harp, two violins, a viola, harpsichord, virginals, and a grand piano. The study had three overstuffed chairs, a pair of hassocks, four tables, and an efficient stove to hold the winter at bay.

"I'm sorry to inconvenience you at such a late hour," said Nikolai Alexandreivich Romanov as he nodded in response to Ragoczy's old-fashioned bow. His greatcoat was dusted with snow and a few flakes clung to his beard; he brushed these away impatiently and turned to his host.

Ragoczy gestured to indicate his lack of concern. "I am often up late into the night; an early morning call might be less readily accommodated." He signaled to his manservant to take the Czar's greatcoat and hat.

Nikolai shrugged out of the garment and handed his hat to the sandy-haired, middle-aged man who accepted them and withdrew from the study. "Then I will not apologize, since the hour suits my purposes so well. I forget precisely where I am supposed to be at this hour, but I am sure one of my aides will tell me, or Sunny will." This mild joke brought an amused crinkle to the Czar's eyes, but it faded quickly to be replaced by a more somber expression. "I am grateful to you for saving this time to receive me." He was not a man who smiled easily, but he did his best. "At three in the morning, who will notice I have come here? Or that I am in Petersburg at all?"

"Your escort? My manservant?" Ragoczy suggested with a touch of amusement in his dark eyes. "The gates of my house may be watched, of course. They usually are." Unlike the Czar, he was clean-shaven, his dark, slightly wavy hair fashionably cropped. Though less than average height, he gave an impression of being tall; he possessed a presence that compelled without being intrusive. When he spoke his voice was well-modulated, his Russian unflawed but for a faint, unidentifiable accent. His movements, from his stride to his posture in a chair, were commanding and graceful, in accord with his elegant surroundings. He wore a long smoking coat of black brocade with lapels and lining of deep dull-red satin, though he indulged in neither pipe or cigarette. Beneath it, his pin-tucked white silk shirt was open at the neck, black tie discarded, his black woolen trousers of fashionable Parisian cut, designed for formal evening wear: all revealed his recent return from the theatre or ballet. His shiny low boots were flawless black, their soles and heels thicker than current tastes approved.

"Not tonight," said Czar Nikolai.

"Ah. And your men?" Ragoczy inquired more out of good form than genuine doubts.

"The two men will say nothing," Czar Nikolai declared, and took a chair as Ragoczy indicated the most elegant of those around the small stove at one end of his study. "I have employed them confidentially in the past, and have never had cause to regret it."

"Then I will not mention the matter again," Ragoczy said, waiting for the Czar to give him permission to sit.

It was accomplished with a single flick to his hand. "For God's sake, Count, we are not at court. There is no reason to bother—" He stopped. "But this is not the issue." For a long moment he scowled at the tiles around the stove. "It's Dutch, isn't it?"

"Yes," said Ragoczy without any sign of discomposure. "I had it shipped from Antwerp four years ago."

"Very pretty," said Czar Nikolai in a distant tone. His meticulous evening clothes were not quite enough to banish the insidious presence of the storm; he pulled the chair a bit nearer to the stove. "Better."

Ragoczy regarded his guest carefully but unobviously; in time the Czar would tell him if the reason for this private meeting at this unusual hour was the one Ragoczy supposed it to be. In the meantime it was useless to try to hurry him. Watching Nikolai, Ragoczy was reminded of another winter night, more than three hundred years ago, when another ruler had commissioned him to secure relations with a difficult neighbor: then the king was Istvan Bathory, the Transylvanian reigning in Poland, and the ruler Ragoczy had been sent to negotiate with was Ivan Grosny of Russia. Concealing a swift, sardonic smile, Ragoczy leaned back in his leather-upholstered chair, saying, "There is no reason to be uncomfortable, not in this room. If you like I will bring a lap rug for you. Or I can add more coal to the fire, if you are not warm enough. I am not often cold, and at present, I am more snugly dressed." He nudged a brass scuttle with his foot to indicate there would be no disruption to their privacy for such a service.

"This will do," said the Czar. He sighed again, the sound wistful as well as tired, and stared around the room as if he had never seen it before. "You have some wonderful things, Count."

"Yes; I do." He knew it was foolish to claim otherwise. He glanced at the walls and the shelves, his eyes lingering on a few pieces which possessed still-potent memories—a small painting of a jester done by Velasquez, a screen of translucent alabaster, a Chinese jade lion with one paw clouded by myriad cracks in the stone—until the Czar recalled them both to the purpose of his visit.

With a single nod for emphasis Nikolai began, "Your reservations were well-based, and I appreciate your expressing them. Sadly, I fear you were closer the mark than I: there is no shared wish for the agreement we have discussed; it has been apparent to me for some time that my cousins have other . . . obligations that could interfere with this one. Austro-Hungary and France are the most troublesome. I have taken the advice of my ministers into account, but I do not think the cause is as hopeless as they do. I am determined that the attempt must be made. So. About your . . . trip to England . . . " He hesitated while tapping his fingers on the arm of his chair.

Without any apparent change in his outward demeanor, Ragoczy listened closely, attentive to every nuance of speech and manner. "I am prepared to leave as soon as you give the word, Czar." He was almost relieved to know the mission would begin soon, for in the last year he had become aware of the increasing danger of war.

Nikolai ducked his head. "Yes. And I am pleased to hear it. But you see, I have decided to extend your activities on my behalf, and to achieve the full measure of accord we will need. I want you to stop in Germany on your way back here. The Kaiser must be included in what we do, as much to convince him that this agreement is not an effort to undermine German interests, or to pay him in his own coin for that treaty he foisted on me . . . " His brows drew inward at the recollection of his humiliation at the hands of his German cousin. Shaking off this unwanted memory, he said more briskly, "I assume that will present no difficulties for you? It will be useless if only Edward and I agree to limit the production and sale of arms in our countries; Germany must also support our efforts. Wilhelm will need to exercise the same constraints on his countrymen as we will on ours, or the efforts we make will be for naught." He managed a wan smile. "This may be the one time in my life when I regret that Franz Josef is not a cousin, as well."

"And France? Austro-Hungary? Italy? Spain? Turkey?" asked Ragoczy, his voice steady as he reminded the Czar of the nations that might be expected to engage in arms trade if Russia, Britain, and Germany did not. "What of the Americans, North and South? Or China? Or Japan? What of the Arabs? Arms are made in other places than Russia and Germany and Britain."

"The three of us can exert pressure on the rest; two cousins and an uncle ruling powerful empires," said Nikolai with such conviction that Ragoczy was unable to think of a way to counter his resolve. "They will have to accommodate our demands, not only for reasons of diplomacy, but to protect themselves as well." He clapped his hands together, locking the fingers. "If we lead the way, the rest must follow."

Ragoczy wished he could share the Czar's certainty, for his long, long years of experience had taught him how fragile peace could be. Yet no matter how difficult its maintenance was, he had spent centuries dedicated to its preservation and had yet to regret those attempts. That most of the work he had done had not kept war from coming, he had learned to buy time, which was what he hoped he would be able to do in his mission for the Czar. He kept his doubts to himself, and said, "I will do all that I can to bring it to pass. You have my Word on it."

"So you have said before," Nikolai reminded him. He yawned suddenly, and looked a bit sheepishly at his host. "My wits will go wandering shortly if I . . . I would like a glass of tea, if you will provide it."

"At once," said Ragoczy, and picked up a small bell on the table beside his chair; the summons was answered promptly, and Ragoczy asked for tea and boiled eggs with caviar, lemon, and shaved onions to accompany it.

"Vyelichyestvo." Roger bowed to Nikolai and departed on his errand at once.

"He is reliable, your manservant?" the Czar inquired carefully.

"I have always found him so," Ragoczy replied. "He has been with me a long time. I have had occasion to be thankful for his reliability." That the time he had spent with Roger was measured in millennia he did not mention.

"Good. Good," said Nikolai. "That is important." He stared down at his linked hands. "I would like to be able to rely on my servants so confidently."

"But, Czar, I am simply an exile. My native land is in the hands of conquerors—it has been for a long time. I have no position there any longer." This was not quite accurate; he knew that explanations could become awkward. "Who has anything to gain through me? Not the Hungarians in Transylvania, nor the Turks, nor the Greeks, nor the rest of them. My manservant comes from none of those places. You are the ruler of a huge country, and those around you cannot forget your state in the world; it makes them vulnerable." He stretched out his legs to the hassock, crossing one over the other at the ankle as he propped them up. "And there are more crosscurrents in Russia than anywhere else I have traveled in recent years."

Nikolai laughed once, sadly. "Crosscurrents. An excellent euphemism. My own ministers would do well to use it."

"What word would you rather I use, Czar?" Ragoczy gestured to show he was not arguing with Nikolai. He received no response and expected none.

"They are terrible men, some of those who advise me, but I would be a fool to fail to listen to them. They speak for many who are of the same mind as they, and without their endorsement, the agreement will not—" He held his hands out to the stove, as much to unlink them as to warm them. "What you have said is true; there are crosscurrents and many clandestine motives working in Russian government and among the aristocracy. I cannot deny it. I have given them the Jews to hate, but they want more." He paused to be certain his next words were given special attention. "Which is why I want you rather than any other, to arrange this agreement for my cousins and me. I hope it will prove an example for the world to follow."

"It will be my honor," said Ragoczy with feeling; he had lived long enough that the ferocity of the pogroms did not surprise him—he had seen the slaughter wrought by Attila and Jenghiz Khan first hand, and the terrorism of the Turkish invaders of Europe—but he still had the capacity to be appalled by it.

"I trust you will say the same thing when all your duties are completed." He turned his tired eyes on Ragoczy, looking for something in the foreigner's countenance; he must have found it, for he nodded in satisfaction. "Five years ago, we saw what could happen in our own streets. Our case is not isolated. There are places in the world where there is as much conflict as we have in Russia. If Europe does not help to stem the tide, I fear what all of us will face."

"Bloody Sunday at the Winter Palace?" Ragoczy wanted to be sure they were speaking of the same events.

"I did not understand. They wanted my help. That's what I've been told. I did not know it at the time. They were suffering and they came to the Czar, to the Little Father to receive relief from that suffering. If I had listened to them, it might have been averted. If only the Guards had not shot." He put his hands to his face. "I should not have given them permission to shoot, had I been there. I would like to think I would not have become so frightened. I never thought it would get out of hand as it did. I thought a few shots would scatter them all; the priest they followed was ready to martyr himself, but who would have expected the rest . . . " He stared at the draped windows, his eyes fixed on the events in his memory. "I thought the Guards had more sense."

"They were frightened, as you would have been," said Ragoczy, not making it an excuse. "With all the political turmoil, they feared you would be killed. It was irresponsible, but it should have been expected."

"It was worse in Moscow," Nikolai said quietly. "But it could be nothing, if all Europe ignites, or England. Let that spark turn to fire and we may all perish in the flames." He got up from his chair and began to pace. "Tell me that there is still time. Tell me that we are not acting in vain."

"I would certainly prefer not to think that," said Ragoczy carefully. "But I know that agreement and compliance are two different matters, and it will take more than three signatures to bring about the thing you desire. I will not expect everyone in Europe to cooperate simply because they say they will. That would be rash." He was not certain that even a show of support would be possible, but that he kept to himself; instead he asked a more awkward question. "How will your own army behave if you are able to limit arms sales in the world?"

"I fear the army would like a war. The . . . upheavals of the last few years have given the officers a taste for it."

"They are not the only ones," Ragoczy warned Czar Nikolai. "The Germans will not want to compromise their position, not with the unrest in the Balkans threatening everything they have sought to gain. If the Serbs and Croats continue their disputes, it could spill over into Hungary. Kaiser Wilhelm and Emperor Franz Josef know this better than any others. As much as that conflict could bring difficulties to you, Czar, in the Ukraine, it could bring far worse developments to Austro-Hungary and Germany."

"So I think, so I think," said Nikolai. "And that is why we must have this agreement now, before events intervene that would make it impossible to achieve any control on the proliferation of arms."

Ragoczy said nothing for a short while, then observed, "There are those who will suspect you are self-serving in trying to achieve such an agreement at this time. You have unrest in Russia, and they will claim that is your reason."

"So there are, and such men are not entirely wrong," Nikolai said at once. "And they are probably right. I would not like to have another uprising like the one we had five years ago, and we will have if war comes to Europe, of that I am convinced. So. It is not in the interests of Russia to have war now, either on our own soil or close at hand. Since Nikolasha threatened to shoot himself unless we instituted the Duma, I've known that our country is at risk. My position may isolate me, but I am not so isolated that I do not understand this. We have become too much a tinderbox to withstand any upset of the order in Europe. If it should happen that we have to undertake to preserve our borders with the West, it would be more than—" He was about to go on when there was a discreet knock at the door and Roger came back into the study bearing a large silver tray of eighteenth-century French design on which stood several covered dishes and an English teapot next to a Russian tea glass. He placed this on the largest of the occasional tables and offered its contents to Czar Nikolai with an appropriate bow.

"Please," said Ragoczy. "The tea is very hot. You may want to eat something while it cools a little."

Nikolai had learned from youth how to change subjects without any sign of doing it. "What is most distressing about winter is the lack of exercise one can get easily. In the summer I ride my bicycle daily, and walk every morning, but with this"—he waved his hand in the direction of the covered windows—"stepping outside is a monumental effort. I cannot wait for spring to return, so that I may once again be active."

"What you say is true, unless shivering counts as activity," Ragoczy said, taking the Czar's example.

With a polite laugh, Nikolai spooned caviar onto half of a boiled egg, added a little of the shaved onion, and bit into the whole of it. He managed a look of approval as he chewed. "Excellent," he said once he had swallowed and run a napkin under his mustache.

"I am pleased you find it satisfactory," said Ragoczy, who had never tasted it.

"What else would it be? In this house," said Nikolai. "I can see you have high standards. I know your hospitality." He took his glass of tea in its porcelain holder and sipped carefully. "Another minute or two and it will be perfect."

"Thank you, Roger," said Ragoczy to his manservant. "This is just what was wanted. I will ring for you when we are through here. Please see that the men who came with the Czar have food and drink, and that the coach horses do not stand in the cold." He watched Roger bow once more and depart.

"I am depending on you to plead the case of peace for all of Europe and Russia, Count," said Nikolai as if there had been no interruption. "The English will listen to reason, I am confident of it. They are aware of how much could be lost if war comes, I think. You have only to show them that we are willing to share the responsibility for such an agreement, and they will be more than happy to give us their support, if for no other reason to preserve their position in the world."

Privately Ragoczy was not so sanguine as the Czar; he contemplated the far side of the room, saying, "Is that your faith in your family, or is it something more?"

"Do you mean have I received any family communications from Uncle Bertie or Cousin Wilhelm that would make me confident that either will support this plan? No, I have not; not beyond the entente we have with England in regard to Persia, and that has little to do with arms sales. So. I have not broached this matter to him yet. The time has not been opportune." Nikolai sipped his tea and nodded his approval, then set the glass aside to go on. "But I know the man, and his prudence is such that we may consider ourselves fortunate. You will find him receptive to sensible argument. He will see the need for this agreement at once, I am convinced of it. He will want some assurance; the Entente Cordiale has been a disappointment. If you will speak with him as you and I have spoken, he must comply with so rational a proposition."

"Very well," said Ragoczy, who was not wholly convinced it would be so easy. "And if there should be difficulties?"

"You will straighten them out, of course," said the Czar as if there was nothing problematic in such a notion. "I know you are capable of doing this; I know all you have done for your workers in your factories, and I am aware of your dedication to your principles. This alone would inspire my confidence, but I know you will be willing to do as I ask to protect yourself." He noticed Ragoczy's narrowed, intense gaze and went on, "I can see you like beautiful things and a life of taste, neither of which are possible during war. Let this consideration guide you: that you will sacrifice these things if war comes. You will act for me to keep from giving up this life you have made for yourself." His face clouded as he reached for his glass of tea. "And if you prove lax, or allow yourself to enter into the interests of others, you have businesses here in Russia that the Duma would not hesitate to confiscate if you embarrass us. If you work for the benefit of foreign governments, no matter

which governments they might be, more than your wealth will be for-
feit."

As if he had not heard the threat Nikolai had made Ragoczy said, "I
trust I will not earn your disapprobation, Czar."

"How very astute you are, Count," said Nikolai, permitting himself
a trace of amusement. "So long as your capacities do not falter, there
should be no reason to fear for your holdings here."

"That is reassuring," said Ragoczy with such irony that Nikolai looked
sharply at him; he half-rose and bowed, saying, "Let me speak candidly:
if you are not satisfied that I will do the tasks you assign me, then it
would be better not to request my help. I do not want to be chosen because you wish someone other than a Russian to fail at this mission. It
is not my intention to seek anything but peace in Europe. If that is in-
sufficient, then accept my most contrite apologies now." It was a risk
to speak so forthrightly, and he knew it, but he was aware that the Czar
would be dubious if such blatant pressure did not go unchallenged.

Nikolai ran his finger under his mustache. "Such indignation, Count.
Most commendable. Now, for God's sake, sit down."

Ragoczy knew he had been right to speak. He did as the Czar bade
him. "I am as eager to see peace maintained as you are, perhaps more
eager, because I have seen what war can do." Over the centuries he had
learned to loathe battle; in the last fifty years, he had come to dread it.
"I thought you accepted that."

"Oh, I do, and I accept your reason—that modern inventions have
made killing too easy and too efficient; soldiers no longer have to see
the enemy when they fight," said Nikolai, taking up his tea glass again;
he stared over the rim, his eyes seeing something other than the study
where he sat. "But a man in my position is told many things, all with
great conviction, and half of them are lies. The rest must be suspect."
He glanced at Ragoczy, wholly recalled to the place. "You are a very persuasive man, Count, which is a quality in you I admire, and one I hope
to exploit for the world's benefit, but it is one I must not succumb to as
readily as you may wish." He drank the tea, finishing half the glass before he put it down.

Concealing his annoyance, Ragoczy responded flatly, "I can think of
nothing to say that will convince you of my—"

"Honor?" Nikolai interrupted, and drank the last of his tea.

Ragoczy nodded. "If you like."

"I have found that men who proclaim their honor usually have little
to boast of." Nikolai sighed heavily. "It is not a question of your honor,
Count, but of your ability to persevere. In this instance you have the

advantage over many others: I know at least a dozen men whose honor is unimpeachable because nothing has ever tested it." He selected another boiled egg and reached for the caviar spoon, then stopped. "As one who has lost much and traveled more, I am hoping you will not be put off by protocol and courtesy."

"I have survived thus far," Ragoczy said with a quick smile. "Often in spite of protocol and courtesy."

Thinking he understood Ragoczy, Nikolai completed putting caviar and shaved onion on his egg, and, preparing to devour it, he said, "Then I am confident you will know how to manage this mission."

"I will endeavor to do my poor best, Vyelichyestvo," said Ragoczy with an elaborate show of courtliness; his use of the Czar's formal honorific title emphasized his intent.

Nikolai was chewing on his egg and so could not laugh; he compromised with a closed-mouth smile and a gesture of amused approval. As the clock in the library behind them sonorously chimed the half-hour, Nikolai swallowed his egg, poured himself more tea from the china pot, and said, "Your credentials will be ready for you in two days. I will have all the material you need delivered to you by a private messenger. Keep them safe. They will come at an hour much like this one, so alert your manservant to be prepared to receive a late-night visitor, so that none of your servants can speak of the delivery, or any watcher know of it. This is not an idle precaution, nor an act of unnecessary anxiety. It will be important to have the packet delivered in complete secrecy. There are too many who would try to compromise the agreement if they learned of it, in England and Germany as well as Russia." He set down the pot and held his hands to the stove again; Ragoczy noticed that two of the Czar's nails were badly bitten. "And, as you are aware, there are rumors already."

"I will make my travel arrangements as soon as the messenger delivers your packet to me, Czar," said Ragoczy, feeling a rush of sympathy for Nikolai, who had never been taught to deal with such complexities as those confronting him now. "If there is anything I can do to better insure the success of this agreement, you may rely on me to do it."

"Yes, I believe you are sincere in what you tell me; that is a comfort," said Nikolai, a little sadly. He took a long sip of tea, watching Ragoczy over the rim of the glass. "You have no children, have you, Count?"

"Not that I am aware of, no," said Ragoczy carefully; those of his blood continued the line in other ways. Any child he might have had would have perished four thousand years ago.

"Then you cannot share my apprehension. I believe you must be a parent to have the concerns I do, and the determination." He coughed once to hide the emotion this admission evoked in him. "I think of my children, and I cannot endure to imagine what would become of them in war. I am not afraid for myself, but for my children. And Sunny"— he shook his head at the mention of his cherished wife—"she is of so delicate a temperament that the slightest suggestion that war may come fills her with anguish for our children's sake."

The subject of the Romanov children—particularly the hemophillac Czareivich Alexei—was always a touchy one for Nikolai; Ragoczy considered his response before saying, "If I may, Czar—it is not war alone that troubles the Czarina. She has much more to—"

"No. No. You are right. It is not war alone." Nikolai put his tea aside. "But Otyets Grigori Efimovich has given us all much comfort. How we managed before he came, I cannot think." He sighed. "With him, we have hope. Without him—" He lifted one hand to show how devastated they would be without their precious Otyets Grigori Efimovich Rasputin-Novyhk.

Ragoczy had met Rasputin once, at a reception in Moscow. He had said little to the Siberian priest with the burning eyes and unwashed garments, remembering the times in the past when he had encountered other such magnetic personalities whose influence was as much madness as inspiration. "A most remarkable man: it is said Rasputin has done the Czareivich some good," he observed, doing his best to keep his voice neutral.

"Yes," Nikolai responded eagerly. "After all the mystics and charlatans who flocked around the family, it was deliverance itself for all of us to have Otyets Grigori Efimovich come to us. If he had not come when Alexei was four, I cannot conceive of what would have happened to my son. He was failing, and we were afraid to pray for mercy, since it might take the child from us." He looked directly at Ragoczy. "Otyets Grigori Efimovich healed him when he was bleeding. A pity Stolypin does not trust him."

The story was a familiar one, often repeated and embroidered, yet Ragoczy only said, "Rasputin saved your son, or so I have been told."

Nikolai was quiet for a short while, his eyes brooding. "We did not succeed at The Hague; too many of the powers who came had grudges against others, and we tried to do too much. There is still time, if the leaders will but see it. I can do little, and what I say is suspect. But you, *you*, Count, will bring this agreement to fruition."

"I have said I will do my utmost, Czar." He frowned slightly, his fine brows flicking together. "Your conference in The Hague did not entirely fail, and certainly not through any act of yours."

"I called it. It was my intention to make all of the nations see that China was not alone in its problems, that we as the leaders of the world had to change our policies so that similar unrest and rebellions should not overtake us all. We had the chance, but the rest would not let themselves see what was obvious—" His voice had risen slightly, and there was a tension about him that was not often so noticeable as now. "This agreement must be ratified. The future is unimaginable without it. You must convince Edward and then Wilhelm. You *must.*"

"I will do my utmost," Ragoczy repeated. He shifted in his chair so that he could meet Nikolai's eyes directly.

"Yes." Abruptly the Czar rose. "Put your affairs in order, Count, and leave for London as soon as the weather permits. You must make haste. Every week of delay brings us nearer to the conflagration." He looked about as if he feared they were overheard. "It is time I left."

"You need not worry, Czar," said Ragoczy, deliberately taking his time getting to his feet. "I do not keep servants who listen at doors." While that much was true, he knew there were spies in his household, as there were in every foreigner's household throughout the world. He reached for his bell to summon Roger. "Your carriage will be at the side entrance shortly."

"Good, good." Nikolai began to pace, his restlessness revealed in the urgency of his stride. "I will prepare the packet tomor— today." He pulled his watch from its pocket and stared down at the face. "You will be able to arrange your booking for London before the end of this day. You will have a day to put any necessary instructions in your business-agent's hands. That should be sufficient."

Ragoczy had already prepared most of the material his agent would require; he bowed slightly. "Yes. That will do."

There were two raps on the door and Roger entered the room, bowing to Nikolai and then to Ragoczy as custom required. "I have sent word to the stable, and I have your hat and greatcoat at the door, Vyelichyestvo. If you will give me the honor to escort you?"

"I will accompany the Czar," said Ragoczy quietly.

Roger inclined his head. "The greatcoat and hat are in the vestibule. On the brass rack." He bowed again to Nikolai and left the room, leaving the door ajar.

"Whoever trained him trained him well," said Nikolai as he halted near the center of the room.

"Thank you; I will tell him," said Ragoczy as he opened the door fully for Nikolai to leave. "He will make sure you are unobserved as you leave."

Nikolai nodded curtly, his mind on other matters. As he passed through the doors, he said, "Let me remind you, Ragoczy. If you fail me through any fault of your own, you will regret it. Count you may be, and Prinz you have been, but it will avail you nothing if you do not turn your full capacities to this."

Ragoczy remained unperturbed. "For more reasons than you suppose, Czar. I want peace in Europe, too; perhaps not as ardently as you do, but as profoundly. Believe this." They had reached the top of the stairs and were starting down, Ragoczy a step behind the Czar, when Nikolai halted and rounded on him.

"You will keep me informed of all you do, Count, from the most significant discussions to the least entertainment. I expect you to tell me everything that transpires. Keep a journal for my review, and send me regular reports. Let no detail go unrecorded. I will want one dispatch a week from you at the least. Sent privately. Do not use any of my ambassadors; they cannot be wholly trusted, not in this regard. They all have relatives." He glared at Ragoczy. "My authorization of your mission will be quickly rescinded if you fail to do as I order."

"As you command, Czar," said Ragoczy, following as Nikolai again resumed his progress down the wide staircase. As he went, his memory from more than three hundred years ago of the far more capricious and dangerous Czar Ivan Grosny rose in his mind; he banished it at once, consoling himself with the realization that Nikolai II was not of the same character as Ivan IV. He indicated the door to the vestibule as they reached the main floor. "If you will permit me?"

"Yes." He waited while Ragoczy fetched his hat and greatcoat. As his host helped him to dress for the frigid night, he relented enough to say, "I am grateful to you, Count, and if there were not so much at stake here, you would hear more of it from me. As it is, you must be willing to forego my thanks until there is something settled."

"I understand, Czar," said Ragoczy as he ushered Nikolai through the side door to his waiting carriage.

Half an hour later, Roger found his master once again in his study, this time with a leather portfolio in his hands. "Is everything all right?" Ragoczy asked in the Latin of Imperial Rome as he slipped three more sheets of paper into the portfolio.

"Yes, my master," said Roger in the same language, going to remove the tray and its contents from the side table. "I presume we are going to England shortly. Should I pack your trunks for you?"

Ragoczy's smile was wry. "Yes, old friend, you presume correctly. We will have to sail, worse luck, but it cannot be helped." He set the portfolio down. "This will have to be delivered to Piotr Dmitrovich Golovin, before noon if possible." The mention of his business-agent, a minor cousin of a high-ranking noble family, caught Roger's attention.

"Shall I carry it?" Roger asked. "And deliver it privately?"

"If you would, please," said Ragoczy. "If he has questions, tell him to come around tonight after supper. If my written instructions are adequate, he need not venture out."

"Are there any verbal instructions you would like me to relay to him?" Roger inquired, taking care not to intrude on Ragoczy's thoughts.

"It would be wisest, I suppose, to tell him that I will not be easily available to him for a while. Let him know I will write to him as business permits. Say nothing about the Czar." He noticed the rebuking glance Roger gave him; he went on at once, "Not that I think you would. It is this court. There are so many plotters at work. I can sense them all around us."

"And all eager to influence the Czar," Roger finished for him.

"Or the Duma," Ragoczy amended. "Or both."

Roger said nothing as he picked up the tray. When he reached the door, he remarked, "There are crates of your native earth warehoused in London. That is one thing you need not be troubled about. I will arrange for shipments to Berlin and Munchen as well."

"All the forgotten gods be thanked," said Ragoczy, and went back to writing out instructions for his factory managers to follow in his absence.

Text of a letter from the Countess Amalija Romanovna Khormanskaya to Franchot Ragoczy, delivered three days after Ragoczy's departure for London.

Jylkkaniemi, Suomi
February 3, 1910

Count Franchot Ragoczy
Daum Saint-Germain
Nevsky Prospekt
St. Petersburg, Russia

My dear, dear Franchot;
Of course I am devastated that you will not be joining us here at the dasha. Not that Finland is any place to be in February. All one can do

*is hunt or hide indoors, and I am no hunter, not at my age. So I long
for entertainment other than my nephew's children. They are sweet and
naughty by turns, which delights Leonid and Irina more than me—I
confess it. I was looking forward to your coming. I long to speak with
an adult about books and opera and art and the ballet, anything that
does not involve toys or nursemaids or schools. I will do what I can to
fill the hours with the piano, but it does not keep tune well in this cold,
and I will probably miss you more when I have finished playing than
before I began.*

*Tell me the instant you know when you are returning. Send a telegram
and it will be brought to me, never mind a letter, which will take much
too long to present its good news. I will return to the capital if I am not
there already and invite everyone worth knowing in St. Petersburg to
a gala to welcome you back, if I do not die of boredom before then. We
will have an orchestra and champagne and dancers and the party will
last until dawn. Anna Vyrubova will be furious, of course; she has set
her stock in that charlatan Rasputin, who is not a suitable guest for most
galas, while you, my dearest Count, are more than a hostess could wish
for. It would please me to annoy her again, and you are the best excuse
I could ever have to show her up as an ambitious woman currying favor.
Let me have the gala, I beg you. And if enough guests come, you and I
can leave by midnight and no one will notice.*

*You should be pleased with my restraint: I will not probe for the rea-
son for this hasty departure, but you cannot keep me from speculation.
If my speculations have any bearing on the truth, I will pray for you,
for if you are embarked on such an errand as I suspect, you will need
all the hosts of Heaven to aid you. It is my observation that the Hosts
of Heaven keep far away from international politics, not that you must
be engaged in such activities. Knowing you, you will say nothing no matter what the situation may be, and I have better things to do with you
than try to wheedle secrets out of you. Besides, I do not wish you to lie
to me, and I fear you would have to do that if I pestered you too much.*

*It would shock my nephew and his wife to know how much an an-
cient like me can miss your kisses. Yes, I lie awake nights wishing I could
hear you tap on the window, and dreaming of what would transpire
when I let you in. Naturally I keep such fancies to myself. They—my
nephew and his otherwise-sensible wife—assume passion deserts the
flesh at forty, never to return. I will try not to scandalize them in your
absence. This dasha is lovely in the spring, when I will turn forty-nine;
I will be happy to bring you here then, when Leonid is once again posted
to St. Petersburg. We will have it all to ourselves, and my staff is dis-*

creet. The Finns, whatever else they may be, are not talkative.
With my prayers and my lonely kisses while you are away, and my
hope for your swift and safe journey—especially the swift part.

With longing for your touch,
Amalija

2

"But it is important," protested the butler from the other side of the door.

"I told you not to disturb me, Schmidt: what is it?" Baron Klemens Manfred von Wolgast demanded of his butler as that long-suffering individual was given access to the Baron's private apartments.

"There is a message, Sir," said the butler holding out a small sealed envelope in a hand that quivered only slightly; he combined obsequiousness with efficiency nicely.

Baron von Wolgast snatched the envelope away from the butler and tore it open while he looked over his shoulder and called out affably, "I will be with you in a moment, Herzog Persuic. Forgive me for this delay, but the press of business . . . " He drew the folded sheet out of the envelope and read it quickly, his small blue eyes, deep-set in a fleshy face, hardening. He shoved the paper back in the envelope and said to his butler. "There is no answer but thank you and a gratuity for the messenger. I will see Madame Nadezna later tonight and discuss this with her then." He disguised his petulance with a blunt sort of smile.

His guest wore a Hungarian uniform, bore an Austrian title, and a Czech Christian name, but was, in fact, Croatian. He was tall and straight, with a mass of thick, tawny-brown hair over a strong brow and hazel eyes; he had an uncompromising jaw. As he set aside his cigar, he said, "I hope it is not bad news."

Von Wolgast waved the envelope in the air as if to demonstrate its unimportance. "An inconvenience, nothing more. Do not worry: it will not intrude on our evening." He put the offending envelope into the pocket of his formal jacket and resumed their discussion. "About the field artillery: I can see no difficulty in meeting your request. You will be able to attend the demonstrations, will you not? You will see the im-

provements for yourself. I am convinced you will not be disappointed."
He coughed diplomatically. "We will have to have a partial payment in
advance, naturally, to cover a portion of our expenses, and to be certain of your . . . ah . . . serious intentions. You do understand the need
for this, I trust?" His laughter was a bit forced, but on this Prussian, who
carefully cultivated his slight resemblance to Otto von Bismarck, from
his clothes to his modified muttonchop whiskers, a little force seemed
wholly appropriate. "We would be well-advised to begin work quickly,
to ensure your advantage in weapons."

Herzog Persuic managed a humorless, vulpine smile. "The sooner
we can act, the better it will be for Croatia. We cannot permit the Serbs
to gain the upper hand." He was slimmer than his host, and half a head
taller; he stood parade-erect. He stubbed out his cigar and rose to pace
the long withdrawing room lined with trophy heads of stags, boars and
bear. At the far end he paused and regarded the impressive collection
with approval. "Yours, I suppose?"

"Most of them," said von Wolgast with self-satisfaction evident in
every aspect of his manner. "The stag with twelve points was my father's;
he brought it down in '71. So was the boar over the gun cabinet." In
actuality, almost half of the heads in the withdrawing room were his father's, but von Wolgast had appropriated the majority when he came
into the rest of his inheritance some nine years ago.

"Have you ever gone after big game? Cape buffalo? Lions? Elephant?" Persuic asked, his eyes alight at the prospect.

"Alas, no," said von Wolgast with a sigh. "I have a business to run;
perhaps when I retire I will go to Africa to hunt." He would do nothing of the sort and he knew it; Africa was a furnace, or so he had been
told, full of dangerous diseases and horrendous insects, and populated
by filthy black savages who regarded white men with undeserved contempt. No, he thought, in spite of the lure of elephant and rhinoceros
and lion, he would keep to Europe for his hunting, where people knew
how to show respect, and where the animals were formidable enough.

"The hunting in my country is very good, Baron," said Persuic. "You
could find many things to . . . shoot at." His implication was broad
enough for a public entertainment, but von Wolgast laughed anyway.

"Isn't that why you have come to me, Herzog?" He reached for another cigar, smelled it and lit it. "My guns should bag real game for you."

"Game indeed," said Herzog Vaclav Persuic, his eyes alight with anticipation. "And the hunt long overdue. The land is filled with . . . vermin." He regarded von Wolgast with curiosity. "Does it ever trouble
you—the uses your guns are put to?"

"No," said von Wolgast. "It bothers me when my guns *aren't* put to use. When that happens, I will be bankrupt." He grinned wolfishly.

"I understand," said Persuic. "This is the German good sense that the whole world admires."

Von Wolgast managed a modest shrug. "It is the way to run my business. If men are determined to go to war, why should I take the blame for it? With or without guns, there will be war if men are prepared to fight. They will find weapons, if only the stones in the field. The world is full of gun suppliers. If no one wanted guns, we would not exist." He made an eloquent gesture of acceptance and turned toward the campaign desk supported by stacks of antlers for legs. It had stood in the family hunting lodge until von Wolgast brought it to Berlin. "This was my father's favorite piece. The top was used in the Crimea. The antlers were trophies from hunting."

Herzog Persuic was not impressed. "You say this to tell me what?"

"That our guns are reliable and have been for nearly a century. I am certain that this improved firing mechanism we are currently testing will be to your satisfaction." He studied a painting on the far wall. "And if it is not to your satisfaction, it will undoubtedly be so to others."

"I understand you, my friend." Persuic rubbed at his clean-shaven chin as he nodded. "I will relay your messages to my superiors, of course. They will make their decision based upon the report I submit."

"And I trust the report will be favorable," said von Wolgast, doing his best to appear confident.

"If your field tests are as impressive as your descriptions indicate, I would be a fool to do less than recommend the purchase. The field tests will be the most persuasive argument you can offer." He glanced up as the clock over the mantle struck the hour. "You mentioned entertainment?"

Von Wolgast hated being pressed, but he did his best to appear cordial. "Yes. So I did. I have arranged for a private supper for us, at the establishment of . . . a friend." He pursed his cupid's-bow mouth lasciviously. "You will not be disappointed, I think."

"Excellent," approved Persuic, determined to take full advantage of his position as buyer. "One hears so many things about Berlin—I am looking forward to the evening unfolding."

"Very good," said von Wolgast as he fingered the watchfob crossing his white satin waistcoat. "I shall send for the carriage directly. In the meantime, have some of this kirschwasser"—he poured a little of the clear, potent liquid into a sherry glass and held it out—"to mark this occasion."

Persuic took the proffered glass and watched while von Wolgast prepared a second for himself. "Prosit," he said, lifting his glass in salute. "Prosit," answered von Wolgast as he prepared to drink. "This is my private stock." His pride was justified; the liqueur ran down his throat like a hot finger.

"Superb," said Persuic, willing to be generous. "If your artillery is as good as this kirschwasser, we will prevail."

It was folly to ask which *we* Herzog Persuic meant: von Wolgast tugged on the bellrope to summon his butler. "Consider this an indication of my standards," he told Persuic before he drank again.

"Promising," Persuic conceded, not wanting to promise too much. He made a last nod to their business. "I am favorably impressed with the designs you have shown me. I am certain you have a superior device. You will have your deposit when I have seen your field tests. We will establish a delivery date when the deposit is made."

"This is most welcome, Herzog Persuic." Von Wolgast knew better than to appear too satisfied. "I look forward to our continuing association."

"As do I," said Persuic, setting his empty glass aside. "Shall we be off, then?"

To von Wolgast's annoyance, his butler had not yet answered the summons of his bell. He tried to cover this lapse with the offer of another drink. "It is a cold night, Herzog. I would not want you to be chilled when we arrive at . . . our destination."

"Nor would I," said Persuic, his expression revealing his eagerness to be off at the night's entertainment. "If it is all you claim."

"I venture to guess you will be as pleased with the evening as you will be with the guns." Von Wolgast turned as his butler came to the door. "About time, you dolt," he burst out, his face darkening. "We will want the carriage at once. At once. The side door."

"I have already sent word to the stable," said his butler, his features expressionless. "If you will come now, the carriage should be ready."

Von Wolgast was torn between annoyance that his butler should so overstep himself as to give orders before receiving any from him; at the same time he was pleased that he did not have to ask Persuic to wait any longer than absolutely necessary. He compensated by asking brusquely for his cloak and Persuic's greatcoat. "We want to leave at once, Schmidt. See to it."

"Helmut will have the carriage at the door," said the butler, who answered to Schmidt, but who had been born Hovarth. He helped von Wolgast into his cloak, then held the door open as the two men descended to the street level of the house. There he brought Persuic's greatcoat.

"Very good," said Persuic as he donned the garment. "It might snow tonight."

"Sleet is more likely," said von Wolgast with evident distaste. "The streets will be fairly empty, at least."

"They should be," agreed Persuic as he stepped out the side door to where the double-sprung berlin waited, the coachman swathed in a multi-caped driving coat, holding the four steaming Oberlanders, their flaxen manes and tails kept long against their liver-chestnut coats. "A fine team," he said as he climbed into the berlin and made himself comfortable facing front.

"Thank you," said von Wolgast, taking the backward-facing seat with ill-concealed annoyance. "They are the pride of my coaching stable." He retrieved the fur lap-rug from under his seat and offered it to Persuic. "It will take us twenty minutes to reach our destination."

Persuic took the fur rug without hesitation, opened it and spread it over his legs. "Raw weather."

"And we will make a late night of it," said von Wolgast with a smile admixed with a leer. "You will want to be comfortable, coming away."

"It may be, too, that I will not be so well-dressed then," said Persuic, matching von Wolgast's salacious grin.

"Precisely." He tapped twice on the ceiling of the carriage as a signal to Helmut to set out. There was a second, woollen lap-rug; von Wolgast used it as the carriage moved forward, turning into the street at a solid trot. "They say the automobile will rule the streets eventually."

"For drudgery, perhaps," said Persuic absently. He was looking out at the night, an appreciative shine in his eyes. "But why should anyone give up the elegance of carriages? What man would prefer one of those noisy, dangerous contraptions to this?"

Von Wolgast shrugged. "They say—" He stopped as he caught sight of two uniformed men riding by. "A hard night to be out on the Kaiser's business."

"It is their duty," said Persuic, an implication of criticism in his tone. "It would not be fitting for them to refuse because they are cold."

"True; very true," said von Wolgast, curious about a man willing to plot against the state and still regarding the Kaiser's soldiers with military demands. Since he could think of nothing he felt was safe to say, he kept quiet, hoping that Persuic would change the subject so that he would not have to. He leaned back as the berlin bowled along toward the private house near the famous studio of ballet run by Nadezna. It was not the newest part of town, but it possessed a fading grandeur that complemented the grand theatres and the Oper that made the district famous.

"I am concerned," Persuic said a little later. "If anyone should learn of our dealings, it could be difficult for both of us."

"You may be assured of my discretion." Von Wolgast sat a bit straighter. "A man in my profession would not long survive in business if he allowed the details of his agreements to be known beyond his office."

"But surely," said Persuic, expressing himself carefully, "you have certain obligations to . . . shall we say make available? the records of your dealings to any official of the government? Mightn't you have questions asked of you if the situation in the Balkans was to change?"

This was an issue of some delicacy, and von Wolgast knew it. "It is possible. But that would depend."

"Upon what?" The question was immediate and sharp.

"Upon the nature of the inquiry and the position of the inquirer, and the reason for it," said von Wolgast. "If the order does not come from those sufficiently powerful, then I refuse all demands, until the request came from an office that had the authority to make demands of me. It would not be prudent to do otherwise, for I have no wish to become embroiled in the machinations of politicians, which would be the case if I honored every petty summons presented to me. There are enough military men in the government that this does not often happen. They are no more eager to have their activities scrutinized than I am to reveal what my . . . clients would rather not have known. You may be confident of my discretion." He managed to smile, though it was an effort, and the result was more of a grimace. "I have never been so—" He stopped as the carriage swayed heavily and the steady trot was interrupted.

Overhead Helmut swore colorfully and comprehensively as he strove to restore order among the horses.

"There's a body in the street," Persuic remarked as he glanced out. "The man's been shot, by the look of him."

"How can you know?" asked von Wolgast without thinking.

"His blood and brains are smeared all over the paving stones," said Persuic with little interest. "The horses aren't used to the smell of blood, are they?"

"They aren't warhorses, if that's what you mean," said von Wolgast testily. "I have not thought they needed to be." Their steady progress resumed; the body was quickly left behind.

Again Persuic said nothing as they continued on. Finally, as they slowed to a walk and entered the narrow alley leading along the back-streets to their destination, he remarked, "They say we'll have revolution here soon, as they did in Russia."

"It's possible," von Wolgast responded carefully, not knowing Persuic's opinion of such an event.

"A wise man could turn a revolution to his benefit." He gave von Wolgast a measuring look. "There would be a need for experienced men, men who could provide many things the new leaders would want."

"I suppose that is true enough," said von Wolgast studiously. "The requirements may prove . . . expensive. Revolutionaries are not often wealthy."

Persuic coughed for emphasis, making a point of not looking directly at von Wolgast. "But there are always men with means who can bring the new leaders the things they want. And new leaders often want many, many things."

"Which are provided in return for a few . . . concessions," said von Wolgast, giving a nod he hoped looked decisive; in a swaying carriage, it was difficult to make appropriate gestures.

"I am pleased we understand one another," said Persuic, his handsome features marred by a cynicism that startled von Wolgast, who had expected zeal instead. "Most of those who are in my position have been foolish enough to go to Krupp with their proposals, but I am not one of those." He cocked his head to the side as if listening to a distant song. "I have thought the matter out thoroughly. Krupp may choose among many buyers and ask prices that are as high as fools are willing to go. You, I have learned, will make adjustments in the payment for the chance of eating into the business now dominated by Krupp. You can only do this with a superior product and moderate prices, and prompt delivery. You also cannot select those whom you will permit to purchase your guns: you must accept any buyer who can meet your price. So, we will deal well together, I trust?"

This meticulous summing up of his predicament surprised von Wolgast, but he was experienced enough to reveal little of his emotions. "There is truth in what you tell me," he responded carefully, wanting to expose no weakness to Persuic. "How does it affect our dealings?"

"That remains to be seen," said Persuic, concentrating on the buildings they were passing. His manner grew brisker. "That new mechanism of yours will be the crux of the matter."

"Ah," said von Wolgast with a knowing nod. "Of course. You will want to be certain you can outfire your opposition."

"That is the purpose of artillery, or so I have been taught," said Persuic primly, as if discussing horticulture instead of guns.

Again there was a brief silence between the two men. Then von Wolgast rubbed his thick hands together and said, "Enough of such matters. We are almost at our destination. Less than five minutes now. Let us put these considerations behind us until we return to my house." His small, bright eyes were alight with carefully concocted enthusiasm.

Persuic showed his teeth. "There are lovely women, you say?"

"Dancers," von Wolgast confirmed; his face glistened as he went on, his cheeks becoming flushed. "They are not children, not most of them, but not hags, either. There are ten of them living in the house."

"That means they are skinny; dancers always are," said Persuic, not quite pleased. "A man likes something to hang onto."

"Skinny, yes. But willing. And very supple. They can do the most amazing things with their bodies." Von Wolgast licked his lips licentiously.

The carriage swayed as if to underscore this observation. It was the last turn on their journey.

"Yes, there is that." He laughed, and the fur rug slipped a short way down his lap. "I hope we will arrive soon. I will not want to contain myself much longer."

"We are almost there," said von Wolgast. He felt the Oberlanders slow their walk, indicating they had passed through the arch into the private courtyard of the house they were going to visit. "At last."

"A discreet place," said Persuic. "Like that place you keep your wife."

Von Wolgast winced. "Hardly comparable. There are no nuns here." And no lunatics, he added inwardly.

"Where are we, precisely?" asked Persuic.

"Near the Oper," said von Wolgast, deliberately vague. "The establishment is private."

"Gambling?" Persuic gathered up the laprug as the carriage came to a stop and Helmut scrambled down from the driving box to open the doors and let down the stairs.

"Heavens, no," said von Wolgast. "That would attract the notice of the authorities."

Persuic went down the steps ahead of his host and peered up into the darkness of the three-storied house. The lamps at the door were bright with gaslight, and a servant stood on the threshold to welcome them; he bowed to the two arrivals.

"I will have the horses in the stable, Baron," said Helmut as von Wolgast descended from the berlin. "I will need twenty minutes to be ready to depart."   *

Von Wolgast nodded as he followed after Herzog Vaclav Persuic to the entry of the house. He gave his cloak to the servant, saying, "Thank you, Pflaume," as much to establish his credibility with Persuic as to show any courtesy to the majordomo.

"Nadezna is expecting you," said Pflaume, who long ago had been the costumer for Nadezna and had become her majordomo when his fingers lost their agility to arthritis. "In the withdrawing room." He nodded in the direction of the stairs but gave no further instructions.

"Nadezna!" exclaimed Persuic with the first show of astonishment. "I saw her dance—what?—ten years ago, shortly before she retired. She must be thirty-five or more now."

"This is her house," said von Wolgast with a show of nonchalance as he climbed the stairs to the main floor.

"But I thought she had become a teacher, and choreographer," said Persuic, revealing his fascination as he came up behind von Wolgast.

"She has. But she has dancers who depend upon her, and she does not teach every hour of the day. Nor will she teach forever. Her patron will not care for her then, and she has grown used to living well." Von Wolgast glanced back at Persuic, assuming the fun of sharing private knowledge. "This place is a well-kept secret. Even that patron of her school knows nothing of it."

"So she is making money for herself," said Persuic, not quite approving. "A woman of her sort must look to her old age, as you say."

Nadezna herself met them at the top of the stairs, her crimson mouth widened in a smile, her dark hair done in a dancer's knot on her head. Her slanted eyes were emphasized with kohl as they had been on the stage. The mauve satin dress she wore was a nice blend of high fashion and *Giselle*, the nipped waist raised; when she moved a deep inverted pleat down the center of the skirt revealed a panel of densely pleated silken gauze dyed to the same shade as the satin. The capped sleeves were shorter and more puffed than the current German mode required, but her famous, expressive arms were revealed, so this French affectation was not too extreme. Her shoes were also mauve satin, hardly more than ballet slippers with a minimal heel. Her long neck was emphasized with a wide choker of pearls, peridots, and diamonds, the gift from a wealthy lover who was said to have been killed in a duel for her favors. She had never been classically pretty; her beauty was more exotic than that of soft, blonde German girls. Now that she was in her early forties, the angles of her face were sharper than twenty years ago but this could be faulted by only the harshest critic.

"This," said von Wolgast unnecessarily, "is Nadezna."

"Ah, Baron," she exclaimed in a deep little voice, her Russian accent as carefully maintained as her body, "We have been waiting for you." She stood on tip-toe to kiss him.

"My gracious Nadezna, how patient you are with us," said von Wolgast, disengaging himself enough to bow over her hand. He stared hungrily down at her, then recalled his other purpose for coming. "May I present Herzog Vaclav Persuic, Colonel of the Ninth Hungarian Hussars."

"Herzog Persuic," said Nadezna, favoring him with a short curtsy. "No whiskers. Like one of the Child Dragoons." It was not much of a joke, but the two men dutifully laughed.

"Enchanted, Madame," said Persuic as he bent over her hand. "And the Child Dragoons are Austrian, as are all Dragoon regiments. Hussars are traditionally Hungarian."

She reclaimed her hand, slapping playfully at him as she did. "I know that. I may be Russian, but I have lived in Berlin long enough to learn a bit about the military traditions. Although I can never recall which Hussar regiment has the red braid and which the gold." She was canny enough not to remark on his Croatian name. She took each man by the arm, and walking between them, led the way into her reception room.

It was a grand apartment, glowing with gaslight that showed the splendid murals off to advantage. The most spectacular was a fine allegory of the seasons, with four women arrayed in garments and colors appropriate to each; all four women resembled the mistress of the house in face and bearing.

There were nine women waiting, as if providing a court to the aging ballerina, all of them in gowns similar to Nadezna's. The two fairest women were in black, the rest in wonderfully soft, greyed hues ranging from straw to tea-rose, to celadon. One woman, with a knot of Titian hair and a Renaissance face, was in a filmy gown of apricot lace over a peach underdress, with a wide golden silk sash just under her breasts, the short bodice embroidered with gold thread. Until two years ago she had been the featured ballerina at the Oper, when her career had ended abruptly in scandal. She caught Persuic's attention at once.

"That is Pier. She is from Belluno." Nadezna saw Persuic's interest at once, and signaled to the Italian.

"Belluno is in Friuli, isn't it?" Persuic said as Pier approached. "We are neighbors."

"It is in Veneto," Pier replied as she offered her hand.

"Then we are rivals," was Persuic's gallant response.

"Or possibly allies," said Pier archly. "Against the Austrians."

"We will have to determine which," said Persuic, his eyes moving boldly over her body, as if he could see through the fabric she wore. "There is much to discover before we have a truce."

"I will give no quarter," said Pier, undaunted by his temerity. "And I will ask none."

Persuic moved a little nearer to Pier and slipped his hand around her waist. "I think we both know the rules of engagement." He gave a quick glance to von Wolgast, as if to be certain his wit was being appreciated. "If you do not, I will explain them to you."

"You must decide how that will be done." Pier flashed a practiced smile.

"Herzog," said Nadezna, enjoying his title, "if it suits you, Pier could serve as your companion tonight. Would you like that?"

"Most certainly," he answered with alacrity as he placed his free hand possessively over Pier's. He glanced around. "We are the only guests?"

"Yes," said Nadezna, with an inclination of her head in von Wolgast's direction.

"A very generous act, Baron," said Persuic, his eyes lingering on Pier. "I will remember it in future."

Von Wolgast bowed slightly, ignoring the cynicism he sensed in his guest. "A good omen, then, for our future dealings." He pointed toward the open sliding doors on the far side of the room. "Supper is laid out, and the wine decanted. No reason to keep these lovely ladies waiting for their supper, is there? Go along with them, Persuic. I will join you directly."

"Gladly," said Persuic, and went off with Pier, the other women following after.

"Now," said von Wolgast in a low voice when he and Nadezna were alone in the room. "What was so urgent that you sent me a note about it?"

She disengaged his hand and moved squarely in front of him. "It is Ragoczy. I have had a telegram from him."

At the mention of her patron, von Wolgast stiffened, his face darkening. "Is he coming here?"

"I think he may. He tells me the Czar is sending him to England. He is planning to stop in Berlin on his return. Why would he inform me of this if he didn't plan to visit me?" Her annoyance made her angular features craggy. "I should send a response to England. He does business with a firm in London where he can receive messages. I have the name somewhere." She scowled. "What do I tell him?"

"As little as possible, until we know more of the reason for his visit. If there is to be a visit. Do you think he is telling you this so you will understand why he cannot be reached in Saint Petersburg?"

"I don't know," Nadezna admitted. "And I can hardly demand an explanation of him, and I may not be able to persuade one from him. I cannot afford to lose his support, not yet." She folded her arms and stood before him, the embodiment of petulant rebuke.

"Did he happen to say why the Czar was sending him to England?" Von Wolgast pulled on his lower lip, his brow beetled with thought; Nadezna's display was lost on him.

"It is a private commission; that is all he told me." Nadezna flung out her arms to show her dissatisfaction as she had done on stage to express despair. "Why does he have to come now?"

Von Wolgast shook his head. "I don't like it."

"And you think I do?" she challenged. "The school is still doing well enough, but if he found out about this place, I could say farewell to his support. I fear he would not understand why I have it." She sighed. "Where will I find another patron willing to give so much and ask so few questions."

"Not in Berlin," von Wolgast finished for her. "Why could he not have remained in Saint Petersburg?"

"The Czar—" Nadezna began, only to be interrupted.

"Yes. The Czar has sent him to England. Then damn Nicholas Romanov is all I will say." He took two short strides away from her. "Did he tell you when you might expect him?"

"No," she admitted.

"Well, he will not get to England overnight. That's something. And if he is dealing with King Edward, it will take some time." He rounded on her. "Do you suppose he will telegraph you before he arrives?"

"He always has in the past. So that I can arrange a recital for my students." She could feel heat mount in her face. "Luckily I have Ursula this year. He will be impressed with her."

"Ursula has a gift," said von Wolgast carefully. He knew that any mention of a talented younger dancer could awaken many conflicting emotions in Nadezna; her mercurial temperament was most unpredictable in such instances.

"Thank God for it," she said. "He has already seen Axel and Lilli. He will want to see improvement in them both. I have given them more to do, but they are not yet at the point where they are entirely confident." Again she made her irate, despairing fling of her arms. "And Magda isn't good enough yet. In a year, perhaps she will be ready. She has some promise but she does not concentrate."

"She must learn that from you," said von Wolgast with asperity. "You are not thinking at all; your dancers are not the issue here, your patron is." Then he held up both hands to forestall an argument. "We haven't time for disputes, Nadezna. We must decide how we are to deal with this."

"I will close this house to visitors while he is here, of course," she said, her mouth pursed sourly. "And I will tell my girls not to speak of it. Most of them are afraid of me. They will do what I tell them."

Von Wolgast knew this was true, although he did not understand the power Nadezna exercised over her students. "Good." He paced to the mural of Summer, with her flowing, vaguely Greek cerulean robes and a wreath of oak leaves and lavender in her hair. "If only he would tell you what his purpose is."

"He rarely confides in me," said Nadezna, her face set. "I don't know how to persuade him to talk to me. I've tried before." It was an admission she did not like to make.

"Seduce him," von Wolgast suggested.

"I . . . haven't been able to." She turned away from him, drooping gracefully. "He told me when he became my patron that he would not be my lover." Her voice became more quiet. "He has never changed his mind."

"He's mad. Or he's keeping boys." He chuckled with certainty. "That is why he loves the ballet."

"I don't think so," said Nadezna, touching her hair as if the gesture would restore her confidence.

Von Wolgast shrugged. "Then he's married to a demanding woman."

Nadezna frowned. "He has said nothing about a wife. Or children. Or mistress."

"Why would he?" von Wolgast inquired. "You are not—"

"He would tell me," Nadezna insisted, unable to conceal her vexation. "He would."

"It's not worth discussing," von Wolgast decided aloud. "What we must discover is why he is coming here and what he is doing for the Czar. Then we can decide how to deal with him." He put his big hand on her shoulder. "You were right to tell me of this. I will give it my attention tomorrow, and when I have made up my mind, we will arrange to receive Ragoczy on his return from England."

Although Nadezna's face brightened a bit, she continued to look apprehensive. "What am I to tell him? I will have to telegraph him in London."

Suddenly von Wolgast smiled. "You will tell him," he said, relishing the idea as it filled his mind, "that you have three students who will need to prepare special material for the recital, and that you will need to know when to expect him so that they will be well-rehearsed. It's reasonable enough. He will think nothing of it. He may even, in fact, be glad of your consideration. And we will know where we stand. I will find someone to help us deal with Ragoczy. That will be my contribution." He bent and kissed her. "There. We can celebrate now."

"With that Croatian trouble-maker," said Nadezna, her disapproval showing in everything about her.

"My beloved Nadezna, my family manufactures artillery. Trouble-makers are our source of income." He ran his hand down the satin of her dress. "We will not have to endure him long. Let him get some wurst and some champagne into him and he will be looking for sport. He will want to be alone with Pier or one of the others. Or perhaps he will want to surround himself with women: he seems the sort who would. Then we will have our hour or two together. And we will not have to spend the time with any thought but pleasure."

She knew he expected her to be delighted at this prospect, so she kissed him before she tugged at his arm. "Come, then. The caviar is cold and I have eels in wine-and-pepper sauce. You like that, don't you?" She gave him no opportunity to reply; he permitted her to drag him in to supper.

Text of a letter from Horace Saxon of San Francisco to his grand-daughter Rowena Pearce-Manning of Longacres, near Chalfont Saint Giles, Buckinghamshire, England.

San Francisco, California, USA
February 16, 1910

Rowena Pearce-Manning
Longacres

My darling grand-daughter;
I just got a note from your mother. It seems she's all upset again about that painting of yours. She's worried you'll get a reputation for being fast if you keep up with it. I can't see the connection, myself, but your mother's convinced you'll never get any kind of a husband if you go on much longer. I don't mean to speak against your mother—she's the only

child I got left, and I love her. Don't you ever doubt that, Rowena. She's got notions, though, and when she takes one, there's almost nothing anyone can do to cut her loose of it. She was that way about your father. She made up her mind to get herself a title and an estate, damn the expense. Lucky for me I got more than enough to buy her your father six times over without pinching, or making much of a dent. He might not like having a father-in-law who made his fortune selling supplies to miners in the Gold Rush, but he's not too proud to take the money I provide. I'd probably get along with him better if he did.

I don't suppose I'm going to come to England again, and not just because it's a long way for a man of seventy-eight years to go. It wouldn't be worth the trouble for an old codger like me, and I don't mean just the trouble of getting there. Your mother isn't interested in having me show up—I'd remind all her friends where she came from, and she's worked so hard and so long to have them forget, it wouldn't be kindly done of me. Besides, I get all the fog I can use right where I am. If you take it into your head to come to San Francisco, I'd be glad to have you. Or Augustus, or Penelope, for that matter. But I reckon you're the one most likely to do it.

Your mother wants me to talk sense to you, which is what I am going to do, but I doubt she'll see it that way. I can't get worked up about you the way she does, mainly because I'm real proud of you, no matter what. She worries that you're not married, Rowena honey, and it's eating at her, you being the oldest and all. She's afraid you'll be a spinster, which would be hard to explain to her friends. She tells me it would be a real hardship for you to remain single, the way things are in England. So I'm going to do what I can for you, but by my lights, not hers. You better throw this letter away, because if your mother sees it, she won't be real pleased.

If your brother hadn't died when he did, she wouldn't be so stuck about you. But to have him drown made her afraid that everything she's wanted for so long would come to an end. When I heard about Arthur, it fair cast me down, too, and I know it was worse for Clarice. Your grand-mother and I lost three of our children, and each time it was worse than anything. You may be your mother's oldest, but Arthur was her first son, and that made him real special in her eyes, a sign that she had arrived. To lose him was like taking Christmas away from a child. It took her so long to make herself feel like someone, and she wants to enjoy it. You can't fault her for that. So she's pushing for grand-children, and important in-laws. You can't blame her. And I can't complain, seeing as how I have you and your sister and brother.

Anyway, you coming twenty-five, you got her worried. She's afraid you'll run away to Paris or Rome or worse, San Francisco, to keep up with your painting, and husbands be damned. The trouble is, she's been making plans for you since you were born and they didn't include you going off to paint. That would make poor Clarice have cat-fits. She means well, no doubt about it; she trying to do what's best. And you'll never get her to understand about the painting, not if you tried for ten solid years. But I'm telling you, if it's what you want to do, you do it. That's what your trust fund is for, so you can do what you want, without being beholden to anyone. Your mother got to do what she wanted. She's married to a man with an old, old name and that four-hundred-year-old house I paid to fix up for her. That doesn't mean I'm going to do the same for you, not if you don't want it. There's no point to doing anything like that. You aren't your mother, Rowena, and I know it even if she doesn't. So I want you to have whatever you want, no matter what your mother says. I won't go treating you any different than I did her. Fair's fair.

I'm going to write to the lawyers and tell them that you can have your monthly income starting now, and you can use it any way you want, in case your mother tries some stunt to keep you from having what's yours. It'll give you a good hundred fifty dollars a month, nice and steady. It's not lavish. You don't need a fortune right now, and a hundred fifty dollars is enough to be comfortable, as a lady of your upbringing ought to be. Your mother might not like you painting, but she'd like it a damned sight less if you had to scrimp to do it. You'll get lavish when I die, and you can worry about all those things heiresses worry about. For now, you won't have to worry about the rent, or where your meals or your paints are coming from. You tell me where you want the money sent, and I'll arrange it.

That's the best I can do for now, Rowena. I'll be waiting to find out what your plans are. In the meantime, you keep painting, if that's what you want to do. Don't let anybody get in your way. Your mother might not like your doing it, but I'm pleased as a hog in a pit of acorns.

Your loving grand-father,
Horace Saxon

P.S. Your mother told me you're using Saxon to sign your paintings. She's embarrassed, I know, but I'm proud to have you use it. I thank you for not forgetting this old forty-niner. Rowena Saxon sounds mighty fine to me.

3

It was raining, a weepy spring rain that made London seem to be a sepia print of itself. All the buildings faded to an indistinct grey and the tops of them blended with the streaming clouds. A dank chill ate into the bones and penetrated clothing so that everyone on the street huddled into themselves in the hopeless quest for warmth. As Ragoczy left his house, he was grateful for the lining of Astrakhan lamb that made his black woollen cloak better protection than most Londoners had from greatcoats and similar rain gear; the black boots on his small feet were also lined with shearling lamb. His black Florentine gloves were silk-lined and concealed his eclipse signet ring on the little finger of his right hand. His umbrella protected his black silk hat from the worst of the rain. He was pleased to see his new Rolls-Royce Silver Ghost waiting, at idle, by the kerb-side, his hired chauffeur standing beside the open door. Ragoczy went to the motor car, furled his umbrella, removed his hat, and got in, handing a slip of paper to Harris as he did.

"That is our destination this morning, Harris. You need not rush on my account; there is more than enough time to reach our destination in the appointed time." He settled back in the dark red leather of the seat, watching as Harris got behind the wheel and prepared to drive off into the confusion of vehicles that made up the midday traffic in London.

"Will you want me to wait?" asked Harris, anticipating their arrival as they prepared to set off.

"Very likely," said Ragoczy, and added with less determination, "Although I have no notion how long I will be."

Harris, whose face showed the lean, lined results of a youth spent in poverty, handled the Silver Ghost like a lover, his hands caressing all he touched, easing the automobile forward with a mixture of concern and eagerness. "I'll take care of her, sir. You just go about your work." In spite of his best intentions to pay no heed to what this foreign gentleman's work might be, he could not completely banish his curiosity, though he did his best to disguise it. "Takes long, does it? Your work?" He could not be much more than thirty, but his straight brown hair was already touched with grey; he behaved as if he were forty.

"I am not sure; occasionally yes," said Ragoczy, frowning slightly. He glanced out the small rear window. Although Ragoczy owned four buildings in London, three of them houses, all but the warehouse were tenanted. Not wanting to draw attention to his presence, he had arranged to let this house in a small mews between Grosvenor and Berkeley Squares. The main attraction of the house was not the Mayfair location but the vast and empty top floor where Ragoczy could establish his laboratory, and the huge cellar where the crates of his native earth were stored. As the Rolls-Royce pulled away toward Mount Street, Ragoczy wondered idly if he should arrange to purchase the house.

"Piccadilly to Haymarket do, sir?" asked Harris. There was a minor collision at the corner where a horse-drawn delivery wagon had collided with a motorized bicycle. The cyclist was sitting in the street, blood running down his face between his fingers, the drayer off his driving box fussing over his bruised horses. Half a dozen men had gathered at the corner to stare and venture opinions.

"Whichever is the most direct way to the law courts," said Ragoczy, whose last stay in London had been more than two decades earlier. "Should we stop to assist?"

"They'll work it out, sir," said Harris, with the snobbery of one who had escaped that life through the most relentless determination. "Best not interfere."

Ragoczy did not argue, though he felt a quick stab of remembered grief for Hercule, who had been his coachman a century and a half ago; Hercule would have insisted they stop for such an accident: it was one of the many things about Hercule he had admired. He put his hand to the front of his cloak, and felt through his gloves and garments the stiffness of the heavy paper carried in his inner jacket pocket. The paper seemed as unyielding as metal. Three letters were there, all bearing the two-headed eagle seal of Czar Nicolai II, who signed himself Nicholas in English, as his English grandfather had taught him. It was perplexing to have to approach Edward VII so circumspectly, but a direct and formal encounter would bring about the kind of attention Czar Nicholas wanted most to avoid. "Harris."

"Yes, sir?" responded the chauffeur.

"You'd better find a place to keep this motor car out of sight. It is not unknown in London, and my work here is confidential. It is best to attract only mild curiosity, nothing more." He did not like having to tell Harris so much: the man was untried.

"I'll take her 'round to the British Museum, sir, if that will do. Foreigners are always stopping there, and well-bred folk. A Silver Ghost won't seem peculiar there. No one will think anything about her." It was apparent he would take great satisfaction driving the splendid automobile without a passenger.

"Very good, Harris," said Ragoczy, slightly amused by the realization that Harris' greatest loyalty was to the Rolls-Royce. "You may let me out at Fleet Street at Chancery Lane." Being so close to the heart of ever-curious, ever-vigilant British journalism, which was centered in Fleet Street, made Ragoczy uncomfortable and wary, but his behavior did not reflect any of this.

"Yes, sir," said Harris, suspecting that Ragoczy wished to keep his ultimate destination a secret even from him.

They reached The Strand readily enough, and continued on to the beginning of Fleet Street. Here there were more motor cars and fewer horse-drawn vehicles than in some other parts of the sprawling city; Harris threaded his way between the automobiles with expert care. Drawing the Silver Ghost to the side of the street to permit Ragoczy to step down, he said, "Will you need more than two hours, sir?"

"I certainly hope not," said Ragoczy with feeling. "I will meet you at the British Museum when I have concluded my dealings here. I would not suppose that I will be longer than two hours at most. If I am going to be more than three, I will telephone the Museum and have you informed of when to expect me." He had already taken his umbrella and was reaching for his silk hat.

"No offense intended, sir, but you do look a proper toff," said Harris as Ragoczy prepared to get out of the motor car.

Ragoczy paused before saying, "Why, thank you, Harris. I do my best to be." With that, he opened the door and went out into the rain, opening his umbrella as he did.

Harris continued up Chancery Lane, wishing the sky would clear so he could take the top down and all the world could see him at the wheel of Ragoczy's Silver Ghost. He consoled himself with the thought that he had been employed to work a full year—there would be plenty of chances for him to tool the streets in style once spring took hold.

There was an uninformative brass plaque on the side of the Tudor building where Ragoczy had been summoned: #2, *St. Dunstan-the-West Close.* Ragoczy opened the door and stepped into a small, marble-columned lobby of Georgian design. Ahead was a reception desk, and Ragoczy again closed his umbrella as he approached. "Good morning," he said to the lanky young man behind the desk. "My name is Franchot Ragoczy. I am here to see a Julian Sinclair-Howard. He is expecting me."

With this, he handed over a card with his precise signature and title on it, his present address written beneath.

"What is the purpose of your call?" asked the young man with an officious sniff at Ragoczy's card; he did not bother to read it.

"I believe that is something between Mister Sinclair-Howard and me." Ragoczy did not change the tone of his voice nor his posture, but there was something in his dark eyes that stopped the next question cold in the young man's throat.

"I'll tell him you are here," he muttered, glad for the excuse to look away. His fingers reached for one of the jacks on the telephone equipment before him, and connected it to a socket. A moment later he spoke into the bell of the speaker angled out from the array of sockets. "There is someone here to see you." He all but whispered it, as if the visit would be news to Ragoczy.

"The name," the Count said in a low voice, "is Ragoczy."

The young man visibly jumped and duly repeated the name, then relayed the information that Mister Sinclair-Howard would see him in five minutes. He inspected the card before holding it out, attempting to restore his dignity by remarking, "I am a trifle puzzled by your name: I would have thought you pronounced it Rah-go-chee, or something like that."

"My family is a very old one. Rah-go-shkee is the pronunciation left over from several centuries ago. Rah-go-chee, or similar variants, is along the lines of Chum-ley, or Fan-shaw." He deliberately chose two noble English families whose names over time had come to be pronounced markedly unlike they were spelled.

"I see," said the young man, who clearly did not. He put the card down on the desk to his right. "May I keep this?"

"I expected you would," said Ragoczy as he shrugged out of his cloak and draped it over his arm, revealing a neat black suit, white silk shirt, and a deep red damask tie patterned with his device: the eclipse. "If you will tell me where I should dispose of these?"

Again the young man looked nonplused. "There is a cloakroom just under the stairs. Mathews will see to you."

"How good of you, and Mathews," said Ragoczy as he removed his gloves and thrust them into the inner pocket of his cloak. He rubbed his hands together briskly and stepped up to the cloakroom.

Mathews proved to be an ancient servant with a few wisps of white hair smoothed across his bald pate. He took the cloak, umbrella, and hat from Ragoczy, muttering, "Very superior quality, if I may say so," as he found hangers for them. "And the name?"

Thinking of the young man at the reception desk, Ragoczy gave his title instead. "Count Saint-Germain," he said, not wanting to create more confusion.

"A foreign title; don't run into them every day," said Mathews as he scribbled it on three tags. "I will remember."

"Thank you, Mathews," said Ragoczy as he returned to the reception desk. "There," he informed the young man. "I am now wholly at Mister Sinclair-Howard's disposal."

"He will call directly. I have a copy of the *Times*, sir, if you would care to—" he ventured.

"I've already read it." Ragoczy was careful not to be too brusque with the skittish young man. "And doubtless the five minutes are nearly up. If you will tell me where I will find Mister Sinclair-Howard's office?"

"Top of the second flight of stairs, the first door on your right after the lift." He cleared his throat. "There has been trouble with the lift, or I . . . "

"Never mind," said Ragoczy, going toward the stairs. "I prefer to walk in any case."

The marble treads were old enough to be worn, but they were still slick, and made haste in climbing them a reckless notion. The bannister was covered in velvet, also tastefully worn although in excellent repair. Ragoczy went up at a sedate pace, pausing at the top of the first flight of stairs to look down on the lobby with its fine Doric columns at odds with the electric bulbs in the Victorian chandelier that had originally been fitted for gaslights. He ascended the second flight and found himself in a wood-paneled corridor with a number of doors ranged along it, each flanked by electric bulbs covered with translucent shell-shaped lamp-holders. The collapsible brass lift doors carried a notice asking would-be users to take the stairs instead. Beyond that, as the young man had said, was a door with JULIAN SINCLAIR-HOWARD picked out in small, gold-foil letters.

In answer to Ragoczy's single knock, a deep, well-bred voice replied, "In a moment." After a brief silence, there were four muffled steps and then three clear ones—Sinclair-Howard's office was carpeted—before the door was opened and the same voice said, "Count Ragoczy. Right on the minute. Not many foreigners are so punctual. What a pleasure to meet you." He held out his hand. He was fair, blue-eyed, clean-shaven and ruddy-cheeked, less than thirty-five, and handsome in the hale, horsey way many well-born English were, with that lingering air of hauteur that detracted from his outward charm. Although he was dressed in full diplomatic kit, it was easy to imagine him in pink coat and breeches, riding to hounds in the morning and relaxing over port and cigars in the evening.

Ragoczy took the proffered hand, saying with slight diffidence, "Actually, it is Count Saint-Germain, for what you would call the fief. Ragoczy is my family name." He did not add that the Ragoczy title was Prince.

"Oh, yes?" said Sinclair-Howard; he could not conceal his distrust of the elegant foreigner, nor his own sense of ineffable superiority to Ragoczy, whose title was not English and whose accent was unknown to him. "Sorry to have got it wrong. Crosleigh must have been mistaken."

"The young man at the reception desk?" Ragoczy asked, thinking that it was not a promising indication when a man had to put responsibility for so minor an error on another.

"Yes. Mister Crosleigh is recently graduated from King's Cambridge. He has his sights set on an ambassador's post." Sinclair-Howard chuckled to indicate that this was most unlikely.

"It is not important," Ragoczy assured him. "A minor thing at best."

Sinclair-Howard murmured what was probably an apology as he held the door for Ragoczy. "If you will step inside, Count."

"Thank you," Ragoczy said, noticing as he did that the carpet was fine quality Bohkara, in lustrous shades of deep red and intense blue with details in black, ivory, and rose. He turned back to Sinclair-Howard and said, "This is magnificent."

"Wog children make them," said Sinclair-Howard. "Filthy practice, though the results are, as you say, magnificent." He indicated the leather upholstered chair that faced his campaign desk. "If you will."

"Certainly," said Ragoczy, following the young diplomat's suggestion. "This is very nice. It is Turkish leather, isn't it?" The chair was tall-backed and overstuffed; the leather creaked as Ragoczy sat down.

"That's right. English manufacture, of course." He paused, inclining his head inquiringly, like a large dog; he all but sniffed the air. "Can I get you something before we begin? Sherry, perhaps, or tea?" He had walked around behind his desk and opened a cabinet. "I'll have to send for the tea, but sherry, port, and whisky are here. What shall it be?"

Ragoczy considered the offer. "Nothing, thank you." He saw the tightening of Sinclair-Howard's mouth. "But if you would like to have something for yourself, do not let my abstention stop you." He realized that this was not sufficient for Sinclair-Howard to ignore his long training, so he added, "I have a . . . condition of the blood which does not permit such indulgence. I do not wish to impose my limitations on others."

"Blood condition, is it?" said Sinclair-Howard as he turned to pour himself a bit of sherry. "How unfortunate. And what a bore for you. It must be a great inconvenience."

"In some ways," said Ragoczy with a slight shrug. "I have learned to live with it, over time." He directed his dark, enigmatic eyes on Sinclair-Howard. "Forgive my next suggestion, but I cannot help but want to avoid all the required pleasantries: they are tiresome and accomplish little. I realize that they are considered a common courtesy, but I find them more a disruption. Let us, therefore, agree that the weather is dreadful, that my passage was about the usual duration for this time of year"—although to him, crossing water was always an ordeal—"that the press has become insolent as well as intrusive, and that the international situation is hazardous. That should save us some time, and permit us to address the Czar's concerns at once."

"How . . . " He could not think of an appropriate comment; he sat down abruptly, his sherry in front of him, and said, "Very well." He cleared his throat, trying to accommodate Ragoczy's request. "What am I to have the pleasure of doing for you?"

Ragoczy reached into his inner pocket and drew out one of the envelopes there. This he laid on the desk and said, "I am sure you know the seal, Mister Sinclair-Howard. If not, I can provide verification for you."

"Czar Nicholas Romanov," said Sinclair-Howard, doing his best to be unsurprised. He knew that Ragoczy had come from Saint Petersburg when he was first contacted, but had not assumed his mandate came from so high a source; in his experience, exiles rarely were accorded more than token acceptance, but this indicated genuine trust, and a position beyond what most foreigners attained.

"This is for you to read. It will explain my purpose far better than I." Ragoczy sat back in the leather chair and waited while Sinclair-Howard lifted the seal with a penknife and drew out the single sheet of paper where the Czar had written in English what he wished this assistant of Edward VII's secretary and remembrancer to do for him.

At the conclusion of his perusal, Sinclair-Howard drank down all his sherry and went to the cabinet for more. "Most interesting. The proposal is . . . unique in my experience. The Czar must have a great deal of faith in you, Count, if your mission is in actuality the one described in this letter. A great deal of faith. It is a most . . . um . . . delicate one,

But Ragoczy shook his head. "It is not the telephone that troubles me, Mister Sinclair-Howard: it is those who may listen."

Sinclair-Howard rose, doing his best to control his expression. "I assure you that no one in this building would—"

"But it is not just this building that must concern us, is it?" Ragoczy again interrupted, his voice mild. "There are many who may avail themselves of the opportunity to . . . eavesdrop. I recall seeing a report in one of your newspapers only two days ago—not in the *Times*, of course—in which the information had been obtained from an unnamed employee of the telephone exchange." He let Sinclair-Howard have several seconds to consider this. "I would not like to see the purpose of my visit here bruited about in the press."

"No. Certainly not," said Sinclair-Howard. "Very well. I will make an appointment with you as soon as I have something in place. In the meantime, I trust you will find our London entertainments to your liking."

"I always enjoy London," said Ragoczy, remembering the times he had been here, since the place had been a Roman encampment called Londinium. He got out of his chair.

"Perhaps I could arrange an introduction or two, if that would suit your purposes? I have a few connections that may interest you." It was more than his post required, but if Ragoczy was going to speak with King Edward, it would be no harm to have him give a good report of Julian Sinclair-Howard.

"Thank you, but I have some introductions already, through business associates, and a few diplomats I have had occasion to meet in the past." He realized Sinclair-Howard assumed he was not involved in trade. "When one has lost everything but titles, business is necessary to survival, Mister Sinclair-Howard." He did not add his alchemical work had financed most of his commercial ventures.

"No doubt," said Sinclair-Howard, who could not entirely conceal his contempt for such concerns.

"Do not worry," Ragoczy said gently. "I have no disreputable dealings that would embarrass you or Czar Nicholas."

"Of course not," Sinclair-Howard said dubiously. What was it about Ragoczy, he wondered, that Czar Nicholas should be willing to trust him?

As he held out his hand, Ragoczy achieved a brief smile. "If you wish to be certain, you need only consult with my solicitors. Their chambers are not far from here. Cowper, Sunbury, Halliwell, and Melton, in Middle Temple Lane. Speak with the elder Sunbury. I will authorize him to release all relevant information." He was well-aware of the sterling reputation of the firm, and the standing of Carlisle Sunbury.

"Well; Cowper, Sunbury, Halliwell, and Melton. Most unexceptional," said Sinclair-Howard, his old-fashioned expression as much a sign of snobbery as approval: the solicitors had a long history of incorruptible reliability, and as a result their clients came from the upper reaches of British society. "I am sure there is no need to request bona fides of them, not with this letter from the Czar."

"I can give you the names of my men-of-business as well, if you would like," said Ragoczy; he was not above being amused by Sinclair-Howard's apparent awkwardness.

"That is hardly necessary, Count," said Sinclair-Howard rather stiffly, aware now that he was being tweaked.

"Very likely not," said Ragoczy. "Still, if you seek reassurance that I am not some homeless adventurer taking advantage of the Czar to promote my own interests, I will be more than willing to show you that I am well enough off in the world not to require the favor of Kings to maintain myself." His personal fortune he knew to be vaster than Edward himself could boast.

"Yes. Well, if there are questions in that regard—"

"Other than your own?" Ragoczy interjected.

"—I will ask for that information when they arise." Sinclair-Howard was visibly affronted as he finished. He went to the door with Ragoczy to hold it open for him. "I will notify you when there have been developments."

"Thank you," said Ragoczy, then added, "I am sorry if I have caused you any distress, Mister Sinclair-Howard. I would like to think you will not let any personal aversion to me influence your diligence on behalf of the Czar."

"I . . . This has nothing to do with my . . . opinion of you, Ragoczy," said Sinclair-Howard mendaciously.

"Does it not." Ragoczy gave Sinclair-Howard a moment to consider his remark, then said, "Adieu. I anticipate our next meeting with hope."

Sinclair-Howard was relieved to close the door on this most perplexing visitor. He could not help but wonder as he went back to his sherry, how such a poseur had gained the confidence of Nicholas Romanov—a confidence Sinclair-Howard was certain would be abused.

At the reception desk, Ragoczy paused to leave his telephone number with Crosleigh, then reclaimed his cloak, gloves, hat, and umbrella before stepping out into the bustle of Chancery Lane, and turned not north, toward the British Museum, but south toward the Thames and

Middle Temple Lane; it was only a matter of a few blocks to reach his destination. Since his interview with Sinclair-Howard had been more brief than he had thought it would be, he decided to call on Carlisle Sunbury and give him permission to release certain of his records to Sinclair-Howard.

Ragoczy was admitted at once to the elder Sunbury's office, a dark, cavernous room with vast numbers of books behind glass panels. He was given a seat before the hearth, next to the well-used chair Sunbury had long claimed as his own. Behind them, Sunbury's desk was stacked with case file boxes. Carlisle Sunbury, whose long face had been schooled never to reveal anything of his inner perceptions, listened to what Ragoczy had to say, one lean finger crooked under his mouth, his deep-set eyes half-closed. "I will attend to it, Count," he told Ragoczy; in his mouth the title was honorable rather than spurious.

"Thank you; I knew I could depend on you," Ragoczy responded.

"That you may," he confirmed. "It will give me much satisfaction to do this. And I would hope you would permit me to put the word about that you are not the sort of scoundrel, to take advantage of your mission, whatever it may be." He lifted his hand to silence his client before he protested. "Oh, nothing obvious, or too contrived, but enough to take the wind out of Sinclair-Howard's sails."

"Why do I have the impression that you have more reason to do this than preserving my reputation?" Ragoczy asked as he studied Sunbury's uninformative features.

"Yes, you have the right of it." Again he paused, offering no explanation. He gazed contemplatively into the middle distance. "In fact, Count," he went on with a speculative lift to one shaggy brow, "if you were of a mind to accompany me Friday week to a weekend party in Chalfont Saint Giles, I think you might make headway on your own account. It is a private gathering, just the sort that would serve your purposes. Don't worry. You would not have to do more than put in an appearance for the entertainments. But I believe it would do you good."

"In what way?" Ragoczy was not enthusiastic.

"In many ways. For one thing, it will give you a chance to get about. That will dampen any speculation that you are avoiding anyone. Certain closed doors might open more quickly. It will also make the reason for your presence in London less a mystery."

"And is it that?" Ragoczy wondered aloud.

"For some, yes, it is. When a man of your wealth is in London, many are curious as to the reason. If you would get out where you can be seen, you will be able to show you are not a recluse or a schemer." Sunbury pulled out his pocket watch and studied the face, then replaced it. "This weekend party is a fine opportunity for you. I doubt it will be too awkward. I will try to see to it that you need not be pestered about meals."

"Have you an appointment?" Ragoczy had taken note of the watch.

"Not for twenty minutes yet." He returned to the previous subject. "What do you think, then? about the weekend party?"

"Who is the host of this event?" Ragoczy asked, prepared to decline politely. There were too many risks for him in such a setting, no matter how useful it might be.

"Pearce-Manning. He's Brooke's nephew, you know. Used to be poor as a parson's groom, until he married that American woman. Now he's got more of the ready than I'm likely to see in a lifetime, and the promise of more still when his father-in-law dies. They entertain generously, and very casually. Buffets four times a day, and dressing for the evening, but not to sit down. It is considered a coup to be invited, though no one likes to admit it. Longacres is a pleasant estate. You'll not have a dull time of it. The food is excellent—not that you care about food—and the company is usually stimulating. Clarice Pearce-Manning is a woman of eclectic tastes and interests. It is difficult to be bored by her entertainments." He stretched out his legs making his lean frame appear even more attenuated. "You will have the opportunity to make yourself known without display."

"And, I would suppose, with some of the same officials to whom Sinclair-Howard would report?" Ragoczy guessed.

"I am pleased you take my meaning, Count." He sighed once. "You will find that these men do not like to have their opinions formed by the likes of Julian Sinclair-Howard." His normally deep and lazy voice now snapped like a closing trap. He glanced at Ragoczy. "One of those self-important functionaries, is Sinclair-Howard. Oh, yes, indeed: I have had dealings with him in the past. He figured in an estate my son represented, about three years since." The languor came back into his voice. "It was not an edifying experience."

Ragoczy hesitated, then ventured, "I take it that Sinclair-Howard's opinion is not the only one that will be consulted? That young man— Crosleigh, the receptionist? Won't he make a report?"

Sunbury chuckled. "You've always been hard to deceive, Count. Yes, young Crosleigh is probably the most knowledgeable young man for contemporary Eastern Europe and Russia that the Foreign Office has. They're grooming him for an Ambassadorial post at the least. If he had not been satisfied with you, Sinclair-Howard would have been summoned to an urgent appointment and you would never have got upstairs."

"And the old soldier in the cloakroom?" Ragoczy asked blandly.

This time Sunbury slapped his knee. "There is no deceiving you, is there? You're right. He knows every spy who has ever set foot on the good, green isle of Britain. If he had recognized you, you'd be explaining yourself elsewhere by now." He glanced aside. "Julian Sinclair-Howard is the least of your obstacles at Number Two, Saint Dunstan-the-West Close, little though he may be aware of it." He reached into his jacket for the triple-cigar case, drew it out and opened it. "I know you do not indulge, so I will save us both the trouble of a declined offer."

"Good," said Ragoczy with a touch of irony.

Sunbury went through the ritual of examining his cigar, then produced a safety match and lit it, blowing out a rum-scented cloud of smoke. "If you like, you may motor down with my son and me. It is not a very long trip, but it does take more than an hour."

Ragoczy made up his mind. "If I have no appointment with King Edward, then it would be . . . interesting to go with you. I assume I will be permitted to bring my manservant?" He was a bit surprised at himself for agreeing so readily; he would have to ask Roger to plan the trip carefully. "However, in regard to the ride to Chalfont Saint Giles, I would prefer to have my chauffeur drive us in my motor car." He would have to travel by day, and the seats of his Silver Ghost were lined with his native earth.

"If that is what you wish, then Anselm and I will be delighted," said Sunbury. "If you will call for us at half three, we will be ready."

"Half three it will be," said Ragoczy, comforted by the thought that if things went badly he could always return to London; that was another reason to have Harris drive. "You will have to guide us there."

"Of course; in fact, I will send you a map," said Sunbury. "You will not regret it, Count."

"I will confirm this with you on Wednesday," said Ragoczy, rising, and although he was nearly a head shorter than Carlisle Sunbury, he gave the impression of greater presence. "Will there be any difficulty about including me in that weekend party, do you think?"

At that, Sunbury gave a rumbling laugh. "Impossible. It is given by a socially ambitious American. If I know Clarice Pearce-Manning, she will be beside herself to have such a guest as you."

Aware that Sunbury wished to reassure him, Ragoczy said, "You must let me know if she would consider me imposing upon her." As he drew on his cloak, he said, "Will I be able to flag a cab, do you think?"

"At this time of day? Of course." Sunbury regarded Ragoczy. "Are you going back to your house?"

"No; to the British Museum. Harris is waiting for me there." He drew on his gloves as he went on. "Call me when we have more to discuss. I will meet you at your convenience."

"Still uncertain about telephone operators, I see," said Sunbury. "In your situation, I might well feel the same way. A word or two in the wrong ears could make your work here much harder than it already is." He watched as Ragoczy prepared to let himself out of the office.

"Diplomacy is not a speedy art," said Ragoczy.

"No; no." Sunbury stared down at the floor. "I don't suppose it is."

Text of a letter to Baron Klemens Manfred von Wolgast from the defrocked priest Paul Reighert.

> *Chez Noir, Berlin*
> *February 19, 1910*

My dear Baron;

Your generous donation has arrived without incident, and I am now about to put into action the plan we discussed four days ago. It may seem a needless delay, but I am going to find the most reliable men I know of to do the work. You will be pleased to know that two of the men I mentioned to you have already responded to my summons and have declared themselves willing to undertake the surveillance you require. As soon as word comes from my associate in London, it will be possible to commence the thing in earnest. A week from now, I am confident it will not be possible for Ragoczy to make a move without note of it being made.

It may be necessary for me to offer larger amounts than we originally thought would be needed to pay for the service you are seeking. Should that happen I will notify you at once, so that we may have the opportunity to arrange matters to your satisfaction. Bernard in Amsterdam has named a price higher than I anticipated, but I must tell you that his skills are such that it is worthwhile to pay for them. You will not find better for any sum. I do not yet know how much Pollard in London will want, but I advise you to meet it, for no man is better at following without detection than he; I have used him five times in the past and no one has ever detected his presence. Certainly you know it would not serve your purpose to have this observation discovered, and in that case, Pollard is your man. He is also not given to boasting or idle talk, a factor

*nearly as valuable as his skill in watching. You will not want to engage
men who trade upon the confidences of their employers.*

*I am confident that we will have all the particulars on Ragoczy's mis-
sion before summer, as well as details on whatever progress he may have
made. Once that information is obtained, it will not be difficult to
undermine the work he is doing, and compromise him in the Czar's eyes.
I will be at your service then as well as now, to bring about your goals.
If my years as a Jesuit taught me nothing else, it gave me instruction in
craftiness. As long as you are satisfied with my activities I will continue
to devote myself to your cause.*

*Sincerely,
Reighert*

4

In the end, Ragoczy motored to Chalfont Saint Giles with only Harris
and Roger for company: a Friday afternoon meeting with King Edward
had necessitated a day's delay in London while Ragoczy went to Windsor and presented the letter from Czar Nicholas and outlined the Czar's
hopes for a limitation on the manufacture of arms.

"That's all well and good," Edward declared toward the end of the
unofficial audience held in a garden folly on Windsor's grounds where
they would not be disturbed. Their talk lasted longer than the forty minutes that had been allotted to it and the day was drawing on toward
evening and the winter twilight was taking hold of the sky by the time
they concluded their conversation. "I am inclined to support Nichi's
goal, but this situation in South Africa must be completely resolved before I will be in any position to agree to limit the manufacture of arms.
Fortunately most of the matter has been settled. It will not be long before it is completed; Parliament approved the South Africa Act last year.
You will have to tell the Czar he will have to wait a few months, Count,
before I can endorse his efforts. When I am at liberty to do so, I will
be inclined to favor his plan. I am certain all will be in order by summer, and that is not more than three months, four at the most. I know
he will understand; he's my nevvy."

The resemblance between Nicholas and his Cousin Edward was not readily apparent: on a second look it could be discerned, their shared legacy from Queen Victoria. But Edward's color was higher than Nicholas', his body larger, and he breathed with effort. Even in a simple dark suit, Edward had the manner of a man used to attention, and for that reason alone he made an effort to conceal the extent of his physical distress. Ragoczy noticed with concern that even sitting in this garden folly, the British King was not rested. "I will convey your predicament to him, Majesty." He used the most correct title Edward possessed, although he knew many Britains did not; as an emissary and a foreigner, Ragoczy knew that his position did not allow for lapses in form. "And I will await the Czar's instructions."

Edward had a ferocious smile that made his beard thrust forward. "You may want to meet with me again. No reason for us not to arrange the basic terms of this agreement while the situation in South Africa is regularized. None of this is so official that I will have to present it formally, which is all to the good." He leaned forward, hands on his knees. "Nicholas is finding out what it is like, having a government to answer to, with that Duma. Of course," he added mischievously, "it does provide a group to blame."

"Is there some reason you anticipate blame, Majesty?" Ragoczy asked with sudden awareness of danger.

"Oh, there is always someone who will protest, no matter what. The bloody Irish haven't yet finished blowing up English soldiers. They will not welcome peace. Nor would those factions in the Balkans. That has been going on as long as we English have had to contend with the Irish. Damn the Turks."

"It has been going on far longer than the Turkish presence, I fear, Majesty," Ragoczy said, remembering the many outbreaks of regional fighting he had witnessed in the Balkans over the last two thousand five hundred years. "If it were only the Turks, peace would have been negotiated there after the Siege of Vienna."

Edward sighed. "You may be right. It is regrettable, and the risks go beyond the Balkans themselves." He squared his shoulders. "You may rely upon it: the Serbs and Croats don't want peace any more than the Irish do. Any attempt to limit arms production would enrage any and all of them, if they knew of it." He studied Ragoczy a moment. "Tell my nevvy Nicholas for me that although I am unable to do anything official quite yet, I will arrange what I can with you; I will speak with George about this, as well." The mention of his heir was awkward; he cleared his throat. "I assume you will be willing to continue our discussions on a clandestine basis?"

"Whatever will best serve the purpose of the Czar's commission," said Ragoczy, so smoothly that he earned a sharp look from the King.

"You're mighty practiced at this game, Saint-Germain, though you go to some lengths to disguise your talents, which only serves to confirm them." Edward shoved himself to his feet. "I begin to appreciate Nicholas' choosing you for this project of his. At first I was at a loss why he did not employ a Russian for his emissary, but I am beginning to understand. After what happened at The Hague, I can grasp his reasons for a less public agreement, if he is of a mind to delay or prevent war. If my mother had been more determined to have peace then, it might have succeeded." He stared off into the distance, as if remembering Victoria evoked so much he could not give his attention to Ragoczy and his memories at the same time.

"The Hague was not what Nicholas had hoped it would be," Ragoczy said carefully, knowing that he was on poor footing. Any remark he made that could be construed as disparaging of the Czar would earn Edward's immediate disapproval whether Edward agreed with Ragoczy or not.

Edward got up abruptly; Ragoczy did the same, moving more gracefully than the King. "It's getting dark. We'd probably better go in. There will be tea and sherry. I would invite you to join us, but the French Ambassador would be offended. Very touchy about protocol, the French. To say nothing of the nature of your work. We don't want your purpose known or speculated about. I'll have a word with George later in the evening, so he will know what his Russian cousin is doing." He accepted Ragoczy's bow. "I will expect to hear from you within the fortnight. Give my regards to Nichi, and my nephew Willy." Without looking to determine where his escort was, he stumped down the steps and trod heavily off across the garden, paying no heed to the two men who scrambled after him.

Motoring to Chalfont Saint Giles the next afternoon, Ragoczy had leisure to review all he had been told by Edward and to enlarge on the report he was preparing for encoding for Czar Nicholas, which he would deliver to the Russian embassy the following week, to be hand-carried back to Nicholas. He was afraid that what he told the Czar would not encourage him, and that caused him a few qualms.

"Which turn were we told to take?" Harris asked as they passed Chalfont Saint Peter's on Denham Lane.

Roger answered for his master. "The second turn on the left after Chalfont Common on the right. There ought to be a gatehouse." He studied the map Sunbury had sketched for them.

"A gatehouse on the left. Very good," said Harris, who did not like taking instruction from Roger.

The gatehouse had originally been built in the reign of Henry VIII and still showed the half-timbering that was characteristic of the Tudor style. But the roof had been recently ornamented with gargoyle spouts along the edge of the roof-slates and the mullioned windows had modern stained glass inserts of lotus blossoms and blooming wisteria. The gate itself was wrought-iron in a design of roses on a trellis, and was manned by a bored, middle-aged servant who put aside the penny-dreadful he had been reading to inquire who the late arrival in the Silver Ghost might be. "They thought you'd be here sooner, Count. They're having charades tonight, and cards," he informed Ragoczy as he checked the list of invited guests and compared it to the inscribed card Roger handed to him.

"Is that the whole of it? Charades and cards?" Harris asked as they went through the opened gates; he had assumed that among the aristocracy parties would be more interesting, more scandalous.

"Probably not, but it is all he will admit to us," said Ragoczy dryly, doing his best to keep from being troubled by the possibility of scrutiny. If such surveillance was taking place, the ones who would be most keenly aware of it would be the servants. "Roger, if you will, listen to the servants. I am curious what their—"

"Gossip is, yes, my master," said Roger with so little inflection that it was difficult to decide how he felt about such an assignment.

"You listen to servants? Why?" Harris asked, startled at the notion that Ragoczy might have done the same for him. "Not to overstep myself, sir," he added conscientiously.

"Yes, I listen to servants; a man in my position is a fool if he does not. Servants know so much more than most give them credit for knowing. I have come to value what they learn, and to appreciate their opinions." He shifted in the seat as he became aware that Harris was trying unsuccessfully to locate him in his rearview mirror.

Roger provided a distraction. "Be alert, Harris," he said. "Longacres is said to have a herd of deer wandering the grounds. It is late enough in the day that they might well be about."

"Deer," he repeated, and thought briefly that he was being twitted.

"The herd is considered one of the finest of its sort," said Ragoczy, his manner wholly sincere.

Harris shook his head as he tried to decide why anyone would want a private herd of deer. He supposed they were being raised for venison. Obediently he put his concentration on the rhododendrons flanking the road. To be doubly safe, he switched on the lights although it was still light enough without them. He slowed down for extra safety, and was therefore more able to gawk at the impressive mansion that came into view as they rounded the bend leading to a small stone bridge over a stream running next to the flank of the building.

The Longacres house was in the shape of a capital I, its upper and lower cross-beams extended to the east to create a wide, shallow court-yard paved with old stones taken from the original wall that once sur-rounded the place. The central part of the massive house was thirteenth century, the stone worn and uneven except where the ongoing repairs had mended them; scaffolding and canvas drapes indicated the work was not yet finished. The crosses at the end were Tudor, replete with the Tudor kettle arches, with low-relief carvings of the family device— nebule per fess, azure over argent, in bend three martlets volant sable—above them, recalling the time when the Pearce family fortunes had flourished. Most of the windows were new, with art nouveau stained glass panels worked into them. The house had been wired for electricity six years ago and now it sparkled as the lights were turned on for the guests gathering for tea.

"Will you *look* at that?" exclaimed Harris as he brought the Silver Ghost to a halt at the edge of the graveled drive.

Ragoczy who had seen everything from hovels to pyramids, from car-avan camps to the Forbidden City, from the ruins of Persian palaces to the ruins of Incan cities, gave Longacres a swift perusal, finding its ex-uberance and unashamed display oddly endearing. "Let the staff show you where to park the car, Harris," he said as he saw three servants com-ing out to them.

The butler, a thick-bodied, baby-faced man of about thirty-five, wel-comed the newcomer, saying, "You must be Count Saint-Germain. We were told you would be delayed."

"Yes; I am Saint-Germain," said Ragoczy as he got out of the motor car. "This is my manservant, Roger; if you will tell him where to take my things, I would appreciate it."

"Very good, sir," said the butler, and turned to Roger. "If you will fol-low me?" He then glanced at Harris. "Thayer there"—he pointed to the Longacres chauffeur who was coming toward them—"will direct you to the guests' garage."

"We appreciate your service," said Ragoczy. "It would seem I am late. I ought to change for—"

"There is a buffet being laid at seven," said the butler, adding, "We keep countrified hours and dining here. But there will be a midnight supper." This last provided the butler a modicum of satisfaction, as if the midnight supper were a saving grace. He hurried to keep up with Ragoczy, for although the butler was taller than the black-cloaked guest, he did not move as swiftly, or as silently, as the foreigner did.

"Does Longacres keep country hours in the morning?" asked Ragoczy, dreading the necessity of rising shortly after dawn.

"Actually, no," said the butler. "The Pearce-Mannings have breakfast laid at eight in the morning room. About half the weekend guests avail themselves of it." They had reached the entrance to the house which had been improved with a decastyle art nouveau portico, partially concealed by the canvas draping. In the center of the portico was the new porch, almost finished, an unlikely wedding of the gothic style of the original building and the modern art nouveau. The butler ushered Ragoczy through the new double doors of vine-carved oak, remarking as he did, "The electric lanterns are the latest of Madame's trumpery."

Ragoczy smiled blandly as he surrendered his cloak, "I rather like them," he said, taking the butler aback.

Before the butler could think of an answer, a woman about as tall as Ragoczy came up to him; she was dressed in the height of fashion, her pale yellow afternoon dress with elbow length sleeves, a high waist with a belt of deep-blue satin, and matching piping on the long lace peplums curving halfway down the organdy skirt. There was a faded prettiness about her, from her beautifully coiffed dark blond hair to the subtle use of cosmetics, and a determined air of wealth: sapphire drops in her ears and a sapphire choker complimented her sapphire ring on the hand she extended to Ragoczy. "Good afternoon, Saint-Germain; welcome to Longacres. We were afraid we would not see you until after dark. With rain coming, you would not want to be out in the night. I am Clarice Pearce-Manning, and I am delighted you were able to join us." As Ragoczy bowed over her hand, she addressed the butler. "Thank you, Waithe. You may escort the Count's manservant to his master's apartment, and then his own." She had worked to eradicate any American sound from her voice, but some of it lingered in the letter "r" and an occasionally flat vowel.

The butler complied promptly but stiffly.

"Should I address you as Lady, or Missus?" Ragoczy asked as he released her hand. "I would like to know which you prefer."

This was just the right tone to set. She laughed expertly, like the tinkling sound of fountains. "We don't stand on ceremony here, Count. You may call me Clarice."

It was easier, Ragoczy thought, to be on Christian name terms with your guests if you take the lead in the matter. He looked her squarely in the eyes, and said, "Very well. I am Franchot."

"Franchot Saint-German," she said eagerly.

"Franchot Ragoczy, Count Saint-Germain," he corrected her, his manner deliberately gentle.

Color heightened in her face; she ducked her head in chagrin. "Of course. That was a foolish mistake. I beg your pardon."

"Nothing of the sort," he assured her. "It might have as easily been one as the other." And, he added inwardly, often had been.

She did her best to recover. "No doubt you will want to freshen up after your drive down. Your room is on the first floor"—she pointed to the gallery above them surrounding the main hall—"at the end of the corridor on your left." She smiled again. "Waithe will have shown your manservant there already, using the side stairs." As she stepped back, she said, "We are having tea in the south drawing room, if you would like to join us when you are ready. There is just enough light left to see the ornamental lake. The deer come down to the water to drink about this time."

"I think it might be best if I changed for the evening; you will surely be done with tea before I come down," he said, wanting to avoid questions about his failure to eat for as long as possible.

"Carlisle and Anselm will be looking forward to seeing you," she said, "And there are several of our guests who want to meet you."

Ragoczy took this prompting without annoyance, although he found it disconcerting to think of his solicitor as Carlisle instead of Sunbury. "And I them." He bowed slightly. "Well, the sooner I begin, the sooner I will finish."

"Certainly," said Clarice Pearce-Manning. "There's no need to feel hurried. We try to let everyone go at his own pace here."

As he prepared to mount the stairs to the first floor, he said, "Thank you so much for inviting me. As a stranger in England, I am grateful for your hospitality."

She brightened considerably. "No such thing, Coun— Franchot." If she had intended to say anything more, it was cut short by a voice from the top of the stairs.

"All right, Mother. Will this do?" By indication, she meant the dark-russet afternoon dress with a deep-brown velvet bolero jacket over it.

Startled, Ragoczy looked up; the young woman above him was fastening a jeweled brooch to the center of the jacket, her abrupt movements eloquently expressing her state of mind. She was as tall as her mother, but her short-cut hair was strawberry blonde and her eyes were almost gold instead of hazel. Her hands were large, long, and supple, with neat, short-trimmed nails. She was not pretty in the prevailing fashion, but her fine classic features were timeless. "Excuse me," he said, realizing that she was unaware of his presence.

"Gracious, Rowena, must you make such a fuss?" said her mother, doing her best to put a good face on their encounter. "Rowena, this is our guest, Franchot Ragoczy, Count Saint-Germain; Franchot, my daughter Rowena."

She studied Ragoczy briefly, and said frostily, "Good evening," before returning her attention to her mother. "I never thought you would make such a fuss about a cycling costume. I thought," she went on with heavy emphasis, "since we are in the country, it wouldn't matter."

"But, Rowena; for *tea?*" Clarice laughed artificially, and turned to Ragoczy in order to show her concern. "You have to pardon my daughter. She is used to flouting polite convention."

Rowena clicked her tongue impatiently. "Yes. You'd better get up to your rooms, Count, unless you want to witness another family altercation."

"I have no intention of intruding," said Ragoczy, reluctant to push his way past Rowena in order to leave mother and daughter in private.

"For heaven's sake, Rowena," her mother chided her. "Not in front of our guest. Stop trying to embarrass your father and me. Come down and have tea. Rupert is waiting; he came specially, to see you."

Something in her golden eyes told Ragoczy that Rowena was not best pleased with this news. She swept past him as she came down the stairs at last; Ragoczy caught a faint trace of her perfume and saw that she was wearing small rose-shaped cat's-eye studs in her ears; he also sensed her defiance which was barely held in check. "All right. I'm ready. We're off to feed the lions," she said, more for her mother's benefit than Ragoczy's.

"Rowena, Rowena," Clarice chided her, preparing to bustle her off to the south drawing room.

Climbing upward, Ragoczy glanced back once, and saw the two women standing close together at the south-leading corridor, arguing in whispers. Whatever their dispute was, he sensed from the tone of their voices, it was an ongoing one not limited to cycling costumes and afternoon dresses. As he resumed his upward progress, he heard the women's footsteps retreating from the hall. He reached the first floor and paused to look around the gallery; the floor above had been removed and now a vast stained-glass window occupied the top of the hall. It was not light enough to see the window in all its splendor, but the electric lights ranged below showed a fine illustration of an old-fashioned map of the world, with a string of facetted red dots linking the west coast of America to Buckinghamshire, England. He heard the first drops of rain strike the glass and went on down the corridor.

Roger was waiting inside the open door. "Two rooms, and a bath shared with the next suite on," he said as he showed Ragoczy the apartment. "A study and a bedroom. Very luxurious."

"Hardly surprising, given the rest of the house," Ragoczy said. "I was warned it might be a trifle grand."

Long centuries of familiarity with his master made Roger laugh once. "What will it be like when it is complete, do you guess."

"Not as excessive as Versailles." Ragoczy nodded as he watched Roger unpack his clothes; he stood in the doorway between the two rooms, wondering if he had made an error in coming here. It was, he knew, too soon to tell, but past experience had taught him circumspection. "I should change for the evening. It will buy me some time before I meet the rest of the guests."

"Certainly," said Roger. "Incidentally, speaking of Versailles," he added as he came from the bedroom with Ragoczy's evening clothes draped over his arm, "there are four mirrors in the bathroom, one of them full-length, on the door to the other suite."

"And the one over the dresser, I see," said Ragoczy. He drew a long breath. "Well, it can't be helped."

"Should I cover the one in the bedroom?" asked Roger.

"Best not," said Ragoczy. "The chambermaids might remark on it. Leave the mirrors as they are. I will be careful of them." He unbuttoned his jacket and handed it to Roger. "I am going to wash my face."

"Are you in any rush? I can have everything ready in ten minutes," Roger stated as Ragoczy went to the bathroom door.

"On the contrary, I would be grateful of a delay. I am not hankering for tea." His ironic smile came and went quickly; Ragoczy left Roger to finish unpacking.

It was nearing six in the evening when Ragoczy finally left his rooms. He was in evening clothes, his white waistcoat impeccable under his silk-lined wool jacket. The studs in his silk shirt were rubies, and his cufflinks displayed his eclipse device. He had not bothered with gloves nor watch. He wore this elegance with ease and was more impressive because of it. As he reached the stairs, he encountered Rowena once again. "Miss Pearce-Manning," he said, favoring her with a slight bow.

"Oh, blast it," she swore as she caught sight of him. "I'm going to be late again, aren't I?"

"Possibly; I suspect I am early," said Ragoczy, standing aside for her on the stairs to give her room.

"It's ridiculous, this constant changing of clothes. You'd think we were in a play." She stopped two steps below him. "Pray don't be offended, Count, but I can't see the purpose of"—she plucked the deep-brown velvet sleeve of her jacket—"all this bother."

"Perhaps its value," Ragoczy ventured, "is in its lack of purpose."

"Form rather than substance, you mean?" She stared at him as if they had never met before; interest sparked her golden eyes. "You may be right," she said. "But there is so much form and so little substance."

"And that troubles you: I wonder why." His dark eyes rested on her golden ones.

For a moment his penetrating gaze unnerved her, then she regained her composure. "Mother would tell you it is nothing more than my willfulness," she said, and prepared to get by him, taking the next step.

He stopped her with a single question. "What would you say?"

Her attempt at laughter was not a success; she shook her head. "I won't impose on you, Count. It would be bad—"

"Form?" he interjected with a lift of his fine brows. "It may be, but the substance interests me." Because he was a step above her, he looked down into her face rather than directly at her.

Now she was truly disconcerted. "Surely you don't want to know. You are being polite, which is very diplomatic of you—"

"Miss Pearce-Manning, I am not practicing courtesy: I am curious about you, and I would like to know why you are so bothered by this . . . function." He gave her plenty of room to pass him.

As she reached the gallery, she hesitated once again, then swung around to look at him, a challenge in her eyes, as if she expected him to be at the foot of the staircase; this was her test of his sincerity of interest. To her surprise Ragoczy stood where he had been a few seconds before, watching her with an enigmatic expression. "Perhaps," she said, feeling she had to say something, "we will discuss this later. If you are still curious. After dinner, if you like."

He nodded to her. "I shall look forward to it."

Most of the weekend guests had gone to their rooms to change and only Carlisle Sunbury, still in his afternoon tweeds, an abandoned cup of tea on the occasional table beside him, waited for Ragoczy in the south drawing room, sunk comfortably in a plush-upholstered chair. As he caught sight of Ragoczy, he said lazily, "What, no Orders?"

Ragoczy shrugged. "I thought they would be presumptuous."

"Oh, they would be; they would be. But Clarice would be enchanted. Particularly Saint Stephen of Hungary. All those diamonds would thrill her, and the sash." He rose and shook Ragoczy's small hand, and was, as always, startled by its strength. "She'd love to host a diplomatic reception, and may still achieve her goal."

"And offer superior amusements and food," said Ragoczy. "Women who want to make a mark in society always do." He realized he sounded cynical, and that shocked him. "I apologize for that," he added swiftly. "I am not succeeding at my task as I wish to and I am taking it out on others."

Sunbury gestured his lack of concern. "Not that what there isn't some truth in what you say. And you must have had a chance to see such women in many places other than London and Saint Petersburg."

It was not a matter Ragoczy wanted to discuss, for it led to speculations he had learned over the centuries were not to his advantage. "When one travels . . ." He left the rest unspoken.

"I would think so," said Sunbury, hardly noticing when two servants came and drew the heavy draperies across the window, though they gave Ragoczy a sense of relief, for now that it was almost fully dark out, reflections were forming on the glass. "You haven't met the rest of the Pearce-Mannings, have you?"

"Only mother and daughter," said Ragoczy.

"Daughter, is it? I take it you don't mean Penelope; she's only ten and not prepared to take on Clarice." He rocked back on his heels. "Not that Penelope won't be her own kind of handful, one day."

"Rowena," said Ragoczy, not interested in having their conversation wander too far afield, "Handsome woman, in her twenties, modish red-blonde hair? We were introduced shortly after I arrived, when I seem to have stepped into a dispute between her and her mother." He gave Sunbury a long, speculative look, seeing something in the solicitor's usually stoic expression that prompted him to add, "I would not be far wrong, I suppose, if I guessed you know what the dispute is about."

"Painting," said Sunbury succinctly.

"What painting?" Ragoczy asked, intrigued. He had not anticipated anything of the sort: only then did he realized he had been more than idly speculating about the woman.

"Whose painting is more like it. Rowena has decided to become an artist and her mother is beside herself. She's been trying to get Rowena properly married for seven years; Rowena won't have it." Sunbury made a gesture to show he thought the whole thing ridiculous.

"The parents are refusing to support her painting, I gather," said Ragoczy, puzzled. "There seemed to be a degree of animosity that—" "They can't," said Sunbury, cutting in. "Not in any material way. The girl's about to come into a trust fund from her grand-father, so there's nothing much her mother or father can do to stop her. According to what I've been told, Rowena has threatened to take a place of her own and take up the study seriously. The family may not like it, but there is little they can do. She's of age." He coughed discreetly behind his hand. "I'm not betraying any confidence, saying this to you. You'll hear about it soon enough, one way or another. Clarice has been complaining about it since everyone arrived yesterday, and very likely longer."

Ragoczy listened with increasing interest. "Does she have talent?"

"How would I know? I've never seen her work. I wouldn't think so, given what she comes from." He stopped short as he nodded slightly to the man in evening clothes who came into the room. "Good evening, Geoffrey. Let me make the two of you known to each other."

Geoffrey Pearce-Manning was tall, loose-limbed and square-jawed, between fifty and fifty-five, with receding dark-auburn hair going white at the temples, and a neat mustache over a small mouth in a pleasant but unremarkable face. More noticeable than his features were the eye-glasses in tortoise-shell frames he wore, and to further distinguish himself, he sported a deep-blue waistcoat under his black jacket, and a matching silk handkerchief in his jacket pocket. Catching sight of an unfamiliar guest, he held out his hand as he came forward, filled with conviviality. "You're Ragoczy, aren't you? We'd about given you up."

"I am," said Ragoczy, taking Pearce-Manning's hand and noticing the lack of firmness in his grip, so much at odds with the line of his jaw. "I apologize for having to come late, but unexpected obligations kept me in town."

"It is often difficult to break away, especially for those at the beck and call of the mighty. No matter; at least you arrived ahead of the rain," said Pearce-Manning, meaning it. "Saturday evening is generally our best in the weekend."

"I'm looking forward to it," said Ragoczy, realizing there was actually some truth in his assertion. "But I fear," he said, "I do not motor well. It would be wise for me to—"

Again Sunbury interrupted. "What Ragoczy is trying to say is that he has a delicate constitution and coddles it shamelessly. He does not take his meals with anyone, not in all the years I've known him."

"I do not like to impose . . . my necessary tastes . . . on those unwilling to share them," Ragoczy said very quietly.

"Hum!" Pearce-Manning said, revealing he did not know what was appropriate to say. "Dashed inconvenient for you. Well, if you get peckish, send word down to the kitchen. They'll boil up some broth for you, or whatever else you would like." He knew his duties as a host and did what he could to execute them graciously.

"You're good to offer, but it will not be necessary," said Ragoczy. "I will fend for myself, thank you."

"You are of a robust nature, by the look of you," said Pearce-Manning, surveying Ragoczy's compact, powerful body. "I won't bother myself about your well-being." His smile was automatic, revealing little of his thoughts. He took a cigarette case from inside his jacket and, opening it, offered it to Ragoczy.

"He doesn't smoke, either; I used to think he had taken a religious vow," said Sunbury, a curious satisfaction in his eyes.

"I suppose I have, of sorts," said Ragoczy lightly, recalling that night four thousand years ago when the god of his people had given Ragoczy his blood to drink, assuring that he, too, would one day be a god to his people, and provisionally immortal.

"Oriental or Catholic?" asked Pearce-Manning, taken aback, his good manners nearly failing him.

"Nothing so dramatic. It is a . . . tradition for those of my blood." Ragoczy said. "I strive not to impose on anyone in this regard."

"Commendable, I'm sure," said Pearce-Manning, his urbanity firmly back in place.

"No doubt you will want to talk without my interference," said Sunbury, apparently convinced that Ragoczy and his host would find much to discuss. "And I must go change. Cocktails in the main hall in what?— forty minutes or so?" He turned on his heel and loped off, leaving Ragoczy and Pearce-Manning to continue their conversation as best they might.

"My wife tells me you arrived in a Silver Ghost," said Pearce-Manning after he had lit his cigarette.

"Yes. A superior motor car," said Ragoczy. "I also keep a Vauxhall for my manservant's use."

"Good English companies," said Pearce-Manning. "Solid."

"That they are," Ragoczy agreed with the ease of a man long familiar with the rules of small talk, which the English cultivated assiduously.

"You might want to tell Asquith. Or Churchill, over at Trade. It's the sort of thing he likes to hear." His smoothing of his mustache was his single concession to pride. "He's coming over in the morning—Asquith, not Churchill—weather and politics permitting—to do some shooting with us."

"Your wife must be delighted to have the chance to entertain the Prime Minister," said Ragoczy, not making it apparent that he was choosing his words carefully.

"As to that, I've known H. H. for donkeys' years. We were at school together; he was two years ahead of me, but we occasionally spoke; you know, as you do at university." The use of Asquith's Balliol College nickname was not as calculated as it would have been had his wife spoken it, but he had intended to impress Ragoczy, or at least startle him; the foreigner's self-possession unnerved him. "Done a very creditable job thus far, though it's early days yet. Not that I agree with him on all the issues; I'm not a Liberal, myself. This determination he has to limit the power of the Lords could well lead to a ruction in Commons. Who knows what would happen, once they get the bit in their teeth?" Having made his point, he said, "Would you like to meet him?"

"Actually, he and I met briefly seven years ago," said Ragoczy quietly. "I would appreciate renewing my acquaintance with him, if you would be kind enough."

"Certainly," said Pearce-Manning, disappointed that his ploy had not gone as he had hoped. He was spared any more surprises from Ragoczy as the sound of high heels announced the arrival of his wife. With an emotion very like relief, he took half a dozen steps toward her. "Clarice, my dear. I was just wondering what had become of you. You look superb."

"Geoffrey," she exclaimed. "And . . . Franchot." She relished the approval her husband offered her, but wanted to find the same endorsement from her guest. "I wanted to remind you that it is about time for cocktails. In the main hall. Waithe is setting everything out." She came a little further into the room so that the light struck her more fully. Her evening dress was a fashionable concoction of gossamer silk, in tiered, deep-ruffled sleeves to match the tiered, deep ruffled skirts, all in varying shades of rose; the bodice was a soft-mauve satin over which she wore a triple-rope of pearls.

"Do you need any assistance from me?" her husband asked as he regarded her proudly.

"Not really, but I could use your company," she replied, slipping her hand through the crook of his arm. "Will you join us, Franchot?"

Remembering he had several tasks to accomplish over the next twenty-four hours, Ragoczy bowed slightly. "It would be my honor," he said, falling into step beside them and listening courteously as Clarice Pearce-Manning led the way back toward the main hall. She began to recite the history of the family, starting with the alliance of the Mannings and Pearces at the time of the Restoration.

"The Pearces were not staunch supporters of the Stewarts, you know, and when Charles II returned as King, they decided it would be wise to include a more truly Royalist name in their own." She smiled at Ragoczy, the first stirrings of triumph within her.

"A prudent act," said Ragoczy, hoping, as he heard the continuing chronicle of the family, that he would be able to find out more about Sinclair-Howard during the evening, that he would have a chance for a private word with Prime Minister Asquith the following morning, and that he might discover why Rowena Pearce-Manning wanted to be a painter.

Text of a note from Herzog Vaclav Persuic to Baron Klemens von Wolgast.

Trieste
February 25, 1910

My dear von Wolgast;

Let me thank you again for the entertainment you provided during my visit to Berlin; Italian-Croatian relations have never been so fervent, and to have had the privilege of meeting the sublime Nadezna as well: I will not soon forget the evening; I have become the envy of my colleagues because of it.

I have met with my associates and discussed what I have observed of your improved mechanism. They are inclined to purchase the items we reviewed, but my superior wishes to see for himself before our order is official. I trust you will receive him in the same generous spirit you showed to me.

If all goes well, we can conclude our negotiations to our mutual satisfaction before August. At that time, a suitable deposit will be made to guarantee your prompt attention to our order, as well as a speedy and reliable delivery. For us, time is an important factor in our dealings, which I urge you to remember.

With anticipation of a happy resolution in our dealings, I express my confidence in your product and your integrity.

Vaclav Persuic

5

Ragoczy stared down at the telegram in his hand, his attractive, irregular features set in world-weary lines which were softened by the faded evening light coming from the windows of his laboratory at the top of his leased house. Methodically he folded the telegram and put it into his inner jacket pocket before glancing up at Roger, who waited in the door leading to his study. "We are going to Berlin in ten days. Nicholas does not want us to linger here when we might be making more progress with Wilhelm." The slight lift of his brows revealed eloquently his sardonic agreement with this notion.

"Ten days?" Roger asked. "Not immediately?"

"My departure is not to appear rushed. Nicholas tells me to make it known that business dealings are calling me away from London, so that no one will speculate about the reason for my leaving: he includes Edward in that. Apparently he is not as sanguine about his uncle's cooperation as he was when I left Saint Petersburg." He went to the window and stared out through the filmy curtains into the gathering dusk; three floors down he could see Harris returning in the Vauxhall from tea with his sister's family. The headlamps marked his turning into the alley leading to the garage at the side of the small back garden. "Madelaine is returning to Monbussy-sur-Marne in a month. I had hoped to visit her, if only for a day or two, before going to Berlin."

"Perhaps when you return to London?" Roger suggested. "There will probably be a return to London, I should think, and you might reasonably go through France as through Holland." He was stretching a point and he knew it.

"You're right, of course. It would be easier, making most of the trip by train," Ragoczy conceded with a quirk of a smile. "And with any luck we will have the opportunity to—" He stopped. "This is foolish of me."

"Not foolish, my master. You are lonely." Roger had long since earned the privilege of making such blunt observations to Ragoczy. "And you did not visit any of the women at Longacres in her sleep, so you have not had even that to sustain you."

"There are others," said Ragoczy, his voice remote.

"Such as the woman last night? The one who does not talk to foreigners?" Roger's voice was low and respectful, but his disbelief was obvious; though he challenged Ragoczy, it was from concern, not impudence. "Was your visit to persuade her she was wrong about foreigners or to take your sustenance from the pleasure she had of her dreams?" Ragoczy stood silent for a short while, then turned away from the window. "Why it is you always require me to accept my nature so uncompromisingly?"

"I? If I do it is because it is what you strive to do. You are more rigorous than I am," said Roger, his voice level. "Only when you are feeling most isolated do you resort to such risks."

"It is no simple matter to make the required connections to fulfill my needs wholly," Ragoczy said, sad, wry amusement in his dark eyes.

"You have managed it under more difficult circumstances than these," Roger reminded him sharply. "As the Emir's son learned to his distress."

"But never under such constant scrutiny as I am now: not even the Emir's son kept such stringent watch," said Saint-Germain. "Oh, you thought I was unaware of that fox-faced man with the ginger mustache who has been following me for well over a week? To say nothing of the retired soldier who is doing a very poor job of his work?" He turned his small hands upward, to show his indecision. "I suppose the soldier is employed by someone in the British government, possibly for Sinclair-Howard, but perhaps not. The second man, however—he may be employed by the Czar, one of his ministers, or any number of others. I cannot easily determine who employs him. With such attention to my movements, it is not an opportune time to court anyone. So I will limit myself to dreams and the satisfaction I can share with the women I visit."

Roger said nothing for a moment, then remarked, "Didn't you receive an invitation from Miss Pearce-Manning to visit her studio?"

With a crack of laughter, Ragoczy said, "Is my curiosity about her so obvious. Yes. And well you know it."

"Your watchers would not think too much of it if you should visit her—not after the weekend at Longacres. They already know you went there." He studiously avoided looking directly at Ragoczy. "She must have interest in you, as well, or she might not have invited you."

"She might not," Ragoczy said neutrally.

"Where is the harm in going, then?" Roger asked, and prepared to leave Ragoczy to his thoughts and his laboratory.

"Remember, we must leave in ten days," Ragoczy warned him.

"Ten days is ample time—for a great many things. Harris will be in the kitchen by now." He bowed slightly and left the room, closing the door with care.

Ragoczy remained where he was for some little time, then went to his trestle table; his volume of notes on fuel designs lay open, and next to it, a note in his small, neat hand, politely declining Rowena Pearce-Manning's invitation to her studio. The light in his laboratory was almost gone, but his eyes were not hampered by darkness. He picked this up, read it through twice, then tore it in half and drew another sheet of paper from his stationery box. He sat down on the tall stool in front of the table, pulled his pen from his waistcoat breast pocket, and began to write a second note to Rowena, this time accepting her invitation.

The next morning two short letters arrived at Ragoczy's house within half an hour of each other: one, delivered by messenger, from Edward VII, requesting Ragoczy join him for another private conversation that evening at the Duke of York's Theatre for the performance of Shaw's new play *Misalliance*; Julian Sinclair-Howard would be charged with bringing him to the antechamber of the King's Box where they might speak without fear of interruption. Rowena Pearce-Manning's reply, coming with the morning post, was less specific, informing Ragoczy of the times during the next week when he could find her at her studio.

By evening Ragoczy was in full formal wear, but once again without the Orders to emblazon him. "If I am to be inconspicuous," he said to Roger as he prepared to leave for the Duke of York's Theatre, "I should not spangle myself."

Roger held Ragoczy's cloak for him. "I will have your study ready for you when you return."

"Do not worry, old friend," said Ragoczy quietly. "I am not planning to get my hopes up. If King Edward wishes to discuss the rudiments of an agreement, I will think my task has gone well. The Czar may not be entirely satisfied, but I will." He frowned as he drew on his Florentine gloves. "Sinclair-Howard is behaving as if he has been . . . what is the expression? brought to heel."

"You do not sound fully convinced about this," said Roger.

"I am not. And I wish I knew why." He took his tall silk hat, carrying it rather than wearing it. "Well, Harris is waiting," he added briskly, and went out of his house to the Silver Ghost, standing like a metal wraith in the thickening fog.

"Good evening to you, Count," said Harris as Ragoczy climbed in.

"And to you, Harris." He paused as he settled himself, then said, "If you would like to see the play tonight, I will provide you a ticket." He had already arranged for it, knowing he would have to wait until the play was finished to depart; to do anything else would draw too much attention to his mission.

Harris had confined his theatre-going to music halls and the occasional pantomime, and so hesitated. "Will it be very long, sir?" "It may seem so." Ragoczy sighed, then relented. "But as it happens, I am not fond of Mister Shaw's plays, which are more like debates than dramas. You may enjoy it well enough."

"Then, yes, Count, I would like to see it—to be able to say I have." This candid confession of social ambition made Ragoczy smile.

They arrived at the Duke of York's Theatre a scant eight minutes before the curtain was to rise; the fog had slowed their progress through the London traffic. A place had been marked for Ragoczy's Rolls-Royce, which Harris greeted with the gratitude of a sailor sighting land.

"There is a ticket at the box office in your name. Just tell them who you are and then go where the usher directs you." Ragoczy lost no time getting out of the Silver Ghost and striding away into the theatre.

"Count," Sinclair-Howard exclaimed with a great display of courtesy belied by the hard expression in his blue eyes. He had jostled his way through the arriving audience to reach the newcomer. "I was beginning to wonder if you would be here in time. I should not have worried." His blather stopped short as Ragoczy interrupted.

"I would prefer not to keep the King waiting." He softened this with a slight smile, but Sinclair-Howard took it as a rebuke.

"Of course." He was stiff with umbrage. "If you will be good enough to follow me? Mind the stairs."

The King was in high color and tending to wheeze as he greeted Ragoczy in the anteroom. "I wanted to have another chance to speak with you before you depart: I am informed you are leaving shortly for the Continent."

"Berlin. Yes. I have business dealings there that require my attention." Ragoczy had bowed and now accepted Edward's invitation to sit opposite him.

"And, of course, my nevvy Wilhelm is there." There was sly and cynical amusement in Edward's eyes. "I would have thought you had a more creditable excuse than this one. Business dealings!" he scoffed.

Ragoczy was unruffled. "I am the patron of a ballet school there, and I have investments in two Berlin companies, one of them working with Karl Landsteiner to develop more reliable ways of analyzing blood, incorporating the work of Phoebus Levene in America." He recalled his excitement when he had learned of the two scientists' work on blood. "The other company is developing fuels for motor cars and lorries. My solicitor will vouch for this, if you want to assure yourself of these things."

"No doubt he would vouch for you, as any worthwhile solicitor would," said Edward with a sour smile. "All right. For the sake of argument, we will agree that it is business and not Nichi that calls you away to Berlin." He spread his thick hands on his knees. "And speaking of Nichi, we ought to reach some kind of gentlemen's agreement about this arms limitation business, so that we will not have to start all over in the summer, when I will be able to address the question publicly." He kept his voice low so as not to disturb those in the box behind them listening to the play.

"I would be grateful to you, Majesty." Ragoczy began to hope his visit this evening had not been in vain.

"I'm not doing this for you, I am doing it because I can see what Nichi is worried about. He is nearer the problem than I am. That doesn't mean I have no appreciation of the European situation. The signs are everywhere around us, aren't they? The world is changing, and not only in matters of industry and trade. You need only look at Vienna to realize that some changes will come, whether we want them or not." He leaned back in his chair as if to draw more air in when he breathed.

Ragoczy watched the King with increased concern: Edward was definitely worse than he had been a dozen or so days ago. "Majesty, forgive me for saying this, but you appear to be in need of rest." It was the most indirect way he could express his apprehension.

"What King is not?" Edward asked, scowling. "I have heard much the same from my physician these five years and more."

Hearing this, Ragoczy felt real alarm. "How do you mean?"

Edward waved the question away. "It is nothing. Let us devote ourselves to the question of arms." It was much more an order than a suggestion. "You tell me Nichi wants Wilhelm and me to join with him in exerting pressure on the manufacturers of arms in our own countries, that pressure intended to bring about a reduction of development and sales of arms. Probably a sensible thing in Russia, given the political climate there. I am not certain the problem is as urgent here in England, or in Europe." He coughed and went on. "I cannot achieve any useful limitation without the help of Parliament, as Nichi cannot without the Duma to support it, assuming it is possible to do. How does he propose to manage that?"

Ragoczy leaned forward so that Edward would hear him clearly. "I believe it is his intention to present your private agreement to the

Duma as a fait accompli, so that the debates of factions will not enter into the process."

"And if Wilhelm and I do the same, he assumes the deed will be done? That our governments will have to support it?" He pulled at his lower lip. "It might work, if we were all to act at the same time. That way it would not seem that any of us is at a disadvantage in relation to the others. I can't think how you will convince Wilhelm of this, but if you are able, I am willing to make the attempt."

"To endorse a policy of arms limitation," Ragoczy said, in order to be certain they understood each other.

Edward nodded ponderously. "As long as Wilhelm cooperates with us." He wagged a finger in Ragoczy's direction. "You will have your work cut out for you, Count. Wilhelm is not so temperate a man as I can be, or Nichi."

"I have met the Kaiser a few times, and I am familiar with his reputation," said Ragoczy carefully.

"With businesses in Germany and Austria, you must have done," said Edward. "Well, I can give you no advice on how to approach him. In many ways he and I are as different as chalk and cheese. You are probably more able to determine the most persuasive approach than I am." He paused, trying to listen to the dialogue from the stage. "Someone is bound to ask me what I think of this."

"Say it is thought-provoking," Ragoczy recommended. "Shaw would like that."

"Thought-provoking. Isn't that a trifle obvious?" Edward asked, amusement glittering in his eyes.

"Perhaps. But it would be fitting," Ragoczy said drily.

With a breathy chuckle, Edward returned his attention to Ragoczy's purpose for attending. "So you will know what to report: I am willing to request that Parliament adopt an arms-limitation policy so long as Russia and Germany do the same, and at the same time. I will not lead the way, and I do not think the government will be willing to enter into such an agreement after the fact. Tell my nephew that. I trust it will help bring a happy result." He prepared to rise. "Would you care to join us, Count?"

Knowing better than to refuse an offer from King Edward, Ragoczy said, "I would be delighted, Majesty," even as he resigned himself to an evening he had little hope of liking. He consoled himself with the realization that he would have another opportunity to speak with the King before the evening was over.

But by the end of the play, Edward's color was ashen and Ragoczy did not want to detain the ailing King any longer than necessary. He bowed and thanked Edward for his courtesy, and received a brusque acknowledgement as Edward left his box. Julian Sinclair-Howard was waiting at the entrance to the boxes, unctuously watching the departing audience.

"Was this worth the effort?" the young man asked Ragoczy.

"Yes." Ragoczy was not inclined to confide in Sinclair-Howard. "I must express my gratitude at your arranging my first meeting with the King. This evening might not have been possible without it."

"Might not?" repeated Sinclair-Howard with disdain. "It would not have taken place at all if I had not fulfilled your request."

"The Czar's request," Ragoczy corrected with every sign of cordiality.

"All right: the Czar's request. But you are the messenger for him, and you are the man who must answer to him." He could not keep the snide tone from his voice. "And you are leaving England."

"But I will be coming back, I would reckon before the middle of June," Ragoczy said, so mildly that Sinclair-Howard shot him a keen glance, trying to detect any mockery that might be concealed in his bland words. "You will want to know that."

"Are you keeping the house you let?" he inquired, trying to hide the disgust he felt.

"Certainly, since I will be returning." He turned to Sinclair-Howard as they reached the front of the theatre. "My solicitor will inform you of my plans."

Sinclair-Howard all but audibly ground his teeth. "Thank you, Count. I shall look forward to his information." Before he had to force himself to other egregious small talk, he bowed and turned on his heel.

Harris was waiting by the Silver Ghost, his chauffeur's cap at a rakish angle. He opened the door for Ragoczy, saying as he did, "I know a place or two you might like to visit before I take you home."

Ragoczy did not answer as he got into the motor car; he was still troubled by the way Edward had looked and sounded. Only when Harris had repeated his offer did he rouse himself, saying, "Thank you, Harris. Not tonight."

"Then home it is," Harris said with a shrug of disappointment. Without further remark, he drove off into the fog.

They were almost to Mount Street before Ragoczy asked, "What did you think of the play?"

It took Harris a moment to answer. "It wasn't jolly, not the way I'd thought it might be. But it was very . . . grand." That, he decided, was the right word.

Ragoczy finally smiled. "That it was." He stared out the window at the fog, once again distracted by anxiety; it would probably be wise to seek a meeting with Edward's heir George, to find out his views on arms production and limitation. It was likely that some of the negotiations would fall to George if Edward's condition did not improve. Ragoczy frowned. In another time he might have offered Edward one or more of the medicaments he had learned to produce so long ago, in Thebes, and later in Rome, in China, and in Baghdad. But the King of England was not a man to use such things. These reflections were interrupted by Harris, who had drawn up next to the house.

"Would you prefer to get out here, before I put her in the garage, Count?" he inquired, reluctant to cut into Ragoczy's thoughts.

"Yes, thank you, Harris," said Ragoczy, doing his best to give his attention to his immediate surroundings; he realized that for most of the drive back to his house, he had not bothered to watch for the two men following him. He shook himself mentally as he closed the door of the Rolls-Royce, then peered into the fog, telling himself that anyone attempting to keep watch on him would be as hampered by the fog as he was. It did not wholly relieve him, but he was able to enter his house with a modicum of ease.

Two afternoons later, Ragoczy asked to be driven to Rowena Pearce-Manning's studio. He summoned Harris to the informal dining room off the kitchen, as was his habit when giving orders to his small staff. "It is off of Great Russell Street, or so her invitation informs me." He was dressed for a social call, in a black suit and waistcoat, with a flawless white silk shirt and a deep-red tie. He had spared himself the affectation of a cane, though they were much in fashion. The two he owned concealed weapons, one a sword, and one a small, single-shot pistol; neither struck him as appropriate for his first visit to Rowena's studio.

"The British Museum again," Harris sighed. "Well, the Museum Pub isn't that far from it."

"I will probably be an hour or so," Ragoczy said, doing his best to ignore the pointed look Roger offered him from across the lounge.

"Time for a bit of fodder, then," said Harris, his clever eyes brightening. "I'd appreciate it, sir."

"Oh, ample time," Ragoczy said, and heard Roger stifle a crack of laughter.

Harris realized that he was somehow out of his depth. He touched the brim of his cap and said, "I'll just bring the Ghost around for you, Count."

"Thank you, Harris," said Ragoczy, and looked directly at Roger as Harris departed. "Am I under a misapprehension: I believe you encouraged me to take the time to do this."

Roger maintained his composure. "I did. And I continue to do so."

"To lessen my isolation?" Ragoczy said.

"We have discussed these things before," said Roger without apology: he spoke in the Latin of first-century Rome. "You are willing to undertake this burden the Czar has imposed on you, but you will not find solace for yourself."

Ragoczy answered in the same tongue. "The Czar's mission does have something to do with my . . . hesitation," he admitted. "The stakes are very high, and that means a risk beyond what those of my blood require. How could I justify bringing that young woman to harm?" He held up his small, beautiful hand. "You need not remind me of the number of times I have done so before. I am acutely aware of them."

"She is not Demetrice, or Heugenet, or Xenya, or T'en Chi-Yu, or Nicoris, or Oaxetli." Roger gave his full attention to the silver he was polishing. "Or Madelaine."

"No, nor any of the rest. She is Rowena. I am aware of that." He touched the glossy tabletop as if trying to determine what substance it was. His voice was remote. "Don't you think that I have endangered quite enough women in my life, no matter how many centuries I have lived? To drag Rowena into the intrigue around me as well as expose her to the hazard of my true nature—" He stopped and gave a sardonic smile. "But I am going to visit her, am I not?" He saw Roger nod his answer; he returned to English. "And Harris is probably waiting at the kerb to take me to her."

Roger continued to polish the silver as Ragoczy left the house.

Harris was complaining about the traffic as they neared the British Museum. He shrugged once. "That red-haired ferret whose been keeping you in his sights is four cars back now."

"Have you seen the other one?" Ragoczy asked; he had not been aware of the second watcher for the last two days, and was beginning to wonder if he had been replaced by a more capable observer.

"Not today, or yesterday, come to think of it," Harris said. "Maybe they've given up watching you, at least he has."

"Or he has suffered an illness or an injury," Ragoczy suggested, unconvinced himself. "Or has given up his observation."

"There you are, then." Harris made another of his quick, furtive attempts to catch Ragoczy's reflection in the rearview mirror, and was again frustrated. If only the Count were a little taller, Harris decided, he would be visible.

Ragoczy glanced back and suddenly announced, "I will meet you at the Museum Pub in an hour or so." Then he opened the door and stepped out into the inching traffic.

"Count!" Harris cried in consternation. "Count . . . " He could not follow his employer's progress through the automobiles to the sidewalk. As he resigned himself to waiting at the pub, he decided that Ragoczy was more capable than he seemed at first, with his elegant clothing and courtly manner. If the hour grew late, he would go searching Great Russell Street: it was not so long as to make that impractical.

The building where Rowena had her studio was set at the rear of a tiny court; a Regency jewel which had changed from a private house to a more modern facility with a secretarial agency and an importer's offices on the ground floor, and two flats above. Rowena had the upper flat, with a number of tall windows that would provide the entire flat as much light as could be had in this part of London; that much was apparent from the exterior of the building. The vestibule was not large, reduced in size from its original design when the building was converted to its present uses, but the detailings over the doors and staircase indicated this had been a home of some luxury. As Ragoczy climbed the stairs to Rowena's flat, he decided that she was truly interested in art, for if she had been merely entertaining herself, she would have chosen another kind of flat in a different part of London.

Rowena answered the door promptly, flushing slightly at the sight of her visitor. "Count. Thank goodness it is you."

"I said I would be here." His quizzical expression took the anxiousness from her face. "Were you expecting someone else?"

"No," she said darkly. "But it isn't uncommon for Ru—" She stopped, her annoyance vanishing as she looked at him. She was wearing a sensible, attractive ensemble in topaz-colored wool reminiscent of the cycling costume that had so offended her mother at Longacres. Her strawberry-blonde hair was negligently combed, and she wore no jewelry but a single ring in gold with her initial incised on it. There was a charcoal smudge on her chin that she had not completely succeeded in cleaning off. "How good of you to come."

"And how good of you to invite me," he replied as he crossed the threshold. "I'm flattered that you offered to show me your work."

Again color mounted in her face. "Well, you asked intelligent questions about it. How could I refuse?"

"You might have done," he said, a slight, enigmatic smile in his dark eyes.

She drew back, her mouth tightening. In the small entry her disapproval was emphasized by the confines. "Not I. I do not want to be one of those women who is forever implying and never doing, who puts all her attention to ensnaring a man so that her hopes can be forever thwarted. That is what so many women are taught will advance them in the world. Such . . . feminine wiles! disgust me. It is so demeaning, to see otherwise sensible females simper and wheedle—" She made a sudden gesture to show she had not meant to have such an outburst. "Pardon me, Count. No doubt you are wishing me at Speakers' Corner. I never meant to harangue—I can't stop myself, if I am caught unprepared."

Ragoczy studied her face intently but briefly, seeing her determination to be direct and forthcoming. "You do not like the routines of society, do you?"

"Not since I was a child, and was not allowed to have a rowboat like my brother's. I tried everything I knew to convince them I could manage one as well as he, but nothing persuaded them; to do such a thing was unfeminine," she said in a burst of emotion that again caught her unaware. "I've done it a second time. I'm sorry if that bothers you." She had stepped back into the main room of her flat, and now she stood aside so that Ragoczy could see where she worked. "This used to be the ballroom. It takes up two-thirds of the flat. That was one of the reasons I leased it. I have an annual renewal option with a contract for ten years." Her laughter was self-conscious. "My grand-father has provided me a trust fund."

"Your mother's father, I surmise," Ragoczy said, looking around the large, light chamber with two easels set up, and a small dais on which a number of fir branches had been arranged.

"Certainly. My father's family is constantly on the brink of penury. Grand-father Saxon, on the brighter side, is a multimillionaire." She looked away as if this admission of wealth embarrassed her.

"He is American, I have been told," Ragoczy said as he noticed the wide shelves standing at the back of the room; there were a good number of large sheets of paper lying in them, many with protective tracing paper on top of them.

"Yes. In San Francisco." She made a quick, impulsive gesture. "I must apologize. I'm nervous. I am not used to showing my work to others."

"You have nothing to fear," said Ragoczy, remembering the many times he had called upon artists at their studios over the centuries, and how often the artists had been apprehensive. "I respect the work you do, whether or not it is to my taste."

Once again she looked him directly in the face in her candid way. "Thank you," she said simply.

There was silence between them lasting nearly a minute as the pale northern sun streamed in on them, and then Ragoczy broke the spell by remarking, "What would you like to show me first?"

She went to the window and looked down on the street. "Damn him," she said under her breath.

Ragoczy was startled to hear her swear. "I beg your pardon?"

"Oh," she exclaimed, turning away from the window. "Not you, Count. My current beau, as my grand-father would call him. He watches this place, to be certain I am not taken advantage of." She clicked her tongue impatiently. "I wish he would not."

"Have you told him so?" Ragoczy inquired, regarding her with growing interest, and reminding himself that this unknown suitor could make things awkward between them.

"Yes, several times. He tells me I don't know the world as he does—which is unquestionably the truth—and that I need strong protection only a man can give me." She flung her hands in the air. "He thinks I do not know my own mind."

"More fool he," Ragoczy remarked, his dark eyes softening as they lingered on her face. "About your work?" he suggested.

Her nervousness returned. "I don't know if you'll find the subject appropriate—many people don't—but I've done a number of . . . illustrative drawings, taken from *Dracula*." She saw the slight lift to his fine brows and hurried on, "It . . . it is sensationalistic, certainly, but it has a quality about it . . . a power. I don't know if you're familiar with the book—"

"By Bram Stoker. Yes. I read it, years ago, in self-protection." His irony was lost on her, as he intended it would be.

"I can imagine. Everyone was talking about it, I remember, though I was not yet twelve," she said. "My mother said it was not a proper story for a schoolgirl to read."

"But you read it anyway, and found it inspiring." He offered her a slight bow. "But it is an odd subject for illustrations, I would have thought."

"So I have been told," she said, her hands clasped in front of her. "But the images in the story are so . . . compelling. I—" she laughed self-consciously "—I could not get them out of my mind once I read the book. I wanted to explore the pictures I had formed in my mind. I wanted to be authentic." Again she faltered. "I have not been to the Carpathians."

"Neither had Stoker," Ragoczy pointed out.

She went on as if she had not heard him. "I have read the travel guides, of course, and seen some photographs, but I don't know that I have achieved anything of the look of the place."

At this Ragoczy smiled openly. "And you were hoping that I, being Carpathian, might give you the benefit of my knowledge." He realized as soon as he spoke that he was correct and that she was reluctant to admit it. "Dear Miss Pearce-Manning, if I were an artist, it is precisely what I would do, in your situation. Even if you were to go to Hungary and see the place, it would not necessarily represent what is in the book."

She turned to him, trying to recover herself. "You're right. I was hoping you would tell me how I might make the drawings more accurate, so that when I paint the scenes, they will be a good representation of what is in the story."

"I will be honored to." He took a step closer to her. "I remind you that Stoker did what you are doing—as he had not been to the Carpathians himself, he spoke to a man who knew the region, and I suspect, chose those elements that best suited his purpose; anything that did not, I assume he ignored." The accuracy of the representations in the novel, he thought, were not exact to the locations, but the flavor of the images matched the tone of the novel.

"Then I will not be too proud to do the same," she said, and in a sudden burst of courage, went to the wide shelves and drew out one of the covered drawings. Without pause, she carried it to the nearer of the two easels and set up the sheet, as if allowing herself an instant for reflection would result in a complete failure of nerve. She flung back the tracing-paper cover and moved aside so that Ragoczy could see the drawing. "That is where Jonathan Harker arrives at the Borgo Pass."

The drawing was done with charcoal with a few accents in colored chalk: there was the traveler with his bag standing beside a coach of Austrian design, the road behind him falling away into nothing. Beyond the screen of trees in front of him there was an impression of an approaching vehicle drawn by three or four horses. Ragoczy studied it, surprised by the intensity of the work. "Very evocative," he said after he had scrutinized it. "I like the sense of foreboding."

"Like Stoker?" she asked nervously.

"Much more like Stoker than the actual place, in fact," he admitted, and turned to her. "Do not be dismayed. You have caught the feeling in the novel, which is your intention." He glanced back at the drawing. "The road to the Borgo Pass is very like that—steep slopes and shaggy pines, with high crags above. The pass itself is a series of wide, high meadows, where peasants farm and herd, very open, not at all appropriate to the story, or the . . . atmosphere of the story."

Her voice rose a few notes. "Should I change it? Would it make it better if I did?"

"Not on my account," he said gently, and decided to reiterate his understanding once again. "The novel is inaccurate, and you wish to be true to the novel." He stepped back. "May I see more?"

She took the drawing from the easel and went for another. To keep from becoming too upset, she asked, "How is it you know so much about Mister Stoker?"

"Oh, I had the pleasure of meeting him once, when I was last in England." He heard her sharp intake of breath. "I was somewhat acquainted with his employer, and met him through Henry Irving." He enjoyed her excitement at this revelation.

"You knew Henry Irving?" she asked as she came back with a second sheet.

"I met him three times, I believe." The first time, the great actor had been a clerk in a counting house, still John Henry Brodribb, a youth longing for an opportunity to act. He had been of great help to Ragoczy then.

"Did you ever see him perform? I wish I had," she persisted as she lifted the tracing paper, revealing the courtyard of a medieval castle starting to fall into ruin, a shadowy figure standing in a half-open door. "I had only pictures of German castles to work from."

Ragoczy nodded, and moved nearer to the easel. "That part of Hungary has few castles of that period; most of what they call castles are actually fortresses," he said. "The German model is as good as any Stoker knew." He regarded the work carefully, then stepped back, saying, "Yes, I did see Henry Irving perform. I saw his *Faust*, and his *Hamlet*." He had also seen him as Romeo, his first major role, but that had been many years ago. "There was a great deal of controversy about his interpretation of the Dane, as I recall. I was introduced to Mister Stoker after a performance of *Hamlet*. As I recall, we spoke for half an hour or so, while Sir Henry got into his street clothes." The big, red-haired Irish Jew had impressed Ragoczy with his energy and his unstinting admiration of Henry Irving.

"My mother thought it was shocking when Irving was knighted." She ducked her head as if to mitigate what Clarice had said. "The idea of an actor being made a knight offended her. She believed it compromised all titles to give one to an actor." Quite suddenly Rowena laughed, and finally her nervousness fled.

Ragoczy smiled at her for encouragement. "I notice you sign your work *R. Saxon.* Is that because of your mother, as well?"

"It may seem that way, but I do it as tribute to my grand-father." She indicated the room in a sweep of her arm. "I would not be here if it weren't for his trust fund."

"And," Ragoczy went on, "I would think you do not want to trade on your family's name. You would prefer to make your mark on merit, not connections." He knew he was right as she held out a hand to him.

"Yes. Count, that is precisely right." She put her hand briefly on his. "I do not want to be beholden to anyone." Her expression grew troubled. "I am dependent on my grand-father just at present, but as soon as I can manage on my own, I will do so."

"A suffragette?" Ragoczy asked quietly.

"In principle, of course," she said, defiance lifting her chin. Her conviction shone in her golden eyes. "But it is more than an issue of votes. It is time women had real autonomy, a chance to make their way in the world without all the impositions of society and family. That is why I am determined not to marry, although my mother is pressing me to accept Rupert Bowen, since he is willing to have me. He is the one who watches me, in order to . . . 'protect' me." She went to fetch two more drawings, and continued with increasing determination, "Marriage is nothing more than bonded servitude, reducing women to brood mares and unpaid housekeepers. It is only when women can cast away all the things that bind them that any of us will be able to accomplish all that is in us to do. I will not apologize for my stance." She swept the next drawing onto the easel and lifted the tracing paper. She paused in her actions. "I don't know why I'm telling you this. It is not as if we are friends."

"Do you think we might be?" he asked, his tone carefully neutral.

She bristled at once. "I will not place myself in an inferior position, Count."

"Nor should you," said Ragoczy, recalling the many times Olivia had railed at her lost rights and legal protections. "All women function at a disadvantage; I have long been aware of it."

"If you have, you are one of the rare few." She moved away from the easel.

Ragoczy struggled not to laugh as he saw the picture—Count Dracula making his way head-first down the wall of the castle. "I'm sorry," he said at once, continuing with a trace of chagrin. "It is not your work, which captures the moment very well; I had the same response to the novel. You see, I have some difficulty in believing any creature, including a vampire, would be able to do that, or would want to."

"You mean climb down the wall of a castle like that?" she asked, becoming more intrigued.

"Yes." He felt more than saw her excitement kindle.

"Why do you say that?" Rowena asked him, her curiosity greater than her affontery.

"It is a conspicuously unnatural thing to do, and unnecessary in the context." He knew she did not grasp his meaning; he went on, "Any vampire indulging in such behavior—if it were possible—would draw attention to his nature, and he would become more of an object of horror than is already the case."

"Where is the trouble in that?" Rowena cocked her head, trying to look at Ragoczy and her illustration at the same time.

He stared directly at her as he answered. "It would set the vampire apart, more than vampiric nature demands. It makes the vampire more . . . unhuman, and therefore more alien, more monstrous." His voice had dropped and he was now speaking as much to himself as to her.

"But don't you think vampires are monstrous?" she inquired, engrossed in what he was saying.

"Do you?" he countered, his dark eyes meeting her golden ones.

She gave her answer serious consideration. "I think they could be. Count Dracula is monstrous some of the time."

"And the rest of the time?" Ragoczy prompted, waiting for her answer.

"The rest of the time he is . . . is fascinating," she admitted, gazing into Ragoczy's face. "It is the other side of being monstrous, don't you think? I imagine vampires would have to be fascinating, if," she went on, breaking away from the hold of his eyes, "they were real."

"Of course," he responded at once. "If they are real."

Text of a letter from Sidney Reilly to "C", sent in code using Key 17, from Saint Petersburg to London, delivered by courier 4 March 1910.

My contact among the Czar's staff has informed me that Ragoczy's departure for Berlin was ordered by Nicholas, for a private telegram was sent by him to London last week, and not to Edward. It has been confirmed for me, quite inadvertently, by Ragoczy's business agent here

in Saint Petersburg. I assume this is another part of the Czar's commission to Ragoczy, and represents the next stage in the process, whatever that may be: I have made a serious effort to determine it, but without conclusive success. No one on the staff seems to know for certain
what the task is assigned to Ragoczy, although speculation is, as the saying has it, rife. In general it is assumed that the task given to Ragoczy
is in some way related to the cooperation of the Royal Uncle and Cousins
in some endeavor of which the Czar's ministers, and possibly the Duma
as well, would not approve. I cannot venture an informed opinion about
what this may be, but I assume that co-operation is at the center of it.

At the moment it is not convenient for me to leave Saint Petersburg,
but if you are determined to send me there, I will find some cogent reason to go. Fortunately I have taken the trouble to establish the understanding that I have commercial dealings in Germany and France as
well as Russia, not that any of them have become lucrative. If we must
continue this farce of my retirement, I will have to be provided the necessary funds through one of the commercial enterprises I have embarked upon. It would not do to have too many questions asked about
my activities that cannot be explained in terms of trade. Russians, as
you are aware, are suspicious people, doubly so where foreigners are
concerned. Any inquiry into my private affairs must be able to sustain
scrutiny, or I may well find myself persona non grata without the protection of a diplomatic passport. I should think a thousand pounds
would do for a start, as well as supporting invoices to account for the
money.

I will be able to leave for Berlin three days after the funds are in place.
I will endeavor to watch Ragoczy without revealing myself to him. I
have some contacts in Berlin which might prove useful in this capacity
as well, and at my first opportunity, I will do what I can to put their
talents to work for me. My task will be much less obvious if I do not have
to do all of it myself, which could result in unwanted attention. I have
learned that Ragoczy keeps a house in Glanzend Strasse, off Knobels-
dorffstrasse; I will begin by acquainting myself with his staff. In time I
will be able to monitor Ragoczy's actions without the cumbersome necessity of keeping him under constant surveillance, which a man of
Ragoczy's experience might well discern and thus avoid. As soon as I
know what he intends to do in Berlin, I will inform you of it. In the
meantime, I will prepare to depart while I await the arrival of the necessary thousand pounds.

                                                    Sidney Reilly (Capt.)

6

Nadezna swung around, away from the pair of dancers rehearsing on the small stage; the light-spill into the dark theatre made harsh planes of her face. She glared at von Wolgast as she struggled to contain her anger. "And you agreed to this without consulting me?"

Von Wolgast was used to these outbursts from Nadezna, and so he pursed his lips and waited for her to finish. When she remained silent, waiting for his response, he cleared his throat, and said, "Well, are you adverse to the money? He is offering a great deal of money for the privilege of spending the night with you. His position in the world of business is very good. He has much to offer. And if you should learn anything of interest during your time with him, I will reward you for it, as well. You have said yourself that you do not wish to die a beggar." He smiled at her. "It is only one night. You will earn as much as you did in a month at the height of your career. By tomorrow it will be over, and you will not have to think of him again."

She said nothing for a moment, calculating all von Wolgast had said, then asked, "And he would pay how?"

"In diamonds, actually. He has eleven of them, with a certification from a Dutch firm of jewelers. They are yours upon his departure." He had not actually seen this document but had been assured it existed; he leaned toward her, running the tips of his fingers along her shoulder. "I will have them checked here as well, if you would like. But it will insult Sisak."

"Yes," she said, her temper under control once again. She turned back to the stage. "Axel, you handle her as if she were a sack of turnips. You are dancing to Chopin. You should have passion in what you do." She put her hands on her hips. "Pretend she is one of your cherub-faced boys if you must, but make this convincing."

Axel snorted, but did his best to comply.

"That is better," Nadezna said a little later as the *Etude* finished. "Now do it again, and remember what I told you. You don't want to disappoint the patron of this school, do you? He will arrive shortly, and he will judge you, and me as well. If he is not pleased, you may have to leave the school. You haven't enough experience to find good employment yet." This last reminder was for the benefit not only of Axel but the other dance students who waited to rehearse.

She was about to start toward the stage when von Wolgast laid his big hand on her shoulder, and making his voice low, he said, "What you tell them is true for you as well: it would be wise to keep that in mind. You are still at the mercy of those who have paid for your . . . talent. Remember: you will need all you can earn if your patron ceases to fund your school."

"And you are not willing to become my patron yourself, of course, if Ragoczy should decide to withdraw his patronage," was her rejoinder as she continued to watch the stage, doing her best to ignore the weight of his hand on her.

"Consider our positions. If I were to undertake to sponsor your school, it would lead to questions neither of us want," he said, but did not indicate what those questions might be.

"Lilli, extend more. Stretch. You are filled with abandon." She recited this as if reading from an unfamiliar page. "I want all the world to be thrilled when you reach the top of that lift. It is also easier for Axel to hold you if you do."

"But, Madame, how can I when he digs his fingers in so?" Lilli complained as she was lowered to the floor.

"Axel," Nadezna said as if to an ill-behaved five-year-old, "we have discussed this before. You are not to clutch at them, but hold them firmly. You are not a cat playing with a mouse." She shrugged von Wolgast's hand off her shoulder and walked toward the stage, her full attention on the dancers, shutting out everything von Wolgast had said to her. "You are not in a contest but a partnership. Both of you will show to advantage if you assist your partner in doing well. If you attempt to make your partner appear awkward, it will redound to you."

"But she is a cow," protested Axel. "Heavy and plodding. All elbows and knees."

"And he is spiteful! Make him stop," Lilli cried, her hands on her hips. She stood in fourth position as if preparing for a place-turn. The lilting melody continued as counterpoint to their carping.

The accompanist fell silent as Nadezna came up the steps onto the stage. "Neither of you is good enough yet to take on such airs. I am losing patience with your behavior. Watch carefully and learn." She nodded to Hannes, saying, "Start again, please. Adagio."

Lilli and Axel moved aside to give Nadezna room to move, exchanging frosty glances as they did.

"Now pay attention," said Nadezna as the music began. With her arms in third position, she extended her leg in an *attitude*, turning slowly as if drifting on the wind. She was not as effortless as she had been ten, or even five, years ago but she still managed to do it more wonderfully than anything her students had achieved. As she lowered her leg she began a series of *brisés*, followed by a *capriole* to the rear, and then *bourréd* to the rear, coming forward with a *tour jeté*, turning forward with a *sisson* to each side, *jeté*, *tour jeté*, completing the combinations with a *pas du chat*. As vigorous as the steps were, Nadezna gave no impression of being hurried, or of forcing herself in any way.

Watching her, von Wolgast was, as always, transfixed by her extraordinary grace and air of excitement she generated when she moved, the fascination she exercised on anyone seeing her. No wonder, he thought, she had dominated the ballet stage for as long as she had. He licked his lips without realizing it; beyond all doubt, she was an amazing woman.

"There. You see?" Nadezna demanded of Lilli. "You do not plod through it, or march. You are made of thistledown, young woman, light enough to float. You let the music carry you." With that she walked to the front of the stage. "Begin. And Axel, enter on the beat this time."

Hannes began to play again, and Lilli did her best to live up to the splendid display Nadezna had just given. Unlike her teacher, she looked rushed and bothered by the steps of the dance. From time to time she counted audibly.

Nadezna clapped her hands sharply to recall Lilli to her senses. "You must break that habit, child. Count in your head if you must, but do it silently, or you will be doing it during a performance, which is not acceptable." As Lilli faltered, Nadezna ordered her to continue. "You must not let things distract you. Concentrate on what you are doing. Audiences are noisy. There are coughing and whispering and shuffling feet almost constantly. None of that should matter to you. You are here to dance, not to listen to them. If you cannot shut it out, you will never be a real dancer." She pointed at Axel. "Now. Be ready."

Axel did his best to behave as if this were not a reprimand. He launched himself into a spectacular leap, landed a little too close to Lilli and almost bumped into her. Chagrined, he tried to recover his composure as he moved to support her *tour attitude*.

"Sloppy," Nadezna remarked, but did not interrupt the music. Only when the dance was through did she begin to itemize the various improvements she expected from her students. "You are not a credit to my reputation as you presently dance. I rely upon you to improve. You have a week to reach a level of accomplishment that will not embarrass me." She swung around to face the theatre, shading her eyes as she peered into the gloom. "Baron. Are you still here?"

"Yes, cherished one. I am." He stepped forward. "You can leave your assistant in charge for the time being, can't you? We have an engagement, as you recall. I have a private dining room reserved for us." It was assumed by everyone that von Wolgast was keeping Nadezna as his mistress, an assumption he was careful to maintain. He did not add there would be another member of their party joining them.

All von Wolgast had said to her came back in a rush; her posture changed subtly, as if she had lost the lightness within her. Shaking off this despondency, she drew herself up straight and stared into the distance. "Very well. You"—she summoned her assistant, a tall Danish woman of about thirty-five, to her side—"will finish the rehearsal. Mind they practice no less than an hour." She looked around. "Aasa is in charge while I am gone."

Von Wolgast was holding her cape for her as she came down from the stage. "You will want to change, of course," he said, indicating the dancing costume she wore. "I know Sisak would be delighted to see you this way, but the Kreuzfahrer Hof staff would be shocked."

"The Kreuzfahrer Hof?" she repeated as she made her way up the aisle toward the rear doors. "Isn't that a little out of the way? We will not get there quickly." The hotel was luxurious, but it was also more than an hour outside the city, catering to the wealthy and important in search of privacy and discretion, as well as illusion.

"It was Sisak's request. And as he is paying for it, I saw no reason to refuse him. Besides, it is two years since I have been there." He held the door open for her as she stepped into the street where von Wolgast's coach was waiting, Helmut driving.

The day was cold enough that Nadezna was shivering as she climbed into the coach. Berlin, she thought, was miserable in winter, and spring was coming very slowly this year. It would be a month at least before the days began to warm. She sat back, content to watch von Wolgast settle himself opposite her. "Is this going to be an evening or an all-night affair? You said all-night, didn't you?" she asked as the coach started off. "And when are you going to purchase an automobile?"

"When they are as reliable as my Oberlanders," he said brusquely. His distrust of motor cars was well-known, and sprang from the conviction that if anything went wrong with an automobile there was nothing one could do but wait for help, whereas with a team of horses, there were always at least two or three animals which, in an emergency, could be ridden. He folded his arms, staring hard at Nadezna. "If you have objections to this arrangement, tell me now."

"I merely dislike being given so little notice. I have other engagements and appointments, you know," she said petulantly; it was not entirely the truth, for what she disliked most was being treated like a prostitute, available at a man's whim. "What if I had my courses upon me—what then?"

"But you don't. Pflaume told me. He knows when you are not available to men, and keeps me informed." He beamed at her startled look. "Come, come, my dear. You did not think I would be unaware of such things, did you?"

"I . . . " she faltered, not able to think of a sufficiently crushing reply to his temerity. "It never occurred to me that you would intrude so. It is not the sort of thing I thought you wanted to know."

"Why would I not?" he responded quickly. "You would like it even less if I importuned you during your courses, would you not? I am making it possible for us both to avoid that unpleasantry."

"How thoughtful," she said sarcastically.

"It is, though you may not think so now." He reached over and laid his hand on hers. "You are a clever woman, Nadezna, and you will know how to make the most of this opportunity."

"You mean I will find out things you want to know and receive more than diamonds for my trouble?" She glowered at him, her rehearsal clothing suddenly seeming terribly inadequate; she wished she were fully dressed and able to show reserve convincingly. "Since it is a settled thing, I will want the diamonds as soon as we arrive. He might forget them if we wait until morning."

"I am not as gullible as you think, my dear." He withdrew his hand. "I have informed him that I will want to have the diamonds and the jeweler's certificate upon our arrival at the Kreuzfahrer Hof. He agreed."

"You said that I would have them upon his departure," she reminded him sharply.

"And so you shall. I will hold them for you until then." He wagged one finger at her. "You do not want them with you, surely? He might decide to take them back, and what then? No, no. It is safer if I keep them for you."

She again had to shake off the unpleasant sensation of being whored. Until recently, her ventures into the realms of supplying pleasure had seemed a sensible way to shore up her financial future, as well as giving those dancers who had passed the point of keeping up with the demands of the profession some way of augmenting their dwindling savings—if, indeed, they had any. Now she felt she was becoming a commodity, a trophy for von Wolgast, to be exhibited and lent out as suited his purposes. Suddenly it became more important than ever that Ragoczy continue to support her school, for without his support, she would be wholly dependent on von Wolgast: it was not a prospect to reassure her. As she gazed out the window at the traffic, she a felt an intense pang of loneliness. She had come so far from Zitomir, from her youthful wonder at Kiev, and the certainty that she would never see a grander city anywhere. What age had she been then? Eight? Nine? How proud her parents had been to have a child enrolled in the dance school there: a baker's daughter, to dance in Kiev. Her father had boasted to all his friends that Nadezna Sychenko would be famous one day. "He was right," she murmured. It had been more than twenty years since she saw him last, and then he was an old man, his fingers gnarled with age, his eyesight failing, but still rising before dawn to make the dough for morning bread.

"Who was right?" von Wolgast said, cutting into her reverie. He waited for her answer with more attention than usual.

"Oh, no one," she said, making herself smile. "It was something from long ago. It came to mind, as such things occasionally do. He is probably dead by now, in any case."

Von Wolgast pursed his lips, his eyes crinkling. "We never do forget our first lovers, do we?"

She turned to face him, shocked. Then she managed to restore the smile to her lips. "No, I suppose we do not."

At her house she ordered Pflaume to fill her bath and have Charlotte, her maid, set out the burgundy satin, with gloves and her diamond necklace with the baroque pearl drop. "And see the Baron has some of that goose-liver paté while he waits." With that, she rushed up the stairs, trying to choose which perfume would be most seductive.

Her bathroom was modern, white tile on walls and floor, her bathtub standing on ball-and-claw feet, the fixtures in gleaming brass. The brass hot-water heater stood beside it, the blue eye of a gas flame showing through the grille at the bottom. Steaming water was already pouring into the tub, wispy clouds of it beginning to obscure the mirror over her sink.

Calling for Charlotte, Nadezna flung aside her cloak and began to peel off her clothes, noticing that she stank like a sweating horse. All dancers did; it was part of the work. She looked up as Charlotte came in from the bedroom. "Good. There you are."

"I'm setting out the burgundy satin, as you asked." Charlotte Milch was of undetermined middle age who had been Nadezna's dresser at the ballet until age crabbed her spine. Now she tended Nadezna in her home, grateful for the work.

"Very good," she said without much interest. "Now tell me, jasmine and what else? Sandalwood? Roses? I can't make up my mind."

"Jasmine and sandalwood are always satisfactory," said Charlotte, her voice neutral as always. "I will make a sachet of it for you, if you like."

"Please; after you put the oils in the bath." She was naked now, and she stretched as sensually as a cat, trying to work the tightness out of her body, and knowing that this time it would not be an easy thing to do. "You choose which shoes will be best. And I will want my seal coat, I think."

"I've already taken it out, Madame." She bobbed a clumsy curtsy before going to the tall, white chest beside the door, opening it and taking out two small vials. At the tub, she poured a few drops of each into the water before turning off the taps. The fragrances welled up around her; she paid no heed. "I will be waiting to help you, Madame, as soon as you have finished your bathing."

Nadezna gathered her hair on her head, fixing it in place with two long hairpins, then got into her bath, reveling in the hot water. She reached for her sponge with one hand, her soap with the other. When the sponge frothed with lather, she set about washing herself thoroughly. If von Wolgast was going to make a whore of her, she would do it as well as she could. She would not let him make her despise herself. As she scrubbed at her long, lean body, she wondered what else von Wolgast might demand of her. The possibilities slipped away from her like the bar of soap adrift in the tub; never quite within her reach but always present, nudging against her flank or her thigh as she washed.

Charlotte brought her a towel and shook her head as she looked at what the steam had done to Nadezna's thick, black hair. "I will have to make a knot of it," she declared. "If we had more time, I could make proper curls, but . . . " She finished her thoughts with fussy plucks at Nadezna's hair.

"It doesn't matter," said Nadezna, preferring the knot in any case. "Use one of the jeweled combs, and it will more than suffice. I don't mind."

"Perhaps you do not mind," said Charlotte, preparing to guide Nadezna back into her bedroom for dressing, "but I do. You have entrusted your appearance to me."

"And you maintain it admirably," said Nadezna, going into her bedroom with Charlotte. "I regret that I must leave so soon." She hoped that the full intent of her words was not apparent. "But you know what the Baron is."

"Oh, yes," said Charlotte bleakly as she reached for the corset set out with the gown. "I know." Without revealing her thoughts further, she added, "I've packed you a case for morning. Pflaume will give it to the Baron's coachman. You will not have to come home in an evening dress."

Forty minutes later Nadezna descended the stairs, a striking figure in the splendid gown of burgundy satin with short frilled sleeves, a valentine neckline, a high waist accented with a wide beaded belt, and a long, sleek trumpet skirt in three layers. Her shoes were made of black satin with spangled bows; her silk stockings had designs worked into them. Long burgundy-dyed kid gloves reached almost to her sleeves. Her diamond necklace and earrings glittered as she moved. Her face was meticulously made up, with her eyes rimmed in kohl, her mouth glistening red.

"As always, my dear, you take my breath away," said von Wolgast with the ease of long familiarity. "And in good time, too; I was afraid you would need much more time to get ready, and then we should be late. I know Sisak will be delighted."

Pflaume appeared with her seal-fur coat, holding it for her to don. She permitted him to slide it onto her shoulders, thanking him in an off-handed way. "I will be back tomorrow. Tell Aasa to begin the rehearsal without me."

"Yes, Madame," said Pflaume, holding the door to permit von Wolgast to escort her out to the coach.

Helmut gestured his relief at the sight of them. "I don't like keeping them standing so long, not as cold as it is." He looked at Nadezna. "I have your case, Madame."

"Couldn't be helped," said von Wolgast, ignoring the last, in a tone intended to put his coachman in his place. "Kreuzfahrer Hof."

"I know where you are going." Helmut was not impressed with von Wolgast's arrogance. With a practiced snap of his whip, he set the Oberlanders moving down the alley toward the narrow street.

They turned past the Hedwigkirche, bound for Friedrichstrasse and the bridge over the Spree. Carts, automobiles, carriages, wagons, and delivery vehicles of all sorts made their way through the streets. The clatter and rush of traffic made conversation difficult, and Nadezna was grateful that she had more time to think, to try to discover how she had allowed von Wolgast to gain such power over her that she was now permitting him to sell her body in this appalling way. To be at the beck and call of von Wolgast and his associates was demeaning. Not that she had been a model of chastity in the past—for that was hardly the case—but she had chosen her lovers before now, and had made them grateful for the privilege of catering to her whims and demands. It had been that way with von Wolgast at first: he had fawned and panted like the others, presenting her with gifts, lavishing demonstrations of his devotion upon her in the forms of evenings out, bouquets of roses in winter, her portrait in oils by Gustav Klimt, hanging now in her private drawing room. She had taken it all, never realizing that this was a honied snare, that he was not her willing servant as he had claimed, and she was in no position to protest his plans for her, not if she wished to keep her house and her jewels. Galling though it was, she knew she had to comply with his wishes. She sighed in exasperation, as much with herself as with von Wolgast.

"Something troubles you, my dear?" von Wolgast asked, leaning toward her solicitously.

"Nothing in particular." She knew he would not be satisfied with this, and so went on, "It is Axel. Try as I will, I cannot persuade him to . . . I despair of ever teaching him how to express an emotion he will not feel."

"Desire for women?" von Wolgast guessed. "You have known such men before. Your old partner, Rene Kranz, was such a man. Or so you have told me."

"Yes, he was," she said, grateful to have him to speak of. "But he was able to dance as if he longed for a woman. On the stage it did not matter that he went home to Dietrich." She drew her sealskin coat more tightly around her.

"What did he die of, your partner?" asked von Wolgast, trying to encourage her conversation.

"Pneumonia, as I recall. It began as a cough and he got steadily worse. Poor Dietrich was beside himself." She shook her head once. "Dietrich moved to Paris after Rene died. I suppose he is still there."

"He had a show here, didn't he? I seem to recall one," Von Wolgast did not actually care what the answer was; he wanted only to shake Nadezna out of her pensive mood before they reached their destination.

"Yes; five years ago. Most of it was sculpture in bronze, although there were a few works in wood, and one in stone." Thinking back, she had to admit most of Dietrich's work was not very good. At the time she attributed this to Rene's death, but now she began to suspect that Dietrich was not a very innovative sculptor.

"How did you manage with Rene? Would it work with Axel?" von Wolgast asked, hoping her explanation would restore her good humor.

The carriage lurched as Helmut narrowly avoided an altercation between the driver of a horse-drawn van and a man in a Benz motor car. The vehicle swayed precariously, then thunked solidly onto all four wheels again.

Nadezna all but slid from her seat. As she recovered herself, she remarked, "I do not know what to tell you. No one had to explain to Rene. There were things he was born knowing. He understood what the dance was supposed to show, and he did it. He enjoyed it, as if his personal taste were his favorite secret." She was more ruffled than she let von Wolgast see. "I don't know how such things are taught."

"But you intend to try," said von Wolgast. "In order to impress that patron of yours."

"I must," she said simply. "If I do not, he may decide to cease his patronage." And then she would be completely in von Wolgast's toils. Since that was intolerable to her, she felt a grim determination to convince Axel of the necessity of his achieving a semblance of passion for Lilli.

"You expect him soon?" asked von Wolgast.

"In five or six days," she confirmed.

"You will be able to do it, a woman like you." Von Wolgast's voice was heavy with implications that made Nadezna want to scream.

She made herself gesture dismissal of the matter. "There is nothing I can do now, in any case."

"Yes, my dear. I want you to put your mind on Sisak. Think of ways to indulge him. You're good at that. I want him begging to kiss your feet, so that he will be willing to divulge anything we wish to know." He put his big, thick hands together with a delicacy that seemed impossible. "He is venal. You may have to show some . . . how shall I describe it? imagination in what you do with him."

Without revealing the alarm she felt at this, she said, "What, exactly, do you mean, Baron?"

Von Wolgast regarded her with the air of one contemplating an approaching storm. "I mean, my dear, that he will not become your lapdog as readily as other men have. You will have to do more than tell him how to please you. This time, Nadezna, you will do the pleasing, no matter what it means to you."

She knew her face was darkening; she could feel the vein in her neck pulse with anger. "You are ridiculous!"

"No, my dear, I am not. I am making the gamble of my life and I will not let any scruples or vanity of yours stop me from achieving what I must have." He took her chin in one hand, his fingers hard against her skin. "You will be compliant and gracious to this man, or you will have to deal with me, and I will not be willing to make allowances for your pride. If you fail me, I promise you, you will regret it bitterly."

Nadezna was not so shocked that she could not speak, but she was able to hold her tongue. She stared down at her hands, wondering if she ought to demand to be taken home; it was tempting, but she hesitated, knowing how much greater would be her despair if he should refuse. Better to wait, she decided, reminding herself she had never been to the Kreuzfahrer Hof and had long been curious to see this legendary retreat.

Von Wolgast recognized the signs of capitulation and said, relishing the moment, "You have always been a sensible woman, Nadezna, not to be swayed by the emotions that so cripple other women."

"You are too kind," she rejoined icily.

They reached the Kreuzfahrer Hof twenty minutes later, having exchanged less than a dozen words during that time. As the carriage lumbered through the massive stone archway into the wide, cobbled courtyard, von Wolgast nudged Nadezna with his arm.

"We have arrived at our destination; this is Kreuzfahrer Hof," he told her as Helmut drew the horses to a stop and clambered down from the box to open the door and let down the stairs for them.

"So I see," she responded with dignity, preparing to descend from the carriage. It was still and cold, making the vast stone building look like an image emerging from a dream of vanished knighthood: there were turrets at each corner of the octagonal courtyard, and one tall spire above the main part of the building. It was someone's vision of the Middle Ages, rendered comfortable and clean. Incongruously bright electric lights made the windows stand out from the stones.

"Reception is this way," said von Wolgast, taking her by the elbow and guiding her into the cathedral-like interior. They trod up the wide, deep-red carpet to the front desk, a massive wooden structure with elaborate wood carving in medieval motifs ornamenting it. The man behind it was in a monkish robe with a large black Maltese cross square on its front, and he welcomed von Wolgast in sepulchral tones.

"Good evening, Baron. Mister Sisak is waiting for you in the dining room. He has reserved private room number nine. Werner will escort you," the desk clerk said as von Wolgast signed his name, adding *and guest* for Nadezna, although he was fairly certain she was recognized.

A strapping young man in a costume like the desk clerk's came forward and bowed slightly to the arrivals. "If you will follow me?" he offered.

Von Wolgast kept Nadezna's hand through the crook of his arm by placing his free hand on it. "We would be delighted," he told Werner, adding to Nadezna, "I'm surprised they don't insist the staff be tonsured," referring to Werner's thick blond hair.

"Some of the patrons might not like being reminded of baldness," she answered, letting her words cut; she knew von Wolgast was dismayed by his thinning hair.

"Of course," he said, acknowledging her barb. "Isn't this an amazing place?" he went on, pointing out the deep Oriental carpets on the stone floors, and the fine tapestries hanging on the walls, ensconced by electric lights in fixtures designed to look like torch flames. Above them the ceiling was painted a deep blue with large golden stars spangled across it, the constellations picked out in fine silver lines. They followed Werner along a corridor decorated with murals of Teutonic legends: "Seigfried and the Dragon, Brunhilde asleep within a ring of fire, Loki approaching Baldur, Wotan and Urda in confrontation, Thor summoning stormclouds, Kundry attempting to seduce Parzifal, Undines drawing the Knight into deep water with drowning embraces, the Rainbow Bridge with heros passing across it to Valhalla.

"Strange paintings for a supposed monastery," said Nadezna, as much to annoy von Wolgast as to point out the inappropriateness of the murals.

"Think of Wagner, my dear," von Wolgast reminded her, refusing to be drawn into any dispute with her. "We're almost there."

The dining room turned out to be a vast hall where a number of men and women in evening clothes watched a young woman in somewhat medieval dress play on an old harp while singing a lament about the Crusader who left her to find glory in the Holy Land.

Werner indicated a line of carved oaken doors at the far end of the room. "Number nine is on the right side, third from the end."

"Very good," said von Wolgast, standing aside as two waiters in page's garb carried out trays of roast pork and veal sausages. "I'm getting hungry. And you, my dear?"

Food was the last thing Nadezna wanted now, but she nodded, thinking that at another time she might enjoy the fantasy and display of this place, but now it only made her feel more cheapened and betrayed. She glanced once at the singer and noted with satisfaction that her long, cascading locks of yellow hair were a wig. It confirmed her cynical view of the place.

"Be careful. There are two steps up here," Werner warned.

Von Wolgast and Nadezna did as he recommended; she said, "I suppose this is more difficult at the end of the evening, when the wine and beer and champagne have done their work."

Werner glanced back at her and showed her a quick, sarcastic smile. "Occasionally it has been . . . " He left her to imagine what it had been.

The door to private dining room number nine stood slightly ajar. As they reached it, Werner flung it open, revealing a room done on Oriental themes, with a peacock fountain in the center, and numerous divans upholsted in brocade Chinese silk around it, each with its own low hammered-brass table. The whole chamber was draped in long panels of heavy irridescent silk from India, so that the room looked to be more of a tent than a stone apartment. Lamps in the shapes of tall lotuses glittered in clusters of two or three at various places about the room.

"Ludwig the Mad would be envious," said Nadezna, who had seen the Bavarian King's fabulous palaces when performing in Munich.

A stoutish man of about forty in a loose robe of deep-rose damask silk turned around from the brass filigree bar and gestured a greeting. "I agree, lovely lady." His German was Bavarian-accented, his manner polished to the point of contempt. His expression was worthy of a Parisian man-about-town, worldly and jaded, detracting from the air of bonhomie he was striving to achieve. There was something about his eyes, however, a covetousness that belied his apparent charm. He held out a tulip glass to her. "If you will be good enough?" He swung around to Werner. "Take their wraps, if you will." He poured a second glass of champagne, offering it to von Wolgast. "Baron?"

"Good evening, Herr Sisak," said von Wolgast, making the most of the moment. "How good of you to invite us."

"It is my pleasure, Baron," he replied as his green eyes lingered on Nadezna.

"Ah, yes," said von Wolgast, taking his cue from his host. "This is Nadezna." He put his hand on the small of her back and urged her forward a few steps. "Our host, my dear. Tancred Sisak."

She moved the tulip glass into her left hand and extended her right. "Mister Sisak."

He bowed over her hand, and did not release it when he straightened up. "I have been anticipating this evening ever since my friend Herzog Persuic told me about the superb hospitality he was given at your house, Madame."

"You know Herzog Persuic, then?" she said, standing as if preparing to dance the Black Swan.

"We have been engaged in various business dealings, yes," said Sisak, as if unaware of the hauteur Nadezna displayed. "I thought it would be an honor to meet you, and to enjoy your company, since I am told it is a rare experience."

Nadezna took a long sip of the champagne, hoping its bubbles might infuse some gaiety into her, but for all the response she felt, she might have been drinking cold, weak tea. She summoned up a practiced smile. "It is often difficult to live up to such high expectations, Herr Sisak."

"Very likely," he said, his tongue flicking over his lips. "But you have always striven for perfection, haven't you? I saw you dance many years ago, and I thought it was impossible for any human to be so weightless, so ethereal."

"That would have been . . . *Rosamunda?*" she guessed, remembering the triumph she had had in the role. How she had relished her adulation then, and how hollow it seemed to her now. Her next sip drained her glass.

"I was breathless for days afterward," he confessed with a chuckle. "But I was very young." The lascivious implications of this last were so obvious that it was an effort for Nadezna not to laugh in scorn.

"The choreography was very good. And Rene Kranz, my partner, was excellent. I was fortunate in both." Both these things were true, but saying them in this company, she felt they were lies.

"Yes. I would have given half my savings to have changed places with him. A most satisfying work, I thought." He reached for the bottle and refilled her glass.

"I'll never forget it," said von Wolgast, lifting an eyebrow to signal her. "Very generous with his praise, isn't he, my dear?"

She nearly choked on the word. "Very."

If Sisak was aware of her discomfort, he said nothing about it. Instead he gave a winning smile and continued with the utmost cordiality, "I will arrange for another bottle and our . . . private entertainment, if you will excuse me? It will not take long. I will return in just a moment."

As soon as he was gone, von Wolgast rounded on her. "You are going to have to do better, my dear. Much better."

"Do you think so?" she countered hotly, the champagne finally reaching her blood. "I think he wants the aloof, remote dancer, not the woman you know. He thinks of me as Rosamunda, not Nadezna. He is determined to return to that magic he felt in his youth." She stopped his questions before he could pose them. "Do not argue with me, Manfred. I have much more experience in these matters than you do; I have seen this before, this yearning for a dream from the stage. Often."

Von Wolgast shrugged. "If you think your way will get the results we both see . . . " He bowed to her. "I will defer to your experience, my dear. But remember," he added with an edge in his voice, "I have certain information I seek, and I depend upon you to garner it for me."

She shook her head, doing her best to conceal her distaste. "I will do what I can, whatever it may be."

"And I want him *grateful* to me for this evening, grateful enough to make concessions in my favor." He loomed toward her. "Am I making myself plain enough?"

"I said I will do whatever I must," she repeated, her defiance less confident now.

She hated herself for asking, "Why are you doing this to me?"

The smile he gave her was without a spark of warmth. "Because I can." He touched her chin with one finger. "Never forget that, my dear."

"I will remember," she said quietly, hoping to quell the panic deep within her.

"You certainly will, or you will not—" He was not allowed to finish: Sisak bustled back into the room followed by two liveried waiters bearing trays of silver serving dishes filled with caviar, flaky meat pastries, pork loin stuffed with apples and raisins, broiled oysters, eel soup, pickled onions, fruit glacée, and a large bowl of sour cream, a concession to Nadezna's heritage. There were also two bottles of champagne in a large silver bucket, and a bottle of schnapps, as well.

"Your dinner is waiting, von Wolgast. They have reserved you a seat at the high table, near the Deputy Minister for Foreign Affairs, as you requested." Sisak beamed again, his best salesman's smile. "He has said he is looking forward to your company. I am certain you and he will find something to talk about. Before you go, there is one more matter." Then he held out a dark velvet jeweler's case, large enough to contain a necklace or brooch and earrings. "Let us get this out of the way, so that we may concentrate on other things."

"Thank you," said von Wolgast, taking the case and shoving it into the inner breast pocket of his claw-tailed jacket. He glanced once at Nadezna, his expression significant, containing both a threat and a challenge. "I will arrange to have the carriage ready at . . . shall we say ten? In the morning?"

"Ten will be very good," said Sisak before Nadezna could protest. "If you would like to breakfast with me, Nadezna will be able to restore herself in peace." He moved toward her possessively. "Come, Madame. Our supper is waiting."

The two page-costumed waiters had left the private room and it remained only for von Wolgast to depart. He went to Nadezna, bowed over her hand without kissing it. "Until tomorrow, my dear."

"As you say," she answered distantly, looking at the supper as if she saw rotten bodies instead of food. Sisak was very nearly touching her; she could smell his cologne, and under it, the stink of stale sweat.

Von Wolgast nodded to Sisak. "Enjoy yourself, my friend."

Sisak said nothing as von Wolgast left them alone. When the door was closed, he took the last step. He wrapped his arms around her from behind, bending to kiss her neck while his hands explored her breasts through the satin of her dress; she felt his erection pressed against her buttocks.

Nadezna tried to laugh off his impetuosity. "Herr Sisak, you will ruin our supper. Be patient and we will manage better." This had worked with others in the past.

"It doesn't matter," he said in a tone of voice that chilled her; she knew what obsession sounded like, and what it meant for her. He let her go, but only to pull her around to him. "Take your clothes off. Take them off."

"How can I?" she asked, trying to keep the fear out of her voice. "You're holding onto me."

"Oh. Yes." He released her and stepped back two paces; his eyes were fevered. "You should have another glass of champagne."

"That would be . . . nice," she said, thinking frantically about how to delay what was going to happen. If he had only adored her as so many of her lovers had, she could make him do as she wished. But those who had made a fantasy of her, a dream image, she knew she could not control. To keep him from becoming too insistent, she began to unfasten her dress, unfastening the hooks and eyes under her left arm so that the dress was no longer clinging sleekly to her. "I should have my maid here, to help me." Usually Charlotte would take the shoulders of the dress, and as Nadezna bent over, she would pull it smoothly off her. Without Charlotte, it would be awkward getting out of the dress.

"I will watch you," said Sisak, suddenly reclining on the nearest divan, adjusting the drape of his robe to draw attention to his penis as it pushed the rosy cloth upward. "Leave your gloves on."

"What?" She had been about to remove them, and this order surprised her.

"Leave your gloves on," he repeated in a tone that brooked no opposition. "I will tell you when you can take them off."

"As you wish," she said, and began the awkward process of struggling out of her evening dress, bending and wriggling as she worked first the bodice and then the trumpet skirts over her head.

"Leave it on the floor," he told her as he drank more champagne. "The stockings next, and then the corset." His voice was becoming hoarse, low, urgent.

"If I took off my gloves, I could—" she began.

"No. Leave them on." He propped himself on his elbow and continued to watch her.

At least, she thought, she had the good sense to wear a modern corset, one with hooks and eyes down the front instead of laces up the back. She unfastened the garters holding her stockings to her corset, and rolled them down her legs, first right, then left. Seeing his gesture, she dropped the stockings on her dress, then went to work on the corset. "What will you want after this?" she asked as she began to unfasten the hooks and eyes.

"I will tell you then," he said sharply.

She relented at once, recognizing the compulsion behind his instruction; she continued to unfasten her corset. When she was done, she dropped it with the rest of her clothes. "My drawers?" she asked, and was given a terse nod of consent.

"Give them to me." He held out his hand for them, and kissed them as she gave them to him.

Standing naked but for her long gloves, she watched him caress her silken under-drawers. Her spine went cold as he rolled onto his back, her underwear over his face. He sighed luxuriously. Without moving, he said. "Get on your knees and crawl to me."

"What?" she demanded, shocked out of her compliance.

He half-sat up. "I said to get on your knees and crawl to me. Do it."

She flinched at the sound of the words. "I . . . I don't understand," she protested, although she did, and only too well.

He regarded her with steely eyes. "Listen very carefully: you will crawl to me. You will lift my robe. You will suck me until I tell you to stop. If you speak to me again, I will break your jaw."

Nadezna wished then she could go numb, that all of this would fade away as the nightmare it was. There was no doubt that Sisak meant what he said, and in a place like this, who would come to her rescue if she resisted him, or tried to get away? Where would she go? She got onto the floor and began to crawl.

✿   ✿   ✿

Text of a letter from Franchot Ragoczy to Rowena Pearce-Manning, delivered by his chauffeur, Timothy Harris; read by Clarice Pearce-Manning upon its arrival.

London
March 9, 1910

Rowena Pearce-Manning
Longacres, Buckinghamshire

Dear Miss Pearce-Manning;
or Saxon, if you prefer;
Let me take this belated opportunity to thank you for showing your work to me. I found it evocative and innovative, and I look forward to seeing more of it in the future, if you will consider showing it to me.
I regret, however, that the press of business which I mentioned to you is taking me to Germany very shortly, and I must therefore decline your gracious invitation to visit the gallery you spoke of, at least for the present. The appointment I had with His Majesty has been postponed, and I now have to advance the time of my departure by two days. I trust this will not prove an inconvenience to you. Currently my plans call for a return to London within six weeks, and it is my hope that you will still be of a mind to show me this gallery. I do not say this idly. I am convinced that the work of women artists is not a mere curiosity, as some have called it, but as much a contribution to the world as any accomplished by males. To see such a gallery is a most intriguing prospect.
Please extend my remembrances to your parents; I passed a very interesting weekend as their guest at Longacres. When you return to London next week, I would count it a personal favor if you would be willing to send a note to my house. I will not receive it until I return, but it will be a welcome I would deeply appreciate; should this impose upon you over-much, I ask you to disregard it. If there are any alterations in my plans, I will send you word so that my commitments will not put you at any disadvantage.
Again, Miss Saxon, I am obliged to you for your kindness in permitting me to visit your studio; I hope you will permit me to do so another time when it suits your convenience.

Most sincerely,
Franchot Ragoczy
Count Saint-Germain
(his sigil, the eclipse)

7

Lowering clouds promised rain, and cold gusts of wind punctuated the threat, but a few determined strollers in the Tiergarten huddled into their coats and did their best to ignore the ominous skies as they wandered through the paddocks and cages, lawns and larger plants; Berlin was showing tentative hints at spring coming, and the Berliners were making the most of them.

Among the visitors to the Tiergarten was a long-faced, sharp-eyed, full-mouthed man in a Russian greatcoat in the company of a short, weedy fellow of about thirty with a Viennese accent. They made a point of keeping to the less-frequented paths where few visitors stopped to stare at the shrubbery in the hope of seeing an exotic bird or hidden animal. They were not obviously avoiding others, yet certainly making no effort to seek them out. Neither paid any attention to their surroundings beyond the effort to maintain privacy.

"So you see my problem," Sidney Reilly said to the Austrian, his manner serious and his intention plain. "I need someone who is absolutely reliable. It will not suit the problem if I worry or doubt. I, and my associate, must watch this man without being recognized, or revealing my purpose, and without betraying my presence while doing it. I must also," he went on, cutting off anything his companion was about to say, "discover if anyone else is engaged in watching this Ragoczy, and if so, at whose behest, and to what ends. There is also the possibility that Ragoczy himself may be watching someone. If I carry out the surveillance wholly on my own, it will probably not be possible to accomplish it all." To emphasize this, he glanced back over his shoulder as if to point out a feature of the Tiergarten to the man walking with him. "So far I have not been aware of anyone assigned to observe me, but it will come, without doubt. It is probably inevitable that this will happen."

"Why do you say so?" the Austrian asked, a slight whine in his voice that went with his threadbare greatcoat.

"Because I am not wholly unknown in Germany," said Reilly, not without satisfaction. "I have undertaken various projects in this country before now. I would like to keep my presence as unremarkable as I can. The authorities do not forget such activities, and when they realize I have returned, they will have questions to ask. Once questions start, well—" He shrugged.

"Why should questions start? For what reason?" The Austrian all but bolted.

"Lukas, Lukas, Lukas," said Reilly at his most placating, "if I can avoid being recognized, it might not happen. If we prepare, if we anticipate, there might not be any questions at all. Or they will be asked only of me, and I will know what to say. You need not concern yourself."

Lukas Strauss was not convinced; he persevered, an annoying note of cowardice in his words. "Who would question me? Tell me. I have to know."

With utmost patience, Reilly said, "No one will, if we work out our plans now. That is why we are talking." Wind snapped at his greatcoat; he shoved his gloved hands into his pockets. "Listen to me, Lukas. We have work to do, and we will do it best if undetected. I can do some of it, certainly, and without attracting suspicion. Ragoczy and I both have businesses in Saint Petersburg, and it would follow that I might have need of his expertise. I will not ask you to do anything more than watch him. You will not have to deal with contacts other than me." He made sure Lukas heard that. "If we do not expose ourselves, we should be largely undetected. Which is why I need you to be willing to be the observer of Ragoczy's automobile. We must know where he goes. One more student on a bicycle will not attract much attention—"

"Late at night, I would," Lukas protested.

"I do not expect you to follow him late at night. It isn't safe." He let Lukas put whatever interpretation he liked on the last.

"I'm too old to be a student," said Lukas, growing more desperate. They were alone on the path now, and he remembered that Reilly was a very dangerous man.

"Not if you dress the part." Reilly resisted the urge to shake him. "You're an actor, aren't you? Making yourself look enough like a student to convince the average passerby that you are one shouldn't take much more than a slight change in your . . . costume." He saw a semblance of pride in Lukas' eyes and made the most of it. "I've been told you are skilled. That is why I came to you." That, and the information that Lukas was also a petty thief and desperate. "Of course, I will pay for any clothes you may need. And a bicycle as well." The funds sent from England would handle these expenses, Reilly knew, but made no mention of this to Lukas; it would only spur him to more questions which would demand greater assurances.

Lukas walked more confidently, his head up, his face calmer. "You're right. I should be able to do as you suggest."

"And no doubt you will have a use for the money," added Reilly. "It should go a long way to helping you out of your current predicament." This reminder, mixed with the appeal to Lukas' vanity seemed to Reilly to be enough to set the hook.

"I suppose I can do it for a week, at least," Lukas conceded, making an effort to look confident. "At the end of it, we will negotiate again." He stopped walking and repeated. "We will negotiate again."

"Certainly, certainly," said Reilly as he halted, confident that he would be able to make Lukas capitulate on every point if he had to. "We will both know more about Ragoczy and that will make it easier to decide how to deal with him."

"Yes, that's it exactly," said Lukas, taking on the suggestion of jauntiness now that he had been reassured by Reilly. "I will need to purchase a bicycle and some clothes tomorrow." This last was almost a question, a testing of the waters. "You'll have to give me money to do it."

"With pleasure," said Reilly as cordially as he could. "Will cash do, or do you want a bank draught?" He knew what the answer would be before it was spoken.

"Cash would be best." He was becoming excited now, revealing his avarice more blatantly than he realized.

Reilly had put a small roll of bills in his greatcoat pocket; he handed this to Lukas, saying, "Is this sufficient?"

Lukas riffled the edge of the bills with his thumb, eyes widening as he did, then did his best to appear unimpressed. "It will do." He pocketed the money before Reilly could change his mind.

"Fine," Reilly said, and resumed walking, knowing that Lukas would follow him. "You will do your best to observe his house the day after tomorrow, so you will know his servants' faces, particularly his chauffeur. Whenever he drives out in the day, you will follow him on your bicycle."

"What if he has a fast automobile, and I cannot catch up with him?" The whine was back in his voice again as he tagged after Reilly.

"That is why you will learn who the chauffeur is, so you can encounter him if you need to, and find out where his employer has been." Reilly saw hesitation in the Austrian's eyes. "You may, for example, ask for help with a punctured tyre, or for directions. You may speak to him to thank him for any minor service he might perform, such as showing you a map." They came to a crossroad and paused briefly. "I will meet you at Glanzend Strasse, across from number forty-five, at two in the afternoon. Tomorrow. Have your clothes and your bicycle by then, and arrive in your student character. Decide before then what that character will be, and maintain it." He narrowed his deep-set eyes. "If you fail to show up, you will regret it, I promise you."

Lukas was not able to conceal the fear that ran through him. "I will be there. You have no reason to doubt me, Herr Reilly."

"Of course," said Reilly, and looked back over his shoulder in the direction of the largest cages. "We will meet by the leopards promptly at nine in the morning each day, and you will tell me all—*all*—that you have observed. Do not consider anything trivial or unimportant. Forget nothing. Carry a notebook, so you will not omit one item or person."

"But," Lukas said, trying to sound reasonable, "don't you think that would be too risky? Someone might notice."

Reilly shook his head once. "That is why you are to dress as a student. No one thinks twice if a student is seen taking notes. Students are expected to do that." He realized he was being too stern with Lukas, and held back the sarcasm he wanted to heap on the Austrian.

"Very well, Herr Reilly. I will do as you tell me." He ducked his head as a show of contrition. His voice was muffled; he was not a skilled actor but he had a good deal of native talent. "I didn't think."

"No, you did not," said Reilly. "And you had better start thinking right now." He nodded once in Lukas' direction. "Leave by the south entrance. I will go another way, in a while. It will not do to be seen together too often."

"Then why meet here every morning?" Lukas asked.

"We will arrange other places if they are necessary. Many people take morning constitutionals through the Tiergarten. Provided we do not arrive together or leave together there should be no problems, at least not for a week or so, when we may decide to make other arrangements, if they are needed. By then we will know how long Ragoczy will be in Berlin." He moved a few steps away from Lukas. "So," he said more loudly, "you will find what you are seeking down that path."

"Danke," said Lukas, and hurried away with mixed emotions, and a growing certainty that he would be a fool to treat Reilly with anything but careful respect.

Reilly watched Lukas go and sighed once. He disliked having to use such unreliable tools as the Austrian so clearly was, but he had not time enough to put a more dependable operation into effect; any extended efforts to bring that about would lead to the scrutiny he was hoping to avoid. His stay here was supposed to be brief, and he intended it would be. Frowning slightly at his own troubled thoughts, he made his way out of the Tiergarten and ambled in the direction of Unter den Linden. He would have to call on Meyer to find out who was working in Berlin just now. It was an exposure he did not welcome, but it was safer to go directly to Meyer than to have Meyer come to him.

By five that afternoon he had located Renfred Meyer; a contact-of-a-contact had supplied the information for a hefty fee and the assurance that Meyer would not be harmed. Reilly made his way to the address scrawled on the grubby slip of paper, doing his best to take the most circuitous route possible, so that a walk which would ordinarily take fifteen minutes required that Reilly spend slightly over an hour to complete it. He entered the rundown building cautiously, making his way up the steep, unsteady stairs with care, his hand in his pocket gripping a small Borchardt automatic pistol. At the landing he paused to look upward before continuing to the floor above.

"Who is it?" demanded an ancient female voice from the other side of the door, in response to Reilly's double-pause-double knock.

"Sidney Reilly," he answered truthfully, knowing that Meyer would not accept a lie, least of all from him.

There was a short, whispered conversation within the apartment, then the door was opened just enough to permit Reilly to squeeze inside.

"Give me the pistol while you are here; I know you carry one," the old lady demanded, her hand extended for the weapon; Reilly surrendered the Borchardt at once.

Renfred Meyer's apartment was a dark warren of trails through stacks of books, newspaper, magazines, and unbound sheets. Ancient curtains over the windows muted the fading winter light to a faint glow. The man himself, middle-aged, balding, stooped, and cocooned in a shapeless, colorless cardigan, greeted Reilly tersely. "I heard you were back."

"Not for very long, I trust," said Reilly, following Meyer through the chaos of his sitting room to a small desk with a single lamp above it. "If you can help me, my visit here will be shortened. That should encourage you."

"Possibly," Meyer allowed. "It will depend on how you use the time you are here." He adjusted his glasses on his nose. "You have your ways, Captain Reilly."

"I have no wish to bring about trouble. In fact, I want to be as invisible as possible." He strove to give Meyer a sense of his mission without revealing much. "The matter is not deadly, only complicated."

Meyer made a derisive noise that was part snort, part bark. "So you say."

"Why else would I seek your help after the last time?" Reilly expected no answer and received none. He went on smoothly, "If you do not like what I ask, you have only to refuse to help me and I will go away."

"My mother will bring you tea," said Meyer as he sat down, making no gesture for Reilly to do the same, though there was a rickety chair set across from the desk.

"It isn't necessary," said Reilly, deciding to sit down.

"Well, she's getting some for me. If you want a cup, tell her." Meyer adjusted his glasses on his nose and glanced once at Reilly. "What do you want to know?"

Long acquaintance with Meyer had taught Reilly to take no offence at the man's brusqueness. He cleared his throat. "I have been sent to observe Franchot Ragoczy, Count Saint-Germain. But I'd like to know if anyone else is doing the same thing."

"Ragoczy. He's the one in Glanzend Strasse, isn't he? Foreigner with lots of money; there's been some talk about him in important circles. They say he has investments in fuels." He squinted as he took a cigarette paper and began to fill it with dark Turkish tobacco. "Questions are being asked, and not from the usual quarters. There is a man, Paul Reighert, defrocked Jesuit, very dangerous in his way, works out of the Chez Noir. That's a brothel near Apostel-Paulus-Kirche." He licked the paper and rolled it shut.

"Who is he working for, do you know? The former priest, not Ragoczy." Reilly waited for his answer while Meyer fumbled for a match, lit his cigarette and exhaled.

"Word is that von Wolgast is paying him," said Meyer.

"Von Wolgast," mused Reilly. "He's a Baron, isn't he? What would an arms manufacturer want with a man like Ragoczy?"

"Ragoczy has that fuel business," Meyer said quietly, enjoying his cigarette. "It may be that von Wolgast wants the fuels Ragoczy has developed."

"Why not approach him directly?" Reilly asked. "Why bother with this former Jesuit who works in a whorehouse?"

"Why take the risk if the man is not what he seems?" Meyer countered. "Better to know what he has before you try to buy it. And it may be Ragoczy has sold his fuels already." He coughed twice, and spat out a bit of tobacco. "It may be that von Wolgast is worried about Ragoczy's connection to the Czar, whatever it is."

Reilly concealed his interest well; he did not rise to the bait offered.

"What else could von Wolgast want from Ragoczy?"

Meyer sounded disappointed. "Well, von Wolgast has been keeping Nadezna for three years now, and Ragoczy is known to be the patron of her ballet school. It could be that von Wolgast is afraid Ragoczy is going to want an expression of her gratitude."

"Do you think that's likely?" Reilly inquired, waiting to return to the matter that interested him most.

"It's possible," Meyer allowed. "But I don't think it is Ragoczy's purpose for his visit." Then he realized that Reilly had caught him.

Reilly's smile was as sweet as his severe features would accommodate. "And what do you think that purpose is?"

Grudgingly Meyer said, "Very clever. I should have realized what you were doing. I must be getting old." He tapped his fingers on a stack of photographs. "I think," he continued with full deliberation, "I think that Ragoczy is here on the Czar's business. I think von Wolgast would like to know what it is, so that he can make the most of it with his arms sales. I don't believe there is any connection between Ragoczy and Franz Josef, no matter what your friends in Saint Petersburg may think, but there is no reason to suppose that Ragoczy is working only for the Czar, either. His knowledge—whatever it may be—could command a high price." He stared distractedly at Reilly. "It is being whispered that the Croats have arranged to buy field artillery from von Wolgast: he will need fuels if he is going to sell to the Croats and Ragoczy has fuel. No one is certain that this will happen, but since Tancred Sisak was seen with von Wolgast in the last ten days, that is a reasonable assumption. Sisak has made no secret of his activities. His intentions are obvious, what with his history." He straightened up as his mother approached carrying a tray with two tall glasses of black tea on it. He did his best to clear a space for it on his cluttered desk.

"Drink it while it's hot," said the old woman. "It's already sweetened." This last was for Reilly's benefit.

"I didn't realize Sisak was still in business," said Reilly very carefully as Meyer's mother left them alone once more. "I heard he was persona non grata all over Europe."

"Yes, that's true, as far as it goes. He has been in Greece for a year or two, and in Egypt before that, while Mustapha Kemal was alive, but he has continued his work no matter where he lives. The government in Turkey threw him out just last year, for dealing with the Armenians and the Georgians." Meyer took one of the two glasses of tea and began to stir it with a pen-holder. "It was only a matter of time before he resumed his work in Austria and Germany."

"But isn't there still a price on his head?" Reilly asked, curiosity finally exceeding his reserve.

"Technically, yes, I suppose there is. But realistically, he is safe unless he does something flagrant. It was Bismarck who was his enemy, and now . . . " He turned his palms up to show how little it mattered now with Bismarck out of power. "There are many who welcome men of his talents, and seek to exploit them for their own ends. Not only the factions in Greece and the Balkans have use for his services. There are many in Poland who do not want their guns traced, Bohemian Separatists who are still trying to preserve thier country. And with the Austrians in Bosnia and Herzogovina, the Croats will want to protect themselves. Sisak will—"

"—deal in arms to anyone willing to pay him: Croat, Serb, Bosnian, Turk, or Hottentot," Reilly finished for him. "And von Wolgast manufactures arms for anyone who can afford them."

"That's about the way of it," said Meyer, holding the rim of his glass and drinking in small, practiced sips.

"Then why does Ragoczy's presence matter to von Wolgast, if he has made a bargain with Sisak?" Reilly was thinking aloud, and for once he did not care that Meyer overheard him.

"That I do not know," said Meyer, reluctant to admit such defeat. "I have been wondering about it myself." He set his glass of tea down carefully.

"Do you have any guesses you would care to make?" ventured Reilly, leaning forward, elbows planted on the edge of the desk.

Meyer took a short while to answer. "It depends on what the Czar wants. And you are more apt to know that than I am." This last was a deliberately pointed observation.

"If only I did," Reilly confessed. "But I have not been able to find out what Nicholas wants Ragoczy to accomplish, or why. Usually someone is willing to talk, but as far as I can determine, the only two men in Saint Petersburg who know what the Czar has ordered Ragoczy to do are Nicholas and Ragoczy themselves. Not that there hasn't been speculation." He directed his gaze to the dusty curtains across the window. "And that troubles me."

"It troubles me, as well," said Meyer. "When I was at the Ministry, I was always hearing things I was not supposed to. Everyone does. Men talk, some of them to boast, others to complain." He did not add that he had sold such gleanings to the highest bidder until he was caught; Reilly had been one of his most reliable customers. "The Czar appears to have kept this between Ragoczy and himself; it may be that Nicholas delivered his orders personally, but I cannot determine when they might have had occasion to do it. It must have been done clandestinely, for no one can say for certain when the arrangements were made, assuming any were made at all. However it was done, it was not through the usual methods. Otherwise someone would have said something— a minister, a secretary, someone." He made a travesty of a smile. "At least that knowledge is useful. Having it can save one from prison, for any trial brings to light such scandalous things." He was speaking of his own experience and both men knew it.

"What do you think the Czar is trying to do?" Reilly pursued, not allowing Meyer to wander too far afield.

"If I didn't know better, I would think he was trying to make peace," said Meyer caustically. "Ever since that disaster in The Hague, he has had bouts of conscience about peace. Not even the trouble five years ago was enough to change his mind. His ministers do not agree about peace, as you know better than I. How can Nicholas search for peace if his own government will not endorse it? What routes are open to him if the usual negotiative channels are closed?" The question was obviously rhetorical. "He might choose a private messenger, outside of his government and as free from the influence of other political leaders. Why not use someone like Ragoczy?"

"But peace?" Reilly asked sarcastically. "Why employ a messenger at all? Wouldn't it be easier to make a mutual support pact, one that would supersede their various treaties, many of which are mutually contradictory in any case." He waited for Meyer's answer with an air of exasperation.

"You wanted to know what I think. I've told you," said Meyer, drinking more of his tea. He regarded Reilly seriously. "It may be as you say, but I don't think so. Whatever the mission the foreigner has undertaken is one the diplomats would shun. Think, Sidney. There would be no need to employ a foreigner with funds of his own to undertake the task if it led to power and influence. That would have to mean a return to the old order in Russia, as you are certainly aware, which many of the Ministers would endorse, no matter what they say in public. Men of high military position in Russia are itching for war, if what my . . . associates tell me is correct." He put his fingertips down on the photographs once again. "Peace, however, is a less popular cause."

"After everything that has happened in Russia, I would not think the Czar would be willing to run the risk of peace-making. Russia has been near anarchy more than once since this century began." Reilly tried not to frown. "What good would it do for him to make a private peace treaty now?"

"It would keep his son from having to fight," Meyer reminded him. "That must always be on Nicholas' mind. That crazy priest cannot work his sorcery on the boy forever. And the Czar will listen to him only so long as his son thrives." He shook his head at the thought of Rasputin.

"Yes, I take your point," Reilly snapped. "Very well. I will not argue that point with you. And in the meantime, we know that von Wolgast is watching Ragoczy. That makes me eager to learn all I can about this development. I know you will be able to help me." He reached into his pocket and drew out an envelope; he laid this on the photographs next to Meyer's fingers. "Here. With your dismissal I understand you lost your pension. This should mitigate your expenses. And when you provide me more information, there will be more money for you."

"Just as there was before I was discovered," said Meyer in a sour way. "A pity you were unavailable when I most needed your concern." The envelope vanished into the recesses of his cardigan.

Reilly took one more sip of tea, then got to his feet. "I was in Siberia, as you must know. And had I been here, what could I have said to protect you? My testimony would have done more harm than good. What would have been the use?" He let the question serve as his leave-taking, making his way to the front door of the squalid apartment where Meyer's mother gave him back his pistol. "Thank you," he said as he pocketed the weapon once again. "I will see you in three or four days."

"With more money. Twice as much," she muttered as she opened the door slightly in order to permit Reilly to leave.

Making his way down the creaking stairs, Reilly could not keep from flinching at the filth around him, and the persistent atmosphere of decay. He had been in worse places, but few had left him with as strong an impression of helplessness and despondency as this building to which Renfred Meyer had retreated in his disgrace. The cold wind that greeted him was welcome, chasing away the sensation of dankness that clung to him. Recalling that he would have to return to this place, Reilly was filled with distaste, and for that reason walked away from the building in a more direct course than he had used coming there.

By the time he reached his borrowed flat, he had already decided on how to broach the matter of von Wolgast, although it was against his initial choice and entailed more exposure than he wanted to risk. But in his position, he thought it might give him an advantage he would otherwise lack. Long experience had taught him that the most direct approach was often the most successful. He had every reason to call on the Baron in person. Reilly knew that von Wolgast would be more than willing to meet with a man of his reputation—and Reilly had few illusions about his reputation. It was simply a matter of arranging an encounter and making the most of it. He entered the flat by the back garden stairs and took the time to inspect his various protections to assure himself that the place had not been violated in his absence. Nothing was disturbed, or it had been done so skillfully that he was unable to detect it, which was unlikely. He gave a short sigh and removed his coat, putting it neatly over the back of the sofa: its presence on a peg by the door might alert any watcher to his presence and his intention to remain in for a time. He took his satchel from under the large chair before the hearth and pulled his pad of notes onto his lap, content to review the scribbling there—scribbling which he intended to be incomprehensible to anyone but himself.

More than an hour passed before he was ready to leave the flat again. It was dark outside, and the air was very cold. As he wrapped himself in his greatcoat, he strove to ready himself for the icy night and the long hours before he would be ready to return to this flat. He pulled his hat down over his ears and muffled his lower face in a long woollen scarf. Then he put his protections in place as he left for the evening.

His first stop was the small restaurant four blocks away where he met with the man from "C", a reputed Swiss of about thirty-two or -three with a vaguely professorial look about him who had a copy of the *Astronomical Journal* and an old issue of *Intermediate Chess* set out on the table where he waited, though neither was open. He was sitting in the far corner, nursing a glass of red wine, his greying beard making his face look rimed with frost.

"Excuse me," said Reilly as he approached the table, "but I was wondering if you might be interested in a game of chess." His German was faultless.

"I'm more interested in games of chance," the fellow answered in the same tongue, following the recognition code carefully. "When there is something worth playing for."

"It is harder to find good partners for those," said Reilly, drawing out the second chair. He took off his hat and sat down, holding out his hand, while saying in English, "How is everything in London?"

The man shrugged, changing back to English as well, "I only know what 'C' tells me, and that is very little; it is on his orders that I am here with a packet for you," he replied, tapping the chess journal. "But I gather all is not going as well as he would like."

"No," said Reilly. "It never is, not that I can recall. Well, tell me what you have for me. We might as well get this done." With that he signaled for a glass of wine and a plate of bread and cheese.

"I have a general report on the current state of diplomatic posts throughout Europe and in Russia. There is more, in response to your last communication." He finished his wine and signaled the approaching waiter for another; the waiter turned around and went to get both men's food and drink at once. "I have the material for you, as you requested." Again he put his hand on the journal.

"For God's sake, don't bring attention to it. You don't know we aren't being watched, do you?" Reilly had kept his voice down but the reprimand stung, as he intended it should.

"Sorry," the man said, averting his eyes. "I haven't done this before. I'm usually kept busy translating reports and breaking codes."

Concealing a sigh, and wondering what sort of men were coming into the service these days, he said, "Then do your best to stay alert. Alert, but not obviously alert, for that only exposes you to others, who are more experienced than you are. You will need to be careful." Reilly glanced casually around the place as if no more than mildly curious. When he was satisfied he looked back at his contact. "All right. Now. About Ragoczy. What has 'C' learned about his stay in London?"

"As should be apparent, not as much as he wanted to. An attempt will be made to learn what Ragoczy told Sunbury, but solicitors are always chancy in regard to clients and he may not be as forthcoming as we would like. There is some record of Ragoczy's movements. He has been to Windsor on one occasion that we know of, but his discussion with the King was not . . . noted"—by which he meant overheard—"by any of 'C's men. It is supposed his nephew, the Czar, made the King willing to see him so . . . irregularly. Apparently Ragoczy has been to a private estate called Longacres in Buckinghamshire for a weekend party, and has since called on one of the family of that place in London. The girl's an artist, or so they say."

"An assignation?" Reilly asked, his attention sharpened.

The answer supplied disappointed him. "Apparently not. Ragoczy is a patron of many artists, and this is thought to be a similar . . . venture." The supposedly Swiss intellectual coughed once and changed to German as he saw the waiter coming with a tray. "It would seem that the Spanish have lost their edge in chess. The Russians, however, are—"

Reilly handed the waiter more than enough for the food and wine. "We will want coffee, black, in twenty minutes. Until then, please do not disturb us." He waved the waiter away and looked again at his contact, saying swiftly and softly in English, "I don't want you to tell me your name, but tell me what I am to call you. Make sure it is not a translation of your name."

The man blinked, staring off in the direction of the kitchen doors. "What about Angebot? That's my mother's maiden name."

"Then you're not apt to forget it," said Reilly. "All right, Angebot it is. What for a first name? What was her father called?"

"Eduard," said Angebot. "I will not forget that, either." His tone was not quite snide but angry enough to catch Reilly's attention.

"Listen to me," he told the other man, "this is not an entertainment. Missteps can cost more than a single life. You may not think it is necessary to take these precautions: I assure you it is. There are any number of dead men who would agree, if they were able to speak." Why, he asked himself as he thought back to the morning's conversation with Lukas, did espionage attract such creatures? He knew of men who had counted on rogues and dilettantes and paid dearly for their trust. He did not want to number among them.

Angebot turned sulky. "I will keep that in mind, Captain Reilly."

"For both our sakes, see that you do." He reached for his glass of wine, tasted it and set it down. "I am going to need the exact time of Ragoczy's arrival here in Berlin. I know it is in two or three days, but I want specific information." He rapped his knuckles on the tabletop, then slid the two slips of paper from the chess journal without anyone, including Angebot, noticing what he had done. "And I will need a ticket for the ballet tomorrow night."

"What is the program?" asked Angebot.

"I have no idea. I don't care. I will not be paying attention to it, whatever it is. But I want a very good seat, not far from Baron von Wolgast's, if you please. And if you can learn when the Baron will be attending, I would appreciate it." He saw the doubt in Angebot's eyes. "Do it."

"But the reason? Good seats are costly. I will have to explain the expense . . . " He watched Reilly slice off a wedge of cheese as if he feared the small knife might pare into him next.

"You have nothing to explain. I must make the acquaintance of Baron von Wolgast; this is the easiest way to do it, and, although you mayn't believe it, the least costly. If I am seen at the ballet on two or three occasions, it will almost constitute an introduction, and that will save lavish entertaining, which is not only more expensive, but takes longer and is more hazardous." He bit into the cheese, studying Angebot, his expression hard to read.

"Ballet tickets, then, and information on Ragoczy's time of arrival. He is traveling by ship, so I will have what you need by tomorrow." He was doing his best to make up for his earlier failure. "I will also bring you any of the information that might come in for you in the next twenty-four hours."

"Good," said Reilly around the cheese.

"Is there anything else?" Angebot asked, taking a long gulp of wine. "If not, I will leave."

"Nothing I can think of at the moment," said Reilly. "I will tell you more tomorrow." He drank again, and returned to German. "It has been a pleasure to meet you, Herr Angebot. I am delighted to have made your acquaintance."

"And I yours, Herr—" He broke off, afraid to use Reilly's name.

"You have forgotten already? Herr Morgenstern," he said as Angebot rose hastily from the table, taking the astronomy magazine, but leaving the chess journal.

"Morgenstern; yes. How thoughtless of me." His contact pulled on his hat and buttoned his coat against the evening chill. As he started to leave, he was visibly dismayed to hear Reilly call after him.

"Herr Angebot, you have left your chess journal behind." He held up the publication, and waited while Angebot retraced his steps to retrieve it. To think, he observed inwardly, that his life was in the hands of this cricket player.

"There is something in it—" Angebot whispered hurriedly.

"Not anymore," Reilly assured him, then added, more loudly, "I look forward to seeing you again. My regards to your father."

Confused, Angebot lowered his head. "Danke. I will tell him you asked after him."

"I appreciate it," said Reilly, and watched Angebot's disorderly retreat with ill-disguised distress. He swung back to the table and set about finishing his supper, knowing he had a long night ahead of him.

A few minutes later the waiter returned with two cups of coffee. "Your friend has left?"

"Regrettably, he could not linger; another engagement, it would seem. I will take both cups," he said, and again handed the waiter a generous amount of money. "If you would bring me some mustard?"

"Of course," said the waiter, setting off to comply at once, anticipating more tips when the man calling himself Morgenstern returned.

Reilly cut more slices of cheese and then halved the chunk of dark rye bread he had been served, preparing to improvise a sandwich. A small crock of butter stood next to the cheese, and he used this on the bread, waiting for the mustard before putting the cheese into place. All the while his thoughts were preoccupied with the house on Glanzend

Strasse and the foreign gentleman who was about to occupy it. He had learned much, but it was not enough. There were many more things he would need to know if he were to complete the assignment "C" had given him. With time so short, he would have to press forward with his task, less prepared than he would have liked to be, and with fewer assistants in place to support him. Anyone looking at Reilly would have been struck at how much at ease he appeared to be as he sipped alternately at his wine and coffee. His mind raced behind his laconic demeanor, all attention given over to Franchot Ragoczy, Count Saint-Germain.

Text of an informal letter from Czar Nikolai to Franchot Ragoczy, written in Russian and delivered by messenger in Berlin.

March 20, 1910

My dear Ragoczy;

I must admit to a degree of disappointment in what you reported in your last communication to me. I had hoped you would be able to explain to my Uncle Edward how great our shared risks are, and how much both he and I stand to lose as men and as rulers if the spread of arms continues unchecked. I believe you have made an effort, but demonstrably it is not sufficient to the task you have been given, and this makes me most apprehensive in regard to your success. I hope you will not become disheartened by your mission and abandon it. That, I am forced to remind you, would be the height of folly, and would undoubtedly bring about consequences you would not want.

It is still my most heartfelt wish that the rush toward war be slowed, if not halted, so that men of good will and governments with integrity will be able to reason with one another to the mutual benefit of all. You may say as much to my Cousin Wilhelm, and remind him that I am no longer a naïve young man on a yacht. His notion of honorable treating is not an example I seek to emulate. You may also tell him this, if it will advance your purpose there.

I have been asked by Stolypin to extend the land reform he initiated a short while ago. I will give him no answer, not yet, preferring to see how much you can achieve, for if the threat of war is not as pressing as it has been, it is my hope that he will not demand such drastic reforms in so little time. Of course it is important to return land to the peasants who work it, but not in this abrupt way. There are legal and traditional considerations that ought to be considered, so that in giving the land to its people, we do not create greater inequities than they have suffered in the past. I have said something of this to Stolypin, and he pretends to agree, but I can tell he is not inclined to accept any delay in these measures, for he is afraid there may still be another outbreak of violence by the people. There are so many firebrands about, stirring up the people with their rhetoric, and this troubles the Duma and Stolypin as well. My suggestions for gradual changes go largely unheeded.

You remarked to me once, some years ago, that the French Revolution failed to achieve its reforms because it fell into the hands of the most extreme radicals, men who were unwilling to endorse any power but their own. Such is the clarity of hindsight. Unfortunately I can see a similar disaster overtaking Russia if we do not now prevail in the cause of sense. Peace is a pragmatic good for all of us. Why is it so difficult for the world to grasp this simple truth? We have just begun to taste the fruits of progress: if war comes it will all be sacrificed to the generals. I have sought to do those things that will make peace not only achievable but desirable, and it seems that my intentions are everywhere misunderstood, not only in my homeland, but among the members of my family. I would not like to discover at this juncture that you are as cynical as the rest and have abandoned any hope for peace.

I look forward to the news you have from Berlin. Once Edward is in better health, he will most certainly be willing to let you speak to him again on my behalf. For the time being, I urge you to continue on your course with Wilhelm. If only I were in a position to enlist Franz Josef in our cause as well, we might hope for a just and lasting peace by 1915. As it is, I am determined to see this task accomplished by no later than 1920. With your genuine efforts, this should be within our grasps.

Most sincerely,
Nikolai Alexandreivich Romanov
Czar of All the Russias
of that name the second

8

As Geoffrey Pearce-Manning rose to welcome his visitor, he said, "What a fine surprise. I wasn't expecting you until Friday evening."

Rupert Bowen took the hand extended to him and shook it forth-rightly. "I hope I am not intruding," he said diffidently, accepting the offer of a chair in front of the library hearth, where the beauty of the park beyond could be glimpsed through the four tall windows which had been one of the many changes wrought at Longacres with Saxon millions. "I wanted to speak to you before Rowena arrives, and I understand she's expected later this afternoon."

At the mention of his oldest daughter, Geoffrey frowned. "Yes. She's driving herself down from London." This rankled with him, and he allowed himself to complain of her, aware that Rupert Bowen knew the worst. "It's her grand-father's fault, of course, letting her have all that money. Well, you know what she is. Ever since she bought that Daimler, she has been racketing about the country in a most . . . " He let the criticism trail off. "Yes, she is expected before six."

It took Rupert a long moment to realize he was expected to speak. He cleared his throat and shifted in his chair; had he been standing he would have shuffled. "This is rather a delicate matter, in regard to Rowena. Pray do not hold it against me if I cannot summon the eloquence I need."

"What eloquence is that?" Geoffrey asked, although he had already grasped the drift of Rupert's intent.

"I . . . this is very difficult for me . . . You see, I . . . I want to obtain your permission to ask her to marry me." Now that he was over the first hurdle, he went on with what he had rehearsed. "I am sincerely attached to your daughter, and have been for well over a year, which I suppose has not escaped your attention, sir."

"No, it hasn't," said Geoffrey Pearce-Manning.

Rupert swallowed hard and plunged on. "You know my family, of course, and you must be aware that although I am not yet established, I have excellent prospects, besides what I will inherit from my grand-father—not that I live on expectations—which is more than a compe-tency, though nothing like the fortune I understand Rowena and her brothers and sister will inherit." He stared down at the toes of his shoes. "Not that I am doing what they used to call 'hanging out for a rich wife.' That would be unacceptably crass, and I hardly need to do that." His chuckle was a little too high and rushed to be as convincing as he wanted it to be.

Geoffrey Pearce-Manning gave Rupert a nod of encouragement. "I am a younger son; I know how such things stand." He made a quick gesture. "Not that I am not fond of my wife. Clarice is a wonderful woman, and, frankly, I would have been in the soup without her father's generosity; I am thankful that we were able to make the arrangements we did." He coughed once, and directed his stare at the glossy paneling between the tall, glass-fronted bookcases. "I would not fault you if you had Rowena's fortune in mind, providing you did not intend to treat her shabbily."

"Oh, no; never that; I would not think of it, I assure you," said Rupert, his fair skin flushing so that his neat moustache seemed suddenly out of place on such a youthful visage. "She is a most wonderful girl."

"And she is something of a handful," said her father, as if admitting to poor conformation in one of his hunters.

Now Rupert's laughter was more confident. "As to that, I am sure it is only the want of an establishment of her own, and her own family, that gives her such starts." He cocked his head. "She may want to continue with painting for a time, and I have nothing against that."

"You're a generous fellow, Rupert Bowen. Not many men would be willing to marry a . . . girl who has shown herself to be so . . . headstrong as Rowena has." Geoffrey Pearce-Manning sighed. "It's her grandfather's influence, I've no doubt."

"That's as may be," Rupert allowed, "but once she is married and has her own hopeful children, she will think her grand-father less romantic than she does now. Not that I intend to cast aspersions on him, for then she would be duty-bound to defend him, and I do not want such a rift in the family." He gazed into the fire, his green-hazel eyes seeing the domestic success he anticipated.

"She will still have that trust from Horace Saxon, no matter what husband she chooses," Geoffrey Pearce-Manning warned Rupert; seeing the slight surprise in the other man's face, he explained, "Old Horace set it up so that her control over the money will remain in place no matter what her married state might be. He said he does not want any of his grand-children dependent on anyone for their support. The Married Women's Property Act will uphold the terms of the trust." He made a gesture of annoyed resignation. "I would like to think that you will not try to break the terms of the trust, for then there might be difficulties in the property settlements."

Troubling though this revelation was, Rupert felt his hopes raise. "Then you will not object to my proposal?"

"My dear young friend, if I objected we would not be having this conversation." Geoffrey Pearce-Manning smiled faintly. "Of course, you will have to persuade Rowena, for neither her mother nor I have the means to compel her to marry you or anyone. More's the pity." He rose, holding out his hand, "I wish you every success in doing so, Rupert. I think you are just the man to exercise a steadying influence on my daughter. With the wisdom you can bring to her, and the guidance, she will certainly come to a more realistic . . . It would be a privilege to welcome you to the family."

Rupert scrambled to his feet, wringing Geoffrey Pearce-Manning's hand gratefully. He struggled to find the words to express his gratitude and satisfaction. "Thank you, sir. Thank you very much. I say, this is most encouraging. I can't say how awfully happy this makes me." Self-consciously he released Geoffrey Pearce-Manning's hand. "It means a great deal to me, your approval."

"As to that," Geoffrey Pearce-Manning said as he went to the small bar set in the middle of a case of leather-bound travel books, "I am most relieved that you did not think the lot of us as harum-scarum as Rowena can be."

"Her spirits are what drew me to her in the first place. There is so much vitality in her, so much . . . verve. And she is a true beauty, beyond pretty, and with more countenance than some women twice her age. She's not one of those pale, eager young things one sees everywhere, only on the lookout for a husband and a name, ready to endorse anything if it will serve the purpose of acquiring a suitable alliance." He blushed again, this time less like a schoolboy and more like a man with a nasty secret. "Rowena would never stoop to such banality. And yet she isn't one of those suffragettes. She confines her activities to painting."

Geoffrey Pearce-Manning had finished pouring two brandies and held one out to Rupert. "Here. Shall we drink to your acceptance?" he suggested as Rupert took the snifter.

"I should think!" Rupert exclaimed, lifting the snifter before carrying it to his lips. "First rate."

"Another benefit of Horace Saxon's influence," said Geoffrey Pearce-Manning, an edge in his pleasant voice. "The cellar is the envy of half the neighbors." He took a long sip of the brandy. "If Horace offers to pay for the wedding—and he will: Rowena's his favorite—let him."

"I don't know . . . It may be premature to consider . . . " Rupert sputtered over the rim of his snifter. "It would have to be . . . "

"I will deal with the particulars, if you prefer," said Geoffrey Pearce-Manning. "For the time being, you convince Rowena to marry you. Once that's done, then we will see about enlisting her grand-father's help. The old man is richer than Croesus, and with no one to leave it to but Rowena, Augustus, and Penelope. He has all the papers completed and filed." He set his snifter down on the mantel and directed his gaze to the fire. "Sometimes this concerns me, knowing my children will have so much wealth to command. Augustus is not the sort of boy who will squander his money, but Penelope, she is . . . well, a bit reckless in that regard."

"When you say wealth, what do you mean?" Rupert inquired, adding quickly, "Not that this is a factor in my interest in Rowena."

"It should be, if you are going to marry her." He said nothing for a short while, then told him, "Each of my children stands to inherit about twelve million dollars. Given Horace Saxon's investments, it might well be more."

Rupert calculated swiftly. "I had no idea. That's more than one million, seven hundred thousand pounds," he declared, "at seven dollars the pound."

"Yes," said Geoffrey Pearce-Manning numbly, "I know." He drank the rest of his brandy in a single gulp, then stepped away from the hearth, his demeanor cordial and reserved. "You'll have your dinner with the family, of course. And when Rowena arrives, Clarice and I will arrange for you to have some time together."

"That's very good of you, sir," said Rupert, also tossing back his brandy. He set the snifter down on the end table by his chair. "Let me assure you that my feelings for her are profound, and my nature is constant. I have never met a girl who so moves me as Rowena does."

"Yes, yes," said her father with a touch of impatience. "I know what you want to say. I was a suitor once myself." He was getting ready to leave the room, but stopped, looking squarely at Rupert. "Not that your situation is anything like mine. I know it is not."

This admission of Geoffrey Pearce-Manning's previously straitened circumstances was more embarrassing to Rupert than anything else they had discussed. "I am sure your affections were engaged when you married Lady Pearce-Manning."

"Oh, yes. She was such a fetching, refreshing girl. I didn't mind her American ways—calling us Mister and Missus instead of Lord and Lady, having the generator installed for electric lights, buying phonographs and telephones and all the rest of the American gadgets—but occasionally I find her enthusiasms a trifle hard to take. She is determined that Penelope have what she calls a real education; that's her most recent decision. She has said that it isn't possible for it to happen in Britain, not to her satisfaction, in any case." He shrugged. "Penelope doesn't want to go to America to attend university, but she is beginning to talk about being a journalist." He made a single, grim nod. "She is young enough that this does not worry me. Two years ago, she wanted to go on the stage, but the impulse passed."

"It's her youth, and her mother's indulgence," said Rupert with all the understanding of his twenty-six years.

"Oh, yes, and the freedom a fortune can give." Geoffrey Pearce-Manning began his march to the door once again. "Not that I despise the money; far from it. But it can cause certain difficulties you may not suppose now could arise."

Rupert tagged after him. "I should think so. Having the purse strings in the wife's hands is never easy nor is being beholden to the distaff side of the family for . . . " He recalled he was describing Geoffrey Pearce-Manning's situation. He broke off and resumed with more restraint, "That is why I hope to convince Rowena to put her money in trust for our children and grandchildren, following her grand-father's excellent example. She is sensible girl. She will see the advantage in the plan." He paused while Geoffrey Pearce-Manning pulled the draperies across the windows.

"Perhaps. But she might not like that notion," Geoffrey Pearce-Manning warned him. "She is certain that she can direct her fate for herself."

Made confident by her father's approval and brandy, Rupert said, "I think I will be able to show her otherwise."

They stepped out into the corridor and made their way to the main hall, Rupert still a few steps behind his host. The shell sconces glowed with the steady brightness of electricity, and the fine carpet underfoot had been installed less than two months ago, a belated Christmas gift from Horace Saxon.

Clarice Pearce-Manning had just changed for dinner, although the meal was more than two hours away, and the hour unfashionably early for her clothes. She was clad in a lovely damask-silken frock of a deep claret color, with a beaded, square-necked bodice, raised waist and long sleeves that flattered her figure and complexion; her hair was expertly coifed and she wore a topaz ring on her right hand. She smiled at Rupert, holding out her hand to him and regarding him expectantly. "There you are; I was told you had arrived." She smelled of lily of the valley and roses. "It is very good to see you, Rupert."

Rupert bowed over her hand, prepared to flatter her if necessary. "It is always delightful to be here, Madame."

Clarice laughed. "Madame indeed. You are not going to take that tone with me, young man. You will call me Clarice, as you have done this last year." She gave him an arch glance. "And I assume that I am to consider you more than a visitor tonight? Waithe told me he had put you in the Hunter Room—he has a high regard for you."

"When a man is well-thought-of by the staff, he has reason to be happy," said Rupert, falling in beside Clarice as she began to make her way to the other side of the house where sherry would be waiting for them.

"You are seeking more than the favor of servants, or you may call me a Dutchman," said Clarice. "I know you and my husband have been talking."

Rupert found this direct speech disconcerting, but endured it with good humor. "I would not want to disagree with a lady," he said gallantly.

"Especially now," she agreed, doing her best to tease him affectionately.

This time Rupert did not know how to make a recovery. He looked to Geoffrey Pearce-Manning for guidance.

"Don't tweak him, my dear," said Geoffrey Pearce-Manning in a laconic way as he ambled along behind them. "He is marshaling his courage for the contest to come."

"Geoffrey," his wife chided him, "you make it sound as if he is going into battle." She looked up at Rupert through her lashes. "Not that Rowena cannot be a challenging girl when she chooses."

"That she can . . . Clarice," said Rupert, wishing that the subject would change.

"We are expecting her within the hour," said Clarice with ruthless good humor. "Not that she will be on time."

Geoffrey Pearce-Manning finally came to Rupert's rescue. He went into the salon, his manner unruffled, and reached at once for the bellpull. "Then let us discuss something else, or we will run out of conversation well before Rowena arrives."

"Whenever that will be," said Clarice darkly.

There was a sudden squeal from the door as Penelope, decked out for dinner in a frock of pale peach organdy in a style about three years too old for her, rushed into the room, going directly to Rupert; she was tall for her age and came up almost to his shoulder. "It *is* you! Waithe said you were here, but I didn't believe it. Oh, how wonderful!" She nearly threw herself into his arms, but held back at the last instant in response to a loud click of her mother's tongue. She responded at once with the assumption of proper manners. "It is good to see you, Mister Bowen."

"It must be," said Rupert, teasing her as the two shook hands.

"I thought I told you this evening was for adults," said Clarice, trying to summon a sternness she did not truly feel.

"I knew you couldn't mean it," said Penelope with her most winning smile. "So I decided to join you while you have sherry."

"You are incorrigible, young lady," said her father, his expression more doting than her mother's. As Waithe came into the room bearing the tall butler's table with glasses and bottles on it, Geoffrey Pearce-Manning went on, "I think we shall have a glass for Miss Penelope, as well, Waithe, since she has taken it upon herself to join us."

Waithe, who did not find Penelope's precociousness as acceptable as her parents, merely nodded to show he understood. He set down his table and began to pour out sherry, starting with Clarice Pearce-Manning, who asked for shooting sherry.

"It tastes so much like hazelnuts," she said, as if this explained her choice.

"Dry sack, my lord?" asked Waithe of Geoffrey Pearce-Manning, knowing the answer and already pouring.

"Yes, thank you, Waithe," said Geoffrey Pearce-Manning, accepting the offered glass with a nonchalance his wife would never achieve.

"Mister Bowen?" asked Waithe, putting off the moment when he would have to give sherry to Penelope.

"Dry sack for me as well, Waithe," he said, knowing what was expected of him.

"And I'll have some cream sherry," said Penelope with an assumed hauteur that made everyone but Waithe smile.

Waithe poured half the amount of cream sherry that he had poured for the rest into a pony. He handed it over reluctantly, thinking that this child belonged in the nursery instead of being here with her parents and their guest. He also disapproved of her obvious flirtation with Rupert Bowen, believing that such attachments ought to be rigorously discouraged. He looked around the room, then bowed slightly. "If that will be all, Madame?"

"Certainly," said Clarice. "Please decant the wine for dinner. Two bottles, I think." She gave Rupert an encouraging look as she raised her glass. "Well, chin-chin everyone."

This toast was recited by the other three, and the first sip of sherry taken; Penelope tried not to make a face, knowing it was too childish, but her nose wrinkled.

"How is London?" asked Clarice, addressing Rupert. "I have been wanting to get up to the theatre for a month and more." She stared down into her glass. "I have been trying to prevail upon Geoffrey to take me to see the Divine Sarah when she next performs here. I have seen her before, of course," she added hastily.

"I don't know that Bernhardt is expected to perform again in England any time soon," said Rupert, who did not completely approve of women on the stage; not even brilliant actresses such as the world-famous Frenchwoman could wholly overcome his feelings on the matter. "They say her mother was a Dutch Jewess."

"My father saw her in Paris," said Geoffrey Pearce-Manning, rather hurriedly, "opposite Jean Mounet-Sully, in *Hernani*, I think it was. Said it was—"

"She is astonishing," Clarice declared. "Even now, though she is not young, there is something about her."

"She wears . . . trousers," said Penelope with a gulp of laughter. "I saw her photograph." Emboldened, she added, "It's because she lost . . . part of her leg."

"She paints, too, so they say," added Rupert as if this last were the most damning condemnation. He stopped himself from saying more.

"Those theatrical sorts often aspire to other talents; Caruso is said to make sketches of his colleagues," said Geoffrey Pearce-Manning, and was spared having to say more by the sound of an automobile arriving. "Ah. Rowena is only twenty minutes late," he said, glancing once at Rupert as if to assure himself of the young man's purpose.

"At least she is home safe and sound, which is the most important thing," said Rupert, putting down his sherry and looking toward the door to the hall. "I wonder, should I . . . " He nodded in the direction of the door to finish his thought.

"Let her change first," Clarice urged with a swift glance of complicity at her husband. "She will be smirched from the road. Let her freshen up and change."

Rupert allowed himself to be persuaded, remarking, "What woman likes to be seen when she is not at her best. You're right, Clarice. I have waited for many months for this day—I will wait a while longer."

Penelope's eyes sparkled, and not entirely from the sherry. "Oh, Rupert." She was young enough to find it thrilling to use his Christian name. "Are you going to *propose*?" Without giving him time to answer, she added wistfully, "My sister is the luckiest woman in the world."

"I hope she thinks so," Rupert said to Penelope with an indulgent smile. "We'll have to see."

"But she must," said Penelope as simply as possible. "How could she not?"

"It is her decision to make, and one she should not make lightly," said Rupert. "She must know her heart and mind are in accord."

"They will be, I know they will," said Penelope, her cheeks flushing. "I know I would marry you in a moment."

"Penelope," her mother reprimanded her gently. "This is not becoming."

"But it is *true*," she protested. "I *would* marry him if I could. If I were older, I would be jealous of Rowena for having Rupert care for her. And I think Rowena would be an idiot not to accept him." She put down her sherry and frowned at her mother. "I can't help it if I—"

The front door opened; Rowena's steps rang out as she rushed toward the stairs. "Bring in my bags if you will, Waithe, and tell my parents I'll join them in fifteen minutes, after I repair the ravages."

"Very good, Miss Pearce-Manning," Waithe announced.

"Fifteen minutes," said Clarice. "Well, she will have time for a little sherry before we sit down. You may consider the time, if you like. I know it is foolish to keep country hours when we entertain during the week, but we are in the country, after all, and . . . " She looked down at her glass. "Well. There will be time for a little more."

"When Rowena comes down," agreed her husband.

Waithe presented himself at the door to the salon. "Miss Pearce-Manning has arrived."

"Yes, Waithe; we know," said Clarice, doing her best not to make this a reprimand. "Tell her we will wait for her to join us here, when she has changed."

"That I will, Madame," he said, and withdrew once more.

In the silence that followed, Penelope reminded everyone, "I will be eleven in three weeks." She looked directly at Rupert.

"Gracious, Penelope," said Clarice, doing her best to recover the tone of the evening and trying not to sound upset. "One would think you were raised by prospectors, the way you talk."

"Well, I will," said Penelope belligerently. She lifted up her small portion of sherry and drank a little more.

"And you shall have a party to celebrate," said Rupert.

"Probably," said Penelope. "If you and Rowena don't spoil it."

"For Heaven's sake . . . !" Clarice protested, going and taking the glass from her daughter's hand. "That is enough sherry for you, young lady. Until you can learn to master yourself. This is not appropriate behavior."

But Penelope was not about to give up. "If they have an engagement party, everyone will forget about my birthday."

"Not at all," Rupert soothed her. "For one thing, we don't know if Rowena will accept my proposal. I haven't had a chance to make my offer to her yet." He looked pleased at Penelope's single scornful snort. "And if she does accept me, there are a number of arrangements that must be dealt with. We will not have everything done before your birthday, I can promise you that. You may celebrate without fear of our plans overshadowing your event."

Penelope sniffed; she was beginning to feel chagrin at her outburst. "I didn't mean I would not be happy for you, of course."

"I know that," said Rupert. Had Penelope been a year or two younger, he might have ruffled her hair; as it was, he patted her shoulder.

"You must think me quite *boorish*." It was a word she had enjoyed using for the last year, one that made her feel very grown-up.

"Never that," Rupert promised her.

Clarice cut into their conversation with sudden determination. "Tell Mister Bowen you are sorry for that display of yours, Penelope. You may be getting a modern education, but it does not excuse such behavior. Ask his pardon for your lapse."

Rupert glanced at his hostess. "Clarice, it's hardly necessary—"

"If she is to behave well in society, it is," said Clarice firmly. "Penelope."

Turning her eyes up to Rupert, Penelope said in her most fetching way, "Oh, Mister Bowen, will you forgive me for making such a display of myself? I didn't mean to offend you, or cause you any distress."

"Apology accepted, but not—" Rupert assured her.

Again Clarice interrupted. "Thank him, Penelope."

"Thank you, Mister Bowen," said Penelope, going on winsomely, "And truly, Rupert, I did not mean anything wrong. I . . . couldn't help myself."

"Don't trouble yourself, Penelope," he said very seriously. "I must admit I'm flattered. I hope your sister shares your good opinion of me." He reached out and patted her hand.

"She must," said Penelope, staring at Rupert with all the longing of her nearly eleven years.

"Now, then, Penelope," said Clarice, hoping to calm down her excitable youngest daughter before Rowena arrived; it would not do to have the child blurt out Rupert Bowen's purpose in coming to Longacres. She lifted her glass to Penelope. "May your good wishes inspire your sister."

There was a soft, relieved chuckle all 'round. Geoffrey Pearce-Manning beamed at Penelope. "You're your mother's daughter, no doubt about it."

Penelope colored from her neck to her scalp. "I just want Rupert . . . Mister Bowen in the family."

"I'll keep that in mind, in case your sister refuses me," said Rupert gallantly, winking at Penelope. "You're so artless and unspoiled, I may prefer you one day."

By the time Rowena came down, still fussing with the topaz velvet of her long skirt, to join them, the rest were on their second glass of sherry and the announcement of soup being served had just been made: Rupert's proposal would have to wait until the end of the evening, for the idea of interrupting dinner for anything less than immediate disaster was unimaginable. So when all the china had been taken, and the napery and silver were waiting to be taken to the kitchen, Clarice rose from the table saying, "Let us leave the gentlemen to their port and cigars."

Rupert intervened. "Actually, I would like a word with Rowena, if I might." He was pleased to see the minuscule nod from her father.

Rowena frowned slightly. "Can't it wait until morning?" she asked him, making no excuse for her brusqueness.

"I'd rather not wait, if you don't mind," said Rupert, being as polite as he could. He did not like being put off, particularly at a time like this. "I won't need much of your time."

"Oh, very well," said Rowena, her face without expression. She looked at Clarice. "I will join you in the lounge shortly." She did not meet Rupert's eyes. "This won't be long, will it?"

"I don't know how long I will need." Rupert sensed he was losing what little advantage he had. He took hold of Rowena's elbow and guided her toward the door. "I think the morning room will do."

"At nine-thirty at night?" Rowena said impishly. "Rupert, how daring of you." She fell in beside him, saying, "I wish you would not hang onto me so."

He shifted his grasp to her lower arm. "I beg your pardon." They started down the corridor to the octagonal room on the southeast corner of the house.

"Oh, Rupert," she exclaimed in exasperation as she tugged to get free, "it's not a matter of . . . courtesy. If you hold my elbow that way, you put me off balance, and in evening shoes, it is—"

He regained some of his optimism. "I understand," he told her at once, increasing his hold on her lower arm.

Behind them at the far end of the corridor, Waithe glanced out of the rear kitchen door, and ducked back in as soon as he saw the couple.

"Then let go, will you? I am not an invalid, needing someone to shepherd me through the halls of my family home," she said testily. "Thank you," she added when he complied.

The morning room was dark, its many windows with garlanded ornamentation in stained glass showing nothing but night beyond; Rowena twisted the light switch and the room came alight, the windows serving as mirrors. Rupert made his way around the breakfast table to the wide benches under the windows. "Come here, Rowena. I need to talk to you."

She went toward him, dreading what was coming. "What is it? I'm tired."

He patted the needlepoint cushions. "Sit down, if you will." When she did not comply at once, he said. "Please."

"Very well," she said, and sat, just a little out of reach, but not so far to be obvious about it. "What do you want?"

"I must assume you can guess the reason for my wanting to be alone with you?" His smile was indulgent, showing that he credited her with knowing his intentions.

"I have some idea," she answered, wishing she were almost anywhere else.

"No doubt." Again his smile, now tinged with nervousness, and his well-rehearsed words. "This conversation cannot be wholly unexpected, not after all the time we have known each other." He inched nearer to her and reached out for her hand, patting it as if it were a puppy when he finally dared to touch it.

"You have not hidden them from me," she said, staring down at her knees. There had been many times, she thought, when she wished he had been more circumspect, or more willing to trust her judgment. She had known this moment was coming, and now that it was here, she began to anticipate relief at putting the whole behind her. She started to pull her hand away, but his fingers tightened.

"You have no reason to be apprehensive. It must be difficult for a girl your age to believe that a change in her state is still possible." Rupert decided things were going well. "Then it will not surprise you to know that I spoke to your father this afternoon, and obtained his permission to—"

He was cut short. "You've already spoken to my father? Oh, how very like you, Rupert. Have you negotiated the property settlements yet, or would that be precipitous?" she demanded, the flare of her temper unnerving her. "How dare you talk to him before you talked to me?"

Rupert's expression was non-plussed. "Of course. I had to get his—"

"Permission," she finished for him, her tone sarcastic. "Like a boy wanting to ride in his first hunt." She rose to her feet, her golden eyes shining with feverish intensity. "If you want my consent, you must have it from me, not my father, not my mother, and not my goose of a sister. From *me*." She was astonished at the fury coursing through her now, at the passion of it. Little as she wanted to admit it, in a very odd way, she was enjoying herself.

This sudden eruption of anger took Rupert aback. He lurched to his feet, reaching out for Rowena, trying to grapple her to him. "Rowena, calm yourself. You aren't considering—" He did his best to press his mouth to hers.

She turned her head away, striking out at his shoulders with her hand that was not pinioned. "Let go of me!"

He managed to get one arm around her tightly, and made another valiant attempt at a kiss, only to feel his lips slide to her jaw. "Rowena, you mustn't be afraid of me."

"Afraid?" she repeated, shoving him hard enough to break free. "Is that what you think? That I am afraid? I am *disgusted!*"

This blighting rebuke stung him; his ardor vanished as if by conjuration and he took a step backward, almost falling as his leg struck the bench. "Rowena . . . I know I ought to . . . "

"To what? Apologize? I have told you again and again that I do not want to marry. Not you, not anyone. I thought you respected my wishes." She was running her hands down the front of her dress as if to rid it of contamination.

"I do. You must believe that I do. I could not do anything else." He took a few uncertain steps toward her only to see her raise her hands to keep him at bay. "Surely you understand that everything I have done has been for—"

"—the antiquated rules that would keep me chattel and you the over-lord." She overrode his calming, sensible words. "I've told you I will not marry. So you perform this underhanded, cowardly, unprincipled strat-agem in the hope that I might be coerced into being your wife—" Her outrage silenced her at last. She stood with her back to the door, pant-ing with wrath.

"Nothing like that, I promise you," Rupert said at his most placating. "You're . . . beside yourself, Rowena. Think of what you are saying."

"Blast your eyes, Rupert Bowen, I know what I am saying." She saw his shock at her language and felt fierce satisfaction. "I am not hyster-ical, though if you continue to treat me as if I were an imbecile, I might become so." She turned on her heel. "I will not marry you, not now, not in a year, not in a century." As she left the room, she resisted the urge to slam the door: the servants would doubtless have more than enough to gossip about already. She gathered up her skirts and would have gone to her room, but the sight of Waithe at the far end of the corridor brought her up short, and she made for the lounge, doing her best to keep from running.

Clarice was in a high-backed leather chair bent over a copy of *A Room with a View*, squinting at the page. She did not look up as the door opened, but said, "I meant it, Penelope. You must go to bed now."

"It isn't Penelope," said Rowena through clenched teeth. Now that the fine tide of temper was ebbing, she felt chilly and slightly sick.

"Rowena!" Clarice shut the novel with a snap and rounded on her daughter. As she caught sight of her, she nearly held her breath. "Gracious. Rowena . . . what is the matter?" She came toward her oldest daughter, feeling very much at a loss. "What did he do? Did he try to—"

"He proposed. As I would think you and the entire household knew." She began to cry, not from weakness, but as a last expression of her rage.

"Well, yes," said Clarice, wondering why Rowena was so distraught. "But we have been expecting him to propose for Methuselah's years," she said, trying to cajole her daughter out of her perplexing bout of tears. She came closer to Rowena, not quite willing to touch her while she was in such a state.

"I *won't!*" Rowena insisted through her weeping. "I will not marry anyone, least of all Oliver Rupert Dominic Bowen!"

Clarice shook her head. "I knew it. I knew it. You're fascinated by that foreigner, Count Saint-Germain, and you mustn't allow yourself to be taken in. When I read the letter he sent you, I knew how it would be, with his polish and courtesy. All that flattery about your art . . . Let me tell you, my love, men of his sort never marry, and you may stake your fortune on it, he would not offer for you, unless he is not as wealthy as I have heard, and then he would seek you for your grandfather's money." She felt tears well in her eyes in sympathy with Rowena's distress.

"Mother, don't be ridiculous," said Rowena, at last bringing her crying under some control. "I've said I will not marry anyone, and I meant it. I will not change my mind, no matter who proposes." She looked about for a handkerchief and felt relieved when her mother handed her one. "Thank you," she muttered as she mopped her eyes with it.

"You don't mean that, Rowena. You know you don't." She put her arm around Rowena's shoulder. "You're a handsome young woman with a generous inheritance coming to you—"

"So it will not be necessary for me to marry." She sniffed forcefully, gave a last, purposeful swipe to her eyes before giving her mother back her handkerchief. "I have never said I would marry."

"But surely you . . . you will want children of your own," said Clarice, being drawn back into an argument they had begun more than fifteen years ago. She released her hold on Rowena so that she could face her directly.

"My work will be my children, Mother," said Rowena, sounding fatigued. "I will not let my work be stifled by the impositions of society. What is the use of my fortune if it will not buy me liberty to do as I wish?" She stared at Clarice. "I know you don't understand. I've stopped expecting you to. But I wish you could believe I know my own mind." She sighed heavily once.

Clarice worried the handkerchief, unwilling to look at Rowena. "You will regret your decision. When you are older, you will look back and . . . People say the most . . . awful things about spinsters. My love, you have no idea how cruel people can be." Her cheeks were wet again, rivulets of powder marking the wrinkles she had wanted to disguise. "It's all very well to say it will not matter, but it will, it will."

"Then I will have to hope my family will not spurn me," Rowena said with a lightness at variance with the somber expression in her golden eyes.

"Oh, Rowena," exclaimed Clarice, sobbing in earnest. "You make everything so difficult."

"I did not," Rowena countered sharply. "Rupert proposed, and he knew I would not accept him. I have told him time and time again that I would refuse him, and he was not honorable enough to respect my wishes. So he chooses this underhanded way to gain his ends. He was a poltroon to try to use Father so disgracefully."

"Your father!" Clarice gave a little shriek. "What will he say when he hears about this? I don't know how I shall face him."

A formality came over Rowena, a sense that she was among kindly strangers. She turned away. "Tell him to talk to me—before I leave; I will explain it to him myself," she told Clarice dully, and withdrew before her mother's distress could wear away at her determination more ruinously than Rupert's courtship ever could.

✧ ✧ ✧

Text of a dispatch from Julian Sinclair-Howard in London to Franchot Ragoczy in Berlin.

London
April 6, 1910

Franchot Ragoczy, Count Saint-Germain
45, Glanzend Strasse
Berlin, Germany

My dear Count;
I have the duty to inform you that it will please King Edward to receive you at Windsor on the fifteenth of this month. I realize that the time is short, but you are no doubt aware that His Majesty is not in the best of health and so has to ration his time. If it should be impossible for you to arrive here in time for the audience, then I cannot tell you when it may be rescheduled, for it is not possible to anticipate what activities the King will have to curtail while he is on the mend.
This may prove some inconvenience to you, for which I, of course, apologize, although there is nothing more I can do to assist you in your mission on King Edward's nephew's, the Czar's, behalf. No doubt you will want to arrange transportation at once; when you have done so, I would appreciate being informed of your travel plans in order to confirm your audience with King Edward. If you cannot reach London a day before the scheduled interview, I would be grateful of notification to that effect so that other petitioners may avail themselves of the time currently assigned to you.
In the hope that I will see you in London directly, I remain

Most sincerely yours,
Julian Sinclair-Howard

9

Harris wisely refrained from saying anything as he drove Ragoczy and his manservant from the train station to the house; the afternoon traffic was sufficiently heavy to give him ample reason to watch the street. He could sense his employer's urgent determination, and realized he would not welcome any distraction from his thoughts. Only when they neared his leased house did Harris remark, "The weather's been mild."

"April in England," Ragoczy mused, thinking of Browning's poem. "In this northern light, spring is very pretty." He glanced out the window of the Silver Ghost at the clinging mist which washed out the city with a milky opalescence.

As he turned into the alley leading to the rear of the house, Harris said, "Is there anything more you will be needing of me tonight, sir?"

"No, Harris, I do not think so," Ragoczy answered, sounding a trifle distracted—between the sun and the Channel crossing, he was aware that the native earth in his shoes was seriously depleted and would have to be replaced before tomorrow. No matter how diluted the sunlight, it was beginning to prove enervating for him. He made himself concentrate on the duties before him. "But if you will be good enough to wait while I review what mail I have received?"

"Right you are," said Harris, pulling the Silver Ghost up at the rear entrance to the house. "The housekeeper's waiting in the study, she said to tell you."

"Very good; and Harris," Ragoczy said as he prepared to get out of the motor car, "I appreciate all you've done for me."

In spite of his determination not to be impressed by the short, deepchested foreigner, Harris could not quite keep from a glow of pride. "Why, thank you, sir," he said. "I'll help Roger bring your bags in, if you like. That trunk looks pretty heavy."

"I'm afraid it is," said Ragoczy as he stepped onto the stone walkway. "Roger will certainly be glad of your help."

"That I will," Roger agreed as Ragoczy started toward the side entrance to the house.

Loretta Nowell was in the study, as Harris said she would be; she was neatly dressed in a severely cut suit of dark grey which nearly matched her hair. She stood as Ragoczy came into the room and bobbed a slight curtsy. "It is good to see you back again, Count."

"How kind of you, and how inaccurate," said Ragoczy without sarcasm. "I truly did expect to be gone longer than I was, but press of circumstances have called me back." He looked around the study with apparent mild interest; in actuality his perusal was acute and he quickly satisfied himself that there had been no significant disturbance in the chamber. "I imagine there has been little change since I left." He removed his coat and laid it over the back of the largest armchair in the study. "I have not been gone very long, have I."

"There are a few letters for you, and a note from that Mister Sinclair-Howard. I set that one aside, as you instructed me to do." She indicated where the letters lay in the eighteenth-century formal secretaire. "The others are piled in order of dates received. All accounts, of course, have been settled but for the new billings which arrived this last week." She did her best not to be nervous, reminding herself inwardly that Ragoczy had never given her any reason to fear him.

Ragoczy had already opened the front of the secretaire and was flipping through the envelopes awaiting his attention. The letter from Sinclair-Howard demanded his most urgent attention. "I will want Harris, after all," he said thoughtfully as he read through the politely self-serving instructions for Ragoczy's scheduled audience with the King.

"Shall I fetch him, Count?" asked Missus Nowell. She found herself confused by her elegant, aloof employer; she attributed this to his being from the Carpathians, for she could not help but think that the people were all very strange there.

"Yes, if you would," Ragoczy said, drawing a cream laid sheet with his eclipse sigil embossed at the top from its small drawer. "I will want this taken to Saint Dunstan-the-West Close at once." He was writing as Missus Nowell left the study.

By the time she returned with Harris, there were two envelopes, neatly sealed and addressed in Ragoczy's small, precise hand ready to be delivered. Ragoczy held them out to Harris. "There you are. One for Sinclair-Howard, confirming my audience day after tomorrow at Windsor. The other—and I hope it will not inconvenience you—is to go to Miss Pearce-Manning. You know where she lives in London. There is no reason to wait for an answer for either. When you have returned the Silver Ghost, you may consider the evening your own." He included a half crown with the envelopes.

As curious as she was, Missus Nowell knew she ought not to linger, listening to her employer's business. Anything she wished to know she could pry out of Harris over their tea the next morning.

"Very generous of you, Count, I'm sure. By the by, the trunks are in your apartment upstairs, sir, stowed just as Roger instructed," said Harris as he took the envelopes and the coin. "Now, you may rely on me: I'll get these in the hands you want them quicker than you can say knife." He all but backed out of the study, leaving Ragoczy to examine the rest of his mail.

It was not quite an hour later that Roger found his master, still in the study, engrossed in the last three editions of the *Times*. "Is everything all right, my master?"

Ragoczy sat back and sighed; the paper was held negligently, half-open in his hands. "I am not sure, which troubles me."

"Is it the King?" asked Roger, knowing how great Ragoczy's concern for Edward was. "Is he . . . worse?"

"I believe so, reading between the lines," Ragoczy said, frowning. "I suppose I should ask Sunbury; he will know more."

"Too ill to act on the Czar's proposal?" Roger pursued, his faded-blue eyes showing increasing distress.

Ragoczy nodded once. "And probably too ill to persuade anyone to go along with the agreement if he was able to make it. I suppose I will have to speak to his heir—the one who looks so much like his cousin Nicholas, the Prince of Wales." He managed a sadly ironic smile. "I would feel more sanguine if I could be certain their resemblance was more than an accident of family and face." He looked down at the front page one last time. "I will have to make the appropriate arrangements, very discreetly. It will not be easy. Perhaps Sunbury can assist me there. It would not be wise to make it appear that I anticipate the worst." He recalled Edward's high color and strident breathing from their last meeting and knew he did not expect the King to live much longer. "I have no wish to offend Edward or those closest to him."

"I will make inquiries, if it would be helpful," Roger offered.

"It certainly would be; you know to whom to talk, and how," said Ragoczy. "Thank you, old friend." He set the newspaper aside. "You will be pleased to know that I have answered Rowena Pearce-Manning's invitation to see her latest work."

"You will call upon her," Roger said, between an inquiry and an order.

"If she is willing to see me, yes. I gather from her letter there has been some difficulty; she indicates she has left Longacres completely, against her family's wishes." He lifted the letter in question from the small portfolio where he had put it with the others he had reviewed. "It was bound to happen eventually, given her ambitions."

"And her mother's," Roger added. "They say in the servants' dining room that Lady Pearce-Manning opens all her daughter's correspondence; they thought it was because Rowena is—by their lights—a little wild."

"She told me about the letters," Ragoczy confirmed. "And I would say that Rowena Saxon is the least wild young woman they'll ever meet. She is the diametric opposite of wild, to my thinking: she is dedicated."

"Her painting," said Roger knowingly. "The servants at Longacres are certain all artists are wild."

"And possibly mad," Ragoczy added. "It is unfortunate that her family shares the opinion of their servants on that matter." He put the letter aside.

"You will need sustenance soon," Roger reminded him after a brief silence. He took Ragoczy's coat from the back of the chair and folded it over his arm.

"Yes; and I know it should be more than the ephemeral gratification obtained through dreams. I've had more than enough of that of late." He pinched the bridge of his nose. "I am sorry I do not have the luxury of time to develop the kind of affections that would make a knowing acceptance of my needs and my nature possible; with what I am engaged upon, I would welcome it sincerely. Amalija is a long way from here, and much as she might be willing to travel, I doubt she has any desire to chase all over the capitals of Europe and Britain."

"Might not Miss Pearce-Manning—" Roger began.

"Have some interest in my nature? Why would that be? Because she admires *Dracula*? That is a fable, something to feed the imagination." His voice dropped although it remained musical; his dark eyes were enigmatic. "Can you imagine what she would do if she were to confront this real vampire?" He put his small beautiful hand to his chest in a self-mocking gesture of protest.

"No, I cannot, my master. And neither can you," said Roger more sharply than before. "She may be an artist, but that does not mean she must be credulous. Or capricious, as you've said."

Ragoczy got to his feet and busied himself closing the secretaire after placing the portfolio inside. "It may all be moot in any case. I have only sent her a note. She may decide not to see me at all."

"It is possible, of course," Roger said, unwilling to believe it. He went to the door and let himself out, leaving Ragoczy alone with his thoughts.

The next morning a messenger arrived at eight with a note from Rowena Saxon (as she signed herself) inviting Ragoczy to take tea with her any afternoon for the next week. She would expect him at her studio on whatever day it was convenient. Ragoczy was thinking over when he would call on her when a confirming note arrived from Julian Sinclair-Howard, indicating that the audience for the next afternoon was confirmed, and requiring Ragoczy to present himself at Windsor promptly at three in the afternoon, where he would be allowed to see King Edward in an unofficial capacity for no more than thirty minutes, on order of the King's physicians.

Ragoczy spent the day in his laboratory amid his equipment including the beehive-shaped athanor, to emerge an hour after nightfall with a stoppered bottle of opaque white glass. This he put into a velvet-lined box and set out for his visit to Windsor the following day. "Edward may not be willing to take the tincture," he remarked to Roger when the two met in the door to the withdrawing room, "but I felt I would be remiss not to offer it. He is in need of something to regularize his heartbeat, of that I am certain."

Roger nodded once, then said, "I talked to Asquith's man today, as you wanted me to do. It would be possible to arrange for a private meeting with Edward's heir." He paused and went on apologetically, "It may require meeting on a boat."

"By all the forgotten gods!" Ragoczy swore softly. "Why are these leaders forever holding meetings on water?" Even with his protective native earth in the soles of his shoes, being on or over water made him queasy.

"There is safety on water, as you yourself have demonstrated in the past. It is not easy to ambush someone on water." Roger chuckled. "England is not Crete, my master."

"No; nor is this the sixth century." He recalled himself. "Well, see what can be arranged, and I will send a note to the Prince of Wales when it is appropriate."

"Very good," said Roger, and went off to his own quarters. A short while later he heard the Collard & Collard square grand piano in the withdrawing room; Ragoczy was playing Haydn, Rameau, Paganinni transcriptions, and some of his own work. The music lasted for well over an hour, giving Roger a sense of hope for the first time in two months that Ragoczy no longer wanted to be isolated.

At Windsor the following afternoon, Ragoczy was informed that Edward was unable to see anyone and that the audience would be set for a time when the King was more himself. Ragoczy bowed his acceptance of this, all the while aware that Edward's condition must be deteriorating rapidly. He considered briefly consigning the white-glass bottle to Sinclair-Howard, then decided against it, for if the King was truly dying, as he now reckoned he was, providing medication might be seen as hurrying, not delaying, his demise.

"I am sorry you were forced to come back from Berlin in vain," said Sinclair-Howard, making no effort to conceal his unctuousness, though whether it was caused by the honor of being at Windsor or from the inconvenience to Ragoczy was not readily apparent. He was in full formal dress, his swallow-tail coat and striped trousers a contrast to Ragoczy's black superfine frock coat, wide silken burgundy tie, and black trousers as suited a private and unofficial audience, yet Ragoczy had about him an air of elegance that Sinclair-Howard had not achieved.

"I will remain in London for a few days, possibly as long as a week." Ragoczy's manner was unruffled. "Perhaps the King will improve and I will be able to see him. On the Czar's behalf."

"Perhaps," said Sinclair-Howard in visible disbelief before turning his back on Ragoczy, leaving the footman to show him out.

"That's a right disappointment," said Harris as Ragoczy got back into the Silver Ghost. "Bringing you all the way back to England and then slamming the door in your face, so to speak."

"Yes, it is a disappointment; it is also intended to put me in my place, I suspect," said Ragoczy, frowning as Harris drove out of the gates. He sat back, staring blankly out the window for the greater part of a mile, then said, "Harris, I've changed my mind. I want you to drive me to Miss Pearce-Manning's studio, if you will. There will be nothing more I can do today in regard to the King, and I confess I would be glad of her conversation."

"Conversation, is it?" said Harris, then realized how impertinent his remark was. "Meaning no disrespect."

"Yes, Harris, it is conversation, little as you may think it," Ragoczy said wearily. "After this . . . this disappointment, conversation can be very . . . soothing."

"Don't bother about what I think, Count. It's not—" He stopped as a delivery van turned into the street ahead of him, demanding his full attention. "Look at that, will you? The driver's a right lob-noddy for fair."

Ragoczy smiled slightly at this unfamiliar aspersion. "A lob-noddy. Sounds dreadful: what does it mean?"

"It means a foolish chap, one who's noddy—half-asleep—in his head." Harris had assumed a public school accent for his explanation.

"I thought it must be something like that," said Ragoczy, and returned to his purpose. "So, if you will take me to Miss Pearce-Manning's studio and wait until I discover whether it would be convenient for her to receive me"—he thought back to her note and found himself wondering if it were good manners or interest that inclined her to send it—"for an hour or so."

"A lot can be done in an hour," said Harris under his breath, going on more loudly, "I'll do that, sir."

"Thank you," said Ragoczy, and fell silent once again until they reached Great Russell Street. "If she is prepared to entertain me, I will be admitted to the building and you will be free to take the motor car back to the house. Circle the block once; if I am still in the building, drive on. Please tell Roger where I am. I will find my own way home." He rubbed his brow. "The walk will do me good."

"It's quite a distance, sir, and some of it not through the safest streets, if you take my meaning," Harris warned him.

"I am aware of that; and I appreciate your concern," said Ragoczy as the Silver Ghost began to slow down. "But I think I can fend for myself."

"If you say so," said Harris dubiously. "I could nip down to the Museum Pub and wait there for an hour or two. I could have shepherd's pie and a pint or two, no trouble."

"Unnecessary, I assure you," said Ragoczy. "And if you want a drink and your supper, wouldn't you rather have it in your local?" He prepared to get out of the automobile.

"Count," said Harris, "I don't . . . Wouldn't it be better if I waited?"

Ragoczy paused in the act of opening the door. "I may be a foreigner, but London is not wholly unknown to me." His acquaintance with the city went back two millennia, but he did not mention this. "To return home, I go along to Oxford Street either by Tottenham Court Road or Bloomsbury Street, west on Oxford Street to Davies Street, south on Davies Street to Mount Street and from there—"

Harris gave up. "Right you are, sir. That's the most direct way. I won't fash myself about you getting lost. I'll circle once, as you've told me to do." He glanced at the traffic ahead. "Be careful crossing, sir."

"As you wish, Harris," said Ragoczy as he left the Rolls-Royce, closing the door decisively. He stood on the kerb while Harris pulled away, then crossed the street, bound for Rowena Pearce-Manning's studio.

She opened the door promptly, the frown vanishing from her features as soon as she recognized her caller. "God in Heaven. Count Saint-Germain." She smiled. "I should have heard you on the stairs, shouldn't I? I was just finishing work, you see. But then, I did not expect you so soon . . . I'm babbling; forgive me. I'm not usually such a dolt. Do come in," she said as she stood aside, holding the door wide to admit him. "I am sorry about the smock. And I'm afraid you will find the studio in a bit of a mess. I was cleaning up—"

"It is I who should beg your pardon for interrupting your work," he said quickly. "As to the smock, you need not remove it on my account." His smile was fleeting but warm. "I should have sent word—"

"Oh, no," she protested. "I did say any afternoon this week, and I meant it. But I occasionally lose track of the time," she went on, stepping back to have room to close the door, "and today was just one such, I fear. No doubt I ought to have put my materials away half an hour ago. Working by artificial light is always a risky thing to do."

"Also it is impractical to stop work and ready yourself for a guest who

may or may not arrive; yes, I agree. And artificial light can be decep-
tive." He stopped to put his coat on a clothes hook by the door. "It is
good of you to see me on such irregular notice."

She gave him a direct look, and a hint of a smile. "Well, any man who
is interested in the art created by women must be cultivated and encouraged, mustn't he?" She made no move to escort him into the main
room of her studio.

To her surprise, he did not show any amusement in his reaction. "I
am not indulging you with my interest, Miss Pearce-Manning. You do
not need to . . . cultivate me." He regarded her with steady eyes.

Rowena flushed. "I . . . didn't mean anything to your discredit,
Count."

He shook his head. "It is not to my discredit; I do not like to see you
or any woman make herself seem less than she is in the name of acceptance. It not only belittles you, it belittles me as well." His stern expression softened. "If you take your work as seriously as you claim, you
need not hide your dedication from me."

It took her a while to answer as various responses jumbled in her
thoughts. Finally she decided he was being candid. "You're right. I was
trying to make light of what I do in the hope that—"

"—that I would not disparage your work, since you had already done
it," he finished for her.

"Yes," she admitted, pointing the way into the studio. "Come in, why
don't you? I was about to put the kettle on for tea, or I should have done,
twenty minutes ago."

He walked beside her into the studio, noticing that the windows
were not covered although it was nearly dark outside, and his reflection was absent from them. He quickly selected the settee with its back
to the expanses of glass, saying, "It is still cool in the evenings. I would
appreciate a little warmth."

As she sat down in the high-backed wicker chair across from him, she
said, "That is the only complaint I have about the windows: they make
the studio impossible to keep warm. Except in high summer, when the
heat is stifling, or so I have been warned. I will find out in two or three
months, won't I."

Ragoczy glanced over his shoulder at the good-sized oil painting set
on her nearest easel and could not keep from recalling the many artists
he had watched at work in the past: the Egyptian temple artists color-
ing the huge low bas-relief records of the events at the temple; the
Greek sculptor shaping the idealized likeness of Alexander of Macedon;
the brass worker on the Irrawaddy polishing the guardian dogs for the

palace; the illustrator in Shiraz applying paint with a brush of a single hair; the mosaic artisans in Rome and Seville, setting glorious shapes into the floors of grand houses; the half-dozen apprentice monks ornamenting the chapels of towering cathedrals; Sandro Felipeppi, who was called Botticelli, struggling with the *Massacre of the Innocents;* Velasquez putting the finishing touches on his *Death of Socrates.* There were many more, but he resolutely put his attention on Rowena Saxon's work. "I like the composition in this."

She made an effort not to deprecate her work. "It is done from a sketch I did on a trip to Scotland, made in the fall of the year. I found that old fortress at the edge of the lake too . . . too fascinating to ignore."

He said nothing for a short while as he contemplated the work. "You are a visionary, aren't you? It is apparent in this, more than in your illustrations; here you have given yourself free rein. You have taken your vision on its terms, not on yours." He paused again, his eyes still on the painting. "You have captured something remote and feral about that place without resorting to trickery or painterly theatrics; your style is distinctive without being intrusive, which is something not many artists achieve, and rarely so early in their work." Then he leaned forward, his gaze leaving the painting; now his eyes were directly on hers.

Her breath came a little faster. "Thank you, Count." She had to force herself to break away from his disconcerting gaze. What was it about his eyes? she asked herself as she recovered her self-possession once more, and would she ever be able to capture it? She got up abruptly. "I will tend to the kettle; it will not boil on its own. Would you like China or India tea?"

"You need fix nothing for me. I have just come from Windsor." He let her make whatever assumptions she wished from the last. "But do not hesitate to make what you want for yourself."

"Windsor?" she repeated, her head cocked to the side. "You have business with the King, or one of the Royals?"

"Yes, but not my own," he told her, aware that her father knew more than that. "Sadly, Edward was not able to give me the time he had scheduled originally."

"Oh, dear," she said as she went into the little alcove that served as a kitchen. "Is his health still poor?" She filled the kettle and set it atop the stove, then lit the burner with a long kitchen match.

"So it would seem," said Ragoczy carefully. He took advantage of her absence to go and pull the heavy draperies across the windows, saying as he did, "This will hold in the warmth."

Rowena stood in the kitchen door, her eyes fixed on him. "It was the oddest thing, Count." She laughed a bit, nervousness making the sound breathless. "Just now, while you covered the windows"—she gave an incredulous shake of her head—"you appeared to have no reflection."

He came back to the settee. "I suppose it was the angle." He sat down again, and in a moment said, very gently, "I was sorry to hear about your . . . estrangement from your family."

She shrugged. "It would have come eventually, I accept that." She sat down next to him. "But I was not as prepared as I thought I was."

"Is there any difficulty?" he asked carefully, at pains to keep her from thinking he would take advantage of her situation.

"Financially, you mean?" she asked. "Oh, no. My trust fund is not administered by my parents, but by my grand-father. And I know how fortunate I am to have it." She lowered her eyes. "No, that was not my meaning. I meant that . . . the circumstances which . . . " Her hands knotted and unknotted in her lap. "My parents want me to marry. My father . . . accepted the offer of Rupert Bowen and he expected I would consent." This last was filled with an emotion that bordered on repugnance. "I have said I would not marry, for years and years, and they still do not believe me. They think I must want a husband, if for no other reason than it would give them grand-children."

"A great many parents want that," he said soothingly, remaining very still beside her.

She sighed. "If I did not have my painting, I might be tempted to set aside my principles and marry to please them. A number of my friends have done, choosing to take the safe path. Not that I blame them." She turned to him again, and found disastrous sympathy in his dark eyes. "But I know that I could not be a good artist and a good wife at the same time; one or the other would have to suffer. So I had to leave before they succeeded in wearing me down with their promises and disapproval." She tried to smile, and very nearly did. "My sister Penelope is mad for Rupert. If she were ten years older, she would be a perfect bride for him. To hear her, flowers sprout from his footprints and birds go silent to listen to him."

"Truly?" Ragoczy said. "And what possessed him to think you would be cut from that cloth."

The kettle shrilled in the kitchen; Rowena leaped up, apologizing as she rushed to tend to the tea. "I have a little wine, Count. If you would like it?"

"Thank you, Miss Saxon, no; I do not drink wine." He followed her to the kitchen, saying, "Will you permit me to carry the tray for you?"

"It is what?—ten feet to the table?—and I have done it often and often." She warmed the large earthenware pot before putting in the loose leaves of strong Assam and filling the pot with boiling water.

"Nonetheless, I hope you will allow me to do this for you," he said as he picked up the tray. "Is this all you were planning for yourself?"

"Two scones and lemon curd," she said as she put both of these onto the tray. "If you feel you must, then you must," she went on, letting him bear the tray to the table in front of the settee.

As he put the tray down, he said, "How has it been, being on your own as you are?"

She did not answer at once; she went back to her chair. "Often it is invigorating, as I knew it would be. I think often of my grand-father, whose father gave him a dollar, a new pair of boots and sent him out to seek his fortune. It is like something out of a fairy tale, except it truly happened to Horace Saxon. When I find myself overcome with doubt, I consider how much better off I am than my grand-father was when he first began to make his way in the world; he is now a fabulously wealthy man." She sat down. "I know painters do not become fabulously wealthy, or very few of them do."

"I was about to mention something of the sort," Ragoczy said, resuming his place on the settee.

"I do not paint for wealth. I am extremely lucky that money need not trouble me." She took her serviette from the tray and spread it on her lap. "Redundant over a smock," she remarked. "It is an old habit."

"And theoretically, men do not need ties to protect the throat from sword-thrusts, but we continue to wear them," Ragoczy pointed out, amusement in the back of his eyes. He waited briefly, and said, "You were going to tell me why your suitor is so determined to marry you when it is plainly not what you wish to do."

Her brows flicked together. "He has formed an idea of me, and he desires to obtain that idea, to possess it." She fell silent. "I shouldn't discuss this with you."

"I will not repeat what I hear," he promised her.

"I don't doubt you, Count. It is not fitting that I should . . . presume upon our acquaintance in this way." She reached for the potholder to grasp the handle of her teapot and placed the strainer atop her cup. "Are you certain you do not want any?"

"Quite certain," he said, continuing to watch her.

"I hope it may be possible to have love, of course," she went on, concentrating on pouring her tea. "But not at the expense of my art. The love must not make such demands of me, not and be genuine. I cannot let myself be restrained or confirmed by anyone, especially Rupert

Bowen, who thinks that I will gladly give up painting for the delights of motherhood. He is eager to have heirs."

"Which you do not want to give him," Ragoczy said kindly.

She put the teapot down so forcefully that the whole tray rattled. "Certainly not. I do not want to give anyone heirs." She was about to speak again when Ragoczy startled her by saying, "Indeed, why should you?"

Now that he had her full attention, he went on, "Any unwelcome bond, no matter how pleasant, is a prison."

"That is it, precisely," she said, staring at him in astonishment, remembering her mother's warning about this man. How hard it was to doubt his intentions with his penetrating eyes on her own. "More for women than . . . than for men."

"I agree," he said at once, and again was subject to her scrutiny. He leaned back against the cushions. "And before you exhaust yourself wondering, I will admit that I am not wholly disinterested in your situation." He was mildly surprised that he had spoken so bluntly.

Her reserve returned. "And I suppose you would like to make an arrangement for an affaire with me?" She hated herself for feeling so disappointed, particularly since she had said so much to him. "One of those clever—"

"No, I am not," he said, his voice flat.

She blinked in astonishment and chagrin. "Oh."

He went on persuasively, "I do find you attractive, as much for your independence as your looks, and more than either, for your talent. You are a rare woman, Miss Saxon, as rare for your determination as for your obvious gifts." He paused, wanting her to look at him. When she finally did, he continued. "And if, at some time you should decide that you might want what love I offer, I would be deeply honored to have such an opportunity. But what I am more immediately concerned with is how your work can reach the discerning public."

She could not take in all he had said; nothing had prepared her for any of this, and she had an instant of annoyance, that he should catch her so unprepared. Then she told him, "I have work hanging in the Gallery of Women Artists: they tell me I can have a show of my own there in a year or so."

"In Dean Street; yes, I know." He leaned forward again. "Where you are thought to be an oddity among oddities, an aristocratic woman among the Bohemians and the naïve. It is a safe place where women may be relegated without serious attention being given to their abilities." He saw he had injured her. "I do not say this because I think it is so, Miss Saxon, but because I think it is not."

Her face was somber. "I wish I could refute you." She took a hurried sip of over-hot tea and put the cup down again, and looked at him, at once direct and reticent. "What do you want of me?"

So many times in the past he had heard that question in one form or another. His answer had always been the same: "Whatever you want for yourself, Miss Saxon," he replied, the words deep and musical.

She stared at him, her tea abandoned on the table. "Whatever?" It was foolish to think, she told herself as she rose, ignoring her serviette as it dropped to the floor. Ragoczy was on his feet as she went into his arms, into a searching kiss that made her body thrum. When she finally broke away from him, she was as light-headed as if she had been drinking champagne too fast. She was about to apologize when his small, beautiful hand touched her mouth.

"Whatever you want for yourself, Rowena, is what I want of you, and with you," he said again, making no attempt to embrace her again, although there was no mistaking the passion in his compelling eyes. "Nothing more, nothing less."

She put her hand on his arm as if to steady herself. "I wish I could tell you what that was," she said, so honestly that she felt fear wash through her in the wake of her confession.

"You need not," he said. "It will change, in time." He read alarm in the quick look she threw him. "That does not mean what you want is not genuine, only that even the most genuine, intense desires modify during life." He raised her hand from his arm to his lips. "Do not be too angry with yourself when it happens: many wonderful things are ephemeral."

Looking at him, her desire intensified; she reached out and brushed her fingers along his cheek. "I don't think I've met anyone like you before."

"Probably not," he agreed, a hint of irony in his tone.

Rowena was less than two inches shorter than Ragoczy, so when she met his eyes now she did not need to raise her head. She held her breath for a dozen heartbeats, then said, "You may stay, if you wish."

He took a step back from her. "I will. When it is truly *your* wish, as well as mine." He took her face in his hands and kissed her again, his mouth tantalizingly light on hers. "Do not rush yourself into something you are uncertain of. I am a very patient man." He gave her a rueful smile. "And I will do what I can to help you with showing your work no matter what you decide about anything between us."

She stared at him. "You do not think I . . . I kissed you to ensure your help for my work, do you?"

"No, I do not," he said with conviction. "And I hope you do not think it of me, either."

Her growing stiffness evaporated in an engaging smile. "How did you know that I was starting to—"

"It is a . . . skill those of my blood possess," he said. For a long moment they were silent, neither willing to break the spell working between them. Then Ragoczy turned away from her. "I will be in London for about a week, then I must return to Berlin. Send me a note if you would like me to call again, for any reason. I will tell you how to reach me in Berlin, as well."

"What . . . " Rowena blinked as if awakening from sleep. "Is there something wrong? Count, why are you leaving," she asked, doing her best to gather her scattered thoughts. "If I have done anything to offend you . . . "

"Nothing in the world. Quite the reverse, in fact: you have paid me a great compliment." He had taken his coat from the hook. "I do not want to . . . abuse the gift." He put his hand on the latch, but continued to look at her.

"You need not leave on my account," she said, the polite phrase sounding hollow in her own ears.

"Then I leave on mine," he said, and went on in a low voice, "Rowena, you must be sure that you want what you think you want, otherwise you will harm yourself, and I would not be able to forgive myself for being party to harming you. When you are sure, tell me what you have decided." Impulsively he bowed to her, his form elegant and graceful. Then he was out the door and on his way.

He had almost reached Oxford Street, his thoughts preoccupied with all that had transpired in the last hour, when he heard someone behind him call his name. He halted at once and turned to see a tall young man getting out of an Arrol-Johnston, his hat pulled low over his face. "Are you speaking to me?" Ragoczy asked him, wondering why the fellow seemed familiar.

"Yes, by God, I am," he declared indignantly.

Then Ragoczy recalled what Rowena had told him about a suitor; he gave the younger man his most affable smile as he stepped up to the automobile. "Mister Bowen, isn't it?" He held out his hand. "We met at Longacres, I believe."

Rupert Bowen declined to take it. "Well, what have you to say for yourself, Count?" He turned the title into an insult.

"About what, Mister Bowen?" Ragoczy asked, his voice carefully neutral.

"About you visiting my fiancée!" he exclaimed. "What sort of adventurer are you, sir?"

Ragoczy was noticeably shorter than Rupert Bowen, but his bearing was such that he dwarfed the taller man. "I am not an adventurer, as you are well aware. I can see you are in the grip of strong emotion, and I will not require the apology I would if you were cooler-headed." He gave Rupert a moment to master himself. "As to Miss Saxon, she has not told me of your engagement to marry."

"Her father and I are agreed," said Rupert haughtily.

"I see," Ragoczy said. "Well, when Miss Saxon informs me that my visits are unwelcome or inappropriate, I will cease to make them. Until then, I will be honored to accept her invitations."

"Her name is Pearce-Manning, damn you," Rupert informed him. He glared at the Sunbeam driver who dared to hoot at him.

"Not according to Miss Saxon," said Ragoczy, and resumed his walk toward Oxford Street.

Text of a letter from Baron Klemens Manfred von Wolgast to Paul Reighert; delivered by personal messenger.

Berlin
April 11, 1910

Reighert;

Let me congratulate you on your industry in finding men in the government willing to be persuaded to stand between Ragoczy and his mission. Whatever the Czar is attempting, it is an abeyance for the moment, and with a little industry on your part, it may remain so. With Ragoczy returned to England without having had an audience with the Kaiser, we have much to be pleased about; it is most fortunate that Ragoczy was not in Berlin for long, given his place in the world which surely would have brought him to the attention of Wilhelm before many days had passed. I believe we must make the most of his most providential absence. If you can assure me that upon his return here, Ragoczy will be unable to obtain any access to the Kaiser, then you will earn the bonus we have discussed. I remind you of this so you will not be tempted to abandon your purpose.

I would like you to take your dealings in regard to the foreigner one step further than what you have already accomplished: I want you to see that Ragoczy is discredited. Nothing blatant, nothing that might be brought into court and formally refuted, but enough to make the men he seeks be unwilling to receive him or advance his cause. Let it be known that he is debauched, or degenerate, and most of those hypocrites serving the Kaiser will run from him, for fear of having their own failings discovered. You will know best how to accomplish this task.

With Ragoczy returning to Berlin, it would also be an opportune time to discover the extent of his wealth; if he is truly as rich as they say, it would be worthwhile to find a way of employing some of his money to our benefit, for surely he will never miss it. I think I may try to enlist Nadezna's help in this as well as yours, for having him as her patron might well provide her with information that might otherwise be hard to come by. Nadezna is afraid that his return to England indicates that Ragoczy is no longer willing to be the patron of her dance school, and for the time being, it is just as well that she think so, for it will cause her to be willing to extend herself to assist me in my work. It would be inconvenient to have her have her own way just now, and her love of her school is perhaps her most enduring emotion. Given that her fears have made her more malleable in my dealing with her I would not like her to think otherwise than what she does; for now, she is committed to allying herself with me and my cause. She is going to be most useful, I think.

Report to me soon. I know your creatures will keep track of all Ragoczy does, where he goes, those he sees. I will want to know everything you learn in this regard, the better to make the calumny we employ more credible. Be sure you admonish those you have retained to find any lapse in Ragoczy's conduct that might be interpreted in an unfavorable light, or any idiosyncrasy that might be seen as dangerous or reprehensible. There is enough money to pay for most of this enterprise enclosed with this missive. I do not mind the cost, great though it is, if it buys the results I seek. If I do not achieve my ends, however, you will have to explain to me how this has come about and determine who is responsible for the failure, so that some adjustment of the fee for your services may be arrived at. I trust this will not be necessary, but I remind you it can occur.

> *In anticipation,*
> *von Wolgast*

10

When he finally opened the door to the insistent knocking, Pflaume was visibly relieved to discover Ragoczy instead of von Wolgast waiting. "Oh. It's you. Come in, Count," he said, standing aside for the well-turned-out foreigner. He favored Ragoczy with a faint smile of welcome. "We did not expect you."

"Then thank you for admitting me at this time of night," said Ragoczy, handing his black silk hat to Pflaume, along with the cane he carried. "It was Mozart at the Oper, at a very energetic pace. The violinists had trouble keeping up." His sympathy was genuine, for he played several instruments expertly, the violin included, and had more than once supported himself through music.

That the performance at the Oper would have ended more than two hours earlier elicited no comment from Pflaume, who was inured to the vagaries of the men who called on Nadezna, her patron included. "Just so." He coughed delicately once. "Madame retired a short time ago. I don't think she's asleep yet. I will announce you, if you like. Do you want to . . . speak to her?"

Ragoczy gave Pflaume a reassuring smile. "Yes. I do. Would you send word to her that at her convenience I will be waiting in her private drawing room?" The room had long served as a kind of study, and guests were rarely admitted to it. "I know the way: the end of the corridor on the right."

Mildly startled that the late-arriving guest did not expect to be escorted to Nadezna's bedchamber, Pflaume ducked his head in a compromise between a nod and a bow, then went off to tend to Ragoczy's hat and cane; he made no effort to take the long black cape that covered the formal wear expected at the Oper: doubtless Ragoczy had his reasons for keeping it with him.

As he climbed to the main floor of the house, Ragoczy noticed the many expensive additions that had been made to the establishment since he had last been there: the chandelier was more elaborate and larger than the one he remembered, there were a number of expensive antique chairs in the corridor, and two new murals had been added to the ones he had originally commissioned for Nadezna. He entered the door at the end of the corridor and saw that Nadezna's extravagance had extended itself to this small chamber as well, with its two portraits of the dancer and an Italian writing desk of satin-finished rosewood. He drew up one of the brocade-upholstered chairs and sat down to wait for Nadezna to arrive, using the time to review the puzzling developments of the evening, hoping that his review of them would shed a more encouraging light on what had happened than he had been able to believe thus far.

Upon his arrival at Frederick the Great's opera house, Ragoczy had been pointedly snubbed by Otto Bleuler and Alfred Kraft, both of whom had always been cordial to him in the past, willing to talk about advances in chemistry and the latest entertainment. Yet tonight neither man had acknowledged his greeting. The faint quality of nostalgia Ragoczy had experienced as he entered the Oper where he and the flute-playing Emperor had met often, a century and a half ago, vanished in the chill reception he now received. Eugen Dreiwald had done nothing more than glance once in Ragoczy's direction, after which he pointedly avoided any contact. When Ragoczy had bowed to the Graffin von Binghen, she had turned away sharply, as if she were insulted. The Count's note to the Chancellor's box, carried by the box usher at intermission, went unanswered. Ragoczy had met Theobald von Bethmann-Hollweg before he became Chancellor, and had found the man's personal chauvinistic arrogance off-putting, but he had not expected to be so wholly ignored. He was still considering the ramifications of these responses when Nadezna came through the door in her negligee, dark hair in a braid down her back. Ragoczy rose to greet her. "I hope you will forgive the lateness of the hour," he said, bowing over her hand.

"Inconvenient and unlike you," she said curtly. "If you wanted to talk privately, you might have sent a note and I would have put myself at your disposal."

"So I might," he agreed, waiting for her to sit down, "but then I would have been followed by at least two men, which I would rather not be. Now I am reasonably certain I am unobserved."

She stared at him. "Followed? You? Why?"

He answered her questions in order. "Yes, I have been followed. I must be of interest to someone, or more than one someone. I do not know why, which is the reason I have come here so late. The thin, jumpy fellow on the bicycle is not on duty at this time of night, nor is the stalwart with the scarred knuckles and broken nose who is right now dozing in a delivery van at the end of Glanzend Strasse, or was when I left

to come here. If there are any others I have not yet detected them."
He saw the disbelief in her eyes. "If you will like, I will return tomorrow and point them out to you. They are both very real, I give you my
word."

"That will not be necessary; I will take it as verified," she said hastily
as she took her seat behind the beautiful desk. "As to why you are here
at any hour, I presume you wish to review my accounts. I have them in
these two ledgers, and—"

He stopped her in the act of reaching for the bound volumes. "I
would like to see them, of course, but not just at present; perhaps in a
day or two, when I am better informed as to the reason for all this surveillance. I am not concerned about the money just now. At the moment there is something more pressing I must ask of you." He sat down
opposite the desk, looking directly at her. "I know you often hear rumors when you entertain." The shock in her eyes was almost ludicrous.
"Oh, yes, I know about your . . . soirées. Do not try to convince me you
do not have private . . . meetings here, for I would not believe you. Von
Wolgast attends many of them, I understand. I do not care what you
do on your own, Nadezna, so long as you continue with your school. I
told you that when we began this arrangement ten years ago, and I have
not changed my view."

She held herself very straight, thinking that she should have taken
the time to dress instead of coming down en dishabille; that way she
would have had more dignity to draw upon. "All right. Occasionally I
do have a few . . . guests here with some of the women who have
danced with my troupe."

"Yes. And doubtless you hear gossip. Which is why I am coming to
you now." He leaned forward. "I have no wish to put you in an awkward position, but I have so little time to . . . " He knew better than to
mention his mission for the Czar. "If anything is being said of me, anything detrimental to my reputation, I must know about it: what is being
said and who is saying it. If I know as much, I may be able to determine
why these things are being said."

Now she was flustered; she knew only too well what von Wolgast had
been saying about his plans for Ragoczy. It had seemed prudent to support him; but with Ragoczy asking her of the matter in this direct fashion, she decided she had not been prudent to agree with this scheme.
Thinking quickly, she did her best to plead ignorance of the rumors.
"One hears so many things, Count—" she began.

"And I need to know what those things are," Ragoczy interrupted her.

"I do not care whether you give the things you hear credence or not; I have reason to think there are others who do." He folded his hands and waited for her answer.

"I . . . I wish I could describe to you the things I have heard, but that would give the innuendos too much . . . shape," she began uncertainly. "They are not very . . . specific, as such vilifications usually are. And since it is generally understood that you are my patron, not everything being whispered is repeated to me. The worst of the aspersions are not repeated here." She tried to compose herself and found the effort greater than she had anticipated.

"Um," he murmured. "I accept that you are not fully informed on this matter, and I believe you do not hear the worst. Tell me what it is you do hear, if you will."

She stared up at the elaborate lighting fixtures flanking the small fireplace and wished she had refused to come down. "All right: I have heard it said that you go to the slums and pay destitute families for their most beautiful children. It is being said that you maintain a brothel of children in Russia. Or France."

"Or Italy or Hungary or Greece or Poland or Turkey," he said with a deep fatigue. "Anywhere but Germany, of course." He shook his head. "Why do these mendacities always follow the same predictable patterns? I would like it much better if some imagination were used. Why not claim that I . . . oh, that I poison the water with disease, or that I practice cannibalism? Or that I leave no alms for lepers? Or that I doubt the immortality of Pharaoh? Or tie red woolen offerings on the branches of hollow trees?" In his long millennia of life he had been suspected of all five crimes. "Nine centuries ago, they would have said I defecated on the cross or did not prostrate myself before edicts of the Vermillion Brush; today they say I make children into prostitutes."

"It is a dreadful accusation," said Nadezna dutifully; she held onto her elbows with either hand as if suddenly taken cold.

"There is probably worse said, as well," Ragoczy conceded, getting to his feet and going to the hearth; he spoke to the embers there, his voice sounding tired. "I am a foreigner in exile, and so it is more readily accepted that I would have to practice some discreditable act in order to maintain myself. Of course, foreigners are always suspect, simply by being foreign."

Nadezna adjusted the lace ruffles at her elbow and leaned forward, elbows on the desk. "You are a wealthy man, Count. Some of the men in Berlin are jealous of wealth, no matter who has it."

"Truly." Ragoczy turned to face her. "I hope you do not make the mistake of defending me."

Her brows rose in surprise. "I . . . I say I know of nothing that disgraces you." She faltered now, her knuckles whitening as the grip on her elbows grew stronger. "I should have said more, but . . . " She could not find words to explain her necessary accommodation of von Wolgast.

"No, you've done very well. If anything, you could have said less." He realized she was puzzled by this; he came back across the room to her. "If you defend me, you will only condemn me in many men's eyes."

"You mean that as a dancer depending on a patron, I would have to speak for you? You would expect me to defend you, no matter what your crime?" she guessed. "Some might think so: men who are as cynical as Kraus of *Die Fackel.*" She had to suppress an intense feeling of disgust.

Ragoczy managed a sardonic smile. "Cynics, my dear, are not always wrong just because they are cynical." He held up his hand.

She paled. "Do you mean . . . " Again her words trailed away.

"That I keep brothels?" He laughed once, his amusement colored with sadness. "Of course not. I would have to be a great fool to do something so obviously despicable. But you and I both know that there are men of good reputation who have few credentials to support that high opinion they enjoy; no doubt I am considered to be one of them now. And any direct protestation I make against the rumor will only serve to confirm it." He sat down once again. "I want to ask a favor of you, if you will?"

"What is it?" she asked, her apprehension showing through her carefully maintained facade of calm.

"I would appreciate it," he said, watching her more narrowly, "that the next time you hear some disparagement of me, that you do not deny it, but instead admit that you have always had some reservations about me; if you can, hint that you would like to know all you can about what is whispered about me, to confirm your own fears. Let those repeating these tales reveal as much as they wish. This will accomplish two things: you may avoid being tarred with the brush being used on me, and you may be able to learn more of the imputations currently—" He got no further.

With a cry, Nadezna pushed herself to her feet. "I don't want to be dragged into this, Count." She put her hands to her face. "No. I'm sorry, but it is hard enough listening to slander without conspiring to enhance it." As she made herself look at him, she said, "I don't know what else to tell you, except that I cannot be party to any more attacks on your character."

Ragoczy made a gesture of respect. "I am grateful for your loyalty, Madame. But in this instance, you would serve my reputation better by helping me to determine the extent of the damage done to it."

She shook her head vigorously. "I'm sorry, Count; I can't."

"It would be very useful to me," he said, his tone steady and determined. "I would not hold anything you tell me against you, if that is your concern."

"I can't," she repeated, fearing what would happen to her if von Wolgast began to suspect she was aiding Ragoczy in any way.

"It would not harm me, and I would not be angry to hear what you tell me, or if I am, I will not be angry with you." He thought this would soothe her, and was mildly alarmed when he saw it did not.

"Please, Count, don't ask this of me. I have . . . too high regard . . . " Her worry lost her in a tangle of half-completed words.

Ragoczy cut in, doing his best to put her at ease again. "I do not seek to have the defamation compounded, you understand; nor do I want to know who believes the tales. I only wish to determine the full extent of it, and how long the campaign has been going on. I will trace the calumny to its origin, and you will not be implicated in any of it." He gave her a little time to consider this. "You may laugh off anything you hear, if it would make you less anxious about—"

"No." She was shocked to feel herself trembling.

At this, Ragoczy relented. He stood, bowing slightly. "Then I must thank you, Nadezna, for your high opinion of me. I will not trouble you again on this matter. I am grateful for what you imparted to me, and I promise you that none of this conversation will be discussed with anyone outside of this room, save my manservant. I am sorry to have disturbed you." He started toward the door, but paused to say, "I did not mean to frighten you."

Her blunt answer told him far more than she had intended to reveal. "You didn't."

"Ah." His dark eyes softened. "How good of you to let me know that much," he said before he opened the door and left her alone in the study while he reclaimed his hat and cane from Pflaume. "I'll find my own way out, Pflaume," he said, handing him an English shilling as a tip.

Nadezna listened to hear the front door close. After several minutes, she decided Ragoczy must have left through the kitchen, a notion that leant credence to his assertion that he was being followed. Perhaps, she thought, it was the fate of all foreigners—herself included—to feel apprehensive in Berlin. She went back to her desk, her thoughts in turmoil, as she tried to decide if she should inform von Wolgast of

Ragoczy's visit. It was not an easy decision to make: if Ragoczy were truly being followed, and if it was on von Wolgast's order, the Baron would expect to be told of Ragoczy's unusual visit and would hold it against her if she failed to mention it. But if the tale of being watched were nothing more than a fiction, then telling von Wolgast of it would surely result in her being found out. Either way, she exposed herself to disapprobation and possible repercussions that would be costly; both men were expecting too much of her, she decided. She was a dancer and a teacher, not a spy. At that moment she hated von Wolgast and Ragoczy equally for putting her in such an untenable position. She swore comprehensively in Ukrainian, and decided it was better to keep silent unless von Wolgast challenged her in regard to the visit; that would give her time to come up with a plausible explanation for her failure to send von Wolgast a full memorandum at once. Satisfied that she had averted disaster for the time being, she left her study, only to find Pflaume waiting outside, his wrinkled features set in a semblance of an encouraging smile.

"Madame," he said, his eyes bruised with fatigue, "it is very late; do you have anything more you need of me tonight?"

"No," she said, drawing herself upright and tossing her head so that her long, dark braid swung across her back. Her demeanor was imperious although her mouth was unhappy. "I am going to retire. I have a full day tomorrow." Then she added, "You are not to tell anyone of Ragoczy's visit here tonight. Do you understand? Not anyone."

"Of course," he said, already planning to include a report on as much of the conversation as he had overheard in his regular accounts of household activity, which he presented weekly to Baron von Wolgast, who paid him well and who had assured Pflaume of a pension when Nadezna could no longer afford to employ him.

"If anyone else comes tonight, I don't want to see him," said Nadezna, as if this single order could keep out the anxiety she felt. "I will want to be awakened at eight."

"Certainly," said Pflaume, recognizing the distress in Nadezna. "The school?" he ventured to ask as Nadezna fled down the hall toward the stairs.

She stopped. "The school?" she echoed. "Oh. There is no trouble that I am aware of. That was not the reason for the Count's visit." Then she resumed her hasty rush to the safety of her own room and the bastion of comforters that would guard her disquiet dreams.

Pflaume was left to try to puzzle out what Ragoczy would have to discuss with Nadezna at this hour of the night that did not involve the ballet school. Ragoczy had always kept late hours, he knew from the past, but this late a call was unusual even for him. Perhaps, he thought, Ragoczy was seeking a mistress and had asked for Nadezna's assistance: that could account for her apparent distress; it was a position she would want for herself, and had Ragoczy suggested such an alliance, he would not have left the house that night. Pflaume was convinced that von Wolgast would want to know as much as possible about that private interview; he decided that tomorrow he would do his utmost to learn what Ragoczy had said to Nadezna.

The big man with the scarred knuckles was still hunched behind the wheel of his delivery van when Ragoczy slipped past him half an hour after he left Nadezna's house. It was tempting to deepen the man's sleep and search him, but Ragoczy knew it was more risky than useful—if the man were a hireling there would be nothing on him to reveal who employed him: if he were a professional, all means of identifying him would be missing. He noticed a camera on the seat beside the dozing man, and managed an ironic, one-sided smile, knowing that all exposures of him would be blurred, no features discernable, just as his reflection was entirely missing.

As he entered his house through the service door, Ragoczy found Roger waiting for him, his faded-blue eyes alight with concern. "You spoke with Nadezna."

"Yes," Ragoczy said as he handed over his hat, cane, and cape. "For all the good it did."

"She could not help you," Roger inferred as he started toward the rear stairs.

"Actually," said Ragoczy in a steady tone, "I suspect it is more a matter of she *would* not help me; either that, or she is more frightened of me than I realized."

"Why would she be frightened?" Roger asked as he followed Ragoczy up the stairs.

"There are any number of reasons," he answered; he had been thinking this over all the way back to his house. "I think she may be . . . on the horns of a dilemma. She is dependent on me for funding for her school, and she may fear I will cease to support her if I dislike what she tells me, though she knows that to remain silent exposes me to a continuing impugning of my . . . honor." That, of all the possibilities, was the most palatable. "It is also likely that she has some other, more pressing, reason to feel as she does, one that increases her personal danger if she warns me. I have assumed from the first that she must have lovers. If one of them has decided to undermine me—"

"Why would he want to do that?" Roger did not wait for Ragoczy to speak. "What if the trouble isn't German at all? I suppose you have thought about the chance that Czar Nicholas may have changed his mind? Or his intentions been found out? You would then be a hazard to the Generals of the Czar's armies, and—"

"Yes, I have thought about all of it, old friend." He held his hand up as he reached the door to his rooms. "Whatever the case is, we will not solve the matter tonight, try as we might. Rest assured that I will do what I can to find out who is influencing Nadezna. I might then discover who is spreading rumors about me, as well." He pressed the latch and was about to go in when he added, "I should call upon Shaller tomorrow morning; or, this morning, considering the hour. He is expecting me at ten-thirty. If the rumors have not wholly eroded my position, I should be able to secure a little time with Kaiser Wilhelm before the end of the week."

"Not before?" Roger's austere features showed no sign of worry, but there was a change in his eyes that Ragoczy knew was concern.

"No; I do not think it could be arranged so quickly. I understand that every passing hour increases the chance that some part of the rumors may reach the Kaiser, which would probably mean I would not be able to reach him at all, not even informally." He lowered his eyes, not liking to admit the defeat such a response would be. He stepped inside his room, leaving the door open for Roger.

The outer chamber was a neat apartment, with two large bookcases flanking the tall window on the east wall. Opposite that, a large breakfront wardrobe of eighteenth-century Dutch marquetry was standing open for Roger's convenience. Between them, a Louis XV chaise longue upholstered in burgundy damask provided Ragoczy a place to stretch out while reading. Three new floor lamps with frosted, lotus-shaped bowls provided illumination as Roger took a robe of black brocaded silk from the wardrobe and traded it for Ragoczy's tailed coat, white brocade waistcoat, and foulard tie with the ruby stickpin that had secured it.

As Ragoczy shrugged into the robe, Roger said in a neutral way, "It has been some time since you—"

"Took nourishment? Fed?" Ragoczy suggested. "Yes, it has been. As you have often reminded me." He tightened the sash around his waist. "You still think I should have accepted the opportunity Rowena Saxon offered me."

"Your attention would have been welcome, from what I observed of her. She would not have been likely to refuse you," Roger said carefully.

"Welcome is not quite the right word," Ragoczy said. "I will allow she is fascinated, in that way that artists are captivated by that which intrigues them. I am a symbol of . . . I suppose escape is the best word, to her. She is not yet ready to . . . to know my true nature; she has an aversion to bonds of any kind, and it may well include the bond of blood. Enough is being imposed upon her now without me adding to her burdens." He went to the nearer bookshelf and took down a leather-bound copy of *Recherches sur la Probabilité des Jugements*. "I had hoped that last evening I might have . . . called upon the Graffin von Binghen once she was asleep, but—" He stopped with a slight nod. "Other problems seemed more immediate."

"You should not go so long without sustenance." Roger had admonished Ragoczy about this so often and for so many centuries that it was now a ritual between them.

"No, and I should have a knowing partner, not one in profound sleep, and I should share full passion with my lover. She should have fulfillment from me so that I, too, could be fulfilled." He rubbed at his chin. "I will need a shave in a few more days."

"And your hair trimmed in a month," Roger added, accepting the diversionary tactic for what it was. "I will see to it."

Ragoczy turned to smile at him. "When have you not?" he asked. "I have been churlish. I apologize."

"You have been preoccupied and fretful," Roger corrected him. "It is hardly surprising you are brusque." He finished putting Ragoczy's clothes away. "Shall I draw a bath for you?"

"In the morning, I think," said Ragoczy. "I have too much on my mind just now; I will have to reconsider my options before I decide how to proceed." He paused. "And thank you for not taking me to task. You had every reason to."

Roger paused in the door as he left. "Why need I bother, when you did it so well without my help?"

The amused half-smile that lit Ragoczy's attractive, irregular features faded as soon as the hall door closed. The frown that replaced it would have confirmed Roger's worst suspicions, had he been in the room to see it. He did not like the prospect of failure on the Czar's mission, but it was looming ever larger in his efforts. No matter what he tried, it seemed he could not gain the endorsement Nicholas sought. Few emotions so aggravated him as frustration; he understood that his indecision was due to lack of information regarding the opposition he faced, but he could not discern how to gather that material without increasing his risk of exposure or confrontation, neither of which would serve the Czar's purpose, or his own. After more than three hours of trying to concentrate on Simeon Poisson's work, he noticed the window beginning to pale; sighing, he returned the book to its place on the shelf and went into his private room, a spartan chamber with a single trestle table at the foot of his narrow bed made over a chest of his native earth. He did not bother to undress, although a black silk robe was laid out, neatly folded, at the end of the trestle table. With a second, deeper sigh he lay down upon it and gave himself up to the annealing power of good Transylvanian soil that had nurtured him for more than four thousand years.

Roger wakened him at nine with the announcement that his bath was ready. "The thin man on the bicycle is back. And the fellow in the van has left. I think there is a rabbity, middle-aged man in a loden coat who has taken his place."

"Who are these people? Why are they watching me?" Ragoczy wondered aloud as he rose from his bed. He was feeling invigorated for the first time in days, and his questions were clear, precise in their enunciation and intention. "I think it may be time we found out, before any more mischief is done."

"Where would you like to begin?" Roger took the robe, the shirt and ruby studs Ragoczy gave him as his master returned to his outer room.

Ragoczy stepped out of his trousers and laid them over the end of the chaise longue. "I think it might be best if we try the newest one first. He will be less familiar with the workings of this household and can be counted on to make certain mistakes." He laid his hand over the top of the scars that covered his abdomen. "See if you can make him reveal himself, will you?"

"Certainly," said Roger, his eyes glinting in anticipation. "I will attend to it while you are out."

"Do not frighten him too badly. If possible, the man should be persuaded to remain . . . on his post, so that we may avail ourselves of what he learns. It is time we found a way to have the advantage in this game. Pay him; money is more likely to convince him than threats are, and to make him more loyal, if we outbid his current masters." He drew a large Turkish towel around himself, then opened the hall door. "I will be out in twenty minutes."

"Your clothes will be waiting," Roger assured him. "Will you need me, or can you manage—"

Ragoczy laughed once. "I will fend for myself, thank you. Do not think I will disgrace you: I won't."

Roger considered this levity a sign of improvement in his employer but was wise enough not to remark upon it. He watched as Ragoczy crossed the hall to the bathroom, then went to set out the proper clothes for an informal diplomatic morning visit.

Reclining in the warm, bath-salted water set over a long, narrow chest of his native earth, Ragoczy found his thoughts again drifting to the problems he had encountered. He was more convinced than ever that he was facing deliberate attempts to sabotage any agreement, private or public, to limit the development and sales of arms. He could come to no other conclusion. What he had to determine was if the actions were directed against the Czar himself, or against his aims. There were many powerful men in Germany and England who did not trust the Russians, just as there were many who would profit from the sale of arms, should the efforts of diplomats fail. The question was, which motive was undermining his work. Once he knew that, he would be much closer to identifying those behind it, and to ending their interference in his mission.

"The Bianchi is fueled and ready," Roger announced as he came into Ragoczy's room half an hour later to find the Count putting the final touches on his clothes—a small lapel pin in silver with his device—a disk with raised displayed wings, all in black—inlaid upon it in a single black sapphire. "Who do you want to drive you? I will need to deal with our watchers."

"Yes; you will." Ragoczy took a pair of black Florentine gloves from one of the wardrobe drawers and pulled them onto his hands. "I'll drive myself. It may make your task easier."

"And what of guarding the motor car while you're with the Chancellor's undersecretary? Surely you will want someone to look after it," Roger asked, deliberately avoided Ragoczy's compelling gaze.

"I will arrange something." He chose a day-wear hat with a modified crown; placed it on his head, then turned to Roger. "Will it do?"

"It will," said Roger.

"At least we no longer have toes so long and pointed that we must remove them to climb stairs, or sleeves that must be knotted to avoid dragging them on the ground," he remarked as he went to the door.

The 1909 Bianchi 20–30 was pulled up at the front of the house, its engine idling as Ragoczy came out to get into it. His steward, Erich Rotscheune, held the door for him and stood on the curb until Ragoczy reached the end of Glanzend Strasse and turned onto Knobeldorff-strasse. A weedy, anxious man on a bicycle pedaled furiously after the Bianchi.

Although the air was still cool, there were many harbingers of spring throughout the vast, grey city. Flowers in bud poked out of window-boxes and trees showed furls of new leaves. Overhead white puffs of cloud grazed the sky like a herd of celestial sheep. Traffic moved well along the streets and people on the sidewalks were becoming jauntier in their conduct; men on cycles raced to keep up with the automobiles, darting among those vehicles drawn by horses and the occasional pedestrian attempting to cross the street. While not so insouciant as Vienna, Berlin seemed to be striving for the levity of the season; it achieved a ponderous kind of success.

Ragoczy pulled into a side street near the large government building where he was to meet Herr Shaller; it was near the Ludwigskirche, away from the most important Ministries, a place relegated to those who filed forms and maintained the records for the Chancellor and the Kaiser. There was space enough for Ragoczy's automobile halfway down the block where the street joined an alley at an angle, creating a small Platz with a number of shops on the ground floors of the buildings fronting it. He glanced about, looking for someone who would guard his Bianchi. Finally he spotted a boy of about eleven outside a bakery; his morning work done, he was lounging at the door of the shop, worrying a pastry. Ragoczy crossed the street to address him. "Good morning," he said cordially.

The youth looked up. "Are you talking to me?" he said, not believing that such an elegant foreigner would have any reason to speak with him.

"Yes. I was hoping you would be willing to help me." He reached for his wallet and drew out two banknotes. "I will compensate you for your time."

"Oh, no," said the boy. "I am not so desperate that I need to—"

Had everyone in Berlin heard the rumors? Ragoczy asked himself, his teeth clenched to keep from protesting aloud. He shook his head. "It's nothing like that." He waited while the boy thought this over. "I want someone to watch my automobile for me."

"Is that all?" asked the boy dubiously.

"I have an appointment in that building, and I do not want any harm to come to my Bianchi. If you will watch it while I am gone—and it should not be longer than an hour or two—I will give you this for your trouble." He went out of his way to be affable in order to offset any lingering doubts the boy might have about him.

The boy took the banknotes, doing his best to be unimpressed with the amount. "It is the black Bianchi, right? With the dark-red leather seats?"

"Yes. It would serve my purpose best if you were not too obvious about it; I think someone is attempting to steal it from me, but I have not yet discovered the identity of the man. I want to find out who this thief may be," he added, hoping to give the boy a sense of adventure as well as profit.

"I'll be wise how I do it, Mein Herr." He gave Ragoczy a half-salute and went back to his pastry.

Karl Shaller was not at his desk when Ragoczy arrived; his assistant offered Ragoczy an uncomfortable wooden seat in the outer office, and explained that Herr Shaller would be somewhat delayed.

"I have time at my disposal; I will not be put out by waiting," Ragoczy said with an unconcerned gesture; inwardly he feared that he had made the call for nothing. "I have allotted two hours for Herr Shaller and I do not mind using them in this way." He did not bother to read the papers set out—they were all three days old at least. Instead, he put his hat on his knees and allowed himself to reflect on the developments of the last two days.

At eleven-thirty, the assistant left his office for a short while, then returned, his demeanor apologetic. "Herr Count?" He had used the foreign title instead of the German equivalent of Graff, as all the Berliners did, to remind Ragoczy that he would never be one of them.

"Yes?" Ragoczy said politely.

"I have a message from Herr Shaller. Just now." He coughed once and his cheeks turned plum color. "It seems he will not be able to meet with you today. He regrets that an unexpected obligation makes it impossible for him to spare any time for you."

"I see," Ragoczy said evenly as hope leeched away from him. "What time would be convenient for him, then? Did he tell you that?"

The assistant blushed more furiously than ever. "He did not . . . I have no instructions from him about . . . another appointment . . . I am sorry—"

Ragoczy held up his hand. "I will spare you further embarrassment," he told the young man as he got to his feet. "Please tell Herr Shaller that I would appreciate hearing from him when he has time to see me. Although I may not be in Berlin for much longer."

"Certainly, Herr Count. I will do that," said the young man with several earnest nods, as if assuring himself that he had done his work properly.

"If my plans take me away from here, I will notify Herr Shaller at once." He placed his hat on his head and went out of the office, returning to the side street where he had left the Bianchi. He got into the automobile and waited.

Ten minutes later the boy emerged from the bakery. "I'm sorry," he said as he came up to the automobile. "We're starting the afternoon bread." He held out flour-whitened arms as proof.

"No matter," said Ragoczy. "Did you notice any trouble with my automobile?"

"Yes," said the boy with mild surprise. "I thought you were only being cautious, as foreigners often are. But you were not gone five minutes when a thin man on a bicycle came up and inspected the automobile." His eyes brightened as he recounted the incident. "He circled the street twice, and then went off; he came back twenty minutes later, and a third time about fifteen minutes ago."

"Ah." Ragoczy cocked his head. "Was anyone else interested in the automobile, did you notice?" He got out of the Bianchi, preparing to turn the ignition crank to start it. He was no taller than the baker's apprentice, but the youth had the impression of height; he let Ragoczy go to the front of his automobile. "Well?"

He paused, frowning. "I'm not sure. There was a big man, looked to be some kind of tough, with a broken nose and scars on the backs of his hands. I didn't want to stare too long. You know . . . " He looked down at his apron.

"I think you did precisely the right thing," Ragoczy approved as he gave the crank a single, powerful twist: the engine fired at once. "You drew no attention to yourself, as I asked you. And I thank you for all you have done." He held out a mark to him as he climbed back into the driver's seat. "For your efforts."

The boy hesitated. "You've already paid me, Mein Herr, more than two days wages."

"Well, consider this a second cup of chocolate," he recommended as he started the automobile. "I am grateful for what you have done."

"Danke," the boy said, ducking his head as he took the money. He stepped back from the Bianchi as Ragoczy prepared to drive off, then called out, "The big man, with the broken nose?"

Ragoczy halted, putting the gears into idle. "Yes?"

"I think he was carrying a pistol," he blurted out, then turned and ran back across the Platz to the bakery.

Ragoczy watched him go, his eyes fixed on a greater distance and the warm spring day had a chill in it that had nothing to do with sunlight.

○   ○   ○

Excerpts from a report prepared for the Russian Prime Minister, Piotr Stolypin, by the Foreign Minister Alexander Izvolsky.

. . . The Serbs have asked for our assistance against the Croats, who are said to be purchasing arms to use against them. They say this is not another Pig War with Austria, but something far more serious. These Serbs, sharing our Orthodox faith, are willing to make concessions to us in guarantees of wheat, meat, and wine if we will help them to prepare for the conflict they hourly anticipate with their ancient Catholic enemies.

Traditionally we have come to the aid of the Serbs, but it is reported in the Duma that it would be an unnecessary risk in these difficult times to give arms to those who could turn them on us or on those with whom we have treaties. It is also acknowledged that Austro-Hungary would look upon such a gesture as a threat to their borders and the integrity of their empire. Inaction may buy us some time to assess the ramifications of some help to the forces that support our goals in that region. It is unlikely that the Duma would agree to permitting the Serbs to purchase arms from us, and it would also provide another ground for dispute in a body already in the throes of dissention.

The leaders of the armies do not agree. They believe it is only through a great show of force that the Germans may be kept from aggression. Ever since that disgraceful incident aboard the Standart, and the appalling so-called treaty the Kaiser foisted upon the Czar, the generals have been certain that Germany has designs on the whole of Europe and Russia. It is thought that the German ambitions in the Ottoman Empire will soon clash with our own, and if there is war in the Balkans, it might well catapult the Turks into full defeat. That is what the Generals have sought since Sevastapol.

. . . In regard to the Czar's revelation that he has a personal envoy working to secure a private peace with his English and German relatives, we must suppose that this is a ploy to keep the Duma and the generals from clashing. Nevertheless, if such efforts truly are being made, it would doubtless be in our best interests to wait for any developments this envoy can secure us before making a final decision in regard to the Serbs. Unless the Croats obviously intend to take the offensive, we will do well to wait for the time being. Should this supposed envoy fail, it will provide us with an object of blame for our inaction, which will placate the Generals as well as the Duma.

. . . Reports from the operative Reilly tell us that there have been at-

tempts to secure this private agreement, or so he believes. Of course,
the man is a former British spy, and his observations must be regarded
as potentially slanted, but it would appear that someone is trying to
carry out Czar Nikolai's mandate. Further intelligence is needed before
an evaluation is in order . . .

11

In the vast, flat, empty fields beyond his factory Baron Klemens Manfred von Wolgast had set up an artillery range to demonstrate the improvements in his new guns this fine, breezy April morning. He was
seated on a platform put up on the highest ground available, with half
a dozen potential customers, including a representative of Franz Ferdinand, Franz Josef's heir—Alois, Graff Lexa von Aehrenthal, the
highest-ranking official in the viewing party. Next to him, Vaclav Persuic was in full Ninth Hungarian Hussars uniform, his handsome face
and straight military bearing showing to advantage amid the rest of the
observers. Tancred Sisak was dressed conservatively, looking more like
a banker than an arms dealer. From Russia there were two delegates:
Mikhail Illyich Plehev, a nephew of the repressive Viacheslav Plehev
who had been murdered six years earlier; and Colonel Georgi
Gavrileivich Spalavsky of the illustrious Preobzhensky Regiment. The
sixth man was a soft-spoken, fifty-year-old Swiss named Moritz Vinadi:
no one was certain whom he might represent, nor did he give any indication.

"As you can see," von Wolgast shouted in order to be heard over the
rushing wind, "we have set up a number of small buildings, three storeys
high for visibility, all made of stone and brick, all of them with walls of
varying thicknesses. The distances to the targets vary, as do the locations—some are upslope, as those farthest ones are, some down. A few
will only be seen with binoculars, which we have provided, so you will
be able to see how well the shells hit their various targets." He pointed
these out with a sweeping gesture to make sure they all noticed the appropriate structures, then swung back to address the men on the platform again. "You all agree that speed is important in artillery. You also
know that accuracy is crucial. Thus far, you have had to settle for one

or the other. That is now a thing of the past!" He flung his arm out again in the direction of the big field where a line of railroad track had been laid for this demonstration. "I know it is thought wise to save the most impressive for last, but I want you to see how our developments have improved our biggest gun first, for it will show you more clearly than any of the others what we have achieved here. This four-hundred-twenty-millimeter howitzer is the largest gun we produce. It can be broken down into component parts for shipping by rail. It requires an eleven-man crew and delivers a shell that weighs nearly a ton. Krupp has nothing to match it." Inwardly he added *yet.* "It can demolish any building that stands in its way." He signaled the crew of the gun. "Prepare to fire."

Persuic leaned forward, attentive to what was happening around the big howitzer. He hardly noticed when the Swiss observer moved a little nearer to him, lifting binoculars to his eyes.

"There are three houses, out there at the edge of the salt-marsh," said Vinadi in Swiss-accented German, startling Persuic.

"So von Wolgast told me when he asked me to come to this demonstration. He has promised to demolish fifteen buildings in all."

"You will all agree that a shell should hit its target directly," von Wolgast declared loudly. "And the cannon should reload and fire quickly as well. This innovative design makes both things possible." He glanced over at his crew, shading his eyes against the morning sun. His collar now felt several sizes too small; if he could not get any of these men to purchase his guns, he would be facing the total failure of his business. Even that suggestion had the power to make him tense; this trial-by-ordeal was his most difficult morning of the last decade. Only six men would decide his fate. Suddenly he was not certain it had been worth the risk he was taking. He forced himself to take several deep breaths as he wished passionately for a schnapps. To his dismay his voice cracked as he called out, "Gentlemen, when you are ready?" He turned once again to the six men on the platform with him. "You may want to watch this through the binoculars, given the distance."

The engineer aboard the base of the howitzer showed von Wolgast a sign, then pointed to one of the distant buildings, then another, then another.

With the sound of massive chains breaking the big gun fired, and the air shuddered. A moment later one of the most distant buildings burst and collapsed. Around the gun the crew rushed to clear and reload as the alignment of the barrel was adjusted by the gunner. The men on the platform had set aside their binoculars and were holding their hands to their ears as the gun fired a second time, and another distant building—this one of brick—flew apart. There was another flurry of activity around the gun, and it fired a third time; a moment later the third building, the most distant of the three, was reduced to rubble.

On the platform the observers broke into applause, interrupting this only to adjust their binoculars, the better to inspect the destruction.

"At the conclusion of this demonstration," said von Wolgast, "you will have the opportunity to inspect all the target structures." That would give his men time to remove all signs of the explosive charges he had had placed in the now-ruined buildings to enhance the effect of the artillery shells.

"It would appear you have increased the initial velocity of the shell," Sisak called out. "How long a range do you think you can achieve with that?"

"We haven't established that yet, not in terms of absolute accuracy of the sort you have just seen, but we are hoping for ninety-five to one hundred kilometers, in the next three years. That would require a longer barrel, and higher speed of the shell fired, of course, and probably less speed in reloading, but we are working on just such a siege gun." He let them think about this for five seconds. "We have hit a specific target at sixty-six kilometers, with this gun. Those structures are less than half that distance."

"That's amazing, if the speed of reloading can remain beyond three shells fired," approved Spalavsky. He was certain the report he would present to his superiors would be enough to convince the Czar that military preparedness was essential to preserving Russia from Germany.

"Thus far, the speed has been good for up to twenty-four shells," said von Wolgast. "And if speed is of the essence, we have developed a machine gun, with armored mounting, suitable for armored cars or trains, that has a new design in the cooling jacket of the barrel which allows the gun to be fired longer and at greater speed." He signaled his next team, who drove up in an armored Mercedes, the machine gun mounted above the rear seat. "Those two nearer structures will be your target," he announced grandly. "If you can, cut the brick one in half."

The gunner saluted briskly, then shouted to the driver and the automobile lurched away across the uneven ground.

"I haven't seen an automobile armored in that way before," said Sisak, his eyes calculating.

"It is a design of my engineers; they developed it especially for this machine gun. I bought five Mercedes and had them adapted to this use." Von Wolgast considered Sisak a moment. "You might want to offer for the complete unit, automobile and gun, as a maneuverable unit. We have taken the problems of such a weapon into consideration, and have added two extra tires to the rear axle for increased stability; otherwise the machine gun would make the vehicle top heavy. The space under the platform has been protected as well, so that ammunition can be stored there. Fully equipped, one of those armored motor cars and the machine gun with it, can deliver more than ten thousand rounds without need of resupply."

"And the petrol consumption?" Sisak asked shrewdly.

"Ah," von Wolgast conceded. "There we have a problem; I admit it. We have converted the boot to a second petrol tank, because with the extra weight, the efficiency is reduced." So was the speed, but his engineers were designing a modified transmission that they hoped would make a difference; he went on about the more obvious problem. "We are planning to modify the engine somewhat, to make it run more efficiently. We expect to have our first armored automobile prepared by September. I have ordered another five Mercedes to adapt. If orders justify it, we will develop individualized motor cars for specific needs." He did not add that he had argued with the aging Wilhelm Maybach about adapting his White Jewel to this use. "We are trying to find ways to improve the whole design, of course, and may eventually produce an armored automobile wholly of our own design—we will have to see how much demand there is for this one. But what we have achieved already is impressive."

Sisak motioned von Wolgast into silence as the armored Mercedes neared the first target building. "Let me watch this, Baron, if you will?"

"Mitt Vergnügen," said von Wolgast sincerely.

The rattle of the machine gun cut across the morning more sharply than the wind. The Mercedes was steady enough to support the constant firing of the machine gun without having the steering compromised: the automobile kept on a steady course around the brick building while the machine gun continued to spit bullets at a steady rate.

There were three minutes of silence while the gunner reloaded, and then the noise began again. This demonstration, von Wolgast knew, was the most compelling of all. The mobility of the motor car combined with the firepower of the machine gun would be of greater interest to all but two of the men watching. The Croatians would want weapons that could be deployed rapidly, which the howitzer could not. Sisak's customers were more often seeking adaptability in their guns than long-range firepower. The Russians would probably find the howitzer the more attractive of the two. What the Austrians might want would be nothing but guesswork until and unless an order was placed.

Finally the Mercedes completed its course and came thundering back toward the platform, its transmission moaning, its tires leaving deep ruts in the wild grass.

"Most impressive," said Sisak to von Wolgast. "And very clever."

"How do you mean?" von Wolgast asked, trying to keep the apprehension out of his voice.

"Oh, nothing to your discredit, Baron," he soothed. "I am only aware that you began by showing us a piece of artillery few can afford or have the skilled soldiers to use, and having established that you have the most accurate and rapid-fire howitzer, you then show us something we are all likely to want. It was particularly wise of you to mount the machine gun on the automobile. The Russians would worry about their rail width if you had run the gun on a train."

"They would realize they could adapt the mounting to their own rolling stock," said von Wolgast, as if Sisak's notion had never occurred to him. "It struck me that there are many places where rails do not reach. The Orient Express, for example, does not cover all of the Balkans."

"Indeed," said Sisak, and took a long breath. "This was more than I anticipated, I confess. I had supposed you were imitating Krupp, but that is not the case. Is there anything else in your new arsenal we are going to be shown?"

"Yes, two things more," said von Wolgast with a dawning satisfaction. "First I have a new quick-fire field gun—using the same firing mechanism used on the howitzer. The firing rate is thirty percent faster than those new French field guns. We are modifying an armored tractor to carry the field guns. We anticipate having a working unit in six months." The armored tractor was nearer readiness than that, but he wanted to provide for the licensing from the manufacturer to come through.

"And the last?" Sisak inquired, running out of patience.

"Something new, for a single soldier. It shoots a stream of flaming petrol. The greatest distance we have achieved thus far is only twelve meters. And the weapon itself is quite heavy, in large part due to the shielding needed to protect the man carrying it." He did his best to look encouraged. "But for small forces fighting in isolated areas, it could be useful."

"That it could," Sisak agreed at once. "When does that get demonstrated?"

"Shortly," said von Wolgast, annoyed at being pressed when he was beginning to think everything was going well. "When we have shown the field guns. You will be impressed with their speed of firing; the same mechanism we use on the howitzer can be made to fire even faster in these seventy-fives." He got to his feet. "Gentlemen, if you would care to inspect the machine gun and the armored Mercedes?" This would give his staff time to put the howitzer back in its assembly building, clearing the tracks for the smaller, lighter field guns.

The men on the platform prepared to climb down, permitting von Aehrenthal to go first, as befitted his rank. Von Wolgast brought up the rear, taking pains to pull Colonel Spalavsky aside just before he started down the stairs.

"I was wondering if I might have a word with you, Colonel? Bitte? It will not take long," von Wolgast said politely, taking care not to stand too close to the Russian. "Not about this"—he waved his hand to take in the whole arms display and the expanse of fields—"but something else. Actually, some*one* else."

Colonel Spalavsky regarded von Wolgast speculatively. "Who?"

"Franchot Ragoczy, Count Saint-Germain," said von Wolgast, trying not to rush. "He is in Berlin just at present and—"

"I have met him a few times," said Colonel Spalavsky. "The exile from the Carpathians. He raises some splendid horses. His house in Saint Petersburg is very grand. I have not seen the one he keeps in Moscow. I have been told it is very elegant." His German was educated but formal, as if he were preparing for a school examination.

"Are you aware of any . . . any special position the Czar has awarded him?" This was a risky question, but von Wolgast decided that the direct approach would seem less suspicious to the Russian.

"Why do you ask?" Colonel Spalavsky inquired, his manner becoming more reserved.

"I ask because it is said that this man is attempting to undermine the efforts we are making in establishing the security of Europe." Von Wolgast did not have to summon up much indignation to appear the troubled modern patriot. "If there is some reason the Czar would seek to—"

"The Czar seeks peace. Plehve and I are here only to see what we will have to confront if there is war. And to consider what we may need to ensure our domestic integrity. Nicholas has been adamant about maintaining peace with our European neighbors." He broke away from von Wolgast and hastened to join the others around the Mercedes.

Von Wolgast descended at a more leisurely pace, watching the men inspect the automobile with as much interest as they gave the machine gun. This pleased him. He was proud of what his engineers had accomplished, and knew at last that his pride was not misplaced; his gamble was going to pay off, he was confident of it at last. He kept back from the motor car, not wanting to intrude when these men were convincing themselves of the superiority of his products.

Then von Aehrenthal detached himself from the others and strode over to von Wolgast. "Pardon me, Baron, but I thought I heard you mention Ragoczy to Spalavsky."

"You did, Graff." It bothered von Wolgast to realize he had been overheard.

"Is this the Ragoczy also called Count Saint-Germain? A man about forty-five, of less than middle height, with a deep chest, dark hair and arresting dark eyes, elegant of manner and intelligent?" von Aehrenthal pursued, his clipped beard and moustache bristling.

"I believe they are one in the same, yes; that is certainly an apt description," said von Wolgast. Dreading the answer, he asked as blandly as he could, "Do you know him?"

"Oh, yes," said Franz Ferdinand's deputy. "I met him in Saint Petersburg when I was Ambassador to Russia. A most accomplished man, of great erudition and culture. I cannot imagine him ever embarking on any scheme that might disrupt the peace of Europe. It would be wholly unlike his character to do anything of the sort." His keen eyes held von Wolgast. "That was what you were implying, was it not?"

Von Wolgast straightened himself and looked directly at von Aehrenthal. "I do not know what to think of the fellow, and was hoping to better understand his purpose here. He is known to have a chemical company outside Munchen where fuels are developed, and a few of them might well be useful in war. He is an exile from the Carpathians, by his own admission, and we are all aware of the terrible potential there. If he is increasing the production of fuels, it strikes me that we Germans should know his motives before embracing his work."

"If you will forgive me for saying so, Baron, such caveats from a man whose family business has long been arms has more to consider from his own inventions than fuels which are said to burn more efficiently and give more power than most of what is presently available. His major buyers, I have been informed, are lorry makers, whose vehicles need more reliable fuel than they can often obtain. I had reports on him, six years ago, that confirm all this. He has commercial holdings, or so I understand, that flourish with the regular delivery of goods, which inclines him to put his efforts toward the same goals as lorry makers." He looked squarely at von Wolgast. "It would pain me to hear anything to his discredit."

Doing his best to recover what he might have lost, von Wolgast ducked his head. "I am relieved to hear this from a man who has something other than rumors to form his opinion. I will put my mind at rest, then." He coughed diplomatically. "It is probably my business, as you point out, that makes me doubtful of others. I deal in war, and it makes me assume many others do the same." He was about to turn away, when he added, as if the idea were new to him. "If you knew him in Saint Petersburg, you probably know if he enjoys the confidence of the Czar."

"I am not aware of an especial favor that Nicholas has shown Count Saint-Germain, at least not during my time as Ambassador," said von Aehrenthal, choosing his words with the precision born of long years in foreign courts.

"But it is not impossible that he might? There have been changes in Russia—might not Nicholas repose more confidence in the man now that so much has happened? I cannot believe that the Czar is so without supporters in his own country that he would be driven to employ someone like Ragoczy unless he were convinced that the foreigner might act with more . . . leeway than a Russian might," von Wolgast persisted. "I am not asking from caprice; I have had it on excellent authority that Ragoczy has undertaken a mission of a private nature on the Czar's mandate. I know that Ragoczy has tried to see the Kaiser to deliver a message on his Russian cousin's behalf." He had paid Reighert a handsome sum for this information and was beginning to wonder if it was worth it.

"I know nothing of this," von Aehrenthal admitted. "But I cannot think of any man in whom Nicholas might repose more confidence than Franchot Ragoczy." He scrutinized von Wolgast's features, to be certain the Baron understood him.

"Yes. I see. Most interesting, Graff. I am grateful to you for telling me this." Von Wolgast cursed inwardly even as he managed to show von Aehrenthal his best cordial demeanor. "I will keep it in mind, in future."

"That is sensible of you, Baron," von Aehrenthal said. "I would like to feel that the matter is settled."

"You may do so, at least on my account," von Wolgast said, noticing that two of the other men were watching them—the two Colonels, Persuic and Spalavsky, both with ill-concealed interest.

"Very good. For I would hate to have to tell Franz Josef that so capable a fellow as you was a poor judge of men." Von Aehrenthal made the most of his opportunity. "And if Ragoczy *is* acting for Nicholas, I know the Czar will be well-served by him."

"Just so," said von Wolgast, achieving a sour smile. His full satisfaction for the day had been tarnished, but he strove to make that unapparent, even going so far as to remark at the end of the demonstration, when they had returned from inspecting the demolished buildings, that he was much relieved to know that Ragoczy was a man of such unimpeachable character that he might now discount the rumors circulating about him.

"You might make an effort to dispel them," von Aehrenthal suggested as he prepared to depart in his chauffeured Benz tourer. His condition now offered, he added, "I am sure Franz Josef will be eager to recommend your machine guns and the field guns. I will describe your howitzer, but I will not make any suggestion one way or the other in its regard." He climbed into the automobile, adding as he did, "This was a most illuminating day, Baron. I congratulate you on your accomplishments."

"Danke schoen," said von Wolgast, all propriety, the words sticking in his throat.

"Bitte," said von Aehrenthal, and closed the door.

"Do not let him trouble you," said Colonel Persuic. "He is in an awkward situation, with Franz Josef on one side and Franz Ferdinand on the other. It is a pity that Franz Ferdinand is not as capable an heir as Rudolf was."

"A libertine and a suicide, that was Rudolf," said von Wolgast, dismissing Franz Josef's son. "A self-indulgent—"

Persuic stared at von Wolgast incredulously. "You don't really think Rudolf committed suicide, do you? You can't be that gullible. The man was murdered, and his mistress, for his support of Hungary." He shook his head, regarding von Wolgast somberly. "Still, don't give von Aehrenthal cause to turn against you."

"I had not intended to," said von Wolgast stiffly. "I listened to him, didn't I?"

"Yes," said Persuic. "And it might be wise to take his advice, at least until you have an order from the Austrians."

"Which you will endorse?" von Wolgast challenged.

"Of course," Persuic replied as if the matter were already settled. "I foresee a need for your weapons, and I would like to be supplied with them before some of the other . . . buyers get wind of them. I predict you will have more business than you ever dreamed possible. The firing speed of all your weapons is nothing less than remarkable." He had gone to his Daimler, saying over his shoulder as he went, "Will I see you at the charity concert tonight? At seven-thirty, as I recall. Haydn's *Creation,* isn't it? I have been told everyone will be there."

Was there a hint of the snide in this observation, von Wolgast wondered. "Naturally," he said at his most affable. "I am to escort Nadezna, as you might expect."

"I should have realized," said Persuic with a lascivious grin. "I will look forward to sharing a drink with you during the reception, over the pastries. We will talk more then."

"Excellent," said von Wolgast, and turned away to bid farewell to the other four.

"That Swiss bothers me," Sisak remarked sotto voce as he shook von Wolgast's hands. "I wish I knew what he is doing here. He is too closed-mouthed." He glanced over his shoulder to the departing Oakland.

"I wish I knew who really sent him," said von Wolgast. "I trust I will learn, in time. When he presents an order on behalf of his masters."

"Whoever that is must pay him well, and if his silence is any indication, get value for money. He can afford an American motor car," Sisak pointed out. "He is no pauper or errand boy, not driving that."

"Well, he is Swiss, and the Oakland is known for its climbing; what better automobile in the mountains than the Oakland," said von Wolgast, doing his utmost not to be impressed with the most silent of the observers.

"It is convenient, of course, and confers virtual anonymity, for it is not likely that the Americans are interested in your weapons. He gives you no indication of whom he represents in anything. And I do not trust the Swiss, with their so-called neutrality," said Sisak darkly. "When you learn who employs him, I would like to know." He watched Plehev and Spalavsky drive off, their Rolland-Pilain motor car lurching along the uneven road. "Russians. Clumsy boors, the lot of them. They will never learn how to manage automobiles."

"That may be the least of it, learning to drive; they are clumsy in all things, just like their precious bears," said von Wolgast. "Their country is on the brink of anarchy, and they think I do not know why they are here to see these guns. It is the Generals' way of controlling the people, no matter what the Czar may think. They are expecting more uprisings and they intend to stop them." He spoke with obvious relish.

"There are those in Russia other than the Generals who will want your guns, Baron," Sisak reminded him.

"And when the time comes, you will sell to them, won't you?" von Wolgast countered. He indicated Sisak's Alpha. "Is this new?"

"Yes; I confess it is," said Sisak. "One of their most recent designs. The sign of my success, or so I am told."

"Very handsome," he approved, and pointed to an Italia Palombella. "As you see, I have succumbed. Helmut is disgusted with me, but I do not think he is surprised."

"You did not purchase a Mercedes," Sisak marvelled. "I would have thought, after what I have seen today, that you would. May I ask why you didn't?"

"I liked the Italia rather better; I think black is more dignified than white," said von Wolgast, neglecting to add that he had wanted to thumb his nose at Wilhelm Maybach for his attitude toward having his Mercedes armored.

"Have you found a reliable driver?" Sisak asked, a shade too quickly. "If not, there is someone I can recommend."

"Thank you," said von Wolgast, unwilling to allow one of Sisak's associates into his household. "But I have hired that young man, over there." He pointed to a tall, stalwart youth in a Prussian-blue uniform. "Dietbold has come highly recommended."

Sisak took his strategic defeat philosophically. "Very good." He gave von Wolgast a mock salute. "I will be contacting you next month in regard to orders for your various guns, Baron. I am certain that you will be pleased." With that, he ambled away to his waiting motor car.

Von Wolgast stood, his eyes shaded, as the six men departed. He was convinced now that he would soon have more than enough business to shore up his fortunes. If his good luck held, he might well become as gigantic as Krupp was. It was a heartening thought to accompany him back to Berlin.

But he might have been less sanguine if he had known of Moritz Vinadi's destination—the rented flat of Sidney Reilly.

"Herr Morgenstern," he said in German as he was admitted by the backstairs. "I took the precautions you required."

"Very good," said Reilly, in the same language, showing Vinadi into the study; the shutters were closed and only two of the desk lamps were on. "Please sit down. May I get you anything?"

"Schnapps would be pleasant," said Vinadi, doing as he was ordered. Once he was comfortable, he began politely, "It has been a most interesting day."

"I want to hear your account, in detail, as we agreed," said Reilly, handing Vinadi a balloon glass with two fingers of schnapps in it. "I trust this is to your liking; I have found it quite acceptable."

"And I, Herr Morgenstern." He took a long sip, then gave Reilly direct attention. "The guns were impressive. Very, very impressive. I know there will be eager buyers for what von Wolgast is making. That new firing mechanism is markedly faster than anything I have seen before. I thought the howitzer a bit too large and unwieldy to be of use to all but the mightiest countries. But the machine gun and the field guns, particularly when mounted in an armored automobile, are bound to create a stir. With all the trouble brewing in this part of the world, I do not want to guess how long the generals will be able to resist trying them out on one another."

Reilly poured a smaller amount of schnapps for himself, then began to pace the room. "I was afraid that might be the case. Who was there? Other than von Wolgast?"

"Six in all, counting myself as one. Two Russians," said Vinadi, his eyes distant, as if looking over the two men in question. "One probably from the secret police—a nephew of Plehev's. The other a Colonel in the Preobzhensky Regiment, Georgi Spalavsky."

"The military is not willing to support Nicholas in his search for peace," said Reilly. "That much we may be certain of."

Vinadi pursed his lips. "Franz Ferdinand sent von Aehrenthal himself to inspect. I must suppose both wish to present opinions to Franz Josef."

"Franz Ferdinand is a heavy-handed dolt," said Reilly, tasting his schnapps. "He has no concept of what he is dealing with."

"Yes," Vinadi agreed, continuing with the voice of long experience, "But he is devoted to the cause of Austro-Hungary, and he is determined to continue the support of the Serbian Obrenovics as long as the Russians support the Karageorgevics, and the Serbians will exploit his dedication to their own ends. He will want to be ready to enforce Hapsburg claims." At last he sipped the schnapps and sighed with satisfaction. "It is my impression that Franz Ferdinand is sincere in his stated desire to grant equality to all the peoples of Austro-Hungary."

"Which he will promulgate with guns," Reilly appended. "That does not surprise me." He lowered his head in thought. "I suppose von Aehrenthal will report on the Russians."

"Certainly," said Vinadi. "He will have to do it." He made a gesture of grudging approval. "He has restored the foreign policy of Austro-Hungary. He will not rest if he thinks his country has foreign enemies working against it."

"And when he reports to the heir, Franz Ferdinand will draw his own, obvious conclusions, and do the obvious thing," said Reilly heavily. "If Ragoczy is truly trying to bring about a private agreement of arms limitations, I doubt he will be able to succeed now, not once the Kaiser gets wind of what happened at von Wolgast's factory today. Who else was there?"

"Colonel Vaclav Persuic of the Ninth Hungarian Hussars. I suppose his purposes were more Croatian than Hungarian; he certainly makes no secret of his personal inclinations." Vinadi lifted his free hand. "He tried twice to learn for whom I worked, and not very cleverly. I let him assume it was the French, as I let von Aehrenthal suppose it was the Spanish. The Russians hardly said two words to me, so I have no notion of their thoughts, if they have any. When I contacted von Wolgast, I did as we discussed, and implied I had a client who did not wish to be identified, but was probably Greece. Von Wolgast had no reason to doubt me. Given the disarray in the Ottoman Empire, it is not unlikely that the Greeks would want to be prepared for the worst."

"And they were all convinced?" Reilly asked, thinking again how useful this self-composed Swiss was.

"Convinced enough to be careful what they said to me," Vinadi told him. "Von Wolgast did not press his curiosity too far, and the others took their cues from him." He smiled faintly, then frowned. "Oh, and one other thing: I overheard an exchange between von Wolgast and von Aehrenthal about Ragoczy, when the demonstration of the machine gun was complete. The two Colonels were foolish enough to let it be seen they were listening."

"You did not," Reilly said, certain of the answer.

"No. Of course not. The exchange was an interesting one, and I reckon von Wolgast was not pleased at the outcome." He had more of the schnapps. "It seems von Aehrenthal knew Ragoczy when he was Ambassador to Russia. He has a great deal of respect for the foreigner, and said so."

Now Reilly was deeply interested. "And what was von Wolgast's response to this?"

"He pretended to be grateful to von Aehrenthal for setting the record straight, but it was apparent that he was much annoyed by these developments." He set the snifter down and laced his fingers together.

"Ragoczy has a powerful enemy in von Wolgast."

"Yes; he is having Ragoczy followed here in Berlin. He might have agents in other cities as well, if he is determined to cause trouble for the Count." Reilly thought back to his conversation with Eduard Angebot about Ragoczy's recent fast trip to England; he had been unable to say what Ragoczy had intended to do, but he reported that his private audience with King Edward had been canceled at the last minute. Was it due to Edward's health or the continuing rumors impugning Ragoczy's honor that had brought this about? Reilly scowled ferociously as he considered the ramifications of both possibilities. "Anything more? You mentioned two Russians, von Aehrenthal, Persuic. There must have been one other."

"There was: Tancred Sisak," said Vinadi flatly.

"Bloody hell!" Reilly swore in English, then shifted back to German. "I would not have thought von Wolgast would be so stupid as to let himself be seen with that viper; it smacks of profiteering."

"From what I observed, Sisak intends to be one of his most reliable buyers," said Vinadi. "The two of them were the last to leave the demonstration this afternoon. Von Wolgast made no secret of his readiness to sell to Sisak."

"What did the others say—anything?" Reilly asked; he knew Sisak's opportunism increased the chance of regional conflicts, and hence, the change of all Europe igniting in whole-scale war.

"I doubt if Plehev knew who he was, although Spalavsky certainly did. Von Aehrenthal made no comment, but he did not speak to Sisak, either. Persuic may well be one of Sisak's customers, on behalf of the Croats, if what one hears is true." He reached for the snifter again and finished his schnapps. "I made an attempt to speak with him, but he was having none of it. I assumed he had decided we are business rivals."

"And you encouraged this," Reilly said approvingly. "You did not feel compromised by—"

"I had a task to do, Herr Morgenstern. I did it as best I could." He put the snifter down and rose to his feet. "Do you still want me to go to Vienna?"

Reilly considered the question. "Let me send you word tomorrow morning, after I have had a chance to look over von Wolgast for myself."

"You will see him?" Vinadi asked in some surprise.

"Yes; tonight. There is a charity concert, and I have secured a ticket for it." He did not mention that Angebot had objected strenuously to the price, but had made the arrangements when informed by "C" that Reilly required it.

"And you are planning to speak with von Wolgast?" Vinadi looked askance. "Don't you think that could be dangerous?"

"It is a necessary risk. I have been making myself visible to him for a while and I now intend to presume on our shared entertainments." He ran his finger under his lower lip. "I think a word or two during the reception should be a beginning. I will not do more than exchange pleasantries about the music. In two weeks, he should be willing to boast to me."

"Which is what you seek," said Vinadi, appreciating Reilly's skill. "I take your meaning, Herr Morgenstern."

"I hope von Wolgast will not," said Reilly devoutly.

Vinadi regarded him seriously as he got to his feet. "I share that hope, for your sake, Herr Morgenstern. I do not think that Baron von Wolgast is a man who would forgive an abuse of his hospitality, however he displayed it."

"I think, perhaps, you are right," said Reilly as he handed over a small envelope. "I will contact you tomorrow, before noon."

"Unter den Linden," said Vinadi. "I will be there at eleven." He slipped the envelope into his coat pocket, his eyes crinkling as he did. "I wish you a pleasant evening with the Baron."

"Thank you," said Reilly, and prepared to show his visitor out through the rear entrance. "If you hear of anything you think I should be aware of—"

"I will contact you at once, of course," said Vinadi. "You may be certain of it." He paused at the top of the stairs. "I am Swiss enough not to relish war, Herr Morgenstern, and I am willing to help those who share my qualms."

"I welcome your support," said Reilly.

"It is not so much your support, as support for what it would seem Ragoczy is doing. If I should learn peace is not his purpose, I will no longer be willing to assist you, not for any sum." He bowed slightly, and went off down the stairs.

Reilly thought this over as he dressed for the concert. He had been aware that Vinadi was an idealistic man, the worst sort for this kind of work, in his experience. He had not realized the extent of the man's zeal. Now that he had seen the extent of Vinadi's commitment, he was more uneasy than ever. With these reflections for company, he set out for the charity performance of Haydn's *Creation*.

He had one more unsettling moment that evening, when he had exchanged a few remarks over the champagne served at the reception with Baron von Wolgast and the magnificent Nadezna who accompanied von Wolgast, Reilly had turned around and met the inquisitive, penetrating gaze of Franchot Ragoczy: for two seconds, their eyes had held, and then Nadezna's laughter had recalled Reilly to his purpose, and he made himself look away, but not before he had the disquieting sense that Ragoczy had recognized him from Saint Petersburg and knew exactly what he was doing in Berlin.

◊ ◊ ◊

Text of a dispatch from Czar Nikolai II in Russia to Franchot Ragoczy, Count Saint-Germain, in Berlin.

April 25, 1910, European
by courier

Franchot Ragoczy, Count Saint-Germain
Berlin, Germany

My dear Count;
Through no fault of your own that I can determine, it would appear your mission has not succeeded, and I must now resort to less agreeable methods to enlist my uncle and my cousin in my cause. I find I have no reason to be displeased with your attempts, except that they have not prevailed. I exonerate you of any deliberate wrongdoing, although I would be less than candid with you if I did not admit to extreme disappointment.

Therefore I am recalling you to Saint Petersburg at once, with the admonition that you are to discuss your activities with no one, and to keep to your own society for at least a month; you are not to be seen at any public or social functions during that time. I have no wish to place you in an awkward position, which I am cognizant would be the case if you had to maintain the usual schedule of calls and invitations that are so much a part of life in Saint Petersburg.

The credentials you have been issued are now officially canceled, and you will be required to surrender them immediately upon your return. The courier delivering this to you will present you with the official termination of your mission. I will expect you to call upon me within a fortnight to present an account of what you have done, after which you will be at liberty to go on holiday for the time being. You are not to travel to any foreign country during this four weeks I have instructed you to set aside. When I perceive the need of your efforts, I will inform you of it, and you may once again take up residence in your house on the Nevsky Prospekt.

With my gratitude for your efforts, and with truly genuine sympathy at your failure,

Most sincerely
Nikolai Alexandreivich Romanov
Czar of All the Russias
of that name the second

12

For some reason the small, elegant handwriting blurred on the eclipse-embossed stationery; Rowena Saxon did not realize her eyes were filled with tears. She had not known until now how much she looked forward to Ragoczy's return. He had all but promised to visit her before the beginning of May, and now the month was only two days away and he was going back to Russia, on the specific orders of the Czar—if she believed what he was telling her in the letter. His apology was eloquent, phrased with regret and what seemed to be affection; it did not change the main point of the letter; he would not be able to come to England until mid-June at the earliest. She wiped her face with her smock and only then became aware that she was crying. Putting the letter down, she covered her face and began to weep in earnest at what she felt to be the loss of her only true ally.

A short while later she got up from her chair, gave herself a stiff, inward lecture about her lack of determination. "After all," she said to her reflection as she stared at the ravages of her tears, "you were the one who told him you wanted no bonds. You said that nothing was more important than your art. And you meant it; you mean it now. So why are you being such a ninny? How can you be surprised that he took you at your word, and respected your decision. It is what you wanted him to do, isn't it." She saw her lip tremble, and continued her admonition, "No more of these tragic airs, Rowena. Remember that your grandfather has assured you funds in any part of Europe you may wish to visit. Why not think about those possibilities. And do not," she added sternly, "take a notion to track Ragoczy down. Inform him of your plans once you have them and let him decide what is to be done. If anything." This last melancholy thought made her eyes fill again, and she glared at herself. "That will be quite enough of that."

On the easel her latest work stood, a third finished: a landscape of the wild Welsh cliffs over the sea, but with the grandeur of them changed to something more sinister. She made herself pick up her brushes and begin to apply color with full concentration on what the brushes did. Umber and raw sienna were applied by turns to the headlands above the iron-grey sea. Her own desolation of spirit communicated itself to the paint on the canvas, and within the hour she was fully caught up in her work.

The arrival of Timothy Harris, shortly before teatime, caught her unaware, and she went to admit him as if she had just wakened from sleep. For once she did not apologize for her appearance, but instead blinked twice before she understood that Ragoczy's chauffeur had a small, oddly shaped package for her. "How very kind," she murmured automatically as Harris gave it to her, touched the brim of his cap. "I had a note from your employer this morning. I was . . . saddened to learn he had been recalled to Saint Petersburg. I confess I was disappointed to learn of it; I was looking forward to his return." She stopped herself before she said anything more—such admissions were unseemly, even in artists.

"And he as well, Madame," said Harris.

"I don't suppose you know what's in this?" she prompted, indicating the package.

"Something the Count would like you to have, Madame," Harris responded. He did not want to guess what someone like Ragoczy would give a young woman the likes of Rowena Saxon.

She glanced quickly at him, and saw there was no trace of impudence in his attitude. "It was good of you to bring it."

"Just doing what my employer wants." He was trying to figure out what Ragoczy saw in this impulsive Miss Saxon. Calling herself by a name other than her father's. She might as well be on the stage, he thought.

"Then I thank you on his behalf," she said, surprised he had not yet left.

"Anything you need me to do for you, Madame?" Harris asked abruptly, going on to explain, "The Count said as I was to inquire if you needed anything done?"

She shook her head. "No. I don't think so."

"You're taken care of for food and the like then?" Harris pursued, following Ragoczy's orders most scrupulously. "He said artists like yourself don't always stop working for meals, and if you wanted, I should be happy to—"

At last she smiled. "No, thank you very much, Harris," she said.

"The Count wants you to know he is very sorry he couldn't bring the package himself, but the Czar himself wants him back in Russia. You don't mess about when Czars give the orders." He folded his arms, giving Rowena time to change her mind if she wanted to.

"Yes, so his note informed me," she said, her formality returning. "Well, if you will return tomorrow, I will have a response for him, which

I would appreciate if you would forward to him. He tells me he will not be at his house in Saint Petersburg through all of May, and I must suppose you know where to find him."

"As a matter of fact, I am told to send everything to his business agent in Russia. Chap by the name of Peter Golovin; he'll do the rest. Seems a sensible gentlemen, from what contact I've had with him." He felt she wanted to know more, so he added, "I've been told that the Count is going to be traveling, and this Golovin will know where he is."

"You mean you cannot contact him directly?" Rowena found this disturbing. "How very . . . odd."

Harris shrugged. "Those Russians take mad turns, now and again. And that Czar isn't any different, for all that our Vic was his grandmother. It could make it worse, if you ask me, him looking reasonable, like the Prince of Wales, and then going barmy. Beg pardon for saying it." He coughed delicately. "I'll return then, tomorrow at this time, if that will suit?"

"It will," said Rowena, her optimism returning gradually, fueled by her amusement. She looked at Harris and told him impulsively, "Thank you so much. I can't tell you how relieved I am. It was good of you to do this, Harris."

"Glad to be of service, Miss Saxon," said Harris, liking Rowena a bit more that she was not acting in that high-in-the-instep way most women of her class did. She was not typical of any woman he had ever met, including actresses. Perhaps that was why Ragoczy was taken with her, being something of an oddity himself. "That's it, then." He turned and prepared to descend the stairs when one parting remark caught his attention.

"If you meant it about running an errand for me, I would appreciate it if you would stop at the art and drafting supplies shop on Tottenham Court Road your way tomorrow and pick up a can of rabbit-skin glue. I have two canvases that need sizing." She knew she was blushing, and did not know if it was for taking advantage of Ragoczy's instructions to his chauffeur, or because she still felt awkward about being set on her art career at last.

"Rabbit-skin glue," Harris repeated, his opinion of such a peculiar substance concealed in his polite manner.

She called after him, "It should run you a couple shillings, no more. I will reimburse you, naturally."

"Not to worry, Madame," he said, for Ragoczy had left him ten pounds to cover any incidental expenses he might incur on Rowena Saxon's behalf. "It's taken care of."

"Oh!" she cried, "But there's no—"

"Taken care of," he said a second time as he reached the landing below. "Teatime tomorrow. Rabbit-skin glue." He seconded his own perception: artists were a strange lot. But not as strange as the Russians.

Left alone again, Rowena went back into her studio, the package Harris had given her still in her hands. She was eager to open it, and at the same time she dreaded it, wondering if her mother had been right about Ragoczy all along, and that he was not to be relied upon. Her hands shook as she removed the brown paper wrapping Loretta Nowell had insisted on supplying; beneath it was a box of carved chalcedony, about four inches long and three wide, shaped like a frog. Rowena held it in her hands, astonished at the quality of the workmanship, and delighted with the implication she thought might well be intended. The gold clasp was at the mouth; she opened it and gasped: on the dark-green velvet interior there lay a necklace and earrings of gold, in the same frog shape, with topazes for eyes. She lifted the necklace out and held the inch-and-a-half-long frog leaping to the right on the filigreed chain up to her face. "Will you become a prince if I kiss you?" Gingerly she unfastened the golden links of the necklace and carefully put it on, fumbling with the catch before securing it. The frog gleamed against her smock and she laughed at the incongruity of it. Next she removed the simple pearl drops from her ears and put the two sitting frogs in their place.

The gold flattered her skin and eyes, as Ragoczy must have intended they should. She smiled at her reflection, liking the gift more and more because it was so unusual. She did not remember seeing its like before. Where had Ragoczy found such a suite? she wondered. She could not imagine that he had taken the time to commission it, although he must have done. The truth—that he had made the whole of it, including the gold, himself—did not occur to her.

Suddenly she was sorry she had nowhere to go that evening; she wanted to show off this most remarkable gift. The Gallery of Women Artists was not open after six in the evening. Besides, she would probably not get the response she was hoping for from the women who frequented the place. No, what she wanted was a modish establishment where jewelry was noticed. The least scandalous place would be a restaurant, she decided. Did she dare to go out on her own? Were there reputable restaurants where she could be served if she arrived without escort? If she were her mother's age, they might—not that her mother would ever consider doing anything so shocking. If she was dressed in full mourning, she might be able to command a table, but otherwise her lone presence was not apt to be tolerated: a few bold suffragettes had made such attempts with unpromising results. She decided she had to try, if only to discover for herself that it could not be done.

Rowena went and stared into her closet, aware that a proper appearance was an absolute necessity for her adventure. She would have to look unexceptional if she was to have the least chance of achieving her goal. As she picked her way through her clothes, she tried to imagine how she would feel if she succeeded.

Finally she chose a conservative ensemble in a faded-wine shade, the gown of matte-finish peau de soie with a Juliet-neck and lily-skirt, with the front of the hem a good five inches above her ankle, the back just brushing the floor. The matching coat was of sculptured velvet, with the same lily hemline as the dress, and a high, turned neck. She selected lacy stockings and black-satin shoes with a Louis XIV heel. As she transferred four ten-pound notes and a handful of coins to her beaded evening bag, she began to enjoy herself. Pausing to check her hair in the mirror, she gave herself a mischievous smile as she approved of what she saw. She was satisfied that the frogs showed to dramatic advantage.

Although her Daimler was garaged nearby, she knew it would be more discreet to arrive by cab, and so she descended to the street and went to flag one down on Great Russell Street. It did not take her long to secure one. As she got in, she said, "Please be good enough to take me to the Savoy." Although the hotel had certain associations with the theatre, it was not a place for low company, and, given its modern conveniences and safety features, quite acceptable to all but the highest sticklers, Rowena thought: opera divas dined there, and royalty, and the kitchen was world famous. It was the most likely place she could think of where she had a chance of being allowed to dine alone.

The cabby let her out in front of the hotel, took his fare and tipped his cap as Rowena stepped out. "You have a care, Miss," he said as he prepared to drive off.

"Thank you; I will." She went up the stairs at a good pace, neither lagging nor rushing. As she stepped into the lobby, she resisted the urge to stare; that would surely mark her as a woman of no sophistication or breeding and would make her expulsion certain. Collecting her wits, she continued through the lobby. As she recalled, the restaurant was ahead and to the left; she went toward it with purpose, although she felt increasing apprehension.

The maître d' hesitated only a moment; he recognized the handsome young woman asking for a table, and said smoothly, "Ah, yes, Miss Pearce-Manning. I suppose you are meeting someone?"

Knowing it was cowardly to do so, but taking advantage of the opportunity presented, she nodded. "Yes. I am expecting . . . a relative. Who has been delayed." That was vague enough to permit her to castigate herself only mildly for her lie; it would also put the maître d' on notice that she was doing this with the approval of her family, reducing the chance of him denying her service. She did her best to look unconcerned, as if she did this every day of her life.

It was somewhat irregular, but the maître d' knew better than to embarrass the oldest daughter of one of the wealthiest men in England. He nodded once. "If you will follow me, Miss Pearce-Manning?" he invited, and led the way to a table somewhat behind a pillar: he ignored the stares Rowena earned as well as she did. "Your party will ask for you?"

"Oh, yes, I should think so," she said, remaining calm although her pulse was fast. "There was trouble with making a connection with the London train. With things so unresolved, I may go ahead and order, if that will not inconvenience you."

This was plausible enough for the maître d', who gave her a menu and said, "How unfortunate; I will send your waiter over in ten minutes," before he returned to his station at the reception podium.

Rowena sat back in her chair and resisted the urge to cheer. To have managed this! She wanted to congratulate herself, to boast to someone of what she had done. The only person she could think of who might understand her pride was Franchot Ragoczy, now en route back to Russia. Tonight would be a much greater triumph if Ragoczy were able to share in it. Well, she told herself, she would include an account of the evening when she wrote to thank him for his splendid gift.

Opening her menu, she discovered that the prices were higher than she remembered—not above what she could afford, but dear enough to make her understand why so many people complained of them. The selections were as lavish as they were costly, and it was with a sigh that she passed over the eggs *á la Russe* with imported caviar. She decided on the truffled-goose-liver paté and then the turtle soup to start, the broiled salmon with mayonnaise for fish, the duckling stuffed with chanterelles in port wine for her main course, with a salad of new asparagus; side dishes she left to the chef so long as none of them were turnips. She would choose her sweet later, at the conclusion of the meal. Tempting as it was to order champagne, she decided on a grey St. Emillion for the soup and fish, and a Côtes du Rhône for the duck. When the waiter appeared, she gave him her order, saying, "When my friend arrives, please return. I'd like to speak to your wine steward."

"Of course, Madame," said the waiter in a vaguely Continental accent, and went away to put her order in at the kitchen, and to inform the wine steward that the young woman dining alone had an order for him.

The somallier—for so he liked to think of himself—went at once to Miss Pearce-Manning's table, and received her selection with a mixture of umbrage and respect, telling those willing to listen that she was not wholly a novice in regard to wine.

The paté was delicious, smooth of texture and savory. Rowena was almost sorry to have so little of it, except that with what was to come she did not want to gorge herself at the start. She was halfway through the bowl of turtle soup when she heard someone speak her name and glanced up to see Oliver Rupert Dominic Bowen standing across the table from her, his features rigid with disapproval.

"Have you taken leave of your senses?" he demanded in a voice quiet with rage. "Well, have you, Rowena?"

Her initial shock gave way to a reserved calm that surprised her as much as it provoked him. "Good evening, Rupert. I didn't know you would be here."

"I should think not! Your pranks are not at all worthy of you, let me tell you," he said in the same restricted tone. "What is the matter with you, doing so reckless a thing?"

"As waiting for my cousin to join me for dinner?" she asked confidently.

"What cousin?" he scoffed. "With your father decrying your wild ways, who among your family would encourage you to greater outrages? Do you expect me to believe such a farrago?"

"This is not the nineteenth century, Rupert, it is the twentieth, and women are no longer content to live under the restrictions of the past. My family does not wholly condemn my actions as you are determined to do," Rowena improvised, all the while maintaining an outward calm that made her feel light-headed. "My cousin Juliana. The eldest of my father's sister Elizabeth's brood. She is nearly thirty, and she is coming to London to take up a post as a private tutor in French and Italian." She smiled winningly at Rupert. "Surely you remember her. She's the one who looks like an owl."

"An owl!" Rupert expostulated in disapproval. "Really, Rowena, you must not speak of your cousin in this way."

"Why not?" Rowena inquired politely, then glanced at the approaching waiter. "Rupert, please go away. I don't like the attention you are drawing on me."

"The attention I am drawing?" he huffed. "I am not drawing any attention. You are the one who is—"

"You are the one who is making a scene," she pointed out coolly.

"I am doing no such thing," he said indignantly. "A fine thing when a man cannot look after his affianced wife—"

"I am *not* your affianced wife," she corrected him, some of her tranquility deserting her.

"Your father and I are agreed—" he began, trying to placate her. He held his hand out as if he was prepared to pat her shoulder.

She interrupted him without apology. "My father may have been willing to listen to you, but I will not believe that he would expect me to consider your offer seriously, not given what I have said about marriage since I was ten. The fact that you are not willing to accept my decision is indication that we would make a very poor match indeed."

"There's no need to cause a scene," he reprimanded her.

"I am not causing it. I was sitting quietly until you arrived and took it upon yourself to correct me, a thing you have no right to do." She had to struggle to keep her voice from rising. "If you are so worried about attracting attention, you had best leave me at once, before I am driven to empty this excellent soup over your head." The golden frog lying in the frame of her gown's neckline felt hot on her skin.

He narrowed his eyes. "Have you had too much wine, my dear?"

"No," she said firmly. "I have only tasted what is in this glass. Not that it is any business of yours."

The maître d' approached the table, his thoughts divided. "Excuse me, Miss Pearce-Manning. Is there any trouble."

"Yes, thank you, there is," she said, her manner affable but for the hard glitter of her dark-gold eyes. "Mister Bowen is under the mistaken impression that I am in need of his company."

Rupert colored to the roots of his hair. "This woman is engaged to marry me—"

"I am not," she countered at once. "Mister Bowen is suffering from a misapprehension."

The maître d' could not make up his mind. If he had walked into a lovers' quarrel, he wanted to get away as quickly as possible. But if this was something different, he did not want it said he permitted a patron to be abused. He remembered why he did not like to permit women alone to dine in his restaurant.

"Her father gave his permission for me to address her," Rupert informed the maître d', standing very straight.

"Which I refused," said Rowena, doing what she could to hold her temper in check. "Mister Bowen is determined to rake through the coals again. This is the reason I would prefer to wait for my cousin undisturbed."

Rupert glared at her, his breathing becoming labored. "Why would you decide to have dinner with a relative you describe as looking like an owl?"

"Not that I owe you any answer, but as my cousin has traveled on the Continent, I was hoping to get her advice," said Rowena, wanting to shock Rupert into leaving her alone. He had almost succeeded in ruining her victory.

"The Continent, is it?" Rupert challenged her. "Not content to get up the nose of everyone you know, you are thinking about the Continent. Let me tell you, my girl, you would be well-served going there, with war coming."

"You will not frighten me with bogeymen of war," she said, affecting a languor she did not feel.

"Everyone says it will flare up one of these days," Rupert persisted. "Rowena, please. Stop talking in this unwomanly way. Permit those wiser than you to choose your course for you."

The maître d' came to the conclusion that he would have to intervene. "Little as I wish to offend you, sir, I must ask you to leave Miss Pearce-Manning to wait for her cousin without you." He did not go so far as to take Rupert by the arm, but his expression was stern enough to suggest he was prepared to do so.

"But she's—" Rupert objected.

"Whatever it is, you will have to deal with it somewhere other than here," said the maître d'. "I apologize, Miss Pearce-Manning, for this importunity."

"You haven't importuned me," she said to the maître d'. "You have no reason to apologize."

"This isn't finished, Rowena," Rupert warned her. "I'm going," he said to the man. "You needn't put yourself out on my account." With that he turned on his heel and strode across the room.

Little as she wanted to admit it, Rowena was shaken. She glanced up at the maître d' and said, "Thank you; that was very awkward."

"As you say, Miss Pearce-Manning," he agreed.

"He is remarkably tenacious," she remarked, trying to make light of the whole unpleasant encounter. She had to resist the urge to rise and leave. But such a defeat would be too ignominious; she could not abandon her plan. What business had Rupert to speak to her in that egregious way? she asked herself as she tried to concentrate on the turtle soup. Her only satisfaction was the shock she saw in his face when she informed him she was going to the Continent. She had said it only to upset him, as he was upsetting her. But now, as she finished the last of her soup, she gave the notion serious thought, as she had from time to time over the last month. With her trust fund to draw on, she might set up anywhere, and still keep the studio in London, in case the climate in Europe turned out to be as sadly deteriorated as Rupert had claimed it was. Not that she trusted his judgment in such matters. If only, she thought wistfully, Ragoczy were in London still, or even Berlin, to advise her.

Her salmon arrived, and her appetite, which had threatened to evaporate in the wake of Rupert's castigation, returned. The aroma of the dish was so intense it was almost edible on its own account. The mayonnaise was ladled over the pink flesh of the fish and garnished with capers. She smiled briefly at the waiter, took another sip of her wine, then began to enjoy herself once again, deliberately shutting out all sense of the presence of Rupert Bowen.

By the time she left the Savoy, two hours later, she was replete. The meal had been superb, and the service impeccable. As she paid, she remarked that she was disappointed that her cousin Juliana had not yet arrived, and hoped there might be a message waiting for her at the desk.

"It would have been brought to you at your table, Miss Pearce-Manning," said the maître d', who had kept an eye on her, and on the small group of diners on the far side of the room where Rupert was seated. "I trust there is nothing wrong."

"Oh, I shouldn't think so," said Rowena, trying to sound concerned. "You know how train connections can be. In some of the more remote locations, there are not more than two trains a day. My cousin is in a somewhat more frequented spot, but it is not easy to reach London quickly." She left the full amount—an outrageous twelve pounds six—and added a half crown for service. "The meal was excellent, thank you. And your tact is much appreciated."

"That young man, if you will pardon me mentioning it," the maître d' said as he escorted Rowena to the door, "may prove difficult."

She sighed. "He already has. More than once."

The maître d' nodded. "I will try to keep him here until you are well-away." He did his best to look reassuring.

On impulse, Rowena asked, "Why have you done this? In many another place, I would probably have been asked to leave after such an unpleasant encounter."

"The Savoy is not like other hotels, Miss Pearce-Manning. We are the most modern hotel in London." He continued at her side until they were halfway across the lobby. "How would it look if our notions were antiquated when our design was not? How could we permit the likes of Mary Garden and Nellie Melba to dine here and exclude less illustrious females?" He smiled at her. "Women alone have nothing to fear at the Savoy." He bowed once and returned to his post.

As she rode back to her studio, Rowena continued to give Europe her serious consideration. Much as she wanted to go to Paris, or Rome, she knew her mother would be distressed beyond measure, certain that vice lurked in every alcove, and that priests waited to snare Protestant souls into the clutches of the Catholic Church. She would have to begin more modestly. If she could get her family used to the idea that she did her painting in Europe, she might be able to work her way by stages to Paris, or the south of France, to the marvelous shores of the Mediterranean. She drew herself up short. "That is for later," she told herself as the cab turned into Great Russell Street.

"You say something, Miss?" the cabby asked.

"Nothing of significance," she assured him, and drew out the money for the ride.

Alone in her flat, she turned off the lights in her studio and went through to the L-shaped bedroom, where she began to undress, hanging her clothes with care. The last thing she removed was the frog necklace and earrings, the very items that had started her evening. Only now did she realize that no one had noticed them—or if they had, they had said nothing. She drew on her simple nightgown and set about brushing her short-cropped hair, trying to decide where she would go on the Continent. Wild scenery suggested Switzerland or the north of Italy; she was drawn to grand vistas. For beauty and culture, she had thought of the gorgeous hills of Tuscany and the endless richness of Florence; she also knew that the presence of all those Titans of art might well prove intimidating: Florence would be for later, when she had credentials enough to go there. She promised herself a visit in five years, as a reward for hard work. There was also her fascination with water. The south of France offered both. But being a foreigner and a woman alone, it would make more sense to find a suitable place in the city, where she would not have to depend on country folk who might not want to acknowledge her. But what city? With the possibilities filling her mind, she slipped into her bed and drifted off to sleep.

By morning, she had settled on Amsterdam. It was close enough to England to reassure her father, but distant enough to permit her some freedom. Her family would not like it, of course, but they would dislike it less than any other place that she could think of. In an emergency, she could return home in hardly more than twenty-four hours. The Dutch were known to be sensible people, and Amsterdam a city of some culture. What had decided Rowena upon it was its system of canals: if she could not have wild cliffs and pounding waves, she could have endless reflections and patterns of light and water.

As she made her breakfast—simpler than usual in the wake of last night's extravagance—she did her best to make up her mind how best to inform her family of her decision. It was tempting to write them a letter, but her parents deserved better than that, she knew; whatever she told them, it would have to be face-to-face. A visit to Longacres seemed out of the question: it was too isolated and she was certain to be at a disadvantage there. Perhaps an invitation to London for a concert or other welcome entertainment would allow her to inform them of her intentions. Her mother would not be too distraught if they were not in private.

Rowena was halfway through a letter to her grand-father, having completed one to the bank administering her trust, when she heard impulsive footsteps coming up the stairs to her door. It was too early for Harris to arrive—he would not call upon her for her note to his employer until around four and it was not yet eleven. Quickly she slipped her pen and writing materials into the central drawer of her campaign desk and put the blotter over the letters, wiped the ink from her fingertips, then rose and went to answer the two decisive knocks on her door.

She was not much surprised to find Rupert Bowen, red-faced and thunderous, his overcoat unbuttoned and his tie not quite correctly knotted, on the landing. "Good morning," she said coolly, keeping the door close to her. "I must suppose if you are here you have come to apologize." She did not make any sign of being willing to admit him to her flat.

But he pushed past her and slammed the door closed. "Apology!" he burst out as he rounded on her. "I should think not!" He took her by the shoulders and shook her.

"Let go of me!" she ordered him sharply, adding with great precision, "If you do not, I will kick your shins."

Very slowly he unfixed his fingers. "Very well. There. You see?" He took a long, deep breath. "What came over you, Rowena?" he demanded as he stepped back from her, his hands raised and palms out in an attempt to show he would not harm her.

"In what regard?" she asked, slipping away from him and returning to her studio.

"You know damned well," he said. "And I will not apologize for my language, not given the provocation you offered me."

"I do not recall offering you any provocation, Rupert. If you permitted yourself to be provoked, that is another matter." She watched him carefully, wondering how long it would be until she could ask him to leave.

He hesitated at the archway into the studio. "Why do you insist on embarrassing me?"

"I was unaware that anything I do reflects on you," she pointed out.

Rupert favored her with a condescending smile. "What man does not have the conduct of his future wife—"

He got no further. "But you see, Rupert, I am not your future wife, and so I am at liberty to do as I wish, within the law, without any ramifications for you." She did her best to keep her voice level. "We have been through this last night. Nothing has changed but the degree of your impertinence in coming here, as if you had authority in my life."

"Your father and I are agreed," he reminded her.

"How very nice for you and my father. But I am not a minor, nor am I incompetent, nor am I dependent on my father for my livelihood— thank God fasting—and your agreement with him has no bearing on me." She did not quite shrug but she lifted her left shoulder to show her lack of concern. "If you will not believe me, I will be compelled to have my grand-father's solicitor explain how things stand."

"A very modern woman, aren't you?" he teased her affectionately. "All right; you've made your point. You have shown you can stretch your wings, and received some notice for it. If you will only be content with that. But if you continue on this mad course, there will be those who say I cannot afford to support you in the style to which you are accustomed—"

"And can you?" she challenged, knowing the answer.

"Not as lavishly, but my fortune is not paltry. You will want for nothing any reasonable woman would." He raised his head. "I would hope you will come to your senses before everyone is too shocked by you to—"

Rowena would not let him continue. "Rupert, try to understand me; if you have any real affection for me. I am not going to marry you. I am not going to marry anyone. I will not give up my painting simply because you think it casts a shadow on your position, or because my parents do not approve, or because it is assumed I will never sell anything

I paint." She saw him wince. "Oh, yes; I know what you think of my work, and how it distresses my parents that I should prefer this life to the life they have made for me. I am sorry they cannot see that this is what I want. But fortunately, I do not have to accommodate them, or you. I am in the privileged position to be able to afford to live any life I decide to, without the consent of anyone but myself. And it *is* my life I will live, not what you think I ought to, or my parents wish I would."

"You don't know what you are saying; you haven't considered what your selfishness—for I can call it nothing less—entails," he told her as she fell silent. "Why must you pretend to abhor the protections of our society?"

"I neither pretend nor abhor," she said stiffly. "And as for protection, I do not see that making myself subject to your will affords me anything but loss."

Again his color deepened. "If you disdain marriage, and think of it as loss, what sort of invert are you?"

To her astonishment as much as Rupert's, Rowena laughed. "I see; I see. If I do not want to marry you, it must be that I prefer women to men. There can be no other explanation in your mind, is that it?" Her face grew serious. "If that is your opinion of me, why do you persist in your courtship?"

"Marriage is the lot of women in life, as the family is the kingdom God has made for them. And no woman is so . . . enamored of her own sex that she would choose to live without her own children. You are not so unnatural as all that." Rupert studied her. "In time, you will come to prefer a man."

"By which you mean yourself," she said with a nod.

"I am the one who is willing to marry you in spite of what I know of you." He frowned deeply, his eyes not meeting hers.

Rowena sighed, wishing now she had kicked his shins when she had the chance. "I am grateful for your candid speech, Rupert. Truly, I am. It makes it easier for me to accept my own decision." She walked directly past him to the door. "And now that you have said all you have come to say, I will have to ask you to leave."

"But I haven't said all—" he began.

"Oh, yes you have," she said firmly. "If you do not go, I will be forced to summon help." She opened the door and held it wide for him. Her long training took over; she kept her voice polite. "I wish you a very pleasant good day."

As baffled as he was angry, he tried to make one last point. "You will come to deplore your stubbornness, Rowena, and I pray God it will not be too late when you do," he said as he came up to her. "By continuing in this recalcitrant way, you are thrusting away the very persons whose duty it is to look after your well-being. You are consigning yourself to a lonely old age, without family or friends to support you."

She smiled sweetly. "Better a lonely old age than wasted youth," she said, and hoped that she meant it.

"Your father will be very put out when he learns of this," Rupert said as he went through the door.

"Doubtless," said Rowena, instead of screaming at him. She remained in the doorway as she watched him descend the stairs, to be certain he had left the building. Only when she heard the entryway door shut did she step back into her flat. She remained leaning against the door for several minutes, shaking with vexation and outrage.

When at last she went back to her desk, it was to read through the letter to her grand-father and to affix a postscript describing the unwanted, ongoing attentions and plans of Rupert Bowen, then to finish the letter to Ragoczy, informing him of her determination to find a suitable place in Amsterdam, where she would be happy to receive him at his convenience. Only when she had disposed of this welcome courtesy did she turn her mind to the far more delicate task of inviting her parents to visit her on the tenth of May, for the purpose of telling them of her plans—which would by then be in motion, if not complete—to leave England for Holland in pursuit of her art.

A memo from Tancred Sisak accompanying an order for guns to Baron Manfred Klemens von Wolgast.

Zagreb
May 9, 1910

My dear Baron;
As always, it has been a pleasure doing business with you. My bank draught included will cover the first half of payment for the specific order, the balance to be paid on the delivery of 50% or more of the order.
The matter of the armored automobiles will probably need more discussion before a final price may be decided upon, and I am willing to continue negotiations as my specific requirements are likely to change while my clients decide on what their uses for the machine guns will be.
You have said that you will have sufficient ammunition to fill the order I have placed within six months. If you can deliver at least 30%

of that total as soon as possible, my position will be favorable not only for my current orders but for future orders, as well.

I have had word from Colonel Spalavsky, who has indicated he has not yet persuaded his regiment to purchase more than one howitzer, and so your production of the three I have ordered may be given highest priority. I would appreciate receiving regular reports on your progress of production. The field guns are the most urgently needed, even more than the machine guns, and if you must deliver one part of the order before another, the fifty field guns should be placed at the head of the list. I am certain that as word of the superiority of your products becomes more widely known, you may rest assured that you will have more orders than you now anticipate; the Balkans alone could keep you in full production for two years and more. If you have not made plans for expansion, it might be wise to begin them now.

In three days I will leave for Belgrade and Sarajevo, where I have a number of appointments with prospective clients. I do not yet know what will be ordered then, but I assume, with the Croats and the Serbs both purchasing new weapons, that the Hungarians and the Bosniaks will want to do the same. I also have plans to visit Poland in June, where I am certain to garner more orders still, particularly if the Russians end up purchasing more than a single howitzer and half a dozen field guns.

Of late, I am being told that even those most pacific diplomats who, but a year ago, said war was as impossible as it was unthinkable, are now beginning to plan for it: your new guns could not be more providential.

I will plan to visit Berlin once again in July, when I trust we will both reap the rewards of prosperity.

Sincere regards,
Tancred Sisak

P.S. I would appreciate it if you could arrange for another evening with the incomparable Nadezna. I have not enjoyed myself so much in many years; I will, of course, pay you a commission for such an arrangement, and will see that she has compensation for her time.

PART II

FRANCHOT RAGOCZY, COUNT SAINT-GERMAIN

T ext of a report from Sidney Reilly in Berlin, sent in Key 21 code, to "C" in London, delivered by courier May 14, 1910.

I wish I could say that everyone in Germany is shocked and saddened to hear of King Edward's death, but that would not accurately state the case. For all his expressions of grief, it is said that the Kaiser is pleased to have his uncle gone at last. He is of the opinion that his cousin will be much easier to handle, and more willing to support German aims in the world. His Ministers have been inclined to the same opinion; the Chancellor is absolutely certain that George will be willing to endorse German goals: he has been heard to say that the House of Hanover is more German than English, for all the efforts Victoria made to be English, and has more in common with Hohenzollern, or Hapsburg, for that matter, than with Stewart and Tudor. It is a tactless remark, but von Bethmann-Hollweg has never been noted for his tact. Wilhelm has said he will show respect for his uncle by mourning him, but will not be too disappointed if George V should be more reasonable than Edward VII. When the Kaiser says reasonable, he, of course, means in accord with him.

From what I have been able to determine, it is unlikely that Ragoczy's mission was successful—assuming it was to establish a private agreement between England, Germany, and Russia about some sort of limit on the development and/or the proliferation of arms. Never has that been more wholly abjured than by the munitions-makers of Germany. Krupp is working constantly to improve their products, and Krupp is not the most aggressive of the lot. I have learned through two of my associates that several of the Balkan groups are purchasing German arms through the agency of Tancred Sisak. Baron von Wolgast, who has had men watching Ragoczy and who has been at pains to discredit the Count, has of late received a large order for his new weapons. He has an improved firing mechanism, which is faster than anything being manufactured elsewhere in Europe. He has also produced an armored motor car which serves as a mobile platform for his newest machine gun. I assure you that this information is accurate, and taken from firsthand observation and not from rumors or boasts of those employed by von Wolgast. I would think that Ragoczy's inability to bring about the agreement it is supposed that Nicholas wants can only increase business for von Wolgast, who stands to profit from the tinderbox climate of the Balkans. With Sisak managing the sales, it is extremely likely that von Wolgast artillery and guns will end up in the hands of Karageorgevics and Obrenovics alike, and all the rest of the Balkan factions who can afford Sisak's prices.

With Ragoczy recalled to Russia, should I consider my assignment here ended, or do you want me to turn my attention to the matter of covert sales of arms? The operatives I have here might be able to continue without me, if you decide I should not remain. I have business in Saint Petersburg I can reasonably use to explain my departure from Berlin, or I can remain here, and monitor von Wolgast and Sisak, who seem intent on doing the briskest business. You may also want to have regular reports on the state of German ambitions, which I must tell you, I doubt your diplomats here are fully able to grasp; they are so used to thinking of the Kaiser as the King's relative and not the leader of an autocratic government. I would appreciate a response from you as soon as it is possible for you to set aside the demands of King Edward's obsequies and the coronation of George V. The attractions of Germany are not sufficient to hold me here on their own strength; I have too many memories that haunt me when I am in this country. If I have no word from you by the end of this month, I will make arrangements to return to Russia.

In answer to your question concerning the coming of war, in spite of the current wisdom, I am not absolutely certain that active conflict may be contained in the Balkans, not this time. The history of all Europe is writ in blood, and this time is no exception. The argument that it has been possible in the past to limit the fighting to the Croatian, Bosnian, and Serbian territories strikes me as irrationally optimistic in present circumstances, for any fighting in that region, given the exist-

ing treaties, would surely drag Austro-Hungary into the conflict, and once that happens, others will be compelled to enter the fray. I view with the most grave alarm the reckless manner in which Germany is pressing the issues of Austro-Hungarian suzerainty, as if encouraging Franz Josef to become more expansionistic; most certainly Franz Ferdinand supports such actions, and as Franz Josef's heir, he has influence. I am convinced that Franz Ferdinand wants to make the Hapsburg presence in the Balkans a more immediate one than it is already.

One other thing: on my own initiative I have notified my operatives in Saint Petersburg to continue the surveillance of Ragoczy, and his man of business there, Piotr Golovin. If there is anything in their reports to me that merit your attention, I will supply you with the material they provide me. You will not have to guess at what the Count is doing: I will tell you.

Sidney Reilly (Capt.)

1

There was a large stone island in the middle of the lake, vaguely equine in shape, with a few spindly and stunted trees clinging to the granite. Pale Finnish spring sunlight glinted off the water, dappling the island with its reflected fretwork shine.

"That's Joukahainen's Horse, according to the local legends," said Countess Amalija to Franchot Ragoczy as they strolled along the rocky shore. They spoke a mixture of Russian and French, both of them expert in the two languages. Her hand rested in the bend of his elbow, her touch easy and companionable; she kept away from the water's edge. "In the story, the same thing nearly happened to Joukahainen himself."

"Local legends, you say?" Ragoczy asked gently. "What had the unfortunate fellow done to deserve such a fate?"

"He took on a powerful magician named Vainamoinen, and very nearly lost the contest," said the Countess as the cool breeze ruffled her greying hair, making tendrils around her face, and teasing a few strands loose from the braided coronet. "He would have done had Joukahainen not had a pretty sister."

"Ah," said Ragoczy with a knowing nod. "Of course. They struck a bargain, the sister being the deciding factor; a fairly traditional arrangement. That still doesn't explain the horse."

"Vainamoinen restored Joukahainen to full life, but left his horse stone, to remind Joukahainen of what nearly happened. You may think of it as a kind of object lesson." She laughed, the sound far more youthful than her face was. "Nilo explained it all to me during the interminable winter: Finns sing their magic, or so I was told. They certainly sing their traditional poetry, if you call two-note chanting singing. Vainamoinen was the stronger singer, with more knowledge in his songs."

"Music and knowledge instead of thunderbolts and mayhem; how very . . . sensible." Ragoczy halted, not to look at the stone in the lake, but to face Amalija, his dark eyes on hers. "And is this the only lake in Finland with Joukahainen's stone horse standing in the middle of it?"

"Probably not," she allowed, her smile growing wider. "Only consider the number of lakes in the country—there must be other places making the same claim."

"Still," he said as they resumed walking, "it is a charming story."

"It is, isn't it?" she said, looking up at the sky, determining the time of day from the angle of the sun. "Leonid and Irina should be here shortly. They are bringing their children. I think you will like them; I cannot say how they will feel about you. Leonid can be a stickler at times."

"I will be prepared," Ragoczy promised her.

She plucked his sleeve. "You've had experience, dealing with such men, haven't you?" She did not let him answer. "No, you don't need to tell me. In four millennia, you must have."

"It would be ungallant of me to contradict you," he said fondly. "And untrue, as well. I have dealt with far worse than sticklers."

"You must tell me, sometime. Not the very worst, of course, but the most . . . colorful." She sighed with contentment. "I could not live as you have, for so long, and in such peril. Losing my husband and children to war and fever has been all I can endure." She patted his hand. "You need not worry about me. I have arranged for full embalming. My nephew is troubled that I insist upon it."

He indicated the path through the pines leading back to Countess Amalija's dasha. "And since you mention your nephew and his family . . . If you expect them soon, shouldn't we—"

"Shortly. I want to spend a little more time alone with you while I still can. I know what it will be like later. Once my nephew and his family arrive, there will be fewer opportunities: their children are delightful but they are also generally underfoot. Do not fret. Nilo will take care of settling them into their rooms; I will leave the fuss to him. Leonid and Irina have been here often enough in the past that I need not trouble myself with formalities. Thank goodness; I am at an age when formalities have lost their significance, at least with relatives." They walked a short way in silence; then Amalija said, "My nephew knows you are my lover. I don't . . . anticipate he will be difficult about it, but he might."

"I have dealt with such problems in the past," he said kindly. "I will not take offense at anything he wishes to say against me. But I will protest if he speaks against you."

Her laughter now held a touch of cynicism, the legacy of her long years at Court. "He will not do that, since he will not want to endanger his inheritance. I have named him and his children in my Will, and he is aware of it. I am certain he will not want to make an issue over my . . . pleasures. If you had no fortune, it might be otherwise, but under the circumstances . . . " She gestured her fatalistic acceptance.

Ragoczy did not speak at once. "He would not be so tolerant if he knew my true nature."

"Oh, my dear, dear Count," Countess Amalija said, shaking her head, mirth bubbling in her voice. "My nephew is a thoroughly modern man, who knows that vampires are the stuff of legends—like Joukahainen's Horse, out there in the lake. He would never believe that one could exist, and definitely not as his aunt's lover. He may wonder about your intentions, but I will take care of any impertinences on his part." She studied the swath of pebbled shore ahead of them. "Leonid is aware that you have been sent here by the Czar. He may have questions."

"Which I will be unable to answer; Nikolai has told me I am not to disclose anything about my mission, and I gave him my word I would not," said Ragoczy, his determination more in the clipped delivery than his actual tone. "I will not make an exception for Leonid because he is your nephew: I have an obligation to Nikolai and I will maintain it." He had learned, more than thirty centuries ago, that one in as precarious a position as he often was had to keep his word or lose what little protection integrity granted him. "I hope it will not be necessary for me to be rude with your nephew, but if I must, I will be."

"Yes," she said. "I will inform him that you are not at liberty to discuss your commission from Nikolai, or the Czar's reasons for wanting you to absent yourself from Saint Petersburg."

"Not that I know what they are," said Ragoczy slowly, although he had a fairly good guess: Nikolai did not want his Ministers or Generals to pry information out of Ragoczy. By sending the Count on an enforced holiday, the Czar was making certain the men around him did not have an opportunity to discover Ragoczy's purpose for visiting London and Berlin.

"Leonid is not a complete idiot," said his aunt with great affection. "Give me a moment with him and I will ensure he will not pester you." A sudden flutter of wings across the lake caught her attention. She pointed to the small, plump partridges with grey breasts and barred wings. "Leonid will have something to hunt; that will please him. I was afraid we would have to play cards all the time."

"And if he bags a few of the birds, it will make for an extra dish at dinner," Ragoczy added.

"Not that you will notice," Amalija teased him. "Although that ghoul manservant of yours might enjoy a fresh fowl."

Ragoczy took up her bantering tone. "I will tell him you said so. No doubt he will welcome the change from venison and pork. And you are right—we will not have as much time to ourselves." He stopped again, and this time kissed her; it was a long, slow, languorous kiss, enticing without urgency, stimulating and tranquil at once.

When she could speak again, she said, "I do not know what to make of you, Count." Her smile was light, but tinged with a deeper sense of disquiet.

"Where is the mystery, then?" he asked, his arms still around her, his handsome, irregular features relaxed.

Her answer was more serious than her question had been. "I don't know why you should bother with me, or any of us, for that matter." Her wide brow puckered as she frowned. "You don't have to, do you?"

"You mean it is not necessary to have such intimacy for survival? As a vampire, all I need is blood?" he asked, touching her face gently, his face shadowed by melancholy. "That, my dearest, is a question of definition more than necessity. It is true I do not need this nearness to remain . . . alive; but if life is to be more than mere sustaining of . . . life, then—" He kissed her again, deeply and tenderly.

Her Asiatic eyes filled with tears. "Then you must often be lonely. That is what I could not bear."

He nodded. "Occasionally ferociously," he admitted. "That is why I treasure those few of you who are willing to know me for what I am, and to accept my nature. There are not many of you in the world; now or ever." His dark eyes were distant, as if caught in his memories. "Of those rare few, fewer still are willing to become one of my blood: in all the time I have been . . . alive, only nine have been capable of living as those of my blood must live. Fourteen have come to my life, but five of them"—his voice dropped as those five came vividly into his mind: Aenath, Nicoris, Padmiri, Heugenet, and Demetrice—"chose the true death for themselves rather than live as we must live. Of the nine, only two are alive now. The rest . . . have died the true death by misadventure or . . . deliberate slaughter."

"Do you miss them? those two?" Amalija asked, so simply that Ragoczy realized he could give her a direct answer.

"One, yes; very much." As he said this, the image of Madelaine de Montalia as he had last seen her almost twenty years ago, filled his mind, with a longing as intense as it was futile. "The other, hardly at all." Decades would go by without any thought of Csimenae; she had made herself remote from him thirteen hundred years ago, when his warning had proved all too accurate, and continued her self-imposed isolation—as far as he knew—to this day, eking out a penitential existence high in the Pyrenees. He achieved an ironic smile. "All those who died the true death I miss now and will miss until, I, too, join them. The bond of blood holds me, and will hold me all my . . . life long. You see, Amalija, they are all a part of me, because they knew me."

"The blood does that," she said, repeating what he had told her when he first became her lover, four years earlier.

"The blood and the knowing," he said.

She cocked her head to the side. "But if there are these few other . . . vampires, why not be safe and continue with them? Why do you want someone like me?"

"Well, you see," he answered, his eyes distant, "what vampires seek with the knowing is life; it is the one thing we cannot give one another."

"You mean that once your lover is like you, you cannot be lovers any longer? And I had thought you were seeking . . . variety, as I have," she said, her face suffused with sympathy. "Oh, sweet saints, Count, that's very sad. I had no idea that—"

"Yes. But it is the way of our blood." He was about to say more when a shout came from the path leading to the dasha and two children raced toward their great-aunt. The girl, although slightly younger than the boy, held the lead.

"Ludmilla," said Amalija, her demeanor changing swiftly from deep concern to joviality. Bending down and holding out her arms to the child, she hugged her great-niece as the youngster careened into her. She looked over her great-niece's fair hair to the boy. "Evgeny. Welcome; welcome."

Evgeny, suddenly aware of the stranger with his great-aunt, slowed to a walk, doing his best to appear calm as he sauntered up to Amalija. "Good afternoon, Great-aunt," he said with the careful social grace of his eight years.

"And to you, Evgeny," said Amalija, taking care not to tease him. "I take it your mother and father are back at the dasha?"

"Yes," he said, adding in disgust, "Ilya was sick in the automobile. Mother is making him change clothes."

"Well, I should think so," said Ragoczy, dropping down on his heel and holding out a hand to the boy. "I am Franchot Ragoczy, a friend of your great-aunt's."

Evgeny took Ragoczy's small hand and shook it firmly once, his large eyes somber. He was slightly accusing as he went on. "My father said you would be here. He said you are a foreigner. He said you are a Count."

"Yes, I am—a foreigner and a Count," Ragoczy responded, and noticed that Ludmilla was staring at him.

"He said," the boy persisted, "you are from some place in Hungary."

"Yes, that's true. Just now the place I was born is within Hungarian borders," was his careful answer.

Ludmilla freed herself from Amalija's embrace in a sudden, impatient burst of energy. "I know where Hungary is," she announced.

"Silly," said her brother, not quite shoving her, adding scornfully "Everybody knows that."

"Not everybody," Ludmilla insisted, shooting a dark look at her older brother. "Ilya doesn't know."

"Ilya's three. He doesn't know anything," Evgeny declared, settling the matter to his own satisfaction. He swung toward Amalija. "Nilo said you are having venison tonight."

"If Nilo said it, then I am sure we are," Amalija responded at once. "Nilo would not say it if it were not true."

"I like venison," said Evgeny.

"So do I," Ludmilla seconded at once, as if liking venison were a contest. "I like it a lot."

"Then it is just as well we are having it tonight, isn't it?" Amalija chuckled in response to the children's eager nods, then motioned to Ragoczy to rise. "It is time we were getting back to the dasha," she said, a degree of regret in her words. She compensated for this at once by catching the children in her arms and giving them a hearty hug. "There, now." She let them go as Evgeny started squirming. "Do you want to run back and warn your parents we are coming?" she suggested.

"Oh, yes," said Ludmilla, grinning wickedly at her brother. She was off in the next breath, her starched skirts whisking around her white-stockinged legs; Evgeny went pelting after her, shouting a challenge, his longer stride overtaking her before they reached the trees.

Shading her eyes to watch the children go, Amalija said wistfully, "Do you remember what it was like, having such energy?" Then she looked over at Ragoczy, about to apologize. "Oh, Count. I didn't mean—"

"Yes, Amalija; I may be old, but not so old that I have entirely forgot what it was to be a child," he said, meeting her gaze steadily. "Occasionally it comes back to me, even now." What he remembered most was a night, four millennia ago, when he had gone to the sacred grove in the darkest hour to taste the blood of his god in order to share his nature. "Although you are right: it was a long time ago."

She took his confession as a sign that he was not angry with her. "I find it is increasingly difficult to recall how new the world was when I was young. I know it must have been, but it is hard to—"

"To forget the intervening experiences," he finished for her when she faltered.

"Yes. That is precisely it; the intervening experiences color everything, and we no longer see the world in the sharp relief of childhood. Try as we may, we cannot truly recapture it, can we," she said, and took his arm again, setting their ambling pace back to her dasha. She stopped again, and looked back at the lake. "I know you will be good to them, to my nephew and his family. If you think you would prefer to use the guest-house, at this time of year it is very pleasant; in the winter, it is unlivable."

He studied her profile. "What are you saying to me, Amalija? Do you want me to go to the guest-house, or would you rather I did not?"

She motioned impatiently with her free hand. "I have been unable to decide for myself. I was hoping you would make the choice for me. In the guest-house we could be more private, more alone together. In the dasha itself, there could be interruptions. If you are in the guest house, my absence from my own room would probably be noticed, by Nilo if no one else."

"Which would be less awkward?" he asked. "Yes, I take your point." He had been wondering about dealing with her family since he learned of Leonid's family's visit.

"Moving you now might be thought . . . obvious, but with the children and all, you could prefer your privacy," she said, addressing the matter obliquely.

"Would the children visit the guest-house?" Ragoczy inquired, trying to discern her thoughts.

"Yes, they probably would. But they would make a great deal of noise coming, and you and I would have time to . . . prepare for them. They would not be able to intrude suddenly, as they might in the dasha." She flushed a little.

"Of course," he said. "Then by all means, let it be the guest-house. I will have Roger move my things over from the main house; I will tell your nephew it is my preference. I suppose there are quarters for Roger in the guest-house as well?" This last was an assumption, but it seemed a reasonable one.

"Yes. And he will be able to . . . take his meals there without fear of disturbance." Her voice was muffled, as if admitting so much knowledge of Roger's ghoul-nature was suddenly and unexpectedly embarrassing.

"You mean the children will not burst in while he is quartering a partridge? Or you will not be faced with trying to explain why I do not eat with you?" Ragoczy was able to be amused at the prospect. "Tell me, Amalija: has this family visit been causing you so much apprehension?"

"Since this morning," she confessed. "I have wondered how we are to manage. He will notice that you do not eat, if you are under the same roof. I know he will."

"The guest-house is a very good solution," he said, knowing she would be more comfortable with the separation of her family from her guest; it would certainly be easier for him to be out of their way. "You can say that as a widower, I find the presence of families brings back painful memories, if you must provide an explanation greater than that I think it a reasonable courtesy to surrender the house to blood relatives. Or leave me to account for it."

She did not quite laugh, caught by his first revelation. "You can't be a widower."

"Oh, but I am," he said, his words light and somber at once. "And my wife, dear Countess, was Russian."

"I don't believe it," she said, and then saw the expression in his dark eyes, and apologized at once, becoming flustered in the process. "No, that's not what I meant. I'm sorry. I should not have mentioned— But you see, it never occurred to me that you—of all people—might have been married."

"It was some years ago." The marriage had been a political one, commanded by the Czar; it had become something more over time; he still felt the loss of Xenya with an intensity that had the power to surprise him. He laid his free hand on her shoulder. "Never mind, Amalija. I didn't mean to distress you."

She resumed her steady pace, going along the path twisting through the pines, her boots more appropriate to riding than walking making sharp heel marks in the sandy soil. "I am not distressed. I am abashed. My remark was inexcusable. I should have known better than to make such assumptions about you."

"You mean that because I am a vampire, I cannot marry?" he suggested, and went on gently, "Not that you are entirely wrong. And I have only been married once. In general, I would rather not bring such . . . obligations upon myself, or consequences upon those I love."

"You think that your love is risk enough?" she asked, smiling to reduce the barb in her words.

"Something like that." He could see the dasha ahead, a thick-walled, two-story structure with bright yellow shutters, open now for spring, surmounted by a modified cupola on the steep roof. The wide veranda wrapped around the south and west sides of the dasha, and was ornamented with elaborate wood carving under the eaves and down the pillars. The stable, with big box stalls for four horses—now occupied by a matched team of Orlov trotters—was on the east side of the dasha, with Nilo's house behind it, and a short distance beyond, Nilo's sauna. The guest-house was on the west side of the dasha, a single-story, half-sized version of the dasha itself, with a yellow door to compliment the shutters, and a smaller porch without the gingerbread carpentry. Just at present, Ragoczy's two-year-old Dupressoir was parked between the dasha and the stable; next to it, Amalija's Renault type X, series B double-tourer stood, and behind them, a dusty double-phaeton La Buire was being unloaded by a stoic Nilo, assisted by Roger and a young man in servants' clothing.

The front door of the dasha banged open and Leonid Yureivich Ohchenov strode out to greet his aunt, his big, square face wreathed in smile-creases. "My dear pigeon," he called out, raising his hand in greeting. He had taken off his wheat-colored jacket, and now in waistcoat and shirtsleeves he seemed quite at home.

"Leonid, my pet," Amalija answered, letting go of Ragoczy's arm and hurrying up to her nephew. "It is so good to have you here."

He hugged her enthusiastically. "I swear," he said as he took a step back from her, "you are looking younger and prettier than ever."

"Flatterer," she chided, obviously pleased at his compliment. "How was the trip here? Did you have any trouble on the road?"

"Only the usual—bad roads and scarce fuel. We had a meal, of sorts, at an inn near Lahti; the fish was good. And Ilya was sick, but at his age, I expect that." He kissed her cheeks. "And where is your other guest?"

Ragoczy had hung back, trying to determine how best to deal with Leonid Ohchenov; now he stepped forward, his hand outstretched. He was aware that Leonid might find his black hacking jacket and black riding breeches and boots a trifle too casual, but he gave no indication of it. "I am Franchot Ragoczy. It is a pleasure to know you. Yet I believe we have met once before, Captain Ohchenov, in Saint Petersburg." He chose to use Leonid's military rank rather than his title, hoping this would remind him of their one previous encounter.

Taken unaware, Leonid grasped Ragoczy's hand out of habit. "We may have: I was posted there for three years. And you are Count, are you not? From Hungary? My aunt has mentioned you often." He gave Ragoczy an appraising scrutiny and apparently found nothing to dislike. "I am retired from the Guard, as of last month. They will only recall me in time of war. My youngest brother will be a cadet, come fall."

"Don't speak of it," Amalija told him. "I want to hear nothing of war."

"You think if you say the word, you can make it happen?" Leonid teased, and was interrupted by Ludmilla and Evgeny, who rushed out of the house.

"There! You see? We said she was coming," Evgeny announced, as if Amalija's arrival was his doing.

"So you did, so you did," their father told his children, ruffling his son's hair and patting his daughter's shoulder.

"I think," said Ragoczy to Amalija, "that I will begin to move my things over to the guest house, if it is convenient? That will allow you to set up in the room I have been using as well as the others."

Leonid shot him a hard, curious look. "Move your things?"

"So you and your family can be with your aunt without feeling you must deal with an . . . outsider," Ragoczy said smoothly. "I am aware how important it is for families to be able to be together without having to accommodate guests. It is not as if I am going all the way to Helsinki—I will be fifty strides from that veranda, as easily reached as the stable, which is near enough for any visitor. If I remain in the dasha, you will tend to try to entertain me when it is far more important that you enjoy the company of your aunt. I've had three weeks already in her company. It is more fitting—don't you think?—to relinquish her to you?"

With all his objections adroitly dismissed, Leonid could only say, "This is very gracious of you, Count."

"Hardly," said Ragoczy with sincerity. Then he gave a slight bow to the woman who came out onto the veranda. "Your Duchess, I presume?"

Leonid turned, and his face softened at the sight of his wife. "Yes. Irina."

She took a deliberate step toward Ragoczy. "You are Count Saint-Germain; I am Duchess Ohchenova. It is a pleasure to meet you."

Ragoczy kissed her hand. "And to meet you as well." Then he went on, stepping back down the stairs as good manners required. "Traveling can be exhausting, don't you think; I have always found it so."

"I think it is the most enervating necessity in the world. It puts the whole family into upheaval." She gave Leonid a gentle tweak, saying, "When we go to the hunting lodge near Riga, that is the worst: I always feel ill-used, because I do not like to hunt. The sound of the guns gives me a headache. But it is a fine place for the children; all that open countryside to run in. The lodge is pleasant, and unusually large, more of a country house than those rustic boxes so many families have."

"And you do not like having bird feathers drifting around the kitchen," Leonid reminded her in what was obviously a traditional argument with them.

"I like the hunting lodge," Evgeny announced, as if his liking settled all argument on the matter.

"Hush, Evgeny," said Leonid, the reprimand gentle.

"But, Papa," he protested, and was waved into silence.

"No, I don't like the whole sport of hunting. My brothers despaired of me long ago." She paused. "And in the winter, the Latvian countryside can be very bleak." This was less of an amusement to her than the first teasing condemnation had been. "The snow blows and everything is raw and bitter."

"I know something of the region," said Ragoczy, who had spent the greater part of a decade as a wanderer in the lowlands along the Baltic Sea, from the Vistula to the Dvina, which was called the Duvna, twelve hundred years ago; and the winter months at Leosan Fortress, three centuries later, had been equally severe. "The winters can be . . . unrelenting."

"Then you understand," Irina said, and looked to Amalija. "I have installed Jeronim in the second servant's room, if you do not object."

"Of course not; although the first one will be available shortly, if your man would prefer it," said Amalija, who, after a single, worried perusal of Irina was now determined to show her the utmost cordiality. "You know that this is your home as much as mine. You will do as you like, and Nilo will—"

"Grumble," said Leonid, and chuckled.

"Certainly," said Amalija merrily. "Nilo loves to grumble." She studied her nephew's face for a moment; she recognized his silent plea to change the subject. "You said that Valentin Tschinsov went to London with the Czar's delegation for the coronation of George of England?"

"Yes. He will return in two weeks or so. We are all quite envious. He was chosen out of all my mother's nephews because he speaks English so well." He smiled broadly, as much to thank his aunt as to show his appreciation of his cousin's good fortune.

"I think I will go in, to check on Ilya," said Irina and, after kissing her husband's cheek, left the veranda.

"I'll go, too," Ludmilla declared, and went to follow her mother.

Evgeny looked up at his father. "Can I go help unload the automobile?"

"If you don't make yourself a nuisance, you may," said Leonid, and watched as his son bounced down the veranda steps and disappeared around the corner of the house. He looked down at his aunt, and said, "Thank you for having us."

"As if I could refuse you anything," said Amalija, laughing.

But late that night, when Amalija had come to the guest-house when all her family had gone to sleep, she said, as he closed the door to his room, "You know, I worry about them. They're all I have left in the world."

"I know," Ragoczy said as he helped her out of her cloak to reveal the satin peignoir she wore beneath. "What worries you just now?" He bent and kissed the nape of her neck before hanging the cloak over the back of the taller of two chairs in his room. He had changed from his hacking jacket, breeches, and boots to a short smoking jacket of burgundy velvet and black woolen trousers, and although he behaved casually, his presence created an air of elegance.

"If war comes," she said as she turned to face him, "I think I could not bear it." She frowned at the table lamp where the flame had been turned down to a shaving of flame. "Promise me, if war comes, you will look after them for me." She rested her head on his shoulder, her fingers holding the lapels of his smoking jacket.

"You have my Word." He laid his hand on her hip, taking pleasure in the warmth of her, and the smoothness of the lavender-colored heavy satin; he could feel her apprehension beneath her desire, and began to soothe her.

"Promise," she insisted.

"You have my Word; my promise would not be more binding," he remarked, lifting his hands to loosen the coronet-braid.

"I suppose so," she said, anticipating his kisses.

"What do you want for tonight, now that you have my—" Ragoczy said, with a nod toward the clock on his dresser. "We have several hours before you will be missed."

She chuckled, the sound tight in her throat. "Wouldn't that be interesting, watching them search the dasha for me while I am here with you?"

"Interesting, perhaps: it would definitely be awkward. It is far more pleasant to have our time all to ourselves, for no one's satisfaction but our own." He held her, feeling her nervousness begin to go out of her.

"How can you tell so much about me?" she asked as he kissed her brow and then the corner of her mouth. "Is it the blood?"

"It is you in your blood," he answered gently; her hair spilled down her back, sliding through his fingers like old-silver silk. "I know the whole of you."

"Then you must know what I am thinking," she said, a little breathlessly. "Do I have to tell you?"

"I would like it if you did," he said quietly. "So you will be wholly fulfilled." He began to unfasten her peignoir, starting at the top.

"Don't you know by now what pleases me?" she chided him lovingly, her body tingling as he brushed her exposed flesh lightly with the backs of his fingers. She shivered in anticipation, her eyes half-closed.

"There may be things you would like that we have not done," he said as he dropped her peignoir to the floor; she wore no nightgown beneath it. "As much as I am capable of, I will try to do." For a fleeting instant the memory of Estasia demanding that he rape her on the altar of San Lorenzo returned to him, so forcefully that he could hardly move.

Amalija realized something had affected him. "What is it?" she said as she put her hands over his.

"Nothing," he said, shaking off the intrusion from the past.

"Truly?" She moved his hands around her, then released them.

"Nothing that need concern you." He drew her to him and kissed her, relishing the kindling passion within her. "It was long ago," he added when she flung her head back.

"I guessed as much," she said, and slipped her arms around him. "What did she want of you?"

He paused before he answered, realizing she needed an answer. "Something I would not have done had I been able to." He regarded her steadily, the low light burnishing her features and casting his own into shadow. "There is nothing you need fear from me, Amalija, not now, not ever."

"I know that," she admitted, and held him closer. "I wish," she said as she pressed her face to his shoulder so that her confession was muffled in burgundy velvet, "I could have you love me slowly, very slowly, and at the same time I long for a spasm that is quick and intense."

"You may have both, if it is what you wish," he said quietly, stroking her back.

She held onto him as if to keep from falling. "How? Can you?"

"If it is what gratifies you, it is what gratifies me, as well," he reminded her as he bent to kiss her breasts, and felt her tremble. Lifting his head, he swung her up in his arms and carried her to the bed; it was wide enough for three. As he lowered her onto the flawless expanse of linen, he reached for the comforter he had thrown back before she arrived.

"No," she said. "I don't want to hide, not from you."

He smiled as he bent over her. "Nor I from you." Then his hands began their persuasive, tantalizing journey, setting out a path for his lips to follow; Amalija let all her present concerns fall away until all the world was only her ecstasy and Franchot Ragoczy.

Text of a letter from Rowena Saxon, in Amsterdam, to Franchot Ragoczy, via his man-of-business in Saint Petersburg.

Amsterdam
May 19, 1910

F. Ragoczy, Count Saint-Germain
in care of Piotr Dmitrovich Golovin
77 Volnyj Street
Saint Petersburg, Russia

My dear Count;
  As you see, I have done it. I am now in Amsterdam, looking to let a charming house built in 1610. You may reach me at the Amstel Hotel for Women in Beethoven Straat for the next two weeks. I have been informed by the administrators of my grand-fathers' trust that there should be no difficulty in securing the lease for me: they have been authorized to pay a year's lease on the house, which should put to rest any objections that might be raised against my occupancy.
  My mother, as you may expect, is quite dismayed at my decision. She has implored me to reconsider in daily letters. Her most recent argument is that it is not suitable for a well-born woman to leave England while the world is still mourning the loss of Edward VII. She has said nothing about our English celebration of George V, I would guess because it takes away from her perceived ill-use.
  In all the years I have been pursuing my art, I have never felt as truly committed to it as I do now. I have at last decided that my dedication is not merely the protestation of a dissatisfied woman—as my mother has long contended is the case—but the true response to the requirements of talent. There. I have said it. I accept that I have talent, and that talent has a price. I will try not to think myself boastful for using such a word, although I cannot fully escape that apprehension, or not yet. In time, I hope to become accustomed to such acknowledgement.
  If you were sincere in your offer to find me gallery attention, I would certainly appreciate your efforts at this time. Now that I cannot easily exhibit at the Gallery of Women Artists, I would prefer an Amsterdam gallery for my work. I realize this may be presuming upon you, but I

confess I am at a loss as to how to achieve a place for my work without someone to endorse it. And although you mayn't believe it, no matter how you decide, I hope you will consider sitting for me when next you are in Amsterdam. I think you would be a most interesting subject for a portrait. And frankly, if you are willing to let me paint you, there may be others who would be inclined to commission their own portraits once they see what I have accomplished with yours. If any of these requests offend you, I beg your pardon and ask you consider them unasked.

Two days ago I received a telegram from Rupert Bowen, who claims to be determined to continue his suit; I have informed him more than once that any engagement he may believe exists between us is a fiction; that my father cannot grant or withhold my affections, no matter what Rupert would like to think. I may not be able to avoid him entirely, but at least I have put some distance between us, and that may serve to diminish his supposed ardor.

As soon as I have moved into the house, I will send you the address. I will also leave instructions with the hotel to forward all mail to me, so that you may be assured that any communication from you will reach me, wherever I am. In time, I hope to move to Paris or Rome, but that will take at least two years' work here. Then I will be ready to test the waters of those splendid places. In the meantime, Amsterdam will do very well for a first venture. I have already learned my way around the environs of the city and I am beginning to explore the countryside a little. By the time you arrive here, I will be delighted to serve as your guide, if you need one.

In anticipation of our meeting again,

Cordially,
Rowena Saxon

2

As he poured out a generous amount of schnapps into a cut-crystal glass, Baron von Wolgast did his utmost to conceal the satisfaction he felt at the shocked expression on Egmont von Rosenwiese's lean, aristocratic face. "Here," he said, holding out the glass. "You look as if you need it."

"Mein Gott," von Rosenwiese muttered as he took the glass and drank down its entire contents in a single gulp. "Those letters— How did you—"

"That is not important," he said, enjoying his position over the younger man. "The point is, I have the chance to secure the letters in question, before they could do any damage." He had paid handsomely to obtain them; he was beginning to think it was money well-spent. He was not willing to tell von Rosenwiese that he had them in his possession, not yet: let the young idiot twist in the wind a while longer. "I know it would not help your career if it was ever learned that you had—shall we call it an affaire? yes?—with Bishop Kalthaus."

"That was six years ago," von Rosenwiese protested feebly; his tall, athletic body seemed to have shrunk in the last few minutes, and he began to fiddle with his cufflinks. He turned his head quickly at a sudden hooting of horns in the street below, as if the sound were intended for him, and not erring motorists.

"Of course, of course. But it would still be a scandal, if it were known, wouldn't it? Affaires of that sort are not as readily forgotten as those we have with women." Von Wolgast's smile was full of counterfeit goodwill. "You are a lucky man that I was the one who happened upon the letters, that the seller brought them to me. I understand the danger they represent to you, to say nothing of your father and older brother. If anyone else had come upon them—" It was, in fact, the former Jesuit Reighert who had discovered their existence, but von Wolgast knew better than to mention this. "Many another would have gone directly to the Minister, or to the press. Or to the Church." He took the glass and refilled it. "Here. Have some more. Steady your nerves, Egmont. You are in safe hands."

Von Rosenwiese took the glass. "Danke."

The drawing room was fashionably cluttered, with two large suites of settee-and-chairs surrounding a large cocktail table. End tables flanked the two suites, each one with a lamp on it. The prevailing color was the glossy oaken sheen of the paneling and furniture, and a rich forest green. There was a trestle table behind both settees, each with its own display of expensive trinkets, including a collection of porcelain figures from the previous century. It was not quite noon and the room was warmed by the mid-June sunshine streaming in the south-facing windows. All in all, the drawing room ought to have been welcoming, but it was not.

"Think nothing of it," said von Wolgast, his eyes brimming with amusement; he tried to look downcast, and nearly succeeded. "I thought it would be best if I came to you directly, Egmont, instead of reporting this to your superiors, as I know it is correct for me to do. Let us say that men of our station in society owe one another more than they owe the masses." He poured a schnapps for himself and sat down in the chair opposite Egmont von Rosenwiese, leaning forward as if to show his deep regard for the tall, blond Deputy Minister for Foreign Affairs. "I was not only thinking of you, but of the Bishop, of course. A shocking thing like this might well—well, let's not dwell on it, shall we?" He sipped and watched his companion squirm.

"It is not only the Bishop," said von Rosenwiese after a short time. "My family would be . . . unable to cope with this, I fear. You are right about that." He finished his schnapps again, and then coughed as the alcohol struck him.

"Would you like some more?" von Wolgast inquired, rising already to take the glass. "At times like this, you do not succumb to drink as readily as others. The shock prevents intoxication. Or, I have always found it so," he said as he again poured out a generous amount and handed it back. "There you go."

"I don't know . . . " said von Rosenwiese as his fingers curled around the glass as if around a floating spar after a shipwreck.

"We will have to make an arrangement, you and I, in regard to these letters, so that they will not fall into the wrong hands," said von Wolgast smoothly. "We must come upon some way to protect you and ensure your . . . privacy."

"And Hugo's, as well," said von Rosenwiese, unaware that he had used Bishop Kalthaus' first name. "He has as much to lose as I, if news of this gets out. The Church would punish him; make an example of him. The Catholics are like that." He put his free hand to his eyes, squinting down into the contents of his glass as if he could read something in it. "We were younger then, and so many things seemed possible."

"Your wife would be distressed to hear of this, I presume," said von Wolgast, doing his best to maintain his sympathetic facade. He glanced up as he saw Schmidt at the door; he abruptly motioned his butler away.

"I don't know," said von Rosenwiese distantly. "She is not a woman much inclined to . . . physical expressions. She has often apologized to me . . . She might be relieved if she knew that I was not as disappointed in her as she fears." This time his sip was more judicious, although his words were already beginning to slur and his clear blue eyes had lost their sharp focus.

"Well, that's something, at least," said von Wolgast, glowering down at his feet; he had wanted to have more than one means to control von Rosenwiese, which now seemed impossible.

"My father, however, would be horrified, and my brother as well, if they discovered anything about this, and my uncles would want my father to disown me. It's happened once, to my cousin Heinrich," von Rosenwiese admitted in a rush. "He went to America; I've no idea where. Thank God my mother is dead. She would have not been able to bear the gossip."

This was more to von Wolgast's liking. "I will do what I can to ensure your protection, and the protection of your entire family. I think men of our rank owe one another that much loyalty, don't you?" He drank a little more, and was pleased to see that von Rosenwiese did the same. "The Ministry would not be willing to keep you on, would they? If any of this comes out?"

There was a shine of sweat on von Rosenwiese's fine brow. "I would be completely disgraced. No part of the government would employ me." He shuddered at the very thought. "I probably could not secure so much as a teaching post, either, not after a scandal like this."

"Then we must be certain it doesn't happen: no scandal will ensue," he said, and went on more energetically. "I do not have the letters to hand, but I know who does. I know the fellow is asking a high price for them. Now," he went on, warming to his deception, "I will purchase the letters for you—"

"Von Wolgast!" von Rosenwiese exclaimed. "I couldn't possibly permit—"

"Well, you cannot afford to do it, can you? Not on your salary. I can, and I would consider it a worthwhile investment." That, at least, was the truth.

"But why—?" He was not yet so drunk that he had lost all sense of danger.

"Because you have the capacity to do so much for Germany, you as a man, and you as a man of your position in the world," said von Wolgast with feeling. "You are born to those who have led this country through every battle, every campaign, every war since Otto the Great. Without men like you, von Rosenwiese, we are no better than the Dutch. We cannot waste men of your . . . heritage, not now that the Turks are in disorder and the whole of Russia may dissolve in revolution. Such catastrophe must not befall Germany. You can achieve much if this . . . youthful mistake is not brought to light. You may well receive the attention of the Chancellor, if not the Kaiser himself. There are too few men of your character in government. Most of them are ambitious hacks, with no sense of patriotism." He was doing his best to seem modest about his own claims to patriotism, and was nearly successful. "You know the sort I mean."

"Oh, yes," said von Rosenwiese, eager to find anything that would ally him more completely with von Wolgast.

"If they are not seeking to make profit for themselves, they are rooted in the past, clinging to the verities of the last century, and to von Bismarck's notions of maintaining our place in European affairs." Von Wolgast saw he had as much of von Rosenwiese's attention as he could give after so much schnapps. "It is up to men like you—and perhaps like me—to claim our place in Germany, to make it plain that Germany is not content to rest on the laurels of the past, but is forging ahead into the new century with strength and vision." He got up, as if in the throes of fervor for his country. "I would like to see Germany assume the mantle of European leadership. Oh, not that we have lagged, but we have not done all that we might."

"I know; I know. There are still those in high positions who are committed to negotiating with the French and the English and the Austrians and all the rest of them, as if talk ever settled anything. Look at the miserable alliances between France and England—historical enemies. They assume a piece of paper will negate ten centuries of rivalry. Ridiculous." Von Rosenwiese tripped over the last syllables, and scowled at the glass in his hand as if he had not seen it there before.

This was almost too easy, von Wolgast thought, and reminded himself that he would have to fire his guest sufficiently for his nationalistic dedication to survive his hangover. "We must prepare to advance the cause of our country," he declared.

"Ja. We must," said von Rosenwiese, going on owlishly, "The Austrians are trying to upset the balance in the east, moving into land the Turks had controlled, fifty years ago. And the Russians are letting it happen."

"Russia, as you have so astutely said, has trouble of her own. She is in no position to interfere with Austro-Hungary." Von Wolgast was not going to let von Rosenwiese be distracted from his purpose. "We must make certain that Europe does not go the way of Russia. We must also try to keep our government strong—none of this parliamentary nonsense to muddy the waters."

"I should hope not," von Rosenwiese agreed, trying to strike the arm of his chair, and missing it. He blinked at his hand, then peered at von Wolgast. "Look what has happened to England. And with George on the throne, well!"

"Exactly." Von Wolgast was not sure what von Rosenwiese meant, but he knew better than to question him in this state. "The whole of Europe needs German leadership, to keep it on course," said von Wolgast as if the prospect were a grim responsibility. "We cannot shirk our obligations to the world, not at this time."

"True, very true," said von Rosenwiese. "I could not . . . " He faltered and strove to recover his thought. "It is right that Germany take the lead."

"And those of you in Foreign Affairs are the ones who must make the policy and set the tone for the rest of the government; too many of the men in power do not grasp the danger in which we stand," said von Wolgast, hoping he still had enough of von Rosenwiese's attention to convince him. "You, with men like me and Krupp, will be the ones to bring Germany to the preeminent position that has so long been denied us."

"Jawohl," exclaimed von Rosenwiese. "In ten years, all Europe must have the stamp of Germany upon it." He raised his glass to toast this prospect.

"It is the destiny of our country," said von Wolgast, keeping his statement as simple as possible.

"That it is," affirmed von Rosenwiese. He had slid down in his chair, but now made himself sit up as straight as he could. "No one can deny that Germany deserves to be first among the nations of Europe."

"My point exactly," von Wolgast encouraged.

"And we must not forget it." Von Rosenwiese wagged an index finger at his host. "If Europe is not capable of understanding this, she must be made aware. Anything else is madness."

"That she must. We are the bastion against the perils of the East," von Wolgast reminded him.

"And the West," added von Rosenwiese. He nearly dropped his glass.

Von Wolgast got up immediately. "Here," he offered. "Let me refill that for you. It has been quite a hectic morning."

"I shouldn't," said von Rosenwiese as he held his glass out for more. "I will not be able to return to the Ministry this afternoon."

"You may stay here, if you like; there is a daybed in my study," said von Wolgast, who had no intention of allowing von Rosenwiese to leave while his tongue was so loose. "I will want to show you some of the new designs we have put into production at my factory. Considering our discussion, I would think you would want to familiarize yourself with them." He neatly topped off von Rosenwiese's glass, saying as he did, "You have dealt with a potentially ruinous problem. Who can blame you for taking advantage of the hospitality I am more than willing to offer?"

"It's very good of you," said von Rosenwiese, his drunkenness not obliterating his sense of manners. "It is probably foolish of me, but I do need . . . " He had a long sip of the schnapps and smiled.

"Nonsense," said von Wolgast. "Every man needs to let himself indulge from time to time, and you have been through more than most of us; you owe yourself a respite. I imagine that you have lived in dread of discovery from the day of your first promotion. And now, given how far you have risen, the anxiety must be very great." He smiled with all his teeth.

"I *was* somewhat worried, yes," said von Rosenwiese. "Knowing that you will have the letters relieves me more than you know."

"And me, as well," said von Wolgast, resuming his seat across from von Rosenwiese. "Tell me, Egmont: how much influence do you have on your colleagues? Will they listen to you if you propose any policy change?"

Von Rosenwiese considered his answer with the ponderous concentration of a fuddled mind. "I should think so," he decided at last. "They did, in regard to Poland."

"And what about the government in Prague? Have you any insights where the Czechs are concerned?" Von Wolgast already knew the answer but he waited while von Rosenwiese answered; how candid the younger man was now would give von Wolgast an opportunity to evaluate von Rosenwiese's judgment.

"I don't know; I've never tried to address the issue of the Czechs. Poland and Hungary are my two primary areas of concern." He cleared his throat noisily. "I am having dinner with von Moltke on Friday. I could speak to him about the Czechs."

Von Wolgast nodded emphatically. "Find out if he still endorses von Bismarck's belief that Germany is a European power, not a colonial one, and how far he is willing to go to secure Germany's position in the world." He had been unable to sound out the Chief of the General Staff on anything but the question of increasing the size of the army. "Any inquiry coming from me will be seen as the ambitions of an arms manufacturer, not a German seeking to promote Germany. I can hardly fault him for his circumspection, but I do wish to know his views; in his position I would predicate my expectations on the same assumptions. He will surely give you the more helpful answers."

"Of course, of course. Of course. I would be pleased to do it; such a small thing, after all you have done for me." Von Rosenwiese's smile was lopsided, but he did his best to maintain it. "I will call upon you on Saturday, if you will allow. It is the least I can do, Baron, with what you have done for me."

"Alas, I will be away from Berlin from Friday until Tuesday; at my factory, as it happens." He needed to review the progress on the orders from Sisak; there was no need to mention that to von Rosenwiese or anyone else in the government. "If you are available a week from today, I would be delighted to hear your evaluation of the General's remarks. With your experience in the Ministry, you should be able to analyze his meaning, and bring about the possibility of more discussions."

"With pleasure," said von Rosenwiese, suddenly sounding half-asleep.

"You are exhausted, my friend, and small wonder," said von Wolgast, rising again. "Let me send for Schmidt. He will prepare the bed for you." There was a bellpull by the fireplace; he rang this and waited while he watched von Rosenwiese begin to doze.

Schmidt arrived promptly, but not quite quickly enough to earn him more than a hard stare from von Wolgast. He glanced at von Rosenwiese and sighed. "The study or one of the guest rooms, sir?"

"The study; the daybed. He will not feel he has been irresponsible if he sleeps in a daybed. He is still able to stumble up the stairs. You will not need help to get him there." Von Wolgast spoke quietly, yet he was reasonably certain that von Rosenwiese could not hear or understand him.

"As you say," Schmidt conceded, disliking the prospect of lugging this sot up the stairs. He went to help von Rosenwiese out of the chair, draping the taller man's leaden arm over his shoulder and securing him around the waist before leaving the drawing room to Baron von Wolgast.

Two hours later, while von Rosenwiese snored on the floor above him, von Wolgast sat over coffee in his drawing room, savoring his sense of victory and planning how he would extend his influence over von Rosenwiese. He was startled by the sound of the front knocker, and shortly thereafter, Schmidt's announcement that Nadezna had called and wished to see him.

"Did you tell her I am in?" von Wolgast demanded accusingly; he was in no mood for the dancer's histrionics.

"She knew. I could not deny you." He had made no effort to, either. "She says she will wait until you are finished if you are tending to business, but she must and will see you today." Schmidt revealed nothing of his sentiments, but inwardly he hoped that Nadezna would give von

Wolgast a hard time; he already felt ill-used and wanted to pay von Wolgast in some of his own coin.

"Damn the woman," said von Wolgast, more annoyed than irate. "I might as well get it over with. Show her into the parlor. And make sure she is offered refreshments. Tell her I will join her there directly." He did not want to give anyone—least of all Nadezna herself—the impression that he could be summoned on a whim.

"As you wish," said Schmidt as he bowed and withdrew.

Left on his own, von Wolgast tried to imagine what had brought Nadezna to his door. Whatever it was, he was not going to encourage her to come here again. He had to admit it was unlike her to disturb him at his house; that alone was distressing to him, for it could mean that there was unanticipated trouble. The chance that he might have overlooked something significant to his efforts made him angry. He refilled his cup and added more sugar, stirring it slowly as he reflected on what might have brought her here. When half an hour had gone by without any answer suggesting itself, he put the remainder of his coffee aside and wandered down the hall to the parlor, as blue and pale-rose as the drawing room was oak and green.

Nadezna had sunk down on the settee, her gorgeous steel-grey cloak flung out around her, making a splendid frame for her graceful posture and many-layered gauze summer frock, like one of those sylphs in the Mucha paintings. She turned her head as von Wolgast came in, and favored him with a petulant stare. "You kept me waiting."

"You did not tell me to expect you," he said, walking over to her and bending down to kiss her brow. "But since you are here, I must presume that whatever the matter is, it cannot wait."

"No. It cannot," she said, her voice dropping to a near-whisper. "It is Sisak."

Von Wolgast smirked. "You have made a conquest of him, have you?" He selected a cigar from the humidor kept on the desk against the far wall, snipped its end and prepared to light it. "Why complain of that?"

"The man is a . . . beast." She made the last an accusation.

"Yes," said von Wolgast, unwilling to be provoked. "I suppose he is. But he is a rich beast."

"What does that matter?" she demanded with a sweeping motion of her arm to show that his money meant nothing to her. "He treats me like a gutter whore."

"Does that surprise you?" von Wolgast asked her, preserving his unruffled calm. "I would have not expected him to do otherwise."

"And you brought him to me, knowing that?" she said incredulously.

"You understood what kind of . . . creature he was, and you still—"

Von Wolgast held up a hand to silence her. "Spare me your indignation, if you please. You are not some abused innocent, are you?"

"I do not deserved to be so badly treated," she insisted, her mouth set in petulant lines. "I want no part of him."

"That is too bad, my pet: he wants to continue with you. He told me so not four days since. In his own way, he is besotted with you." He smiled, his eyes flat as pebbles. "And as long as it serves my purpose to indulge him, you will make yourself desirable for him. Do you understand me?"

Nadezna rose to her feet, her movement as lovely and pliant as a willow in the wind. "I do not want to. He makes me sick."

"Don't assume you can win me over with a performance," he warned her. "I have known you much too long to be swayed by your theatrics. Spare me, I beg of you." His tone was more bored than pleading.

"Why?" she said, moving to confront him. "Because you do not want to deal fairly with me? I know he has been paying you for arranging our . . . trysts. He told me as much last week." She made a face that blighted her loveliness. "I cannot endure the thought of him. He smells. He . . . he humiliates me. And he *delights* in my humiliation." There were tears standing in her eyes, and she caught her lower lip in her teeth.

Von Wolgast was unmoved by her display. "You are being very well-paid to suffer his petty demands," he reminded her. "If you are willing to give up the money, then there is nothing more to say."

"Oh, yes there is," she countered. "Since I know how much he pays you—in diamonds—I have decided that I want a larger share of the jewels. I don't want to have to be subjected to Tancred Sisak's horrible—" She read von Wolgast's expression, and abandoned the catalogue of Sisak's despicable acts. "If you want me to continue with that barbarian, you will pay me half again as much as I have been receiving from you. If you will not do this, I will cease to receive that man in any way."

Regarding her through narrowed eyes, von Wolgast gave himself a moment to consider his options. He could not afford to have Nadezna reject Sisak at this time of delicate negotiations; he would have to make some gestures of compensation to stop her from denying herself to Sisak. Accepting his unwelcome predicament, he said, "Very well: I will give you thirty percent more of the diamonds than I have done, but not fifty percent."

"It isn't enough," she said bluntly. "If you had any idea of how he behaves, you would not wonder at why I must have more."

"Let us see how these terms work out. If you are not satisfied, we can discuss it again, at a later time. We can reach a more equitable arrangement when times are better." He had no intention of permitting her to dictate the terms of their agreement; he had to make it appear he would.

"Thirty percent is not enough." She placed herself in front of him, her hands on her hips in a show of defiance.

He pursed his lips, trying to find the means to calm her without capitulating to her demands. "For the moment, it must be. I have had very high expenses; the factory has needed refitting and that is costly. In a month or so, when the first orders have been delivered, there will be more money for us both." He put his hands on her shoulders, letting her feel the weight of them. "Be patient, and together we can achieve our goals without rancor or suspicion."

She was not to be cajoled. "I have no desire to be patient with Sisak. I want to hurt him. I want to repay him for what he has done to me."

"There, there, my pet," said von Wolgast, leaning down to kiss her brow. "It will not be much longer and then you and I will both be free of him. Is that really so much to ask? Hm?" He waited a moment, making sure she would not have another outburst. "And when this is concluded, I will be very, very grateful, I promise you." He tightened his hands on her shoulders, to remind her what he could do if she failed him.

"I can't take much more of him, and all his tyrannies," she said, ashamed of herself for confessing so much. "When he puts his prick in my mouth, it's all I can do not to bite it off."

Von Wolgast winced, and his brow drew downward. "Don't say such things, not even in jest."

Realizing that she had struck a nerve, she smiled mischievously. In her best coquetting style she pursued, "Do you think I couldn't do it? Oh, Baron, I can; take my word for it."

"That is not an issue," said von Wolgast stiffly. He moved away from her, disgruntled by her increasing merriment. "I don't want you—"

"Does it worry you?" she interrupted with exaggerated sympathy. "Do you become afraid, thinking I might one day do it to you?" She came up behind him and put her arms around his thick waist. "It wouldn't be—"

As he rounded on her he brought up his hand, striking her backhanded and thrusting her away from him all in the same movement. *"No more!"* he bellowed at her, taking satisfaction in her awkward sprawl over the back of his eighteenth-century library chair. He came up to her, standing over her with hands tightened into fists; he was panting with exertion and some sensation he did not dare to name. "Do not make it necessary for me to do anything more to discipline you. You don't want bruises all over your body, now do you?"

Nadezna righted herself, her face already showing the mark of his blow. She schooled herself to a compliant manner, saying, "I did not intend to offend you."

"I am not offended, I am revolted," he said and made himself put a little space between them; it was too tempting to hit her again when she was so close. "Christ! Listen to yourself! You call Sisak a barbarian."

"Because he is," she said in a small voice. She flicked her tongue over her lips and left a small smear of blood behind; the inside of her mouth had been cut by her teeth when he struck her.

"And then you— You're as much a barbarian as he." Von Wolgast tugged at his jacket, not willing to look at her.

She made an effort to conceal the fear she felt as she watched him. "Baron. I apologize." Her voice cracked. "I didn't—"

"I don't want to hear anything more about this. Not a single word." He folded his arms. "You forget who you are dealing with, Madame. I will not tolerate such remarks from you or anyone. Is that clear?"

She put her hand to the side of her face he had injured and nodded. She would have to put ice and raw bacon on her face as soon as she got home or would have to keep within doors for a week while the bruise faded. "I mean it about the money, Baron," she said sullenly.

"No doubt you do. I told you what I am prepared to do and I will abide by it, no matter what I may think of your lapse here." He shrugged, trying to lessen her fear of him. "I will see you have thirty percent more now, and when I have been paid all that Sisak will owe me, I will make sure you share in that harvest."

"Thank you," she said without emotion.

"I think you will find you will not have to worry about your old age, not when we have achieved all that we can from Sisak and Persuic." He felt his pulse begin to slow at last; he went a few steps closer to her. "I did not mean to hurt you. If you had not provoked me, I would not have."

"I've apologized," she reminded him. "I don't want you to hurt me again."

"If you don't make it necessary, I won't," he said, and went to summon Schmidt. "I will have him fetch a cognac for you."

"No, thank you," she said, standing fully upright at last. Her head ached and her hands shook, but she managed to look resolute in spite of these factors. "I will tend to that when I am back in my own house. Charlotte will tend to me."

"All right," he said placatingly. "I won't force it on you."

She gave him a scornful, speaking glance. "How thoughtful; how contrite."

Reluctantly he added, "If you must consult a physician, will you let me choose which one? I would not like you in the hands of—"

"Of someone who might tell the authorities how I came to be hurt?" she suggested. "Do not worry, Baron; no matter what I said, the police would pay no heed to me if you denied it. We both know it."

He stiffened; she was so accurate that it troubled him: was he really so transparent? "It's not that at all," he said feebly. "I only mean that . . . that there are physicians who would take advantage of your reputation to enhance their own." He contemplated the spot on the carpet where a bottle of Bordeau had been spilled during the holidays: a small red stain still remained in spite of the best efforts of his servants.

"I am sure you did," she replied with mendacious sweetness that concealed her increasing fright.

He tried to undo some of the damage he had done. "Look, Nadezna, my pet," he said, using the same persuasive tone that had worked so well on von Rosenwiese earlier that day, "it will not be much longer. We will soon be able to set our own course, without having to cater to Tancred Sisak, or any of the rest of them. If you will only consent to help me for a few more months, you will be rewarded, I promise you."

"If you mean the thirty percent, it is not sufficient. I will expect you to provide me extra money for each month from now until I can tell Sisak to go away and never touch me again. I loathe him. He is hideous," she said, her voice beginning to rise.

"Now, my pet," von Wolgast soothed, unwilling to endure another round of arguments with her. "I said I will make it worth your while, and I will. I have been reliable before now, haven't I? You may be certain that I will not leave you without any recompense for what you have done." He lifted her cloak from the settee and put it around her shoulders. "I would feel better, knowing you were home and resting. That bruise—I cannot sufficiently apologize to you for forgetting myself so completely—will rebuke me for days to come." He put his hand on the small of her back and propelled her toward the door. "Remember, you are to send me word if you decide to consult a physician."

She stopped abruptly. "One other thing, Baron," she said, making up her mind to reveal this additional news. "Ragoczy will be back in July." She saw the startled look in his eyes, and said, enjoying his distress, "I had a letter from him this morning. He has been recalled to Saint Petersburg and the Czar has asked him to visit Europe again. If his plans continue as he supposes they will, he should be here on or about the tenth." She gave von Wolgast a look bordering on triumph.

"Ragoczy," said von Wolgast, making the name a curse. "In July?" He swore under his breath. "Did he say why he is coming back?"

"Only that the Czar has asked it of him. He would tell me no more than that." She wanted to smile at him, if only to contain her trepidation.

"I wouldn't expect him to," said von Wolgast, sighing in disgust. "Well, I will have to keep an eye on him."

She dared to be bolder. "I think you ought to thank me for telling you so much. I think I deserve payment for informing you." It was dangerous to push him, now of all times, but she held onto her courage and met his hard gaze steadily.

"All right," he muttered after a brief, silent contest of wills. "I will see that you have a few more marks to spend."

"I think I should have double the usual amount," she told him, lifting her chin not only to show her determination but to remind him of his attack.

"Yes, yes; very well. Double it will be," he promised, and continued to guide her to the parlor door. "Schmidt will see you to the automobile."

"Pflaume will want to know why my face is . . . " She ended with a gesture. "I will have to tell him something."

"Say you fell; say I have a clumsy butler; I don't care what you say, so long as I am not implicated." He made sure she understood his meaning. "If word gets out, I will not be as generous as I will be if it does not."

"I expected as much," said Nadezna as she stood in the open parlor door. "I am sorry that I will be indisposed for three or four days. If you must speak with me, you may find me at my school." She flung the end of her cloak over her shoulder and sallied off down the hall, doing her best to show a confidence she did not feel.

It was after seven when von Wolgast accompanied von Rosenwiese home, shepherding him up his steps and putting him into the care of his house steward with admonitions to take care of him.

"Back to your house, Baron?" asked Dietbold as von Wolgast closed the door of the passenger compartment.

Von Wolgast considered his answer. "No; not yet. Take me to Chez Noir. The side entrance, if you will."

If Dietbold was startled to have his employer ask to be taken to so well-known a whorehouse, he did not say so. He put the Italia in gear and headed off to the south side of the city. Along the way he pointed out a party of strolling officers in Hungarian uniforms; this brought no response from von Wolgast, who continued to ride in solitary thought, head down, brow brought low.

At the Chez Noir—a slate-colored house with black shutters and door—von Wolgast emerged from his motor car, saying to Dietbold, "I will expect you back in ninety minutes. I will be waiting. Do not be late."

His chauffeur touched the brim of his cap before he drove off, already planning to spend the time having his supper in a nearby cafe.

Heloise, the tall, loose-limbed, large-breasted madame of Chez Noir came up to von Wolgast; she was wearing a tight corset of red leather and a long skirt of shining taffeta of the same shade. Her long black hair was gathered in an untidy knot on the top of her head, and when she spoke, her words were more slurred than her French accent required. "Good evening, Baron. We didn't expect to see you tonight. I am afraid Aurore is busy."

"I'm here to see Reighert," said von Wolgast curtly, wanting no part of Heloise tonight. He often despised the woman for knowing his tastes and acknowledging them so blatantly. "Where is he?"

"He is with Dulcie and Maxim just now. He will be available shortly." Heloise smiled at him, winked, and ambled on into the main room of the Chez Noir.

"Where should I wait for him?" von Wolgast called after her. "This is urgent, woman."

She stopped and turned back to him. "You may go into the dining room. He will want some refreshment when he is finished. Food and a cigar." Her laughter was gentle and poisonous. "I will have Phoebus tell him you are here, if you like?"

"I would appreciate it," he said through a tightened jaw. He saw Phoebus in the main room—tall, supposedly of Greek descent, but with an obvious admixture of Turk or Arab—carrying a platter of fruit and cheese, his muscular body encased in a kind of black leather rig that left only his arms and penis free. "Degenerate," von Wolgast whispered. As he watched, Heloise went up to him and murmured something in his ear; Phoebus nodded. Von Wolgast escaped to the dining room, where a lavish buffet was being laid out by girls of no more than ten, clad in sheer linen chemises and white leather collars. The light was low enough to make it difficult to identify the men seated at the tables around the walls, but von Wolgast recognized three of them; none of them exchanged greetings.

For the next twenty minutes von Wolgast nursed a plate of excellent ham, butter, and mustard, all the while increasing his sense of ill-usage so that by the time Paul Reighert emerged from his evening's debauch, he found the Baron glowering and sulky.

"I was told it was urgent," he said, sitting down opposite von Wolgast. His thinning chestnut-brown hair was wet and his clothes were neat to the point of fussiness; although he was now soft of body and slack about the waist, Paul Reighert still had the remnants of handsomeness that had served him so well before the Church defrocked and excommunicated him. His most striking features were his large, blue-green eyes and a full, sensual mouth.

"It is," snapped von Wolgast.

"Well?" said Reighert. He reached over and took a slice of ham from von Wolgast's plate, rolling it into a long tube. "Tell me about it."

Von Wolgast stared as Reighert ate the ham, thinking he had rarely seen anything so obscene. He cleared his throat. "There are two things. The first is that Ragoczy will be returning next month, or so Nadezna has been told."

"My people will know what to do." He seemed unimpressed with this news. "Shall I put them to watch his house now, before he arrives, or later?"

"Sometime the first week in July should be fine. The house steward—"

"—Erich Rotscheune," Reighert supplied.

"Yes; if he can be persuaded to talk, that would be useful, providing it does not put him on guard." He leaned a bit closer to Reighert, and lowered his voice. "The second thing is more difficult." He paused, to be sure of Reighert's full attention. "It's Nadezna."

"Oho," said Reighert, licking his lips.

"She is becoming greedy, and dissatisfied." He hesitated, this time to sort out his words. "I am worried that she is no longer to be trusted, and I am afraid to try to buy back her loyalty; it might well prove too costly."

"I see," said Reighert, encouraging von Wolgast to enlarge on his theme.

"Yes. Yes." He wiped his mouth with his serviette, a nervous gesture that Reighert did not miss. "Something will have to be done about her."

"How soon?" Reighert asked, as if it meant nothing more than issuing a warning.

"I'm not sure. It will depend on her." Von Wolgast took a deep breath and revealed his favorite idea. "If possible, we should wait until Ragoczy is in Berlin."

Reighert's eyes brightened. "You mean so that he can be implicated in her . . . loss?" He did not wait for an answer. "Very, very good, Baron. Keep thinking like that and I'll make a Jesuit of you yet."

It rankled with von Wolgast to have Reighert speak to him with such disrespect, but he held his pride in check, saying only, "I think you might want to consider how best to do this. I want everything ready by the time Ragoczy is back in Berlin."

"Certainly," said Reighert, unconcerned. He helped himself to more of the ham. "Heloise has an excellent kitchen—wouldn't you agree?"

"Yes. Excellent," he answered brusquely. "About Nadezna—"

"Let me think about it," Reighert interrupted, still chewing. "This isn't the kind of thing you can do off the top of your head. I will have to make sure it will all fall into place. We don't want the police to arrest the wrong man, do we?"

"No," said von Wolgast, reaching for the large glass of white wine at his elbow.

"Once I talk to my . . . operatives, I will know how to arrange . . . the event." He grinned. "Thank you, Baron; I was beginning to fear that summer would be dull." He clapped von Wolgast on the shoulder, very nearly causing him to spill his wine.

Von Wolgast put the glass down. "Just one thing, my friend," he said, his voice low and stern. "I do not intend to trade one leech for another. Do I make myself clear?"

"Oh, very clear," Reighert assured him. "Very, very clear."

Text of a letter from Julian Sinclair-Howard in London to Ludwig Kesselmann in Berlin.

> *#2, St. Dunstan-the-West Close*
> *London, England*
> *May 28, 1910*

Ludwig Kesselmann
Ministry of Foreign Affairs
Berlin, Germany

My dear Kesselmann;
I should think you and the Kaiser have nothing to fear from George V; he is inclined to listen to his advisors in regard to European mat-

ters, *and in spite of his inexperience, he is not without knowledge. In my opinion, he will be less likely to take an extreme stance in regard to military commitments, either for or against them. In two or three years he may not be so malleable, but just at present, he is feeling his way, and you may rest assured that I will do all I can to keep the ship of state from rocking too much while George is at the helm.*

I concur with your assertion that the interests of Germany are the interests of England, far more than of France or Russia: the Czar and George may look more like brothers than cousins, but you may rest assured that it is the House of Hanover that exerts the strongest influence on George.

There are those in government here who are determined to bring about the Russo-French alliance with England joining it in mutual support. I do not suppose that it will be anything more than a cobbled-together farce, for all it is being proclaimed the way of the future. No, I am willing to stake my reputation on England's maintaining close ties to Germany, and therefore to the Kaiser and his government, and you may assure your superiors of my continuing endorsement of German preeminence in Europe.

Sincerest regards,
Julian Sinclair-Howard

3

Ragoczy was mounted on one of his grey horses, a Lipizzaner whose fading dapples indicated his nine years; beside him, Nikolai rode his bicycle, pedaling steadily along the dusty road leading to his temporary summer retreat. It was early enough in the day that the last of the morning breeze cooled them as wraiths of dusk swirled behind them, hanging on the air and glistening before settling back to the earth. In another hour it would be hot. Even so far north the sun weighed heavily on the Count.

"I wish Uncle Bertie had lived six months longer," said Nikolai to Ragoczy, his resolution to speak of other issues long forgotten. "We might have achieved something then. He would have understood. I know he would have joined with me in the limiting of arms sales, if not their production."

"You have the agreement of two years ago," Ragoczy reminded him. "Surely it is a good beginning." His native earth lining the soles and heels of his boots offered some respite from the sun, although it was becoming uncomfortable to be so exposed.

"And thank God for it; you would have made no headway at all without it," Nikolai exclaimed, leaning more firmly on the handlebars to show his sincerity. "I know it is some protection, and better than nothing at all, most certainly. But it does nothing to limit or reduce arms, it only provides for our mutual assistance, and such." He sighed bluntly. "I don't think that is enough, not with what I have been told, not only by you, of the increase in arms production in Europe, especially German." His face clouded. "I hope Cousin Wilhelm knows what he is doing, letting Krupp in Essen and von Wolgast in Prenzlau step up their production. It seems reckless to me, but the Kaiser has always thought first of Germany and second of any other country. As he must. As we all must. But with an eye to our mutual obligations. That is why we sign treaties." This last was emphasized with a pursing of his lips and a closed-mouth smile.

"It troubles you, doesn't it?" Ragoczy asked, holding his grey to jogging trot to match Nikolai's slowing progress. "That Germany is advancing its production of arms to sell to foreign powers?"

"Yes; of course it does. You need not ask. It was the very thing I've hoped to avoid, this competition and expanded sales in arms. Probably nothing can be done to stop the development of arms, but their production and sale is separate question. I know that Wilhelm's explanation for his current policy in this regard is that the situation in Austro-Hungary is deteriorating and that Germany needs to be prepared to deal with the coming collapse by being militarily strong. But the unrest he so laments is bolstered by the increasing supply of German arms flooding into the Balkans." He stopped for a moment and looked out over the expanse of land to the south of him. "You would think that Wilhelm would know how risky his gamble is. I cannot help but think if you had been allowed to speak with him, you could have persuaded him that he is courting disaster."

"Perhaps he does have some sense of it; he is not a stupid man," Ragoczy suggested, preparing to swing out of the saddle to show his proper respect for Nikolai; the Czar waved him permission to remain mounted.

"What do you mean? Are you saying that Wilhelm is trying to destabilize the Austro-Hungarian Empire?" He did not look as shocked as he felt he ought to. "He would not be so . . . contemptible."

"Possibly, but there are those around him who are eager to take advantage of any upheaval in Hapsburg territories. There is much rancor still about the way in which Germany dealt with Austria fifty years ago, and men of titled and landed families do not readily forget such things, no matter what lip-service they pay to unity and accord. They are determined to maintain Germany's power, and they encourage Wilhelm to act in their interests." That Wilhelm was the most arrogantly chauvinistic of the lot, he did not mention. "Those same men would not be adverse to seeing that trouble spill over your borders, Czar, or into France, or Italy, or Poland." He did not want to soften the blow, for that would provide Nikolai with an excuse to ignore the trouble in Europe. "You have much to contend with here in Russia, and I do not suggest that you turn away from your country to the problems of foreigners, but I suspect that much of what is fueling your . . . situation here is tied, directly or indirectly, to the developing conflicts in Germany and Austria, with the Balkans serving as flashpoint."

"All the more reason for George and Wilhelm to join with me in limiting arms and negotiating terms of arms sales. No matter what they may think, none of us can afford war. I remember an American General saying there will be no more small wars."

"General Sherman, I believe." Madelaine de Montalia had repeated this to Ragoczy not long after the American's death.

"Yes. I did not think so then, but now I fear he may have been right. I would not like the Balkans to prove his case." He studied the road ahead, frowning.

"And that is becoming more likely each day," Ragoczy agreed.

Nikolai began to pedal again, increasing his speed as he neared the summer house. "They are going to start cutting down the trees on the northeast side of the house tomorrow," he remarked, cocking his head in the direction of the trees in question. "I think they are quite nice and I do not want to lose them, but my Generals advise me that they give too much cover for anyone approaching. They are afraid that what happened to my father will happen to me. I did not learn at Professor Pobedonostsev's knee as my father did; I do not intend to devote my rule to nationalism, Orthodoxy, and autocracy, but to guiding the country on a middle course." His mild features became sad. "I don't think anyone will make the attempt, but they are afraid, so—" He coughed, adding, "Pavel is quite annoyed." The steward of the summer house was known to be prouder of it than its royal owners.

"Is it possible some danger may exist?" asked Ragoczy, who for once agreed with the Generals. He pointed back down the road to the Mixed Guard soldier standing in front of the gates to the estate, rifle in hand. "You have accepted some protection already. Why refuse more when it would mean increased safety."

"I don't like to think that my safety is so illusory," said Nikolai. "If there is an assassin looking to kill me, a few trees more or less will not stop him. I will not let fear of such a man make me a prisoner of the Generals."

"Do you think the Generals would agree?" said Ragoczy, surprised at how acute Nikolai's assessment had been.

"Nikolasha, perhaps," he said thoughtfully. "Perhaps Grand Duke Sandro, if he had cared to express an opinion. The rest—" He shrugged. "If they thought it would increase their chances of my favor, they might."

"But with your family here, isn't this precaution of theirs wiser? If the Generals have their way, your family will not . . . " Ragoczy let the rest of his caution go unspoken.

"You mean that I may have enemies who will take so great a chance as to attack my children instead of me?" His front wheel swung out at the edge of a rut and he had to concentrate on keeping his bicycle on the road. "If they want me, I suppose there is not much I can do about it; if it is God's Will, then I accept it, as I must. But I would begrudge them one drop of my family's blood." For a compliant man, Nikolai's face grew suddenly obdurate. "I will not permit my family to come to harm through me."

"No honorable man would." Ragoczy did not want to remind the Czar that if such an action were to come Nikolai's feelings would not be consulted. Instead, he said, "What else do the Generals recommend? Other than cutting down the trees?"

"It is foolish of them," said Nikolai. "They want to enlarge the army and establish posts from Finland to Manchuria; they see enemies—of mine and of Russia's—the world over. Nothing anyone tells them will convince them otherwise." He did his best to negotiate his way between two deep ruts where the road began to curve around the summer house gardens. "There is also the question of cost. It is too expensive, enlarging the army, and the Duma would never stand for it."

"Possibly not, but they may be willing to increase industry in the East. It is one of the few things most of the delegates agree on, that more industry is needed. Wasn't it Count Witte who recommended expanding the Trans-Siberian Railroad?" Speaking of the ousted Sergei Witte was tactless, but Ragoczy hoped it would not earn him a reprimand.

Nikolai frowned. "He did. But if you think developments in Austro-Hungary have made Wilhelm uneasy, anything beyond the Urals could give him apoplexy. He is certain that Jenghiz Khan is coming again, to overrun Europe, and if I should begin to lure the Chinese by increasing factories and railroads in the East, he would presume I had thrown in my lot with the Orient. He has told me often enough that it is the duty of Russia to be a bastion for Europe against the Yellow Horde."

"This is not the thirteenth century, and the Mongols do not rule in China. Even if they did, it would not constitute a military threat to Europe. China may be enormous, but it is also impoverished. It would be reckless beyond any justification for the Chinese to attack the West," Ragoczy said, thinking back to what he had seen at T'en Chi-Yu's side, seven centuries ago.

"Wilhelm does not agree," Nikolai said drily.

Ahead on the road was an Italian donkey cart, the five-year-old Czareivich Alexei, dressed in a miniature version of a navy uniform, holding the reins in his fists, his face flushed with effort and set in studious lines from concentrating on his driving. He noticed his father approaching with Ragoczy, and halted the donkey, waving his hand, his smile mitigating his pallor. "I was coming to find you, Papa!" he called out.

The smile Nikolai answered his son's with was tinged with worry. He pedaled faster, coming up beside the cart quickly enough to cause the donkey to put back his long ears in alarm. "You shouldn't be by yourself. What are you doing out on your own? Why are you alone?" he demanded, trying not to sound angry.

Now Ragoczy dismounted, leading his grey up to the cart as Nikolai got off his bicycle. He watched as Nikolai put his hand on his son's shining red-gold hair, and he could not keep from feeling sorrow for the Czar and his family: to have a child so desperately and dangerously ill was beyond his experience, but he had seen enough of death to know that the boy lived forever in its shadow, and that nothing could be done to change his condition. As much as the family might pray for and protect him, the Czareivich would probably be dead before twenty; few children with his affliction lived half so long. Seeing Nikolai with Alexei, he once again understood how Rasputin—by saving this fragile child not once but twice—had won the endless gratitude and unswerving loyalty of all the Romanovs.

"I haven't gone far," said Alexei defensively; he was getting to an age when he chafed at the endless restrictions placed upon him. "And I did it right, Papa."

"You certainly did," Nikolai approved, and glanced at Ragoczy, his concern overshadowing his affection for the child. "But you should have someone with you, you know, if not Derevenko, then one of your sisters; Derevenko cannot be everywhere at once. Your mother would be upset if she knew."

"I won't tell her," said Alexei, defiance and supplication mixed in his tone. "I won't tell anyone, Papa. I won't even tell Derevenko." This last was his plea to have an adventure of his own, the one thing he was regularly denied; he was too resigned to sulk, but he could not keep his mouth from turning down in disappointment. "I wish the new palace at Livadia was ready. They are taking so long to rebuild it. I want to go swimming in the sea again."

"Soon, my child, soon." The anguish in Nikolai's eyes was unmistakable. "Next summer for sure." To console his son for the lack of their palace near Yalta, he said, "We will have the White Nights for a while longer; we can have midnight supper out-of-doors. And we can go to the Gulf of Finland, if you want to see the ocean. For your birthday, perhaps: how would that be?"

"We don't swim there," the Czareivich said, putting an end to the matter. Noticing Ragoczy, Alexei grinned, relieved at having someone to witness his independence, however fleeting. He realized that Ragoczy was watching, and made the most of it. "The King of Italy gave me my donkey, and the cart," he boasted, making a grand gesture to encompass the whole equipage. "Do you like it, Count?"

"What a fine gift," Ragoczy said, impressed that Vittorio Emmanuele III had such good sense; possibly one of his aides had been the source of the inspiration. "He looks to be a very good donkey."

"For an Italian donkey," said Alexei, assuming the hauteur he saw around him.

Ragoczy smiled slightly. "But anyone can have a Russian donkey in Russia," he reminded the child. "How many have Italian donkeys?"

Nikolai gave Ragoczy a look of gratitude; he was pleased that his son was being reminded of the favor his pet represented. "And where is your sailor?" he asked his son. With Nagorny away to visit his ailing mother, Derevenko had the full responsibility of looking after Alexei, of the two men, Derevenko was the more patient with the Czareivich, and more understanding of the severity of his disease, treating the child with affection and sympathy.

"He is having a glass of tea with Pavel." The boy's eyes filled with delight. "He doesn't know I've got away. I slipped out through the terrace doors, and went to the stable without being seen."

"He will tell me how it came about that he was not with you." He touched Alexei's hair again, as if assuring himself the boy was all right.

"I harnessed the donkey, and everything," Alexei crowed, once again happy to have had this brief moment of freedom. "My sisters are with Gilliard, talking French; Olga and Tatiana are helping him with Marie and Anastasia," he went on. "Mama is at prayers. She has been praying all morning."

Nikolai began to push his bicycle along, compelling his son to turn back toward the summer house; Ragoczy brought up the rear, his horse walking at his shoulder, listening to the child talk to his father, asking questions about everything that caught his attention, from bees to the mare's-tail clouds overhead; Alexei was a curious boy, still young enough to be filled with wonder by the world around him. As they reached the summer house, a dark-haired, mustached man of about twenty-eight or -nine in an adult version of Alexei's uniform, came rushing around the side of the house, his haste indicating his worry.

"There you are!" Alexei cried out, waving merrily.

Derevenko stopped, relief in every line of his body. After a moment, he came down the drive, saying, "You are a proper scamp—do you know that?"

Tremendously pleased, Alexei beamed. "You didn't know I had gone, did you?"

"No," said Derevenko, exchanging an uneasy glance with the Czar. "And it was wrong of you to do it. I would have come with you, had I known you wanted to go out."

"But," Alexei protested, assuming all the dignity he could, "I wanted to go alone, and I couldn't do that with you, could I? You won't be angry with me, will you?" He turned his blue-grey eyes up at his guard and beamed angelically.

"You're not supposed to be alone, Czareivich," said Derevenko, looking fond and stern at once. "If my boys had come with me, they would have insisted on coming with you; you would not have managed this alone."

Alexei's pleasure turned to smugness. "I know," he confessed.

Ragoczy was aware of how precious these few moments of liberation were for Alexei, and said, "You were clever to plan so well, Czareivich."

"I was, wasn't I?" the boy asked, relishing this implied approval.

"It was very wrong of you, to worry us all so much," Derevenko scolded fondly. "But you did it very well." He gave the Czar a second, more apologetic stare. "Pavel was certain that Alexei was out in the garden."

"I like to look at things," the boy announced. "I think about what I see."

"That you do," said Derevenko. He carefully took the donkey's reins from the boy, and assumed the task of handling the animal and its cart. "But it's time to have a bite to eat and a little time to lie down." He lowered his voice as he spoke to Nikolai. "I am sorry this happened. I will be more careful in future."

"I have faith in you," Nikolai said, and patted Derevenko on the shoulder once; he was awkward doing this ordinary thing, and that made the gesture the more genuine.

"Come along, Alexei," said Derevenko, speaking up for the boy's benefit. "I'll give you a hand with the harness."

Alexei's sigh was not completely from exasperation. He sat back in the cart and let his guard lead him away. Only when they had reached the corner of the house did he turn and wave to his father.

"Poor boy; I wish we did not have to guard him so constantly, but with his condition being what it is—" said Nikolai as the cart disappeared in the direction of the stable. "It is very difficult to have so many restrictions on him, to be guarded day and night, to have doctors and nurses around him wherever he goes. But if we did not, he would . . . be dead now. At least his temperament is not volatile."

Aware that he was on delicate footing from the few previous times he had brought up the question, Ragoczy said, "It is a disease of the blood, is it not. His blood does not clot readily." He had been aware of the nature of Alexei's illness from the first sight of the boy, but had not spoken of it so directly in the past; the policy of the family was to say as little as possible about the Czareivich's health, and even less about the specific nature of his ailment.

"Otyets Grigori has stopped the bleeding when all else failed," the Czar said, coming as close as he ever did to identifying his son's condition.

"I knew it had to be something of the sort." In response to the sudden expression of alarm in Nikolai's gaze, he went on reassuringly, "Oh, I doubt most people recognize the gravity of his illness; but as you know, I have some knowledge of things medical, and Alexei symptoms are—"

"Sunny does not want it talked about—ever," said Nikolai. "I should not be telling this to you."

"Do you think her reservations might be too . . . stringent? He is a boy who needs to discover his limits for himself, don't you think,"

Ragoczy suggested, remembering as he did that Nikolai generally deferred to his wife in such matters.

"If they are strict, it is only from her love that she makes them so. She is trying to ensure his well-being, as are we all." Making an effort to speak of something else he went on in fluent English, "You know, when I saw Georgie at Cowes, last year, he asked me if I would like to trade places—Britain for Russia. It was said in jest, of course, and we both had a good laugh about it. But now there are times I think I should have." His self-deprecating chuckle told Ragoczy laughter was permissible.

Ragoczy knew that it would not please the Czar to discuss his son again, so he said in the same language, "England is a very pleasant place, is it not. So green and prosperous."

"Lovely, and far more orderly than here. I could find it in my heart to envy George his navy. But the island is so small," said Nikolai, "after Russia." He made his way along the side of the house, continuing in Russian, "Let me send for one of the grooms to take your horse. It's time you and I had a discussion."

Ordinarily Ragoczy cared for his own horses when he could; now was not such an occasion. He inclined his head. "I am at your disposal, Czar."

Ten minutes later they were in the summer house, in the parlor. "The library is being used for tutoring," Nikolai explained as he sat down and motioned his approval for Ragoczy to do the same. "Thank goodness Gilliard is Swiss; who knows what Wilhelm would say if this man were French."

Ragoczy sat down in a high-backed chair and readied himself for what Nikolai would say. Since being summoned from Finland, he had been aware that the Czar had more for him to do. As he stretched out his legs, crossing them at the ankle, he said, "Have you had word from Germany?"

"Of course. And from England, not that any of it is to the point." Nikolai leaned back, staring up at the ceiling, his expression remote. "If only I knew which of them would be willing to take the first step. On the face of it, you might think George is the more likely to see the danger and support my plan. But he has only recently taken up his duties, and he has a strong Parliament to contend with, and Asquith to shape the course of his government, so whether or not he is willing to limit the production of arms in the British Empire may be a moot point; he is not likely to be able to act swiftly, even if he is in accord with my hopes. Wilhelm has, on the surface, a stronger reason not to agree with me, unless he sees his arms manufacturers as a threat to the stability of Germany, in which case he will want to support my efforts, and will not need the endorsement of so many as George would."

"You wish to try to secure the private agreement—still?" Ragoczy asked, and recalled the fragile son Nikolai adored; the Czar would do anything to keep Alexei from physical danger—his repetition of this plan was his way of showing the depth of his purpose; it was the one weapon he had had in his youth against the overpowering tempers of his uncles. Of all the attributes of an autocrat he lacked, Nikolai possessed obstinancy in abundance.

"Certainly," Nikolai said, unoffended by Ragoczy's tone. "I trust we have not yet reached the point where negotiation is useless." He was quiet for a short while, then added, "If it isn't possible to get anything in writing, at least they might be willing to agree in principle: that would be better than nothing."

"If you wish," said Ragoczy, keeping his reservations to himself.

"With Montenegro's independence assured, the Balkans may yet achieve balance. I am certain that—" He stopped as his second daughter came into the room. "What is it?" he asked, undismayed by her interruption.

Grand Duchess Tatiana Nikolaivna was a dark-haired, pretty girl who had turned thirteen a matter of days ago, with intelligent eyes and a quickness of movement that promised beauty in adulthood; her white, pin-tucked blouse and gored skirt were fashionable country wear. She saw Ragoczy and paused. "I thought you were alone. I'm sorry." She was about to leave the parlor.

"What is it?" her father repeated. "Ragoczy does not mind the interruption."

"Oh." She came back toward him. "Pavel wants to serve luncheon outdoors, like a pic-nic, in an hour or so. He tells me he has everything ready. I told him I'd ask if that was all right with you."

"On such a lovely day it would be a shame not to," said Nikolai. "By all means, let us have a pic-nic."

Tatiana blew a kiss to her father, turned away and rushed out of the room.

"She is a thoughtful child, not as rambunctious as Anastasia is turning out to be." Nikolai beamed with fatherly pride. "They will all marry well, my girls. Sophie Chotek has already corresponded with Sunny about the possibilities; her own children are not in the succession for Austro-Hungary, but she had a few recommendations to make. Sophie's family may be impoverished, but there is nothing wrong with her heritage, and she knows better than most the importance of a good match, to say nothing of her understanding of the political climate in the world." He laughed indulgently. "I've said it is early days yet, but Sunny is set upon making plans. She tells me they will be grown and ready for husbands before we know it."

"There are a few years yet, before that happens," Ragoczy said, feeling a gulf between him and Nikolai that was as gaping as an open wound. What was it like, he wondered, as he had many times before, to have children, to plan for their futures, to invest such hope and such despair in them?

"Yes, but they do grow up so fast. It seems only yesterday that Tatiana had her first lessons and could not tie her shoes without biting her tongue." He sighed, frowning again. "We must not give them a legacy of war."

Particularly, thought Ragoczy, the Czareivich Alexei, for whom battle was unquestionably fatal. "Let us trust not."

"We must do more than trust; we must deserve our children's trust in us," said Nikolai with decision. "That is why I depend on you to resume your mission." He sat forward, his concentration on his inner vision. "And this time, we must begin with the Germans, for I have considered it, and I have decided that I made a mistake in sending you to Edward first: Wilhelm wants to be first in all things. To be anything else makes him feel slighted. If he understands that he is the one on whom all depends, he might be willing to receive you on my behalf. If you can approach the necessary men around the Kaiser so that they will understand I have no underhanded intentions in my goals . . . " He looked to Ragoczy to go on.

"You may rest assured that I will do my best. But I have told you that someone has managed to call my character into question in Berlin," Ragoczy reminded him, bristling in spite of his best intentions. "I think it may be necessary to deal with that before I can accomplish your mandate."

Nikolai shook his head. "I have not ignored your trouble there. I think you might accomplish the most at your Schloss in Bavaria." His smile was wider than usual, showing his poor teeth more than he generally did. "You thought I had forgot about that, but I hadn't." He put his elbows on his knees, resting his chin on his interlaced fingers. "If you were to set up a long weekend at the Schloss, for hunting, perhaps, you might find that in such a setting these men who have looked upon you askance in Berlin will be less inclined to snub your efforts. Germans are always genial when hunting."

Ragoczy was not certain he agreed with Nikolai's assessment of the

German character, but realized it would be folly to challenge the Czar. "It could be done," he said slowly. "But I doubt the Kaiser would accept my invitation."

"Not the Kaiser, Ragoczy—no; you will want to have one or two of his Ministers, who are willing to hear you out in the evening over schnapps, and carry their observations back to Berlin. Then it is possible you will be allowed to see my cousin. The only other way would be to send you to him directly, which would mean using the whole diplomatic panoply. That would obviate the privacy I wish to maintain in regard to any agreement we achieve. So this oblique approach will be the preferable way."

"It may not succeed at such a remove from the Kaiser; he will not have reason to consult those I invite unless he decides it is in his interests to question them," Ragoczy warned Nikolai. "And with so many second parties involved, it will probably be impossible to keep my mission wholly private." This was the most obvious flaw he could find in the plan, and the one Nikolai was most likely to endorse.

"I have thought about that, too; and I appreciate your reservations. You confirm my trust in you with so much insight." He unlaced his fingers and leaned back, once more staring up at the ceiling. "It would be best to single out one or two of your guests—the ones with the most direct link to Wilhelm, and sound them out, and to determine where they are willing to act and where they are not. If they are among those advocating the strengthening of the German army and navy, then it would probably be of no use to talk to them, but it would let you know where the greatest resistance to arms limitation is within the German government, and that in itself is valuable information. It is an opportunity that may not come again." He was clearly enchanted with his plan, and did not want any opposition to it.

"If it is what you want, then I will do it." Ragoczy said it conversationally, as if he were discussing the state of the spring planting, but there was no mistaking the force of his intent.

"Count, why do you do this?" Nikolai asked suddenly.

"What do you mean, Czar?" he countered, the question taking him by surprise. "Why do you ask?"

"I mean that you are not my subject. You are an exile, with no obligations to me beyond one titled man to another. Yet you have done all I asked you to do: you could refuse my commission and have no fear of repercussions from me. So there must be some greater reason that you take this on." He paused, and when Ragoczy said nothing, prompted, "What is it?"

"I abhor war." His mellifluous voice was low and his dark eyes distant. "I have seen it too often. All it ever brings is death and ruin."

"Your country was conquered," said Nikolai, as if this completed the explanation.

"Mine is not the only one." His Carpathian homeland had been overrun more than thirty-five times since his own father had been conquered by Hittite-sponsored invaders, four thousand years ago. "Russia has had more than its share of—"

"Conquerors," Nikolai finished for him. "And yet my cousins wonder why I fear war and want to stop it." He sighed. "Well, if you are not so discouraged that the attempt seems useless, I hope you will undertake a second mission to Willy and Georgie. If you cannot persuade them to see sense, then at least determine how much preparation for war is ongoing, so I will know what to believe when my Generals talk to me. If I cannot supply information that supports my position, they will not listen to me."

"But you are Czar; yours is the authority," Ragoczy reminded him, thinking again that Nikolai, honorable and conscientious as he was, lacked the autocratic temperament his position demanded.

"Tell my Uncles that. The Grand Dukes still think I am at school, and need their tutoring if I am to decide anything." For a moment, Nikolai's face was clouded, and then he shook off the self-indulgent emotion and resumed his theme. "If you are able to see the Kaiser, tell him that I would count it as a personal favor, and would regard myself in his debt. It is a position he would like me to be in, and if it will serve my purpose, I do not begrudge him that satisfaction." He frowned briefly. "I would appreciate it if you would not remain in Saint Petersburg too long."

"You perceive the situation as urgent? Should I plan to leave at once?" Ragoczy asked, already convinced it was necessary to act immediately if any portion of the Czar's desires were to be achieved; he was no longer certain that the arms limitation Nikolai sought so ardently could be achieved, but he kept his opinion to himself.

"I think that there are many men around me who would bedevil you for information about what I intend you to do in Europe. It would serve no purpose to let it be known to any of my Court that you are trying to establish the agreement I seek." He considered Ragoczy out of the corner of his eye.

"No one will learn the particulars from me, Czar: believe this," Ragoczy promised, his dark eyes intent.

The Czar made a gesture of assent. "I do, my friend, but I also know how persistent my 'boyars' can be." He chose the old title deliberately, to reveal his view of them. "All of them will try to take advantage of anything they can pry out of you." He stood up suddenly; Ragoczy rose out of courtesy. "My own brother is trying to get me to tell him my plans. Mikhail is a good man, but he is too much inclined to speak of what he knows, and to those whose purpose is not always beyond reproach."

Ragoczy had a different opinion of the Grand Duke Mikhail Alexandreivich, but kept it to himself. "You cannot blame him; he is always in your shadow, Czar, no matter what you or he would wish to have otherwise."

"That may be," said Nikolai. "I would not want to put him at a disadvantage, in any case." He paced the length of the room, his dusty boots leaving a faint mark on the carpet to mark his progress. "I must rely upon you to carry out my instructions without fully revealing them to anyone but my royal German and English cousins; I do not want the particulars revealed to anyone but them. I realize this is an imposition that limits your discretion more than may be prudent, and I apologize. It may be difficult to gain support while witholding so much, but it is necessary if we are to keep our enemies from learning about this plan, and doing their utmost to subvert it before it can be undertaken." He stopped, giving Ragoczy a wistful smile. "Your reticence may well save my son; there is nothing dearer to me in the world."

"I am aware of that, Czar," said Ragoczy quietly; he did not add that he was fairly certain that his mission was not so secret as Nikolai hoped, for surely someone was working against him in Germany, interfering with his approach to the Kaiser as surely as if he had constructed a brick wall.

"Be sure to keep it uppermost in your mind, Count. I have the protection of my family and my people in my heart always," Nikolai told him, slapping at his cycling breeches to rid them of the dust clinging to them. "If you flag in your efforts, my son may well pay the price for it."

"I hope that will not happen," said Ragoczy, certain that Alexei would never be permitted near any battle.

"You must do all you can to be sure it does not; I am determined that my children shall be spared from all danger," Nikolai told him emphatically. "I don't question your dedication, but I insist that you not become disheartened. I have done that once already, and through my discouragement, I have lost valuable time, which I deeply regret. I was a fool to think you were at fault." He coughed as the dust reached his nose. "Sunny is so certain that we can stem the tide, and I want to share her conviction. If you will strive to make this possible, our debt to you will be above all repayment, but you may repose total confidence in my continued support, and the support of all my family for as long as you have any ties with Russia."

"I thank you for that, Czar," Ragoczy said. "I appreciate your . . . encouragement, but it is not necessary. Intending no disrespect, I must tell you that what I do, I do as much for myself as for you."

For the first time Nikolai looked pleased. "You relieve me."

"That was not my purpose, either," Ragoczy admitted, pausing as the sound of young laughter and pounding footsteps came from the corridor; a loud squeal was followed by a scuffle mixed with giggles. "Do you want to attend to that?"

"It is only Marie and Anastasia playing," said their father. "They will be gone shortly. Unless one of them shrieks, nothing is wrong."

As if to punctuate Nikolai's reassurance, the two rushed off down the hall, one vowing to catch the other. "No you won't!" was the delighted answer.

"In the country," Nikolai explained, "Sunny indulges them. They have so few opportunities to romp at Court."

Ragoczy listened to the girls running. "They do not have an easy life, your daughters."

"It is not so hard as my son's life," said Nikolai, unaware that he had agreed with Ragoczy in his response. He went to the curtained window and looked out at the broad expanse of fields where the Russian army occasionally held maneuvers. "God entrusted Russia to me, and I will do His Will for Russia as long as I breathe. But I fear that God cannot intend so frail a boy as Alexei is to assume my burden when I am no longer here to bear it; my cousins will not help him, and the Grand Dukes, my Uncles, will not welcome such a Czar as Alexei must be. It may be that my brother Mikhail will be named to succeed me, or Olga's husband, if she marries an acceptable man. I must balance my devotion to my country against the interests of my son, and that is a constant . . . " He turned around to Ragoczy. "It is hard for Sunny to admit, but I know the Duma would not be willing to place Alexei on the throne without a . . . lieutenant they can support." He was silent for a short while. "I trust you will keep my confidence, Count; I could not impart such reservations to any Russian noble."

"I can understand why," said Ragoczy, recalling how many whispers at Court referred to the Czareivich; speculation regarding the nature of his malady were rife, some suggesting that the boy was not, in fact, ill, but insane. "You have no reason to fear me, Nikolai Alexandreivich: you have my Word on it."

"So I hope," said Nikolai, coming away from the window. "In four days, I would like you to depart for Munich. If you will take the time to prepare invitations to the men I will specify in my written instructions, I believe you will be able to arrive prepared to entertain your guests at your Schloss. I want you to act swiftly. Delay now will bring about nothing but difficulties. It is my intention to have you in Wilhelm's presence before autumn." He said this as if it were a foregone conclusion.

"Do you think you might approach the Kaiser directly?" Ragoczy suggested, aware that this was futile, but wanting to speak of it in any case. "He would be willing to receive your private envoy, would he not?"

Nikolai sighed heavily. "It would not be as private as I would like, having him know of your purpose. I know enough about my cousin to know he would let it be known you were acting for me, and then you would know no peace." He flung up one hand in exasperation. "If it were possible to do as you recommend, I would have begun that way. This oblique approach is as frustrating to me as it is to you. But I will not expose your mission to the prying eyes and wagging tongues of the Kaiser's government. It is as riddled with spies as my own." He took two deep breaths. "I don't want to make your task more difficult than it must be, Count. However, I would rather have it difficult and successful than an easy failure."

"Certainly," said Ragoczy. "I will do what I can during the hunting party, but it is apt to take longer to reach the Kaiser."

"But if you have the favor of his Ministers, then he will no longer think that I am alone in my goals," Nikolai told Ragoczy with the confidence of desire. "Once my cousin knows that I have allies even among those near him, he will have to reconsider his posture regarding arms."

"I may have to be more candid with his Ministers than you would like," Ragoczy warned him. "They will not support what they do not understand."

"Well, you must do as you think best," said Nikolai, going on briskly, "If you will leave for Saint Petersburg this afternoon, you may begin your preparations to leave for Germany at once. You know what you are to do; we have established that. Your authorizations will be brought to you by courier in two days time, late at night, as before. Be ready to receive them." He nodded, not in dismissal but slight apology. "I have never known you to take a meal in company, so I will not ask you to join us."

"Thank you," said Ragoczy in form. "My manservant and I will be away before three."

"Excellent. Excellent. Then"—he held out his hand—"Godspeed, Count."

Ragoczy's small hand closed on the Czar's slender one. "Amen," he said.

Text of a letter from Sidney Reilly in Berlin to "C" in London, set in Key 29; delivered by diplomatic courier on July 9, 1910.

It would seem Nicholas is again the one behind Ragoczy's return to Germany; my contacts in Russia tell me that whatever the Czar wants from the Kaiser, he has not yet given up his efforts to achieve it. The consensus continues to be that a private agreement in regard to arms is the chief item sought on the Czar's behalf. My operatives do not often err in these matters, and although I do not dispute what your staff has learned, I am not thoroughly convinced that their assumptions are correct. According to what Renfred Meyer has found out, Nicholas has been consistent in his desire to stop the development and sales of all sorts of weapons. He demonstrated his concern at The Hague eleven years ago and there is no indication that he has altered his opposition to the development and sales of arms.

Since Ragoczy is taking up residence in his Schloss near Munich, it would be useless to use my Berlin operatives to observe him. I have a very reliable Swiss agent who will blend in more suitably in Munich than my two Berlin operatives might: I have assigned him the task of surveilling the Schloss and Ragoczy, and to report to me daily. I understand that Ragoczy is planning a week of hunting and has asked a number of men occupying high positions in the various Ministries of the Kaiser's government to join as his guests. I plan to remain here, in case Ragoczy should come here, as well as to take advantage of what Meyer can glean from those who attend the hunting party. If the men themselves are closedmouthed, their servants may not be. I still have one of my operatives here watching Ragoczy's house in Glanzend Strasse, and my other has been given the task of monitoring Nadezna's house, to determine what persons call there, and in what company. It is obvious that Baron von Wolgast calls often, and occasionally brings others with him. If we assume that we know the Czar's purpose in sending Ragoczy to Germany and England, then I find it ominous that von Wolgast should maintain so close an association with a ballerina whose ballet school Ragoczy finances. It may be a coincidence that these two men have dealings with Nadezna, but I cannot make such an assumption without finding proof that it is or is not accurate. I would fail in my duty if I did otherwise.

Your recommendation is reasonable on the surface, but I am reluctant to approach Ragoczy directly myself; he has seen me in Saint Petersburg and here as well, and I fear he may have recognized me, at least to the degree of knowing he has met me before. The only name he can put to me here in Berlin is Oertel Morgenstern, but if he does recollect our discussion in Russia, he might well conclude that I am not what I appear to be. I am absolutely certain that he would not ignore such a deception once it came to his attention, and therefore I am resolved to keep out of his way, and to do nothing that might draw his attention to myself. It is more sensible to be prudent in these situations than to tempt fate and hope that the risk will not exceed the benefits inherent in it.

Your man here, the one I have designated Eduard Angebot, is proving difficult to deal with: he thinks this is some kind of game we are playing, and that there are no more serious consequences than a black mark on a record book. I have tried to explain to him that men's lives are at stake, but he has no conception of the brutality of the contestants. I would very much appreciate it if you would set him to rights as soon as possible—I fear for the lives of my operatives if he continues to blunder about as if this were blind-man's-bluff. If he cannot be taught, then I request you assign another intermediary to me at once, before anyone gets killed.

Sidney Reilly (Capt.)

4

Near the Schloss there were birches; on the rising flank of the mountain were oak, larch, and pine, all vibrantly green in the August heat. The sky overhead was unrelenting blue, but towering clouds far to the west might well bring rain before nightfall, at least that was the opinion of Bertram Grunbach, the Deputy Minister of Finance, who was the first of nine guests to arrive.

"They are saying at the Hausham station that the road to Starnberg is being repaired; there is gravel everywhere. If it rains, it could be closed. I stopped there for instructions to your Schloss." His long, lugubrious face made any observation seem to have tragic meaning. Behind him, his squat Swiss valet struggled with two large bags.

"I had not planned to go to Starnberg, so the condition of the road is of little importance to me, although I am grateful for the timely warning," said Ragoczy calmly. "Thank you for coming, Herr Grunbach. It is a pleasure to welcome you to my Schloss."

"No doubt," said Grunbach, looking about the entry hall with a critical eye. "What is this place—two hundred years old?"

"Closer to three hundred twenty, as I understand; completed in the late fifteen hundreds, according to the records." Ragoczy did not allow Grunbach's superior attitude to offend him. "It came into my . . . family in 1735, I believe." He had been in The Netherlands, establishing a private press and studying botany for the years immediately previous to his purchase of the Schloss, and before that he had spent two decades traveling about Europe making a reputation for himself playing the violin; having a place of his own had become irresistible. He indicated the nearest staircase. "My manservant will show you to your rooms, if you would be good enough to follow him? Then you may join me in my study. It is on the north side of the Schloss; the second door along the corridor on the left."

Bertram Grunbach scowled, but did as Ragoczy suggested, saying to his valet, "You will have to find your own quarters, I suppose."

"I will show him," Roger assured Grunbach from his place on the landing. "Do not concern yourself."

This implication that he might let a servant's predicament bother him annoyed Grunbach, who climbed more quickly, calling back over his shoulder that he would be down again directly and leaving his valet to pant after him, Grunbach's luggage making him clumsy as a bear.

Twenty minutes later Euchary Apfelobstgarten—tall, pale and muscular—arrived in a two-year-old 20–30 Spyker, followed within minutes by Johann von Traunreuth of the Ministry of War, and Leopold Oberstetten of the *Berliner Morgenblatt,* whose political connections made him almost as powerful as the Ministries he reported on. As soon as these men—both middle-aged and portly—were escorted to their rooms, a Benz tourer pulled up, and three more guests got out—Volger Kraftig, Lothar Teich, and Paul von Nordlingen, all from the Chancellor's office: Kraftig was fretting from the journey, his lank hair fallen over his brow; Teich affected a sophisticated languor; von Nordlingen was open-faced and eager. Their servants arrived a short while later in an older De Dion Populaire, crammed in among suitcases and trunks sufficient for a safari.

Von Nordlingen made a point to address his host with courtesy and to compliment him on the quality of restoration done to the Schloss since his great-great-great-grand-father had ruined himself at gambling and had sold off all the holdings he could in a vain effort to recoup his fortune. He did his very best frank smile as he said, "I don't know how your ancestor knew to pay half the money to Fredrich's wife, but without his prudence, I shudder to think what would have become of us."

"I am gratified to accept your thanks on his behalf," said Ragoczy with a hint of a bow and an ironic light in his eyes.

"Your . . . was it great-great-great-uncle? . . . is the preserver of our family," von Nordlingen continued.

"I am a trifle vague on our exact degree of relation," said Ragoczy smoothly, remembering precisely how he documented his claim to the Schloss he had purchased from the bankrupt Fredrich von Nordlingen. "By now I am sure any obligation is . . . diluted, for both of us." There had been many times in the past when he had come to realize that gratitude and resentment were two faces of the same coin and he had no desire to evoke such an emotion in Paul von Nordlingen; the hunting party would be tricky enough without that.

The guests had all gathered in the study for sherry and schnapps when the last two invited men arrived: Koenig Einlass, and Werner Hohepfad, both functionaries in the Ministry of War advising on scientific developments, both intellectually energetic, both striving to make a mark in their work, both young enough to know they had not yet proven themselves. They and their manservants had been driven up from the station at Hausham, having shared a compartment on the train from Berlin. By the time they arrived in the study, the generator in the wine cellar was operating and the lights had been turned on, bringing a glow to the long summer twilight; all the rest of the guests were on their second drink and were enjoying the hot Hungarian sausages that Roger had just brought from the kitchen. A small fire burned in the hearth more to show hospitality than to provide any needed warmth.

"Good evening, gentlemen," said Ragoczy, coming to greet the new arrivals. "What may I pour for you?"

Hohepfad surprised the others by saying, "Scotch, if you have it."

"Certainly," was Ragoczy's urbane response. "Single malt?"

"If you have it," Hohepfad repeated, taken aback by the offer. He generally requested the drink to show his sophistication and rarely actually had to drink the stuff. Knowing any hesitation would embarrass him more than Ragoczy, he held out his hand for the squat glass the Count offered.

"There will be a light supper laid out in the dining room at eleven," Ragoczy went on when he had finished pouring drinks and handing them to his guests. "I recommend getting a good night's rest, for we hunt at six in the morning. I have asked the local wardens about boar."

"Boar!" exclaimed Grunbach. "Now that is a prey worth going after. I haven't hunted boar in . . . oh, it must be three years now."

A spurt of lightening flickered across the tall windows, followed a few seconds later by thunder.

"What about the rain? Won't that interfere with hunting?" asked Oberstetten.

"It should not last more than an hour or two, not in summer," said Hohepfad, wanting the rest to take note of his expertise.

"But if the ground is too wet, we will not have a good—" Lothar Teich protested, turning to Ragoczy for additional information.

"I have hired a few men to accompany us—men who know the terrain better than I, and who are willing to guide us." Ragoczy saw a quick exchange of looks between Lothar Teich and Koenig Einlass. "I have guns for those who need them," he added, wishing he knew what his two guests had conveyed to each other.

"I . . . did not bring anything more than birdshot," said von Nordlingen. "I thought, well . . . you see, I thought that this was not going to be . . . sporting. I assumed, given the company, that we would be expected to spend the time in discussion." His fair cheeks reddened.

"I do not anticipate our hunting will last more than three or four hours each day; certainly no longer than five at most if we have to go any distance from the Schloss. You will have plenty of time for relaxation and talk, if that is what you prefer," said Ragoczy. "We do not have to stock the winter larder with our kill." Three hundred years ago and further back, the hunt would have been more demanding and purposeful. Now it was a recreation, and Ragoczy was not wholly convinced the change was for the better; these men had learned to enjoy hunting for its own sake rather than for necessity, an appetite he had lost three thousand years before.

"No, indeed, if what my man told me is right," said Leopold Oberstetten, rubbing his wide hands together. "This is what a hunting box should be—not like that comfortless place of von Wolgast's. I understand you have a . . . larder to envy. He said that your cook is preparing a truffled goose for midday dinner tomorrow."

"What a treasure, to have a fine cook," exclaimed von Traunreuth. He put his hands over the front of his waistcoat and smiled. "Such a cook makes eating worthwhile."

"I am told that Martin is very accomplished." Ragoczy leaned back, bracing his shoulders against the mantel, his arms lightly folded. "I trust he will show you why he has his excellent reputation."

There were murmurs of satisfied anticipation, and then Hohepfad remarked they were out of sausages. "We appear to have inhaled them," he added with a trace of chagrin. "They were so delicious."

"I will ring for more," Ragoczy offered, his manner unruffled. He reached for the bellpull to summon Roger. "Would you like cheese as well?"

Two or three of the men demurred, but Einlass grinned. "That would be wonderful," he exclaimed. "I don't know why sitting down in a moving vehicle should be so wearing, but it is. I am always famished at the end of a journey."

"It is exhausting," agreed Oberstetten, continuing smugly, "We newspapermen find we must develop a tolerance for such travel or we cannot perform our tasks."

Roger tapped once on the door and stepped into the study. He looked directly at Ragoczy, waiting for instructions.

"More of the sausages, if you please, Roger; and a tray of cheeses as well," he said, indicating the men gathered in the study. "And two bottles of the Mosel."

"Very good," said Roger, and withdrew from the room.

As the night came on tongues loosened; Oberstetten became more provocative in his remarks; von Traunreuth and Teich spoke adamantly about the future of Germany—neither of them expressed any desire for peace in Europe—Grunbach, Kraftig and Hohepfad all had some accomplishment still recent enough to excuse boasting of them; Einlass and von Nordlingen contributed their observations—Einlass' sarcastic, von Nordlingen's idealistic. Only Apfelobstgarten remained as silent as Ragoczy, watching the others narrowly as the hour grew late.

When the party was summoned to supper, von Nordlingen remarked that the time had passed too quickly; the rest seconded his enthusiasm as they rose and allowed Ragoczy to point out the way to the dining room. Only Apfelobstgarten lingered behind, taking stock of everything in Ragoczy's study in a series of knowing glances.

"Is there anything you seek?" Ragoczy asked politely from the door.

Apfelobstgarten hesitated before he spoke. "You have eclectic tastes, Herr Count."

"I am curious by nature," Ragoczy said, waiting in the door for this last, reserved guest. "And I have the luxury of time to indulge myself."

"A luxury indeed," said Apfelobstgarten, not quite cynically. He turned on his heel and left the study.

Ragoczy watched him go, wondering what the man had been looking for, and why. He followed after his guests at a leisurely pace, knowing that Roger would attend to the buffet. It would draw undue attention to his abstention if he went to the dining room now and did not eat, so he continued on his way to his music room and sat down at the ormolu-embellished Erard grand piano. He played from memory, with enjoyment and flair, melodies of Haydn and Bach and Scarlatti. Long after his guests went to bed, he remained at the keyboard, letting the music envelop him in its happy sorcery.

The morning was bright, everything fresh from the rain of the previous evening; a rich, loamy scent filled the air as Ragoczy met his guests not long after sunrise near the excavation at the rear of the Schloss. He was dressed for hunting, his high, thick-soled black boots glossy with polish, his twill breeches as black as his boots, his dark-burgundy coat over a black collarless shirt. He carried a shotgun in the crook of his arm, and a cartridge box of black leather hung from a belt over his shoulder.

Most of the others were in similar garments, though few of them wore black; it being summer, tan, deep green, and brown were the preferred colors; four of them—Einlass, von Traunreuth, Kraftig, and Hohepfad—wore gaiters instead of boots. They had just come from the light breakfast laid out for them.

Only Euchary Apfelobstgarten had donned a black jacket; his had a collar of dark green over a tan roll-neck pullover; his face looked unusually pale, as if he had become ill, though he was able to greet Ragoczy heartily. "I had the coffee and almond roll. Very good."

"So did I; truly excellent," said Teich, his approval sounding sycophantic instead of genuine. "I remain impressed."

"Thank you; I'll tell Martin," Ragoczy said, glancing up at the wooded slope. "Renke should be here shortly, with his assistants," he added. "He is the warden I mentioned to you last night."

Oberstetten put his hand up to shade his eyes. When he spoke his voice was gravelly; he was not yet fully awake. "I am always astonished at the good humor of those whose custom it is to rise early."

"Do not fault us, I beg of you," said von Nordlingen with such earnestness that Oberstetten groaned.

Bertram Grunbach appeared to have recovered from his travels; his stride was jaunty as he joined the men. "What on earth are you planning for that hole, Count?" he asked, hitching his shoulder in the direction of the excavation.

Ragoczy smiled slightly. "I am putting in a swimming pool," he said blandly; he said nothing about the thick layer of his native earth that would line it, to protect him from the enervating effect of the water. "My villa in Rome had one; I've learned to like them." He did not add that he had built the villa when Claudius was Caesar.

"A swimming pool," Teich marveled, and would have gone on, but was interrupted by the arrival of Renke with three other men, all of them in heavy jackets and knee breeches. Each carried a shotgun and each glowered with purpose.

"Good morning, Herr Count," said Renke, putting his hand to his grisled hair.

"And to you," said Ragoczy. "What are our prospects, would you say?"

"We've been out since an hour before dawn." Renke scraped his stubbled chin with his thumb. "There are boar, if we can search them out."

"Excellent," enthused von Nordlingen. "Just what we want."

Koenig Einlass grinned. "Let us start at once." He glanced once at Ragoczy. "If you permit, Count?"

"Of course," said Ragoczy. "Stay in pairs and listen to your warden," he reminded them. "We will gather here again no later than noon. Dinner will be waiting."

"Truffled goose," Volger Kraftig said in anticipation.

"Delightful," seconded Oberstetten. "And I suppose we must earn it."

"I would not put it so harshly," said von Traunreuth. He pointed to Grunbach. "Why don't we hunt together this morning?"

"Delighted," said Grunbach, "so long as you do not want to discuss financing for weapons. Or anything else."

In a short while all the guests were off in pairs with wardens; Oberstetten made a point of having Ragoczy for his partner, saying as they set off, "Why don't you tell me the real reason for this hunting party now, so that I need not pester you constantly?"

"How do you mean, 'real reason'?" Ragoczy asked blandly.

"I mean," said Oberstetten, "that there have been rumors about you for weeks. I can't believe that all of them are the products of gossip." He fell into step beside his host, moving with spritely speed, his thick legs working steadily as they set off up a narrow trail, Renke slightly in the lead.

"What rumors are those?" Ragoczy inquired in the same unconcerned way.

Oberstetten shook his head once. "All right; if you insist, I will be specific. I do not mean those ridiculous tales of children's brothels, nor do I mean the whispers that you are a spy. No. I am not as gullible as many others—"

"Journalists rarely are," said Ragoczy at his most affable. Ahead the pine trees crowded the trail and they were forced to walk single file until the trees thinned at the edge of a clearing.

As they went on, Oberstetten kept talking, growing breathless with unaccustomed exercise, making his remarks deliberately blunt in the hope of startling Ragoczy into a revealing remark. "I am referring to the rumors—and they are rife—that you have been charged with the task of making some sort of private agreement with the Kaiser on the Czar's behalf."

"If that were the case, you must know I would not be at liberty to discuss it," said Ragoczy. He paused at the edge of the clearing in response to a signal from Renke. "What is it?"

"Deer," said Renke softly. "Two fawns and a doe." He pointed to a fallen log at the edge of the clearing; the deer were on the far side of it. At the sound of their voices, the doe raised her head, ears turning. An instant later the three bounded away through the underbrush.

"You must know that I am here to find out about this," Oberstetten persisted, unimpressed by the deer. "The *Berliner Morgenblatt* did not send me to Bavaria to hunt boar."

Ragoczy turned to Oberstetten. "My friend, I am sorry to disappoint you, but it would be best for all of us if you did hunt boar."

Undeterred, Oberstetten persisted, "You're assuming I can do nothing but print stories in the paper, but I have more influence than that. It is not difficult for me to reach some of the men you have been trying to gain access to; I could, if I knew more about your task. There are men whose private sentiments are not the ones they express in public. In that regard, I am in a position to aid you. If you would tell me something of your intentions, I might be able to suggest to you which of your guests would be inclined to support your purpose. I have assumed from the first that this little gathering was for more than hunting, and I am fairly certain that the rest are of a like mind. It would save you time, talking with me now, and it would also serve to reduce the risk of being exposed to those opposing your mission."

Ragoczy turned directly to Oberstetten. "My mission—if I have a mission—is a private matter." He did not raise his voice to speak, and when he was done, he gave his full attention to Renke.

"But you cannot imagine—you are working against opposition you cannot overcome," Oberstetten protested.

"Am I." Ragoczy provided no indication of his state of mind in either his tone nor his stance.

"Gott im Himmel!" Oberstetten swore. "You are worse than the bloody Turks!"

In answer to Renke's signal, Ragoczy moved off again, letting Oberstetten come after him. "Quietly, Oberstetten; quietly."

"As you wish," said the journalist, accepting his thwarted purpose for the moment.

Three times that morning they heard gunfire, and twice came the signal of a kill. By the time the sun was nearly overhead, Ragoczy was glad to turn back toward his Schloss.

"Tomorrow we'll find our boar, unless you would prefer to hunt something else, in which case we will still bring it down," Renke promised, his face chagrined; he was embarrassed that Ragoczy had not been able to make a kill this first morning.

Ragoczy shrugged. "I would be a selfish host, to deprive my guests the satisfaction of getting their kills first." He motioned to Oberstetten, who lagged after him. "Come. It is time for dinner."

"Not an instant too soon," Oberstetten grumbled. He lowered his head, concealing his face reddened with sunburn and effort.

"As you say," Ragoczy agreed, beginning to feel the impact of the sun; it was time to be indoors.

"The dinner was a triumph," exclaimed von Traunreuth when Ragoczy joined his guests in his parlor shortly after four in the afternoon. "Magnificent."

"A pity you did not join us," said Grunbach pointedly. "I hope you did not deprive yourself on our account."

"No; and I beg your pardon for that." Ragoczy said. "I have a . . . project I am engaged upon. It has to do with fuels, and it required my prompt attention. I have to deliver my findings to Professor Rieman in Munchen before I return to Berlin." He hoped that Isidore Rieman's reputation was sufficiently impressive to keep his guests from asking more questions.

"Something you are funding?" asked Teich pointedly.

"In part. I am not . . . unknowledgeable in chemistry," Ragoczy replied, wondering what these men would make of his alchemical laboratory, where he had spent the last few hours making improvements on his athanor as part of his experiments on petroleum.

"Reviewing what Rieman wants funded, no doubt," said Einlass, chuckling at his own sarcasm.

Ragoczy did not respond to the implied challenge in Einlass' jibe; he sat down and stretched out his legs, resting his heels on the nearest hassock. "Do not tell me that the Ministry of War is not developing fuels."

Einlass coughed. "I wouldn't know about that."

"I would," said Hohepfad, precariously near boasting. "All the world is working to make more efficient fuels, if they have any resources to use: Germany is no exception. And since we have superior scientists, I assume we are making advances beyond what others are accomplishing. It is the only prudent thing to do, with the shadow of war growing wider and darker every day."

Apfelobstgarten glared at him. "You are as loose-tongued as your wife."

Stung, Hohepfad straightened up in his chair. "You will not say that about Isabel," he declared. "And I doubt that anyone in this room is unaware of what Germany has achieved in this realm."

"What about Ragoczy?" asked Kraftig, making no apology for the insult his question delivered to their host.

"If he is working with Rieman, he probably knows more than the rest of us combined," said Einlass, dismissing the matter as he deliberately changed the subject. "What do we hunt tomorrow? More boar?"

Ragoczy accepted this ploy without comment. "If you would like. We brought down two today, which is more than we will eat. I have already given one to Renke, to be divided among his helpers. I told him that tomorrow any boars shot would be his. As it is, Martin will have his hands full with the one in the kitchen."

"Perhaps there will be other game?" suggested Apfelobstgarten.

"Perhaps," said Ragoczy, and was relieved when Roger appeared with a tray of cheese and wurst.

By evening, Ragoczy's guests were discussing their families, trying not to brag of their children's abilities and their wives' devotion.

Von Nordlingen was the one who asked Ragoczy directly, "Where is your family, Count?"

"My parents, and my brothers and sisters are all dead," he replied carefully and honestly. "Killed by our enemies when they overran our land."

"No wife, no children?" he pursued, as if determined to put Ragoczy at a disadvantage. "Not even a bastard or two, somewhere?"

"Paul; we're guests here," Teich admonished him, speaking the reprimand the others only thought.

Ragoczy answered the question. "My wife died . . . some years ago."
He folded his arms and waited for the next intrusion.

It never came. Leopold Oberstetten said, "To lose so many. That is
very sad, Count." In the next breath, he mentioned a minor feud going
on between factions in the Office of Procurement, and let Apfelobstgarten explain the reasons for the rivalry.

At the end of the evening, while his guests amused themselves with
cognac and cigars, Ragoczy found a moment to pull Roger aside.
"Well?" he asked, his voice low and with an edge of urgency.

"None of the servants are willing to say much. They know their masters will not tolerate any breach of confidence. But I do think it would
be good to be cautious of Apfelobstgarten; his servant carried a note
down to Hausham today." Roger reported in Latin, in the same steady
manner that he discussed household accounts.

"Did you happen to notice an address?" Ragoczy inquired in the same
tongue.

"The note was going to Switzerland, to a Moritz Vinadi," said Roger.
"It was a private address, I think; there was no business title on the address, in any case. Do you want me to make inquiries about this Vinadi?"

Ragoczy sighed. "Then I suppose I must discover as much as I can
about this Swiss; yes, make your inquiries, but carefully. We do not want
to make matters worse, not if we can help it." He glanced over his shoulder. "Have you any other impressions?"

"Only that none of these men seem much inclined to peace, not if
their servants' attitudes are indicative; they are all making cryptic remarks about the possibility of fighting within two years," said Roger,
pausing a moment before adding, "And they are not here out of goodwill. I don't think most of these men trust you, your motives, or your
invitation."

"So I've realized," said Ragoczy with an ironic turn to the corner of
his mouth.

Roger's faded-blue eyes grew steely. "It is probably useless, but I feel
I should warn you, my master, that one of these men may mean you
harm."

Ragoczy did not seem alarmed by this warning. "What makes you say
that, old friend?"

"Nothing specific," Roger admitted. "But when servants are tight-
lipped and jumpy, I assume it is not from fear of volcanos—not in
Bavaria."

"I see," Ragoczy said, taking a long breath. "Do you think it could be
from pride? or prudence?"

"The silence might be; this is something more." He looked down at the fine Bokhara carpet. "I know it may be nothing, but—"

"Yes; precisely. But." Ragoczy went back to speaking German. "Very good. I appreciate your telling me."

"You are going to the laboratory later?" Roger had raised his voice slightly, so that anyone listening could overhear without effort.

"Yes. I must complete my work tonight. I want to be ready for the hunt tomorrow." He put his hand on Roger's shoulder. "If you will set out my things, I will not need to trouble you."

"I would rather it were deer than boar," Roger said, knowing Ragoczy would understand his intent.

Ragoczy nodded, saying, "No doubt Martin would do well with venison." The expression in his dark eyes was not nearly so off-handed as his words. He gestured dismissal to Roger and went back to his guests, filled with more qualms than he had been the previous day. If Roger's apprehension was realistic, then he had little hope of achieving the prize Nicholas sought, for none of these men would be willing to help him pursue his mission to the Kaiser, no matter what authorizations he carried.

By early morning, Ragoczy had decided to focus his efforts on von Traunreuth, Koenig Einlass and Werner Hohepfad, all of the Ministry of War; if he could not learn of German intentions regarding arms proliferation through them, he doubted the others could or would. With this resolved in his mind, he went to prepare for another morning tramping about the woods.

Renke was early, his three deputies flanking him as they came up the drive at the side of the house. He regarded the six men waiting for him with amusement. "Too early for city-folk, is it?"

"It is early," said Volger Kraftig, still heavy-eyed from the previous evening's cognac. "The Count may be right not to drink."

Renke laughed, enjoying Kraftig's discomfort. "Stick with beer, sir, that's the sensible thing to do." He noticed that two more men were coming out of the house. "Lazy fellows."

Oberstetten took the teasing in good part—his fellow journalists often said much worse to him—but Teich was offended. "You men may know the game in these woods, but you wouldn't last an hour in Berlin."

"That is why we do not live there," said Renke. He concealed his satisfaction by lighting his pipe. "There will be time for a smoke before you are all ready."

To Ragoczy's surprise, Euchary Apfelobstgarten made a point of becoming his partner for the hunt, although Ragoczy gave him no encouragement beyond what good manners required. "It is your land; if anyone has an advantage, it is you. Yesterday was a disappointment for me. Today I intend to find game to my liking."

"Then load for deer, not boar," Ragoczy reminded him, and gave Renke a nod of approval. "We saw a doe and fawns yesterday. Perhaps today we can find a buck or two." He looked around. "I don't want any does or fawns killed. Bucks only."

"Trying to preserve your herd?" asked Grunbach, making this sensible notion sound questionable.

Von Nordlingen answered. "Anyone with an estate like this would do. I know I would, if it was still in my family. It's the only reasonable thing." He was not quite as effusive as he had been the day he arrived, but his good humor had not deserted him completely. "I'll wager ten marks that we get at least three bucks today."

"I'll take that wager," said Oberstetten, reaching into the pocket of his jacket and pulling out a roll of banknotes. "Ten marks says we will get two or one."

For the next few minutes there was an enthusiastic exchange of bets, and then they prepared to set off into the forest once more, out of the sun and into the dappled shadows of the trees; Renke again walked with Ragoczy, shotgun tucked under his arm and a cartridge case hanging from his belt. His steady, swinging stride set the pace as they made their way up the slope and around to the east. The others moved off in parallel paths to the one Renke chose, two groups going higher up the mountain, one going lower.

"The deer will be active for about three hours more; we will have plenty of time. They rest through the heat of the day," said Renke. "It is not sporting to shoot them while they sleep."

"Can you get close enough to do that?" asked Apfelobstgarten. "I should have thought the deer would waken and flee."

"Men from the city, like you, cannot. You go through the forest like herds of swine." Renke put a hand to his chest. "I can walk within four strides of a sleeping herd of deer and not startle them."

"And Ragoczy? What of him?" Apfelobstgarten persisted. "How would you rate his skill?"

"I would reckon that the Count could pass through a herd while they slept and never waken one of them." His respect was clearly genuine, bordering on awe. He did not look at Ragoczy, preferring to keep his eyes on the trail ahead.

"High praise indeed," said Apfelobstgarten, glancing once at Ragoczy.

"And from a man of your experience, warden, I must assume you have reason to know his abilities and to assess them."

"I have hunted with the Count," said Renke, his face becoming closed; he had realized belatedly that he had said too much and now wanted to keep from being drawn into more indiscretions.

"So I gather," Apfelobstgarten said, speculation narrowing his eyes as much as the occasional shards of brilliant sunlight piercing the forest.

Ragoczy realized that to interfere with Apfelobstgarten's questions would only serve to draw attention to them; he remained silent as they continued to go further into the dense growth of pine and oak. Gradually he put some distance between himself and Apfelobstgarten, allowing the man from the Office of Procurement to stay near Renke. He wanted to avoid more conversation with the man. His own company was disheartening enough, he thought, now that he anticipated he would have to inform Nicholas that he had been unable to bring about the support the Czar had envisioned. He was far enough from Renke and Apfelobstgarten to be out of sight, although he could hear them moving along the narrow track. His passage was nearly silent; Renke had been right about Ragoczy's ability to move soundlessly.

Something flickered at the edge of his vision; Ragoczy started to turn even as he heard the noise of gunfire and felt what seemed to be a hot fist slam into his side, catching him just below the ribs on the left. He took half a dozen faltering steps before his legs went out from under him, leaving him sprawled between an oak and a moss-covered stump of a long-vanished pine. When he clapped his hand to his side, it came away bloody. He sat still, trying to absorb the pain which now had him in its clutches. His spine was not damaged: he would recover.

"Oh, Mein Gott!" shouted Apfelobstgarten as he came plunging up the slope, Renke close behind him. "You're—"

"Shot," said Ragoczy. "Yes. I am."

"Who on earth—" Apfelobstgarten began, only to be interrupted by a shout from up the hillside. A moment later, von Nordlingen and Einlass came pelting through the trees, their warden behind them.

"I never, I never, never, never thought—" von Nordlingen was protesting. "I thought it was a *deer*. I was sure it was a deer. I *never* would have fired if I—" He reached the place where Ragoczy lay. "Count. I can't find words. How can I apologize?"

"Someone might get me back to the Schloss," Ragoczy said dryly, adding as two of the men bent to lift him, "*Not* carried, if you please.

I'm bleeding quite enough without that." He saw the shock on the faces around him. "*Renke. Now.* Before I faint."

Oberstetten and von Traunreuth were gasping for breath as they stumbled up. "We heard a shot . . . Didn't think any . . . thing of it," Oberstetten said between gulps of air. "Then—"

"I will go for aid," said Renke, as if coming out of a dream. "Do not move him until we can bring a stretcher."

Ragoczy closed his eyes as he heard his warden hasten back down the slope. "Someone give me something to press against my side." He was shocked to hear how thready his voice was. Looking up, he realized the men expected him to die; the wound must be worse than he supposed it was. He wondered vaguely how difficult it would be to account for his survival.

Apfelobstgarten removed his hunting jacket at once, and, wadding it up, handed it to Ragoczy. "I don't want to make . . . it any . . . " His words faded as he stepped back from the wounded man.

"Christ!" von Nordlingen exclaimed, dropping his shotgun as if had caught fire. "It was an *accident!*"

"An accident," echoed Einlass, then turned on von Nordlingen. "You fired without being sure of your target."

"I know, I know," said von Nordlingen in a steady way, as if repetition would bring real understanding. "I should have made certain. But I saw . . . and he is . . . not so tall. I supposed it must be a deer. He was by himself." He looked around at the others. "You know how it is, don't you?"

It was von Traunreuth who answered. "This is a tragic accident."

Ragoczy's thoughts grew muddled; his side was agonizing now, and it took all his scattered concentration to keep from crying out. He no longer tried to listen to the voices around him, but let himself slip into the twilight of semiconsciousness while the others waited for Renke to return with a stretcher. "Roger," he said, doing his best to make his manservant's name distinct.

"What is it, Count?" asked Oberstetten, bending nearer, one hand cupped to his ear.

"Roger. Will know." He was certain that the journalist heard him.

"Right you are," said Oberstetten with the false cheerfulness of one expecting the worst. "We'll put him in charge."

"Good," said Ragoczy, but in the lost tongue of his people, who had vanished more than two thousand years before. His voice was so soft that none of the men around him paid any attention to it; they were occupied by the continuing protestations of Paul von Nordlingen, who adamantly insisted on his innocence of intent in the shooting, and to demand understanding from those around him.

"Poor devil," said Grunbach as he came up to the rest. It was impossible to tell if he meant von Nordlingen or Ragoczy.

Text of a report from Sidney Reilly to "C", sent in code using Key 56, from Berlin to London by diplomatic courier, delivered September 1, 1910.

I have at last spoken with my agent's man who witnessed the shooting, who declares that in spite of what the police have decided, the shooting was no accident, and that von Nordlingen was determined to shoot Ragoczy from the first day. His report says that von Nordlingen has harbored a grudge against Ragoczy for living on the estate he has long felt he deserves to own, and would have owned if one of his forefathers had not gambled away the family fortune. I have never met Paul von Nordlingen, but Renfred Meyer informs me that von Nordlingen has coveted all his family owned long ago, and has been known to express certainty that he will, in time, restore his family to the glory Fredrich von Nordlingen has lost. Until now, these claims have been regarded as the vanity of an ambitious young man, but now it is possible he has attempted to remove one of the obstacles from his path. Meyer is convinced that if Ragoczy had no will, or if he had no direct heirs, and had not survived the injury he suffered, that von Nordlingen would make a claim on the Schloss and its surrounds.

As to Ragoczy himself, I have learned that he has gone to Amsterdam. To the surprise of everyone, he did not die of blood loss, nor of any infection, although with such a wound, it might have been expected. He left the Schloss two days after being shot, in a private railway car, accompanied only by his manservant, who said it was his intention to consult with one of the physicians in Holland. Apparently he did not feel entirely safe in Germany, at least that is what Oberstetten has been saying in public, and he was on the same hunt, although not in Ragoczy's company when the shooting occurred. He does not believe that von Nordlingen fired on purpose, but he has stated that he thinks there are those who might want to take advantage of Ragoczy's incapacity.

I am sending the man I have named Eduard Angebot to Amsterdam, with the hope that he will not be too incompetent to keep track of Ragoczy there. Given the severity of his injury, I would expect Ragoczy to remain in that city for some time; his recovery will not be an easy one, not after such a massive hurt as the one he suffered. I have already ascertained that Ragoczy has rented a house there, and that should make the task easy enough, even for Angebot. What troubles me the most about him is his continuing lack of comprehension of the stakes of this work we do. He is not willing to take the necessary steps his duty requires. It appears he still thinks spies are gentlemen, and that he must keep to the rules of the cricket field. I trust you or someone in your office will be able to persuade him that this is not the case. If I am not satisfied with his performance, I may well go along to Amsterdam myself for a day or two, to see what can be done with that chap.

Tomorrow I am meeting with Leopold Oberstetten in private, to determine how much of what he is saying is speculation and how much is knowledge. When I am through with the interview, I will be more able to analyze what I have learned thus far. I am absolutely convinced that there is more to this shooting than avarice and envy; in fact, I am now assuming that someone played upon von Nordlingen's malice for reasons other than those that have been proposed. He is too obvious a figure to be the only one who might benefit from Ragoczy's death. If I am fortunate, I will be able to discover from Oberstetten all who attended the hunting party, and then, with Renfred Meyer's help, I may be able to determine what purpose Ragoczy's wound serves. When I know this, I will inform you of it. Until then, I will keep my reports to a minimum, so as not to draw attention to what I am doing, or who I am watching. If Ragoczy has enemies in Germany, there may be others elsewhere as well. And Germans take trains to other countries regularly: Ragoczy will not be safe in Amsterdam if he is not safe in Berlin. So I will continue on my guard for the time being.

Sidney Reilly (Capt.)

5

Ragoczy turned away from the window and let the curtain fall back across it. "Thank all the forgotten gods that we do not overlook a canal," he said in Byzantine Greek, half in jest, to Roger. "It would sap what strength I have just dealing with the water. At least we are far enough north that the sun does not wear on me, as it did in South America."

"The water troubles you? Even now? You are much improved." It had been three weeks since they arrived in Amsterdam, and the wound Ragoczy had suffered was now nothing more than an angry red weal atop ancient white scars. For ten days Ragoczy had kept to his private quarters, lying atop his chest of native earth in a kind of stupor while Roger had tended him.

"Yes, even now. But not as it would have done at first; then the water would have been . . . overwhelming. If it were not for Anna, on the floor above, I would not now be so . . . restored. I am obliged to her, little though she may know it." His smile was wintery; he fingered the square sleeve of his dressing gown of black satin. In the lucid September light filling his parlor he was splendid darkness.

"She has enjoyed her dreams, has she not?" Roger asked, knowing the answer.

"Of course; and she has not lost more than a pint to me, over two weeks, and her dreams have been sweet. I think she has surprised herself with her dreaming. She will take no harm from me." He folded his arms. "You need not worry, old friend. I am aware of my state: believe this."

"I have no doubt," said Roger dryly. "It is what you plan to do about it that concerns me." He paused, his attention fixed on the art nouveau settee at the edge of the carpet. "Do you want to change your residence yet?"

"You mean that I would attract less attention in an older part of the city, where foreigners are not so . . . obvious?" Ragoczy suggested.

"Something of the sort, yes. Leonardo Straat will do for a while, but there will be questions if we continue on here much longer," Roger agreed in Latin. "At least the buildings are new enough that your modifications are not noteworthy. With new construction all around us, it makes anything done here unremarkable."

At that Ragoczy smiled, and switched to Latin as well. "I might still occupy the old press building. I own it." He looked out at the street once more. "But that could lead to questions in official quarters I have not had the chance to prepare to answer, such as which of my relatives I am to be."

Roger said nothing, but there was a look in his faded-blue eyes that revealed relief. "You don't want to make it too easy for those hunting you to find you."

"No; I do not, until I am ready to be found. No doubt they have followed me, but they have not yet resumed watching me; I would be aware of it if they had," Ragoczy said, his voice cautious, his eyes less so. "Which is one of the reasons I am still a trifle reluctant to visit Miss Saxon at her studio. I do not want to expose her to risk through my presence."

"But you will." Roger was not as confident of this as he sounded, but as he spoke, he saw Ragoczy nod once. "Today?"

"Tomorrow, I think. I've prepared a note for her. If you would be good enough to carry it 'round to her?" He indicated his tall, Louis XVI secretary on the far side of the room. "It is in the top drawer."

"You know where she lives, then?" Roger asked, making the question almost an accusation.

"I know where she paints," Ragoczy corrected him mildly. "It is the place you went last week, if I am not mistaken." He paid no attention to the look of chagrin that crossed Roger's features. "I do not know if she lives there or elsewhere, although I would suspect the former, but I do not know for certain, since I do not know if the address she provided is the same as the house she was going to let. I will find out when I see her, at her studio." He glanced back at the window to watch a tortoiseshell cat amble across the street, tail up, fur glossy with health. "Now there is an animal to admire," he said.

At this Roger looked startled. "You want to keep a cat?"

"No: not when their lives are so brief; it is hard enough keeping horses," said Ragoczy sharply. "But I can admire the creatures, and I do." He came away from the window, pacing the room in measured steps, the heels of his thick-soled shoes making a muffled report on the antique carpet. "When you take that note to Rowena Saxon, will you also visit the press? Be alert as you do, in case you are followed. I would like van Groot to know I am here. We will have things to discuss when I am more fully recovered. The press is in need of improvement."

"If you wish," said Roger, puzzled by the request.

Sensing Roger's bafflement, Ragoczy went on, "I will want to have a reason for being here, one that will not alert those—"

"Trying to kill you?" Roger supplied. "They will not be pleased to learn of your recovery."

"No, they will not, whoever they are." Ragoczy stopped still, as if listening for stealthy footfalls. "But if they are watching me, they will expect me to return to Germany if there is no obvious thing keeping me here."

"Why not assume the Czar has ordered it?" Roger went to the secretary and opened it, pulling out a letter with the double-headed Romanov eagle embossed on it. "Surely they know you have had correspondence with Nicholas since you arrived?"

"If the Czar ordered me anywhere, it would not be to Amsterdam; he has few connections here that would be useful to his plans for me," Ragoczy declared. "He would send me to England, or call me back to Russia."

"Are you certain of that?" Roger asked. "In his letter, he told you to remain where you could receive the best treatment for your injuries."

"So he did," Ragoczy said. "That does not mean he will not send me back to Germany when I am . . . shall we say well enough? to resume my mission. The danger is greater for his family than for me. He has a stricken child to protect. What is a foreign exile, compared to that?" He went to Roger's side and handed him the note written to Rowena Saxon. "Here. If you will, wait for her answer; tell me how she reacts. Your observations will give me some notion of the reception I will receive from her."

"Of course, my master," said Roger, taking the note as an indication their discussion is over.

Ragoczy gave a single, apologetic laugh. "I am going back to my quarters, to lie down a while." He put his hand to his side, the single indication of pain. "I'm . . . not so much restored as I like to think."

Alarmed, Roger reached out to steady Ragoczy. "Is there trouble? Do you need anything—"

Ragoczy shook off Roger's hand. "I am not that incapacitated, thank you." His manner changed at once. "And I ask your pardon for being brusque with you. I had no reason to be so churlish." He rubbed his face with one small, beautiful hand. "I am fatigued; more than I realized."

"Yes," said Roger, putting the note into the inner breast pocket of his coat. "I will attend to this at once." He started toward the door, then stopped for a moment. "If you don't mind, I will convey your personal greetings to Miss Saxon."

"The note already does that," said Ragoczy, wondering why Roger should be so specific about this.

"Nevertheless, I will reiterate." He let this sink in before he added, "If you could see yourself, if you had a reflection, you would know how pale you are."

"And you want to be certain Miss Saxon will want to accept . . . what I offer?" Ragoczy asked sardonically. "Well, I hope it hasn't come to that, though you may well be right. I do not like to be so much in need of sustenance. It wears on me." He watched Roger depart, then slowly climbed the stairs to his private quarters on the floor above, seeking the sanctuary of his bedroom and the succor of his thin mattress atop the chest of his native earth.

By late afternoon, Roger had returned with notes from Rowena Saxon and Jo van Groot. He was waiting in Ragoczy's dressing room when the Count emerged from his bedroom shortly before sunset.

"You look pleased with yourself," said Ragoczy with a smile that echoed Roger's. "I gather it all went well."

"It did," Roger confirmed, proffering the two notes he had brought. "Miss Saxon was delighted to hear you are well enough now to call on her, at her house where she has taken a two-year lease. It is nothing grand, but it is far from shabby. Her studio is on the top floor, and she has had skylight windows installed; she says her grand-father paid for the renovations. She is anticipating your portrait sittings with what I can only call eagerness." His expression was smug as he watched Ragoczy open the envelope and pull out the note. "She was happy to know your wound has healed."

Ragoczy's expression was a mixture of satisfaction and irony. "You must have painted a very bleak picture the first time you called on her." He read the brief note, clearly written in haste. "So," he said as he put it down. "She will expect me tomorrow at three."

"And van Groot will see you Friday." Roger gave him the second note. "He was not so glad as Miss Saxon to know you are coming to see him."

"You astonish me," said Ragoczy with faint amusement in his dark eyes. "I, too, am looking forward to seeing Miss Saxon more than I am to my interview with van Groot." He sat down, looking at the brushes and basin set out on the dresser. "Yes, I suppose it is time to be shaved again."

"It would be advisable," said Roger, and began to strop the razor.

Aside from his pallor, Ragoczy appeared wholly restored and at ease as he arrived at Rowena Saxon's studio; he was in a neat suit of superfine black wool, with a dull, deep-burgundy waistcoat edged in black twist over a white silk broadcloth shirt and a black silk tie with his eclipse-sigil worked into the pattern of the silk. He went up the stairs to the door of the narrow house, doing his best to ignore the enervating presence of the canal behind him.

Rowena herself opened the door, her short-cropped strawberry-blonde hair looking particularly stylish. She was dressed for afternoon tea in a dress of muted gold wool crepe a shade lighter than her eyes, with a square neckline and full, elbow-length sleeves covered in ecru lace. The high waist was not so tight as fashion decreed, and the double-pleated skirt was an inch or two shorter, revealing neat brown pumps and silk stockings. Around her neck and in her earlobes she wore the golden frog jewelry Ragoczy had sent her. Her smile at the sight of him was more revealing than she knew. "Count," she exclaimed as she stepped back to admit him. "Come in, please."

"With pleasure, Miss Saxon," said Ragoczy as he crossed the threshold. He bowed slightly as she closed the door behind him; the faint vertigo the water had caused him ceased.

"I can't tell you how good it is to see you," she said in good form, making more room for him in the small, white-painted entry.

"I am very happy to be here," said Ragoczy, and smiled, his penetrating dark eyes on hers. "I have been looking forward to seeing you again."

"I haven't had the opportunity to thank you for these wonderful . . . frogs. They are marvelous. And unique. I have not seen anything like them."

He smiled courteously. "I am glad you like them, Miss Saxon."

"They are treasures." She looked away, her small talk becoming labored. "I . . . I am so . . . so *gratified* to have you . . . I wasn't sure you would be willing to . . . " Color mounted in her cheeks as she strove to regain her composure. "I hope you do not think me terribly forward for asking you here. I realized after I sent the note that you might well think I had gone beyond the bounds . . . "

"I am not Rupert Bowen, Miss Saxon, nor am I your mother," Ragoczy reminded her gently, and lifted one of her hands to kiss it. "I do not think you forward; far from it. I do, however, think you have flattered me by wanting to paint my portrait."

Her color brightened. "Well, I do," she said almost defiantly. "And I cannot do it in a single afternoon."

"I did not suppose you could," Ragoczy responded, and waited for her to speak again.

She made a quick, impulsive gesture encompassing the house, which served to restore her sense of self-possession. "Welcome, then. And let me show you around before we begin."

"Thank you; I would appreciate that." He nodded his encouragement.

She started down the hall, occasionally walking backward as she pointed out various features of the house she wished to bring to his attention. "As you can see, it is not very wide; just twenty-three feet. I am told that when these were built, taxation was based on width and number of stairs to the front door. It is quite deep, however. This ground floor is just over seventy feet long. The corridor runs the length of the house on the first two floors. The top floor is open. It was servants' quarters once, and then an attic. Now it is my studio." She was talking too fast, but she could not stop herself. "The parlor is in front, through the double doors, with a withdrawing room behind; it is very dark, having only one small window. Then there is the dining room, and behind that, the kitchen. The stairs are opposite the dining room." She began to walk toward them, her strides long and quick. "I have two bedrooms and a bath on the next floor; it is not so long as the ground floor, so that the skylights in the dining room and kitchen keep them from being like tombs. The rear bedroom has a small skylight, which makes it very pleasant." She started up the stairs, looking back down at Ragoczy as she climbed. "I have turned the front bedroom into a sort of study, and the second one is . . . where I sleep."

"That would seem a practical arrangement," Ragoczy said, to indicate he was paying attention.

"The bath is between the two bedrooms. I am using the maid's room as a dressing room. I have a housekeeper three days a week, so I don't need a place for a maid. My housekeeper is not here today." She began to climb the second, narrower flight of stairs. "As you see, I have found some prints from the last century; they were in the market by the bookstalls." She pointed out the framed works on the walls. "I find looking at them puts me in the right frame of mind to paint."

"Then they are an excellent investment," said Ragoczy, following her up into her studio. He looked around the sunny expanse with approval, looking up at the four large skylights, and then at the three tall windows at the rear of the room. "Very good, Miss Saxon."

"Do you really think so?" she asked as she turned around to face him. "I've curtained off the window over the canal, to keep the activity out there from distracting me." She indicated the window in question. "They used to have a small crane out of that window, to unload barges." Then her eyes grew anxious again. "Count—do you really like this?"

"Oh, yes. This is very, very good." He indicated the two draped easels in the middle of the large room. "New work, I trust."

"Part of a series of paintings, actually." She swallowed hard and nodded. "Studies of the canal. They may seem a trifle obvious, but I find the—" She fell silent as she came up to him.

"You need never deprecate your work to me, Miss Saxon; I thought we had established that, last spring." His dark eyes were somber but there was no rebuke in his voice; he took her hands in his.

"Yes," she said. "Yes, I remember." She stared down at their joined hands, noticing with some surprise that his hands were smaller than her own. "Forgive me for being a ninny. It's just that I have not yet grown accustomed to . . . having anyone accept what I do so readily."

"Does that frighten you?" he asked kindly.

She tried unsuccessfully to smile. "I rather think it does," she admitted.

"You have no reason to fear me, Miss Saxon; neither my opinions nor my actions," he said softly.

"Oh, God," she murmured, and pulled her hands away from him. "This is very difficult." She made herself face him. "You see, I have been fretting. I have been wondering if you expected something . . . After how I behaved, that time at my studio, in London, I was certain you would have . . . assumed I was . . . trying to make a trade with you, and—"

"As I recall, I expressed the opposite. I do not bargain in that way." He put his hand under her chin and turned her face to him. "I do not make it a practice of lying, or of coercion, Miss Saxon."

This assurance was more flustering to her. "I did not mean that you . . . But you see, when I . . . when I—"

"Kissed me?" he said for her. "You paid me a great compliment, Miss Saxon."

She stepped back from him. "How can you say that?"

"I can say it because I mean it," he replied calmly. "I am honored that you showed me such high regard."

"Is that what it meant to you—that I respect you?" Her confusion was annoying her. "Nothing more than that."

"You know that I would be glad of more, if you wanted it. I have told you so already." His musical voice betrayed no hint of dismay as he watched her. "I have not changed."

"You expect something from me because of it, don't you?" she challenged. "You assume—"

"I assume nothing. When you have lived as long as I have, you learn that such assumptions are more trouble than they are worth." His voice was low and steady. He remained at the top of the stairs while she went down the length of her studio as if to put as much distance as she could between them.

Rowena cocked her head and studied him. "I still do not know what to make of you, Count."

"What troubles you?" he asked; he made no move to approach her.

"I don't know. Perhaps everything." She flung this at him to see what he would do. When he remained quiet, she relented. "No. That has nothing to do with you. It has to do with me."

"Tell me," he encouraged her; he still did not stir from his place at the top of the stairs.

"Every time I have been with you," she began, then faltered as the immensity of her feelings rushed in on her. "I . . . don't know if I can explain."

"You need not upon my account; if you would rather not, then say nothing." He continued to watch her, his enigmatic gaze following her as she wandered restlessly about the studio.

"But I know I . . . owe you an explanation for—" she said, breaking off as suddenly as she began.

"Miss Saxon, you owe me nothing," he promised her, the gentleness of his voice all but taking her breath away.

"Then I owe myself one," she said.

"Ah. That is another matter entirely." He gave her a slight bow. "I will listen to whatever you decide to tell me."

She walked away from him, deliberately avoiding his eyes. For a short while she said nothing, but finally she was able to speak. "All the times I have been with you—and there are not that many of them— you have made me aware of things I want for myself." For an instant she glanced at him and saw a flicker of a smile on his lips. "I don't mean jewels—not to make light of your gift, for I don't."

"No; I did not think you did," he said when she seemed unable to go on.

"No, I don't." She took a deep breath. "When I say 'things,' I do not mean objects or possessions, I mean something else."

"I know," he told her, so compassionately that she was able to look at him without having to glance away.

"How can you?" she asked candidly. "When I hardly know myself?"

"Will you trust what I tell you?" He saw the skeptical angle of her chin as she nodded. "I know there is a wildness in your soul: I have felt it. It is in your work, in your eyes." Ragoczy saw her shake her head in doubt. "You are made of passion, and you have yet to learn to embrace it."

"It is not an easy thing, to trust," she confessed, adding in a rush, "When I kissed you, in London, I . . . I would have given more, if you had asked for it." She could feel her cheeks go scarlet.

His demeanor was unchanged. "I told you then and I tell you now that when you know what you want of me I will—"

Rowena did not let him finish; she rushed into his arms, holding his shoulders as she pressed her lips awkwardly to his. Only when his arms went around her, supporting her and caressing her at once, did she release her grip on him. As the kiss grew longer and more involved she wrapped her fingers around the back of his neck, sighing as she drew a little apart from him. "There."

Her cheek was soft under his fingers. "Well?"

She took a long breath. "I know that I want you. To make love to me. Now."

"You are certain?" he said, his need rising to match her own.

"I am certain I want you; that I want you to love me. I have wanted you all along." Her voice became more deliberate. "I am just as certain that I do not want to be your wife or bear your children." She shivered at this admission. "If you seek to establish a family, Count, then—" Her hands fell away.

"No; I do not seek either wife or children. For those of my blood, children are . . . impossible." He whispered this, his compelling gaze on her. "If you wanted them, you could not have them of me."

She was so startled she almost broke from him. "What do you mean?"

"I mean I am not quite what you think me," he said, feeling his own alienness as acutely as he had felt the buckshot tearing through his side.

"It is not some . . . disease, is it?" She winced at the word.

His chuckle was more reassuring than his answer. "No; not the way you mean."

"Do not tell me that you . . . prefer men. I won't believe it." She was breathless now, and she pressed close to him, sensations in her body she had never experienced so intensely before.

"No, I will not tell you that; the injury that caused the . . . condition is an old one." He kissed her again, his mouth opening hers, his hands spread over her back to touch as much of her as possible at once, longing for the feel of flesh instead of cloth.

She clung to him. "I don't care what it is, so long as you desire me, and you will show me how much."

There was a sadness at the back of his eyes that tweaked her curiosity as it roused her more fully. "I hope so."

"Let me find out," she urged him, daring to slip her hands under his coat. "Perhaps we should go down to my . . . bedroom. It would probably be more comfortable in my bed." Saying this aloud astonished her.

"If you wish," he said, feeling his first true pang of esurience; his sense of her grew keener as his desire increased.

"I do wish," she said, becoming bolder now that she had committed herself. She leaned against him, finding his strength comforting. "I have wished this ever since I came to Amsterdam."

He stroked her the length of her spine, her frisson of response making him tremble. "Ah, Rowena."

Rowena pulled away from him, but only far enough to start down the stairs, holding her hand out to him. "I'm not a virgin," she warned, but did not add that she had only made love twice before, and both attempts had been fumbling, her partner—the same man both times—as inexperienced as she.

"It isn't important," he said, his words like music to her. "Your fulfillment is all that matters."

She paused halfway down the flight. "I don't . . . I haven't . . . if there is such a spasm as I have been told of, I . . . "

His gaze was mesmerizing. "Then you have something to discover."

"Perhaps," she allowed dubiously as she continued down to the corridor below, then turned toward the back of the house. For a moment it seemed to her that the distance to her bedroom was vast and impossible to cross as the deserts of Arabia. Then she began to walk toward it, and in a few steps was through the door.

The afternoon light did not touch the windows, giving the room a luminous dusk; the sheets were opalescent as Rowena tossed back the covers. She did her best not to think, afraid that if she permitted herself a rational second or two, she would not be able to open herself to what Ragoczy offered. She nearly froze as he came up behind her and put his arms around her, his hands coming to rest over her breasts; she held her breath as he bent and kissed the nape of her neck just above the clasp of the necklace he had made for her. "Count," she whispered.

He had removed his jacket and hung it over the back of a grandmother's chair; the silk of his shirt was enticing as she touched his arms, as much to keep his hands where they were as to stop him. "Rowena."

They stood together, unmoving, for the greater part of two minutes, then Rowena turned in his embrace, seeking his mouth with her own as her senses grew more acute in answer to her longing. At last she moved enough to reach the underarm closure of her dress. "I should get out of this."

He said nothing, but the tenderness in his dark eyes made the breath catch in her throat. It had not struck her until now how awkward it was to unfasten the hooks and eyes concealed under the seam. She felt graceless as she struggled with them, her fingers clumsy with need and impatience. Then she felt, more than saw, Ragoczy take over the task. A moment later he helped tug the dress up and off her, leaving her in her satin slip and half-corset. She pulled the slip up and flung it away as soon as it was clear of her head. There were the laces and hooks of the corset; she wanted to scream with vexation until Ragoczy gently began to loosen the laces for her. It took only a few seconds before she was able to cast away the restricting undergarment, leaving her naked to the waist.

"Shall I take these off?" She indicated her pale silk drawers with the garterbelt over it, holding up her silk stockings.

"When you are ready," he said, drawing her into his arms, beginning light kisses on her brow, her closed eyes, the corner of her mouth as his hands sought out the beginning of her gratification; his ardor so precisely matched her own that she quivered in anticipation, dawning hope filling her that she might at last experience what she had only read of before and had supposed was a romantic fiction.

"What are you doing?" she whispered as his tongue touched her breast; the nipple was suddenly sensitive and erect.

"Something to please you," he answered as his hand cupped her other breast, awakening new responses.

"Not here," she murmured, stepping out of her shoes at last, and bending to remove her stockings, garters and drawers. She faltered, half-inclined to hide in her covers, half-preening as she saw how he looked at her. Never had she stood naked in front of a man before; never had she thought of her body in anything but pragmatic terms. She raised her arms slowly, then languorously and deliberately fell back across her sheets. "This is better."

He had cast aside his tie and waistcoat, but he removed no other clothing but his thick-soled shoes. As he stretched out beside her, he saw the bewilderment in her face. "This is for you, Rowena."

"But you—" She did not know how to go on.

"Never fear; if you are fulfilled, I will be also." His hands moved down over her hips and thighs, tantalizing and reassuring at once.

This was nothing like her two previous encounters with Clive Washbourne, when everything was hurried and disappointing: this was glorious turmoil of flesh and feeling that caught her unaware, a revelation she had not considered herself capable of achieving.

At the first persuasive movement of his fingers between her legs, she sighed, certain now that all the lovely evocations would quickly end; Clive had plunged into her as soon as he had tugged her drawers off. But Ragoczy continued his ministrations without haste, with no indication that he intended to climb atop her; his hands gave exquisite attention to every nuance of voluptuousness. When she was convinced that no greater ecstasy was possible, she lay back; he startled her afresh by moving down her body to taste the sea-shell-scented folds. "Count?"

He raised his head. "Do you dislike it?" he asked softly.

". . . No," she told him.

"Then I will continue." He bent his head once more, finding the hidden place that trembled and jumped.

Passion gathered in Rowena, coiling like a spring; when the release came it went through her like storm-driven waves, tremendous and rapturous at once, so engulfing that she no longer noticed the texture of the sheets and coverlets beneath her, or heard her own soft cries. Gradually she realized Ragoczy was holding her, his lips pressed to the curve of her neck. Flushed with elation, she sank her hands in the loose waves of his hair. Now she felt the buttons of his shirt against her skin. As he lifted his head, she beamed at him. "Oh, Count. *Thank you.*"

He kissed her softly. "It is I who should thank you," he told her with utter sincerity.

"No," she insisted. "You had nothing for yourself."

He put his finger to her lips. "Oh, yes, Rowena," he said gently but in a tone that stopped all argument, "I had all that you had."

"But—" She rolled onto her side in order to face him, preparing to ask something that now seemed impossible to speak aloud.

"Those of my blood . . . only receive what we give." He waited for her to consider what he told her.

"But . . . how?" she asked, adding, her voice becoming teasing, "Not that I disapprove. But why?"

"That is our nature." His smile was loving, but tinged by irony. "Your fulfillment is my own."

"If that is true, then I am thrilled," she said, taking his hand and putting it over her breast again. Now that she had discovered the richness of her passion, her own boldness was no longer confusing to her. "Can you feel how much?"

His dark eyes were luminous in the fading light of the ending day. "Better than you know."

Questions rose in her mind, but her lingering delight kept her from asking them. She kissed him soundly. "In that case," she said, happiness coursing through her as her orgasm had, "this portrait may take a *very* long time to complete."

His laughter surprised them both. "As long as it brings you pleasure, so be it," he declared, and wrapped her in his arms again. "You have done more than I can tell you, Rowena."

Again she set aside her questions, although she knew that they would persist long after this apolaustic glow. "It's useless to begin today; I wouldn't be able to hold any concentration at all." Her expression was mischievous. "Tomorrow, perhaps? At the same time?"

Her offer was tempting, but he was not willing to risk taking blood from her again so soon. "The day after, if you please." He reached behind him and tugged on the edge of the coverlet, pulling it over them both.

"Are you cold?" she wondered aloud; the movement of the air sent chills over her, leaving a trail of gooseflesh.

"No; but you are," he answered.

"I don't mind," she said as she snuggled close to him, making herself comfortable against his deep chest.

"I do," he said as he cradled her. "It would gall me if you should take any harm from me."

"You said that before," she reminded him, drowsiness coming over her. "In London."

"I meant it then and I mean it now," he murmured.

Several seconds went by before she spoke again; this time her voice was muzzy. "You couldn't . . . hurt me." She yawned once, then tucked her head into the curve of his arm.

"I will explain everything when you waken." He kissed her shining hair, and lay still so that she could sleep without his presence disturbing her.

Text of a letter from Paul Reighert to Baron Manfred Klemens von Wolgast.

Chez Noir, Berlin
September 16, 1910

My dear Baron;

I pray that what I have to report will mitigate your anger somewhat. My man in Amsterdam, Bernard, has found where Ragoczy is living in that city, and he reports to me that apparently the foreigner has recovered from the wound he received. Either the injury was not so severe as you were told or the man has remarkable powers of recuperation. I realize you do not agree with me, but I still say you should have chosen a more reliable instrument than von Nordlingen to deal with Ragoczy, no matter how eager he may have been. If you had let me find a marksman, he could have waited in the forest. I am also certain he would have got clean away, so you would not have to worry whether or not you might be implicated in Ragoczy's death. As things stand now, you have someone who knows of your complicity in the plan and Ragoczy is still alive; a very poor state of affairs, wouldn't you agree?

Bernard in Amsterdam has offered to find someone experienced and reliable to waylay Ragoczy and dispose of him in any of a number of ways that would suit your purposes. He has employed men in such endeavors in the past and is aware of the risks involved. If you would like, I will tell him that my employer will pay well to have Ragoczy put out of the way. He is more able to find someone who will not talk than anyone I know in Amsterdam, and you may rest assured that he will not return to you time and time again for payments for continued silence. The prices are high, but you will get value for your money, as you did not with von Nordlingen.

Bernard also reports that there is someone else watching Ragoczy. The man uses a German name but is clearly English, and it is Bernard's opinion that the man has come to Amsterdam to protect a woman calling herself Rowena Saxon. She is, according to Bernard, who learned it from the Englishman calling himself Angebot, the daughter of a very wealthy English nobleman who fancies herself an artist, and has come to Amsterdam to paint. Bernard discovered that Ragoczy has commissioned this Englishwoman to paint his portrait, and has thus far visited her studio three times. He has spoken to the housekeeper, who told him that the Englishwoman is indeed preparing a canvas for the portrait and has done a number of sketches in preparation. If Ragoczy has other purposes in visiting this artist, the housekeeper knows nothing of it, and the Englishman watching Ragoczy has said he is certain that such a woman as Miss Saxon would not involve herself in anything of a clandestine nature. It is Bernard's opinion that this so-called Angebot is a fool and a danger to his colleagues. If half of what he has reported about the man is true, I would have to agree with him. Bernard has also been told by Angebot (apparently in confidence) that a meeting is being set up between Ragoczy and certain key government men on behalf of King George, to take place in or near Liege, sometime late in October. It is Bernard's opinion that this may well be false information, being used to test him, but I think there may be some truth in it; given the many attempts Ragoczy has made to reach the English King, this would seem to be a means to accomplish that end. It would also explain why the Czar has not ordered him to leave Amsterdam. So long as he is, in effect, halfway between Berlin and London, he is well-situated to bring about the private dealings you believe it is his task to do. Bernard has made arrangements to follow him to Liege, when and if Ragoczy leaves Amsterdam for Belgium.

In any event, Bernard is planning to continue his surveillance on Ragoczy for another two weeks, at which time he will need to be paid if he is to keep on. The forty guilders a day he asks for may be high, but I think you will agree it is worth the price. His commission for finding someone to do away with Ragoczy is twenty percent of what you pay the assassin. Again, the price is high, but the results are well worth the money. It has long been my experience that Bernard is the most accomplished private spy in all of Holland, and I think you would be foolish to permit the few extra guilders to keep you from employing him.

While Ragoczy is sitting for his portrait, it would be possible for Bernard to get into his house. There is just one servant, the middle-aged valet who was with him in Berlin, and he should not be difficult to handle, if it comes to that. My own advice is to wait a while until we have exhausted other approaches to the man. If you authorize this venture, Bernard will probably be able to discover a great deal more about Ragoczy, which I know you wish to do. But Ragoczy is no fool, as you have already discovered. He might take it into his mind to retaliate for actions taken against him. He might also decide to leave Amsterdam if he believes that he is the target of your investigation, and that could create trouble of another sort. It is my recommendation that you continue to have Ragoczy watched but do nothing more until his activities warrant it.

In closing, let me reiterate one thing: your anger at what you call my failure to eliminate Ragoczy is uncalled-for. You were the one who insisted on using von Nordlingen. You thought such a man would create less suspicion than an experienced assassin. You may rail all you wish, it does not change the fact that your methods were ill considered and turned out to be ineffective. In future I urge you to keep in mind that you want distance between yourself and your agents, and that like it or not, I am still the most capable man for such things. If you think you can find better in Germany, I wish you luck. If you want to bring about the things you claim to want, you cannot find anyone better than I am. That is not a boast, dear Baron; it is a simple fact.

Awaiting your response,
Reighert

6

Four automobiles ahead in traffic, a lorry had collided with a streetcar, making it impossible for any vehicles to pass without running up onto the sidewalk. Dietbold turned around and signaled his helplessness to von Wolgast, who was hunched in the Italia's passenger compartment, scowling at the jumble of automobiles, carts, wagons, lorries, bicycles, and pedestrians, aware he would be late for his meeting with Persuic; the Croatian was expecting him at two, and that was minutes away.

It had been a most unsatisfactory day for the Baron: his meeting earlier with Nadezna had proved to be acrimonious, and he had ended by storming out of her house, swearing to end his dealings with her. Then he had had coffee with Reighert, and was forced to comply with the defrocked Jesuit's demands in regard to both agents and money. If Persuic did not have good news for him, he thought he might well leave Berlin and go to his factory until the end of the year. Then news had come from the nuns that his wife had taken a turn for the worse. He did not want any more trouble.

"Baron," said Dietbold apologetically. "There is nothing I can do. There is no way arou—" He made a futile gesture at the windscreen.

"Yes. That is apparent," said von Wolgast through the half-opened connecting window. "It is one of the things I like least about automobiles. Everyone is driving them, and no one has any respect any more. No wonder the Americans love them." He thought fondly of his coach, with his spectacular team of Oberlanders and his family arms on the door panel: no one would dare to hinder their progress through the streets. His Italia Palombella only told the world that he was rich.

"There are two policemen sorting it out," Dietbold said as he peered into the confusion ahead. "We should be underway again shortly."

"Good," von Wolgast grumbled. He made himself sit back against the pale leather cushions and wait with the air of one who is being inconvenienced; he considered what he would have to do if Persuic did not bring him the news he wanted. The possibility of another meeting with his banker made von Wolgast feel more resentful than ever; that he should have to explain his business to a glorified clerk verged on intolerable. It was time to put pressure on von Rosenwiese.

"Finally," said Dietbold as he put the Italia into gear and inched forward. "It will not be much longer, Baron."

Von Wolgast grunted to indicate he had heard.

It took more than five minutes to go two blocks, so that by the time the Palombella drew up at the Empress Elizabeth Hotel in Schillerstrasse, von Wolgast was seething with indignation. He let himself out of his automobile before Dietbold could set the brake and tend to that duty. "I will want you in an hour," he said. "If I am to be longer, I will send word to the front desk. Do not be late." With that he swung round on his heel and trod up the wide stairs to the lavish entrance to the hotel.

"Colonel Persuic is expecting you," said the receptionist, indicating the wide staircase at the rear of the lobby. "Room three-twenty-nine."

"Very good," said von Wolgast, and went up the stairs, in a hurry to reach his goal; he rehearsed his explanation with every step.

Vaclav Persuic was seated at the dining table in the parlor of his suite, finishing off a platter of Rebhuhn mit Trauben, the partridge placed neck-down so that its legs pointed straight up, in the traditional style; black and green grapes flanked the bird, with brussels sprouts, creamed onions, and potato dumplings accompanying it. As von Wolgast came in, he waved negligently and indicated the chair across from him.

Von Wolgast was in no mood to be received so cavalierly. He drew himself up and strode toward the table, full of purpose. "I assume you have news for me."

"Yes, Manfred, of course I do. I wouldn't have invited you here if I did not," said Persuic with an indulgent smile. "I started without you, as you can see. Sit down and have some of this excellent meal. I can't do justice to it myself." There was another place set, and von Wolgast took the seat grudgingly.

"What is it? I warn you, I am in no humor for games. The traffic coming here was at a standstill." It was all the excuse he was prepared to offer for his tardiness. Little as he wanted to admit it, the sight of the half-eaten partridge made him fiercely hungry and he could not make himself refuse it. He allowed Persuic to cut some of the meat for him, and to select the grapes and vegetables to augment it.

"A pity about the delay, but no harm done. We have much to discuss. This meeting is no game, Manfred, it is the most wonderful opportunity, one we have been waiting for," said Persuic, and as he handed the plate to von Wolgast, got down to business at once. "Events are moving more swiftly than any of us anticipated, and we are trying to prepare to make the most of them. At the moment, the signs are fortuitous. You are aware of the situation in Albania, are you not?"

"I do read the papers, Persuic. They are calling it a revolution: it is probably nothing more than a revolt," said von Wolgast as he picked up his fork and began spearing onions with it.

"You are probably right, but that shouldn't make any difference to you. Between the establishment of Montenegro as a kingdom and the upheaval in Albania, the time is coming when Croatia may achieve the independence we have sought for so long." It was clearly a rehearsed speech, and he delivered it very convincingly. "You have probably made plans in this regard."

"Sisak has sold my guns to the Albanians; I do not anticipate they will want to purchase more during this rest of this year. Sisak says they cannot afford any more. He has just left for the Union of South Africa to see what business he can create there." Von Wolgast was fairly certain that Persuic knew of Sisak's activities as well as he did. "If you have nothing more to tell me than that Croatia may decide to take some action against Austro-Hungary, then we have nothing to discuss; I do not deal in vagaries." He chewed vigorously, liking the food in spite of the occasion.

"It is not a distant prospect anymore, my friend," said Persuic. "Between the Serbs and the Bosnians, the Balkans are ready to erupt, and the instant they do, it will be our signal to act. We Croats have been biding our time." He sat forward, his well-cut features shining with purpose. "We will wait until Serbia and Bosnia have become embroiled again, as they will, and then, when Franz Josef has their insurrection to deal with, we will strike and claim our country as our own at last."

This was more promising than von Wolgast had assumed it would be. "And when do you expect this to happen."

"Three years, perhaps four at the most." He waved this aside. "That is not so long as it seems. Three years is hardly sufficient time for your company to manufacture the guns we want. We must prepare now, and that is why I have invited you here, to begin our arrangements for the materiel we will have ready. I have received authorization to purchase weapons from you, quite a few of them. We will have to arrange for indirect delivery, of course."

"Of course," von Wolgast seconded.

"You will be satisfied with the order, I am certain," Persuic said. "The delivery, perhaps less so."

"And why is that?" von Wolgast asked, watching his host narrowly.

"It is cumbersome, but the guns will have to go by ship to Trieste, and go overland from there." He saw the look of ire von Wolgast shot him, and went on smoothly. "We will pay for the shipping, naturally."

"You certainly will." Von Wolgast sliced off a morsel of partridge, impaled it on his fork and held it to his mouth. Before he ate, he observed, "You will be using ships of what registry?"

"Greek," said Persuic promptly. "It is all arranged. The authorities will not question such orders from Greece, will they?" He was clearly very pleased with these arrangements and made no secret of it. "In fact, I would guess that Kaiser Wilhelm would be delighted to know that the Greeks are preparing to throw off the last vestiges of Ottoman rule. What else would the government assume?"

"I don't know," said von Wolgast around a mouthful of partridge. "I am the one who will have to answer those questions, should any arise."

"Yes, we are aware of that; there are officials who will need to be placated," said Persuic. "And we are prepared to compensate you for any additional risks you may incur in this regard. Here"—he held out a bottle of dry Tokay—"have some of this. It is Hungarian, but it is very good."

"Yes, if you insist," said von Wolgast, extending his glass to be filled. "How much are you paying me, and what are you buying?"

"The draft is for thirty thousand marks. It will be delivered to you by messenger tomorrow morning, along with the specific purchases we intend to make. The draft will be dispatched as soon as my endorsement is received by the intermediary here in Berlin. You will find that the company giving you the draft is in Prague, one with an impeccable reputation. That is to throw any government inspectors off the track. The company in Prague is owned by a Croat with a Hungarian name. He is one of our main supporters, and he will be the agent to handle the financial arrangements." Persuic carved the last of the meat off the partridge and made a neat stack of it on the platter. "Whenever you are ready, help yourself."

"Danke," said von Wolgast, feeling more cordial now that he had been assured of thirty thousand marks. It was not a staggering sum and would not purchase large numbers of guns, but it was a respectable amount, sufficient to put his factory to work on whatever Persuic wanted. Once he had the draft deposited, he would feel vindicated: Krupp would be envious, and his father—were he still alive—would be proud. He selected a potato dumpling and cut it in half before eating it, his hunger less sharp than when he arrived.

"I have a written order for you. It is the first. We will undoubtedly order more in the next year." He spoke as if he were purchasing blankets instead of guns. "We will need to have delivery dates as soon as possible."

"Very good. I suppose the orders will come from Prague, as well? From the same account? Wouldn't that be best, if there is any official scrutiny?" He tasted the wine, finding it a bit too flowery for his taste but nothing so bad as to be undrinkable.

"Naturally. We want to make the whole transaction look as legitimate as possible." He leaned back and propped one leg on the table next to the platter. His glossy boot looked to be quite new, given the state of the sole.

"A sensible decision," said von Wolgast, and concentrated for a short while on his meal.

"We are not amateurs, Baron. This operation is the result of long planning." He popped a grape into his mouth.

"If you are willing to give me so sizeable an order, I must assume you are prepared in other ways as well." He ate a few bites more.

"We are military men; we know what must be done," Persuic said a bit stiffly.

"You may rely on my discretion," von Wolgast declared.

"If we could not, this conversation would not be taking place." Persuic poured more wine for himself and, having sipped it, remarked in a deliberately casual manner, "I suppose you have heard about the meeting in Liege."

"I have had a few reports," von Wolgast replied carefully as he sipped his wine, letting the partridge in his mouth modify the sweetness of the Tokay. Why, he wondered, did the Hungarians and their neighbors like such infernally sweet wines? Not that he liked the French ones any better, with their oak and flint flavors: no, give him good German wines, spicy and fragrant. He decided he had better pay attention to what Persuic was saying.

"—British officials will be staying at a private estate not far north of Liege." He looked smug at having this news and he rubbed his hand on the serviette before he picked up his wineglass once again.

"I did not think that had been settled," said von Wolgast, aware he had missed too much.

"It is all Ragoczy's doing, of course. He made the arrangements with the estate's owner—some kind of nobleman; I forget which—for the use of his villa. Ragoczy himself will stay elsewhere and will motor to the villa each day." Persuic grinned in unabashed triumph. "Your spies are behind the times, Baron, or so it appears."

Von Wolgast frowned. "Possibly."

"I had this information not two days since. It has been done quickly, and with greater secrecy than one would expect. Your friends in the

Chancellor's office may not yet have learned about it." His pretense at soothing had precisely the opposite effect, as he intended it should.

"My friends in government are not my only source of information," von Wolgast snapped, and immediately chastised himself inwardly for giving so much away.

"So I told my . . . associates. I informed them that you were not so naive as to rely entirely on your friends in high places." He took the bottle and poured more wine into von Wolgast's glass.

"No," von Wolgast said. "I do not. And the others I employ are cautious; they do not approach me directly." It was not quite the truth, but Persuic would believe it.

"Yes. I have assured the others that you cast a wide net." He ate another grape. "Your contacts in government cannot always be relied upon, can they? Kesselmann, for instance, is often watched by his superiors in Foreign Affairs; he must be prudent in how he reports to you. And it would not be wise to use von Nordlingen for a while—don't you agree?" Persuic was amusing himself now, taking delight in von Wolgast's discomfort. "His inquiries about Ragoczy might alert the authorities and cause them to have questions they have not pursued thus far."

"I had not planned to speak to von Nordlingen," said von Wolgast as if indifferent to the man. "But it would not be thought strange if he should inquire after Ragoczy, as a man inquires after another whom he has inadvertently injured."

"Inadvertently?" Persuic challenged. "That may well wash with the authorities in Bavaria, but you and I know better, don't we, Baron? And if I know, surely others guess." He propped his other leg atop the one on the table, his smile affable. "Not all Nadezna's lovers tell her things of importance, do they? Not all men babble state secrets to their mistresses. And she, herself, may not be as reliable as you would like. There must be others you can employ. Your contacts are not so limited that you have to limit yourself to one or two of them."

"I have ways of discovering what I need to know," he said, privately shocked that Persuic had learned so much about his clandestine dealings. Now he was more annoyed than ever at Reighert for not bringing him the information he needed before he ventured to this part of Berlin. He should have been better prepared. In retrospect, he realized he would have been wiser to see Reighert the night before, when he had called at Nadezna's house, claiming he had an urgent message.

"The *Berliner Morgenblatt?*" Persuic suggested, so mildly that von Wolgast longed to slap him.

"No." That evening he would send word to von Rosenwiese, and to

Reighert. He had let himself become lax out of pique, and that was a foolish mistake. He made himself continue to eat, although the food had lost its savor.

"You don't want to reveal them?" Persuic said in false concern. "Why not? I will not take advantage. From what I have observed, your spies are not nearly efficient enough. They would be of no use to me."

Stung, von Wolgast responded, "So you think; you do not know the whole of it, much as you think you might," and saw derision in Persuic's eyes. He mustered what dignity he could, and declared, "You may not have a very high opinion of those I employ for information, but you are impressed by those engineers who improve my guns. And guns, not rumors, are my business, Colonel."

"So they are," said Persuic, his mocking tone gone. "And in that, you are without peer."

"Which would you rather?" von Wolgast persisted. "That I have superior guns or more spies?"

Chastened, Persuic stared at the shining toes of his boots. "The guns," he admitted.

"I thought so," said von Wolgast, pleased that he had scored his point with the arrogant Croatian.

An awkward silence descended between them. Persuic was the first to break it; he swung his legs off the table and sat up straight in his chair. "I will want to inspect the guns you are making for us, to see they are coming along well enough. We do not want any delays. And we do not want quality sacrificed in the name of haste."

"My plant is not given to slacking," said von Wolgast, so confidently that Persuic was forced to concede the matter.

"Still, I must inspect our order as you progress on it," Persuic stated bluntly.

"I expect no less." He would demand additional payments with every inspection, and realized that Persuic was prepared for that. He finished the wine in his glass, and set it down. "Is there anything else we must deal with just now?"

Startled at this sudden conclusion to their meeting, Persuic was slow to get to his feet. "I don't think there is," he said, unwilling to relinquish his claim on von Wolgast quite yet. "I must prepare my statement for the factor of the Prague company."

"Yes. You must." He held out his hand to Persuic, pleased that his abrupt leave-taking had shaken the Colonel. "Thank you for the luncheon. I would remain a while longer, but I am invited to the Chancellor's reception tonight and I must excuse myself now, in order to be ready." Had Persuic been German he might have clicked his heels, but since he was a Croat in a Hungarian regiment, he disdained the courtesy. "I will expect the draft by noon tomorrow?"

"I will arrange it," said Persuic with less force than he wanted to show.

"Very good." He was about to turn, but added, "You will see to it that the order accompanies the draft, won't you?"

Persuic glowered. "Of course. You will have all you need to begin work."

Von Wolgast bowed slightly, then left without any further remarks. As he went down to the lobby, he thought over all he had learned, and decided that, all things considered, he had come out ahead of Persuic. The only information vexing him was what Persuic had told him about the meeting in Liege; that could mean trouble if it came to anything. He would have to speak to Reighert as soon as possible. Galling as it was, he thought he had best go around to the Chez Noir before returning to his house: it would be foolish to attend the reception without learning as much as he could about the meeting in advance.

Dietbold was surprised to be ordered to drive to the Chez Noir; usually von Wolgast only went there after dark. He put the Italia into gear and eased into the traffic, turning south at the next corner. Occasionally he glanced back into the passenger compartment and wondered what had happened in the Empress Elizabeth Hotel that made this trip so necessary.

Phoebus opened the door to von Wolgast's insistent knocking; he was dressed in a loose robe negligently tied over his naked body. "Oh. It's you, Baron," he said with exaggerated ennui. "I suppose you want to see Reighert."

"If you would summon him?" von Wolgast said as he stepped into the entry and closed the door himself.

"This way," said Phoebus with a smirk. "If you like, Aurore could entertain you when you are done with Reighert." He gestured languidly to the parlor, then sauntered away into the long corridor lined with closed doors.

Von Wolgast was roaming the room like a caged leopard by the time Reighert joined him. "You wanted to see me, Manfred?" said Reighert, dropping into a chair and pulling a cigarette case from his jacket pocket. "Why don't you sit down."

"What do you know about this Liege meeting?" von Wolgast demanded, ignoring the offer of a seat.

Reighert lit his cigarette and blew smoke toward the ceiling. "Why this sudden interest? You didn't seem to think it was important, last night."

"You didn't tell me enough to—" von Wolgast began.

"No; Schmidt escorted me out before I could, as I recall. You said I was not to be admitted again for a week." He tapped the ash from the end of his cigarette onto the carpet. "That will cost you, Manfred."

"We will settle that later," said von Wolgast. "Right now, I must know everything you have learned about the Liege meeting."

With a sigh of ill-use, Reighert began, "All right. There is a villa on an estate—"

"Near Liege which has been chosen as the site for the meeting. Yes, I am aware of that. And that Ragoczy is not staying at the villa, but at another location. What else should I know?"

"Um." Reighert pretended to puzzle it over. "Well, Sir Mansfield Cumming will attend."

"The head of the British Secret Service?" He had not supposed that Ragoczy could command the attention of so important a figure.

"Yes." Reighert relished the astonishment in von Wolgast's face. "Also Julian Sinclair-Howard, and the President of the Board of Trade. As I recall the man's named Churchill."

"Why the Board of Trade?" von Wolgast demanded.

"I would guess it has to do with the ways in which arms limitation could be implemented," said Reighert, doing his best to sound bored.

"All right: Cumming and Churchill and Sinclair-Howard. Anyone else?" The three British representatives were a strange cross section, thought von Wolgast.

"One of King George's personal staff, but I haven't been able to find out who it is. And someone from Asquith's office." He achieved a yawn.

"You do not seem to think that this is an important meeting," said von Wolgast critically.

Reighert gave von Wolgast a look filled with an emotion very like malice. "You were the one who did not want to hear about it, yesterday. Today, you have decided it is worth your attention. In my opinion, if this meeting succeeds, Ragoczy will be able to speak with the Kaiser directly, and whatever little cousinly agreement he is carrying will be signed, and none the wiser." He stretched his legs out and took a long drag on his cigarette.

"And you still think that his mission has to do with arms limitation." Von Wolgast made the statement a challenge.

"We have been over this before, Baron," said Reighert, his voice soft with fatigue. He went on as if reciting in class, his eyes set on the middle distance, the cigarette smoke curling around his head like a malign halo. "It is the only thing that makes any sense, in these times. The Czar could not get his own government to support one if he did not have the assurances of his cousins that Germany and England would do the same. My Russian contacts—such as they are—tell me that the Czar and his military are in disagreement about arms. Nicholas has said he wants to maintain peace for the sake of all Russian children. What else would be his purpose in sending a man like Ragoczy to arrange matters for him?"

"All right; all right," said von Wolgast testily. "I know it is the reasonable explanation. But I had hopes that George would not concern himself with European, let alone Russian, affairs. This suggests he may change his mind." Hearing himself speak his anxieties aloud, he realized how little he wanted any restrictions imposed upon him.

"He may still do as you wish," said Reighert. "There is no reason to assume that the conference will be anything more than a sparring match." He finished his cigarette and stubbed it out in a crystal ashtray. "What does Nadezna know about this?"

"I haven't been able to question her of late," von Wolgast evaded.

"But surely, given who she is, she must have been garnering tidbits for you. Most men cannot resist boasting to the women they intend to fuck." He shrugged. "Surely she knows how to take advantage of this weakness."

"Not nearly enough to suit my purposes," said von Wolgast, his irritation resurging. "I no longer trust her as I once did. She may be holding out information in the hope that she might be able to pry more money out of me."

"You're growing tired of her, as well," said Reighert, so cynically that von Wolgast stared at him. "She is no longer as famous as she was when she was dancing, and her school, while it has had some artistic success, is constantly teetering on the edge of collapse. Without Ragoczy she would be on the street. Without you, she would not be able to live as she has been living. Is she that good between the sheets?"

"She is better than you might think," said von Wolgast, straightening up to show pride.

"I hope so," said Reighert, crossing himself. "My opinion of her abilities beyond *plies* is not favorable. She does not know what is serious and what is trivial." He got to his feet. "Have you gained all you came for?"

"Not quite," said von Wolgast. "I must find out whom else in the Kaiser's government might champion my efforts. I would rather not have to threaten too many bureaucrats. They might start talking. Can you do this?"

"I think so," said Reighert, his eyes narrowing with thought. "There is a man. His name is Meyer. He used to be in the government himself, but left in disgrace. He still knows more about those men, and not only in Germany. He is expensive and cranky, but his information is beyond question the best to be had."

Von Wolgast's brow lowered. "Why have you not approached him before now, if he is as expert as you claim?"

"Because any inquiry I make will also be information for sale, and Meyer is no fool," said Reighert, continuing his explanation with a show of patience. "You are not the only man seeking what he sells. He has other . . . clients who would be interested in knowing what I wanted to know. In time, Meyer would be likely to connect you to me, and then you would be in an unenviable position." His smile was flat, without meaning. "If you do not want the intelligence available—"

"You will tell me what the man says before tomorrow night." Von Wolgast resisted the urge to slap Reighert. The insolence of the man was infuriating. He shoved his hands into his pockets.

"It will be expensive. Meyer will not say anything without money." Reighert folded his arms, waiting for von Wolgast to pay him.

Hating the prospect of spending anything beyond what he already had, von Wolgast capitulated. He pulled out a half-dozen banknotes and thrust them at Reighert. "There. That should be sufficient for half the secrets in all Europe. See that you spend them well, Reighert. I expect more than a few hints and whispers for so much."

Reighert did not bother to count the money; he slipped it into his trouser pocket, his face revealing nothing of his thoughts. "Tomorrow evening. Shall I call at your house, or do you want to come here?"

"Neither," said von Wolgast sharply. "We will meet at the kiosk at the entrance to the Tiergarten. No later than five. See you meet me. If you do not, I will have nothing more to do with you." It was an empty threat and both of them knew it.

"I will be there." He offered von Wolgast a sloppy salute. "You are going to the Chancellor's reception tonight, aren't you?"

"Yes," von Wolgast replied, his suspicions once again activated.

"While you are there, you are going to twist the knife in that fellow? The one who was the Bishop's lover?" He chuckled at von Wolgast's expression of shock. "Well, I wanted to remind you that he's skittish, and when he's frightened, he might say something you would not like."

"Are you telling me to leave him alone?" von Wolgast demanded.

"Nothing of the sort," Reighert replied at his most languid. "I merely suggest that you do not pressure him until he is ready to leave. That will keep him from speaking out of turn and it will give him something to . . . sleep on. If you accost him at the start of the reception, he may decide during the evening to complain about his ill-use, and that could result in questions you would prefer not to answer."

Nodding twice, von Wolgast considered this recommendation, his thoughts racing. "I take your meaning," he finally admitted.

"I thought you would." He ambled across the room and picked up an apple from the fruit dish. "Are we finished now? I have a few things I ought to do before Heloise opens her doors."

Much as he hated being dismissed, von Wolgast accepted this slight without complaint. "I trust you will have all the information I seek by the time we meet tomorrow."

"If Meyer has it, so will I," said Reighert with sudden staunchness of purpose.

"I depend upon it." Von Wolgast's intent matched Reighert's.

"Good afternoon, Baron," Reighert said.

By the time he reached his house, von Wolgast was sufficiently late to have little time to ruminate on what Reighert had told him. He summoned Schmidt as he came through the door and ordered him to find Malpass, his recently hired English valet. "Tell the devil I need to be in evening clothes in half an hour."

"Malpass is at your tailor's, Baron," Schmidt reminded him. "You told him to get your two new suits. He ought to be back shortly."

"He had better be, if he wants to continue in my employ." Von Wolgast had fired three valets in the last four years. He swung around to face his butler, needing to see someone jump at his orders. "I will need someone to help me dress. You will do until Malpass returns. I have to be ready shortly, and if my valet cannot assist me, then the task falls to you. If you argue," he went on with mendacious civility, "you may also find yourself without employment and without my recommendation."

Schmidt schooled his features to a total lack of expression as he followed von Wolgast up the stairs; he reminded himself that he ought to be inured by now to what the Baron required of him, but he could not shake off the feeling of being slighted by this arbitrary command.

"I will want the white waistcoat, and the swallowtail coat." Von Wolgast was stripping off his jacket, tossing it aside as he began to unbutton his waistcoat and the shirt beneath. "I must bathe quickly."

Schmidt had gathered up the jacket, and stood uncertainly in von

Wolgast's dressing room door. "Shall I draw one for you, sir?"

"Yes. And be quick about it." His waistcoat was cast aside; he shrugged out of his suspenders and began to unfasten his cufflinks. "Here," he went on, throwing them to Schmidt. "See you don't lose them. I'll want the onyx studs tonight, and the onyx-and-gold cufflinks." He paid no attention to Schmidt as he continued to undress; he left his garments strewn about, knowing they would be tended to by Schmidt or Malpass. "Get the bath going. I like the water warm."

Schmidt retreated across the hall to the bathroom, and checked the water heater standing behind the tub, to be certain its little gas flame was shining, and the thermometer registered sufficient heat. Satisfied that the water was hot enough, he put the plug in the drain and began to run the water, adding salts and the sponge as the level rose. Schmidt was just stepping back from the tub, von Wolgast's jacket still clutched in his arms, when he collided with the Baron as he pushed the door open.

"Clumsy oaf!" von Wolgast stormed. "Where are your wits, you turd?"

"I'm sorry, Baron," said Schmidt automatically, backing away from von Wolgast, and reaching behind him for the edge of the door. "I should have been more careful."

"That you should. Have my clothes ready in ten minutes. I will shave myself." This last was a great concession. He dropped his robe on the floor and prepared to enter the bath. "Well, man, get on with it!"

Schmidt hastened out of the bathroom, closing the door behind him before going back to von Wolgast's dressing room to set out the garments the Baron had demanded.

Von Wolgast was half-dressed by the time Malpass returned; he favored his valet with a fulminating glance that was not the least mollified by the two canvas cases Malpass carried over his arm. "You're late."

"The tailor kept me. There was something wrong in the hang of the trousers in the herringbone suit," Malpass said, his German strongly accented with English. "I made certain it was corrected."

This was a reasonable enough excuse, and ordinarily von Wolgast would not have minded his valet's taking the time to correct any flaw in his clothing, but this evening he needed to vent his spleen. "It was an idiotic thing to do."

"It was what you instructed me to do," said Malpass sensibly, which only served to make things worse.

"You knew I have to attend the Chancellor's reception tonight." He shoved Schmidt away from him. "Now you're here, you might as well do what you get paid for."

Schmidt and Malpass exchanged glances as the butler left the dressing room; the valet assumed his most soothing manner as he took over the task of making von Wolgast ready for the reception.

There was no fault to be found with von Wolgast's appearance when he arrived at the Chancellor's reception not quite an hour later; his formal attire was as elegant as any in the vast ballroom. Without seeming to, he took careful stock of those who had already arrived, then he stepped into the reception line, praticing an affable smile. He greeted Theobold von Bethmann-Hollweg with an effusiveness that bordered on sycophancy, thanking him for the magnificent evening before it had truly begun.

"May your thanks be well-founded," said the stuffy Chancellor, and gave his attention to Volger Kraftig, who was behind von Wolgast in line.

Satisfied that he had performed his social duties well enough, von Wolgast strolled off across the floor to where champagne was being poured for the guests; he took the tulip glass and lifted it in the general direction of the Chancellor before downing his first sip. Feeling restored, he exchanged a few words with the Italian Ambassador's Undersecretary, then went in search of more impressive company; he noticed the Austrian Ambassador in conversation with Lottelise, Graffin von Bingen, and set out to join them. He had not got far when he was intercepted by Leopold Oberstetten.

"Good evening, Baron," said the journalist affably. "Quite an occasion, isn't it?"

"Yes, it is," said von Wolgast as curtly as was acceptable; he tried to escape Oberstetten without success.

"We're hearing some promising things about your new guns, Baron," Oberstetten went on, linking arms with von Wolgast to keep him from getting away.

"That's very flattering." Von Wolgast spotted Egmont von Rosenwiese with his skinny, vapid wife in tow; he would have to deal with the Deputy Minister of Foreign Affairs later, as Reighert suggested.

"Not flattering at all. I am curious—all journalists are, you know—about your guns. If half what we hear of them is actually true, you stand to make a great deal of money from them."

"That will depend on many things," von Wolgast said, disliking the insinuating tone Oberstetten was taking with him. "Guns are not of much use during times of peace."

"How long can peace last with men like you and Krupp selling arms to everyone from Ukranians to Turks to Serbs? Don't you think your sales might be seen as provoking war? You give Generals new guns, they will want to try them out." He kept up his ruthless smile as he continued. "How do you reconcile your product with your hope of peace?"

"I have a business, Herr Oberstetten, as do you. What I do is not intended to bring about war, but if war comes, we must all be as ready as we can. I am of the opinion that having superior weapons ensures a continuing peace." He drank down the rest of his champagne. "Many Generals share my opinion, as you must know."

"But think, man," said Oberstetten, unwilling to release von Wolgast quite yet. "You have to consider the consequences of such weapons."

"Weapons are nothing more than objects. If men do not use them to kill, they are harmless as andirons." He finally succeeded in pulling his arm free of Oberstetten's grasp. "You journalists may not like rearmament, but you will have to admit that in times such as these, only an imprudent ruler would refuse to arm his country."

"Some journalists are calling for more guns," Oberstetten reminded him politely as he moved away from von Wolgast to corner other guests of the Chancellor.

A passing waiter refilled von Wolgast's glass, and a moment later, Euchary Apfelobstgarten appeared at his elbow. "Good evening, Baron," said the Undersecretary of the Office of Procurement.

"To you, as well, Apfelobstgarten," said von Wolgast; he was eager to be on good terms with this man, and with the Office of Procurement.

"Quite a crowd," said Apfelobstgarten. "I wouldn't have expected so many."

"It is an honor to be invited," said von Wolgast, downing half his champagne. "Anyone would make an effort to attend."

"No doubt," said Apfelobstgarten, his manner faultlessly polite. "I noticed we have had some dealing with you at the Office," he went on. "I have also been told you sell to nations other than Germany."

"In these times, men in my business must," said von Wolgast, being as direct as he could, for he did not want to have any misunderstanding with this man. "But it has never been my intention to put Germany at any disadvantage. In fact, I believe that so long as a German company supplies the arms, our enemies will think twice before they act, knowing how excellent our weapons are, and that once they attack us they can have no more, and we will continue to avail ourselves of our weapons." His mouth hurt from smiling.

"In fact, your sales are gestures of patriotism," said Apfelobstgarten. "I had not thought of it in that light."

"You can see the sense of it, can't you?" von Wolgast asked as if it were obvious to everyone. "What better way to ensure our security than by making the finest weapons in the world and then making sure the world knows it."

"I suppose I see your point," said Apfelobstgarten, bowing slightly to von Wolgast. "I don't know that it is as clear to some others."

This was not the reaction von Wolgast had been hoping for; he straightened himself and gave Apfelobstgarten his most candid look. "If the world were not as uncertain as it is these days, such precautions would not be necessary. But look at Austro-Hungary. Look at the Balkans. Gott im Himmel! We would be contemptible if we ignored the threat they represent."

Apfelobstgarten nodded and allowed himself to be called away by one of the Deputy Ministers, leaving von Wolgast to continue to prowl, so that by the end of the evening, he was satisfied that he had spoken to most of the men he had come to see, and that he had not encountered any outright opposition. He began his search for von Rosenwiese, and found him at last by the balcony door.

"Baron!" exclaimed von Rosenwiese as he caught sight of von Wolgast bearing down on him. "I . . . I noticed you earlier, but . . . I—"

"You have been trying to avoid me," said von Wolgast silkily. "I know that. But now it is time we had a word or two." He secured von Rosenwiese's elbow in a firm grip and guided him away from the small knots of remaining guests. "I need you to do a few things for me."

"What?" von Rosenwiese yelped softly, looking about apprehensively. "My wife is looking for me."

"Don't let her concern you just now," von Wolgast recommended. "Listen to what I tell you: I want the endorsement of the Ministry of Foreign Affairs for a shipment of guns to Greece. You are in a position to be certain that happens."

"I might be able to . . . move things along," said von Rosenwiese, his doubts making him stammer. "I don't have a great deal of authority, you know." It was a desperate attempt to dissuade von Wolgast and it failed.

"You do not have sufficient regard for your post, von Rosenwiese," von Wolgast admonished him. "You need only sign off on the forms and there will be no delays and no questions to answer. I think you would want to do this for me, von Rosenwiese, when you remember all I have learned about you."

Von Rosenwiese went pale. "You would use the letters?"

"If you force me to. I would rather not have to be compelled, of course, but that is out of my hands." He did his best to reassure his victim. "But so long as you are reasonable, I will be reasonable, too." He patted von Rosenwiese on the shoulder. "You and the Bishop have nothing to fear from me as long as I am able to ship my guns without hindrance."

With a numb gesture of consent, von Rosenwiese stumbled away, muttering disjointed phrases of leavetaking.

Von Wolgast watched him go with dawning triumph; he would not have any more trouble from von Rosenwiese, he was certain of it.

Text of a letter from Nadezna to Franchot Ragoczy.

Berlin
October 19, 1910

Franchot Ragoczy, Count Saint-Germain
Leonardostraat, #44
Amsterdam, Holland

My dear Count;
I do not mean to impose on your patronage of my school, but I fear I must do so. We have recently had an increase in expenses that have made it necessary for me to write to you in the hope that you will be able to extend your support a little further than you have done before. I am sorry that I must come to you, for I was convinced that we had secured a degree of sponsorship that would cover our additional expenses. Such has not turned out to be the case.

You have been more than generous, I am aware of it, and I am truly grateful for all your kindness and assistance in years past. You have rescued me from my own stupidity before, and it was my intention never to call upon you in that capacity again. Had I not misplaced my trust, I would not have ended up in this predicament, and would not have to impose upon you: I ask you for this help not so much for my benefit as for the benefit of my students. As you are aware, some of them are nearing readiness to begin careers of their own. If I am unable to continue with them it is possible that they will not have the opportunity they so richly deserve.

I apologize for having to ask you for this. I am most despondent that in my naïveté, I permitted myself to be deceived by one who claimed to wish to encourage me and my students. Now that I have realized how

much I have erred in my judgment, I hope you will not require my stu-
dents to pay the price for my lack of perception.

In supplication,
Nadezna

P.S. Von Wolgast has planned to go to his Austrian hunting-box for ten
days. I would be glad of your answer before he returns from his holi-
day; in that remote place, he will not know what I have done.

7

A swath of burnt sienna was the first paint on the canvas, covering over
the drawing beneath. "Are you certain you have to go away?" Rowena
asked as she glanced up from the charcoal lines to their subject, seated
about ten feet across the studio from her; wan October mizzle turned
the studio a soft, pale grey, with blurred edges to all shadows in contrast to the firm delineations of her brush.

"You know that I must; early tomorrow," Ragoczy replied, regret in
his voice. They were speaking English, although she occasionally practiced her French and Italian on him. "I will not be long. You will have
me sitting for you in fewer than ten days. I promise you." If he was unable to convince the British delegates that King George's support of the
Czar's agreement was essential in a week, additional time would make
no difference.

"And if someone should take a shot at you once again? What will you
do if they try to murder you? You could be at risk, continuing with the
mission." She kept her hand as steady as her eye, although it was an effort.

"You need not worry. Those of my blood are notoriously hard to kill,"
he said, doing his best to assuage her anxiety. "If anything untoward
should happen, Roger will inform you by telegram at once. I do not intend to delay my return."

"You had better not; you will not like how I paint if you do not come
back quickly. I might give you two heads, or something worse." She
daubed up some more of the paint and continued to apply it, her brush

moving as if she were still sketching him; the shape of his head was now haloed in dark paint.

"Ah, the revenge of artists; is there anything more dreadful," said Ragoczy in mock solemnity. "Like Michelangelo and the Pope's secretary."

"How do you mean?" she asked, most of her attention on her work.

Ragoczy knew her focus was on the painting, but answered her anyway. "The Pope had a secretary with whom Michelangelo did not get along—he was one of many; Michelangelo was sharp-tongued and did not suffer fools gladly—and Michelangelo wished to punish him for his interference, so he painted the secretary's face among those in the *Last Judgment* waiting to be judged. The secretary complained to the Pope, who ordered Michelangelo to remove the secretary's portrait from where it was. Michelangelo promptly painted the man's face among the damned; when the secretary complained of this greater indignity, Pope Paul III, Alexander Farnese, told his irate secretary that those damned to hell even the Pope cannot save."

She laughed, shaking her head. "Is that really true?"

"If it isn't, it ought to be," he answered, his dark eyes holding hers for an instant; he gave a single chuckle. "So far as I know, it is true." He remembered how caustic Michelangelo's wit was, and how prickly he could be; the story was typical of him.

"He was a very great artist," said Rowena, sighing. Her brush became still.

"He certainly thought so," said Ragoczy, aware that she was comparing her efforts to those of Michelangelo. "Not everyone agreed with him."

Her grin was like lightning, come and gone in an instant, but all the more dazzling for its brevity. "I suppose he had to have some appreciation of his talents, or he could not have done as much as he did. No one who painted as he did could have been modest about it, could he?" She went back to painting with enthusiasm.

"Not on the scale he worked," said Ragoczy, not meaning size alone, but theme as well. "Do you mind if I move my legs a bit?" He did not have to do this, but he had been sitting in the same position for more than twenty minutes; most models had to break their poses from time to time, and he should be no exception. In addition, he was cognizant of the many questions Rowena still had not asked him.

"Oh, yes." She stood back from the canvas, regarding it critically, seeing the finished work superimposed over these beginning strokes. "I would keep you in that chair for two hours at a time if you didn't remind me."

"It is tempting to try," he said lightly as he rose to his feet.

"You would be a solid knot if you did," she said, matching his tone as she put down her palette and walked over to him and into his arms, welcoming his gentle kiss, and answering it with a more emphatic one of her own.

"You will not finish the portrait until next summer at this rate," he teased her affectionately.

"Would that distress you?" she asked, deliberately provocative.

He was spared the necessity of answering by an energetic ringing of her bell far below. "Were you expecting anyone?" He was surprised at the interruption, and saw that she was upset by it. "Would you like me to answer it?"

"No. My housekeeper will tend to it. But I may have to go downstairs." She shook her head impatiently. "I hate having my concentration broken."

"Hence the kiss?" he asked, amused and ardent at once.

"That improves it; it reminds me of what I want to have in the portrait." As the front door opened, she listened to her housekeeper's barely audible inquiry.

"Let me in, I say. Stand aside," came the brusque command in response in English.

"Oh, damn the man. Why on earth is he—" whispered Rowena as she pulled her smock off; she gave Ragoczy an apologetic look. "It's Rupert."

"Where is she?" The voice below was loud. "Rowena Pearce-Manning!"

"I had better go deal with him," she said, resignation making her look weighted down; she sighed and hung her smock over the newel post at the top of the bannister. "I will be back in a few minutes."

"Would you like me to come with you?" Ragoczy offered, his dark eyes revealing his concern for her. He would be able to send Rupert away quite handily, but knew that Rowena would dislike him doing it.

"No; he would only want to make an issue of your presence, and would linger." She ducked her head and started down the stairs.

Ragoczy waited at the top of the flight, listening intently. Much as he wanted to attend to Rupert himself, he knew that Rowena would not forgive him for interfering in her life. She had made it unquestionably clear that she did not want him as anything more than her subject and lover; he was not permitted access to more than a very narrow part of her life. He sighed once, and remained where he was.

"What are you doing at my house?" Rowena demanded coolly as she faced her determined suitor.

"Do I need an invitation?" he countered; it was a foolish tactical error.

"Yes, you most certainly do. And I do not recall issuing one to you. You are not here through any wish of mine." She shoved past her housekeeper, giving the woman a brief smile to show her irritation was not directed on anyone but Rupert Bowen.

"For Heaven's sake, Rowena," he said, doing his best to be patient with her. "You cannot still want to remain here and paint, do you?"

"No, I don't," she announced, and went on, dashing any hope he might have had. She motioned to the housekeeper to leave them alone. "I want to go to Paris and Vienna and Rome. Where I will continue to paint." She tossed her head defiantly. "And neither you nor my father can stop me. Only my grand-father can do that, and I know he will not. Unlike the rest of you, he is proud of my painting." It would be wonderful to slam the door in his face, she thought, hanging onto the latch to keep from doing it. "No, you may not come in."

"I will not leave you," he told her.

"Yes, you will. Or must I notify the authorities and have you removed by force? I will do it, Rupert, do not think I won't. My housekeeper will carry word for me." She let him consider her words before she went on. "Rupert, understand me: we are not engaged. I am not going to marry you. Go home, Rupert."

"I can't do that," he said at his most indulgent. "You will not want to live this way for the rest of your life. You probably will not want to live this way for another year. I am not as feckless as you seem to think I am. I will not be persuaded by your odd starts; I know you will remember the values you learned as a child, and when you do, I will be willing to help you reconcile with your father and mother."

"How very, very good of you," said Rowena with heavy sarcasm, adding, "When that matters to me, I will attend to it myself. I am not incompetent."

"By then, your reputation may be beyond repair, if you continue to live in this highly irregular manner," he warned her, leaning hard against the door frame. "At least as long as I am near you, I can answer for your conduct. It should keep those who matter from thinking the worst." His earnestness served only to fuel her anger.

"If you don't mind, *I* will answer for my conduct. It is my conduct, after all, not yours. I am busy just now. If you will excuse me." She was getting ready to slam the door when Rupert made one last attempt.

"You cannot want to have it thought that you have lived an abandoned life." He was determined to convince her, and his face was set with constrained emotion.

"If you mean free when you say abandoned, I want nothing more. And nothing less." She leaned on the door with greater purpose. "Leave me alone, Rupert, do. If you have any regard for me whatsoever."

"But you cannot understand what you are doing—" he began, making ready to launch into another series of admonitions.

"We have discussed this before. There should be no reason to repeat myself, but apparently I must: I do know what I am doing. It is what I have said I was going to do since I was a child. I am not acting on caprice or with the intention of disgracing my family." She took a long breath. "Difficult as it may be for you to grasp, I am very happy, Rupert. I want to remain that way."

He shook his head. "Then at least take down the address of my hotel. I will be there for at least six weeks. If it is necessary, I will remain longer."

Rowena's eyes widened in dismay. "You can't," she said, and faltered in her determined efforts to close the door on him.

"I can, and I am going to," he vowed. "If you have no regard for your welfare, I do, and I intend to preserve your good name no matter what you do to ruin it."

"Rupert, please. Do not bedevil me any longer. Go back to England. Find yourself a wife who is the kind of woman you want and marry her, with my blessing." She stared at him, as if she could move him with the weight of her eyes.

"You know I can't do that," he chided her. "I have already found that woman."

"You certainly can, as soon as you realize I am not the woman you think I am. The sooner you do that, the better it will be for all of us. I am not going to marry you. How often must I tell you?" She gave the door an abrupt push, and had the satisfaction of seeing him stumble back a step. Her eyes hardened as he tried to regain his position. "I want you to stay away from me, Rupert."

"I will leave this house now, since you insist," he said, making an effort to recover his dignity. "But I am going to call again tomorrow, and every day thereafter, until you come to your senses."

"I wish you would not," she said, keeping her voice level and reasonable. "You will do nothing to advance your cause with me if you try to wear me down." Her temper flared again. "You will gain nothing by it but my disgust."

He started to protest. "Be grateful that I am not like most men, who would take you at your word and leave you to—"

She slammed the door, cutting off the last of his words. When she had thrown the bolt into place, she swung around to see her house-keeper standing in the shadow of the parlor door. "Do not admit that man. In fact, do not open the door to him," she ordered as she started for the stairs once more.

"I didn't realize what . . . " the woman said softly, her English over-laid with Dutch.

"My dear Yseut, do not fret. You had no way of knowing what sort of overbearing lout Mister Bowen can be." Rowena did her best to reas-sure the older woman as she paused on the second step. "I am aware that your duties require you to receive callers. In the case of that man, however, I am instructing you to refuse him entrance to the house, and to deny me to him whenever he is so inopportune as to call here."

"As you wish, Miss Saxon," said Yseut, looking relieved.

When Rowena reached her studio again, she glared at Ragoczy, her annoyance with Rupert increasing. "Did you hear? You must have done. How *dare* he? What is he *thinking* of, badgering me in this uncon-scionable way?"

"He thinks you are someone he wants you to be, not the person you are; you are right—that is what he is seeking," said Ragoczy as gently as he could; he did not move toward her, realizing she did not want com-forting but vindication.

"When have I ever given him the least reason to suppose I would change my mind and marry him?" she went on without truly hearing Ragoczy's words, her voice rising now that she could give free rein to her ire. "What have I done, ever, that made him think he could—" She flung her hands in the air to show her disgust.

"He does not know you, Rowena. And regrettably, he does not want to know you." Ragoczy saw her hesitate in her outrage; he kept on. "He knows his idea of you."

Ragoczy's words stopped her. She put her hand to her face, conster-nation in every lineament of her being. "Dear God. Yes. His idea." Her demeanor changed, becoming disheartened. "What if he's right? Is that all any of us ever know of one another—what we suppose the other is? What we hope the other is? What we want the other to be? Is that all we *can* know?"

"No, Rowena, it is not," he said, and something in the deep note of his voice caught her attention and held it. "I know you as you are. In my case, there can be no deception, even if you wished to deceive me."

She stared at him as if seeing him clearly for the first time. "You mean because of the blood?"

"In part; it is the core of you. The rest is found in what we have together." He chose his words cautiously. "It is what forges the link between us."

"Link?" She frowned, her hands locked fretfully. "I've told you before, I will not be held by you, Count, or by any man."

"The only one held by it," he reminded her with a look of such kindness that she wanted to flee from him, "as I've told you, is I myself. You will know the bond only if you become one of my blood."

"One of your blood. It sounds so . . . theatrical." She made a gesture to minimize offense. "That isn't going to happen, is it?"

"Not yet. When you have knowingly let me love you six times, then—" His smile was sad. "You will have to make arrangements to prevent changing, when you die. Unless you decide you want to live as—"

"As a vampire? No," she said, shaking her head. "And I will not be obligated. I know what you told me, but I will not hold you to it. You need not feel any bond or link or whatever else you wish to call it, with me."

"Too late," he said lightly. "The die was cast the first time I tasted your blood." He studied her. "I explained then. The damage is done."

"I wish I knew if I should believe you," she said, cocking her head as she began to put Rupert out of her mind. "It seems so . . . absurd, to have one taste of blood—"

"Which do you disbelieve? that I am bound to you because I truly know you, or that I am a vampire?" He spoke easily enough, but there was a flicker of apprehension in his steady, dark eyes.

She smiled a little. "I reckon I would be best served to doubt it all, but I cannot bring myself to do it. You are very convincing, but . . . " As she reached for her smock, she went on, "What sensible person would think that vampires roam the world today?"

"Seeking whom they would devour? Climbing headfirst down castle walls?" he suggested. "If that was truly our nature, we should not survive long." He watched her as she tugged her smock back on. "Do you want me to sit again?"

"Yes, if you would, please. I must take advantage of the light while I can." She had retrieved her brushes and now reached for her paints. "It changes so quickly."

Ragoczy knew it was not the light or her work that lent her urgency, but he complied without any contradiction, aware that she needed time to reassure herself that she had not escaped the fantasies of Rupert Bowen only to fall into a greater delusion provided by Ragoczy. He sat down and resumed the pose she had asked for, saying only, "Will this do?"

"Yes; thank you." All her attention was on her work once again, and she went at it with determination, as if the way in which she put oil paint on canvas would somehow convince the world of her dedication to her chosen profession.

"Would you like me to stay?" he asked when she finally released him from sitting; it was growing late and long, muted-purple shadows angled across the studio.

She moved into his arms and kissed him, then pulled back almost at once. "You must have things to get ready tonight."

"Roger attends to my packing," said Ragoczy quietly as he touched her face with the backs of his fingers. "But if you would rather be alone you have only to tell me."

It took Rowena a few moments to answer. "You'll think me past praying for, but I am afraid that Rupert has quite taken the—"

He took her hand in his. "I thought he might have bothered you."

Her laughter was brief and apologetic. "I didn't realize how much he had upset me." She looked at him. "You did, didn't you."

"Shall we say I sensed something of it?" His one-sided smile was kind, without any condescension or indulgence.

"From the blood?" Her curiosity was real; Ragoczy's intimacy intrigued and worried her, and never more than now.

"Among other things," he said, trying to reassure her.

"You aren't angry?" she asked him nervously.

He did not answer until she looked directly at him; then he spoke quietly and gently, his steady, compelling gaze never wavering. "I wish I could convince you that I want no accommodation from you, only that which is genuine. Anything else would serve no purpose.. There is no benefit for either of us if you decide you must sacrifice yourself to indulge me."

"But you will be gone for more than a week," she protested, as much for herself as for him.

Now his amusement was more apparent. "And you fear I will become a ravening beast, creating mayhem wherever I go? I am no Dracula, or Mister Hyde, for that matter." He welcomed her slightly guilty chuckle. "Perhaps I might have done so, if this were thirty-six hundred years ago. But it has been a very long time since I made such a . . . disastrous—"

She held up her hands in protest. "No. You could not do anything of the sort. Do not joke about it."

"Not now," he agreed somberly. "The provocation would have to be . . . extreme."

They parted twenty minutes later at the front door, Rowena glancing nervously out at the narrow street and the canal beyond. "To hell with Rupert Bowen. And I will *not* excuse my choice of words. I hate the thought of him watching me."

"Better him than some others," Ragoczy said, lifting her hand to kiss it. "I will be back shortly. We will be able to resume our sitting then."

"Yes." Her formality was made awkward with apprehension. "Send me word as soon as you return." She leaned forward and whispered to him quickly, "I want to kiss you and embrace you."

He released her hand, saying very quietly, "I would like that very much. But it might be wiser to wait until we may be private awhile. When I return."

"Rupert is out there," she said fatalistically. "You're right."

Inwardly he hoped that Rupert Bowen was the greatest of her worries, but he said nothing as he bowed formally to her, saying, "Until next week," and then made his way down her steps carefully, the nearness of the canal making him queasy; he dared not look down into it, for he had accepted long ago that his lack of reflection was more bothersome to him than to others. At least it was after sunset and dusk was wrapping Amsterdam in its darkening folds, the western sky fading upward from gauzy, mist-silver to mauve to purple. As Ragoczy made his way through the streets, he was aware of being watched and was fairly certain that it was not Rupert Bowen who shadowed him.

Roger was putting the last of Ragoczy's papers into a valise of black Florentine leather when the Count arrived back at his house in Leonardostraat. He indicated the two chests standing near the vestibule, one filled with clothing, the other with Ragoczy's native earth. "We are ready to leave at any time. I will summon the porter, if you like. The station has notified me that your private car has been positioned for the journey to Liege."

"Let us wait a short while for that; we have hours before we leave for the station. There is no need to reveal our plans," Ragoczy advised in Imperial Latin. "I had . . . company on my way back here." The sternness of his features belied his mild words.

"German?" Roger suggested in the same language.

"Possibly." He went on a trifle sardonically, "It wasn't that young fool who is trying to wear Rowena Saxon into being his wife."

"Is he here?" Roger asked in some surprise. "I wouldn't have thought he would take such a chance."

"He is. He presented himself at her house today, claiming to be attempting to save her reputation. He has appointed himself her savior." His smile was harsh and there was a shine in his eyes that boded ill for Oliver Rupert Dominic Bowen. "The man has got it into his head that all he need do is lecture her sufficiently and she will become the woman of his dreams." He chuckled. "Of his nightmares, should he succeed."

"Why his nightmares?" Roger wondered. He locked the valise and put it with the other luggage. "You are pleased enough with her, and she with you. Why should she be a nightmare for Bowen?"

"Because the person he wants Rowena Saxon to be is not the woman he has assumed she is. What he has decided about her is all he wishes to know of her. She is far more than he has thought she could be, and of another character than the one he has invented for her; he wants a biddable woman, and that is one of the last traits he will find in her." He walked over to the waiting chests and rested the tips of his fingers on one of them. "He thinks that Rowena Saxon does not know her own mind, or that she has no grasp of the consequences of her decision to be an artist."

"He has no understanding of her, if that is the case," said Roger bluntly. "I have small acquaintance of her, but I would not have made either of those assumptions."

"It is what he wants her to be: capricious and unaware," said Ragoczy slowly. "He has got his way in most things, and now he is attempting to do the same with her." He shook his head. "He may never accept that she is not painting as a ploy."

"What use would such a ploy be?" Roger shook his head in a show of dismay that only served to baffle Ragoczy as well.

"I cannot read the man's mind, not on that point, in any case; I must assume it is all part of his image of her. I was not encouraged to deal with him myself." He glanced toward the curtained windows. "Whoever is out there, I am fairly certain it is not Bowen."

"Then I take it we are still being watched," said Roger without any outward sign of distress; his faded-blue eyes flicked toward the window and back again.

"Yes. If only I knew who was doing this, I would feel much more"— his ironic smile vanished quickly—"sanguine than I do."

Roger indicated the two gas lamps burning in the front room. "Should I turn them down?"

"No. That would only imply we are aware of the watcher, and that would not be prudent, not just now." Ragoczy gave a slight shrug. "I am going to change clothes for our journey. Then I will spend a while in my laboratory. I have received some new material from P. T. Levene in America; I want to review his findings on nucleic acids. He is doing such remarkable work with blood."

"Your traveling suit is laid out in your apartment," said Roger, aware that Ragoczy was eager to look at the information from America. "I will speak to the staff. Do you still intend to leave at midnight?"

"Yes," Ragoczy said over his shoulder. "I will attract less attention, and anyone watching will be more conspicuous; and my strength will be at its greatest, although I hope I will have no need of it. Have the motor car ready at eleven."

"Do you wish to be early to the station?" Roger inquired, following him to the stairs.

"I wish to have time to inspect the train car thoroughly. While I do not anticipate anything dangerous, there may yet be problems we know nothing of; the car has only been locked, not guarded. There might have been all kinds of mischief done. I am in no mood for surprises." He shook his head once and went up the stairs. When he came down again it was nearly eleven and he was dressed for traveling, a neat, dark suit appropriate for the negotiations he would be attending when he reached Liege; his heavy coat over the rest was trimmed in curly black Astrakhan lamb, as was the Russian hat he had donned.

Roger also had changed to warmer clothing, his suit a conservative dark-pewter, his long, dark-brown coat of heavy Scottish wool double-caped. He signaled Ragoczy and nodded in the direction of the window. "Someone is across the street, in the shadow of the doorway."

"I was afraid of that. Well," he said with a gesture of philosophical resignation, "it will not be the first time we've been followed."

"No, it will not," Roger agreed, and went to fetch the handcart for carrying the chests.

"A nuisance," said Ragoczy as he lifted the heavier chest onto the handcart with ease. "But it would be unwise to put our watcher too much on the alert."

"He does not know how heavy these are," Roger pointed out as he moved to open the door.

"And I do not want him to start wondering about them, given their size," Ragoczy said, cocking his head in the direction of the window. "It might be difficult to explain how a man recovering from a bullet wound in the side can lift an earth-filled chest so soon after his injury." He glanced out into the street, making sure they would attract very little notice as they departed. "Very well. Let us leave, old friend."

They reached the railway station without incident; the inspection of the private car revealed nothing more dangerous than a small pile of cigarette ash near the door into the second chamber where Ragoczy's austere bed stood, covered in a spread of burgundy damask that matched the draperies on the windows.

"Very sloppy," Ragoczy remarked in Russian as he swept the ash away with a scuff of his thick-soled boot. "Either that, or they wanted me to know they had been in my private car. It all depends on the expertise of whomever was sent to see this." He unbuttoned his coat and slid out of it, hanging it on the brass rack near the door; his hat was put above the coat.

"It may have been a railroad employee," Roger said, also in Russian while supervising the placement of their luggage by two sleepy porters. "Someone who was curious about a private railway carriage; nothing more."

"I suppose it could be." He frowned as he considered that. "It is never easy to decide these things; I do not like wearing myself out with needless speculation."

"You will not learn by fretting," Roger reminded him as he saw the last of their luggage brought aboard and placed in the closet designed to hold it. He paid the porters and tipped them, following them to the door of the car, then removed his own coat and hung it beside Ragoczy's.

"No; you're right about that; all fretting will do is distract me, which is not what serves my purpose just now." He went to the simple couch set under the window and stood over it as if undecided. "I wonder who is on this train?" he mused as he stared out onto the ill-lit platform. Finally he raised his head. "Tell the stationmaster that we are ready to go."

"The train is getting into position now; so far as I can tell, we are not being observed," Roger said, looking out of the car from the door leading onto the platform. "We will be away on time."

"Excellent," said Ragoczy, and deliberately switched from Russian to French. "Then our followers are either aboard the train, or have lieutenants in Belgium." He shook his head once to dismiss the matter. "I am told an automobile will meet us, courtesy of Verviers; I am grateful he is willing to let us use his villa. It would not be prudent to stay with the others, although having to travel to the meeting daily is inconvenient; it is preferable to giving our opponents too many targets in the same place. The Czar is going to send Verviers a formal letter of appreciation for the loan of his villa." He sat down in the Turkish chair, stretching out his legs as the joints of the chair adjusted to him. "Verviers, at least, shares Nicholas' conviction—and mine—that war in Europe would not be containable, which would lead to catastrophe."

"Must it come to that?" Roger knew the answer but asked the question anyway; he had been with Ragoczy long enough to realize when the Count wanted to prepare himself for dealing with the opposition.

"If we cannot stop it, I fear it will. There are so many who are moving toward it, and their numbers are increasing. I hope I have gathered enough material to present an argument that will not be dismissed as alarmist." He began to sort through the papers in the envelope. "Although how anyone can look at these figures of arms sales and not be alarmed, I cannot imagine."

"You have done all that Nicholas could expect of you. He cannot fault your efforts." Roger closed the door to the platform and put the bolt in place, and saw the sardonic look in Ragoczy's face. "Very well: the Czar may demand more of you, but that is another issue. We are about to get underway." He held the grip by the door as the car lurched at the first contact with the rest of the train.

"I will stay up until dawn; then you can keep watch, if you will, although I am damned if I know what either of us is to watch for." Ragoczy reached out for his valise which Roger had placed near him. "That's the worst of it, not knowing who has been set to surveilling us, or why. If I could be certain about that, I would be better-prepared to negotiate." He tapped the thick envelope he had taken from the valise. "As it is, I have a great deal to do before we arrive."

Roger nodded and left Ragoczy to his work as the train pulled away from the station; in a short while Amsterdam lay behind them and they bowled along through rich fields and small, darkened villages. Across the flatlands of Holland the train sped on, heading south to the tumbled hills of Belgium. There was a single stop, near dawn, at Eindhoven, where two more cars were added to the train behind Ragoczy's private car. One carried mail coming from Germany and beyond, the other was a sleeping car, bound for Torino and Genova in Italy.

"It will take a while to uncouple all this in Liege," Ragoczy remarked to Roger, who had been wakened by the disruption brought about by adding on the extra cars.

"Does that trouble you?" asked Roger, inspecting himself in the mirror.

"It probably should, but since this car is going to remain on a siding at Liege, we will not have to stay with it while the maneuvering is going on. I am grateful for that." Ragoczy stood up and stretched.

"What automobile is Verviers sending, do you know?" Roger inquired.

"A pale-blue Hispano-Suisa, according to his telegram," said Ragoczy, steadying himself as the car rocked. "That should be the last of it."

"On to Belgium," said Roger, a slight pucker to his brow.

"Yes," Ragoczy said, understanding Roger's reservations. "On to Belgium—not Hainaut or Brabant, and not in the fourteenth century." He pronounced the names as they had been spoken almost seven hundred years ago.

Roger nodded, accepting the point being made. He waited while Ragoczy began to put his papers back into his valise. "Do you want to bathe, my master?"

"I don't think so, not in a moving train, thank you," Ragoczy said after a brief silence to consider. "I will do that when we reach the villa, where the floor will be steady, and we can slide a layer of my native earth under the tub. I will want to be fresh when I present myself at Chaudfontaine for the official start of these unofficial talks." He started toward his bedroom, accommodating the rocking movement of the train with the length and rhythm of his stride. "I confess I am not looking forward to seeing Julian Sinclair-Howard again. He is part of the pro-German faction in King George's government, the ones who want to leave Europe to the Kaiser and trust him to maintain order."

"Are you certain of that?" Roger asked.

"If the information Leopold Oberstetten provided me is reliable, then yes, I am certain." He shook his head once. "In this instance, I hope he is wrong." With that, he went into his bedroom and closed the door.

Jacques d'Ais, Vicomte de Verviers' pale-blue Hispano-Suisa was waiting at the cathedral-like train station in Liege. The uniformed chauffeur approached Ragoczy's private car as the train came to a halt, removing his cap in spite of the light rain that had begun an hour earlier. "I am here for le Comte de Saint-Germain," he said, a bit uncertainly as Roger stepped onto the platform.

"I am his manservant," Roger said, holding out his hand to the chauffeur. "I am Roger. My master will be with you directly."

The chauffeur could not conceal his pride as he said, "I have already driven Sir Mansfield Cumming, Mister Sinclair-Howard, and an impatient fellow named Churchill to Cascade-en-Foudre at Chaudfontaine." He put his cap back on; drops of moisture hung on his face and straight brown hair. "Two other men arrived from England yesterday morning; they say one is the assistant to the Prime Minister. I did not have the honor to drive them to the villa. You will be staying at Sainte-Amienne, as he requested. It is a trifle old-fashioned, and not as grand as Cascade-en-Foudre, but not uncomfortable There is a staff of three. Oil lamps, but the plumbing is fairly new, and the drive is graveled. It takes less than ten minutes to cover the distance between the two villas. There was a convent on the site of Sainte-Amienne, long ago." He offered this last information as if could make the place more acceptable.

"Hence the name. I am sure the Vicomte and my master arranged everything to their satisfaction," said Roger, coming down the last metal stair to the platform.

The chauffeur glanced back at the steps. "Do you need help with the luggage? Or an umbrella?"

"We may," said Roger calmly. "If you will summon a porter?"

"Oh, yes, of course." The chauffeur hurried off down the platform, one hand raised to summon assistance.

"What do you think?" Ragoczy was on the car behind Roger, his coat thrown negligently over his shoulders, heedless of the rain.

"Aside from the chauffeur, there is a vendor with newspapers at the far end of the platform and a dustman across the road," Roger reported.

"Whose hands are remarkably clean," Ragoczy agreed. "And who knows who may be in the station. With Cumming here, I would assume we are being watched by some of his men. If there are others, the British may discover them." He came down from the train and seemed disinterested in his surroundings, although his dark eyes made a single, comprehensive sweep of the place. "At least the old market square seems much the same," he observed to Roger in an under-voice.

"If you discount the automobiles, lorries, and bicycles; and the streetlights," Roger remarked, noticing the chauffeur returning with a porter tagging behind him. "There are two chests, two suitcases and a valise," he instructed the men; it was not expected that Ragoczy would address such menials directly. "We will wait for you in the motor car," he went on, handing coins to both men.

Ragoczy led the way to the Hispano-Suisa, his expression unreadable. As he climbed into the automobile, he said, "If all goes well, we may conclude our work quickly."

"You said you did not expect it to," Roger reminded him as he got into the front seat next to the chauffeur's.

Ragoczy nodded once, and looked out the window toward the southeast; he seemed a bit distracted. "Monbussy-sur-Marne is not far away."

"No," said Roger carefully.

Ragoczy laughed once, his tone remote and ironic at once. "You don't need to distress yourself, old friend. I miss Madelaine, but I know there is nothing to be done, now that she and I are of the same nature." He paused as he moved back squarely on the seat; his attitude changed, becoming brisker and a bit self-mocking. "With a memory as long as mine, nostalgia is a luxury I can ill-afford: it would be too overwhelming to indulge in it."

"So you've said," Roger told him, signaling him that the porter and chauffeur were coming.

"Um." He put his small hands together, staring down at them. "Let us get on with it. The sooner we begin, the sooner we will finish."

Roger recognized Ragoczy's overly pragmatic tone for what it was: a disguise for despair. "You may succeed," he reminded the Count.

"So I may," was the only response Ragoczy offered as the porter began to load the trunks into the boot of the Hispano-Suisa.

Text of a letter to Sidney Reilly in Berlin, sent in code using Key 11, from Sir Mansfield Cumming from Bruxelles, Belgium, October 23, 1910.

I would appear to be the only official at the meeting with Ragoczy who was convinced his work for Czar Nicholas is sincere and his fears well-founded. His reports on the escalating purchase of weapons as well as the capacities of the weapons was consistent with all we have learned from other sources. Sinclair-Howard led the opposition to Ragoczy, and succeeded at every turn in discounting everything Ragoczy offered to support his contention that without arms limitation, war would erupt before another five years have gone by. Even Churchill, who is no staunch advocate of peace for peace's sake, told me later that he thought Sinclair-Howard must be receiving largesse from the arms makers for so adamant an endorsement of their products. Why it should be that Sinclair-Howard dislikes Ragoczy so obdurately, I have not yet determined, but I am convinced that patriotism is not his only excuse for his aggressive determination to stop all Ragoczy proposed. The assumption held by the rest of His Majesty's representatives is that the Czar wants to be free to act against his own people without any European interference: if Nicholas limits his arms purchase and manufacture along with the rest, I do not comprehend how he is supposed to achieve this end.

So it looks as if we will have war, no matter what the Czar would like.

Our efforts at Liege were for naught but the excellent meals served at Cascade-en-Foudre. If your information is correct, Ragoczy is unlikely to be able to get Kaiser Wilhelm to endorse the Czar's plan, and since King George's advisers have set themselves against any such clandestine agreement with Czar Nicholas, the opportunity to contain the development and proliferation of arms has been lost. In the end, no one was willing to make concessions to benefit Nicholas until either Russia or Germany has done so, which is not apt to happen at this time. Your claims that Ragoczy has powerful opponents, which at first I thought were exaggerated, now seem reasonable. Sinclair-Howard claimed to have reliable reports from Berlin that cast serious doubts on Ragoczy's honor. But from what I was able to observe of his character, in concert with what you have told me, these claims would appear to be fallacious.

Your account of the hideous murder of Renfred Meyer and his mother was most distressing reading. I concur that such deliberate slaughter was intended to do more than silence the man. It is as obvious to me as to you that his death was a message to many using his services to abandon their activities or face a similar end. I am relieved to recall that you have more than one source of information in Berlin, and that your agents are not connected to Meyer but through their dealing with you. Assuming you have been as careful as you have been in the past, the others should be safe. Still, it might be wise to pay attention to the warning and take extra precautions. To that end, I am posting the man you call Eduard Angebot to Oslo, where I hope his loose tongue will not be as dangerous as it has been.

Incidentally, I share some of your impressions of Ragoczy. He is a very capable man, and more intelligent than one would expect of a man in his position. Undoubtedly well-educated, erudite, and cultured, but I had a glimpse of the strength of his character during our talks, and I am inclined to agree with you: for all his courtliness, he is a formidable presence, which we would do well to remember. At first I was dubious about his decision to stay at a villa away from Cascade-en-Foudre, but when it became clear that our negotiations were to be acrimonious, I revised my opinion of his tactics. I applaud your caution in observing him, and in your continuing duties, I recommend you become even more circumspect in regard to Count Saint-Germain. In the past I have not been much impressed by those men Nicholas charged with duties, but this Ragoczy is of another stripe entirely. For once, I am confident that Nicholas is well-served.

Remain in Berlin. I will authorize your continued expenses there, and whatever you need for your agents in Berlin, in Munich, in Amsterdam, and in Saint Petersburg. The funds are not limitless, but considering how much material Ragoczy presented us regarding arms, it would be folly to ignore what he has discovered, and it would be dangerous to be unaware of his activities. Use your own best judgment in regard to surveillance of the man, so long as you monitor his travels. I will expect your regular report in four days.

"C"

8

It was cold in Leopold Oberstetten's study; his fireplace put out a little warmth from the last of a smoldering log, but it was not enough to stave off the dank chill that accompanied the low-lying evening mist holding Berlin in its gelid embrace. Oberstetten himself compensated for the weather by wearing four layers of wool: a high-necked brown jersey under a dark-green woolen waistcoat beneath a heavy loden boiled-wool jacket, and topped by a vast, mahogany shawl; his trousers were rust-colored twill hunting breeches. He peered over his snifter at his visitor in the chair on the other side of the hearth, and shook his head in sympathy. "I hear the rumors, of course. Who does not? But I have not been able to trace them to their origin, and that bothers me. I have done what I can to mock them, but not enough, it would appear. You know more keenly than anyone, I am certain, that the rumors are continuing." He propped his elbow on the mantelpiece and did his best to look nonchalant.

Ragoczy, elegant in a black suit appropriate for an evening at the theatre, shrugged away this apology. "I didn't think you would do as much. Thank you."

"Yes." He looked down at his shoes in an effort at misdirection. "Rumors aside, I still say that—ah—accident of yours was not what it appeared to be. Incidentally, you seem recovered."

"I am mended. As to your doubts about the accident, you've indicated them before," Ragoczy said dryly. "The Bavarian authorities do not share your suspicions, which may be just as well."

Oberstetten looked peeved. "If you were German and not a

Carpathian exile, they might reassess their position." He did not get the reaction he was hoping for.

"So they might. And if someone were not blackening my reputation, there might be more diligence. There are many factors to consider, but the deliberate slandering of my name—" He lifted his gloved hands in resignation. "I know those things are all factors, but I suspect the rumors have done the most damage. Until I can track the calumny to its source, I will keep encountering barriers. After, who knows?"

"Barriers created by whom?" Oberstetten prodded, hoping to find an opening. "Are they the Czar's opponents or yours?"

"I have no way of knowing and guessing serves no purpose," Ragoczy said affably, his eyes serious.

"They tell me things did not go well with the English," Oberstetten speculated, changing the subject deliberately.

"The meeting could have had better results," Ragoczy conceded.

"And they say it was the English who balked at the proposition you presented—whatever it was." He leaned forward a little, listening closely. "The rumors are that you are authorized to negotiate a private peace with the European and English powers on the Czar's behalf. What else would it be, if not a private peace agreement?"

"With the exception of Cumming, I was not able to persuade them to support it, whatever my mission might be, so that is unimportant." Ragoczy gave a tiny shake to his head, the only acknowledgment of his inner consternation at his rout.

"It may interest you to know that Ludwig Kesselmann over at Foreign Affairs has been boasting that he convinced one of the English to stop all progress toward peace, to let Germany take the lead." He did his best not to look directly at Ragoczy, aware that such obvious interest might put him on the alert.

Ragoczy realized he was being pumped for information, and decided to give a little in order to learn as much as he could from Oberstetten. "One of them did appear to be against the proposal I presented from the first."

"According to Kesselmann, the man's name is Sinclair-Howard; I have ascertained that there was a Sinclair-Howard at your meeting," said Oberstetten, trying to shock a reaction out of his guest.

"Sinclair-Howard," Ragoczy said, unperturbed, "was not willing to support any terms enforcing peace, no."

"According to Kesselmann, Sinclair-Howard believes that the future of Europe is in German hands, and that England will thrive as long as the English make no move to interfere with German activities in Europe. You wonder how I verified this, don't you? I had a second report, from one of the servants at the Cascade-en-Foudre." He triumphed momentarily. "Yes," he declared emphatically. "I have discovered where the meeting took place. According to the servant, Sinclair-Howard had a second argument in opposition to any private peace agreements: apparently he persuaded the rest of his delegation that to enter into any agreements with Germany would fatally compromise the Entente Cordiale with France, and the rest agreed with him, with, as you remarked, the exception of Cumming. Or they said they did in order to have a reason to refuse any peace agreement with Russia and Germany. Kesselmann is taking credit for the whole thing, including Sinclair-Howard's high opinion of Germany." He had not intended to reveal so much, but he wanted to gain some confirmation from Ragoczy in regard to Sinclair-Howard's participation.

"Kesselmann may think he has influenced Sinclair-Howard if he wishes," Ragoczy allowed, his expression still cordial.

"What is your opinion?" Oberstetten asked bluntly.

"Since I have no knowledge of Kesselmann, I have none: Sinclair-Howard did not confide in me, although I will confirm that he did not like the terms of the agreement I put forth." He smiled slightly at the journalist. "Give it up, Leopold. I will not be badgered or trapped into reckless statements."

"As I can attest, and not from this evening alone; you were tight-lipped about being shot. And about your recovery. Not that I wish you ill, but at the time it appeared you would have difficulty staying alive; I am somewhat surprised to see you so . . . ah, hale now." Oberstetten said, hitching his shawl-swathed shoulder to show he did not begrudge Ragoczy his reticence.

"Appearances are deceiving," said Ragoczy, knowing better than to change the subject, for that would make Oberstetten more dogged than ever.

"My very point," said Oberstetten with the suggestion of a sigh. "The question is, who is deceiving, and why?" He got no answer, and continued, "I cannot help but congratulate Nicholas on having so honorable a deputy; I trust your mission deserves such uncompromising dedication, for it is most unusual to find an envoy who is willing to remain silent. Is it because you are an exile, I wonder, that makes you so reserved?" He paused long enough to take a deep breath. "I cannot, however, speak as highly of most of the representatives of the Czar I have encountered in the past."

"I have gathered something of that," said Ragoczy, willing to discuss what was common knowledge.

"What am I to do?" Oberstetten burst out. "You have given me nothing I can write about, Count."

"I know." Ragoczy smiled fleetingly again.

The last log in the fireplace broke in half, sending ashes into the air, and a few, dying sparks onto the hearth.

Oberstetten looked down, punctuating this with a sneeze. "I should have fresh tinder laid."

"You need not on my account," said Ragoczy, who was far more impervious to cold than to the rays of the sun; he dressed for the climate out of strategy, not necessity.

"Then I will on mine." He reached for a bell to summon a servant.

"Are there any other rumors you think I should know of?" Ragoczy asked as Oberstetten went to the door to pass on his orders for a new fire.

"Damn you, Count," said Oberstetten with genial annoyance, "I am the one who ought to be wringing information out of you, not you from me."

"Still," said Ragoczy, and waited.

"Oh, very well," said Oberstetten as he came back to the hearth. "I will tell you some of what is being whispered, although why I should, I cannot think." Having made his point, he went on, relishing this opportunity to display his vast knowledge of secrets. "I have been told that one of the arms dealers has paid a handsome bribe to a foreigner in order to have free access to the Balkan markets. The arms involved are not rifles but field guns and canon. It is said that the dealer has large orders from the Serbs and the Croats." He held up his hand. "I have no confirmation on this, of course, but it is persistent enough to have some basis in fact. I do know it is not Krupp who is selling the weapons, because they are huffy about the rumors."

"True or not, it is the sort of thing that would be suspected," Ragoczy said. "Who is the source of that rumor?"

"Probably Egmont von Rosenwiese, from what I have been able to glean," said Oberstetten, looking down at the hearth again. "I tried to find out from him, but he refused to see me, and has avoided me ever since. I take that to mean that he must know something of the matter."

"Ah, the suspicions of journalists," said Ragoczy, rising from his chair. "And you wonder why I tell you so little. Do you think that von Rosenwiese would see me if I called at his office?"

"I would doubt it, since he has not been willing to talk to me," said

Oberstetten with a shake of his head. "He will use the rumors about you as his excuse, of course. But I have it on excellent authority that he is seeing no one without an approved appointment. Those approvals are rare."

"Which provides you another confirmation that he has something to hide," Ragoczy ventured.

"Let us say that it gives me reason to suppose," Oberstetten remarked, his features schooled to innocence. "I am curious about a man in his position suddenly trying to vanish from the world, as he has done."

"And that, I assume, will keep you on the scent." He laid his hand on Oberstetten's shoulder. "I must thank you again for all you have done. I hope you will believe me when I tell you I regret I am not at liberty to tell you anything more of my duties here in Berlin. If I were, I would be glad to answer your questions." It was a half-truth, but sufficient to the occasion.

"I gather from this effusion that you are about to leave?" said Oberstetten. He held out his hand. "Let me thank you for calling on me. Little as you have told me, I am grateful for the opportunity to speak with you."

"Alas, I have other calls to make," said Ragoczy, starting toward the door.

"And you will not tell me on whom, will you?" he asked, continuing before Ragoczy could reply, "No, don't bother. I know you well enough, Count, to know that you will not reveal such things unless they are of no importance whatsoever; I have observed you for long enough to recognize the habit."

Ragoczy smiled as he stepped into the corridor. "In that case, I will tell you I am going first to call on Nadezna." He bowed slightly. "Thank you again, Leopold. I may not be able to tell you as much as you wish, but I appreciate what you have done for me."

Oberstetten waved him away, calling to his servant to let his guest out before laying the logs for his fire.

Berlin was sunk in twilight, the low-lying fog making the city appear to be floating in a calm white sea. Ragoczy made his way to his automobile, his vision unhampered by the dark or the thickening mist. He swung the ignition crank with more than his usual force; the Bianchi 20–30 rumbled into life. As Ragoczy got into the driver's seat, he noticed a weedy man on a bicycle emerging from an alley across the way. He sighed as he pulled into the street; he was still being watched.

Pflaume admitted Ragoczy promptly, saying as he did, "Welcome,

Count. It is a pleasure to see you again. You and Madame may be private. The rest of the staff is off tonight."

"Thank you," said Ragoczy, adding as an afterthought. "As long as you are on duty you might let me know if you see anyone watching this house."

"I will be taking my supper shortly. I will not be here." He managed to make this sound like a major occurrence.

"If you see anyone before then, make a note of it, if you will." He held out two coins and waited for Pflaume's nod and then inquired, "Is Nadezna—"

"She is expecting you. In her study." Pflaume indicated the stairs. "You know the way."

"Very good," said Ragoczy as he handed over his coat. "I have no idea how long I shall be. I will let myself out." He started up the stairs, noticing as he went that the porcelain figurines of dancers were no longer on the trestle table under the mirror. His brow drew down as he considered what this might mean as he continued on to Nadezna's study door; if she were selling possessions, she must be far more desperate than her letter had revealed.

"Good evening, Count," Nadezna said at her most gracious, rising from her desk to greet him, her hand extended for him to kiss. She was in a splendid, mauve-lace-festooned wrapper in ecru satin, her dark hair done up in an artless knot on her head, as if she had not expected any caller this evening; the lamplight was low enough to make her skin rosy.

Ragoczy kissed her hand obediently. "Good evening, Madame. I must apologize for taking so long to answer your summons, but circumstances intruded." He waited until she sat down again to choose a chair across from her. "I gather you are having trouble. That is what your letter gave me to understand."

She managed a modest smile. "Yes. I . . . I have been foolish." She looked directly at him. "I realize I should not have permitted myself to be deceived, but I did not realize how great the villainy was of those I trusted."

"This sounds quite dreadful," said Ragoczy, his tone carefully neutral.

"It is," said Nadezna, her lovely face taking on a tragic cast, as if she were in the last act of *Swan Lake*. "I don't know how to explain . . . it came about so . . . I should not have let myself become caught up in this, but . . . I do not know whom else I can turn to, if not to you." She made a gesture with her arm that was exquisite. "I let myself be lulled into a sense of ease that was folly." She paused to give him an opportunity to speak. When Ragoczy said nothing, she went on. "If I had only put myself at risk, I would not be distraught. But I let my school become a part of the matter, and that has led to this . . . embarrassment. In order for me to rid myself of the . . . complications which have arisen, I would have to sacrifice my school. It is not truly mine to sacrifice, of course. It belongs to the students, and you are its patron." She hesitated, finding his penetrating gaze unnerving. "I would not mind bearing the burden myself, if I were in any position to do so, but as I am not, I had to turn to you."

"I see," he said, and indicated for her to go on, revealing nothing of his thoughts.

"Yes. Yes. It is very difficult for me to have to come to you this way, as much because I am ashamed of my own credulity as because of my . . . financial blunders. You see." She put her elbow on the desk and propped her chin in her hand, head angled becomingly. "You see, Count, I wanted so much more for my students, that I allowed myself to be persuaded that . . . certain—well, I cannot call them gentlemen—men would help me to expand my school, bringing more students and more performances than I have been able to offer before now. I . . . I wanted this so much that I let them commit a portion of my money to their project, with the guarantee that I would have a significant profit in fairly short order."

"This should end your trouble for a few months. If you still have difficulties, we can discuss them then." Ragoczy withdrew a roll of banknotes still secured with a bank collar from his inner breast pocket and handed them to her. "By the way, Nadezna: how much of that tale do you expect me to believe?"

She froze, her hand on the money. "What do you mean?"

"I mean that while I have no doubt that you are short of funds, and that because of it your school is suffering, I am not convinced that you were compromised in quite the way you describe it." He closed her fingers around the bills. "Don't worry. I am not asking you to tell me what really happened. That is your private life, and I have no part in it; your school is what concerns me, and I will do my utmost to help you to maintain it and its quality. But I will not continue to support your caprices if your students have to pay the price." He regarded her amiably. "You like living well. Who am I to blame you? I like living well myself. However, if you wish to continue in this style, you cannot continue to use the school to support your extravagances. I don't mind paying for better facilities, or for more rehearsals, or for more performances. I do mind paying for your soirees."

"Soirees?" she echoed, her cheeks flushing as she put the money into her capacious sleeve, taking care to refasten the button at the wrist. "What are you talking about?"

"I am sure you know: those elegant private parties you have here for the benefit of your influential friends. You have some of your former dancers here, women who are willing to entertain the men you invite. The gatherings where you hear the rumors about me that distress you so. The ones you began four years ago." His affability was now colored with sardonic amusement. "You are not the only one to hear rumors."

"You are despicable!" she cried before she could check her impulse. "How can you make such accusations?" She half-rose from her chair, her confusion abandoned. "They are *lies*, all lies!"

"Do you deny that you have such gatherings?" he challenged. "I have spoken to several men who tell me they have attended your parties. I am told by your students that they are occasionally asked to attend them. Are they lying?"

"Those who say you have brothels for children are lying," she reminded him sharply.

"And men lie about women all the time. Yes, I am aware of that." He watched her bring her temper under control. "If that were the only source of information I have, I would extend you the benefit of the doubt; men desire lovely women, and you are lovely. Even the students might be jealous. But Aasa Bjorngard has confirmed many of the stories. Are you saying that your assistant is lying, too?"

"She spoke against me? Aasa?" Nadezna's thoughts raced furiously. "She must be more ambitious than I thought, wanting my school for herself."

Ragoczy sighed. "Nadezna, use a little wisdom." He had not moved from his chair, but he slid it toward her desk. "I have no argument with you regarding your soirees. That is your business, not mine. But I can and will protect your school. If that is not acceptable to you, tell me now, so that formal arrangements may be made to preserve the school. I do not want you jeopardizing it again."

"Protecting your investment?" she asked him scornfully.

"Of course." He leaned back, his manner still cordial, unmoved by her display of pique. "You may not believe me just at present, but I admire your work as a teacher and a choreographer. I think you have real ability in both capacities. It would be a shame to lose your talents."

"So you say." She tossed her head as she once again took her seat, her eyes bright with fury.

"And I have said all along," he reminded her without a trace of rancor. "I understand why you are not willing to help me in regard to the rumors circulating about me. You do not want it said that you report on what is said by your guests, particularly those who are known to be powerful men." He held out his hand to her. "Nadezna, let us agree that my support is for your school and nothing more."

"Or you will make claims against me in court?" she demanded, unrelenting. "Why should you not? It is your right."

"No, I will not make claims against you in court," he said wearily.

"Then what? If you speak out against me, you will not be believed, not after what is being said of you." Her defiance made her voice shrill. "No one will listen to you, not in court, not anywhere!"

"I would not do that, Nadezna," he said, her venality making him feel very ancient and tired. "I would merely take steps to separate your school from your private life, so that you would have to answer to more than two retired dancers and my banker. I do not want to hamper you with directors of your school, but if you continue to squander your money, I will."

"I do not squander," she said, becoming haughty. "I . . . I am ensuring I will not be destitute in my old age." She moved in her chair and felt the roll of banknotes he had given her rub against her arm.

Ragoczy smiled ironically. "You cannot blackmail them all, Nadezna. Some of them will turn on you, oh, perhaps not this year or next, but in time they will, and you will face worse than poverty."

"Because you will help them." She flung the accusation as if striking his face with a glove. "Because you will encourage them to ruin me."

"No."

This calm denial silenced her. She tried another tack. "I am afraid, Count. The men who come here frighten me."

"So you have said before," he said, watching her. "I find it curious you would continue to entertain these men, if they distress you as much as you claim."

"I . . . I . . . dare not refuse . . . to . . . " She made sure Ragoczy saw the tear on her cheek. "They are very powerful men, and I am helpless to stop them. They demand I obey them. How can I refuse?"

"In other words, you, not they, are being blackmailed. I had not realized you were so much in their thrall." He straightened up and rose from the chair, his fine brows drawn together thoughtfully. "All the more reason to appoint directors for you, so you will not be as easily manipulated by the . . . sponsors you are afraid to disoblige. You will not have to make the decision for yourself, or to expose yourself to trouble. And you would not have to surrender so much to their demands, those gallants who have imposed on you." He studied her face, adding, "At least the fear is genuine."

"What do you mean?" she demanded, her pathos forgotten.

"I mean that you are a far better dancer than you are an actress," said Ragoczy, kindness taking the worst sting out of his words. "I will meet with my man-of-business and make arrangements to see your school is protected. And your old age, as well." This last was offered with a quick smile. "Shall we say a pension, to be paid when you retire from the school, to be continued until your death? I will set the amount in relation to the cost of certain specific items, such as food and woolen clothing, for money has a way of changing its worth over time."

"And you? Will this generosity extend beyond your demise?" She wanted to slap him for his concern.

His smile disconcerted her. "It is not my old age that is worrisome. Do not worry; I will order the thing to your liking. If you wish to have a place among the directors, I will provide for that as well." He bowed to her. "I will not stay to vex you, Nadezna. I have other calls to make."

She blinked in confusion, aware that things had not gone as she had anticipated; she longed to humble him, as she had been humbled. "Couldn't we make another arrangement?" she suggested breathlessly. "A more private arrangement?" She let the flounce on the neckline of her wrapper drop a little.

"No, Nadezna," he answered, his eyes stern and gentle at once. "It would be unwise: believe this."

"How do you know if you will not try?" she prompted, her gesture to him enticing, languishing, and artful.

He shook his head. "No. I prefer not to bargain in bed."

"What are you saying?" she said, her languor gone. "Are you calling me a whore?"

"No, my dear," he replied. "I am trying very hard *not* to. You are the one who has suggested we substitute flesh for business contracts." He bowed again, as an indication he did not intend to insult her. "Come, Nadezna. You knew from the first that our dealings would be about your school, and nothing more. You have been willing to accept such terms from the first. As I recall, you welcomed our formal agreement because it provided you would have the autonomy you said you wanted. And now this. It is not wise of you to change our contract. If I have learned nothing else in my life, I have realized that it is a mistake to conduct commerce and strive for intimacy at the same time: the two are antithetical."

Her mouth was square with outrage. "Is it because you do keep children? Is that what you are hiding? If a woman does not move you, then what does? Are all those stories completely wrong?"

The softness went from his voice, although he spoke no louder than before. "You do not want me for an enemy, Nadezna." He saw he had her full attention. "I will not tolerate threats."

She swallowed hard. "But—"

"If you want me to continue to sponsor your school, you will say nothing more. Is that clear? Not now about anything, and never again about those vile insinuations." He waited until she nodded. "Very good. I will make the arrangements I offered you. Do not stare," he went on as she watched him in amazement. "Whatever my opinion of you may be, I keep my word, and I told you, eight years ago, that I would support your school." He opened the door. "You will be notified when your directors have been selected. I think it would be better if we do not meet again."

The events of the past few minutes had moved too fast for Nadezna. She remained in her seat, her face empty of all emotion, as Ragoczy closed the door. Hearing him go, she had the urge to rise and slam the door in a display of temperament that would restore his opinion of her. But she could not bring herself to move; it was too galling to feel the money in her sleeve. She was annoyed now that she had sent Charlotte Milch away for the night, in the hope that she and Ragoczy might want more privacy than her maid provided. Pflaume would not listen to her tirades; she would not reveal so much to him, in any case. She grabbed a crystal rose from its place on her desk and hurled it at the fireplace, smiling wolfishly as it shattered. She reached for her bell to summon Pflaume, then remembered he was at supper and would not come back from his bierstube for at least an hour. She rose from her chair and began to pace the room, reviewing in her thoughts all that had passed between her and Ragoczy. The more she thought, the more irate she became. Only his assurance that he would continue to support the school kept her from writing a letter to the authorities denouncing him.

A short while later she left her study and went up to her bedroom, cursing Charlotte for being gone. It was no difficult matter to draw a bath, and she decided to do just that. She was always calmer after a long, hot bath.

The bathtub was long and stood on clawed feet, with shiny brass fixtures at the straight end. For Nadezna, it was a symbol of her achievement in the world that all her fine clothes and adoring followers could not equal: all through her childhood she had bathed in an old flour barrel and listened to her mother complain about the decadence of rich people, who weakened themselves by lying in hot water. She added jasmine-scented salts to the water and slid out of her wrapper, leaving it on the floor; Charlotte would take care of it in the morning: the bank-notes Ragoczy had given her lay discarded along with the wrapper. A large sea-sponge rested above the soap, and she grabbed it as she got into the tub, testing the water with her feet and adjusting the spigots to a warmer temperature. Satisfied, she lay back, working the spigots with her feet until the tub was full. The hot water wrapped around her, the air misty with fragrant steam. She closed her eyes and let her senses drift. No Ragoczy, no von Wolgast, no school, just the warm, sensuous caress of the water and the heady smell of flowers.

It was a while later that she heard footsteps in the hall—Pflaume must have returned from supper early, she decided, and was about to call out to him when she heard the door to the bathroom open. She started to sit up, reaching for a towel to cover herself, and wondering why Pflaume had entered her bathroom when she heard a voice above her.

"There you are, Nadezna," said Klemens Manfred von Wolgast as he came up to her, signaling the man behind him to approach. "I realize we are not expected."

Nadezna held the towel more tightly as it began to get wet. "Baron. I hardly know what to say. Pflaume will attend to you—"

"Truly," he purred. "Let me advise you not to lie."

"He will come if I scream," Nadezna said with as much conviction as she could summon.

Reighert laughed, and closed the door, putting the lock in place. "Your servant . . . the one who guards your door? he is still drinking. Unless he has fallen asleep from his drink."

"What do you mean?" Nadezna shrank back as much as the tub would allow, her back pressed against the porcelain surface as if she wanted it to give under her weight.

"I know your schedule, my dear," said von Wolgast. "You are not as secretive as you would like to think. On Tuesdays you are alone at night. This is Tuesday." He folded his arms. "And we have a few things we must settle."

"Get out of my house!" Nadezna ordered sharply. She could not summon the strength to get out of the bath; her bones seemed made of the same material as her sponge; she could get no purchase on the porcelain. "This is not amusing, Baron. Leave. I will forget the intru-sion. But you must leave at once. You and your . . . companion."

"Poor Nadezna," said Reighert in snide sympathy. "You don't like imposition when it is directed at you, but you are willing to impose on others."

"I . . . " She managed to get her legs under her; she reached for the edge of the tub. "You are offending me. The both of you."

"Tit for tat," said von Wolgast with terrible satisfaction as he reached out and slid her hands back. "You have been offending me ever since you refused to see Sisak last month. He is blaming me for your rudeness."

She tried to brazen it out. "The man is a pig. He delights in humiliating me."

"For what he pays, he ought to be allowed to cover you with dung if he wants to," said von Wolgast, no trace of sympathy in his eyes.

At that instant, Nadezna knew beyond all doubt that von Wolgast and the man with him had come to kill her. She strove to climb out of the tub, her body fired by dread. She had swung one leg out of the tub and was levering herself upright when she felt von Wolgast's hand close around her wrist and pull her back again into the tub. Her head knocked on the porcelain and her vision spangled as the pain ricochetted through her.

"Ready?" Reighert asked, reaching under his shapeless coat.

"She's strong," von Wolgast warned as Nadezna summoned up all the resistance she could, kicking and trying to flail her pinioned arms. "I don't know how long I can hold her."

When Nadezna saw the knife in Reighert's hand, she began to scream, only to be shoved under water. She broke the surface coughing, her throat burning.

"Be quick," von Wolgast ordered, his cheeks flushed with effort and excitement.

"No!" Nadezna gasped, one hand reaching out to stop what was coming. It was impossible that the knife was moving down on her, that the weight that she felt across her belly was the cut of the knife. The knife came again and again. The pain hit her a moment later, and took her breath away.

Reighert continued to hack at her torso, from breasts to pubis, turning her flesh to mangled meat, until the bathwater was a murky red, the towel she had clutched was shredded, and the smell of copper and feces completely overpowered the jasmine.

Von Wolgast released his hold on her arm and stepped back. As he looked down at the front of his suit he saw for the first time he was wet, and that the stains were bloody. He looked down at Nadezna's body, her beauty ruined, her grace destroyed. "Well."

Reighert's eyes were glazed. "Do you want to leave her here?" he asked in a strained voice.

"It would be best. If we move her, we might . . . " He gestured to show that they might have to wrap her up.

"Then we shouldn't wait any longer," Reighert warned, using a wash-cloth to blot his hands and face. "It's getting late. If Ragoczy has reached his next appointment, he will be able to account for his time, and that—"

"Will not suit our purpose. I agree." Von Wolgast looked around the bathroom, desperate now for something to dry his clothes. "Hand me that towel, will you?"

"This one?" Reighert inquired unpleasantly, indicating the scraps floating in the bath.

"No, you lunatic," snapped von Wolgast. "One of the clean ones." He pointed to the rack beside the sink.

As Reighert handed over the towel, he glanced down at the roll of banknotes lying with Nadezna's wrapper. "There's a lot of money here. It's a shame to waste it."

"It will not be wasted. The sleeve on it will identify the bank, and the bank will identify the person who received it." There was a gloating light in his eyes now.

"You are assuming she had it from Ragoczy," said Reighert, his statement filled with doubt.

"Who else would give her so much money? Her other callers earlier, according to your associate, were dancers; Pflaume will vouch for that. Why would they give her a roll of banknotes, if they had them to give?" Von Wolgast finished his rudimentary cleaning up and tossed the towel aside. "This way, they will know it is not a robbery. We would not want the police looking in the wrong place for the culprit." He bent over the bathtub again, as if held by arcane spells. "You wouldn't think it would take so little to change her from a desirable, vibrant woman to this, would you?"

"You make guns. They do worse and in less time," Reighert reminded him as he slipped the knife back into the hidden pocket in his jacket.

Von Wolgast gave a bark of laughter. "You're right, of course." As he started to the door, he slipped on the wet tile floor and dropped heavily to his knee, cursing as he went down. "Stupid!" he accused himself.

Reighert helped him back to his feet. "Be careful, Baron. We have to get out of here without being noticed, which we shall be if I have to carry you out." His amusement was angry, for von Wolgast clearly weighed half again as much as the former Jesuit did.

"Right you are," said von Wolgast, limping noticeably as he went out into the hall. "It might be best if you fetch the automobile and bring it here. I don't think I can move very quickly."

Shooting von Wolgast a look of disgust, Reighert said, "If you like."

"It would be sensible," said von Wolgast in a display of petulance that evoked a sour smile from Reighert. "I can manage my way down the stairs, if I take my time." The prospect of two flights made him cringe.

"We do not have much time," said Reighert, the elation of a few minutes ago giving way to growing apprehension. He faltered, then made up his mind. "All right. I will get the Benz. And you had better be on the street when I return; I will not come looking for you."

"Fine," said von Wolgast between his teeth; his knee was throbbing and he was certain he could feel it swell.

Reighert patted his pockets nervously, and drew out his cigarette case, his hand shaking slightly as he pulled one from the container and used a match to light it. "Get downstairs, that's all I can say." He coughed once, then hurried away.

By the time von Wolgast had made it to the front door, Reighert was pacing around his idling Benz, his gestures made abrupt by his nerves. He opened the door for the Baron, then climbed into the automobile and put it into gear.

Neither man noticed the fellow in the overcoat with deep-set eyes who stepped out of the shadows across the way, watching them go; Sidney Reilly glanced at his watch and entered the time of their departure—as he had their arrival—in his notebook using his private code.

Text of a letter from Horace Saxon in San Francisco to his granddaughter Rowena Saxon in Amsterdam.

San Francisco, California, USA
November 9, 1910

Rowena Saxon
c/o Maarten and van der Gelder
Willemstraat, #16
Amsterdam, Holland

My dear Rowena;
 This is coming to you through my lawyers there because I want you to know through them that I am amending the terms of my trust to you—I want you to be able to use it whenever you want, without hav-

ing to answer a lot of fool questions. This way, you will know that I've done it, and the damned lawyers will know that you know. They're old ladies, the lot of them.

The paintings you shipped arrived safe and sound, all three canvases, and I got to tell you, I'm proud as pistols to have them. They're framed in nice gold-leaf frames. I hung them in the drawing room, just over the red settee. You haven't been here, so you can't know how good it looks there. The windows across from the settee face northwest, and it means that the light is best in the afternoon, when I'm most likely to do my entertaining. I show them off to everyone, and you should hear how surprised they are when I tell them my grand-daughter did them. Sometimes people don't believe me, so I show them where you've signed, and then they have to beg pardon, which tickles me.

Your mother has sent me another letter of complaint about you, as if she has nothing better to do with her time. If she's been half as persistent with you as she has with me, I can see why you decided to get out of there. She's my daughter and I love her, but she can try the patience of a saint, and that's a fact. Who is this paragon Rupert she keeps going on about? She says he's been waiting to marry you for years. I got to tell you he sounds like a half-baked Napoleon to me, but your mother is convinced he's the best husband material anywhere. She also carries on about this insinuating foreigner—those're her words, not mine—who she thinks has hornswoggled you. According to her, you've been mooning after this Count since he hove on the scene last spring. I've told her time and time again that you know your own mind, but I don't think it's done any good. She just gets all riled up at me for encouraging you. If you want to tell me what's going on, I'd keep it confidential, but I'd have a better idea about what to say to your mother. I don't mean to intrude, and I'm not telling you what to do, but I'd be able to deal better with Clarice if I knew how much of what she says is sensible and how much is pie in the sky.

You know you can come here any time you want, if you decide you need to put more distance between the family and you. I got plenty of room, or I could get you your own place. I'm not the interfering type, and you won't find me riding herd on you if you show up here; you've had more than your share of that already. I think you've got a lot to chew on right now, but don't think you have to manage it all by yourself. I don't mean you have to do it. Just think it over. There're places in California that are mighty wild and pretty. You'd like painting them, I'll bet. In the meantime, you keep at it, Rowena. You got something special, and I don't say that just because I'm your grand-father; if you didn't

*have an eye, I wouldn't be doing you any service by saying you have.
I've bought a passel of art in the last thirty years, and I know quality
when I see it, even if I don't know the high-brow palaver for it all. You
got quality.*

*You let me know if those lawyers of mine give you any guff. I'll set
them to rights, I promise you. In the meantime, you look out for yourself, Rowena. It would kill me if any harm came to you, and they say
things are fiercing up in Europe again. Don't stick around if any shooting starts. You come here and be safe.*

Your loving grand-father,
Horace Saxon

9

It was always difficult dealing with foreigners, thought Inspector Herbert Blau as he looked over the statement Franchot Ragoczy had just
signed for him: it was the third such account he had provided. It was
more difficult, Blau told himself, when the foreigners were rich and had
the ear of some important Berliners, as well as diplomatic ties to the
Czar of Russia. He read over the three pages, finding the small, neat
handwriting highly legible, if a bit old-fashioned. With a sigh he put the
sheets aside and stared with supreme blankness at the filing cabinets
on the far side of the room. Inspector Blau realized his wife would be
dining without him again tonight or going to their usual Friday concert,
and felt a pang of regret: he missed his evenings with Sophie and their
two children. At forty-three, he had come to value his wife's calm good
sense as well as her Hungarian cooking, and their children's optimism.

If only he were not under such scrutiny. There had been a public out-
cry, of course, for Nadezna was a legendary dancer, and to find her, bru-
tally hacked to death in her bathtub, had created a scandal; for the last
eleven days, the press had continued to speculate about her murder.
Blau's superiors had insisted he get results, and obtain a quick conviction, and all he had been able to do was to detain Franchot Ragoczy for
a third round of questioning, trying to break down the Count's story of
his last visit with Nadezna. So far he had not been able to find a flaw in
the man's report.

The Inspector went over the other statements he had taken, reviewing the subject in his mind: Pflaume, the houseman, had admitted Franchot Ragoczy shortly before he left for supper, which would make his arrival at Nadezna's house at approximately six-forty, or so Pflaume estimated; there had been nothing threatening in Ragoczy's manner, no sign of anger. Pflaume stated that it was well-known in Nadezna's household and her school that her patron was Ragoczy—no one had ever made a secret of it. Pflaume admitted to having lingered at the bierstube longer than usual, for he had become sleepy; he had not returned to the house until after ten, and by then the police had arrived. He had been aghast at what he found, so incoherent with grief that he had not been able to say anything that night; his statement had been secured two days after the hideous act.

The other statements supported what Pflaume had said in regard to time, and so far he had no reason to suspect any of them. He rose slowly and walked the length of his office; it took no more than four moderate strides. Impulsively he rang for coffee and added, "See if Ragoczy wants any."

"He hasn't before," the uniformed policeman said.

"Offer it, in any case," said Blau, lowering his eyes and rubbing his underlip with the end of his thumb. "And tell him I will be with him in ten minutes." He suspected the wait would demand more of him than it did of his prisoner.

"Very good, Inspector."

It was common wisdom that any man in police custody, left alone in an empty room for half an hour or so after writing an official statement, would become nervous and when questioned would betray himself, goaded by the anxiety of his long wait. That had not been the case with Ragoczy, who for the last two interviews had been content to wait patiently as long as it was necessary and remain unruffled and polite when finally addressed; at his first interview, the foreigner had given every evidence of shock and distress, but that might be a deception. What had come after had almost convinced Blau that Ragoczy was either innocent or the most unnatural, depraved killer he had ever encountered. Blau went down the corridor to the toilet, anticipating a long evening. When he got back to his office he found a large cup of sugared coffee waiting for him. He sipped at it and burned his tongue. Picking up the mug, he went along to the room where Ragoczy waited.

"Good afternoon, Inspector," said Ragoczy courteously as Blau came into the room. He half-rose from his wooden chair. "Or perhaps it is evening now." He was dressed with an easy elegance that Blau recognized as aristocratic in its very understatement. From his black suit, dark waistcoat, immaculately white shirt, and burgundy silk tie, there was nothing out of place or anything fussy. The silver signet ring worn on the index finger of his right hand showed a disk with raised, opened wings all in black cabochon sapphire.

"Good evening, Count," said Blau, feeling self-conscious about the cup of coffee he held; he put it down on the small table as if to disown it. "I'm sorry to inconvenience you again, but—"

"But someone murdered Nadezna, and you are doing your utmost to discover who it was," said Ragoczy with understanding, resuming his place. "Because—aside from her killer—I was the last person to see her alive, you need to go over my statement again." He had sat down once more. "I am at your disposal."

"Thank you for your cooperation," said Blau, his delivery automatic. "It is unusual to find someone so willing to help us." He managed to fill this observation with sinister implications.

"And you find it strange that I should be one such?" Ragoczy said.

Blau shrugged in his best noncommittal manner, watching the foreigner out of the corner of his eye.

"Very well, Inspector." Ragoczy leaned forward. "Let us be plain with one another: it is in my best interests to assist you to the limits of my abilities. Like it or not, I am under investigation. That you need not deny, for what other purpose would you have in these repeated interviews, if not to try to catch me unaware? You assume my protestations of innocence are mendacious, as I suppose you must. There are many unanswered questions in this case, aren't there? And all of them are bruited about in print. I don't enjoy the hints that I am the murderer, nor do any of those associated with me. Therefore I will do all I can to help you find the one who did kill her. That was why I gave you all my evening clothes—so you could inspect them for blood. Which you admit you have not found. Surely after such a killing, with all the water and blood on the floor, the murderer's clothes would be soaked in it."

"As you say," Blau murmured. "It is worthwhile to be plain. And you may have disposed of the bloody garments. You are certain we cannot find them, and thus suppose we cannot apprehend you. You are willing to help us so that you may laugh at us. Do not bother to argue with me: I will only think the worse of you if you do." He folded his arms, wanting to look imposing, although inwardly he felt foolish and could not persuade himself Ragoczy did not sense this. "Shall we get on with it? You say you called on her."

"Certainly. As Pflaume must have told you. I arrived and went to her study. She was expecting me, and we discussed certain modifications in our dealings regarding the funding of her school. She was in need of ready cash, which you know I gave her. She had requested it and I provided it; such incidents were rare, but there had been a few of them in the past, which I handled in the same way—the cash she needed delivered personally. You admit you found the roll of banknotes I left with her, and that my banker has confirmed I withdrew those funds that morning. You know anyone killing her by . . . misadventure or with the intention to profit by the act would have taken the money, and so, quite reasonably, when you discovered it, that money led you back to me. And you have remained fixed on me ever since." He had been punctuating his points with single taps on the tabletop; now he leaned back and steepled his fingers. "If I had killed her, I would have removed the money just to avoid such suspicions. Yes, I knew her servants had Tuesday off; Nadezna asked me to come when we could be private. She gave me no reason, but I suppose she wanted our financial arrangements to remain confidential."

"That is just the trouble," said Inspector Blau, his features arranged for stern friendliness. "The arrangements have been so confidential that—"

"My man-of-business has been instructed to supply you with photographs of the contract she and I signed when the school was founded. He will have all the material delivered to you by tomorrow." Ragoczy looked directly at Blau, catching him unaware with the full intensity of his eyes. "I know it is assumed I was her lover, but I give you my Word, I was not. Ask Charlotte Milch. She will know."

Blau picked up his coffee and sipped it; it was almost cool enough to drink. "She has given her statement."

Ragoczy knew better than to prod. He nodded once. "I am relieved to hear that you are taking precautions and being thorough. I would not like the killer to slip away due to your lack of diligence."

With a sigh, Blau conceded. "She confirms your statement. We have taken two statements from her, and her answers from one to the next are consistent. We have corroboration on her statements from others who occasionally entertained with her; dancers from her company who assisted her and her guests. The list is impressive. We are in the process of interviewing each of them. Milch will not tell us who among the guests were also Nadezna's lovers, but she says that you were never one. She also says that your lack of . . . shall we say interest? often aggravated Nadezna."

"No doubt," said Ragoczy. "She liked to have a sense of a man's weak-

nesses, particularly when it gave her strength." This was not said critically, but Blau seized on it.

"And she wanted to know yours! She had found your weakness." He
put his cup down surprised he had almost finished it, as he leaned forward.

"Certainly she tried to," Ragoczy said steadily. "She preferred having men as lovers so she would not feel beholden to them when they
did favors for her."

"You were different," said Blau, hoping that at last he would learn
something not already in Ragoczy's accounts of his dealings with
Nadezna.

"I did not do her favors," he said. "That is why we had a business contract, so that we would know what things each was to do for the other,
and the terms on which they would be done." He regarded Blau with
the same level look he had given from their first meeting. "You will see
for yourself, when the copy of the contract is delivered."

"I am looking forward to receiving it," Blau said, as if he doubted this
would ever happen.

Ragoczy heard the dubious note in Blau's voice, and told him purposefully, "Inspector, understand me: I did not kill Nadezna. I intend
to see her killer found and brought to justice, as much to establish my
innocence as to avenge her death. I am prepared to do anything within
the law to accomplish this, so let us abandon this adversarial stance."
He let Blau consider this. "I am willing to provide you anything that
will end your suspicions of me, if you will tell me what such a thing may
be. Is that clear? If it is not, what must I do to make it so?"

Blau sipped his coffee again, and spoke aloud the observation that
had haunted him since he began work on the case. "You are either the
most cold-blooded murderer I have ever encountered, or you are gen-
uinely indignant, and an innocent man," he allowed as he walked to the
far side of the room, then turned and stared back at Ragoczy, keeping
the accusation out of his voice. "The trouble is, there are those who say
Nadezna was blackmailing you—that your business contract was a
sham to cover the payments she demanded of you."

"If that were true, if she were blackmailing me, why would I be so
foolish as to leave a legal document of the arrangement? It would surely
serve neither her purposes nor mine, having such a record of blackmail,
would it? for it could be called into question. Aren't you doing that right
now?" Ragoczy asked unflustered. "If the purpose of blackmail is con-
cealment of acts, there are far more sensible means at hand to pay it
without making discovery as likely as it is with contracts for it. She may

have blackmailed some, but Nadezna never blackmailed me. Don't you think I would have arranged matters differently if she had been successfully blackmailing me for years?"

Blau acknowledged the accuracy of this. "Perhaps the payment she demanded was the support of her school, not payment to her. That is possible, isn't it? She might have thought with the traveling you do, she needed something to insure you would continue to pay. A contract, properly put together, would guarantee her the money she required. Aren't those considerations reasonable? Wouldn't you have them if you were in my place?" It was unlikely, and both men knew it, but he felt compelled to ask, if only to hear Ragoczy's answer.

"Why would she blackmail me?" Ragoczy inquired levelly. "She did not know me at the time we began our dealings together."

"There have been rumors," said Blau, deliberately vaguely. "She may have heard them."

"If you mean the rumors that I keep brothels of children in various parts of the world, you will discover they only began after the Czar commissioned me as his envoy to his cousins, and so far are centered in Berlin, although that may change, given how quickly news spreads these days." He put his hands flat on the table. "It is my belief that they were started specifically to discredit me with the Kaiser, to prevent my gaining access to him."

"For the Czar's business?" Blau asked, hoping to disrupt Ragoczy's thoughts.

"As I have said before: it is in my statements," Ragoczy replied, unfazed.

"And Nadezna was aware of that? She knew you were attempting to see the Kaiser?" Blau all but pounced on this.

"Certainly she was. She was the first to tell me what the rumors were, but she did not know that few things are more repugnant to me than the deliberate exploitation of children. Of all the acts I might do, prostituting children is not one of them." He recalled the terrible things he had seen in Tunis, when he was a slave, and they still had the power to sicken him with loathing. "Until she spoke to me, I knew only that there had been whispers." Ragoczy hesitated. "She was not willing to tell me what the source of the rumors was, if she knew."

"Then it is possible that she had private information she could use to change her agreements with you." Blau watched carefully for Ragoczy's reaction.

"It is possible, but it was also unnecessary. Our dealings were of long standing. I came to her with the offer, as my man-of-business will ver-

ify. She knew nothing of my interest in her work until I had her contacted through the appropriate legal devices. And before you wonder
if she had not made a secret offer to me before then," he went on, one
hand raised to silence Blau, "I had never met Nadezna when I first contacted her. That you will have to accept as true, for I can give you no
proof that I did not know someone before I first met the person. I doubt
anyone can." He fell silent.

"You may be correct," said Blau after a moment. "I would not like to
have to do so, in any case." He finished his coffee, and considered
sending for more.

"Have you discovered yet who the anonymous caller was? I know the
crime was reported by an unidentified person telephoning the police."
Ragoczy saw that Blau was startled by the question, and took advantage of this. "I have been looking for answers, too, Inspector." His
source was Leopold Oberstetten, who had not revealed his informant,
and Ragoczy trusted him enough to accept his intelligence as accurate.

"How did you—" Inspector Blau was sputtering.

"I said I have been looking for answers," Ragoczy repeated without
rancor or impatience. "And this is one I found. I am puzzled why you
have not mentioned this mysterious telephone call."

"It is strange that you know of it. We have been keeping it secret,"
said Blau, his suspicions flaring again.

"Not as secret as you thought, if I could learn of it." Ragoczy said,
thinking that Leopold Oberstetten had outdone himself with this intelligence.

"Unless you made the telephone call yourself, after you committed
the crime," Blau said, his eyes narrowing keenly. "In which case, you
become a more likely suspect than before."

Ragoczy shook his head. "Wouldn't that be a trifle reckless? Did the
man making the call have an accent?" Ragoczy asked, making no mention of his own faint, unidentifiable accent.

"You could have disguised your voice," Blau said, not as convinced
as he wanted to be by his own argument.

"Surely your police operators are skilled at recognizing different accents, even those the speakers attempt to disguise," said Ragoczy,
adding "If they are not, they should be."

Blau scowled. "We believe that the killer might well have made the
telephone call; he would know to tell the police that the door was
open," he admitted. "If you committed the murder and did not want
to place the call yourself, you might have hired someone to do it."

"Oh, that would be very clever of me," said Ragoczy, nodding in spurious approval. "As clever as arriving at the house while Pflaume was still there when I knew he would be gone in half an hour. Not content with providing you with one witness to my presence, I had another place the telephone call. I would then have a second witness to say what I had asked of him, making me more suspicious than ever. An ingenious ploy, I concede. How can I have overlooked Pflaume? I should have killed him, too. That would give you two bodies, not one. I wonder how I have survived to this age, with such cleverness."

"All right." Blau held up his free hand in a show of capitulation. "I will grant you probably did not make the telephone call. But I would like to discover how you found out about it."

"If I am permitted to, one day I may tell you," said Ragoczy, his demeanor concealing his growing distress. "There was a telephone call. We may consider that a given, may we not?"

"Yes." It was annoying to accommodate Ragoczy, but Blau did it. Then he rang for more coffee.

"I am assuming you spoke with Herr Tauber?" Ragoczy went on. "Does he confirm the time of my arrival at his home?"

"At approximately seven-thirty, yes he does." Blau had not wanted to admit as much, but Ragoczy would surely talk with Tauber, and denying what he had said would achieve nothing.

"And Pflaume left for his supper when—?" Ragoczy pursued. "A few minutes before seven?"

"According to his statement. He arrived at the bierstube at five minutes after the hour; the host knows him well." Blau realized the questioning had got away from him, and he struggled to reclaim it. "How do you come to know of this? Why should you duplicate the work of the police?"

"For several reasons." Ragoczy prepared to enumerate them again, his hand lifted so that he could use his fingers as indicators. "First, to reiterate: I want to find her murderer. Second, I want to assure myself that you have investigated all possibilities, so that the guilty party may be held accountable. Third, I need to know what you have indicating I am the murderer, so that I may counter the information or expose any misrepresentation. Fourth, I may be able to reach certain persons the police cannot so readily approach."

Blau nodded for each point. "If you had said this at our first interview—" he began.

Ragoczy laughed once. "If I had said this at our first interview, Inspector, you would have been convinced of my guilt. Any lack of shock or confusion would have looked to you as if I had some knowledge of the crime. You spoke to me about seven hours after her body was found, to notify me of her death. When I was questioned early that morning, not more than two hours later, I was upset and appalled, which is why my first statement lacks details. Most of us, disturbed in the dead of night with shocking news, do not instantly recall all details. Again, I assure you, I was not party to her death in any way." He stood up for the first time. "Nadezna was a woman of many gifts, and it offends me that she should die so . . . so egregiously. I have no desire to hamper your work, and every reason to want you to succeed." Ordinarily he would have held out his hand, but he realized Inspector Blau would not regard this as anything but an attempt to suborn him.

"If you say that enough, I may be convinced of it," said Blau, opening the door in response to the double knock for his fresh cup of sugared coffee. He handed over his old cup, saying "Danke" as he did; he closed the door on the "Bitte."

"I hope you will," said Ragoczy with intense feeling.

Blau used his pencil to stir his coffee, buying himself a little time with this fussy act. "It is odd for you to be so forthcoming if you are actually guilty of her murder." He held the pencil up to make his point. "Unless you are so confident that you believe you will never be apprehended or tried for the murder, in which case, you are enjoying yourself at our expense."

Ragoczy sighed. "If I help you, I am doing it because I am guilty: if I don't help you, I must be guilty." He shook his head and looked up at the Inspector. "With such constraints, what can I say to you?"

"Not a great deal," Blau confessed. "If only we knew who made that telephone call."

"You can want to know it no more purposefully than I," said Ragoczy. "I do not like these tales about, saying that I was the one to blame for her death, and they will continue as long as no one else is held responsible. Any lingering suspicion will fall on me because I am a foreigner and her patron, which is more peculiar in those who are not German." He glanced down at the floor, then back at Blau. "I would tell you that I want her killer tried and convicted because he deprived the world of a wonderful talent, but that is one of the things that makes you suspect me, isn't it."

"It is a factor," Blau told him, sitting on the edge of the table not only for comfort but so he could loom over Ragoczy.

"A factor," Ragoczy repeated, his sarcasm hardly in check; he was not the least intimidated by Inspector Blau's encroaching nearness. "Yes."

Blau gave Ragoczy a long, thoughtful stare. "There was a murder, four years ago. You probably heard nothing of it; it was not a significant one and the press paid little attention to it." He sipped his coffee, then went on in a distant, conversational tone, "I investigated the crime. A woman—a singer in one of the theatres, considered to be talented and with a following—was found strangled in her rooms. There were many possible suspects at first, but each was finally eliminated, leaving us with no one. She had had a friend, a man a trifle younger than she, who was known to be deeply but platonically attached to her. Because he was not her lover, and because he gave every sign of wanting to assist our inquiries, we had not considered him, for there were aspects of her murder that hinted at sexual excesses." He coughed once. "When her platonic friend finally confessed, he said he had wanted her but could not have her, and when he could bear it no longer, he killed her."

"And you think I may be another, like him, who killed because the woman did not want me," Ragoczy concluded for Blau. "Inspector, how am I to convince you with the ghost of that wretched fellow haunting you?" He cocked his head. "Think a moment. I am not a callow boy, Inspector; I have loved women who refused me—many times. It has been . . . ages since such refusal made me resent the woman who gave it. To hack a woman I deeply admired to pieces—" He broke off.

Blau saw torment at the back of Ragoczy's dark eyes, and he relented. "I am less suspicious of you than I was two days ago." He had more of the coffee. "That does not mean I am not going to continue to investigate you, but that my inquiries are tending to make me look in other directions."

"That is a relief," said Ragoczy, preparing to rise. "Is this the whole of it, Inspector, or have you more questions you wish to put to me?"

"Not at the moment. But I would rather you remain here for an hour or so." He was prepared to leave Ragoczy alone for a while once again, to see if he became rattled.

Ragoczy regarded him with a knowing half-smile as he sank back in the chair. "I will not have anything different to say to you, Inspector, no matter how long I sit here. But if it will make you more willing to accept my assertions, I will not begrudge you the time." He appeared to make himself comfortable.

The Inspector waited a full minute before speaking. "You do not advance yourself with such remarks, Count."

"I intend no disrespect," said Ragoczy at once. "I am only telling you that I am tired of the contest. I would far rather see you asking questions of others." He held up his hand once more. "Which inclines you to suspect me again; I realize that. But since I know I did not kill

Nadezna, why should it astonish you that I would prefer you use your energies in finding the man or men who did."

"Very credible," Blau approved as he went out the door and returned to his office, his brow furrowed in thought. The trouble was, he told himself, that Ragoczy was a very persuasive man, and Blau was finding it hard to remain unconvinced by his protestations. He supposed that Ragoczy had intended to plant just such doubts in his mind as he now possessed. He took his place at his desk and sipped meditatively at his coffee, letting his mind make the connections that had brought him so far in his profession.

"Inspector Blau?" The young dispatcher spoke hesitantly from the half-open door. "I . . . I have something for you."

"Yes?" Blau said curtly, resenting the intrusion.

"It is Ragoczy's servant. He is here with someone from the Russians . . . it's about Ragoczy." The dispatcher had paled as he spoke, as if realizing he was not giving Blau good news.

"The Russians? The Embassy?" Blau demanded.

"I suppose so. There is a courier from the Czar, in any case." He straightened up as if to make this announcement more official.

"With Ragoczy's servant," Blau mused aloud, taking a perverse satisfaction in this acknowledgement. "Extending the Czar's protection, I would guess." He had expected something like this, but was annoyed it had come about so soon.

"I don't know," said the dispatcher stiffly. "But they would like a word with you."

Blau did his best not to sigh as he stood up. "Very well. Send the gentlemen in."

"Shall I fetch Ragoczy?" the dispatcher offered, looking over his shoulder as if he feared eavesdroppers.

"Not yet," Blau decided, unwilling to surrender all his authority at once. "I will let you know." He set his empty cup aside, thinking as he did that Ragoczy has played him expertly, delaying and misdirecting all inquiries about him until the Czar's messenger could arrange for his release; it was another indication of his skill in diplomacy. No wonder he had been willing to be interviewed and to make every show of cooperation; he knew it would never lead to anything but the shelter of the Czar's diplomatic cloak. What struck the Inspector most forcefully was Ragoczy's dogged insistence on his innocence. He would never have to answer for his deeds, so what did it matter? Blau waited by his desk, wishing he did not feel so much like a schoolboy.

Duke Vladimir Arkadeivich Nagoyev was not quite thirty, a bit too taken with himself to make the impression he so obviously desired; his uniform was immaculate, the medals on his chest jingling a little as he stopped to salute Inspector Blau. "Inspector," he said in very good German, nodding once instead of bowing, "how lamentable that we must meet under these provoking circumstances."

"Yes: provoking," said Blau, taking Nagoyev's proffered hand.

"My credentials," went on Nagoyev, handing over a small portfolio of impressive-looking certificates. "You will want to assure yourself they are in order. And these—the reason for my coming." The last was two envelopes, one with the Byzantine double-headed Romanov eagle embossed on it, the other with the address of the Embassy in Berlin.

Behind him, Roger slipped into the Inspector's office, his expression marvelously neutral. He waited in silence while Blau examined the various documents he had been given.

"So." Blau let out his breath slowly. "You are going to take charge of Count Saint-Germain."

"The Czar is recalling him to Saint Petersburg, as you will see," Nagoyev said by way of confirmation. "It is expected that he will leave tomorrow, or the day after at the very latest."

"Tomorrow. I see," said Blau. "How very . . . "

"Very what?" Nagoyev asked sharply, hearing the condemnation in Blau's tone.

"How very predictable," said Blau, sitting down without any apology. "Your Czar wants his man back in Russia. If we do not comply immediately, I am warned that there could be an incident, which none of us want." He looked pointedly at the two envelopes, now open. "So it is, is it not? predictable."

Nagoyev scowled, sensing he was being mocked. He moved nearer to Blau's desk. "I will sign whatever you require."

"You most certainly will," said Blau with feeling. "I will make sure the Czar is aware that his actions have compromised a murder investigation, possibly beyond repair." He spoke bluntly in order to shock Nagoyev out of his smugness.

"Any comment you care to make will be conveyed to the Prime Minister," said Nagoyev stiffly. "If Stolypin feels your complaint needs some attention, he will attend to it. The Czar will not be troubled with matters of this sort."

"Will he not?" Blau asked, as if he were astonished at the information. "I am shocked, truly shocked." He realized he had put himself beyond the acceptable limits of conduct, and he at once took measures to ameliorate the offense he had given. "I mean no disrespect, Duke; the

Kaiser is not one to concern himself with murder investigations, either."

Not sure this had been sufficient apology, Nagoyev said, "Rulers of nations and Empires do not sink to the level of children."

"I suppose not," said Blau, and began to fill out forms as quickly as he could. As he finished the first, he called to his assistant, an eager young man from Köln who had come to Berlin to be at the heart of things. "Here. Use the information on this sheet to complete the applications for Franchot Ragoczy to leave Germany." He handed the material over.

"But . . . isn't he one of the . . . " He could think of nothing else to say.

"Yes, he is a suspect in the murder of Nadezna. But he is here as a diplomat, and as such, his diplomatic position takes precedence over our inquiries." He looked up at Nagoyev. "He will have to return to Russia at once. We can give him a grace period of seven days, but no more. When and if he returns to Germany, he may be once again under suspicion and subject to German laws in regard to it." He issued the warning in a flat tone, as if he had spoken it thousands of times.

"He will be so informed," said Nagoyev, preening a little in spite of his best intentions to remain businesslike.

"If you do not mind, sir," said Roger from his place by the door, "I would like to speak with my master."

The old-fashioned expression *my master* caught Blau's interest, and for the first time he looked at Roger with real curiosity. "I will arrange it," he said, setting the form he had begun aside. "Tell me, have you been with Ragoczy long?"

"Half his life, sir," said Roger with utter candor: he did not mention that half of Ragoczy's life was two thousand years.

"You aren't German, are you?" Blau pursued.

"No, sir. I was born in Cadiz," he said, using the modern name for the Roman city that had been Gades when he lived there.

"And Ragoczy hired you in Spain?" Blau was now alert to any minute change in Roger's voice, any hesitation or stutter that would identify problems.

"No, sir. I met my master in Rome." Again he told the truth.

"So you and Ragoczy are both exiles," said Blau, nodding to himself; some of Roger's devotion must come from this shared misfortune.

"In a manner of speaking," Roger agreed.

"Did we get a statement from you?" Blau inquired, ignoring the glare from Nagoyev.

"Yes, sir. You have two." Roger achieved a polite expression that did not presume to be a smile. "I will prepare another, if you wish."

"No," Blau said, abandoning the scent for the present. "I will have the dispatcher take you back to where your . . . master is." With that he rang the bell by his elbow and gave his instructions to the dispatcher as soon as he appeared.

"Thank you, sir," said Roger to Blau, and prepared to follow the dispatcher. "We will await your summons."

Since the point of keeping Ragoczy waiting was to keep him isolated, Blau relented. "You may both come here in ten minutes. I am certain that Duke Nagoyev and I will have concluded our business by then."

"Very good. In ten minutes," said Roger, and left the office in the wake of the dispatcher. He did not look around him, or pay the least attention to the corridor; he betrayed no sign of apprehension or of bravado; his curiosity was minimal. As the dispatcher reported to Blau a few minutes later, Roger was a middle-aged man walking down a corridor—no more and no less.

Ragoczy was sitting where he had been when Blau left, but his demeanor was intent and his countenance set in lines of concentration. He looked up abruptly as the door opened, and in an instant, his expression changed to one of bonhomie. "Roger. How good to see you."

"My master," said Roger, coming into the room and permitting the dispatcher to close it behind him. "Duke Nagoyev is delivering a declaration of immunity to Inspector Blau at this very moment. You are—"

"—recalled to Russia by Nicholas," Ragoczy finished for him with a gesture of impatience. "Why could he have not delayed for a while longer? I hoped we would have a few more days here."

"But why?" Roger asked, anticipating the answer.

"Because we might be able to find Nadezna's murderer in three days, if we have the opportunity." He made a short gesture of frustration. "The killer must be convicted of his crime, beyond any question." His mouth twitched with ironic humor. "That is what I want to happen."

"You want to stop the rumors," said Roger.

"And the investigation," Ragoczy said, adding in Chinese, "There are things I do not want them stumbling onto in the process."

"You have left troublesome situations before," Roger reminded him in the same language.

"That was centuries ago. Trouble could be headed off with quick action. Now that trouble travels on telegraph wires, we can no longer get ahead of it. Ergo, we must confront it." He made a sign with his hand, reminding Roger they were probably being overheard, and changed back to German. "The only thing I can do, under the circumstances, is to clear my name. If I do not, I will have to go into Asia or the remote Andes once more until this is over and forgotten. Since I do not wish to hide, all that is left is for me to bring the killer to the bar, and let the court deal with him."

Roger also spoke in German. "I fear that will not be easy once you return to Saint Petersburg."

"No, it will not," said Ragoczy. He started toward the door. "Since it is Nicholas' pleasure that I do so, I had better be about it."

"I have already begun packing," said Roger as he followed his master out of the interview room and down the dingy hall to where Duke Nagoyev waited.

Text of a letter delivered by messenger from Tancred Sisak in Cairo to Baron Klemens Manfred von Wolgast in Berlin.

Grand Hotel, Cairo
November 16, 1910

My dear Baron;
Such sad news about Nadezna. I was shocked to learn that the po-lice suspect her patron. For all I could discover, the man is not much more than a eunuch with a fortune. Why should he have her murdered, and in so hideous a way? If he was tired of supporting her school, or thought she had cheated him, there are many other ways he might have exacted vengeance without destroying so remarkable a woman. It would seem to me that those who had something to conceal might well be more likely to kill her, since her living was a risk to them in a way it was not to Ragoczy. Now that the man is being called back to Russia, we may never know beyond doubt that he was the killer. Still, it is convenient that Ragoczy is not German. It makes him so much easier to suspect.
Business is going well here, in fact better than I expected, which means I will probably remain here through the end of the year. I am certain that as the Ottoman Empire breathes its last the British hege-mony in and around Egypt and Palestine will not remain unchallenged. I anticipate orders for those armored automobiles of yours that might well exceed the orders I have already placed. In such an event, I would think you would want to give some consideration to the price you charge me, for with large orders, a certain discount would not be unreason-able, don't you think?
You may look for me in Berlin in February or March. During that

time, I am confident you will arrange a suitable discount for me. I will be bringing you an order that will warrant such consideration. I give you my word.

As I think of visiting Berlin again, it saddens me that I will not have the opportunity to see Nadezna again. I always enjoyed our little evenings together. She had so very many talents, did she not? In our own ways no doubt we will miss her. We must plan to drink to her memory, and to the apprehension of her killer, if that is appropriate.

Yours, etc.
Tancred Sisak

PART III

ROWENA SAXON

Text of a letter from Julian Sinclair-Howard in London to Ludwig Kessel-mann in Berlin.

#2, St. Dunstan-the-West Close
London, England
December 8, 1910

Ludwig Kesselmann
Ministry of Foreign Affairs
Berlin, Germany

My dear Herr Kesselmann;
You may rest assured that His Majesty's government is not interested in any proposal put forth by the Czar in regard to arms or such matters that might be seen to be detrimental to the balance of powers in Europe. Any apprehension to the contrary is flummery. It is the general opinion of the government that no conflagration is likely to occur so long as Germany and Austro-Hungary hold the reins, and we know it would be imprudent to do anything that would shift the military and political equilibrium of the region. We are convinced it would be folly to intervene in what is clearly a minor dispute between hostile factions. We have the Entente Cordiale to keep the French from cutting up rough, and we have been instructed to put our energies to other matters than arms being produced by your admirable munitions industry.
We have therefore prevailed upon the Prime Minister and the King

himself to rebuff all advances from the envoys of the Czar, no matter how innocent their stated purpose may seem. Nicholas seems bent on dragging his cousins into an ill-conceived private pact to stop the spread of arms in Europe; we had long supposed it must be something of that nature, but most of us did not reckon that the Czar was so näive. I have already been privy to one such attempt, in Belgium, and you have my word that all but one of those attending share my view of the situation. Ragoczy officiated at that debacle, and I must tell you that his determination to coerce such an agreement struck me as questionable, and I am proud to say I led the resistance to his efforts. The notion that such an agreement is possible, let alone desirable is ludicrous, and I and those around me will continue to encourage the King to keep well-clear of any notion the Czar may have of coming to some private accommodation.

It is our understanding here in England that the greatest buildup of arms is in the eastern part of Europe, which would understandably dismay the Czar, who has such a long border to defend, reaching as it does from the Black Sea along the Carpathians and the Ukraine, up through the Slavs and the Poles to the Baltic Sea. Were we in his position, we might also want such an agreement as the one he has been proposing. It was represented to us: the Czar's concern that any regional fighting might well expand into Europe and through Russia has been evaluated and rejected as alarmist. It is not the work of England and Europe to come to the aid of Slavs and Serbs.

You may rest assured that this position will remain unaltered. Your development of arms, and their sale, can only insure the continued stability of Europe, and we will help to maintain this as best we may without actual participation. His Majesty is not one to be caught up in the brawls of envious peasants, or of age-old hatreds that are the staff of life of those barbarians in the Balkans. King George has indicated that he regards such squabbles as European intrigue and without any real implication where England is concerned: in fact, it is the view of most of the government that it is prudent of Germany to build up her arms at this time, to remind those less circumspect leaders in the east that they will not be permitted to run wild as they have done in the past. If history has taught nothing else, it has taught that Eastern Europe is a quagmire, whose feuding occupants should be left alone to kill one another off without any burden to the more civilized nations. As long as German and Austro-Hungarian guns are pointed east, you may rely on George V to support your efforts.

Thank you for your kind words, which I value most highly. It would be correct for me to claim I did nothing, but it would be untrue. So, if you will forgive my immodesty, yes, I am very proud that my efforts have helped to bring this desirable conclusion about. It was no small matter on my part to keep Ragoczy from reaching King George. I was unable to stop him speaking to Edward VII, but at least that association was of short duration and the impact was minimal. It is humbling to realize that upon such little acts as mine the fate of great nations may rest.

To you and yours, the best of Christmas tidings, and may we all enjoy a New Year of progress, prosperity, and mutual beneficence.

Most sincerely,
Julian Sinclair-Howard

P.S. Is it true that the police have discontinued their investigation of that ballerina's death now that Ragoczy has be summoned to Saint Petersburg? Quite a damning decision. The man will probably never gets what he deserves, not with the Czar protecting him.

1

Champagne foamed down his arm, wetting the satin cuff of his hunter-green quilted smoking jacket, but von Wolgast did not care; it was the fifth bottle he had opened in the last half hour and he had ceased to concern himself with appearances. The green-and-oak drawing room was already showing signs of disorder, and the celebration had only begun at eleven. Now that it was 1911—by twenty-six minutes—he felt his optimism fizz as merrily as the sparkling wine he poured out for his guests: Vaclav Persuic, in parade uniform, who was drunk enough to have to lean on the voluptuous woman he had brought with him, although she was not much more sober than he; Egmont von Rosenwiese, in full evening dress, who was as morose as von Wolgast was joyful; and Paul von Nordlingen, his dinner jacket open and his deep-blue waistcoat unbuttoned, looking tremendously pleased with himself, although von Wolgast could see no good reason for it.

"To a glorious year!" exclaimed Persuic, lifting his glass so energetically that a little of the champagne sloshed out. "To every wish fulfilled!"

The rest echoed his sentiments with varying degrees of enthusiasm.

"And to our host! May his enterprises flourish!" von Nordlingen cried, sipping his wine before the rest could second his toast. He did not look drunk, but there was a shine in his eyes and a wildness of gesture that belied his crisp speech. The woman he had brought with him was draped on the settee, snoring gently, her lavish taffeta gown in disarray from von Nordlingen's pawing.

"And may my guests have every good thing: good fortune, good wine, good family, good reputation, good standing, and good—" He held the champagne bottle at his crotch and shook it so that more of the spume rushed out as he laughed; his face was flushed and half his shirt studs had been removed; he wanted to think this was intimate attire, not slovenly. He wanted the night to be filled with carousing to justify his own satisfaction at the end of the police investigation into Nadezna's murder.

"This next year will be wonderful," Persuic announced, doing his best to come to attention. "I keep my duty here in Berlin, on behalf of the Emperor, of course, and so the Baron and I can continue—"

Von Wolgast was not so inebriated that he would permit such loose talk. "We will have other occasions," he warned, wagging a finger at the Croat as he went to fill the rest of the glasses. "When we have less reason to be festive."

"Our business is reason to celebrate," Persuic said mulishly.

"And we will have many opportunities to do so," von Wolgast promised him.

"So we will, so we will, so we will," said Persuic, as if the words had caught in his teeth. He drank down the contents of his glass rapidly and grabbed the neck of the bottle for more. "You have a case, haven't you?"

"Yes. Two." Von Wolgast signaled to von Rosenwiese, indicating he should take over as their wine steward. He enjoyed watching the unhappy man drag himself to the copper tub of ice and champagne bottles von Wolgast had had brought to his drawing room at the beginning of their evening. "See that the glasses stay full, Egmont. Including your own."

Von Rosenwiese shot him a look that might have been disgust had he not been afraid and not drunk enough to ignore it. He pulled one of the green bottles from the ice, removed the foil and the guard, and began to ease the cork out with his thumbs. He jumped visibly when the cork popped. "There," he said, holding out the bottle. "Who wants it?"

Persuic's companion held out her glass, her smile tenuous.

The woman on the settee stirred, but not enough to wake up, which made von Nordlingen howl with mirth. "Look at her. What a sot she is." He bent over the back of the settee and slipped his hands into the bodice of her elaborate gown, pinching her breasts, and grinning as she made an ineffective swipe at him with one arm. "Might as well have a sheep to fuck as this one. She'd sleep right through it," he said, suddenly tiring of his amusement. He straightened up and looked at Persuic. "Your company is more to my liking."

"Too bad," said Persuic, unimpressed by von Nordlingen.

"I said, she is more to my liking." There was a belligerence in von Nordlingen now that made him shed all appearances of playfulness.

"And *I* said—too bad," Persuic reminded him, deliberately dismissing him with a single gesture. "You were the one who gave your friend too much champagne."

Von Nordlingen took a step nearer, one hand coming up to shove Persuic. "Let me have a turn with her."

Unsteady as he was, Persuic fell into a pugilistic stance, his slight

crouch and weaving motion as much the result of champagne as box-
ing practice. "You will not." He elbowed the woman on his arm out of
the way, nearly stumbling in the process.

By now von Wolgast had realized the two men were not playing, and
he made haste to intervene. "Come, come, come. None of that. We are
friends here. Friends. You know that fighting at the New Year brings
acrimony." He had, in fact, made that up on the spur of the moment,
but it did the job.

Muttering a few words that might have been an apology, von Nordlingen retreated, the bellicose light leaving his slightly bloodshot eyes. He
stared down at the carpet, sulking. "It's no good with . . . Gretta's drunk."

"No matter; so are you," said von Rosenwiese gloomily as he handed
von Nordlingen a full glass of champagne. "A little more of this, and it
won't bother you or her."

Von Nordlingen accepted the wine grudgingly, but drank it down
quickly enough, and held it out for more.

"That's it," said von Wolgast, trying to encourage more festivity. "Let
us all drink again to the Kaiser."

Obediently they did, although Persuic added, "The Emperor, and the
Austro-Hungarian Alliance," immediately afterward, and giggled as the
rest joined him in the toast. "Franz Ferdinand will be a grand-father
before he sits on the throne, the way Franz Josef is going." He had trouble getting the words out between slurs and sniggers.

"Franz Ferdinand is a pig," said von Nordlingen conversationally. "He
hunts for slaughter."

Sensing that tempers were about to ignite again, von Wolgast said,
"More a butcher, from the look of him. Tie an apron around his waist
and put a cleaver in his hand and who would know the difference?"

This brought a bellow of laughter from Persuic and a snide chuckle
from von Nordlingen; von Wolgast thought the worst was over. He indicated that von Rosenwiese should open another bottle and rang for
Schmidt. "We will have supper now," he announced to his butler. "Is it
ready?"

"As you instructed," said Schmidt, so expressionless that his condemnation was obvious. "Ham, three kinds of schnitzel, baked eel,
game birds, capon, chopped goose liver, rack of lamb, pickles, butter,
whipped cream, mustard, cheeses, breads, and pastries." He recited the
menu in case von Wolgast had forgot what he had ordered and would
criticize what he found laid out.

"Yes. Yes, yes. Very good," said von Wolgast, his hunger suddenly immense. "Come, it is almost one," he enjoined his guests. "Supper is wait-

ing, and if you are not ready for it, I am." He swung around to his butler. "Schmidt. Have the champagne brought to us—at once."

Von Nordlingen hitched his shoulder in the direction of Gretta. "What about her?"

After a moment's consideration, von Wolgast said, "Leave her for now. I will have the servants carry her in a bit later."

Hearing this, Schmidt gave a sour smile. "I will bring the wine first."

"You surely will," said von Wolgast, and raised his hand to signal the advance.

It took them longer than usual to make their way down the corridor to the rose-and-blue parlor; von Nordlingen walked as if he were on the canted deck of a ship, and Persuic careened from side to side as if trying to keep up with an energetic folk dance, dragging his female companion along with him. Von Rosenwiese toddled as automatically as a toy, and he no longer pretended any delight in the evening.

As he went into the parlor ahead of the rest, von Wolgast had a brief, eerie sensation that Nadezna was reclining on the settee. He shook his head and reached to turn on the lights, relieved to discover no apparition as the room brightened; a shawl that was usually spread over the sideboard was now draped over the back of the settee. He leaned on the back of one of the chairs, aware his heart was racing. Then he heard his guests behind him and he lurched around to welcome them.

"It's pretty," said Persuic's woman; then she let out a squeal as she saw the food laid out on the sideboard. "Oh. That's . . . that's *marvelous.*"

"Come in. Have something to eat. The rest of the champagne will be along in a moment. And if we run out, there is more," Von Wolgast rubbed his hands together. "Let's sop up some of the wine, so we can have more."

"Excellent! Excellent," Persuic approved, weaving in the general direction of the sideboard. "I'm famished."

"And I'm . . . sick," said von Nordlingen, leaning over suddenly and vomiting onto the hearth, his hands knotted on the mantle. He righted himself slowly, looking a trifle shamefaced. "I didn't mean—"

"No matter," said von Wolgast quickly, determined to keep the celebration cordial. "Schmidt will clean it up. In the meantime, what you need is food. The chopped goose liver is especially good; there are truffles in it. The lamb ribs you can eat with your fingers, if you like, as if we were in the country. We'll have no ceremony here. The cheese is good. Have some of that on an onion roll. And the ham is smoked, and garnished with tinned cherries. You'll like it." He took von Nordlingen by the shoulder and steered him toward the buffet. "The plates are at the other end."

Von Nordlingen glanced back toward the hearth. "I'm . . . sorry. I would have used the toilet . . . But . . . so sudden . . . "

"These things happen, nothing to distress yourself," said von Wolgast, paying no attention to the skeptically raised eyebrow Persuic offered in silent comment. "After so much champagne . . . " He did not bother to finish.

"Is there any horseradish?" asked von Rosenwiese, looking over the dishes laid out.

"There should be: behind the eel, I think," said von Wolgast, his drunkenness deserting him as he strove to set the evening to rights once again. "If you want something that is not here, let me know what it is. There is more in the pantry, I'm told." He reached for a bottle of champagne as Schmidt tugged the copper tub into the parlor, then indicated the hearth. "That needs cleaning."

"So it does," said Schmidt, trying not to sigh as he stood up. "I will send one of the kitchen staff."

"Whatever you do," von Wolgast said, "do it quickly. The stench is ruining the buffet." He jutted his jaw in the direction of the corridor. "Then have that drunken slut brought in here for von Nordlingen."

"Certainly, sir," said Schmidt, wishing for the thousandth time that he had the courage to leave von Wolgast's employ. The thought of trying to find other work in Berlin daunted him enough to keep him where he was.

"And see if we have any of those little peppers. You know the ones I like—from Italy." He pursed his lips, thinking that the peppers would be the perfect compliment to the game birds. "Well, hurry up, Schmidt. The year isn't getting any younger." He chuckled at his own humor, and poured more champagne for himself.

An hour later the sideboard was a shambles, the remains of the food strewn about carelessly. Plates were stacked haphazardly about the parlor, and all but two of the champagne bottles in the tub of ice had their necks down, empty.

"Wonderful," muttered Persuic as he pronged the last of the sausages with his fork and began to bite one end of it; his supper had given him renewed energy but had only slightly diminished his intoxication. Chewing vigorously, he said to his host, "You know, Manfred, your party is wonderful. The food. The wine. I don't remember a better New Year. Wonderful."

The night's revelries were catching up with the woman beside him.

She did her best to conceal a yawn; her fair hair was slipping out of its elaborate coiffeur, and there were circles under her eyes that made her appear closer to forty than thirty. The carmine color on her mouth was smudged, and she was sagging with the task of propping him upright. She took the last of the pickled onions and ate it, making a face at its tang. "When were you planning to send for your automobile? Your chauffeur is surely longing for his bed."

"He is napping now, no doubt," said Persuic, scowling at the sausage as if it were his hapless chauffeur. "They all do, no matter what they tell you. They nap, they use the automobiles for their own purposes, and they pay too much for parts."

"But it is late," she protested, far more for herself than the chauffeur. "It is time we were . . . alone."

"Hah!" Persuic scoffed. "It is hardly more than two, and New Year as well." Another bite brought his teeth almost to the tines of the fork. "Wonderful."

On the settee where Schmidt and the cook's assistant had set Gretta as upright as they could, von Nordlingen now reposed as well, his arm flung over the end of it, his head against the armrest. Occasionally he gave a stentorian snore, woke himself, muttered an excuse, then slid back into slumber. Von Rosenwiese stood by the fireplace, one elbow propped on the mantelpiece, a half-drained bottle of champagne clutched by the neck in his hand, an expression of utmost misery on his face.

"I'm glad you're enjoying yourself," said von Wolgast, less sincerely than he had said it half an hour ago. He was nursing his champagne now, dreading how his head would feel when he woke next, around noon. "Have more champagne. And help yourself to the food."

"In a moment I will refill my glass." He reached over and fondled the woman beside him. "You think this sausage is impressive, little lamb? I have something better than this for you." He took her hand and laid it on the front of his breeches. "You will feel it from your cunt to your skull," he promised.

She did her best to give him an encouraging smile. "I hope so, Colonel," she said, "I am longing to lie with you. You've filled me with longing for you. That is why I would like to leave." Her sensible plea fell on deaf ears.

"Anything for a bed," said von Wolgast with unusual insight, and realized at once he had made a mistake; Persuic glowered at him. "Not but what the night is still young, and you are not ready to abandon the revels."

Persuic decided to be magnanimous about the remark. "The night is young. Young and lusty," he said, and reduced the sausage by another bite. "A pity about Nadezna," he added as he ate.

"Nadezna?" von Wolgast repeated, his bones going icy within him.

"Yes." He continued to chew as if unaware of von Wolgast's response. "Your friend."

"What do you mean?" von Wolgast asked sharply, spilling champagne on his shoes. Why did Persuic have to mention her? The evening had been going well enough without any reminder of her.

Persuic stared at him. "I meant it is a pity she is dead. She would be a wonderful addition to our party. I liked having her around. So charming and so famous. We could have held this celebration at her house, and she would have had the women for us." He took a last bite, pulling the remaining sausage off the tines while smiling toothily.

"Yes," said von Wolgast, mollified.

"Did they ever arrest anyone for killing her?" Persuic inquired, his attention no longer fixed on the answer.

"No. When Ragoczy left, they stopped the investigation," said von Wolgast with deep satisfaction. It was one of the few delights he had had in the last month.

"Pity," said Persuic. "She was a nice piece." He licked his lips.

"That she was," von Wolgast said, raising his glass to her memory.

"And you would not be alone to bring in the year, if she were still alive," Persuic went on. "A man should have more under him than sheets for New Year."

"He probably should," said von Wolgast with a sigh. "But Nadezna is gone. And sadly, my wife is not available." He made a gesture of fatalistic resignation.

"The devil's own luck, to be married to an invalid," said von Rosenwiese, as snide as he dared to be. "I have been told she is unable to leave her room."

"It is true enough," said von Wolgast with a shudder. He had visited his wife only twice in the last five years. Both times their encounters had ended in her shrieking obscenities at him through the bars on the window of her room; the nuns had hurried him out of the asylum, suggesting that it might be better to come another time.

"How sad for you both," said Persuic's companion.

"Yes," von Wolgast sighed, thinking again that he wished she would die and be done with it. He shook his head. "We must not let unhappy thoughts mar the New Year. Let us drink to happy days and an end of suffering."

"Strange wish, for a munitions maker," Persuic observed as he lifted a new glass of champagne. "Why not drink to a bloody war instead? We do, in barracks. There is nothing like a war to bring promotions."

"Because," said von Wolgast, straightening the sash on his smoking jacket, "war is risky. I would rather see hostilities increasing without actual fighting. Fighting is always costly, and unpredictable." He hoped that von Rosenwiese would remember some of this tomorrow. "If I were to have things precisely as I like, all sides would purchase my weapons, but not actually use them. That is the best possible outcome." It was also the way to the greatest profit, but he said nothing of this.

"Then we drink to that," said Persuic, stumbled backward a few steps, spilling champagne, and fell into one of the Louis XV chairs near the buffet; his companion staggered and managed to remain upright. He stared unseeing at his host. "Lost my footing."

"So it appears," said von Wolgast, oddly relieved that Persuic was finally succumbing to his excesses.

His companion knelt beside him. "Colonel, let us leave now. Before it is so late that all we do is sleep." She kept the desperation from her voice but not from her face.

He tugged on her dress, bringing her down onto his knee. "No. You wouldn't want to sleep tonight, would you, little lamb? You can sleep any time, but you cannot have me between your legs." He fumbled with the spill of lace around the low neckline of her evening gown. "You aren't tired, are you? Little lambiken?"

"Of course not," she lied valiantly.

"Such an eager little bitch you are," Persuic murmured to her, nuzzling her neck. "You know you want me to prong you now, don't you?" He slipped his hand along her skirt and began to lift it. "What an infernal mess of petticoats you're wearing," he complained.

"Then let us go to your flat," she insisted. "You will take them off me, one by one, and I will take your uniform off. Won't that be fun?" She sounded like the nanny she had once been, attempting to get her charge to behave.

"We can do that here. Von Wolgast won't mind." He chortled lasciviously. "You will not be able to walk for three days by the time I've done with you." He took hold of her hair, dislodging a flurry of pins, and tugged her into a kiss. When at last they broke apart, Persuic beamed at her. "Women are so depraved. No wonder your employer's son was smitten with you. I am."

As von Wolgast watched, the woman tried to stand up, only to be dragged back onto Persuic's lap. He decided it would be best to leave them alone, and after checking to be certain that von Nordlingen and the woman Gretta were still asleep, he signaled to von Rosenwiese, and indicated they should leave the parlor. "They will want privacy," the Baron remarked as he heard the thick taffeta of her dress tear.

"This is scandalous," said von Rosenwiese as they stepped into the corridor.

"Egmont, Egmont," von Wolgast chided him. "Just because women are not to your taste does not mean that a private act at a private party is scandalous. I will not say anything. Persuic certainly won't, nor will the woman. That leaves only you." He waited while von Rosenwiese considered what he was being told to do.

"You may rely on my discretion," he assured his host, unable to look at him. "If you are content to have your house used thus, what cause can I have to object."

"Very good," said von Wolgast, indicating the corridor back to the room where their festivities had begun. "We'll be private in there."

Von Rosenwiese heaved a sigh. "If you insist."

"Of course I do," said von Wolgast, trying not to gloat. "We have a few matters we must discuss, and there is no time like the present. Wouldn't you rather attend to this now, than have to call here again in a day or two?" They had reached the drawing room, and von Wolgast permitted von Rosenwiese to enter first, then closed the door. "Sit down. I will order coffee for us in a short while. But there are one or two matters I want to have . . . arranged between us." He stood until von Rosenwiese had selected one of the high-backed chairs; then he went to the settee and sat down, bringing his legs up onto the velvet upholstery. "You recall that I have wanted a stronger position within the Office of Procurement?"

"You have mentioned it, I believe," said von Rosenwiese, cursing himself for not having left an hour ago.

"And thus far, nothing has come of it." His tone was mild, but this was only the first salvo.

"I . . . I have had other demands on my time. The holidays are always filled with official entertainments, and it would make me conspicuous to attempt to press any of the men in the Office of Procurement . . . " His words straggled to nothing.

"There is some merit in what you say," von Wolgast allowed. "And I must suppose you are preparing to launch increased activities now that the New Year has come. Let me tell you, it does not look advantageous for me to have so many orders for my . . . products going out of Germany. If anything should erupt among those to whom I have supplied guns, I could be called to account if I have not been selling to Germany as well. I do not want to be seen as a profiteer. I am a patriot." He put his hand to his chest, only then noticing the large spot of mustard on his half-open shirtfront.

Von Rosenwiese sighed. "There is a man—Euchary Apfelobstgarten—who has been reviewing your sales; he has expressed interest in the orders handled by Sisak. I found that out only two days ago or I would have sent you word of it. I did not want to report falsely." He held up his hands in response to the thunderous look in von Wolgast's eyes. "I have been told the man has some link to Franchot Ragoczy, and has been upset at the intimations of criminal doings laid at his door. It seemed best to explore that avenue before approaching him."

"Apfelobstgarten," said von Wolgast. "I don't believe I know him." He made no mention of his encounter with the man at Chancellor von Bethmann-Hollweg's reception, trusting that von Rosenwiese had not been aware of it. "We may have met," he added cautiously.

"He is something of an independent, or he has that reputation. His degree is in chemistry, I am told, and he is considered a first-class thinker." This offering was made in the hope of diverting the worst of von Wolgast's wrath. "I was planning on seeking him out this next week."

Von Wolgast snorted. "First-class thinkers don't end up in the Office of Procurement. He may have secured good marks at university, but he would be at Farben or possibly Krupp if he was so accomplished."

"Perhaps he is interested in public service," von Rosenwiese suggested. "I don't know him beyond exchanging greetings, but it is possible."

Von Wolgast put the tips of his thick fingers together, trying to force his sodden thoughts into motion. "Does the man have any . . . weaknesses?"

"I have no idea," said von Rosenwiese, knowing where von Wolgast was heading.

"See what you can learn about him," von Wolgast recommended.

For a moment von Rosenwiese's temper flashed. "So you can blackmail him, too?" As soon as the words were out, he hoped the earth would open up and swallow him. He did his best to cling to his evaporating indignation.

"So that you will not be under so great an obligation to me," von Wolgast said smoothly. "You are aware that I will continue to make demands of you so long as I do not have another to do my bidding. You have made it abundantly clear that you dislike your position with me. You need not continue to occupy it." He was almost purring as he continued. "You

can become my lieutenant, von Rosenwiese, and profit from our association. Or you can continue to oppose me and pay the price for it."

"You are despicable," said von Rosenwiese, shocked by the suggestion that he might want to be part of von Wolgast's schemes. "Your
claims of patriotism are nothing more than blatant self-service."

"No; venal, perhaps, but not despicable. Despicable people are usually without influence, and I am not one such. And I am a patriotic German, no matter what else I may be. I know that we must preserve the
Kaiser if we are to have order in Europe, order maintained with German guns: my guns." He smiled faintly. "You have such tremendous
ideals, Egmont. How do you reconcile them to your perversion?"

"I need reconcile nothing," said von Rosenwiese, but without the conviction he had had moments before. "You have no idea—"

"What it is to have a cock up my backside? No, I don't." He folded
his arms. "I would rather have a woman."

"Then your wife must be a double disappointment to you," said von
Rosenwiese, striking back the only way he could. "Mad, and childless
to boot."

Von Wolgast pointed at von Rosenwiese, saying in quiet fury, "Leave
my wife out of this. If you mention her again, you are a dead man."

Von Rosenwiese believed him beyond question. He sat very still,
hardly willing to breathe, as his host paced around his chair. "I . . . " he
ventured when he could stand the tension no longer. "I did not mean
anything . . . "

"Of course you did," said von Wolgast, his tone silky and fatal. "You
wanted to be certain that I recognized the extent of your displeasure."
He rocked back on his heels. "You may rest assured: I do." His next
words were measured. "Just be sure that you recognize the extent of
mine."

"Ah . . . " Von Rosenwiese was finding it hard to breathe; his whole
body sagged. "I apologize, Baron. I . . . I hope you will not . . . "

"Show the letters to anyone?" von Wolgast supplied, his smile oiled
with his pleasure at von Rosenwiese's terror. "No, not yet. That would
make everything easy for you, wouldn't it?"

"That wasn't what I—"

"Egmont, you are an amateur at these games. Leave the field to
those who know how to play." He coughed delicately. "And keep in mind
that I will not tolerate any lapse about my wife again. Is that understood?"

"Yes. Yes. It is fully understood." He began to rise only to be shoved
back down into the chair by von Wolgast. "Is there something more?"

"Yes, Egmont. I am afraid there is." He stared down at his cringing guest and was almost sorry their conversation had to end. "I have been told that someone is watching me. I must know who it is, if indeed it is taking place at all. If anyone in the Kaiser's government is keeping a record of my movements and transactions, I must know. Is that clear? Report what you find to me in a week. Between Apfelobstgarten and the surveillance, you should have your time filled."

"I will try," said von Rosenwiese.

"You will do more than try—you will succeed," said von Wolgast with such conviction that von Rosenwiese was frightened afresh. "When I am satisfied that you have done enough to support my interests, I will return your correspondence to you. In case you should be tempted to be lax in these things, remember your performance will determine if and when you will be free to destroy those very compromising words you were foolish enough to commit to paper." He patted von Rosenwiese on the shoulder. "I look forward to a most profitable year for the both of us."

Von Rosenwiese could think of no appropriate response. He hunkered down in the chair and hoped von Wolgast would get back on the other side of the room. Finally, he forced himself to say, "I hope it may be, as well."

"Wise," von Wolgast approved, withdrawing to a place by the heavy draperies now shrouding the windows. "You will come, I think, to be pleased that I have dealt with you as I have. Many another would have used you and then exposed you, but I will not do that, so long as you continue to assist me. But you are aware of that already."

"Yes. I am aware of that." Von Rosenwiese felt the full weight of the demand come down upon him.

There was a loud bellow from the parlor, and a muffled shriek.

"What . . . ?" von Rosenwiese demanded in a shocked voice.

"Persuic and his companion, no doubt. He has probably exerted himself overmuch with her." Von Wolgast found von Rosenwiese's dismay amusing. "It is illegal to go to her aid, you know. You are not her father or her brother."

"And Persuic is not her husband," said von Rosenwiese, sticking by the letter of the law.

"A fine point," said von Wolgast, not turning his head as the shriek became a wail. "You would not find many advocates to support you in court, if you were impulsive enough to make an issue of it. I doubt the woman would welcome any official attention to her activities." He held up an admonishing finger. "And Colonel Persuic could make any case unpleasant for you, being an officer on diplomatic assignment here. We know how large a cloak diplomacy provides, do we not? The Colonel would be excused much on behalf of Austro-Hungary."

"Yes. I know that," said von Rosenwiese, relieved that no more sounds came from the parlor down the corridor. That such cries could be heard through two closed doors—he did not want to think what their cause might be.

"Then keep in mind that both of you are my guests. I would not want any embarrassment to result for either of you—or for me—from this evening's entertainment." He saw von Rosenwiese nod. "I think we begin to understand one another at last, my friend." He indicated the draperies. "No one beyond this house could possibly have heard anything, and you would have to stake your reputation on the scream of a whore. A poor exchange, I would have thought."

"I take your point," von Rosenwiese said after a short silence.

"I thought you would," said von Wolgast, liking to see von Rosenwiese squirm. He abandoned his sport reluctantly. "So. This next week you will find out what you can for me about Apfelobstgarten's inquiries, and inform me if it appears anything more may come of them. Then you are to discover who may be observing my movements, and why, and this you are to reveal to me as soon as you have any solid information." As he said this, he decided it was time to speak with Reighert once again; for all his faults, Reighert was an invaluable source of reliable intelligence.

"I will: of course I will." Von Rosenwiese scrambled to his feet, hoping the interminable evening might finally be ending. "If you will permit?"

"As soon as you thank me for the hospitality I have shown you; you know how such things are done," von Wolgast reminded him, relishing the stricken look that crossed von Rosenwiese's face. "Oh, Egmont, do not make such a chore of this. Pretend it is part of your work—for in a very real sense, it is." He gave a short, Prussian bow. "I am honored you accepted my invitation, von Rosenwiese. I look forward to our continued association." He beamed. "See how easy it is?"

"Yes." He went through the formal rituals of leave-taking, ending with the phrase, "I cannot tell you what a pleasure it has been to pass the evening in your company."

Von Wolgast laughed aloud at this. "No, Egmont," he said, his spirits once again restored. "I don't suppose you can."

Text of a letter from Carlisle Sunbury in London to Franchot Ragoczy in Saint Petersburg.

January 19, 1911

Franchot Ragoczy, Count Saint-Germain
Daum Saint-Germain
Nevsky Prospekt
Saint Petersburg, Russia

My dear Ragoczy;
How disappointing to have so much effort fail to bring the desired results. I have instructed my secretary to send you the papers you have requested; they will be delivered to your man-of-business, P. D. Golovin, by courier, within the month. That will be sent from the office, all right and tight, and with appropriate releases and signatures. I wanted to express my sympathy in a more personal form, hence this letter from my private study.

I must apologize for my inability to persuade such men in the government as I know share your apprehension about the European situation to advance your cause with HM's government. I had not anticipated such obdurate opposition to what I felt was a very reasonable mission. I am still perplexed as to the cause of it, and I have given many evenings to analyzing how this came about. After due consideration, I must suppose it springs from the growing fear of Bolshevism that has taken the popular fancy just now. Although why anyone should assume that Czar Nicholas is a Bolshevik, I cannot think.

In accordance with your instructions, I have continued to authorize payment on your house lease, and have kept up the salaries of Timothy Harris and Loretta Nowell. While I know you can well afford these expenses, I would be remiss if I did not remind you that you own buildings in London where you might establish yourself with less cost to you. Having said this, I will resign myself to maintaining the arrangement you already have in place. These two individuals have proved most reliable, and I agree it would be time-consuming and costly to replace them on short notice. We both know there are ways to deal with this, but I will not waste my time by reminding you what they are.

I have been led to understand that you have had some contact with Rowena Pearce-Manning in Amsterdam. I impute no questionable purpose to this, but I feel I must tell you that your association with Miss Pearce-Manning has caused her mother great distress. I have promised her I would tell you of her many reservations in regard to you where her daughter is concerned. She is very much afraid that this latest escapade—her word, not mine—will ruin all Miss Pearce-Manning's *chances for a good match. That is her first worry, but by no means her last. She has enumerated them to me many times in the last two months. A young woman of Miss Pearce-Manning's fortune might easily fall prey to those unscrupulous men who batten on women with money. Nothing I have told her has convinced her that you are not one such. She has expostulated at length on the fatal attraction certain foreigners exert over impressionable, well-bred girls. More than once I have observed to Lady Pearce-Manning that her oldest daughter is no longer a schoolgirl, and well able to take care of herself, all to no avail. Clarice has decided you are seduction incarnate and is unwilling to believe you have any goal beyond the ruining of her firstborn.*

You mentioned you may return to London before summer. If you do, let me warn you that you may have to endure a few cold shoulders and other indications of support for Lady Pearce-Manning. Most sensible persons recognize the overblown sentiments of Lady Pearce-Manning as precisely what they are. But a few have combined those distraught diatribes with the failure of your diplomatic mission, and have developed more serious reservations. These may prove to be the more difficult to counteract, and you are well-advised to be prepared to deal with them. I need not remind you, such rumors are Hydra-like—cut one off and two more grow in its place.

Pray do not let these uncharitable aspersions keep you from returning. I assure you most here have goodwill toward you and regard your presence as an asset to the scene. I would enjoy another opportunity to discuss your theories on the language of the ancient Romans. I confess, until you mentioned it, I never considered the matter of dialect and jargon in Roman speech, though it makes sense.

In the hope that your efforts may at last prevail, I remain

Most sincerely,
Carlisle Sunbury

2

In the drawing room half-a-dozen guests gathered in the fading afternoon to hear Countess Amalija's illustrious guest play Chopin and Liszt on her splendid Chickering square grand piano; it was usually consid-

ered a coup to be invited to one of Countess Amalija's salons, but this
one was not as well-attended as many due to the uncertain standing
Franchot Ragoczy was thought to have with Czar Nikolai. As he was
the pianist, many of the high-born of Saint Petersburg thought it wise
to stay away. Fortunately there had been enough of a storm that morning to make excuses readily come by.

"Don't let it bother you," Countess Amalija recommended to
Ragoczy, as she went to greet late-arriving guests, whose motor car had
just drawn up at the coach-door. "It is nothing more than the usual social snobism, and the fear of courtiers to be without favor. We'll tell
everyone it is on account of the storm, as they have told me, and we
can all shake our heads together." She signaled her majordomo, saying,
"We will delay for a few minutes so that whoever-that-is may come up."

"I have played for fewer," said Ragoczy, recalling the many times
music had gained him admission where no other skill would. He retired
to a corner of the room to wait.

"As you wish, Countess," said her majordomo, bowing enough to be
respectful but not so much to be cowed, in accordance with recent re-
visions of servants' conduct in the Czar's household.

"Gennady is a gem, isn't he?" Countess Amalija asked Ragoczy before going to her drawing room door, and lifting a hand to wave to her
nephew Leonid, in the company of his youngest brother Konstantine.

"Sorry to be late, Aunt," said Leonid as he came up the stairs. "Irina
was having trouble with the baby, and . . . well, I couldn't leave her until
the physician arrived and declared all well."

"Commendable," Countess Amalija approved as she offered her
cheek for her nephew to kiss. "I am not going to stand on ceremony
with you. Or with you, Konstantine. And don't you look splendid in your
uniform?"

The Guard cadet blushed to the roots of his tawny hair; he had just
turned seventeen and was still caught in the tumult of youth and striving to his utmost to seem two or three years more experienced than he
actually was. "Thank you. I am proud to have been accepted. There is
always an Ohchenov in the Guards." He gave his oldest brother an ad-
miring look. "Leonid arranged it for me to join a year early."

"With some help from our Aunt Amalija," Leonid reminded Konstantine, and glanced around the drawing room. "A little thin of company," he observed.

"Alas," Countess Amalija agreed with a sarcastic light in her fine
eyes. "The weather is so cold. February is often the harshest part of the
winter."

"I see," said Leonid knowledgeably, "It must be the chill." With that he indicated the large brass samovar on the table across the room. "Konstantine, make yourself useful and get us both a glass of tea, will you?" He showed an expression of concern only after the young man had left his side. "Ragoczy is still regarded as trouble, is he?"

"So it would seem," the Countess admitted. "But I will not let Nikolai Alexandreivich Romanov's freaks change my friends for me. If I were twenty, it might be different, but I am old enough to know how important friends are, and how insignificant a Czar's whim can be." She indicated a dozen empty chairs. "Sit wherever you like. I am grateful you are here, and your brother."

"I am more respectful of an auntly summons than I am of court gossip; after all, I am your heir," said Leonid with a wink, then bowed slightly before going to take a chair, greeting the other guests as he did. A moment later, Konstantine joined him, two glasses of steaming tea in lavishly decorated pewter holders clutched in his hands. "Very good. Now sit down and listen."

Obediently, Konstantine did, smiling at his brother. "I don't understand the music of Chopin," he whispered.

"It doesn't matter," Leonid assured him as he took his glass of tea. "You can like it without understanding it."

"I hope so," said his youngest brother devoutly.

Countess Amalija resigned herself to the small attendance as she stepped in front of the Chickering grand and said, "Thank you so much for coming this afternoon, with the snow falling and the rest of it." She glanced once at Ragoczy standing a short distance away. "Most of you already know Count Saint-Germain from his long residence in Saint Petersburg, but few of you have had the pleasure of hearing him play. I have asked him if he would remedy that, and so he has agreed to perform some of the works of Chopin and Liszt." She turned to him, holding out her hand. "Count, if you will?"

Ragoczy stepped forward and bowed slightly to the listeners. "Allow me to echo the sentiments of your hostess: thank you so much for coming, and in such inclement weather. I think it is appropriate that I begin with Chopin's *Winter Wind.*" He saw Leonid smile, and felt that the afternoon would not be a complete exercise in futility. Flexing his fingers he took his place before the keyboard and began, his small hands working unexpected magic with the long chromatic plunges that characterized the piece. At its conclusion, the applause he was given was more than polite. He turned on the bench, saying. "I would next like to play Liszt's piano transcription of Bellini's opera *Norma.*" It was as difficult for the pianist as the title role was difficult for sopranos, written by Liszt to show off his own consummate virtuosity and to intimidate less accomplished pianists; Ragoczy loved it as much for its demands as for its remarkable musicality. He put his whole attention on the keyboard, and the music he had memorized decades ago.

He was six minutes into the piece when there was a stir in the room and two latecomers sat down at the back of the room, waving away the flurry of attention offered by Countess Amalija and her staff. At the conclusion of the work, the latercomers were the first to applaud.

"Bravo, bravo," enthused Czar Nikolai, while his lovely Czarina continued to clap.

There were exclamations and a buzz of whispers. The other guests rose, the women curtsying, the men bowing. Ragoczy got to his feet and bowed.

"This isn't Court, sit down, sit down," said Czar Nikolai, coming up to the piano to shake Ragoczy's hand.

"Thank you," Ragoczy said sincerely. "And not for your applause alone."

"Let us pretend it is for the applause, or for Countess Amalija Romanovna," said the Czar, going on amiably, "I don't know about you, but just listening to Liszt exhausts me. After such a harrowing piece, I should think you would want an interval, wouldn't you?"

Even if it was not what Ragoczy had planned he knew better than to argue with such a recommendation. "I am at your disposal, Czar."

"And precious little good it has done you, for which I ask your pardon," said Nikolai, pointing to the samovar. "If you will bear me company, I want to get my wife a glass of tea. Come with me."

Ragoczy went with him, noticing the other guests had not yet moved to help themselves to the tea or hors d'oeuvres laid out for them.

"I had no idea you played so well," the Czar went on, determinedly making small talk. "You could be on the concert stage, I should think."

"That is a difficult life," Ragoczy observed as Gennady appeared to pour two glasses of tea for the royal guests.

"It may be. But it is no more difficult than the one I have required of you," said Czar Nikolai, doing his best to make sure they were overheard. "I hold you in no way accountable for the decisions of my cousins. Your conduct was all that was admirable. I had no concept of how adamant my relatives could be." He put his hand on Ragoczy's shoulder, knowing that by this time tomorrow it would be all over Saint Petersburg that Ragoczy was in the Czar's favor once again. "I am sorry it has taken so long for me to acknowledge the great service you have done." He sighed and glanced at Alexandra. "Sunny is so disappointed," he said in English.

"She is afraid for your son," Ragoczy agreed in the same language.

"As are we all. And I thought it was a reasonable plan, beneficial to us and to them. I still do," Nikolai declared, and continued in Russian, "It is a pity that my cousins were unwilling to consider my suggestion, but so be it. I can take satisfaction in knowing I made the attempt. I pray we will not all pay the price for their folly." His face was genial but his eyes were troubled. "Well, however it turns out, I am in your debt, Count." He picked up the two glasses of tea and went back to where his Czarina waited for him, listening to Countess Amalija tell her what the rest of the program would be.

"That was well-done of him," Leonid remarked as he came up to Ragoczy, watching the other guests hover in the vicinity of the Czar and Czarina. "I would not have thought he could be so generous."

"I did not suppose he would have made so public a show of it," said Ragoczy, wondering why the Czar had chosen so open a place to reestablish his regard for his foreign friend. He had supposed that in a month or two he would have been summoned to the Winter Palace for a reception or other court function and received with a modicum of goodwill. To be given such a gesture of approval as attending this private concert was extraordinary.

"Whatever his reason, it was a fine demonstration. No one will doubt Nikolai's confidence in you now," said Leonid, at last looking away from the Czar to give his whole attention to Ragoczy. "You must be relieved to have it behind you; all that traveling and clandestine talks."

"Ah, but it is not behind me, not entirely," said Ragoczy with a curt nod of his head. "I was recalled from Germany with a cloud over me, and I know it would be idiotic to let it remain any longer than absolutely necessary." He saw the astonished look in Leonid's eyes. "I will go back, if Nikolai will permit me to," he admitted.

"Why?" Leonid demanded. "What can suspicions in Germany do to you here in Russia?" He refilled his tea glass. "It's not as if you would have to go to Berlin any time soon."

"I am an exile," Ragoczy reminded him. "And as such, I travel. To be restricted in that regard is more than inconvenient. I have businesses in Holland, Switzerland, and Germany that would make any crimes alleged against me detrimental to my ventures. I may have to return to Berlin one of these years, and if this matter has not been resolved, my hands would be tied both literally and figuratively." He paused and went on more crisply. "And in these days of telegraphs and telephones, and international newspapers, rumors may fly farther than ever they did before. What is suspected in Berlin today may be whispered in Moscow tomorrow."

"Surely it is not so bad as that," said Leonid, though he was much struck with what Ragoczy had said.

"I hope it is not, but I am far from certain of it," said Ragoczy, and smiled as Countess Amalija came up to them. "Flushed with success, you snatch victory from the very jaws of defeat," he said with a mixture of gallantry and amusement, one fine brow lifting as he continued. "Confess it, you are delighted to have the Czar and Czarina here, and not for my sake alone."

"Yes, indeed. I am quite beside myself, if only you knew. I would probably be capering with glee if I were twenty years younger and we were on a picnic. I can hardly wait for tongues to start wagging. By next week, you will be amazed how many people will have been here. This room will have overflowed, if all of the boasts will be believed." She was able to laugh quietly enough to keep from any possible disrespect to Nikolai and Alexandra.

"You're probably right," said Ragoczy, and looked quizzically at her nephew. "What do you think, Leonid Yureivich?"

"I think that Saint Petersburg would do better to pay attention to more important issues than court functions, if you want my honest opinion," he said, with an expression of genuine worry on his face. "I am shocked at the number of sensible persons who are paying no attention to what is going on around them. You may dismiss what I tell you, but I have been listening to what the students are saying, and it is very troubling. This is more than the complaints of discontents, or the shouts of a rebellious few. It is not simply a question of what happened six years ago; there is something deeper and more sinister taking place. I don't say this to frighten you or to make myself a prophet of doom, but because I am convinced we are in real danger. There are firebrands exhorting them to be the forefront of reform and revolution."

"Surely the Duma will deal with them," said Countess Amalija. "That is what the Duma is for, Leonid. You know how students are, wanting the world to fall into accord with the favorite theories."

"Yes, I know that, Aunt," said Leonid, though the vertical line between his brows did not fade. "But students are not the only ones who are demonstrating."

"That's so," she agreed. "And with good cause, if what I read is accurate. And in time it will be possible for the Duma to resolve their grievances. It isn't as if there have been no improvements in the last five years."

"There has been a taste of reform, and the taste whets the appetite, particularly for those who think they have nothing to lose," said Ragoczy, recalling what he had seen in France, slightly more than a century before. "The zealots will shout down the moderates if the government does not move quickly."

"To stop them, you mean?" Leonid asked. "I would think that would make martyrs, and they would become rallying points."

"Exactly," said Ragoczy. "The government would be wise to incorporate as many reforms as possible, as soon as it can, putting emphasis on those things that will improve the lot of the most disenfranchised. Without the reforms, the zealots will gather credibility, and once they find a leader who moves the people, it will be beyond remedy." He recalled what had happened in Fiorenza when Laurenzo died and Savonarola had moved to fill the gap he left. The devastation of Savonarola's four years of power to that most humanist of cities had marked the place for two centuries; Danton and Robespierre had left a similar but bloodier mark on Paris. "No country is immune to extremists."

"But how are they stopped? Would you put them in prison, if you could?" Leonid asked with genuine curiosity.

"Certainly not, unless their offenses were great enough to demand such punishment, and even then, I should take care not to create martyrs," Ragoczy said at once. "I would expose them for what they are, make their intentions known to those they try to influence, show what the consequences of their demands would be." He was aware as he said this that he had tried it more than once in the past and had not succeeded in stemming the tide. "To meet force with force gives credibility to their zeal and disguises their greed."

"Zealots, force: if you must talk about such dire things, I will go attend to my less ferocious guests," the Countess said, and left them.

"Did that happen in your homeland, Count? Did your people come under the influence of an ambitious charlatan?" Leonid inquired, and added with a self-deprecatory laugh, "I do not mean to offend you, but you speak as if you have seen the trouble you describe, and I could not help but—"

"Oh, yes, I have seen the thing I describe," said Ragoczy, his dark eyes flinty with memory, "Not in my homeland, though. Our defeat was the case of a larger, better-armed force with powerful allies opposing us.

Inevitably the larger, better-armed foe won." Their defeat had been accelerated when his father's younger brother had thrown in his lot with the enemy, realizing he would salvage himself from the devastation; Ragoczy had seen the same pattern repeated countless times since his family had been defeated four thousand years ago.

"Is that why you were willing to help the Czar try to limit the spread of arms?" He noticed the reserve that came over Ragoczy, and explained. "I do not intend to intrude, but there has been much speculation regarding your mission. Of all the suppositions, that was the most credible theory. It was all over the Guard since summer that the Czar was seeking an arms limitation agreement with his cousins. We supposed that was what you were doing for him in Europe. Don't tell me we were wrong."

"You will have to ask Czar Nikolai about the particulars, if you want them; I am not at liberty to discuss them. But I will tell you this much: my abhorrence of war did incline me to act on his behalf." Ragoczy did nothing overt, but a distance seemed to widen between him and Leonid Ohchenov.

Leonid understood he had overstepped himself, although he did not know how, and said, "I did not mean to ask anything compromising, Count; that was not my intention. I ask your pardon if I did."

"Your Aunt would require me to grant it even if I were not so inclined," Ragoczy replied, and the gulf disappeared.

"So she would, if I know her," said Leonid, smiling fondly as he looked across the parlor to Countess Amalija, who was deep in conversation with the Czarina. "A wonderful woman, in spite of all the tragedy in her life. I can't imagine how we would have grown up without her."

"Less pleasantly, no doubt," said Ragoczy, and saw Nikolai signal to him. "If you will excuse me?" He did not wait for Leonid to speak. As he reached the Czar, he bowed once. "Nikolai Alexandreivich, I am at your service."

"As I am keenly aware," said the Czar, touching his wife's arm. "My dear, if you will give me a moment with the Count?"

"Certainly, my dear," she said, barely glancing in Ragoczy's direction before pointedly returning her attention to Countess Amalija and a discussion of pearls.

"You will have to forgive her; if we were not at so small a function she would not behave so . . . brusquely," Nikolai said in a lowered voice as he stepped out into the corridor. "Otyets Grigori has unaccountably taken you in dislike, and Sunny follows his lead in all things."

"I am sorry to hear it," said Ragoczy, who had no high opinion of Rasputin. "I have never been aware of offending him."

"He is a holy man who sees many things," the Czar said. "He has done so much for our son—"

"And you are grateful," said Ragoczy when Nikolai broke off.

"Yes. But it is true that Otyets Grigori takes aversions to certain people for reasons that are obscure. You, I regret to say, are one such. He has said that he feels the presence of death when you are near, and the Czarina takes such warnings to heart. And so my wife is wary of you, although I am not." Nikolai glanced at the door to be certain they were not overheard. "I think she is convinced that you are not as . . . as dedicated to preventing war as she would like, and that accounts for the warning Rasputin has given. What else could Rasputin have against you that would make my wife mistrust you beyond that sense?" He took a long breath that was not quite a sigh. "Rasputin has warned us about war, telling us that without peace we will fall. I think the Czarina believes that peace is so sensible that no one would knowingly . . . And if you did not secure peace, Rasputin is right, and death is around you. . . . " He let his words fade away. "Tell me, Franchot Nemovich,"— he used the patronymic Ragoczy had assigned to himself more than three hundred years ago, during his stay in the court of Ivan Grosny— "are you truly determined to return to Berlin and deal with Nadezna's murder?" He did not wait for an answer, hurrying on, "I had a note from Countess Amalija Romanovna, expressing her concern that this was your intention, despite the risk such an action would pose."

Ragoczy did his best to keep his response level. "Yes, Czar, it is what I want to do."

Nikolai shook his head. "My protection cannot be extended a second time. Cousin Willy will not tolerate it. If you go back, it will be without any support from me beyond my personal concern. Do you comprehend this?"

"Of course I do," said Ragoczy, and softened this blunt admission by adding, "I am grateful for your concern, Czar, and I know the gravity of my situation; I do not underestimate the hazards I face. But if it were you, would you be willing to have such a crime laid at your door when you knew that the true criminal had escaped the consequences of his act and left you to carry his burden?"

"I would not want such a thing to happen, no," Czar Nikolai allowed. "But you must be aware that the Germans are far more ready to suspect foreigners than they are Germans, and by your very alienness, you are in danger."

"I have some grasp of this, yes; nor are the Germans the only people to distrust foreigners," Ragoczy told him, as his millennia-long memories jostled in his mind. "I mean no discourtesy when I say this: we will not settle this tonight, Czar, and I have more music to play before this salon is at an end." He nodded to the half-open door. "And I suppose you would rather be more private in our discussions than we can be here."

Nikolai nodded and held up his hands in resignation. "In two days I have time in the evening, after ten. If you will come, we will discuss this more fully."

Ragoczy bowed. "As you wish," he said, knowing he would not change his mind.

"I will anticipate your visit with pleasure." With the skill of long experience, Nikolai assumed a more genial tone as he went back into the salon, saying, "Knowing what a busy man you are, Count, I wonder that you have time to practice your music. Yet obviously, you do."

"I do not sleep a great deal," Ragoczy said candidly. "I have two or three hours most nights when I play."

"How fortunate your servants are, to have so expert a serenade," the Czar remarked, and smiled enough to show this was a joke.

Taking the same bantering tone, Ragoczy said, "I regret to tell you that I have never inquired of them what they think. I have supposed they would rather sleep undisturbed."

"Then they are not deserving of such a master," said Nikolai, dismissing the matter with a shrug.

Ragoczy bowed again, and prepared to return to the keyboard. As he passed Leonid, Amalija's nephew whispered, "Restored to grace."

"In a manner of speaking," Ragoczy replied softly, then resumed his place at the piano, announcing his next selections as the room fell quiet.

When the music was over, the Czar and Czarina did not linger; they gave minimal ceremony to their departure, all the while heaping polite, appreciative phrases on Ragoczy and Countess Amalija. Leaving, they discovered a gloomy evening, with heavy clouds drifting overhead; the last of the winter sunlight had faded two hours before, and the streets were marked by the piles of snow along them. Inside all the stoves and fireplaces were pressed into use to keep off the pervasive cold. The other guests were effusive in their thanks for the whole occasion, one woman going to far as to tell Countess Amalija that she would rather spend the afternoon at this salon than in her box at the ballet.

"And you know that is not true. Rather be here than at the ballet indeed," said the Countess after most of her guests had departed and she was reveling in her triumph with Leonid and Konstantine; Ragoczy listened without interrupting her recitation. "She makes it a point of honor to be in her box whenever she can, and not just so all society will talk about what jewels she was wearing."

"She wants to be included in your next salon," said Konstantine, feeling very sophisticated for recognizing this.

"Of *course* she does," said Leonid. "Marina Gavrileivna is just the sort of woman who finds her greatest enjoyment in reporting on what she has done and with whom instead of in the event itself."

"Think of the frantic life she is forced to lead in order to have new conquests to preen about; there is no end to the demands of being at the forefront of the season," said Countess Amalija, and then put her hand to her cheek. "That was beyond the line, even for me." She was chagrined. "I did not think I could be so catty. I am ashamed of myself."

"No reason to be," said Leonid. "It is what anyone with any sense would think, having seen her here." He grinned impulsively, and wagged his finger in gentle admonition at his Aunt. "You tell me you did not speak accurately, and I will cry shame with you." He was finishing the last of the caviar, spreading it on small rounds of toast and squeezing lemon juice on top of it.

"Well, accurately perhaps, but not charitably," said the Countess, glancing at Ragoczy and then looking away. "I heard her whisper something to Duchess Olga Petrovna about you and it . . . offended me."

"Ah," said Ragoczy. "And what did she say?"

"She . . . she was not surprised that I should be taken in by such a charming imposter as you." Her voice dropped lower and lower with each word so at the end she was barely whispering.

To the Countess' astonishment, Ragoczy laughed aloud. "What perspicacity! I wonder what she would say if she knew as much about me as you do, Amalija Romanovna?"

To Leonid's bafflement, his Aunt joined in the laughter. "My word," he said, looking from one to the other. "Konstantine, what has come over them?"

His youngest brother shook his head, knowing when to stay out of adult matters. He drank down his tea and went to get the last dark, stewed liquid out of the samovar, removing himself from the perplexing turn their conversation had taken.

While Konstantine was on the far side of the parlor, Countess Amalija stopped laughing and confided, "You know, I worry about him, being in the Guard at a time like this. What happens if fighting breaks out again? He's so young."

"I know," said Leonid. "I am concerned for him, too. Anyone with a trace of good sense would be. But it is the tradition, and we haven't fortune enough to establish all the family without gaining some patronage for them." He slapped his knee. "I have tried to think of some way to keep him safe, but short of withdrawing him from being a cadet, there is nothing I can do."

"And he would resent that," said Amalija knowingly. "He thinks himself glorious just for wearing the uniform."

"And with good cause," said Leonid in defense of the Guard. "It is an honor to be part of that service. I counted myself very lucky to have been in the Guard." He noticed that Konstantine was coming back. "So I hope that the Czar is able to establish some peace in Russia if not in the world."

"For his own son as much as for anyone else's," said Countess Amalija. "I don't know what ails the boy, but he is not strong, and I think the Czar and Czarina would rather die than see Alexei go off to battle." She shivered.

"They love their children," said Leonid. "They do not want to see any of them come to harm. And with just the one son to inherit, they will be inclined to protect him more than most children, and would do so if he were hale as a horse, instead of given to fevers." He stared at the platter where the dregs of caviar sat in a bowl surrounded by shaved ice that was now mostly slush. "I think of my children, and I know how it would make me feel, to see them exposed to war. How much more dire it is for Nikolai and Alexandra, whose dynasty rides on the shoulders of the Czareivich."

"You speak as if you think war is coming," said Konstantine, a martial light in his youthful face. "Think what excitement we would have then."

"Think of the calamity," his Aunt admonished him.

"It would make my career, to fight in battle," Konstantine insisted. "It's what we all hope for, a war to gain promotion and notice."

"Providing you survived," said Ragoczy curtly.

"Count," Countess Amalija protested.

"Well, of course I should survive," said Konstantine with the confidence of inexperience. "I may not have seen real fighting, but I have got high marks in my maneuvers."

"Are you certain that war is the same?" asked Leonid, suddenly very somber. "I wish I could be."

"What would be the point of maneuvers if war were not like them?" Konstantine asked, his temper flaring at what he thought was a slight to his honor.

"It could be that maneuvers are intended to give you a context to reduce the confusion of war," said Ragoczy gently. "War is so confusing that without a context, it is easy to become wholly disoriented and thereby do yourself and your men more harm than good." He studied the far wall. "War is also very noisy, and you cannot rely on hearing the commands you expect. The maneuvers you practice give you something that is familiar to all for those times when the guns speak louder than anything else."

"My word, Count," said Leonid with dawning respect, "You talk like a true officer. I would think you must have been in war at the worst. I had no idea the battle for your homeland was so—"

"I suppose all battles have more in common than not," said Ragoczy, recalling himself. "The guns shoot farther and faster than they used to, but that only makes the confusion worse."

Leonid nodded. "True enough," he said in a measured way, the speculative angle of his head indicating he was not yet satisfied that Ragoczy had told him all he knew about the nature of war. He would have asked more, but Ragoczy's daunting reserve had returned, and he could not summon up enough audacity to attempt to break through it.

"I wish you would talk about something more pleasant," Countess Amalija admonished them all. "You may think me a squeamish old woman, but whenever I hear talk of war, I cannot forget all the dead." She gave a wan smile. "Say what you will, the dead are the harvest of war."

"I will not argue," said Ragoczy quietly, but with such feeling that Leonid obediently changed the subject to the controversy surrounding the Paris premiere of Igor Stravinsky's *Firebird* ballet, and the forthcoming new work to be performed in Poland, *Petroushka*. Within an hour Leonid dragged his youngest brother away from their Aunt's house, leaving Ragoczy and Amalija Romanovna Khormanskaya alone.

"Do you think they are lovers?" Konstantine asked Leonid as they drove away.

"I think if they are it is no one's business but theirs," said Leonid pointedly.

Countess Amalija watched the automobile make irregular progress down the icy street, remarking over her shoulder, "Konstantine is growing up so fast."

"Not half as fast as he would like to," said Ragoczy. "He would give an ear to be twenty-five tomorrow."

"And there are times I would give an ear to be twenty-five again," said the Countess, chuckling, and came away from the window. "Are you really going back to Berlin?"

"I think I must," said Ragoczy. "But I will go to Amsterdam first. And possibly to France."

"Amsterdam. Your English artist," said the Countess with a slight smile. "I hope she is as talented as you think she is."

"I will try to bring you something she has done," he promised, coming up to her and laying his hands on her shoulders. "I have not yet thanked you for your determination to restore me to Nikolai's good graces. And do not tell me," he went on as she shook her head, "that the Czar and Czarina simply happened by this afternoon: they were out for a drive and decided to stop in? Truly? That would not convince even a child."

"And you are not a child," said Amalija, making a gesture of concession. "Very well; I did send a note around to the Winter Palace in the hope it might be useful."

He kissed her, offering her more affection than passion. "I am honored that you would do so much for me."

"It was not entirely for you," she reminded him, moving away from him toward the piano. "I have gained much from their visit, and I intend to make the most of it."

"And so you should," Ragoczy agreed, going after her.

"Yes; I think so." She stopped in front of the keyboard and began to pick out the melody of *Sadko's Song of India.* "When were you planning on going?"

"The end of next week, if the weather allows. I will go by sea to Amsterdam." He could not conceal his dislike of travel over water, and made no effort to do so.

"Roger is going with you?" she asked, still playing.

"Yes," said Ragoczy, saying with unexpected humility, "I told him it was not necessary, but he refused to remain here. He said someone would have to handle my affairs if I were incarcerated, and he would be the one."

"He is very loyal to you," said the Countess, sitting on the bench in order to continue to play, now using both hands.

"He is," said Ragoczy. He stood and listened to her for a short while. "Are you angry with me?"

Countess Amalija stopped playing and turned to look at him. "No, Franchot Nemovich, I am not angry," she told him before putting her attention on her music once more, "I am frightened."

Text of a letter from Sidney Reilly to "C" sent in code using Key 49, from Berlin, Germany to London by diplomatic courier, delivered February 19, 1911.

I must tell you again how distasteful it is to me to withhold information from the police that would exonerate Ragoczy from all suspicion regarding any part he might have played in the murder of Nadezna. My records and the records of my agent L.S. can show that Ragoczy was gone from the house by the time von Wolgast arrived, and further, that there was blood on von Wolgast's clothes when he and his accomplice left. This should serve not only to end all suspicion for Ragoczy, it may cause the authorities to resume their investigation of her death. I am certain your cautions are too severe in regard to my speaking with the police. So far as they are concerned, Oertel Morgenstern is a legitimate journalist from Prague, who has been assigned to Berlin to report on the cultural life. They would have no reason to think that I had my own network of spies to protect, and they would understand that as a journalist, I would require a number of sources for my articles. I wish you would reconsider and give me permission to speak to the police, as Morgenstern, of course. I could provide them my notes in such a way that my network will be wholly protected. I know that the murder of Renfred Meyer has demanded greater vigilance in these matters, but I dislike the unnecessary damning of an innocent man all in the name of preserving the network I have developed in Berlin.

I have kept some watch on von Wolgast since that last night, and I am convinced he is one of those working to discredit Ragoczy here in Germany. I can understand why an arms manufacturer might want to promote war for his own profits, but I find it contemptible that this Baron von Wolgast would actively try to ruin a man seeking to bring about a limited peace. It is one thing to engage in open debate but quite another to resort to the subterfuge von Wolgast employs. You may think it odd that I, of all persons, should castigate anyone for taking such steps as this Baron has, but I tell you there is no one more keenly aware of the limits that should be adhered to than I am. If von Wolgast were engaged in espionage, I would not cavil at what he is doing, but he presents himself as a man of business, not a spy. I find such double-dealing and underhandedness reprehensible. Had he not participated in

Nadezna's murder, I would still think him despicable. You may say that I am splitting hairs when I remind you that I am only willing to kill when that death advances the purpose of my mission. Others may think that the differences between von Wolgast and me are minor; I think they are vast. For that reason alone, I want to see von Wolgast answer for his crime. That prosecution of von Wolgast would lift the shadow of suspicion from Ragoczy is an added benefit that may prove useful in future.

I must also tell you that I think having this man removed from his sphere of activities would be of great benefit to Britain. Having guns being sold indiscriminately throughout the world the way von Wolgast has been doing endangers areas of British interests. You are aware, I know, that von Wolgast works extensively with Tancred Sisak, and is party to some of the most questionable sales and transfers of weapons taking place in the world today. If von Wolgast were removed from the game, another might well take his place, but we would have time to put men in place to monitor what he does. I need not point out the use that would be.

I reiterate my plea to be allowed to speak with the police. Inspector Herbert Blau who has charge of the investigation has an excellent reputation for integrity, and I know if I go to him directly he will pursue all the information supplied with diligence and vigor. I can probably persuade him that it would be unwise for me to testify. Since Blau is no fool, he is likely to respect what I tell him. I maintain that the circumstances in this particular instance are extenuating and that Ragoczy would not be the only one to realize worthwhile ends as a result of my actions. Let me have your response quickly, for I fear that von Wolgast might remove himself from Berlin if he learns that his crimes are not as secret as he has persuaded himself they are.

Sidney Reilly (Capt.)

3

At the first sound of the door-knocker, Rowena rushed down the stairs, calling to her housekeeper not to bother: she would answer it herself. "I know who it is, Yseut." She had been anticipating this moment since she had wakened, earlier than usual, at the first glimmer of dawn, her mind swimming with images from her dreams. She had spent most of the morning fretting under weepy skies, discontented with her attempts at work and unable to concentrate enough to remedy them. She had fretted over a dozen sketches and set them aside, annoyed at the quality of work she was doing, and blaming it on the muzzy light the rain created. An hour ago, she had left off all pretense and gone down to her bedroom to dress for Ragoczy's return. She had spent the last ten minutes attempting to read more of Frank Norris' *The Octopus*. Now as she swung open the door, she had to admit to herself that her pleasure at seeing Ragoczy went beyond mere flirtation to an emotion that troubled her as much as it delighted her.

"Rowena," he said, removing his Russian hat and bowing slightly to her. "My cherished one. How good to see you." He was elegant in his black cashmere topcoat, open just enough to reveal the white of his silken shirt and the rich, black silk tie with his eclipse sigil worked in dark burgundy.

Flushed with excitement and the intrusion of cold, she beamed at him. "I've made progress on your portrait, Count. You must let me show it to you," she said, all but dragging him into the house and closing the door. "I don't want to lose all the heat, or let the rain in," she explained as she put the latch in place.

Ragoczy submitted to this flurry of activity until the door was secure; then he took Rowena in his arms and kissed her thoroughly, only drawing back when she moved. "I've missed you," he said to her. "Let me look at you."

She had donned a neat suit in red-amber wool, one with a wide collar and a dropped waistband of russet velvet that clung to her hips, setting off the straight line of the skirt that reached almost to her ankles and the neat rose-brown button-pumps. Beneath it, her blouse of ecru silk had a simple, mannish collar instead of a lace insert, revealing his frog necklace at her throat; her short strawberry-blond hair was newly trimmed and she had touched her lashes with kohl and used lip-rouge on her mouth; she smelled faintly of violet scent. "Well?" she asked.

"Very fetching; I'm truly complimented," he told her, adding, his demeanor gently teasing, "So fetching that I hope you weren't painting in such nice clothes, or that you wore a smock if you did."

"I've quite wasted the morning, waiting for you to come," she confessed. "How was your journey."

"Tedious," he admitted, "as all journeys over water are for those of my blood. We do not relish separation from the earth." He thought of the many times he had traveled in closed rooms or in the holds of ships in order to be atop the crates of his native earth; it helped alleviate the worst of his misery.

"It is difficult to imagine you at such a loss," she told him, taking his hand in hers and then letting it go.

"Be glad you have never had to deal with it. Roger is a hero for what he does when we travel over water," said Ragoczy with great feeling. "I do not say hero lightly."

"Do bridges bother you?" she asked, prolonging the courtesy of the moment. "Amsterdam is filled with bridges."

"Yes; and canals," he confirmed. "It is hard to escape running water here."

"Does that cause you distress?" she inquired, with a stab of chagrin for his discomfort.

"Upon occasion; it is quickly remedied when I am once again on solid ground," he said. "Crossing oceans takes longer."

"And the rain?" she asked with an involuntary glance at the door, as if she expected it to burst open, flooding them.

"It is a mild inconvenience when it is like this. Severe storms are more taxing, but not unbearable," he said. "And neither rain nor storms nor running water would keep me away." As long as he wore his earth-lined shoes, he added to himself.

"Well, water or not, I am happy to have you back in Amsterdam." She laughed, her self-consciousness fading as she saw the ardor ignite in his eyes. "I've been working on your portrait; it's three-quarters done, I think," she said. "And I've done a series of studies of barges on the canals, trying to improve my eye with near and far light. They aren't as good as I want them to be, but they are not too shabby, either. You can tell me what you think when you see them."

"They're probably excellent," he said, shrugging out of his coat and hanging it on the coatrack by the door, then met her gaze steadily. "You, like most artists, compare what you have done to the perfect version you have in your mind, and you find what you have done lacking. As the rest of us can make no such comparison, we are more easily satisfied." His compelling eyes rested on hers; then he took her face in his hands and kissed her again, this time tenderly, all his attention concentrated on her, on the texture and weight and warmth of her.

When she drew back from him, she was somewhat shaken. "You've never kissed me that way before," she said, her cheeks flushed anew.

"You've never wanted me to before," he said, his voice somber and lighthearted at once. The entryway was small enough to feel crowded with two people in it. He nodded in the direction of the drawing room door. "Shall we be a little more comfortable?"

"The drawing room? I thought . . . " She could not keep the disappointment from her face; she did her best to conceal her response. "I thought you would want to go to the studio . . . "

"And so I do," he assured her, inwardly pleased that she had been anticipating their reunion. "But with you dressed so fashionably, I supposed you wanted to follow the social dictates."

"When have I ever followed social dictates? I would be in England raising heirs for Rupert if I gave a fig for society's dictates, wouldn't I?" she asked him scornfully, and flounced off toward the stairs. "I want to show you what I have done. I haven't been frittering away my time, waiting for you to come back. And I want to be a little more private than we are here." She stopped on the third stair and turned to look back to look at him, hanging on the bannister with her left hand so she could lean toward him. "If everything you tell me is true, my wish is your command."

His laughter was soft and genuine. "That is certainly one way to look at it," he said as he followed her up to her studio, suiting his pace to hers, aware of the emotions contending within her.

She felt unaccountably breathless as she reached her studio; she had not raced up the stairs, and she made the climb so often she was used to it. Doing her best to appear confident, she went out into the center of the large room, half-twirling, her arms extended to the sides. "Look around you. I've been busy while you were gone, Count." The sound of the rain on the skylight beat a gentle tattoo, and the muted light made all the shadows soft and blurred.

"So you have," he agreed as he halted at the top of the stairs to look around. The studies of the barges were propped against the walls all about the room. "Fourteen of them?" he asked when he had looked around.

"Fifteen. I have one on the easel," she said, nodding to the smaller of two easels. "The other is your portrait." She paused, trying to gather her nerve to show it to him.

"Are you going to show it to me?" he asked when she made no move toward it.

She hesitated. "I don't know how you'll like it."

He smiled his encouragement. "Nor do I." He tried to soothe her growing apprehension, saying, "And you will be the better judge of your success than I will, Rowena. You have your talent to guide you, and I have . . . nothing. Remember, I have not seen my reflection for four thousand years, and I must place myself in your hands for accuracy. If you want a strict critic, you must show it to Roger." He chuckled. "I've contented myself with paintings and sketches over that time, perforce."

The rain-filtered light from the ceiling windows greyed the colors of everything around them, making the paintings seem less vivid than they were. Rowena was suddenly grateful for this, certain that this muted light would give the portrait a kinder glow than the full brilliance of the sun.

"That's right; you've no reflection, and no photographic image." She nodded in a rush of understanding. "I forgot how it is with vampires," she said, meaning she had not actually believed it.

"So anything you show me will be a revelation," he encouraged her. "Unless you have given me white hair and a beak of a nose, or dripping fangs, for that matter, I will be delighted."

She recognized his description as the first one of Count Dracula in the novel, and shook her head. "None of those." Before her nervousness made things any worse, she took the corner of the drape and tossed it back over the canvas. "It isn't finished," she said quickly, "but it is getting there."

He came up to it slowly. "Ah," he said softly, impressed at what he saw. "I may not know my own face, but I recognize your perceptiveness, and some of your intent," he said after a long silence.

Against a sketchy background of tall conifers and the suggestion of mountains, Ragoczy's face held the eye: the left side of the canvas was light, the right side in shadow, so that half his features were not clear but for the smoldering darkness of his eye, and beyond it, black on dark, was his eclipse device; the details of that side of his face were lost, but the line of his brow, cheek, and jaw could be seen. Although obscured, there was very little sinister in that part of his face. On the lighted side, his strong forehead and fine eyebrow emphasized his penetrating gaze; the tone of his skin was olive-cast but pale. The highlight on his cheek caught something of the angularity of his features, as did the line of his slightly askew nose. The dark waves of his hair were suggested in broad, neat brushstrokes, as was the soft roll of his collar against his neck. There was something in the expression that spoke of compassion and incalculable loneliness.

"I haven't got the mouth right, or the nasal-labial fold," she said, frowning a bit and using the end of a brush handle to indicate these parts of the portrait. "I saw some photos of Etruscan funerary figures," she went on, "and I noticed a similarity in that part of the face; not the smirk, but something about the cast of the features, an angle, something in the proportions, the lines of the skull." She gave a short sigh to punctuate her frustration. "But I haven't got it right yet."

Ragoczy could not quite smile. "It's not surprising that there is a similarity. The Etruscans were the only descendants of my people to survive. They went westward into the north of Italy to escape what we could not. They were unable to escape the Romans, however." He continued to stare at the painting, trying to reconcile what he saw there with what he had come to think about himself. "Rowena? Do I really look like that?" he wondered aloud.

"Well," she said, nonplused by his question, "this is a painted portrait, not a photographic one"—she gave a single chuckle—"and so I have given emphasis to parts of your face that the camera, if it could capture you, would not. The lighting is also not quite what you would actually find in nature; it is too highly contrasted, more what a spotlight would do instead of the sun. The parchment-like quality of your skin is difficult to show, and the kinds of lines in your face are . . . they're like strong lines that have been smoothed or partially erased." She paused, puzzled at her own assessment, then resumed, more confidently. "I have taken advantage of the somewhat Slavic lift to your cheeks and brows, for example, and put more contrast in the shadow of your eyes, but otherwise, except for the mouth, it is a fairly accurate likeness. The color of your eyes is difficult to capture, a sort of blackness that is actually blue, but darker than any blue can be." She shook her head once. "Something about the mouth eludes me."

"Does it." He looked from the portrait to Rowena.

Her pulse jumped to a faster tempo. "Surprising, isn't it?" She did her best to maintain a bantering tone with him. "You would think that I would know it well enough to paint it, but no such luck. Perhaps I know so much that I can't put all of it in the portrait." She tried to make light of this with a flip of her hand, but did not succeed.

He did not reply at first; he looked again at the portrait. "I don't know what to say; I cannot comment on its accuracy, but . . . " He paused thoughtfully, then asked, without turning from the image on the canvas, "Are you showing me what you see in me, Rowena? Or are you showing me what you think I want to see?" The questions took them both by surprise.

She considered her answer carefully. "More the former than the latter, but I don't see how I could escape some of wanting to show you what you want. I am an artist, and you are my lover."

It was the first time she had acknowledged him as her lover, and it took him a moment to think of what to say. "It is a humbling thing, to see a reflection of yourself in another's soul."

"You make it easy to do," she said glibly, to avoid saying what was really on her mind.

He understood her ploy. "You do not need to flatter me, Rowena, not this way, not any way, ever." The deep, musical note was back in his voice.

"I'm not flattering you," she said emphatically. "Not exactly," she appended under the impact of his eyes. "Perhaps I am trying to show what it is that . . . attracts me to you. I don't know if I can paint it, but I am trying."

"If that is for you and not for me, then I wish you every success; if it is intended to sway me, then do not trouble yourself." His features softened as he saw distress come into her face. "Do not assume the worst, my cherished one. That was not my intention. I did not mean to offend you, Rowena. If I did, I apologize most repentantly. You are the one who paints, not I." He had, in fact, occasionally painted in the past but knew that at best he was a skilled dabbler, more gifted at making pigments than applying them to wood or canvas—his real talents lay in music, alchemy and healing, and he had long since come to accept this about himself.

She could think of nothing to say as she put the drape back over the canvas; she began to amble about her studio as if browsing, all the while striving to bring her thoughts into order once more. Finally she stopped walking and said, as she looked out the small rear window to the rooftop behind her, "Since I've been in Amsterdam, I have had my family on my mind a great deal, all my family. Not missing them, exactly—more like trying to sort them out. I've tried to remember about how it was when Arthur drowned, and what it was like when Penelope was born. I've thought a great deal about my mother and her father, of course. This last week I've been remembering my paternal grandmother, for some reason. I never knew my mother's mother but my father's lived with us after she was widowed."

"Oh?" said Ragoczy to indicate he was listening without intruding on her memories.

"She was a famous invalid, and had been for many years." Rowena cocked her head on the side. "She often declared she hated being incapacitated, but I noticed more than once what pride she took in having the whole family accommodate her; all our plans at Longacres were contingent upon her. When my grand-father died, she said that if she had been able she would have danced for joy. Everyone said it was a jest, but I was sure she meant it."

Ragoczy saw the confusion in her demeanor, and he said, "They were not well-matched, your father's parents?"

Her laughter was short and mirthless. "I should think not," she exclaimed. "It was arranged, all quite suitable, except that my grandfather was one of those self-indulgent gentlemen who thought the world worked for his convenience; they were more common in my grand-father's time, men who were lords of the earth, or so they believed. He indulged himself, going through what small amounts were left of the family fortune, and chafing at the restrictions his profligacy brought, blaming everyone and everything but himself for his misfortunes. My grand-mother said he was coarse and brutish. My father said only that he was thoughtless." She tugged at the wide, dropped belt of her jacket. "Why am I telling you this? Why do I always tell you things?"

"If you keep talking, you will probably find out," he encouraged her.

"I do this to you, don't I? burden you with things that puzzle me." She shrugged, her discomfort revealed in the stiffened angle of her shoulder. "Anyway, she complained of him often after he died, and of men in general. She said that it was the punishment of God that women had to bear children as they did, and that her children were her contrition. I told her once that she was being unkind. She said I knew nothing of unkindness, that men were cruel. She warned me to put no faith in men, for they were deceitful and lecherous. 'Let his mistresses put up with his rutting. Let them be the objects of his bestial inclinations', she said, with such disgust that I have never forgot it." She shook her head. "It is silly to dwell on such things."

"If it troubles you, it is not silly," said Ragoczy, taking a step toward her. "She must have frightened you with her anger."

"She said she was never angry, that she pitied him for having fallen so far from grace." Rowena dared to look at him. "She said that religion saved her from anger, that without it, she would have been consumed with rage for what he did to her. God spared her that sin, or so she told me."

" 'One who does not own his anger nurtures a murderer in his heart,' or her heart," Ragoczy quoted, adding the last with care.

"She said he would answer for the wrongs he had done before God; I came to feel that she expected God to provide her vindication, to do to my grand-father all the things my grand-mother had wanted to do." She came up to him. "My parents might be a strange match, but my mother does not loathe my father."

Ragoczy took her hands in his; kissed one and then the other. "Their lives, whatever they may be, are not your life, my cherished Rowena. They are not you. Look at what you have done: you have no reason to fear you will end up like your father's mother. You are not she and your world is a very different place from hers."

Without warning she began to weep; she leaned against him while the tears wrung her. She made no attempt to hold him, relying on him to keep her upright while her unexpected feelings tore through her. "It's hopeless, isn't it?" she asked as she strove to contain her perplexing grief. "My grand-mother was bitter, but she was right that it is hopeless."

"Hopeless? No, I would not say so; difficult perhaps," Ragoczy said as he kissed her hair. "Rowena, Rowena."

This gesture of compassion brought renewed weeping; now she clung to his sleeves, her hands fixed in the fabric as if intent on rending the material asunder; there was nothing she could offer by way of apology. She pushed her head against his shoulder. "How can anyone endure it?"

He did not ask her what she meant; in the last two thousand years he had learned better than that. He stroked her hair and held her while her sobs became shuddering breath and her eyes finally dried. Only when she gave a self-conscious nudge to his chest did he release her. "You have been through a great deal."

She stared at him. "You say that? You?"

"I am the most likely of all to appreciate what you endure. I have seen much more than most what humankind does to itself." He lowered his eyes and paused. "What you are doing takes courage, as much as facing the foe in battle."

"But if it never changes, what hope is there?" she asked, her eyes filling with tears again.

"But the world does change. Oh, yes, very slowly, and occasionally catastrophically, but it does change. I know; I have seen it." He put his arm around her, more companionably than lover-like. "Since you have told me about your paternal grand-mother, let me tell you about . . . an old friend. There was one of my blood who felt the same anguish you do. She came to my life in the first Christian century. The elder Titus Flavius Vespasianus was Caesar." He did his best to put his thoughts in order. "She had survived a husband as bloody-minded as any I have ever encountered, and when she came to my life, she kept her independence, not wanting to be in the thrall of another man again. The law, which had given rights and protections to women in the glory-days of Rome, changed once the Christians became powerful, and over the centuries, she lost land, position, and the control of her fortune. But she endured it, and eventually she found ways to deal with the demands made of her, although she never liked having to. When she died the true death, in 1658, she had begun to reclaim much of what had been lost to her in the previous millennium."

Rowena wiped at her eyes with her fingers. "And you tell me this so I can be grateful that my circumstances are so much improved?"

Ragoczy shook his head. "No, Rowena," he said sadly. "I would not mock you. No; I tell you of Olivia so that you will know that other women have endured what you are enduring. You do not stand alone."

She glared at him, her brow puckered in thought. "You will pardon me if I do not feel this is so, or that I find it less than comforting. Working here I have had time to think." She folded her arms and made herself stand upright. "You make it harder for me, with your kind words and your encouragement. My grand-mother was more honest. She did not tell me that it would be possible for me to overcome the dictates of the world."

"The dictates of the world," said Ragoczy quietly. "Often they are unreasonable and harsh, but they support most of the people; that is why they are respected, and why they are clung to long after their usefulness is gone." He moved away from her, going to the darkest end of the studio. "But they can never accommodate everyone, and I do not restrict my meaning to those of my blood. Those with vision are always beyond the dictates of the world, and you are no exception." He turned around and looked at her, his penetrating gaze holding her as surely as if his arms were still supporting her. "Tell me: why have you continued to resist the life your family wants for you? It is not because they are evil, or bent on your destruction. They do not have your vision, and therefore are not cognizant of how you view the world. They truly have your best interests at heart, so far as they can perceive them. That they are limited by their lack of vision is unfortunate, but not perverse, any more than you are."

"But is it worth it?" she cried out, her determination failing her.

He took two steps toward her. "Only you can answer that; not now, but when you are old. Then you will know your answer."

She cocked her head as she studied his face. "Do you never wonder about these things?"

He gave a single laugh. "Often. So often that I am bored with my wondering. Yet I cannot stop it." He came nearer to her. "It is knowing human beings of vision that make my . . . life valuable to me." At that he held up his hand. "The human capacity for vision continues to fascinate me."

"So you are studying me?" she asked, her voice sharper than before. "I am someone who will supply you with another vision? You will garner as much of the vision as you can, and then seek new ones." She knew she was trying to force him away from her, and she felt powerless to cease.

"No." His face and voice were filled with sorrow. "Three thousand years ago, I might have, but not now."

"Then what?" she asked, no longer offended by his remarks.

"I love you." This simple statement hung in the air between them as if each word were burning.

It was what she had wanted most to hear, but now that he had spoken the words aloud, she had to stop herself to keep from running down the stairs. "Oh, God," she whispered. "You can't. You don't."

"I can," he promised her. "I do."

"But . . . " Her confusion coalesced into a single "Why?"

Ragoczy could not keep back a one-sided smile: how often he had been asked that question over the centuries. At first it had troubled him, but now he recognized it as the sign of trust it was. "Love is not a matter of reason. But if I have to have a reason, it is because you are Rowena: what other reason is there to love anyone than for being who the person is?"

She tried to turn away from him, determined not to succumb to his presence, but was unable to keep from staring at him. "You will expect too much of me. You will want me to be . . . sworn to you. I will not do that; I've told you—"

"I expect you to be Rowena, nothing more, nothing less," he said.

"Or your idea of me," she said, coming to the crux of her fears.

"No," he told her. "I leave such folly to young Mister Bowen." He held out his arms to her. "If you will have what I offer, I will require nothing of you but your fulfillment."

"And my bond," she added, clutching at her elbows to hide the trembling that came over her.

"Only if it is what you want. I will be bound, but until you come to my life—if that is what you want to do—you will not have any tie to me but the ones you create yourself. You cannot be compelled to acquiesce, not in anything between us." He sensed her fright, and lowered his arms, adding, "I do not mean to cause you any distress, Rowena. I would rather remain nothing more than the subject of a portrait than give you any unhappiness."

She stared at him in wide-eyed silence for some little time, then said, "I am almost convinced you mean it."

The pang that went through him was a keener pain than the buckshot had been. "I do not lie, Rowena: what would be the point."

"You need what I can supply," she countered at once, inwardly appalled at the callousness of her challenge.

"Yes," he said.

The candor of his answer took her by surprise. "You do not deny it?"

"No," he told her, his tone low and melodious. "Those of my blood survive on what we gain from the living, but it is not blood alone that sustains us. It is the touching, the knowing, that nourishes us." He looked directly at her. "The touching is rare, and all the more treasured for its rarity."

She blinked, shaken by what he said. "Shall you touch me?"

"If you will be touched," he responded.

"And if I will not?" she demanded. "What then?"

He did not quite shrug. "Then nothing will happen. I can derive nothing of . . . value from coercion, and I do not want your disgust. I experience what you experience, and if that is repugnant to you, it is abhorrent to me: there is no merit for either of us in that." He gave her some seconds to consider what he had said. "Do you want touching? Rowena?"

To her amazement, she heard herself say, "Oh, yes, please." And before she could change her mind, before sanity reasserted itself, she rushed into his embrace, her mouth open on his.

Ragoczy caught her up in his arms, relishing the passion he felt welling in her. He caressed her cheek as she drew back from their kiss, his small hands cradling her face as they kissed again. His senses awakened with hers, his eagerness attuned to her own. He whispered her name as he swung her off her feet with an ease that revealed his strength. "Well?"

"My room is ready," she admitted, her face pressed against his collar. "This morning, I was more certain . . . "

He had begun to descend the stairs but stopped when she faltered. "If you are uncertain, then—"

"No," she insisted. "I know that you are what I want."

"Ah," he said, and carried her down the stairs and along the corridor to her bedroom while she murmured tentatively of her need.

"I want," she began, trying to formulate a description of what she wanted. "I want to know you will . . . you will accept . . . what I want."

"As much as I am capable of, you will have, so long as it gives you joy," he told her as he closed the door to her room behind them, then set her on her bed.

"Oh, Lord," she said suddenly. "Yseut."

"Your housekeeper is here?" Ragoczy asked. "What do you want to do?"

"Yes, she is here. But she has said nothing . . . " Rowena laughed nervously. "If she has said nothing yet, she probably will not disturb us." She unfastened the frog necklace and handed it to him. "Thank you for that. I wear the suite often."

"And you enjoy it?" he asked, knowing the answer already.

"Of course." She looked up at him. "I . . . I'm nervous." Her golden eyes pleaded with him even as she attempted to laugh off her statement. "I don't know why I should be, but I—" Her words stopped as he laid his finger gently on her lips.

"It's all right to be nervous, Rowena; you are taking a risk," he said, and moved to kiss her.

She halted him. "You mean that I may not be as resolute in my independence if I have more . . . contact with you?" She knew that she sounded defensive, and mentally castigated herself for admitting so much.

His smile banished her anxiety. "If you are, it will be what you want, not what I demand of you." Then his mouth met hers, awakening her need; their shared silence was eloquent.

When she could speak again, she said, "But what is the risk, then: it isn't as if we haven't . . . done anything before. We have."

"So we have," he agreed. "But when you took ballet as a child—and do not tell me you did not: no doubt your mother insisted—was not the second lesson after an absence from it more difficult than the first? The muscles were stiffer and the habits of movement had not yet been reestablished. This, Rowena, is the second lesson." As he spoke, she put her arms around his neck and pulled him down beside her on her bed, her lips seeking his.

"I must strive, then," she whispered, "to regain my strength." And she pulled him against her in fierce determination, trying to summon up the courage to set her fears aside.

When he could, he propped himself on his elbows and looked down at her, saying gently, "This is not a contest, Rowena."

She stared at him, trying to reconcile her desire with his compassion. "Then what is it?"

"If we are fortunate," he said in still, deep tones, "it is a revelation."

She gave a little cry and reached for him once more. "I want . . . I want to have that," she said, trying to control the surge of excitement coursing through her, hoping that her desire would not be ephemeral.

Ragoczy drew back, but only to remove his jacket, waistcoat, and tie, which he hung over one of the short posts at the foot of her bed; he did not quite stand. "You will want to take off more than the necklace, I should think," he said with a wry lift to his brows. "Clothes make everything more clumsy."

"Will you do it?" she asked.

He stopped in the act of removing his cufflinks as he watched her unbutton her shoes, "I will help you; I will not do the whole," he said after a short, thoughtful pause.

"Why not?" She sat up on her bed, trying to summon a sense of indignation, without success. "Is that beneath you?"

"Hardly," he said, and answered her first question. "You are troubled by our attachment because you do not want to give up your autonomy; I do not want that, either. If I were to undress you entirely, you might decide that your hard-won emancipation had been compromised. I would not want you to feel that now or any time, and I would prefer not to provide you an excuse to decide it has happened. It is not your subjugation I seek, Rowena, it is your liberty: believe this."

"You cannot know how much I want to," she said as she stood up and began to unfasten the jacket of her suit. When she had draped it over the back of her grand-mother chair, she turned to him. "You're right," she conceded. "I must do this for myself." She unfastened the skirt and stepped out of it as it puddled around her feet. "How did you know?"

"I know you, Rowena," he reminded her, his voice kind and caressing. "The knowing and the love are the same."

Her face and neck flushed as she began to unbutton her shirt; she took her time, using each tiny delay to assuage her doubts. Finally, standing in her slip, she faced him. "I leave the rest to you," she said, and stepped out of her shoes.

His eyes were warm as sunlight on her, and he saw her reserve fade as he closed the distance between them in four steps. "Are you certain this is what you want?"

"Yes, I am certain," she said testily, then repeated, "Yes," in a softer tone.

He lifted her slip without haste, and when he had it off her, he bent and kissed her above her half-corset, as lightly and persistently as the falling rain.

She held him close as he unfastened the lacing of her half-corset, trying to smile as he tossed the undergarment onto her grandmother chair. The silk of his shirt was luxurious, but she suddenly found it disappointing. "Aren't you going to take this off?" she asked, plucking at the collar.

"If you insist," he said, and added, "I had better warn you: I have scars." They were a white swath from the base of his ribs to the top of his groin, tokens of his first, incomplete death. He took her hands and put them over the buttons. "Turnabout is fair play."

This reminder made her giggle; she did her best to unfasten the buttons without moving more than an inch or two back from him. When the shirt was open, she reached behind him and grabbed the back of it, intent on pulling it off. "Straighten your arms. One at a time," she said as she felt his thumbs slide into the tops of her drawers. As he bent to help her step out, she finally got him free of the shirt. When he stood up again, she glanced down. "Lord God in Heaven," she exclaimed.

He knew what caused her outburst. "Do they disgust you?" he asked, waiting for her reply.

"You said scars." She raised her eyes to his face. "I had no idea." Impulsively she wrapped her arms around him. "No wonder you have the ideas you do." She kissed him, her sympathy going out to him. "They look . . . fatal."

"They were," he said.

The full significance of his admission sunk in. With a rush of tangled emotions, she clung to him. "How terrible," she said, certain that her attempt to comfort him was inadequate.

"It was a very long time ago," he said, and bent his head to her breast, ministering to the other with his hand until the aureoles and nipples were rosy with excitement. He continued down her body, his whole being and his esurience fixed on her growing fervor and the wildness in her soul.

She lay back trembling, her body quivering like the strings of a 'cello as he devoted himself to her pleasure; she welcomed the sensations he offered her, and the discovery of responses within herself that were new to her, astonishing and wonderful. Her gratification was more sustained and intense than the first time they had lain together, shaking her with release; she took pride in the fulfillment they shared, in the murmured words of rapture he gave her when her frenzy had passed. When she could trust herself to speak coherently, she asked, "Are you really four thousand years old?"

"Yes," he said, stroking her from her neck to her hip; her flesh moved pliantly with his hand.

"And you have survived this way?" She reached up and touched his mouth.

"Once I understood what survival was, yes," he said quietly.

"It isn't just the blood is it?" she asked.

"It is life," he answered.

"Life," she repeated, drawing him into another kiss. Finally she trusted him.

Text of a letter from Reighert to Baron Klemens Manfred von Wolgast.

Chez Noir
February 27, 1911

My dear Baron;

Once again, in accordance with your orders, I have had word from Bernard in regard to Ragoczy. He has continued to observe him and follow him on his various errands throughout the city. When not at his house, he occasionally visits the press of Jo van Groot, of whom he may be the patron. It also appears he is continuing to visit the artist to sit for his portrait. Bernard has had a few conversations with her housekeeper, a widow named Yseult, who has told him that occasionally Ragoczy and Miss Saxon spend long hours together in her room instead of occupying their time in her studio, and that these visits sometimes extend far into the night, which Bernard has confirmed, at least as far as the hours are concerned. Whether this affaire is an arrangement of convenience or something more Bernard has not been able to determine. I will instruct him to inquire more closely if you decide you want more specific information. If the housekeeper is telling the truth, you may rest assured that Bernard will confirm it in no more than a week.

Since you are determined still to disgrace Ragoczy, I recommend you pay Bernard the sum he has been demanding in order to ascertain the importance of this artist in his life, and he in hers. Ragoczy does not strike me as a cold fish, no matter what Nadezna told you. He may have dealt with Nadezna only for her dancing abilities, but that may have been out of prudence instead of indifference. Perhaps his interests lay elsewhere. If this artist has engaged his heart, she could be used to advantage. Bernard will put one of his men to watch Miss Saxon if you are willing to pay the price for such surveillance, which he will want in advance. I have instructed him to continue to watch Ragoczy and to confirm the nature of his dealings with Miss Saxon, but with a second man, we will know more, and sooner.

Every policeman I have approached tells me that Inspector Blau cannot be influenced or pressured into supporting a case he is not cer-

tain is accurate; his integrity would seem to be beyond question. There-fore, I would not advise trying to interfere in any way in his investi-gation of Nadezna's death. With Ragoczy out of Germany, there is nothing more being done. If you were to appeal to him in any way, it might have the reverse effect desired, and cause him to reexamine what he has learned about her murder. This could lead to questions neither you nor I would want asked, in public or in private. I urge you to keep silent about her death, except to say it was a terrible tragedy, which is safe enough. Let time take care of the problem. As long as Ragoczy is in Amsterdam, or London, or anywhere but Berlin, we are safe.

The Chez Noir has taken in four of Nadezna's girls; it seemed the most sensible thing to do. It keeps them where they can be watched, and guar-antees I will know if they make any attempts to profit from Nadezna's death. Should I learn anything from them, I will inform you at once. From what I have determined thus far, their suppositions regarding her murder are just that—suppositions. The police rarely listen to the spec-ulations of prostitutes, which is in our favor.

Until next Thursday, when I will be delighted to introduce you to Bi-ennot: she is a glorious fourteen-year-old from Trier, very lovely and completely inexperienced. I think you will find her to your liking, and worth the price.

Reighert

P.S. As far as I can discover, there has still been no connection made be-tween the death of Nadezna and the death of Renfred Meyer. Let us trust that this will continue to be the case, for both our sakes.

4

As the train rolled inexorably toward the German border, Roger re-garded Ragoczy with a mixture of worry and aggravation. "It's plain that you left your private railway car behind in order to be less . . . visible in your travels, but, my master, this is not sufficient, nor would travel-ing with the third-class passengers be." He looked at his watch as if ex-pecting it to toll out the hour of doom. "The police will not be content to ignore your presence," he warned, speaking in a combination of Latin and Italianate French they had evolved between them over the centuries. "You will not be able to conceal your presence long enough to do the things you want to do. This isn't a hundred years ago, when you would have had a week without interference. You yourself have said that you cannot outrun the telegraph." He stopped his harangue to shove his watch back into his pocket. "You could end up in prison. Do you recall what prison was like? In China? In Mongolia? In Tunis? In Central America? It will be much worse here, for you will be watched, and you will reveal your true nature, eventually."

"So you have said, repeatedly." Ragoczy sat back against the upholstered seat of their first-class compartment. It was more comfortable with the small case of his native earth shoved under the seat. "You did not need to come, if you are so apprehensive, and pessimistic."

Roger lifted his hand to express his capitulation. "You could not go running off to Germany without someone to keep track of you." He fussed briefly with the map he had been consulting. "At least we will cross the border after midnight, and in bad weather. The inspectors might not be as alert then as they would be during the day. And we are on the fast train, so we will make fewer stops. That should buy you a little time." If he found this reassuring, he gave no indication of it.

"Or they may be more diligent," said Ragoczy in sardonic amusement. "If they are fresh, they will want to show it." He looked at the window, watching the night rush by; only the compartment and Roger were reflected in the glass. After a short silence he said, "I hope I have not endangered Rowena."

"My master?" Roger said in some surprise.

"Oh, not from anything she receives from me—no, I meant that I am afraid those who oppose me may wish to harm her, as a way to strike at me."

"Is that why you recommended she visit her family?" Roger asked, setting aside his map and folding his arms.

"Part of the reason; yes, it was," Ragoczy replied, adding, "I hope she decides to go, not only for protection, but so she can make some peace with them. It is more vexing to her than she likes to admit that the family cannot understand what she is doing: only her grand-father in San Francisco, who is proud of her, endorses her—all the forgotten gods be thanked for Horace Saxon."

"Do you think she will?" Roger indicated his interest by the angle of his head.

"Go to England or make peace?" Ragoczy shrugged, not to indicate any lack of concern but to express his uncertainty. "I do not know if she will do either. She wants to sort out her feelings about her family, that much I am certain of, and she will have a better chance of doing that if she does not rule out all contact with them. Much as she is an artist, she is also a daughter, and she has not been able to forget that. It may be too soon for her to make such a gesture, but in time, I hope she will." He shifted in his seat. "From what she said last night, Rupert Bowen is coming back to Amsterdam in a week or so, providing she does not go to England."

Long acquaintance with Ragoczy prompted Roger to ask another question. "If she is in England, he will see her there, won't he?"

"Yes, he will, and her parents will probably urge her to accept Mister Bowen before it is too late," Ragoczy told him. "He would say the same thing in Amsterdam, and probably be more intrusive, under the mistaken impression he was saving her from herself." He was still for a short while, then said, "They would drive each other quite mad, you know, if they were ever foolish enough to marry. Neither would be able to endure the other. He would find her independence embarrassing and she would find his condescension intolerable. At least she knows it; he has no inkling."

"You talk about these things?" Roger said. "She confides in you?"

"Well, she must talk to someone and her housekeeper is not an understanding woman; Rowena is afraid that the woman gossips. I am not an inexperienced confidant, after all." He listened to the whistle signaling, the train slowing. "I think this is a stop to take on water; as I recall one is scheduled. Do not put yourself to worry. We are not yet at the border."

"That will be another two hours," said Roger, consulting his watch once more. "It is still possible to leave the train and slip across the border through the fields."

"No," Ragoczy said. "If we did that and we were apprehended, we would be in more trouble than if we simply submit our documents in the regular fashion. There would be questions when the train reached Munich and our trunks were not claimed."

"Are you certain you will not consider going into Switzerland? It is near enough to Germany that you can gain the information you seek, isn't it?" Roger asked, repeating a request he had made several times in the last few days. "Why do you expose yourself to arrest when it is not necessary? The police can take you into custody in Munchen as easily as in Berlin, and you will not have Inspector Blau to deal with."

"True enough, but in Switzerland, I cannot pursue my exoneration as I can in Germany." He made himself smile. "Besides, as the owner of Schloss Saint-Germain, I am known and respected enough that the police will think twice before detaining me." He held up his hand to forestall Roger renewing his plea. "We are bound for Germany, my friend. When we cross at Strassburg, we will still be a long way from Berlin, and the crossing reports are sent by rail, not by telegraph. Any processing of documents will take time. I estimate we will have three days at least before we have to contend with Berlin."

"You have said yourself that they will be looking for you," Roger reminded him.

"But there would have to be some pressing reason to make inquiry, and there is none, not obviously," Ragoczy pointed out. "Our papers are in order, and the Czar will vouch for them, if it comes to that. Whatever possessed the Russians to invent passports?" he asked of the air.

"If they had not, the Germans would have," said Roger, amusement in his faded-blue eyes.

"You're right, old friend." He glanced out the window again. "We've almost stopped." As the engine came to a halt, hissing and steaming like some iron dragon out of myth, the first-class conductor came along the corridor, inquiring if any of the passengers wished to order a nightcap.

"We have cognac, schnapps, brandy, and kirschwasser," he informed the occupants of E. "One of the waiters will bring it."

"None, thank you," Ragoczy said, and offered the man a coin for his efforts. "For your service."

"Danke schoen, Mein Herr," the conductor said as he backed out of compartment E and continued on to the last in the car.

"Bitte," Ragoczy responded as the door clicked closed.

In fifteen minutes they were underway again, sweeping through the night, the headlight shining off the freezing rain, spangling all that was caught in its beam.

"We will be at Tubingen before dawn, at about four," said Ragoczy. "They take on coal at Tubingen. Then to Ulm, Augsburg, and Munchen. And you needn't remind me," he went on with one small hand raised, "that we could transfer here at Tubingen to a train bound for Basel."

Roger sighed deliberately. "You have made it clear you do not intend to do anything to prevent your arrest."

"I do not intend to encourage it, either," Ragoczy said as he leaned back in his seat, pretending to enjoy the ride. "If I did that, we would be en route to Berlin, not Munchen."

The official who inspected their documents at Strassburg was young, self-impressed, and sleepy. He examined the Russian passports, frowning at the Cyrillic letters as if by staring hard he could read them. When he spoke, it was very slowly and loudly, as if he thought Ragoczy was hard of hearing. "How long . . . how many . . . days . . . you understand? do you stay in Germany?"

Ragoczy answered in excellent German, "I do not quite know yet. Perhaps three or four weeks, perhaps somewhat longer. It will depend on circumstances that are not entirely within my control." Ragoczy was entirely polite, but he saw that the young official did not trust him. "I own land and businesses here, some in Bavaria, some in Prussia, you see, and they are in need of my attention. It will take a short while before I am in any position to assess all that must be accomplished. I will be near Munchen most of the time, if all goes according to plan."

"Ach, Munchen," said the young man as if this explanation accounted for everything. He took his stamp and marked Ragoczy's and Roger's passports, saying, "Welcome to Germany." Then, handing back the passports, added, "Count."

"You will find six trunks in the baggage car with my name on them," Ragoczy told him, and noticed the young man wince at his omission.

"Six. Very good." He turned on his heel so crisply that is was apparent he was trying to make up for his lapse. Then he was gone.

"He will turn in his paperwork at the end of the day, it will be prepared to go to Berlin, and then tomorrow—more than twenty-four hours from now—it will be placed, with all other forms, on a train bound for Berlin. I expect there will be at least a day before someone in Berlin notices my name," said Ragoczy in their conglomerate language, hoping as he spoke, that he was right.

Roger had nothing to add; he picked up his map again and devoted himself to studying the route their train was taking, through Swabia toward Bavaria.

Sleet mixed with snow was falling by the time they reached Tubingen, an hour later than scheduled. The ancient university town had much the same look to it as it had had a century before, and a century before that; narrow streets and steep slopes above the Necker. Pulling into the station, the train created a sudden flurry of activity in the predawn darkness. Porters appeared out of the night, their coats shining with wet; the stationmaster hollered orders for coal and the unloading of an automobile from the fourth baggage car.

"How long will we be here?" Roger asked, and answered for himself, "Probably forty minutes. And we will be delayed again, getting into Munchen, with the weather what it is."

"Not enough to stop us, I assume; this will teach me to travel in the first week of March, at least in this hemisphere," said Ragoczy, and stared out at the station platform, listening to the shouts and bustle. "There are a dozen passengers getting on here; most of them look like students."

"It is a university town; you will find students everywhere," Roger remarked pointedly as he consulted his watch. "Students are up to all hours, and do not mind taking this train. There is another train due through at ten in the morning. Who else is willing to travel at this hour?"

Ragoczy chuckled. "Who indeed," he said, listening to the train prepare to start up once again.

They reached Munchen three hours late, arriving in a steady snowfall that turned the whole city into something out of a book of travel prints. Snow accented the roofs of the buildings, and with the mountains towering behind the city, it seemed that Munchen was the ornamented hem of a sweeping train on the mountains' cloak.

"Tread carefully," Ragoczy recommended as they left the train. "It's very slippery." He was speaking German now, and heard Roger answer in the same language, "Do you want to hire a wagon to take the luggage to the Schloss? I don't suppose we can hope to go the last distance by train, not in such weather."

"Gregor should be waiting for us," said Ragoczy, drawing on his Florentine leather gloves. "Assuming the stationmaster at Hausham remembered to engage him." He made a self-deprecatory motion of his hand. "I know it is a long way to go, but when I was informed that the spur through Hausham is closed due to damage to the tracks, I thought it best to arrange our transport from here. I wired them two days ago with instructions for Gregor to meet us." Gregor Einsatz was the local drayer for Hausham, and was considered impudent but reliable.

"A horse-drawn wagon. Well. We've done worse for transportation. At least its not llamas or camels. I'll go look for him," said Roger, heading off toward the end of the platform where all manner of vehicles waited for trains arriving and departing.

"Count Ragoczy," called out the baggage conductor, his breath as steamy as the engine's as he approached.

Ragoczy did not bother to correct the man for the misuse of his title. "We are trying to find our drayer," he said to the conductor. "If you will have the trunks taken off and put on the platform, I will undertake to guard them myself." He tipped the baggage conductor more generously than was customary, and saw the man straighten up in newfound respect.

"At once, Herr Count." He very nearly saluted.

"Danke," Ragoczy told him, and went along to the baggage car where his luggage was stored. A few minutes later Roger found him there, four of his trunks standing beside him, lightly powdered in snow. "Two more and we're ready to load the wagon. Is Gregor here?"

"Yes. He has his four Rhinelanders hitched to his wagon. He says they'll get through the snow better than any automobile could do; his wheels have studs on the rims. No doubt we will need them once we leave the city, if the snow is as deep as it looks." Roger stood aside as a porter emerged from the baggage car with another large trunk on his handcart. "He has no shelter on the wagon—he doesn't hold with it, says it saps a man's character."

"He's probably right about his team," said Ragoczy, making no comment about the exposure to the snow. "I would beg to differ about the character-building properties of freezing."

Roger achieved a faint smile. "He told me to warn you that we won't reach the Schloss until late afternoon; the roads are not clear of snow, and there have been avalanches. He expects that it will be slow going once we leave Hausham. The last leg may take the longest."

"That does not entirely astonish me," Ragoczy said dryly, looking up at the steadily falling snow.

"Do you want us to load these up and carry them to . . . " He indicated the general direction of the loading area.

"That would be most satisfactory, yes," said Ragoczy, and gave Roger a signal to return to Gregor's wagon. "Tell him we will be along directly, if you will."

"He's brought fur lap-rugs for us," Roger informed him as he started back the way he had come.

"Very good," Ragoczy said, but he doubted Roger heard him. He noticed that the porter had gone back to collect the last trunk. He took his watch from the breast pocket of his heavy overcoat: not quite noon, and a cold, six-hour trek ahead of them.

"Where do you want this taken?" the porter asked, emerging with the last trunk on his handcart.

"Load up the rest and we will put them in the wagon pulled by four Rhinelanders," said Ragoczy philosophically.

The porter shook his head once, thinking it odd that a fine gentleman who traveled in a first-class compartment and dressed in fine clothes should load his trunks into an old-fashioned wagon instead of a motor lorry. "The one at the end of the platform?" He touched his cap in acknowledgment. "At once."

"Thank you," Ragoczy said mildly, and accompanied him to the loading area where Roger was waiting in the bed of the wagon to help. The Rhinelanders, all shaggy in their winter coats, stood patiently, their thick necks arched, long, taffy-colored manes showing the signs of recent grooming, their harness capped in snow. They had rough-woven blankets spread under the harness along their broad backs, to keep out the muscle-numbing cold, Gregor's one concession to marginal comfort.

"If you don't want to stop for food, we'll get underway now," said Gregor in a tone that implied anyone asking for food would be regarded as a self-indulgent weakling. He lifted the reins in shearling gloves as massive as paws, whistled through his teeth, and they were off.

The streets of Munchen were icy and what little traffic moved along them went cautiously. Even then, there were mishaps; near the Promendeplatz two automobiles had plowed into one another, both sliding up to the Karmelitenkirche, leaving a record of their collision in the snow. Further along on Maximillian Strasse there was a tangle of horse-drawn wagons and carriages, the struggle to extricate the vehicles hampered by the distress of the horses on the slippery street. Other, more minor, problems were encountered: turns had ended in skids, or had left such slushy furrows that those coming after were trapped by the trail.

Once on the Maximilliansbrucke, Gregor permitted himself a satisfied smile. "Not as fast as motor cars, perhaps, but I will put my horses against a dozen automobiles in winter. Two dozen." He glanced at his two passengers, stoically enduring the weather, and remarked, "I am surprised you were willing to ride with me when you could have hired an automobile."

"But you have said that automobiles could not reach my Schloss," Ragoczy reminded him gently.

"True enough, but that would not keep others from staying out of the weather. Most of the high-born are too soft for this life. You are not like them."

"I suppose not," said Ragoczy, and prepared for the long haul out of the city and south into the mountains. "I prefer to remain with my valuables. Not that I mistrust you, Gregor," he went on diplomatically. "I know you are honest to a fault, but in snow, mishaps may happen, and if that should occur, I want to be with my . . . property." He had a fairly good supply of his native earth at the Schloss, but getting there without it would be uncomfortable during daylight.

"I have a flask of brandy under the seat. Use it if you feel cold," Gregor recommended. "I don't want you losing fingers and toes from this day's work."

"Thank you, but we will not need it," Ragoczy said, and accepted Gregor's shrug without argument.

"I left Hausham not long after dawn, Count. They hadn't dragged the roads from last night, and they may not get much done today," Gregor warned. "We won't return any faster than I reached the train station."

"We understand," said Ragoczy.

It was nearly dark when they arrived at last at the entrance to the curving, upward drive leading to Schloss Saint-Germain. Lanterns burning on either side of the open gates marked their way, and more lanterns guided them through the trees to the Schloss, their little wings of flame wavering in the wind; around them pines sagged under the burden of snow on their branches, and bare oaks were limned in white, their limbs like spectral bones. The three huddled on the seat of the wagon were stiff from travel as much as the falling temperature. The last hour had been made wretched by a sharp wind that drove the snow into drifts and obscured the road ahead, making for white wallows in every bend of the way.

"The boys know where they're going. Never fear, they will get you home," said Gregor as he whistled to his Rhinelanders. "That's another thing an automobile cannot do—find its way in the snow."

"True enough," said Ragoczy, who had steeled himself against the cold from the first, and was inured to it by now.

"It is a fine thing, having such horses as these; how can anything with a motor hope to take the place of these animals?" Gregor went on as he turned up the drive. "Is your staff expecting you?"

"They were telegraphed," said Ragoczy, watching the Schloss itself loom out of the wild snow. "You may take us to the side entrance. It will be easier to unload there."

"As you say." Gregor signaled his team again. "I will need to light my lamps before we start down to Hausham again."

"Of course. And come in for hot rum to warm you," Ragoczy offered, preparing to get down from the seat he occupied. "I will tell the cook to make you supper as well, if you like."

"Very pretty of you, sir, but I think not. I want to be getting back to my family." He had reached the side entrance to the Schloss, and was pulling his horses to a halt. "It's good of you to offer, Count. Many another would not."

"I will go summon Gualtier," Roger offered as he jumped down from the wagon, dislodging snow from his shoulders and hat as he landed. "He will help speed these chores."

Gregor shook his head. "Strange folk, the Alsatian," he remarked, in oblique reference to Gualtier Shenk, Ragoczy's recently employed chef. "But they're foreigners, after all."

"By that reckoning, so am I," said Ragoczy, long since used to the insularity of European regions. "Far more than my cook, if it comes to that."

"Ah, but you're Quality, sir, and birth makes all the difference," said Gregor with earnest sincerity. "Gualtier is the son of a butcher."

Knowing that it was useless to pursue the matter, Ragoczy handed Gregor half a dozen banknotes before he got down from his perch. "If you will help lift down the trunks, I would appreciate it."

"That I will," said Gregor. "And I don't want my team standing in this cold for any longer than necessary. They're strengthy, but they feel the ice, like all creatures do. It will do them no good to be chilled."

Gualtier Shenk appeared in the doorway, a portly man of thirty with fussy habits and economic movement who held four feedbags in his hands. "I heard you, and I knew what you would want. For your team," he called out. "Oats soaked in hot water with honey."

Ordinarily Gregor would have spurned such an offering, but his love of his horses overcame his reservations about the Alsatian cook. "They're in need of grain. That's kindly done," he said grudgingly, and accepted two of the feedbags. "You may tend to the on-side."

"That I will," Gualtier said as he set to work slipping the feedbag over the bridles of the lead and then the wheeler on the on-side of the wagon. "Splendid horses, Einsatz. Just splendid. My father had a team of Percherons, but they were as nothing compared to these."

"Percherons!" Gregor scoffed. "Lightweights, to be sure. You need one of those Dutch horses—the big blond ones—to come close to these beauties." He patted the massive flank of the nearest horse, a descendant, in fact, of the very Dutch breed Gregor was praising. "Not that these boys don't appreciate the grain. I know they do." It was as close as he would ever get to thanking Gualtier.

Ragoczy was tempted to tend to the unloading himself, but knew it would attract notice to his remarkable strength, and so resisted the urge to do more than drag the trunks into the corridor that led to the kitchen, the servants' quarters and the hunters' room, where heavy boots and muddied clothes could safely be stowed.

"I am surprised that you chose to come up in such weather," said

Gualtier, puffing slightly as he and Roger laid down the largest of the trunks. "I assumed you would remain in Munchen."

"I prefer my own bed," said Ragoczy. "How have you fared up here? Has the winter been hard?"

"Winter is winter," said Gualtier. "Some years there is more snow, some years there is less, but it is cold and vegetables are in short supply." He paused, as if uncertain how to go on. "I've started a mushroom plantation in the kitchen cellar. I trust you do not object."

"A mushroom plantation," said Ragoczy, resisting the urge to laugh aloud. "Well, why not? Many good things come from the earth."

Gualtier looked relieved, and when he went back to work unloading the wagon, he was whistling.

Not long after midnight Roger found Ragoczy in his alchemical laboratory, frowning over the pages of a notebook by the light of a kerosene lamp. "Gualtier and Lambert have retired; the Schloss is battened shut for the night," Roger announced in their private language, lingering in the door.

He worked up the nerve to say, "I want to apologize for complaining as I have, my master."

"Have you been complaining?" Ragoczy asked him mildly. "I hadn't noticed." Before Roger could interject any further observations, the Count went on, "I have been aware that your concern for my well-being has prompted you to remind me of the risks I am running, coming back to Germany, but I realize that is only well-intentioned advice, not complaint."

"Not complaint?" he echoed. "When I have been critical of everything you've done since we left Saint Petersburg?"

Ragoczy smiled, his dark eyes enigmatic. "Who has greater reason than you to remind me of my capacity for recklessness? You have seen me through more inexcusable temerity than I can easily reckon. You have had to deal with the results of my blunders, and you seek to keep me from another such . . . miscalculation."

Roger could think of nothing to say. He bowed slightly. "Will you be staying up?"

"I think so," Ragoczy said, glancing down at the notebook once more. "I want to review all I have been able to discover about Nadezna's murder, and so be better prepared to make the best use of my time in trying to determine the actual killer." He shook his head once. "I have been trying to decide if I can entrust anyone with the task of consulting Inspector Blau." He saw Roger's eyes widen in alarm. "Blau is a sensible man, old friend. He is not easily gulled. I cannot help but believe that if we could compare what we know, we might cut through much of the confusion that has weighed down this investigation." He sighed once. "I cannot have such suspicions clinging to my name, not in this day and age."

"In time it will be forgotten," said Roger. "If you were to return to Asia, or even to Russia, eventually it would be forgotten."

"Until I went to Germany again, unless I stayed away for . . . what? fifty years? More easily proposed than done," he went on. "I have too many interests in Germany to be able to walk away from them for half a century and hope that they will continue as I intend they should. The research in blood alone would be enough to compel me to return; with the metallurgy and medical patents, my absence would be more conspicuous than my presence. There are too many changes now, and they happen too quickly. Think back fifty years, if you think I overestimate the situation."

"I could argue with you, but I will not," said Roger, his reluctance less set than before. "I am not as convinced as you are that staying away will not serve your purpose, but I do not doubt that you have reason to make your assumptions."

"Thank you," said Ragoczy in his native tongue.

"Remember this, my master: if they hang you, your neck will be broken. No vampire can survive that." Roger let himself out of the laboratory, doing his utmost to keep his apprehensions from showing too clearly. Only when he was in his own quarters and busy with quartering a chicken for his supper did his anxiety return at full force, and left him to lie awake most of the night, his mind prey to all manner of worries that all the good sense and calm assessment could not disperse.

Over the next three days, Ragoczy prepared a number of telegrams which Roger dutifully took to Hausham and sent off; after the third day, there were five replies waiting when Roger presented the most recent messages for transmission.

"Graffin von Bingen, Johann von Traunreuth, Lothar Teich, Leopold Oberstetten, and Urban Seligerquelle," Ragoczy said, reading the names from the telegrams; outside his study window the sun was shatteringly bright off the snow, turning the whole forest luminous. "Very good. I think we may learn something."

"Teich and Oberstetten I understand, and the Graffin and von Traunreuth as well," said Roger. "But who is this Seligerquelle?"

"He is an opportunist," said Ragoczy bluntly. "He is one of those men who are found at the fringes of politics and advance themselves by clandestine means. In this instance, I am gambling that his snooping will lead me to those who might wish Nadezna ill. This man has, on various occasions, been of service to Colonel Vaclav Persuic, who spent some of his evenings at Nadezna's soirees, or so Pflaume has told me. I am hoping he will be able to tell me who was following me in Berlin."

"I'm certain, if he is the sort you claim, he will offer whatever information will bring him the most money, if he has to make it up to suit you," said Roger.

"This is not Vadim de Silenrieux's page, Roger, and I have means of ascertaining the value of what he tells me." He looked up at the ceiling of his study. "Apfelobstgarten told me that the man is reliable, or I would not have approached him."

"You think he will help you to put together the pieces of—" He broke off. "What is to stop him telling the police about you?"

"Nothing," Ragoczy said with such unconcern that Roger regarded him accusingly.

"You expect him to tell them, don't you?" he challenged.

"Well, I am assuming at least one of those I have contacted will do that. Whether it is Seligerquelle or another does not entirely concern me." He tapped the telegrams impatiently. "With any luck, the knowledge that I have returned will give Inspector Blau the impetus he needs to resume his inquiries."

"It might also bring the police to arrest you, my master," Roger pointed out.

"It's possible, but not likely, not in this weather, and with so many questions still pending in Berlin. They had better be ready to make a formal accusation if they come here. I am willing to talk with Inspector Blau at any time, of course, but I will not let them hold me when there are so many . . . loose ends to tie up." His smile had more mischief than Roger had seen Ragoczy display in more than six hundred years.

"And you intend to tie them? From here? Or to compel those in Berlin to deal with them, because it is what you want?" Roger asked, and made a gesture of resignation. "You need not tell me, my master. I understand. But let me remind you that the role of gadfly is not often rewarded with anything other than a slap."

"Yes, I am aware of that," said Ragoczy coolly.

Roger lowered his voice. "You are taunting them, my master. They will not take it kindly."

"I trust they will not," Ragoczy agreed.

"It is hopeless to talk sense to you when you are in this frame of mind," said Roger, and turned on his heel.

Ragoczy shrugged to himself, and set about preparing more telegrams, including one to his banker in Munchen, authorizing a transfer of funds to the account of Urban Seligerquelle. He was beginning to feel the first true optimism he had experienced since he left Amsterdam; it was just possible that his plan would succeed, and he would have the information he required before the police came for him.

Over the next week the snow gave way to rain in the day that brought ice at night. The roads were bordered in dirty slush and marked with deep, muddy ruts that mired progress by day and became treacherously slick once the sun was down. When not pursuing his investigation of Nadezna's death, Ragoczy busied himself with constructing a new athanor in his alchemical laboratory, intending to continue his research with Isidor Rieman as time allowed. More telegrams were sent and delivered, including one from Rowena, who informed Ragoczy that his portrait was almost complete. Then one came from a man signing himself Oertel Morgenstern.

"Who is this fellow?" Ragoczy wondered aloud as he read the page-long message a second time.

"Why not ask one of your contacts in Berlin?" Roger recommended. They were in Ragoczy's laboratory, the half-finished new athanor between them, its beehive shape completed on one side. "Surely they know the man."

"It's possible," Ragoczy mused. "I suppose Oberstetten should be able to find out something, or Seligerquelle." He read the telegram a third time. "Whoever this Morgenstern is, he clearly has more than a passing interest in Nadezna's death. Listen to this: *Saw you depart N's house shortly after servant left stop Saw two other men arrive not long after stop Saw the two men leave hurriedly approx. twenty minutes later stop One of the men looked disheveled stop Had colleague with me to corroborate observation stop Trust you can find other verification stop Am not at liberty to address authorities stop.* Who the devil is this man? and why was he watching Nadezna? More to the point, whom did he see arrive?"

"Is there no way you can ask him yourself?" Roger knew the answer, but could not keep from speaking.

"If I had the means to reach him. At least he tells me I may show his telegram to the authorities, in lieu of his own statement to them." He set the telegram down, apart from the others. "I have a few things I would like this Oertel Morgenstern to explain to me."

"Such as who her later visitors were, and why one was disheveled when they left," Roger suggested.

"Among other things." Ragoczy's voice was distant and his dark eyes were focused on something far beyond the walls of his laboratory.

Roger hesitated, then observed, "Have you considered that Morgenstern may be sending you this to misdirect you?"

"I have," said Ragoczy at once. "And if that was his intention, he has succeeded. It has also occurred to me," he went on before Roger could speak, "that Morgenstern was not watching Nadezna at all—that he was, in fact, watching me."

Text of a letter to Baron Klemens Manfred von Wolgast from Egmont von Rosenwiese, both in Berlin.

March 18, 1911

My dear Baron;

Pursuant to your instructions, I have submitted a fabricated report impugning F. Ragoczy's motives in regard to his mission in Berlin, which should suffice to make useless any further efforts on his part where matters of peace are concerned. The allegations are vague enough that they cannot easily be refuted without exposing more of the Count's dealings than it would be prudent to do. I have also instigated a series of inquiries related to the police investigation of Nadezna's tragic death. Even if Ragoczy is somehow able to show himself guiltless in that crime, the questions will remain in the records of this department, and unless my activities are discovered, they will not be removed. Further, I have introduced records of his businesses in Russia, some of which could be converted to the manufacture of military supplies. With all this mitigating against him, should Ragoczy attempt to present any petition for limiting arms, it will seem that he is intending to weaken the German sphere of influence in order to ensure the Czar's domination of Poland and all of Eastern Europe.

I have also strengthened the recommendations in regard to dealing with the continuing unrest in the Balkans and what it could mean in our negotiations with the Czechs and Poles. The separatist Bohemian faction have proved most useful in this context, since they have been most outspoken over the years, and Prague is such an important city. It did not take much work on my part to make the stability of the region far less certain than it may actually be. That, in turn, lends credibility to my recommendation that men like you be included in the dis-

cussions of the Chancellor's advisors so that the preparedness of the
country for war be sufficient to meet any challenge.

You have made certain promises in regard to my success in these endeavors, and I expect you to honor those promises. This is not a threat,
merely the assurance of one gentleman to another that the terms on
which we were agreed will be kept. I cannot help but worry that you,
having such compromising material in your possession, might desire to
use it to achieve more than what I have done thus far. If that is your intention, then I will have to reconsider my obligations to you and to my
position as Deputy Minister of Foreign Affairs. It would not be suitable
for me to continue to act for you beyond the tasks originally stipulated.
I would feel it incumbent upon me to expose my work on your behalf
and to throw myself on the mercy of the law courts, or in some other
way exculpate myself.

I am curious still about your animosity toward Ragoczy, and while
I understand what he represents in terms of your business, and how you
despised him for his patronage of Nadezna's school, I continue at a loss
as to why your determination to discredit him should be so vehement.
What has this man done that you seek to ruin him so utterly? Is it that
he has more strength of character than I, and will not be coerced by
you? Is it that he is more wealthy than you? Or is it that he is an exile
who has overcome his losses and made his way in the world? Or is it
something else entirely—some antipathy beyond definition? Whatever
it is, I pity him, as I pity any man who earns your enmity, including
myself.

Let me recommend, for your own sake, that you destroy this letter;
its contents are damning for both of us.

Yours to command,
Egmont von Rosenwiese

5

From the drawing room of the Chez Noir came the sounds of energetic
singing, squeals of laughter and an occasional whoop of dismay, the first
prelude to what would be a busy evening; in this small, unadorned, private room at the end of the hall opposite the kitchen that served Paul

Reighert as an office, the voices were as hushed as if in a Confessional.

"You understand what is to be done? We have specific instructions—can you follow them?" Reighert asked the thin, seedy young man in the threadbare coat seated across from him. "If you cannot do this, then the employer will not be pleased, for you have already received a handsome amount from him."

Abalard Dyre stared nervously down at his long fingers, refusing to meet Reighert's eyes. "Do we have to kill her? Is that really necessary? I mean, she's . . . confined. She'll be there the rest of her life. What's the point in killing her?"

"It's what we're being paid to do. If we do this well, there will be other work, and more money for both of us." He held out a dozen banknotes. "Here. This is the second payment."

Dyre made no move to accept the money. "I don't really want to kill anyone—let alone a madwoman. I don't mind stealing, or taking a fool's wallet if I have the chance—that's the way of the world—but this killing isn't like robbing a drunken Pole or raiding a jewel-box if the owners are stupid enough to leave it in plain sight and the doors unlocked. Killing a woman kept in a hospital run by nuns: what's the point?" He winced as he spoke, as if the words made the deed more real. "Isn't there another way? She's locked up, isn't she? Well, where's the danger in her? It's not as if she will be let out."

"What good is she to anyone? What good is she to herself, for that matter?" Reighert asked, assuming his most reasonable tone of voice. "Think about it. She has been confined as surely as if she were a desperate criminal for more than a decade. She is said to be dangerous to herself and others. She has attacked the nuns who tend her more times than I can tell you. She has no friendships with anyone; her family have long since ceased to visit her, except her husband, and he is only permitted to do that rarely. What kind of life is that? She will never be anything more than an animal in a cage." He leaned forward to be heard over a sudden burst of noise. "The money is very good. The woman is miserable and a burden. She has been living this way for long enough, don't you see? What is the matter in profiting from ending her life? Would it be more merciful to ignore her plight and let her continue as she is?"

"Does her husband want to marry again? Or are there children he would like to disown?" Dyre asked with an acuity that took Reighert aback.

"The man is not one to ignore his duties," said Reighert with more sincerity than the statement warranted. "He has been told by the nuns that his wife's condition is worsening and that they are powerless to help her."

"Has he tried everything?" Dyre asked. "What about this Herr Doktor Freud in Vienna? Mightn't he have the means to treat the woman?"

Reighert regarded Dyre with dawning suspicion. "Why should this trouble you? I tell you everything that can be done for her is being done."

Dyre hitched his shoulders up and plucked at a fraying strand of his sleeve. "I . . . suppose I dislike killing anything that is helpless. When it is a woman, it is much worse."

"Ach, ja," said Reighert, recognizing the weakness of the man. "You think that the only dangerous humans are male, that females are soft and biddable, needing our guidance and protection. Well, that is hardly the case with this woman, you must believe me. She has rages and in those rages she is capable of pulling closed doors off their hinges. I myself have read the report the nuns provided of just such an incident. You know that nuns would not give a false report, especially of anything so serious." That was stretching the truth, but he had seen von Wolgast read it, and for the moment that was close enough to the truth to satisfy him.

"And the children? What does this mean to them?" Dyre asked, his gaze once more directed at the tops of his knees.

"The man hiring us has no children," Reighert snapped. "Not that that has any bearing on the case. Women as mad as she do not conceive."

"Then the man wants heirs," said Dyre, looking less apprehensive now that there was some reasonable explanation for the husband's intentions. "Legitimate ones, and who is to blame him? With a wife locked away like that, he must feel himself in desperate trouble. Any child coming from such a mother would not be regarded as competent no matter how hale he seemed. If his wife should outlive her husband, then so much the worse." He smiled nervously in his efforts to convince himself. "I still do not like the notion of killing someone who is mad," he said in an undervoice.

"Do you think God will hold it against you?" Reighert's laughter grated. "I can assure you that God has no concern for such things. Why, He destroys more lives in a single day than any man can, no matter how warlike his actions. And how does the woman come to be mad, but at God's instigation. Could it not be God moving her husband to end her travail?"

Dyre shook his head. "You used to be a Jesuit, didn't you? I'd forgot."

"I was." Reighert glowered. "I am still ordained: that cannot be taken from me. Not that oil on the thumb and first two fingers is anything more than slippery. They chose me as the example to the rest. I was not the only one profaning my vows; I knew of four others who were far more corrupt than I was, but they came from better families. I was defrocked; one of my . . . companions was promoted. He works in Rome now, at the Vatican. The other runs a foundling school in Silesia. To put Ernst Schneide in charge of children!" He spat to show his contempt.

In the front of the house someone was banging out a polka on the piano, and from the thunderous pounding, a few were attempting to dance to it; a few seconds later came the unmistakable rattle of falling chairs.

"You say that the woman is suffering?" Dyre asked after a long, thoughtful moment.

"She must be: she is just sane enough some of the time to know she is mad beyond all healing." He shook his head in counterfeit sympathy. "She has four times attempted to starve herself to death. She has told her husband, when she has not tried to gouge his eyes out with her thumbs, or bite the skin from his cheeks, that she is miserable. When she is not in her wits, she becomes wholly altered. Increasingly she claims to be under the control of angels and devils, all of whom prompt her to unspeakable things. The nuns say that she has been getting worse; occasionally she sleeps for days on end. She will stand in one posture from dawn until dusk. She eats her own excrement. She has gnawed the flesh off the backs of her hands. If she dies by her own hand, it is a mortal sin. If she is killed by another, she will be welcome in heaven as a martyr. Consider what she has endured and decide what is kindest to that poor woman."

Dyre's confusion was so apparent that it might have been amusing if the circumstances were less stringent. "I suppose, if she has tried to die, that it makes a difference." His voice was hardly audible over the noise from the parlor.

"Of course it does," said Reighert, certain he had achieved his end with the young man. "She has had anguish enough in her life."

There was enough doubt remaining in Dyre for him to ask, "And the husband is concerned only for her welfare? He is not planning a new marriage, or . . . or anything of that sort?"

"No," said Reighert, "he has no one he intends to marry."

Dyre fussed with the frayed cuff of his old-fashioned coat. "And it is not that he is unwilling to support her any longer?"

That guess was close enough to the truth that it caught Reighert off guard. He stammered out a denial, hoping Dyre would take this as a sign of indignation on von Wolgast's behalf. He gathered his wits quickly enough. "The man is wealthy, and of very good family. He could easily afford to support her for decades to come, but seeing her in such affliction would break his heart."

"I see," whispered Dyre, then spoke up to be heard over the intruding noise. "When does he want this done? Why has he decided it must be now?"

Reighert had an answer ready for this. "He recently had a long discussion with the nuns caring for her, and they have told him that his wife is unable to recognize those who have tended her for years. She is despondent and is often unaware of her surroundings. From time to time she throws herself violently at the walls of her cell and must be restrained in order to prevent serious injury. The nuns and her physician warned him that she may soon be incapable of remembering any individual for more than a day. The last time he went to see her, she did not know him, called him disgusting names and accused the nuns of drugging her with opium and belladonna." Reighert shook his head. "What would you do, in his place."

"I would not want my wife to suffer," said Dyre quietly before shoving himself to his feet. "All right. It goes against the grain, but I can understand why it is so urgent a matter." This time when Reighert offered him the money, he took it. "Who is this woman, and where do we find her?"

"You do not need to know more than that her name is Antonia; the nuns refer to her only by her Christian name, out of deference to her family. When everything is arranged, I will drive you to the hospital— it is in the country—blindfolded, so that you will not know which one it is, or where." He saw the qualms come back into Dyre's manner, and hurried on. "You will be able to say you do not know the woman, or where she was confined if there are ever any questions asked. I will take the brunt of such investigation, if there is any."

One hand on the door latch, Dyre had one last concern. "This woman's condition: what is the cause?"

"Who knows, in these matters?" Reighert answered with a sigh. "She comes from a fine family, very old and distinguished. Their arms were enrolled in the eleventh century. But, you know, there is often a great deal of intermarriage in the highborn, and the bloodline can become . . . shall we say, too dense? She was the only child of her parents, who were first cousins with one remove. There was more than twenty years difference between husband and wife." He knew this only because of von Wolgast's scathing remarks about his in-laws.

"You are saying that they were too closely related for healthy children?" asked Dyre, who had followed some of the writings about eugenics.

"They, and many of their ancestors. The result was few living children, and then Antonia, who is, as I have told you, mad." Reighert lit a cigarette and let his first exhale serve as a sigh. "Inbreeding inevitably leads to a compromised line."

"Inbreeding could cause such madness?" Dyre asked incredulously. "I have been told that it sometimes results in idiocy, but madness?"

"Madness, idiocy—is there really so much difference?" Reighert asked, expecting no response and receiving none. "You will hear from me within the week."

"Yes," said Dyre, and left Reighert to depart from the Chez Noir through the rear kitchen door, as he had been instructed.

Half an hour later von Wolgast arrived, decked out in full formal attire; after a friendly glass of cognac with Heloise, who was rigged out in a broad damask skirt over a flounced petticoat and panniers with only the tight-laced corset above, he sought Reighert out in his austere room. "How does it look? Is he willing?"

"Oh, he will do it," said Reighert through a halo of cigarette smoke, "but we had better be about it quickly. I do not know how long he will remain convinced that murder is the only path to your Antonia's salvation." The cynicism of his words was as real and oppressive as summer heat in Naples.

"What do you mean by soon?" von Wolgast asked with mild interest. "Tomorrow? A week? A month?"

"No more than a week. Dyre has too many reservations to depend upon his greed and confusion to sustain him longer than that." Reighert finished one cigarette and used it to light the next before dropping the butt on the floor and grinding it with his heel.

"Very well. I will make the arrangements we discussed," said von Wolgast, sitting down in the same chair Dyre had occupied. "And the other matter?"

"Baron," said Reighert with an impatient sigh, "I wish you would abandon your vilification of Ragoczy. What is Ragoczy, that he deserves so much attention? And what use is pursuing him? Soon or late, it will bring questions to you, questions you will not want to answer."

"That's ridiculous." Von Wolgast dismissed Reighert's caveat with a swipe of his thick hand. "There is no reason for that to happen."

"Not yet," Reighert said. "But the longer you insist on keeping the calumnies alive, the more likely someone will trace them to their source."

"And who would that someone be?" von Wolgast jeered. "Who does he know? What Prussian will vouch for him? The most prominent supporter he has is that newspaperman Oberstetten, and he is a sensible man who does not ally himself with unpopular causes or figures, which Ragoczy is rapidly becoming." He leaned back in the chair in order to draw out a tall, cylindrical cigar case from his inner breast pocket. This he opened and sniffed the cigar it contained. "Rum-soaked," he said with a beatific smile.

Reighert cocked a brow, his cigarette dangling from the corner of his mouth. "Well, I have delivered my caution, and you will heed it or not, as you like." He folded his hands. "I have found a source of heroin to use on your wife. If she speaks at all after she is injected, the nuns will suppose it is more of her delusions."

"Excellent," approved von Wolgast. "Did you warn Dyre that she could be dangerous?"

"Yes, of course; I told him she has attacked you," said Reighert, offended that von Wolgast would ask such a question.

"Good. Good. And the truth, as well." His cherubic smile never warmed his eyes. "The nuns have been increasing Antonia's sedatives, which her physician has recommended in case she should attempt to injure herself again. There should be no trouble with her, but it would be best to be on guard, in case she revives enough to realize her danger." He bit the end off his cigar and removed the band. "This is such a pleasure."

"Arranging the death of your wife or smoking a cigar?" asked Reighert sarcastically.

"Why, both," said von Wolgast as he lit up; pungent, rum-scented smoke blended with the harsher odors of Turkish tobacco. "Now, you said you had to speak to me about Inspector Blau? What is the matter this time?"

"He has resumed asking questions about the night Nadezna died; apparently he is not as convinced of Ragoczy's culpability as we assumed he was." He noticed that von Wolgast's brows drew down upon hearing this. "He has asked Pflaume about her soirees, again. Pflaume would like to have a word with you about it."

"I am certain he would," said von Wolgast. "How much does he want?"

Reighert shrugged. "Whatever it is, it will not be the last, dear Baron. Pflaume needs a pension."

"Must he be accommodated?" asked von Wolgast with a significant look. "Dead men do not collect pensions."

"No, but that man dead could reignite the fire the police have been willing to damp. It would be imprudent to have another tragedy occur so nearly related to the case." He felt annoyed with the Baron, and decided to go on. "I begin to think that you like dead bodies: that you make weapons to provide you with more of them."

Von Wolgast sat bolt upright in his chair. "I trust you spoke in jest," he said, so smoothly that he filled Reighert with dread.

Reighert drew back. "Of course I did; what else would it be?" he said at once, and attempted a laugh to illustrate his sincerity. He nearly dropped his cigarette from suddenly nerveless fingers. "You could arrange for him to leave Germany. He must have relatives in America or Canada who would have a place for him if he brought them a small stipend, enough to make him welcome but not so much that he would be conspicuous for it." As he spoke, he became more confident. "The police are not going to cross the Atlantic to ask Pflaume about Nadezna, and once he is gone, the need to pay him also ends. So a single amount would be the best offer, along with a second-class ticket to New York or Nova Scotia, to speed him on his way."

Out in the front of the house, someone with a very good voice was singing one of the Mahler songs about dead children; most of the guests had gone silent to listen.

"America or Canada," said von Wolgast to himself. "It is, as you stated, a long way from Germany." He contemplated Reighert with a degree of interest that the former Jesuit found unnerving.

"And once he is there, he is not likely to return, particularly if you pay him enough to make it worth his while not to," Reighert said hurriedly, and explained himself. "If you do not pay him well, he may become discontented. You want him grateful enough that he will not suddenly take it into his head to send a sworn statement to the police. If you were to give him a generous amount, anything he said about you could be dismissed as the dissatisfaction of a servant, one who is ungrateful for the generosity of his late employer's friend." He was not actually certain this was the case, but he knew beyond all reservation that killing Pflaume would take suspicion off Ragoczy and might well lead back to them. "You could be certain he would be ignored if you—"

"What do you mean by a generous amount?" von Wolgast interrupted.

"Five years' salary, or six," said Reighert. "Based on whatever Nadezna paid him in her best years. He was very loyal to her." It was not the amount he would have recommended, but he thought it was the greatest sum von Wolgast would stomach.

"Why should I spend so much? That is not an insignificant amount of money, is it?" von Wolgast asked around his teeth as he chomped on his cigar.

"For your own safety, of course." He paused, arranging his arguments in his mind and striving to quiet the tension he could feel gathering in his neck and back. "It is nowhere near what you would have to pay to defend yourself in court. It might be just as well to have Pflaume out of Germany in any case. If what you tell me is true, he did not know everything about her business, but he knew how often you were in her company, and he might begin to assume certain things that would be to your disadvantage."

"And yours," von Wolgast said, his mouth sullen.

"Oh, without doubt, if Pflaume knew me. But as far as I can recall, he saw me only once or twice, and not at any time near her death." Reighert let this sink in. "Tell me what you decide as soon as you do," he advised von Wolgast.

"I will," was the answer, given so readily that Reighert braced himself for what would come next. "If you will do something for me."

"What would that be?" Reighert asked, feeling his chest tighten with the question.

Von Wolgast did not answer directly. "Did you know that Ragoczy is back in Germany?"

Reighert was startled and disbelieving. "I have heard nothing of it."

"No; nor had I until I paid a handsome sum to Seligerquelle, who had been contacted by Ragoczy from his estate in Bavaria. He had provided Ragoczy with information that would spur his interest, worse luck. I wish Seligerquelle had come to me before he answered Ragoczy's inquiry. I would have made it worth his while." His glare became a sour smile. "Yes, it would seem he has not remained under the Czar's cloak, so to speak. He has come back." Von Wolgast relished the shock in Reighert's eyes. "I understand from Seligerquelle that Ragoczy is seeking information about Nadezna's death with the intention of apprehending the man responsible for it as well as removing all suspicion from himself." He drew on his cigar again. "I think it would be best to distract him."

"Distract him?" Reighert repeated, knowing he would not like what was coming, and knowing that von Wolgast was already determined on his course.

"Yes. We must provide a diversion. He has been as busy as he has been private, may God strike him blind and impotent for his audacity." His small eyes glittered dangerously. "I won't have it. He will not be permitted to ruin everything, not when I am so close."

"What is it you want to do?" asked Reighert with a fatalistic shrug, aware that whatever it was, von Wolgast would not be persuaded to abandon his plans for Ragoczy.

Again von Wolgast's answer was oblique. "Does your associate Bernard still keep watch on that Englishwoman in Amsterdam?" he inquired as if wanting to know about the weather, or the supper being laid in the dining room.

"Yes," said Reighert, a cold stab of something more than fear going through him.

"Good," said von Wolgast, and resorted to his cigar again.

"Good?" Reighert demanded when von Wolgast said no more. "What the devil have you got planned?"

"Ach," said von Wolgast, tapping the ash onto the rug. "Do you think it would distract Ragoczy if some misfortune befell her?"

Reighert shook his head emphatically. "Not another murder. No. Oh, no. And not of a titled Englishwoman, no matter where she is living." He stubbed out his cigarette on the side of his table and lurched to his feet.

Von Wolgast ignored him. "I have given this careful thought, and I am certain that I can keep Ragoczy from continuing his efforts. The information Bernard has provided you should make it easy to accomplish our ends."

Another singer, a thick-voiced bass, was now beginning the Serenade from Mussorgsky's *Songs and Dances of Death*, lavishing the rocking phrases with sensuality and temptation.

"It will not only be Ragoczy who you will have to contend with if there is another murder. You cannot commit the murder of that young woman and—"

"Not a murder," von Wolgast soothed. "A kidnapping." He beamed at Reighert, his mouth caressing the cigar.

The music filled the hush between them, and the applause that followed.

"A kidnapping?" Reighert echoed, as if in response to the clapping, not to anything von Wolgast had said. "Of the Englishwoman? From Amsterdam?" His thunderstruck silence gradually gave way to consideration; slowly he sat down again.

Von Wolgast permitted himself a satisfied smile. "Yes. It should not be difficult. She lives alone, doesn't she? There should be no problem in taking her on the day her housekeeper is absent, which I understand she is once or twice a week, according to your Bernard. I don't see that it is necessary to kill her, at least not at first. In fact, it is better if she is alive, for that would demand immediate attention from Ragoczy, and he cannot do two things at once. If a ransom is required, it will make the act seem one unrelated to anything Ragoczy is doing in Germany. If she learns too much, we can abandon her in the mountains. She is not likely to survive long if we deprive her of clothes and shoes. That would be a charming sight, wouldn't it? A naked woman of good breeding, forced to choose between preserving her modesty or her life."

Reighert was nearly overwhelmed with confusion. "What mountains? How could this be done?" were the first sensible questions that came to him and he blurted it out. "We are not talking about some insignificant trollop here, we are talking about a woman with important connections. Where would she be held? How would—"

"Calm down, Reighert," said von Wolgast smugly. "I tell you, I have planned it out perfectly." He watched as Reighert reached out and opened the cabinet next to the table and drew out a half-full bottle of schnapps; as Reighert drank from the bottle, von Wolgast went on. "You will go to Amsterdam next week, to arrange matters with Bernard. I want you there so that you can supervise the transporting of Miss Pearce-Manning to the train, and guard her in your journey to Innsbruck." He saw the astonishment come back into Reighert's face again. "I will meet you there, and we will go to my hunting lodge." He gave a nasty grin. "I use it rarely, and never for entertaining. I doubt if anyone is aware that I have it."

"A hunting lodge in Austria?" said Reighert, feeling thick-witted; he drank again, relishing the burn of the liquid as it ran down inside him.

"A remote one. Between Hintertux and Madern, very steep. There will be a great deal of snow still." Von Wolgast tapped off more ashes. "After the lamentable demise of my afflicted wife, no one will think it strange that I decide to spend time by myself, alone, for a while. No one will consider my absence odd, nor will they seek to accompany me, out of respect for my grief." His smile was worse than any laughter could have been.

"Then . . . you want this done . . . shortly?"

Von Wolgast nodded with supreme confidence. "I want it done as soon as you have taken care of Antonia. You will leave within a day of her death. I will arrange your travel for you, in both directions; your tickets will be waiting here when you come back from your . . . errand. If you will pack your bag before you go to the hospital, you need do no more than collect it and the packet I leave for you: it will spare you the inconvenience of working out routes and will keep you to a schedule." He sat forward and balanced his cigar on the edge of the table. "You will reach Austria through France and Switzerland, to avoid any inquiries of the police Ragoczy might instigate. I have worked out the timetables already."

Reighert scowled. "You make it sound as if Miss Pearce-Manning will cooperate in this. I shouldn't think she would." He found von Wolgast's confidence in his plan mesmerizing.

"But that assumes she would have anything to say about it. Now that you have the heroin, you can keep her sedated during your travels, incapable of speaking for herself, or moving, which would account for strapping her into a wheeled-chair, and the necessity for your constant attendance. What official will stop a devoted uncle from bringing his stricken niece home to her family? Think of the pathos of it." He gestured with operatic extravagance.

"Bathos, more like," muttered Reighert.

"Only if you are clumsy," von Wolgast warned him. "Once you have her at Innsbruck, you will not have to drug her, and we will transport her—bound and gagged if necessary—to my hunting lodge. It will be your work to send the ransom telegram and to monitor all the responses, as well as obtain reports about any investigations underway." He stopped. "The money from the ransom can be paid to Pflaume, and that will guarantee that it will be beyond recovery, should any attempt be made to trace it."

"Can that be done?" Reighert asked. "I've heard that it has been, but I've never known it to be successful."

"The numbers on the banknotes are apt to be recorded. Scotland Yard is meticulous about such matters. And if her family in England pays the ransom, you may rely upon Scotland Yard to do their utmost to keep track of the money. The bank will insist upon it if the family does not." He folded his arms. "Imagine what anguish Ragoczy will feel."

"If he cares for her," Reighert appended, trying to find a flaw in the plan. "You have no evidence that he—"

"Oh, I am convinced he does, having encouraged her artistic pretensions as he has done. It suits his purpose to have her away from her family, filling his absences with daubing paint about. Why should he do that, but to put her in a position of obligation to him? It may be only an affaire with him, but you may be certain that any man as proud as he will not stand idly by to see his mistress taken advantage of by anyone but him. And Ragoczy has an unconscionable amount of pride. And it is pride that 'goeth before a fall,' if I remember correctly." He coughed delicately. "With a little finesse we might be able to implicate him in her disappearance. He could not then pursue any inquiries about Nadezna without further embroiling himself in both . . . misfortunes."

From the front of the Chez Noir came a chaotic eruption into *The Looking-glass Waltz,* the guests creating high-spirited cacophony; the pianist had to pound the keys in order to be heard at all.

"It was not his way with Nadezna, to use his sponsorship to bind her to him," Reighert reminded von Wolgast.

"Have you considered Miss Pearce-Manning herself? Nadezna was a woman with great gifts but a common birth. I don't think Ragoczy would sully his exile's name with so lowly a paramour as Nadezna was." His sneer was eloquent.

"And Miss Pearce-Manning is part of a titled family," Reighert persisted, though he was almost convinced von Wolgast would succeed. "You may be right, Baron."

"Of course I am. And while Ragoczy is searching futilely for Miss Pearce-Manning, we will have a chance to discredit him completely. It should not be too difficult to persuade his house steward—"

"Erich Rotscheune," Reighert supplied.

"Yes: Rotscheune," von Wolgast agreed, irritated by this interruption. "He must have a price that would make it possible for us to plant certain of Nadezna's things in Ragoczy's house in Glanzend Strasse. It must be done diplomatically, of course, and in such a way that Rotscheune will not feel he has necessarily acted against his employer. There are one or two things of hers that I would like to have out of my hands and put into his; things that will lend credence to the rumors about his role in her murder." He licked his lips and picked up his cigar once again. "So. As you can see, I have been most thorough in my planning."

"That you have," said Reighert, wishing he could rid himself of the sensation of being sucked by a whirlpool down into the depths of the ocean; always in the past he had been titillated by a new undertaking, but since von Wolgast had begun his pursuit of Ragoczy, Reighert had become steadily more anxious. He said, "It is a very risky plan; I presume you are aware of it."

"Small risk, small gain," von Wolgast paraphrased. "And this will accomplish so much more than removing me from the possibility of suspicion in Nadezna's death: it will put to an end this preposterous notion of limiting the production of weapons. With Ragoczy revealed as a violent criminal, any venture he advocates must be seen as reprehensible. Let the Czar limit his own weapons, if it suits him." His petulance flared at the recollection of Ragoczy's mission. "It cost me half the price of a field gun to learn what the Czar was trying to gain. I begrudge Ragoczy every mark of it."

Reighert had heard this recitation often enough to want to avoid another one. "Yes, and so you shall, if your plan is as flawless as you suppose it must be." He lit another cigarette. "The first thing we must arrange is the visit to your wife. You said you will have the necessary authorizations for me."

Reluctantly von Wolgast gave his attention to his more immediate goal. "Yes. I have asked for a letter from her physician admitting certain family members to see her. I will supply you with identification as her cousins, and a note from her old Confessor, who still believes she will return to her senses, if God is satisfied that she is ready for such an experience. I will include a most heartrending request that she be placed in restraints while her cousins are with her, so that neither she nor they will come to harm. They will leave you alone with her if Antonia is restrained. You should be able to inject her without detection."

"Shall we kiss her? That would be a fine opportunity." Reighert exhaled slowly. "And appropriate, in context; a kiss as a . . . betrayal."

"Whatever you wish," said von Wolgast with studied indifference. He drew on his cigar; his expression was inscrutable. "So long as she dies."

A tick jumped in Reighert's cheek. "She will."

"Very good." Von Wolgast lowered his head and stubbed out his cigar on the floor. "If she does not, you will answer for it. The police would find your presence at the hospital questionable at best."

Reighert swore under his breath, then made himself say, "I am not going to disappoint you, Baron. But I would not like to be cast in the role of coryphaeus."

Von Wolgast chuckled. "This is not going to be a tragedy, Greek or otherwise. Rest assured that you will not have to serve as the chorus, or its leader." He rose, his hand extended. "Then we are agreed? After my wife is . . . departed, you will go to Amsterdam and secure Miss Pearce-Manning?"

Reighert shook von Wolgast's hand. "I think it may turn out to be an unwise move, but I can offer no reason for my opinion other than a chill in my spine—"

"Which is to say that you are growing fearful," von Wolgast interrupted. "Yes, I can see why you might feel that way. But think of how great an attainment you will have when you've overcome your trepidation and brought the woman to me." He waved one arm in the air. "You will be able to demonstrate that you have broken the hold that fear had upon you."

"Possibly," said Reighert, still not wholly convinced. "You may want to work out your strategy more closely." He saw the ferocious scowl that greeted his remark and decided it would not be wise to contradict von Wolgast while he was so rapt in his own plan. There would be time later, he thought, when he could suggest the dangers in the Baron's scheme.

As von Wolgast opened the door, he heard the opening bars of *The Artist's Life Waltz* hammered out on the piano, accompanied by cheers of approval and one or two groans of displeasure. "It is going to be a hectic evening, by the sound of it." He nodded his approval. "Heloise told me she would save me two hours with Aurore. Apparently Biennot is . . . indisposed tonight."

"She is very young," said Reighert, wanting to be rid of von Wolgast so he could make his own arrangements for the night. "Until . . . what day, Baron?"

"I will expect to meet with you again in three days, for a final discussion. You will be here?" The implication that Reighert might flee was apparent in the set of his countenance.

"Certainly," Reighert snapped.

"Excellent. *Excellent.* And we will tend to the matter of Pflaume, as well?" He was about to turn away, but added, "You ought to wire Bernard, to prepare him for what is coming. Don't you think?"

"Of course," said Reighert, preparing to close the door.

"Oh, and Reighert," von Wolgast said with spurious sweetness, "If you plan to ask for more money, I would recommend against it."

Reighert made his face go blank, as if nothing of the sort had crossed his mind. He nodded to show he had heard, and then stepped up to the door. "In three days, Baron. Enjoy your evening." With that he closed the door, standing for several seconds before undertaking the unappealing task of cleaning von Wolgast's smashed cigar butt off the floor.

※ ※ ※

Text of a letter from Euchary Apfelobstgarten in Berlin to Franchot Ragoczy, Count Saint-Germain in Bavaria.

> *The Office of Procurement*
> *Berlin*
> *March 29, 1911*

Franchot Ragoczy, Count Saint-Germain
Schloss Saint-Germain
Nr. Hausham
Bavaria

My dear Ragoczy;

I have, as you requested, been in contact with Inspector Blau in regard to his investigation of the murder of the ballerina Nadezna. I found, as you suggested I would, Inspector Blau to be a thoughtful and reasonable man, who has informed me that he has received an unusually large amount of anonymous information pertaining to the case, much of which he views with extreme skepticism. He has said that when he is given so much information from undisclosed sources, he is inclined to take the opposite view from what the informants advocate, for it is his experience that such persistent activities are intended to obfuscate the issues instead of illuminating them.

I asked him why he resumed his investigation, and he said it was not, in fact, your return to Germany, but the report of an Austrian fellow, a would-be actor who has apparently been paid to watch you and those you know when you are in Berlin. This man, who Inspector Blau identified only as Lukas, apparently claims that after you left Nadezna's on the night of her death, two other men arrived. This Lukas further claims that the man who had paid him for his services also saw the arrival and apparently the departure of these later visitors.

It is now Inspector Blau's intention to learn as much as he can from the statements of this Lukas, and to question the man who hired him, to determine if his observations do, in fact, corroborate what Lukas has told him. As he has not yet been able to contact this man, whom Lukas calls Morgenstern, he is without the substantiation he seeks. Until he has done this, he is disinclined to detain you again, not only because of the possible diplomatic consequences, but because he is increasingly uneasy about the case against you. This may change in the course of his inquiries: for the time being, you may assume you are not likely to receive a call from the authorities.

Your second request is somewhat more difficult to answer. I have not, myself, seen the orders for arms and munitions, but I have it from a reliable source that there is going to be an increase in guns purchased for the army in the second half of the year. Bids have already gone out to Krupp and von Wolgast for their prices, and the General Staff will be meeting to discuss what is needed in June. Von Moltke is determined to have the best-equipped army in Europe, with the most modern weapons. I am cognizant of your hopes in this regard and I am sorry to have to dash them in this way. Let me suggest that you take the same attitude that the Kaiser has expressed—that so long as it is known that Germany has guns enough to keep the peace, peace will be kept. It may be cold comfort, but it is the best I can offer.

I look forward to seeing you when you return to Berlin, and I trust that day will not be far off, when you are wholly exonerated of any part in Nadezna's murder, and all tarnish to your reputation is gone.

> *Respectfully,*
> *Euchary Apfelobstgarten*

6

It was with reluctance that Yseut announced the caller to Rowena. "Mister Bowen is here again, Miss," she said as she climbed halfway up the stairs to the studio at the top of the house. "He says he will not leave without seeing you."

"Damn the man," Rowena said quietly and angrily. "What must I do to convince him I will not—" She broke off as she set her palette aside. "Tell him I will be with him shortly. It would be common courtesy to offer him something, but make it as little as you can: chocolate or coffee or tea. Nothing to eat. He is not invited to high tea. He is not invited at all."

"If you think it best," said Yseut, her tone dubious. "Do you want to encourage him, Miss?"

"Not at all," said Rowena sharply. "But I will not convince him of that by being deliberately rude to him. He has not noticed when I have been." She began to unfasten her smock. "But it is tempting, to say or do something so scandalous that he would be shocked into taking the scales from his eyes," she admitted with a faint smile, then added, "He would probably decide it was incumbent upon him to rectify my manners. So, it would be best to provide him minimal courtesy and then to speed him on his way."

"Yes, Miss," said Yseut, and went down to the ground floor to relay Rowena's unenthusiastic greeting and to offer him the choice of tea or coffee.

"Why, coffee, if you will, with milk and sugar," said Rupert, looking very natty in his new slate-and-tan tweed jacket. His shirt was a pale-blue—a daring departure for him—and his deep-brown flannel slacks were neatly creased. His tie had Corpus Christi colors, and his cufflinks displayed the college's arms. He went into the front room, shaking his head at what he considered the extravagance of a canalside house, and sat down on the Empire couch upholstered in honey-colored linen, two shades darker than the draperies. The butler's table in front of the couch had bright brass fittings—Rupert approved of it, for it reminded him of Longacres. He glanced around at the rest of the furnishings, shaking his head at the eclectic styles represented: a Chinese chest of polished wood on short, bowed legs next to a fifty-year-old Dutch chair; the other chair was of the Queen Anne period, reupholstered in a modern Viennese print; a long Japanese scroll on the south wall depicting a waterfall contrasted with the modern end tables flanking the couch, each with an Art Nouveau lamp on it, and the carpet from Bokhara. Most of these items had been purchased one at a time over the last four months, and each item had been selected by Rowena after careful consideration: what Rupert saw as deplorable inconsistency, Rowena regarded as harmoniously diverse.

Yseut brought the coffee in a tall, white pot with a single cup accompanying it on the tray, milk and sugar already in it. She set this down on the butler's table and curtsied. "Your coffee, Mister Bowen."

"Thank you, Ysabel," said Rupert, unaware of his mistake in her name. "Won't Miss Pearce-Manning be having coffee, too?"

"She did not say so," Yseut answered, continuing awkwardly, "I have work to do," as she withdrew, going back to the rear of the house, and to her continued preparations for supper.

Rupert poured himself coffee, annoyed that Yseut had not put the sugar bowl and creamer on the tray so he could have more than one cup. He sipped at the cup and decided it was a bit too hot.

Five minutes later, Rowena came into the room, still tugging her bolero jacket into place over her blouse. "Good afternoon, Rupert," she said brusquely. She had not changed from the neat, practical gored skirt she had put on in the morning, and the addition of the jacket was as much for the cool afternoon as for appearances; she had small pearl earrings on, but no other jewelry, and there was a faint odor of turpentine about her, leftover from her work. "I didn't expect you." She would not apologize for keeping him waiting, though she knew he considered himself entitled to it.

Rupert rose and extended his hand to her, aware that she expected it instead of anything more familiar. "I've missed you."

She knew she was supposed to say the same thing, but could not bring herself to do it. "Did you have a good crossing?"

He frowned a little. "The weather was mild—as it is here, and we made excellent time." His face softened. "It's good to see you, Rowena."

"I wish I could say the same," she replied at her most blunt. "I did not expect guests. I was counting on having another hour to work." She sat down in the Queen Anne chair. "If you had sent a note, we could have arranged a more convenient time."

"My, you are petulant today," he chided her with an affectionate smile delivered from his full height. "Artistic temperament; I will have to get used to it."

"I don't see why you should," she countered.

"Oh, come now, Rowena," he said indulgently. "You have had your chance to spread your wings, but now it is time to return to the nest." He felt rather proud of this analogy; he had worked it out during the Channel crossing, and was pleased to have found such an adroit way to use it. "If you stay here in Amsterdam much longer, you will be thought eccentric." His smiled faded, "And if you are hoping to encourage that foreigner, I would hope you would have more respect for yourself—"

She slid one leg over the other as she interrupted. "What I do, and where, and when, and with whom, are no business of yours, Rupert."

"Is he still in Bavaria?" he asked innocently. "Oh, that's what I was told by his neighbor when I stopped round at his flat to have a talk with him."

"You what?" she demanded, and could find no words to express the extent of her outrage. "What right—"

"You know what right I have, Rowena," he reminded her. "Do you really think Ragoczy has a Schloss in Bavaria? The address is 'Near Hausham'—whatever that means. This Schloss may well turn out to be little more than a cabin on the mountain."

"*Stop it,*" she said very quietly but with great force. "You have gone too far. I will not listen to more of this petty jealousy, which is wholly unmerited. Say what you want about Ragoczy: you will lessen yourself in my eyes and discredit him not a whit. You and I are not going to marry, and that is not because of Ragoczy. It is my decision. Were he to ask, I would refuse him as well. This is not a whim, or a ploy. I am not trying to catch your attention by being coy. I have done all I can think of to make it clear to you. I wish you would believe me." Her golden eyes shone with ill-concealed indignation. "Go home, Rupert, if you are so interested in nests. Wait a year or two and offer for my sister. Penelope adores you, and she will be thrilled to be your wife. And she will be just what you want her to be, which I never shall."

Rupert sat down once again and added some coffee to his cup. "How can you say such a thing to me?" he marveled, shifting his cup and saucer from one hand to the other, "When you know that you are everything I want in a wife. My family adores you. And yours would like nothing better. And—"

"I am nothing of the sort, and well you would know it if you could bring yourself to listen to me when I talk to you. I am not going to marry anyone, Rupert. I wish you would abandon this suit of yours. You would do better for yourself with another female. I am never more your friend than when I tell you this." She kept her tone steady and her temper under control.

He smiled gently. "You are trying to vex me, but I will not permit it. I know you too well to listen to you when you are in one of your crochets."

"Don't let's start this again." Rowena folded her arms, wishing she had the courage to tell him to leave.

"I am not starting anything, I am offering you a kind of truce," Rupert protested, and offered the excuse he had hit upon for his visit. "My purpose in coming here was to invite you for a ride in my new Darracq. It's an open racer. I understand it will do over sixty miles an hour, though I've only had it to fifty-five. You'll like it."

Little as she wanted to admit it, Rowena was intrigued. "You're offering me a handsome bribe," she corrected him.

"It is not a bribe at all; come, it's parked around the corner. We can be off at once," Rupert said, offense giving way to persuasion. "I know you enjoy automobiling, and I thought, in such congenial activity, we might better resolve our differences. I am trying to settle something that has remained unfinished."

"There is nothing unfinished between us, Rupert," said Rowena firmly. "I have told you my decision, and there is nothing left to discuss."

"But there is, you know," he said, refusing to be goaded into an argument.

"Only in your mind," Rowena informed him, the pleasure at the prospect of riding in an open racing motor car evaporating. "I have spoken to you as clearly as I may without deliberately giving offense."

There was a rattling crash in the kitchen; Rupert looked up. "Good Lord, what was that?"

"By the sound of it, Yseut dropped a bowl again." She was annoyed for the interruption as well as the undoubted loss of a bowl; she hoped it was one of the plain ironstone ones and not any of those she particularly liked.

"Should I go—" he offered, about to get to his feet.

Under other circumstances, that was precisely what Rowena would have done; now that Rupert had implied it should be done, Rowena said, "Why embarrass her? Cooks and housekeepers break things from time to time. So do I. So do you. I cannot recall the number of teacups I have ruined over the years. A bowl is no major loss, after all. Leave her be, Rupert."

He sat down reluctantly. "If you insist. She is your housekeeper, as you have been good enough to remind me. And I am certain you will hold her to account for the price of the item."

There was a scuffling sound at the back of the house. Both Rupert and Rowena were silent for a moment, until the sound stopped.

"What I do and do not do in my own house is my concern, Rupert, and not yours," Rowena reminded him, her efforts to control her temper losing ground to her irritation with him.

"You are too lenient, my dear. Any losses should be charged against her wages. To do anything else encourages laxness." He smiled confidently, and decided to make the most of his opportunity. "Do not jump all over me when I say this: once we are married you will leave such decisions to me."

She sat upright. "We are not going to *be* married. Rupert, how much more plainly can I say it? I am not going to marry you. I will never marry you."

The force of her voice took him aback. "You are overwrought, Rowena. It comes from working too hard—"

A masked figure in nondescript dark clothes appeared in the door; swearing in German, the man rushed into the room as Rupert got to his feet, turning the parlor to chaos in an instant; everything seemed to happen at once, as if time itself had been stunned by the appearance of the sinister man.

Rowena screamed in objuration and leaped up, aghast at this invasion of her home. In an instant she was looking around desperately for something with which to drive the intruder away: it did not occur to her that Rupert might decide to dispatch the marauder. She had just decided on a large Oriental umbrella stand by the door when Rupert, with a roar, dropped his cup and saucer and rushed directly at the man; he overset the butler's table in the fury of his attack, splintering one of the legs and destroying the tall coffeepot as he launched himself directly into the chest of the masked man, fists up and ready.

Their tussle was close-fought and nasty. Both men were determined to hurt each other as badly as possible; Rupert had a slight advantage in height, but the disadvantage of his background, which still enforced certain codes of sportsmanship. His masked opponent had no such compunction, and quickly began to get the better of Rupert, breaking his nose and then driving his knee into Rupert's kidneys while Rupert flailed in a vain attempt to land a sporting blow on the other's face.

Rowena gave herself an inward command to keep her wits; giving way to panic would serve no purpose but the attacker's. She picked up the umbrella stand, and hefted it, finding its porcelain weight reassuring as she prepared to drub the unknown man with it. Then she realized a second man, masked and in the same sort of dark-grey trousers and jackets found on half the workmen in Amsterdam, was standing in the door, a small pistol in his hand. She swung around and with all her strength threw the umbrella stand at the second man.

It struck with gratifying impact, cracking where it hit. The second man, who had been raising his pistol, staggered, cursing in Dutch as he tried to steady himself; he did not drop the pistol.

"Rowena!" Rupert shouted breathlessly, having struggled to his knees. "Run!" He was rewarded for this by a two-handed blow to his chest that rocked him onto his side with an audible cracking of bone.

The man with the pistol was clinging to the doorframe, a patch of blood visible on his mask at the top of his forehead. He thrust out his arm to block any escape from the room. Unsteady as he was, he had the significant advantage of his weapon, and it was enough to make Rowena hesitate.

Rupert's opponent had Rupert down and was methodically kicking him in the ribs and back; Rupert groaned and tried to draw himself up into a ball, but the punishment continued.

"You'll kill him," warned the man with the pistol, and Rowena gave a quiet shriek at these words, and flung herself at the unarmed man, prepared to do what damage she could, as much to save herself as Rupert. Her first assumption of robbery had given way to something far worse.

Reighert rounded on her and struck her a savage blow on the side of her face before she could reach him, sending her reeling. He was panting as he regained his balance and pulled off his mask. "Damn bitch wanted . . . to scratch my eyes out," he muttered, looking down at the pair sprawled on the floor. He rubbed his chin where a bruise was already forming. "That fellow. It's his own fucking fault. He shouldn't have been here."

As if to punctuate this, Rupert moaned and tried to speak through a split upper lip and two broken teeth.

"What about the woman?" Bernard asked in Dutch-flavored German, adding, "I think she cracked my skull."

"Then it's a good thing she's unconscious. We won't have to drug her until we're on the train." He took a deep breath while he made a rapid assessment of the damage Rupert had done: he would have some spectacular bruises and a long cut on his cheek, but nothing of real harm. Still, he would make certain the Englishman did not forget him before he left. Relieved, he straightened up. "Come on. We haven't got much time. We'll miss the Innsbruck connection if we're not on the express to Basel."

"Don't worry. You have the tickets already and we have forty-five minutes yet," Bernard said as he took a step forward, one hand to the growing lump above his brow. He swallowed hard. "I don't think I can bend over. I'll vomit."

Reighert shot him a look of disgust. "Then remain where you are," he said sharply. "I do not want to have three lumps to deal with. Four, if you count the housekeeper. Too bad we had to kill her. At least we can leave the Englishman here. Why did he have to be in this house, of all places? It's on him that he's hurt." He ignored the shambles of the room—the broken butler's table, the overturned Dutch chair, the cracked umbrella stand, the coffee soaking into the crumpled carpet, the spatters of blood on the Chinese chest and the couch, the two smashed lamps which had fallen from the end tables—and reached down to tug Rowena onto her back.

"I'll take care of her after you're on the train with the Englishwoman; it's what was planned," Bernard said, his attention apparently wandering as he glanced toward the rear of the house. "I'll change, so if anyone sees me, they'll recall that Yseult has been stepping out with a new beau, and will recognize me in that context. She has been telling all her cronies that I am courting her, which has the other biddies eaten up with envy, or so she told me. That she should ride in my motor car will surprise no one, assuming anyone notices." His speech was a bit slurred, and he held his head at a strange angle, but seemed coherent enough. "I'll make sure no one finds her, ever."

"Fine," said Reighert, pulling out the rope wrapped around his waist; it had saved him from some of Rupert's most punishing efforts, and now would be used for the purpose Reighert had originally intended. As he began to secure Rowena's hands, he said to Bernard, "The wheeled-chair. Bring it from the kitchen. And make sure the rear door is closed."

"And the blanket?" Bernard asked as he stepped back, swaying slightly.

On the floor, Rupert stirred, and one bloodshot and livid eye half-opened: aside from a single glance, Reighert ignored him. "Of course the blanket. How else shall we make her an invalid without a blanket around her?" He continued to knot the rope, drawing it down the front of her body to her feet; he looped one ankle, then the other. "Well? Get on with it. It's a long way to the Baron's lodge."

Steadying himself against the walls, Bernard went to retrieve the wheeled-chair with the blanket draped over the back of it. He did his best not to look at Yseult's body slumped against the stove. He leaned heavily on the wheeled-chair as he negotiated it around the obstacles in the kitchen and then down the hall to the parlor.

"Took you enough time," complained Reighert as he lugged Rowena into the chair and secured her with the leather belt attached to the chair, making sure she would remain fairly upright. Then he carefully wrapped the blanket around her before looking closely at Bernard. "I'd better drive. You look pasty. And for God's sake, take off the mask. Anyone looking in would see you."

"Oh. Right." He tugged his mask off, revealing the full extent of the blow Rowena had delivered with the umbrella stand: blood soaked the side of his face, his skin was the color of whey, his prominent blue eyes were almost froglike and sunk in ashen shadows that would soon turn to bruises, and there was a small, brilliant stain of red on the white of his right eye, below the bruise and swelling.

"You'll need to have that looked at," said Reighert. "After you dispose of the housekeeper. Say you were struck by a barge crane. That would account for the damage done, and who's to question it."

"Certainly," said Bernard, and held onto the wheeled chair, beginning to push it toward the rear of the house where the Humber waited. He blinked as he walked, to keep his vision steady.

Reighert remained in the parlor long enough to deliver a solid blow to the side of Rupert's head, sending him into an oblivion he was convinced would last until morning, when he and Rowena Pearce-Manning would be far away.

When Reighert stepped out into the rear yard, taking care to close the kitchen door behind him, Bernard was in the front passenger seat of the Humber, the wheeled-chair secured to the rear seats, Rowena drooping in it, the blanket drawn carefully around her so that she had the appearance of being paralyzed instead of unconscious. After checking to be certain the wheeled-chair was not going to shift, Reighert cranked the motor into life, climbed into the driver's seat and edged the automobile along the alley to the narrow, canal-edge street, bound for the bridge that would lead him to the broad avenue and the train station. He patted his dark jacket lying on the seat behind the gearshift, making sure the tickets were still in place. "It's going to be close."

"But you will make it," said Bernard, sounding very sleepy.

As they turned into the loading area in front of the train station, Reighert had to shake Bernard to recall him to his senses; as they wrestled Rowena and the wheeled-chair out of the rear seat of the Humber, Reighert said, "Remember to have a physician look at you."

"Once Yseult is taken care of," Bernard agreed. "I will."

"Can you drive without mishap?" It was more out of concern for the Humber he asked, and the desire to bring no attention to what they had done, than any regard for Bernard's health.

"Yes," said Bernard defensively. "If you have any doubts, stay here and I will take the train with Miss Pearce-Manning."

"No," said Reighert, indicating the boot as he drew on his most respectable jacket and pulled the tickets from the pocket. "Get the bags. The train leaves in ten minutes."

Bernard did as he was told, trying not to grumble as he followed Reighert and the wheeled-chair into the cavernous station, his stride faltering and not for the weight of the luggage alone. He found it difficult to read the platform signs, and had to rely on Reighert to find the right train. When he had bestowed the luggage in the overhead racks, he helped lug the wheeled-chair into the compartment, then turned to Reighert. "You will send the telegrams from Basel, is that right?"

"One to Berlin, one to London: to our employer, and to her family," said Reighert, reviewing their plan. "Yes. I will attend to it at Basel, as we planned." He had taken his seat opposite Rowena. "Your final payment will be wired to you as soon as our employer receives the confirming telegram from me. The money should be in your hands in twenty-four hours."

"Good," said Reighert, stifling a yawn as he glanced down the track as the conductor gave the first of three departure calls. "I'll be going now."

"Considering what we encountered, you did very well," said Reighert mendaciously. "I'll ask our employer to give you a bonus. That's no promise he will give you one, but he should pay attention to my recommendation."

Rowena made a soft sound and her head rolled slackly.

"I'm off," said Bernard, stepping back and closing the compartment door. He very nearly stumbled as he moved away from the train; by the time he got into the Humber, he was feeling queasy. He fought off the discomfort and drove to his own flat to change clothes and retrieve a tarpaulin before returning to Rowena's house for the unpleasant chore of loading Yseult's corpse into the automobile; the body was growing stiff and it was with difficulty that he propped her into the passenger's seat with the tarpaulin under her feet for later use. He considered going back into the house to check on the Englishman, but decided against it; such actions might well attract attention, and if Rupert had regained consciousness, he might well try to put up a fight again. Certain that his decision was the right one, he got into the driver's seat and drove off, knowing he would never return to that house again.

The sound of chimes striking the hour of four brought Rupert to hideous wakefulness. He blinked his eyes, and discovered that one of them was swollen closed. As he tried to move, pain assailed him from more sites on his body than he thought could all hurt at the same time, and for half an hour, he lapsed back into partial consciousness. Half an hour later he was awake again, and this time no kindly fainting saved him from the full realization of his injuries. It took him ten minutes to sit up, and fifteen more to get to his feet. In that time, several things had been brought home to him: he had been seriously hurt, Rowena was missing, he had overheard some mention of Innsbruck, his splendid new clothes were ruined, Rowena had been the target of the masked men for purposes he dreaded to contemplate, the authorities would only bring scandal and delay, a physician would be almost as bad, it was his duty to find her before anything beyond remedy occurred, and all this was somehow entirely Franchot Ragoczy's fault—for which he must be made to answer, and soon. It was obvious to Rupert that the men who had attacked him and carried off Rowena had been working for Ragoczy, undoubtedly with the intention of compromising her in order to compel her into marriage. Burgeoning rage fueling his efforts, he felt his way toward the back of the house, supporting himself on the wall when the pain threatened to overwhelm him.

In the kitchen he dared to turn on the light, and was taken aback by the mess he encountered, including an ominous brownish stain on the side of the stove. At the sink, he used the dishrag to clean off the worst of the dried blood, using the small mirror Yseult had hung near the door to check his face; he winced at what he saw. His eye was puffy with an open cut along the line of his brow, and his upper lip was three times its normal size and purple. He was fairly certain two of his ribs were broken, and possibly his collarbone as well. His hands were stiff, knuckles cracked and swollen, the nails torn to the quick on three fingers.

Fortifying himself with a tot of brandy he took from the larder, he made himself leave the house, using a broom for a kind of crutch. He took care to close the door behind him, wanting to avert any possibility of idle investigation. He had decided he would send a telegram to the Amsterdam police when he reached Metz, for he was determined to seek Ragoczy out at his estate in Bavaria and demand that he shoulder the responsibility for the danger that had come to Rowena Pearce-Manning: if Ragoczy had been foolish enough to have Rowena brought to his Schloss—whatever it actually was—Rupert would demand her immediate release. Cursing that foreign opportunist for the cad he was, Rupert made his way to his Darracq, and after two attempts, cranked it into life, then, ignoring the occasional stares of the early-rising workmen on the street, he drove away from the canals, out of Amsterdam, into the flat, open countryside, pushing the racing automobile to its highest speeds, passing slower vehicles impatiently, determined to cover as much distance as he could before nightfall. He hoped his condition would not demand he abandon his resolution to drive into Germany before stopping to rest. As dawn gave way to early morning, he shut out his growing fear for Rowena and put all his concentration on the road, for the road would take him to Ragoczy, and Rupert could heap excoriations on him for all he had done.

By noon he was in Belgium, and found a bank to change money into French and German notes as well as Belgian for him while he had a hasty lunch of local cheese and cold ham, accompanied by three cups of coffee to keep him awake. His thoughts were black with vengeful intentions as he contemplated what he would do to Ragoczy when he found him, and saved Rowena from her disastrous infatuation with the Count. He purchased some medications at a chemist's shop and affected minor repairs on his injuries as well as taking half a dozen tablets to relieve the pain that surged through him with every movement, including breathing: he could not permit himself to feel anything.

In Metz that night he found a hotel selling petrol. He refilled his tank and purchased two five-litre containers more, in case he should have difficulty locating more on his long drive into Bavaria. He answered the anxious inquiries about his condition by saying "Very nearly had a nasty smash back there on the road from Luxembourg. It was a close thing, I can tell you. The other driver looks much the same as I, and his automobile is badly damaged." He chuckled unconvincingly. "Lost my case, getting out; had everything in it. I'll have to purchase a few new things, I suspect."

The clerk, trying his best to conceal his dismay at Rupert's appearance, said, "Would you want to see a physician?"

"No," said Rupert abruptly, then realized he needed to reassure the clerk or he would draw unwanted attention to himself, "Thanks, but this looks worse than it is. A good night's sleep will do me." As he signed for his room, he asked, as if trying to figure out a puzzle. "Is it faster to Bavaria through Saarbrucken or Mulhouse? I'm afraid I don't know the roads around here."

"With the petrol you've purchased, I would recommend going through Saint Die to Mulhouse," said the clerk, about to hand him a key. "An automobile like yours will handle the roads well, and there is not so much traffic on that route."

"It's rather pressing," said Rupert, just to make his point.

"Judging by your appearance, it must be," said the clerk, too experienced to let his misgivings show.

Rupert decided to ignore that remark. "Is it possible to send a telegram from here? I have to notify some of the others in this . . . competition where I am putting up for the night." One would not be to Ragoczy. That he had decided hours ago: he had also decided during his sixteen hours behind the wheel that if he was questioned, he would claim to be part of a kind of race, and would use his Darracq to prove his point.

"You may arrange it here, if you wish." His regional accent made it difficult for Rupert to understand him; his French was strictly public school.

"You'll tend to it, will you? They are urgent." He took the forms that were handed to him and reached for the pen lying by the register. "How soon will they be able to go off?"

"Tonight, if you pay the additional price. If not, first thing in the morning." He showed the list of charges for the various services.

"Very good; let's go for early morning," said Rupert, handing over the amount. "There will be two of them. This will cover the cost. With something for your trouble."

"Thank you," said the clerk.

"And I will want to be wakened at six-thirty. Not a moment later." He scribbled his messages on the telegram forms and returned them to the clerk. "Not a moment later than six-thirty," he reiterated. "And let us pray for good weather."

"The farmers say there will be rain," the clerk warned.

"Then I hope it will come as late in the day as possible," said Rupert, his manner brusque.

"Will you want breakfast, Monsieur?" the clerk inquired politely as he put the telegram forms into the pigeonhole designated for them.

"Just black coffee and an egg, if you will. Have it ready when you wake me." He tossed the man a couple of coins to ensure this service, then made his way slowly up the stairs, feeling very old, but resolute in his self-determined mission. He did his best to sponge himself off without dwelling on the condition of his body, then wrapped himself in a towel and dropped into bed, his exhaustion overriding his pain; his sleep was more stupor than slumber, and he wakened fired with greater purpose, his soul set on finding Ragoczy before he slept again.

It was near to two in the morning when Rupert Bowen arrived in Hausham, his body singing with aches, his thoughts swimming, but always coming back to his determination to let Ragoczy know just what his cavalier dalliance with Rowena would bring him. He was sorry now that the age of duels had passed: he would have loved to have Ragoczy in the sights of his pistol. Even that would not be enough to salvage Rowena's good name, he feared, but if he could reach her before the unthinkable happened—if indeed he was not already too late—he might contrive to account for her abduction in some acceptable way.

The village was quite dark, and on the streets nothing but the Darracq moved. He found the train station and discovered, as he hoped, a single railway clerk of vaguely middle age tending the station and watching the telegraph in a little pool of light. Rupert's German was rudimentary, but he was able to make it understood that he wanted Franchot Ragoczy.

"The Count, ja?" the man asked, listening closely to Rupert.

"Count Saint-Germain he calls himself, yes," said Rupert, too worn out to be sarcastic.

"His Schloss is out that road," said the railway clerk, pointing out into the night. "There are iron gates, with a disk with wings in the middle of them. The gate is marked with lanterns." He nodded several times as if to encourage understanding.

"Out the road," Rupert said laboriously. "Iron gates, lanterns marking them. How far?" he added.

"Not far," said the railway clerk. "Turn at the inn. To the right. That's the road you want." He scrawled a kind of map on a telegram form and gave it to Rupert. "You see?"

"I'll find it," said Rupert, his voice grim and hoarse.

"Good," said the railway clerk, who was glad of this strange interruption in an otherwise dull night.

"Is he there?" Rupert demanded as an afterthought.

"The Count? Ach, ja. I think so." He watched Rupert find his way out to his automobile, and made a note of the time.

The lanterns were burning just as the railway clerk had said they would be. Rupert turned up the drive, pleased to find the gates open and the roadway freshly graveled so that he was not impeded by mud. He took this as a sign that Ragoczy was as lax about his property as he was about his conduct, an assumption that gave him savage satisfaction. As he emerged from the trees, he saw the Schloss ahead of him, and began to have his first niggle of suspicion that his impressions might be wrong. Such a building was not the property of an adventurer. If, he added darkly to himself, it was truly Ragoczy's property. There was every chance it was not: Ragoczy was not above claiming ownership of a building that had been hired for the purpose of impressing the gullible. He pulled up in front of the main door and lurched out of the Darracq, all but falling against the door in his effort to break through. Propping himself against the iron-bound wood, he pounded with his fists as if the oak were Ragoczy's flesh. He did not consider that he was unlikely to be admitted at this late hour: he was convinced that his arrival would provide Rowena with some comfort, and he bludgeoned away until his bruised hands began to bleed again.

A few minutes later Ragoczy himself opened the door, his burgundy dressing robe over his white shirt and black trousers. "Mister Bowen," he said, startled by the man and his appearance. "What—"

He got no further. "You bloody blackguard!" Rupert howled, shoving his way into the Schloss. "Where is she?"

Ragoczy's affability vanished to be replaced by stern apprehension. "What do you mean, Mister Bowen?" he asked as he followed Rupert into the main hall, increasingly aware of the young man's exhaustion and injuries. "What are you doing here?"

Rupert swung around to face him. "Damn you, where have you got her?"

"Got whom?" Ragoczy asked, and knew the answer. "What has happened to Rowena?"

"You know exactly what happened to her!" Rupert bellowed. "Where is she? Rowena! *Rowena!*" He staggered toward the stair leading to the gallery above. "ROWENA!"

Ragoczy moved up behind Rupert. "Mister Bowen, she is not here." His voice became low and commanding. "What has happened, that you think she was?"

Fatigued, enervated, and groggy from pain, Rupert steadied himself on the newel post and met Ragoczy's penetrating gaze with the last vestige of his strength. "You had her taken. Two men. Your men. Yesterday . . . the day before. In Amsterdam. Deny it if you dare, you swine."

"No, Mister Bowen; I do not have her." Ragoczy began to understand the oppression that had held him in its grip for the last two days. He had assumed it came from Madelaine de Montalia because of its power. Now he knew he had been terribly wrong. "Mister Bowen, tell me what happened."

"You know—" Rupert began, and then broke off. "It had to be your doing," he insisted doggedly. Only that conviction had given him the strength to keep going when weariness had threatened to overcome him. If he had been wrong, he had failed Rowena doubly. He stared at Ragoczy with growing horror. "If not you, then who?"

Ragoczy came near enough to put his small hand on Rupert's shoulder. "If you will tell me exactly what took place, we shall discover the answer," he promised the taller, younger man.

But the weight of the last two days caught up with Rupert. The last of his strength drained away, and with a gentle cry, he slumped to the stairs: never before in his life had he fainted.

Text of a summary report filed by Inspector Herbert Blau in Berlin.

In re: the investigation into the murder of the dancer Nadezna. Records of April 3–6, 1911.

April 3
Interviewed Lukas Strauss once more, and am satisfied that the first account he provided was accurate, for while his second interview was not precisely the same as his first, it is consistent in all significant details. He is willing to swear under oath that he observed Baron von Wol-

gast and a second man enter Nadezna's house approximately fifteen minutes after Franchot Ragoczy left it. His notes indicate they remained inside for about twenty minutes, and he was under the impression that von Wolgast's clothes were wet when he departed. He has given me his word to bring his employer, Oertel Morgenstern, to give me a report day after tomorrow.

Subsidiary remarks regarding Lukas Strauss: according to our police files, the man claims to be an actor, and has appeared in three plays since arriving in Berlin four years ago. He is a native of Vienna, with a secondary education, the child of a carpet-layer, one of four children. He is known to work for various persons engaged in espionage, but is not considered to be a true agent in any sense of the word. His activities are minor, and motivated by the need for money, not any known political purpose.

April 5

Received Oertel Morgenstern at ten; the man was prompt, courteous, and clever. He supported Lukas Strauss' report completely, including that von Wolgast's clothing was wet, as well as stained, very probably with blood. That said, he added some of his own observations in regard to Ragoczy and Nadezna. He stated that he had reason to believe that Nadezna had been blackmailing Baron von Wolgast, and that the Baron had every good reason to want to be rid of her, while none of his investigations could reveal anything that smacked of the illicit, either in conduct or finance, between Nadezna and Ragoczy. He further stated that he—Morgenstern—has been making inquiries about Ragoczy for several months, although he declined to say precisely why or for whom. He was reluctant to testify in court, but offered to provide a sworn statement. It seems that he is concerned that his employer, ostensibly a journal in Prague, would feel his work would be compromised if he entangled himself in legal affairs in Berlin.

His report on the events at Nadezna's house the night of her death provide sufficient reason to consider Baron von Wolgast may be implicated in the crime; surely there is as much reason to suspect him as to suspect Ragoczy.

Subsidiary remarks regarding Oertel Morgenstern: his journalistic credentials are in order, and the journal has confirmed editorial reluctance to have their man at the center of a murder trial; however, I would be remiss if I failed to observe that we have an account from a man known as Eduard Angebot that suggests that Morgenstern is a foreign agent in the employ of the British, possibly known as Sidney Reilly. I would not be surprised to discover this is true, but whether Morgenstern is a journalist or an agent, his testimony is nonetheless persuasive, and he has no reason that I can discern to offer a false account in this matter, for although von Wolgast deals in arms, I have no reason to suppose that this Morgenstern, or Reilly, or whoever he may be, is in any way involved with the procurement of weapons. It is apparent that he is convinced of von Wolgast's culpability in this matter, and is willing to risk his position to give his report to us. I am inclined to believe him in regard to Ragoczy. His notes indicate that von Wolgast has had extensive dealings with Tancred Sisak, which our own police records confirm. Morgenstern also provided certain information regarding a Paul Reighert, whom he states was the man accompanying von Wolgast to Nadezna's house. I have not been able to verify this, for I have learned that Reighert is not presently in Berlin. Upon his return, I intend to conduct a long interview with him, to find out as much as I can what part, if any, he has played in this case.

Subsidiary remarks regarding Paul Reighert: a known procurer for the Chez Noir, the man is a defrocked Jesuit, apparently dismissed from his Order for seducing schoolgirls, although I have been unable to secure confirmation of this from the Catholic Church. He has been seen in von Wolgast's company from time to time. Currently he cannot be linked directly to any of von Wolgast's enterprises, the two men are not strangers, and it is not beyond possibility that their dealings have gone beyond those we have been able to discover.

Subsidiary notes related to von Wolgast: his wife, long the resident of a private hospital was found dead eight days ago, following the visit of her cousins. There is currently no reason to suspect foul play, but I have asked the nuns to provide me with a full account of her death, as well as for any information on her cousins, whom I may want to interview if the nuns' information indicates it would be appropriate. I understand her husband declined to permit an autopsy, saying that her suffering was finally at an end, and that she should have the dignity in death she was unable to achieve in life. I will reserve any opinion in the matter until I speak directly with Baron von Wolgast.

April 7

I have this morning received a telegram from Franchot Ragoczy, who is currently in residence at his Schloss in Bavaria, requesting any information I can provide regarding an apparent abduction in Amsterdam two days ago. The woman abducted is English, Rowena Saxon, also known as Rowena Pearce-Manning. He indicated he would soon have more specifics to aid me in my inquiries. The telegram was sent at three in the morning from the train station at Hausham, with the no-

tation that the case was urgent and required utmost discretion. What bearing this may have on the present investigation I have not yet ascertained. When I have confirmation of this event, I will comply with Ragoczy's request. If there is any commonality from the investigation of Nadezna's death to the alleged abduction of this Englishwoman, I will discover it.

7

When Rupert finally awoke, it was nearly two in the afternoon; his wounds had been expertly treated and bandaged, his ribs strapped, and his arm placed in a sling; a bridge of gauze and sticking plaster protected his newly set nose. He was lying in a comfortable bed in a pleasant room looking out onto a hillside of pine and oak. He blinked his one good eye and groaned, more from inner anguish than from pain, for to his astonishment, the worst of his hurts had been taken away, as had his clothes; he was in a fresh nightshirt of heavy muslin.

"Good afternoon, Mister Bowen," said Ragoczy as he rose from his chair next to the bed. He had changed from the robe of the night before to a neat hacking outfit, all in black; his manner was unruffled; only the smoldering quality in his dark eyes revealed his foreboding. "I hope you are feeling better." He smiled pleasantly. "You are in a guest room in my Schloss in Bavaria. You came here very late last night, much the worse for wear, and began shouting for Rowena."

"How . . . who . . . ?" he asked as he touched the bandage over his blackened eye.

"I think you had better tell me that," said Ragoczy, reaching for a bellpull near the fireplace. "I would like to know the answers to both who and how. You said that Rowena had been taken by two men, men whom you assumed worked for me. Who were these men you spoke of last night? What can you tell me about them?"

"What doctor did . . . ?" Rupert persisted, knowing that his care had been expert. The last thing he wanted now was to be in Ragoczy's debt.

"That isn't important. You will mend; that is what must concern you." He came back to the bed and looked directly down at Rupert. "When you arrived last night, you made a number of statements that trouble me. You accused me of taking—I must presume you mean kidnapping—Rowena. Since I did not, I would appreciate a full account of how that happened."

It all came back in a rush. Rupert turned his head way, chagrin doing what his wounds could not do: he was ashamed. "Oh, Good Lord! How could I have slept?" He muttered a few words of dismay, then realized Ragoczy was still waiting. "I was certain you had done it."

"Yes; I am aware of that," said Ragoczy with an ironic glint in his eyes.

He sat up, his hand to his head as if holding it would control the dizziness that possessed him. "I . . . What time is it?"

"One forty-seven in the afternoon. You've slept roughly eleven hours," Ragoczy said calmly, his own concerns carefully kept at bay while he gained the information he sought.

Rupert glared at him. "Why didn't you wake me?"

"You were . . . not quite yourself for a while," Ragoczy informed him, recalling how both he and Roger had struggled with their unexpected guest when he began to flail about, ranting and delirious, while they were trying to bandage his ribs. "I thought it would be for the best to let you restore yourself somewhat before dealing with the events that brought you here."

"Oh, God," whispered Rupert; his mind raced with ghastly images. "She has been gone so long . . . "

"When was she taken?" Ragoczy asked, his tone a bit sharper in spite of his best intentions.

"I called on her . . . it must be day before yesterday. It . . . it has been my habit to visit her regularly, given the nature of our relationship." He held up his head as if anticipating an argument; when Ragoczy offered none, he went on. "It was slightly after four when I went round to Miss Pearce-Manning's house. I wanted to show her my new racing automobile."

"Ah, yes; the Darracq," said Ragoczy. "Very impressive."

"Yes. She had her housekeeper bring me coffee—" He broke off, suddenly pale.

"What is it?" Ragoczy asked, striving to keep Rupert on the topic at hand.

"I haven't thought about the housekeeper. There was a stain in the kitchen, and she was missing. I . . . supposed she had run away, but . . . they might have . . . hurt her." He looked directly at Ragoczy. "I hope that she has not been . . . " He could not bring himself to speak the word he feared, nor could he speak of his fears for Rowena.

"I will send a telegram to the Amsterdam police to discover what has become of Yseut," said Ragoczy smoothly. "You were served coffee: then what."

"Well, Rowena . . . Miss Pearce-Manning came down from her studio. She was in a rallying mood, and we had a tussle of wills, don't you know, as one does with spirited girls. I reproved her for her lack of management, I recall, and she took it amiss; women do like to think they are sensible. But when I offered to take her for a ride in the Darracq, she was all enthusiasm, and had we only left at that moment, she must have been spared what happened next." His voice dropped and his words came more unevenly. "We were in the front parlor, and something had been broken in the kitchen. I remember telling Miss Pearce-Manning—"

"You may call her Rowena to me, Mister Bowen. She has allowed me to use her given name for some time." Ragoczy was finding Rupert's punctiliousness grating, but kept his demeanor as cordial as possible.

"Very well," said Rupert with evident disapproval. "I told her she would have to deduct the cost of whatever was broken from the housekeeper's wages, to remind her of the need for economy. She has occasionally been lax about such things, relying on her grand-father's generosity to keep her from having to practice needed thrift."

"Is this to the point?" Ragoczy asked, allowing his sense of urgency to make itself felt.

Rupert flushed. "No . . . not truly," he replied, and returned to his account. "I do not recall precisely when I noticed the masked man standing in the door, but it was on me in a flash that he meant no good, and I strove to drive him off." He put his hand to the bandage over his eye. "He gave me this for my trouble, along with the rest of it. Although," he added in self-defense, "I was able to land a few good punches before the second masked man appeared, and I was bested. I did not entirely lose consciousness at first, for which I am eternally grateful. Rowena was in a swoon." He coughed. "The men spoke in German, and one of them said they were bound for Innsbruck, so I could not help but suppose that you—"

"That I had sent two henchmen to abduct Rowena. Merci bien du compliment." His crisp sarcasm had the desired effect.

"I will not apologize," Rupert announced. "What would you have thought, in my position? I was convinced you brought her into danger."

Ragoczy relented at once. "And I fear you may be right, Mister Bowen, although not for the reasons you suppose," he admitted. "How long were you—"

"The first thing I remember after one of the men struck me in the head, some time after we fought, was the sound of chimes ringing four. So I must have lain there all night." He began to fidget with the satin comforter. "When I left the house, I decided I had to find you before any irreparable ill was done. I had to confront you—for her sake."

Ragoczy did not stop himself from saying, "What a very flattering notion you have of my character."

"Well," said Rupert, his swollen jaw thrust out, "you cannot blame me. You have made every effort to encourage my fiancée in exploits that most men would consider unacceptable in their promised brides."

Knowing there was nothing to gain from getting into a discussion of Rowena's intentions regarding marriage, Ragoczy said, "That is a matter for later; I will accept responsibility for the danger she is in. What must concern us now is finding her. You have indicated that one of the men spoke of Innsbruck."

"Yes," Rupert said. "They were going to take the fast train to Basel."

"Which means they would probably have arrived in Innsbruck some time this morning, if there were no delays. Is there anything more you remember?" He had gleaned far more from Rupert's report than the young Englishman realized, and hoped for one last part of the puzzle.

For a moment Rupert was silent, his thoughts in disorder. Then he said, "One of the men said something about the Baron's lodge. That is all I recall, but that they put Rowena in a wheeled-chair to make it appear she was ill."

"The Baron's lodge," Ragoczy repeated, warning himself inwardly against the folly of rushing to assumptions. "Who knows about this kidnapping?" he asked before Rupert demanded to know the reason for Ragoczy's increased interest.

"I sent telegrams from Metz, night before last; one to her family, and one to the police in Amsterdam; I described the incident to the authorities, but I decided to spare her family such distressing specifics. I urged the Amsterdam police to be circumspect in order to avoid scandal. You know how cases of this sort can attract unwanted attention." He shifted uncomfortably; the pain was beginning to return.

"A wise step," said Ragoczy as much to comfort Rupert as out of any conviction that such a request would have any weight whatsoever with the police. He stood up. "Leave this to me, Mister Bowen. You have already done more than anyone could expect."

"I hope I know where my duty lies," said Rupert, a little huffy.

"You do, beyond cavil," Ragoczy assured him, then paused, regarding Rupert with a measuring look. "Mister Bowen, since you and I are equally anxious to preserve Rowena from any more hazard than she has already endured, may I ask a favor of you?"

"I . . . suppose so," said Rupert, leery of Ragoczy's request.

"I would appreciate the loan of your Darracq." He held up his hand to keep Rupert from interrupting. "Neither of my motor cars that I keep here can sustain the speeds a racing automobile can; if Rowena's situation is as dire as you indicate, speed is demanded to spare her."

"Yes; yes, I take your point," Rupert conceded reluctantly; he had no wish to have Ragoczy drive it, but he was aware that he was in no condition to make the attempt. He thought furiously for nearly a minute, and then sighed. "Very well. Go ahead. But it is low on petrol, and I have used the reserves I have purchased."

"Fuel is the least of my worries," said Ragoczy briskly.

"You will not think so if you are stranded," Rupert said.

"Mister Bowen, one of the businesses I am involved in is the creation of fuels for automobiles and lorries. I have four large drums of fuel here, each containing one hundred-ninety litres. They are being readied to—"

"You cannot put that much in the boot," Rupert warned him.

"Then they will be stowed elsewhere, so their weight can help maintain balance and traction, and my gear will go into the boot. You need have no fear that I will fail to reach her for lack of petrol." He held out his hand. "I will leave you in the hands of my manservant, Roger, in whom you may repose complete confidence. I am going to prepare now, and I will depart within the hour. Roger will bring you something to ease your hurts; be sensible and take what he offers."

This abrupt shift from attentive auditor to assertiveness took Rupert aback, and he stared at Ragoczy, nonplused. "You mean to go after her?"

"Of course, Mister Bowen. I should have thought this was obvious." He bowed slightly, then turned toward the door.

"You'd better take a pistol," Rupert recommended

"I will bear it in mind," said Ragoczy as he let himself out into the corridor where he relinquished his affable demeanor; his stride was purposeful, his heels sounding a crisply determined tattoo as he went along to his private apartment.

"Have you determined where she is?" Roger asked without preamble as Ragoczy closed the door.

"Somewhere near Innsbruck, at the Baron's lodge," said Ragoczy curtly. He passed through his outer room and into his bedchamber. "It is close enough for the bond of blood." He remained wholly clothed as he stretched out full-length on his hard, narrow bed; beneath the mattress stood a large chest of his native earth.

"In a way it is unfortunate that she is not yet come to your life," said Roger from the doorway; he held a valise in his hand.

"If she had, this would not have happened," Ragoczy said, his eyes half-closed and his words becoming distant.

"Very likely not," Roger agreed as he continued to prepare Ragoczy's valise. "But you might have found her more easily."

"True enough," said Ragoczy. "Make sure you pack clothing for her. She will want something fresh."

"Do you think she would object to wearing riding breeches?" Roger inquired.

"I think she would probably welcome a burnoose," Ragoczy said with a quick sardonic smile.

"There are four thirty-litre containers of fuel being put into the Darracq, beyond the filled tank; Gualtier is attending to it, and to the packing." Roger said nothing more for a short while, then: "Is the bond strong enough to guide you?"

"It will have to be. At least I know where to begin." said Ragoczy bleakly as he lapsed into a kind of sleep, not unlike the sleep he taught Mesmer. Generally he used this state to control animals, but it could be used also to trace those with whom he had a blood bond; for the next half hour, he remained suspended while he discovered her, bound and in the boot of an automobile, bound for a place called Madern. He felt her anger, confusion, and despair keenly, and lamented that she was not yet vampiric, so that he could communicate some solace to her; as it was, he found her emotions wrenching, and as he came back to himself, he had to shake off her distress in order to concentrate on the things he would have to do.

"Mister Bowen is asleep again," Roger reported as Ragoczy left his bedchamber. "I looked in on him ten minutes ago and he was unaware of it."

"Good. I am not eager to have to deal with him just now." He drew on his black Florentine gloves and took the valise Roger held out to him. "For one thing, I share his belief that I am the cause of Rowena's being kidnapped, but an extended bout of recrimination will do none of us any good."

"You cannot be blamed for all the misfortunes in the world, my master," Roger reminded him with the despondent certainty of long acquaintance that it would make little difference to Ragoczy. He held out a thick muffler and watched as Ragoczy wound it twice around his neck. "You are not the cause; you need not take it all upon yourself," he added for emphasis.

"No; not for everything: but I must accept responsibility for this." He reached out his hand and laid it on Roger's arm. "You know where the necessary documents are if you require them."

"I will not need them," said Roger firmly.

Ragoczy sighed, his voice lightly ironic. "Even vampires die, eventually." His eyes grew somber. "Notify Golovin and Sunbury if there is reason, and go to Madelaine. She will need you."

Roger made a gesture of exasperated capitulation. "If you wish it, I will do it. But it will not be necessary."

"I hope so," said Ragoczy with feeling as he reached for his Russian coat. "I will wire you, probably from Innsbruck, when I have her safe. If you do not hear from me in five days, notify Inspector Blau that I am missing, and tell him where I was going. I'm sure he can work out some proper arrangement with the Austrians if it is necessary."

Roger did not move from where he stood. "I will expect you in four days, my master."

"I trust you are not too optimistic, old friend," said Ragoczy as he left the room.

"Your pistol is in your coat," Roger called after him, hoping it would not be needed; he did not hear Ragoczy's answer, if there was one.

The Darracq started at the first turn of the crank and as Ragoczy climbed into the driver's seat, he took goggles from the pocket of his coat and fixed them in place over his eyes; on a long, cold drive, they would be useful protection. For the few seconds it took him to adjust to the presence of the containers of fuel strapped to the rear of the automobile, he reminded himself the boot was full of his own supplies. He turned the automobile in the flagged court in front of the Schloss, then started down through the trees to pick up the road out of Hausham. The afternoon was cloudy and he anticipated rain by nightfall, when he would be higher into the mountains, at Achenkirch if it rained, or near Maurach if it held off a while. He rehearsed his route in his mind as he left Hausham for Tegernsee: south into Austria, then west-by-southwest to Innsbruck, then south again to Steinach, east to Schmirn, and from there up the slope to Madern. From there he would have to use his blood bond with Rowena to find the Baron's lodge.

The rain began near Jenbach, mixing with snow and sleet as the evening grew colder. Now the road was treacherous, steep and slippery at once. At every turn Ragoczy was threatened with skids and slides that required all his skills to negotiate without trouble. He diminished his speed but only enough to keep from fishtailing on the road. The head-lamps made the ice glisten, and turned the sleet and snow to a shower of jewels coming out of the dark and howling heavens. Ragoczy held onto the wheel and pushed on; by nine he had the road to himself.

Shortly before he reached Innsbruck, he felt the first tug of Rowena's presence, as slight as a fragment of remembered melody; he clung to it, using it as an invisible beacon to guide him. As he made his way through the outskirts of Innsbruck, Ragoczy reminded himself that within the living memory of many in that city such a night would have made all travel impossible. Even the truly desperate would not venture out into such weather. The automobile had changed all that, and made this pursuit he had undertaken possible, at least until an avalanche blocked the road or he ruptured a tire on hidden rocks. Telling himself that such things were impossible, he drove on to the south, his progress becoming slower until the snow—for now it was too cold for rain at this elevation—dwindled and stopped, and for the first time the clouds began to break up.

At Schmirn the Darracq could no longer wallow its way through the drifts, and Ragoczy left it in the lee of a small inn an hour or so before dawn. He thought briefly about securing a horse—one like Gregor Ein-satz's sturdy Rhinelanders perhaps—and as quickly rejected the notion. In snow so deep and on steep terrain, a horse could rapidly become as much a liability as a motor car. Keeping his goggles and coat on, he re-trieved snowshoes and walking staff, both of his own design from the boot of the automobile, strapped the snowshoes on his feet, and took off up the hill, moving at speeds that were well beyond what living men could achieve, with or without snow. His long, gliding stride left tracks behind him as if a massive yet lightweight animal with round, three-toed feet had been there. Now he was being guided by the strength of the bond, bringing him unfailingly to her; he felt Rowena's presence poignantly, and he longed for her to have the capacity to experience the bond as he did, so that she could take succor from him; her fear and loneliness were an endless pang for him. As he made his way up the mountainside, he reminded himself that he had had no link with De-metrice when he found her in prison, and none with Aenath when he had first been commissioned to bring her back from the encampment near Eburacum. If he had been able to reach those two, he could surely locate Rowena.

Dawn came much too soon to suit Ragoczy, who had hoped for an-other forty minutes of darkness; his formidable stamina was somewhat reduced in the daylight even with his native earth lining his boots. He paused on the brow of a long ridge and looked about him: below to the north lay a hamlet he supposed must be Madern. There were no signs of automobile tracks in the snow; only the runners of sleighs had come and gone from the place since the last snowfall. At another time he would have been struck by the beauty of the little village huddled against the rising shoulder of the Geier Spitze with the first promise of spring showing at the edges of the melting snow; this morning it seemed to him to be an arduous landscape filled with obstacles and snares. His goal lay beyond the small valley to the east of him. With a quick, hard sigh, he resumed his trek, making himself move faster, determined to reach his destination by midafternoon. As he began his descent, a pregnant doe who would in another two weeks have a fawn at her side, leaped from the small copse ahead of him, bounding away through the shining morning. Ragoczy watched her go, remaining still for nearly a minute until the doe was well away from him; he did not want any frightened animals to draw notice to his progress. Continuing his journey, he kept careful scrutiny on the slopes above him; as the day warmed, melting shelves of snow could come suddenly loose and drop on whatever lay beneath them. He had no desire to waste precious time digging himself out of any unexpected avalanches when he already begrudged every minute of delay.

By the time he saw von Wolgast's lodge Ragoczy was aching from his long exertions crossing the mountains. It was a little after three, the afternoon mild with cotton-puff clouds floating gradually eastward; Ragoczy was glad of the chance to halt while he took stock of the place: the lodge was in the chalet style with an elaborate balcony above the front porch; there were signs of many footprints around the porch, now turning to muddy slush. The lodge was built in a hollow in the mountain, surrounded by pine trees and birch, ideally concealed and readily defendable. The impression of two runners with horseshoe prints between them indicated that someone had recently arrived by sleigh, which meant that the outbuilding behind the lodge was a stable. He moved a little closer, taking care to remain in the cover of what seemed to be a berry thicket just shedding its cloak of snow. It was tempting to rush directly up to the lodge, pistol at the ready, to demand Rowena's immediate release, but if Ragoczy had learned nothing else over the millennia, he had learned that such assault was an act of bravado, often costing far more than it gained: until he knew how many men were in the house and where Rowena was being held, any precipitate act on his part would be apt to turn her into a hostage or a corpse. So he kept to his place, all his concentration on the lodge and what the blood bond told him of Rowena.

Some little time later, a thin man in a heavy coat came stamping out of the front door and turned toward the stable, his brown hair longer than was fashionable. As he walked he flicked a burning cigarette from his fingers, then went into the stable where a loud whinny welcomed him; Ragoczy suspected the horse was hungry. Ten minutes later, the thin man went back into the lodge, brushing hay from the front of his coat as he went.

The impression Ragoczy received from Rowena was of two men in the lodge, one of whom had kidnapped her in Amsterdam; the other had been waiting in Innsbruck. Both spoke German, of which she had some knowledge, and she was aware she was being used to bait a trap. With care he induced a light hypnotic sleep in himself and began to probe more determinedly for her. When he returned to himself, he was fairly certain she was being held, bound and gagged, in an upstairs room at the rear of the lodge, a location he could not reach straightaway without exposing himself and Rowena to the two men in the lodge. The men inside were undoubtedly armed and were demonstrably inclined to harm Rowena before taking him on. He decided he would wait a while longer, until the hollow fell into shadow and he could move nearer without attracting attention.

A movement at the edge of his vision startled him, and he slid his hand into his pocket to grasp the pistol as he turned and saw a fox staring directly at him, black eyes alert. He stifled a laugh before it reached his throat, let the pistol settle back into the depths of his pocket, and resumed his surveillance of the lodge.

By the time the hollow was shrouded in deep purple shadows, Ragoczy was ready to make his attempt. Lashing his snowshoes and his staff to his back, he slipped forward, keeping to the patches of darkness as he approached the lodge from the side away from the stable— he did not want to take the chance of the horse announcing his presence with friendly neighing. Drawing near the east wall of the lodge, he hunkered down in the shelter of snow-draped pines where he could listen to the voices in the central room on the ground floor. As the day dimmed, his senses grew stronger and he soon began to make out full sentences.

". . . from her family yet," said the rougher of the two.

"Perhaps not. You will have to drive down to Madern tomorrow morning, to see if any telegrams have been brought up from Steinach." This voice was richer, the accent more aristocratic, definitely Prussian;

Ragoczy warned himself again about the urge to make assumptions. He would need to identify the men beyond question before he got Rowena out, or any accusations against them would be suspect, for the testimony of a terrified Englishwoman would have little credibility against a high-born Prussian in a German court.

"Why not the afternoon? If the road is still bad, there will be only one delivery, and it will most likely be after noon." There was a whine in this request, as if this were a continuing issue of contention between the men. "Besides, it's better to have as few tracks to this place as possible."

This last made sense to the other man. "You will leave at one, when the day is warm, and you will pick up my Mors for the drive into Steinach if nothing is waiting at Madern. The road should be passable." His laughter was plummy, mocking. "You have said you like to drive the Mors; why waste this opportunity?"

"All right. Tomorrow I will go to find out if her parents have responded to the telegram." He sounded displeased. "I still say it is reckless to keep her here."

"You would rather take her to Berlin? Here we cannot be approached without knowing about it in plenty of time to deal with her. Why should anyone think to come here, Reighert? Unless they were told about this place, what reason would anyone have to think she was here?" There was a threat in those last words.

Ragoczy strove to place the voice, knowing he had heard it before.

"But Steinach is a small place. If the police are notified, they would quickly learn that the telegram was sent by me, and all they would have to do is wait for me to come again, and then where would we be?" The thin man was fretful; Ragoczy could hear him pacing the room as he continued his recitation of worries. "You may think this place is safe because we can spot people coming, but if we do, where do we go, then? If we take to the mountains, all they have to do is follow our tracks. I don't like it, Baron."

"Will you be quiet?" the other demanded. "Mein Gott, you would think you are a novice at these things. You disgust me, with your carping and dithering. Sit down. Have some schnapps. It is going to be a quiet night."

After a short pause, the thin man said, "What about . . . her?"

"What about her?" came the challenge.

"She hasn't been fed today, and she will want to use the toilet, has asked to since early morning. She needs to do that twice a day at the least." The whine was back in his voice. "She'll be the devil to clean up if she isn't attended to." This grudging admission indicated he knew who would have to do the cleaning, and resented it.

"You can take her to the toilet if you watch her, as you did before," said the Prussian and Rogoczy was certain it was von Wolgast. "If you must, see she has some tea and a little bread. There's no point wasting food on her."

This last statement chilled Ragoczy more than the wind off the high, snow-laden peaks.

"You're not going to kill her?" said the thin man, more from dread that it was what the other planned than certainty that he could not do it.

"Not I: you." The Prussian laughed, an overripe sound, reminding Ragoczy why he had never enjoyed Baron von Wolgast's company on the few occasions they had actually met. Who was this Reighert, he wondered.

"Oh, no," Reighert said with unusual force for him. "I took care of your wife. You want to be rid of Miss Pearce-Manning, you must do it yourself. I will not be the only one with blood on my hands, not for you, not for anyone."

"There need be no blood," said von Wolgast at his most soothing. "I believe I mentioned that she could be abandoned somewhere in these mountains. If we take all her clothes, she will not last a night."

Hearing this callous plan, Ragoczy vowed to himself that one way or another, the Baron would answer for what he had done, and what he intended to do. Public disgrace would be the least of it, though the man deserved ignominy and imprisonment at the least. If the courts failed to punish him, Ragoczy would not let him escape.

"And what if she is found?" Reighert asked. "What if she—"

"You had better go attend to her, since you have not abandoned all your Jesuitical sensibilities, it would seem." Von Wolgast sounded bored and annoyed.

"While you sit here, drinking schnapps?" Reighert turned this to an accusation.

"Anything to dispel the stench of your vile cigarettes," said von Wolgast.

Ragoczy heard Reighert tramp up the stairs, and knew it was time to move. Slipping through the shadows, he made his way around to the back of the lodge, and used his sense to determine which shuttered window concealed her; the growing despair and her ongoing fight against it went through him, and he rebuked himself for having to subject her to the loneliness and despond she had endured. Now that the two men were separated, he would have a chance to deal with them without exposing Rowena to greater danger.

This would be difficult, he knew, for he would have to time it carefully. He was glad now he had waited so long, for it was sundown, and his full strength was returning. Searching out footholds and places to grasp the outside of the lodge, he began to climb toward the window of the room where Rowena was being held. However he dealt with Reighert, it would have to be silent and quick, for he had no wish to alert von Wolgast to their presence. Reaching the window and clinging to the eaves behind the icicles with one hand, Ragoczy was preparing to pull the shutters off their hinges when he heard Reighert come into the room. He went still and listened.

"The Baron says you can have bread and water," he informed Rowena. "Just like a penitent. I'll bring it up directly."

Rowena's answer was muffled; Ragoczy knew she was gagged.

"Get up. I'm taking you down to the bathroom." Reighert paused. "I'm going to untie your legs now. Don't do anything that will make me have to hurt you."

Again an indistinct answer, followed by the thud of feet striking the floor; Ragoczy knew her legs were numb from being tied to the iron frame of the bed.

"Stand up," Reighert ordered, then swore impatiently. "You'd better lean on me," he appended in a tone of ill-usage. "Come on. Let's get this over with."

This was the most hazardous part of his plan; Ragoczy made himself alert to every movement, every sound around him. Stealth and cunning were as necessary now to Ragoczy as his strength: with meticulous care he began to pull one of the shutters off the window. It took great control to accomplish this silently, and as the shutter came free there was a sudden cracking of wood, not loud but enough to be heard inside the room beyond. Ragoczy waited, hoping the noise had attracted no attention. When there was no alarm raised, he flung the shutter away into the trees and pushed the window open, hearing one of the hinges squeak. Again he paused, anticipating discovery, and when it did not happen, he slipped into the room, encouraged to find that the door into the corridor was ajar, so that a slice of light spilled in. That meant he would have to ease it open only once, reducing the risk of his apprehension by Reighert. Moving swiftly, making almost no sound, he went to the door and peered out through the crack between the door and the frame.

Reighert was standing in the hall outside an open door, staring into the room beyond; he held a smoking cigarette between his thumb and first finger of one hand, and a knife in the other. "Hurry up, can't you?" he said with annoyance.

In the next instant Ragoczy was behind him, one powerful small hand around his wrist above the knife, the other pressed into his throat, stopping breath and any movement at the same time. He increased the pressure. "Step back, Herr Reighert," he said, so softly that not even Rowena heard him.

Reighert obeyed at once, his eyes wild as he strove to determine who had attacked him. For an instant Ragoczy released his hold on Reighert's throat, allowing him to take a breath, then the inexorable fingers clamped down again.

In the bathroom, Rowena looked up, and from behind her gag came a sound that would have been a cry. Then she blushed, realizing her situation, and turned away in confusion.

"Herr Reighert," Ragoczy continued in the same steady, quiet way, "I want you to get down on your knees. Now, Herr Reighert."

As Reighert moved to comply, he tried to make a swing with the knife, intending to put this unknown opponent on his mettle. The fingers around his wrist tightened sharply, and then the bones grated together; pain shot up Reighert's arm and his eyes watered. "That was not wise, Herr Reighert."

Rowena had struggled to her feet, dragging herself erect by clinging to the sink. The first sensation was coming back to her legs, heralded by an unpleasant tingling which she knew from her three days of captivity would soon turn into agonizing cramps. She held onto the sink and stared as Ragoczy knelt beside Reighert, his hand still on Reighert's throat, his knee in the small of Reighert's back. Clutching the sink more firmly with one hand, she reached up with the other and removed her gag; she understood the necessity of keeping quiet, so she only murmured Ragoczy's name.

Ragoczy glanced swiftly up at her, taking stock of her condition. Then he leaned back down and whispered to Reighert. "Your wrist is broken, and if I wanted to I could kill you. Do you understand."

The slight sound Reighert made indicated he did.

"Good." His silky undervoice was heard by no one other than Reighert. "Listen very carefully. I am going to tie you up and gag you, as you did Miss Saxon. If you can get out of your bonds, or if help arrives you will live, otherwise you will die." He spoke a little bit louder.

"If you live, I recommend you throw yourself on the mercy of the authorities. Otherwise you may well share von Wolgast's fate."

Spots were swimming in Reighert's limited vision so that when Ragoczy once again permitted him to breathe he could only gasp. He felt Ragoczy's knee leave his back, and a moment later, Ragoczy hauled Reighert to his feet, his hand never leaving Reighert's throat. With an ease that left Reighert astounded, Ragoczy carried him into the room where Rowena had been held, and rapidly tied him down. Suddenly Reighert kicked the floor violently.

"You will have the opportunity to think over what you have done as you lie here," Ragoczy said gently as he secured Reighert's legs. "I recommend you put the time to prudent use."

"You're not . . . going to kill me?" Reighert croaked, unable to raise his voice.

"That would be too easy, and too quick," Ragoczy said with a brief smile that filled Reighert with foreboding. "If you try to escape your punishment, I will find you and you will receive it at my hands."

Reighert tried to nod, but could not make his neck bend. He made a sound that he hoped Ragoczy would recognize as capitulation.

"Count," called Rowena from the hall as there was the sudden banging open of the front door. "He's getting away."

Ragoczy stood upright, listening. There were running footsteps outside, and then the loud whinny from the horse in the barn. Realizing von Wolgast was escaping, Ragoczy flung himself out the window, somersaulting in the air to land on his feet; the pistol fell from his pocket. Wasting no time searching for the weapon, he ran toward the stable door, resolved to prevent this flight. Just as he reached the stable, von Wolgast emerged, mounted bareback on the coach horse, the animal's lead ropes tied to the halter, creating clumsy but serviceable reins. "Von Wolgast!" Ragoczy shouted, and reached out to pull the man off his mount.

But von Wolgast was prepared. He carried a mucking rake in one hand, and this he swung vigorously, burying the times in Ragoczy's side and knocking him down as von Wolgast kicked the horse from a trot to a canter.

Ragoczy careened to his feet as he pulled free of the rake, and using it as a prop, he strove to remain upright while he mastered the agony possessing him. Gingerly he put his hand to his side and was not repelled by the blood he touched. Fortunately it was dusk; he would not be much weakened by the wounds. He glanced down the road, and heard the hoofbeats fading. Tossing the rake away, he made his way back to the lodge, smarting as much from his failure to catch von Wolgast as from his injuries. As he climbed the stairs, he saw Rowena huddled at the top of the flight, Reighert's knife in her hand.

"Oh, thank goodness!" she exclaimed as she dropped the knife and hurtled into his arms.

He held her a while, soothing her and assuring her she was safe. "I could not stop von Wolgast," he confessed when she could bear to release him. "But Reighert will not get away."

Her laughter was a bit wild. "I should think not. You have him trussed like a hog for market," she managed to say before hilarity seized her again. She clung to the lapels of his coat as her glee turned to tears; he held her as she cried herself out, making no attempt to cajole or abjure her to cease, giving her what time she needed to find her own cessation point. Only then did he kiss her, his mouth touching hers with abiding kindness that complimented the passion shared by them both.

When she drew back, he looked directly into her golden eyes, seeing how exhausted she was. "I fear we have a long way to go tonight," he said, and when he felt her worry spring afresh, he went on, "If you cannot walk, I can carry you."

"What?" she asked with shaky amusement, "Can't you fly?"

"Regrettably, no. I agree it would come in handy just now," he said, shaking his head in chagrin. "It is some distance to Madern."

"Can't we stay here?" she pleaded, afraid to undertake what she knew to be an arduous march. "Surely someone will find us."

"You mean that von Wolgast will send help?" he suggested, one brow raising sardonically. He held her close again. "Once we reach Madern, the worst will be over: believe this." He brushed the tangled wisps of strawberry blonde back from her bruised face. "It will not be much longer, Rowena."

She pressed her head to his shoulder and nodded, saying, "What about—" She pointed toward the room where Reighert was tied.

"We will arrange for the police to retrieve him," he promised her. "Come. I want to be driving by dawn."

Only then did she realize he was hurt; she gave a wail of dismay. "How can you do it? You can't . . . " She set her jaw tenaciously. "Leave me here and come back for me. I don't mind. Truly I don't. I have the knife, and there must be guns about."

"And give von Wolgast another opportunity?" he asked. "I would take Reighert with us if I could manage it, but—" he broke off with a gesture of resignation.

She lowered her eyes. "I don't know that I can. My feet are . . . swollen."

"As long as it is night, I can carry you," he told her, with such conviction that she let herself be persuaded.

"Then we had best leave at once, before I change my mind," she said, gathering her courage to face what she knew would be a harrowing several hours.

"Good for you," Ragoczy approved as he started back down the stairs, half-carrying, half-guiding her as their exigent trudge began.

Text of a telegram from Franchot Ragoczy sent from Steinach, Austria to his manservant Roger via Hausham Railway Station in Bavaria.

R Saxon safe stop Inform Blau parents of events stop Advise B must detain von Wolgast stop Returning before midnight stop Have food clothes medicine etc ready stop Thank RB for automobile stop

F. Ragoczy

8

Looking up from the telegram Roger handed to him, Inspector Blau came close to smiling for the first time since his arrival at Schloss Saint-Germain the night before, worn out from a long day of travel. "The Austrians have agreed to hand Reighert over to us. They are satisfied that we have prior claim to him, and to prosecuting him," he announced in English to the study at large; telegrams had been filling the wires between Bavaria and Austria on an almost hourly basis for the last six hours.

"I hope you put him in prison forever," said Rowena with a loathing so intense that she sat back in shock. In her casual gored skirt and pullover tunic of bottle-green twill, with an ivory cotton blouse beneath, she seemed very much like a woman on holiday—or she did until you looked into her eyes or noticed the marks on her face.

Ragoczy came up behind her chair and laid his small, well-shaped hand on her shoulder. "He will." The ache in his side had nearly subsided, and the only sign of discomfort he revealed came more from the midday sunlight streaming in the windows than the now-faded damage the fork tines had done. By the end of the month the impressions would fade, leaving no trace.

"Yes, we will, Miss Pearce— Saxon," said Blau after a quick glance at Ragoczy. "Thanks in no small part to your presence of mind. I have not often encountered a woman of such fortitude as you possess. Your statements have been concise and sufficiently detailed to allow us to find excellent corroboration." He did his best not to stare at the green-edged livid bruise on her face.

"Corroboration; it is hardly enough," said Rowena. "I wish I could testify against him. Against them both."

"With what we may learn from this Reighert, it will not be necessary," Blau said at once; his English was heavily flavored with German and bookish in delivery, but he managed it better than Rowena did German. "I am persuaded you would not want to undertake anything that would bring you notoriety, as such testimony must. Questions would be asked that you would not be able to answer modestly. Your family would not want to see you exposed in open court, your indignities reported in the yellow press. I am sure you would find the whole experience distressing."

Rowena raised her head. "Being held captive by von Wolgast was . . . distressing," she said, throwing the word back at him. "Seeing him answer for it might be unpleasant but the satisfaction of bringing him down would more than compensate for a few snide remarks in print." She stared down at her laced fingers. "They have not found von Wolgast, have they?"

"Not yet," said Blau, the admission feeling like failure. "The Austrians are keeping careful watch, but—"

"But he could have been gone three days ago, as soon as he left his lodge: yes, I know. He could have had a plan to get away from the first, after he had killed me or left me to die. He told me more than once that was what he intended to do: let me die of cold and thirst." Rowena made no apology for her sharp tone, or for going on, "You cannot think a man of his cut would falter at taking shelter with your enemies, or arranging to go abroad where he could not be found, or brought back to stand his trial if he were. You know as well as I that there are those who would assist him because of his standing in the world, and others who would welcome the chance to have him gone from Germany. Between the two, he could be anywhere, with his fortune to buy him speed and secrecy. Why should he wait for the police to come for him, or linger where he could be taken and charged? I'm sure any sensible man would leave the region as soon as he could. By now, he could be at the far end of the Orient Express, could he not?"

"Yes, he could," said Blau, letting his bitterness show.

"But you will find him, won't you? You will not relent because he may get away now?" Rowena demanded, knowing her voice was too shrill. Her outbursts were troubling to her, and this one was no exception. Only Ragoczy's assurance that speaking them now would spare her later suffering kept her from maintaining the semblance of composure. "He is powerful, with powerful friends, and not just here in Germany. Powerful men can demand things the rest of us cannot. He will try to avoid apprehension; it is typical of criminals to want to elude capture, and a rich criminal can put many stumbling blocks in your way. He boasted of how he has been able to suborn men in crucial positions to do his bidding. They might still be compelled to aid him. You will not let him get away because he is Baron von Wolgast, will you? He will be arrested?"

"Of course," said Blau. "We are making every effort." He paused. "Miss Saxon, I realize this is not much comfort, but given the gravity of his acts, his position in life will not be able to save him from the consequences. On that you may repose complete confidence. He will not go free in the world, no matter who he is by birth and fortune. His crimes are sufficiently grave to put him beyond privilege." He gave a short little bow and turned to Ragoczy, speaking in German. "I will have to go tomorrow to take this Reighert in hand. The paperwork will be ready the day after, and I will be there to escort him. From Innsbruck we will go by rail directly back to Berlin, keeping this Reighert under guard and chained for the whole journey. I will not have to take advantage of your hospitality again." He had moved to the corner of the room and lowered his voice, and indicated that Ragoczy should do the same.

"You are more than welcome to command it at any time, Inspector, whether I am here or not. I will leave instructions with my staff to receive you as my guest at your convenience." Ragoczy indicated the door across the study leading into the hall. "And pursuant to hospitality, there will be a luncheon laid on the buffet in the dining room in half an hour or so; I hope you will avail yourself of it. Mister Bowen is coming downstairs today, and will be glad of company at table; at present he and Miss Saxon are not comfortable in one another's company. I believe luncheon is eels broiled with bacon. Gualtier is very good with eels, I am told." His courteous conduct held Blau's attention.

"For a man whom I very nearly put in prison, you're being remarkably gracious," said Blau. "Mind you, I'm not objecting; you're a most helpful fellow and this Schloss is as pleasant a place as anyone could ask for. But not many men would be as well-disposed to the police as you are; I am curious as to why you should be so willing to extend these courtesies to me after what I have subjected you to."

Ragoczy smiled slightly. "Inspector Blau, you strike me, and have struck me from the first, as a fair man, one who is more interested in seeing justice done than in bringing glory on himself. As I have learned in my life, those qualities are lamentably rare. When I discover them, I like to do my best to acknowledge them. Furthermore, it is in my best interests to see that my name is wholly cleared, which is not likely to happen if the real culprit remains at large."

Blau gave a nod of acceptance. "Very noble of you, I'm sure, and very pragmatic." He hesitated. "Yet I am not convinced those are your only reasons."

"No, they are not," said Ragoczy with such candor that Blau stared at him. "I am hoping that by being reassured that Reighert and von Wolgast will be held to account, Miss Saxon will not have to live in fear of either man. If they are not made to answer for what they have done, she will not be free of them, and she will lose faith in justice. She has suffered enough at their hands, and, I fear, on my account." He noticed the faint look of surprise in Blau's eyes, though his face remained impassive. "Do you think she would not be afraid?"

"A well-bred girl, carefully raised," Blau mused aloud. "I suppose she might be inclined to apprehension." He coughed diplomatically. "All the more reason for her not to appear at a trial, wouldn't you think?"

"No," said Ragoczy bluntly. "Quite the reverse, in fact."

"Then on that, we must disagree," said Blau, taking his notebook from his breast pocket and his pen from the pocket of his vest. He unscrewed the cap and prepared to write. "While I have the opportunity, I will want a few matters cleared up."

"Ask anything you like, Inspector." Ragoczy said, knowing the debate would accomplish nothing of use; then he glanced back at Rowena, saying to her in English, "Do you mind if we attend to—"

"Please. Carry on. I think I will go out onto the terrace for a little while. It is such a nice day." Her smile was not quite genuine, and marred by the fading bruise, but she stood up without giving in to her still-aching muscles.

"Pluck to the backbone," Ragoczy said to her, pride in his penetrating eyes.

"I should hope so," she said to him. "Inspector, we will meet in the dining room?"

"I look forward to it, Miss Saxon," he told her.

As soon as she left the study, Ragoczy said to Blau. "You can see my reason for concern for her, can you not?"

"She has been through an ordeal," Blau agreed. "Which is why I would like to spare her a second one, as you know as well as I her testimony at a trial must be." He prepared to write in his notebook. "You tell me you do not know this Oertel Morgenstern, who revealed so much to us?"

"The name is not familiar to me, no. I have thought about him since you mentioned him last night, and I cannot recall meeting anyone by that name. It does not mean I may not have encountered him once or twice, but if I did, it was without an introduction that I can bring to mind." He frowned, his gaze directed at the logs in the copper bucket at the hearth. "And yet: you say he was watching me? For a cultural journal in Prague? I find that baffling, even if it were true. Did he indicate anything more?"

"Such as why?" Blau suggested. "Only in the vaguest terms, I regret to tell you; his discretion is exemplary. There was a kind of excuse he gave, although I doubt he cared if I believed him, which I did not. He said he was observing you for an article on exiles, those who have risen above misfortune." Blau's inflection indicated how little he was convinced by that assurance. "I was certain he had other reasons, although I cannot confirm them, and it is not required of me that I try, for the case is solid without knowing Morgenstern's truth beyond his observations." He scribbled a few words.

"Might not the defense call Morgenstern's statement into question, with so many questions about him as yet unanswered?" Ragoczy asked, thinking it was what he would do, were he defending Reighert.

"I think we have enough information to support everything he told us, aside from his direct observations of the evening of the murder, and for that we have Lukas Strauss, who is willing to appear in court." Blau held his pen poised. "You are aware you were being followed while you were in Berlin?"

"I have been followed in many places, Inspector," said Ragoczy.

Blau sniffed to show impatience. "About Berlin?"

"Oh, yes; two men stand out particularly: one was a thin sort of rabbity fellow, thirty or so, I should say; he kept track of me in Berlin. Most of the time he was riding a bicycle. There was a second man in Berlin: large, brutish, with a face that had seen some brawling. He generally watched my house on Glanzend Strasse, but occasionally followed me when I went out on business."

"And you do not know who these men are, or why they watch you?" Blau persisted.

"Foreigners are often watched, for a variety of reasons," said Ragoczy in a spirit of philosophical acceptance. "I am no longer surprised when it is done." Over the last three thousand years he had ceased to permit such surveillance to trouble him; he had learned to deal with such inconveniences at the Temple of Imhotep, when he rarely left the building but was still subject to occasional scrutiny by the Temple denizens. "I regard it as a necessary evil of my . . . life." At least, he reminded himself, these men were not officers of the Emir's son, or companions of the Vidame de Silenrieux, or familiars of the Inquisition, or Vasilli Shuisky's minions, or members of Saint Sebastien's coven: at the worst these men were spies.

"Do you know if they were foreigners?" Blau persisted, prepared to make more notes. "Was there anything to draw your attention in that regard?"

"You mean Austrian, or something further afield?" Ragoczy inquired, and answered before Inspector Blau could clarify, "No; there was nothing outwardly that made me think the men were anything other than German. I did not have occasion to hear them speak, and their clothes, as you might expect from men in their line of work, were quite inconspicuous."

"You admit to having been in Berlin at the behest of Nicholas Romanov. That has been established, I am convinced. Your mission may or may not be as issue, but we will assume it is a factor. As an emissary of the Czar, you did not think you were being watched by his men, or by those who oppose him?" Blau made an uneasy gesture. "I am anticipating the concerns of the prosecutor."

Ragoczy stared out the window at the trees. "No, Inspector, I did not have any reason to think the men following me were either in the employ of the Czar or of his enemies. And to anticipate the rest of it," he went on with asperity, "no, I doubted the King of England, or any other power, in or out of Europe, had sent men to spy on me."

"I did not intend to offend you, Count," said Blau in a tone that was almost contrite. "You do understand the goals we are pursuing here, don't you?"

"Of course I do," said Ragoczy, his manner becoming more compliant at once. "And I am in sympathy with you, although I am not fond of the method."

At that, Blau was able to chuckle. "I am not enchanted with that myself." He made a few more notes, then put his pen away. "It is not my favorite activity, either." His smile was predatory. "I would far rather be running von Wolgast to earth, but until we have more information, any attempts along those lines would be wasted effort. And it could provide him the very thing we seek to withhold—a chance to slip through our fingers."

Ragoczy glanced at the clock on the mantel. "If there is nothing more, I have a few matters to attend to," he said to Blau.

"Not for the moment," Blau said as he returned his notebook to his pocket. "We'll let the rest go for now. I have a number of telegrams to compose, and then, as soon as luncheon is finished, I will go into Hausham to send them."

"Then I wish you a good appetite," said Ragoczy, preparing to leave the study to Blau.

"You will not be joining us?" Blau asked blandly as he screwed the cap back on his pen. "At luncheon?"

"Alas, no," said Ragoczy. "I have a . . . condition of the blood that limits my diet, and for everyone's comfort, I dine in private." He gave Blau a knowing stare. "As my cook has certainly informed you."

"Ah, yes." Blau had the grace to be embarrassed. "Gualtier Shenk has been most informative, with your permission, he tells me. You are to be congratulated on the circumspection of your staff. He has confirmed everything you and Mister Bowen told us of how you came to go into Austria, searching for Miss . . . Saxon."

"And are you satisfied on that account?" Ragoczy's manner remained courteous, but a quality of distance altered his demeanor in a subtle way.

"Generally, I am," Blau answered more formally. "Although I am not yet certain I understand how Mister Bowen took it into his head to come to you."

"That is a puzzle," Ragoczy said, and turned to leave the study to Inspector Blau; he added from the door, "You will have to inquire of him."

By the time the Inspector went into the dining room for luncheon, he saw Rupert Bowen had come down and was struggling, his arm in a sling, with a plate at the sideboard where the buffet was laid. Blau went to the Englishman's aid, holding the plate for him while Rupert selected the items that struck his fancy. Only when Rupert had taken his place at the long mahogany table did Blau go back for his own food. Sitting down about halfway along the table, across from Rupert, he remarked in English, "You are looking improved, Mister Bowen. It is good to see you up and about."

"I am feeling more myself. I expect I will be able to leave in a day or two, if I put my Darracq aboard a train, and me with it," Rupert said as he attempted to cut his portion of eel with the edge of his fork. His jacket, borrowed from the stationmaster at Hausham, was slightly old-fashioned and too broad in the shoulder, which added to Rupert's uneasiness; he felt terribly conspicuous, both for his injuries and for his sartorial ineptitude.

Blau did not know if it would offend Rupert to offer him help again, so he merely said, "Let me know if there is anything else I may do for you."

"Much appreciated," muttered Rupert, continuing in his efforts. "I've been told one of the blighters who abducted Miss Pearce-Manning is being held in Innsbruck." He lifted his head. "Ragoczy's man, Roger, has been keeping me abreast of developments."

"Yes. The man Reighert is going to be taken back to Berlin," said Blau, tasting the eel, and delighted at how good it was. "I will be one of his guards."

"But the other man is still at large? Is that right?" Rupert put his fork aside to listen.

"As far as I know this morning, yes, I am sorry to tell you he is," Blau replied, and cut another slice of eel.

"I see," said Rupert. The tone of his voice hinted at his desire to say more.

Blau could not resist probing a bit. "We have every hope of apprehending him shortly." It was not the truth, but it caught Rupert's attention.

"You know where he has gone?" he demanded, his cheeks reddening. "You are in a position to apprehend him? You will have him under lock and key shortly?"

"Not yet, but we are pursuing every clue, and we are confident of useful results," Blau said, unwilling to sustain the deception. "As soon as we do locate him, you will be informed of it, in Germany or in England."

"Bloody poltroon deserves to be shot," Rupert said under his breath.

"He has a great deal for which to answer, we are agreed on that," Blau said, but thought that his view of von Wolgast's crimes and Rupert's view would be very different.

"And the other man, the one in Amsterdam? Mightn't he know something of use? Have police taken him into custody yet?" Rupert asked, shifting awkwardly in his chair.

"I have not yet had word from Amsterdam today. I hope there may be some word at the railway station when I go there within the hour; I will be dispatching word of the Austrian decision to let our charges against Paul Reighert take precedence over theirs, and our coming extradition of him." He decided that Rupert needed to hear some good news to make up for the failure to arrest von Wolgast. "We have been able to establish that Ragoczy played no part in Nadezna's murder; there will be no legal action taken against him, and all allegations will end." Rupert did not seem pleased to learn this. He glowered down at his plate as if he had discovered the food was inedible. "How fortunate for the Count. He must be glad to be so conveniently absolved."

Curious and bewildered, Blau went on with his meal while he tried to make sense of Rupert's evident dislike of his host. Finally he said, "I gather I have been under a misapprehension regarding your dealings with the Count. I have assumed you came to him for help. You did a heroic thing, driving here, and in such poor condition, to inform Ragoczy of the abduction. Your timely—"

"I did not come to inform him, or for his aid," Rupert said huffily. "I came here because I was convinced he had arranged the abduction. I expected to find my fiancée here. It was enough to drive me mad when I discovered that in my haste to prevent scandal I had done the wrong thing." Now that this confession was out, Rupert glared defiantly at the Inspector. "You may say what you like about my error, but how could I think otherwise? He had made her the object of his gallantry, even though he was aware of our engagement. He called upon her in Amsterdam, ostensibly to sit for his portrait, but with the intention of playing upon her emotions. I do not absolve him of all responsibility in these terrible events. Had he not encouraged her as he did she would never have been in the hands of such miscreants as von Wolgast and his henchman."

"So he says himself," Blau remarked, and heard a cough at the door; he swung around in his chair to see Rowena standing there, her posture overly straight. Blau half-rose from his chair. "Miss Saxon," he said.

"Miss Pearce-Manning," Rupert corrected him. "Saxon is the name she uses to sign her paintings."

"It is my grand-father's name," said Rowena with great finality. "I am proud to have it as my own." She went to the sideboard and stood looking at the food laid out; she was hungry, but the thought of eating made her queasy; she poured herself a cup of coffee, added milk and sugar, and sat down at the foot of the table, three chairs away from the men. She stirred her coffee absently. "It is lovely outside."

"Yes, I can see this," said Blau, a little too heartily. "I am sorry my duties have not allowed me the chance to enjoy this splendid setting."

He started on his carrots baked with cheese, trying to maintain a degree of friendly chatter as he did. "I am told that the road to Starnberg is glorious at this time of year. Perhaps, when I have the opportunity, I will be able to see for myself."

"And when do you think that will be, Inspector?" Rowena asked, her question remote, as if unattached to her.

"I would like to hope it would be soon," said Blau with purpose.

Rupert seized on this with a tenacity that surprised Blau. "Then you do have some notion about von Wolgast's whereabouts?"

Blau did his best to deflect the onslaught he knew was coming. "I cannot say quite yet. But I am expecting useful information this afternoon." He did not mention specifically what he hoped his various morning telegrams would reap. "I do not want to offer false hope to you, Miss . . . erh . . . "

"Saxon," she informed Blau while staring at Rupert.

"Of course," said the Inspector, and resumed, "I am fairly certain that we will be able to eliminate several points of egress for the Baron, and that will keep us from . . . isn't the phrase 'wild goose chases'?"

"That is the phrase," said Rowena as she took a sip of her coffee. If only she could bring herself to eat, she thought as she stared at Rupert's plate. Had three days' captivity robbed her of her appetite so completely? She had a bit more coffee and thought it tasted like mud.

Rupert went back to work on his luncheon, glaring with the effort of cutting his food with his fork. When he had at last got four sections of eel ready, he shifted his gaze to Inspector Blau once again. "Something has been bothering me, Inspector: perhaps you can explain to me how a man of von Wolgast's stripe has been able to carry on the nefarious activities of the last week without catching any attention? Didn't anyone suspect he might be capable of—"

"Of abducting Miss . . . Saxon?" Blau finished for him. "If you can tell me why we should have made such an assumption, I wish you would, Mister Bowen." He was almost finished with the contents of his plate, but he put his utensils aside in order to give his whole attention to Rupert. "It was not von Wolgast's habit to announce his plans aloud to the world."

"But surely someone must have—" Rupert insisted.

"Who? I gather it was his practice to tell his . . . associates only as much as each individual required to know in order to carry out his part in von Wolgast's schemes." He leaned forward. "Even your Scotland Yard would not have been able to determine what he had planned: I know this, for I have twice worked with Scotland Yard on cases involving smuggling. By comparison with von Wolgast, the smugglers were sterling examples of loquacity." He rose, nodding in Rowena's direction. "If you will excuse me, Miss, I must be about my work."

"Certainly," she said. "I wish you every success." It was an automatic response, but in this instance she meant it as sincerely as she had ever meant anything in her life.

As soon as Blau was gone, Rupert took advantage of the moment to say, "It may not be the most opportune time to point this out, but I trust you have come to realize that this whole unspeakable episode could have been avoided."

"Oh?" There was a brilliance in her golden eyes that should have warned Rupert he was on dangerous ground. "Why do you say that, pray?"

"Well, I should think it is obvious," Rupert declared, taking up some of the eel he had cut. "Had you not made that ill-considered move to Amsterdam, you would not have been accessible to von Wolgast's men."

"So I am responsible for my abduction?" she challenged him, her words keener because she dreaded that some portion of his accusation might be true.

"Well, not responsible, exactly," he said, his indignation fading, "but not wholly without blame. If you had listened to your mother, and to me, and allowed yourself to be guided by us, you would not have encouraged Ragoczy's attentions, and then you would not have suffered. None of us would have." He showed his most indulgent smile. "You let your enthusiasm overwhelm your good sense."

"How idiotic of me, to be sure," Rowena said with a brittle laugh. "I should have arranged to be killed, so you would not have to be ashamed of me."

"You *were* in the hands of those men for three nights," said Rupert critically. "I know what the world thinks of such incidents."

Rowena's face grew rosy. "You think that they . . . raped me? When I have told you and the police that they did not? Or do you require that they have done, so that you may feel more offended?"

"It is not my opinion that we must consider here, Rowena." He stared down at his plate and poked the eel with his fork. "You know how censorious people are. It is the assumption the world will make, and—"

She did not let him continue. "You are telling me that you will give greater credence to gossip—to *gossip*!—than to my word?"

The sound of an automobile starting up in the courtyard reminded them both of Inspector Blau's errand.

"I tell you, it isn't what *I* think, it is what persons of quality will be-lieve that concerns me." He dared to meet her eyes. "If only you had not run off to Amsterdam in that ramshackle way, it might have been possible to maintain your reputation untarnished. But, Rowena, don't you see what your ill-considered escapade has led to?"

"You mean," she said crisply, "that 'persons of quality' will take it for granted that by pursuing my painting, I became a woman who de-served to be abducted."

Rupert's face was a study in disapproval and misery. "I did not mean precisely that," he began.

"No? It sounded very like that to me," she countered, and braced her elbows on the table. "Dear me, I had not known that my painting was so very harmful to my good name—"

"It is what I have been trying to tell you—" Rupert interjected.

"—and that because of it, I might be attacked at will. So it is due to my work that I was allowing, even *encouraging* von Wolgast's men to carry me off to be held for ransom." She opened her eyes very wide in fallacious naïveté. "I should be grateful that I was not sold into white slavery in Turkey, shouldn't I? Or perhaps taken by sinister Orientals to be part of a potentate's harem?"

"Rowena, please," Rupert said sternly. "This is difficult enough for me without your sarcasm."

"Difficult for *you*?" she challenged, getting to her feet so hastily that she overset her coffee cup; the liquid spread across the glossy wood as if aimed at Rupert. "For you?"

"Of course for me," he said. "And look what you have done."

She made a sound in her throat like a growl. "Yes. It is all my fault. And you are the one who has sustained the worst—" She stopped, her anger cooling immediately. "Not to say that you did not endure a great deal for me, and not that I am ungrateful for all you did to help me." Her features were conscience stricken, and she took a moment to re-cover herself. "I fully understand why you are upset, Rupert: I do not think you comprehend why I am."

"There you are wrong," said Rupert with all the dignity he could sum-mon up. "I think your high spirits and overly independent ways have led you to take chances that are not appropriate for you. I am sorry you have had to endure so much hardship, but I cannot hold you entirely blameless, either. Nor will anyone who knows you. And unlike me," he went on with an expression bordering on piety, "they will not be will-ing to extend you the benefit of the doubt. This is not some errant schoolgirl prank you were involved in, after all."

Her hands closed into fists at her sides. "I did not seek it for myself," she insisted, then looked at the spilled coffee, and belatedly reached for her serviette to clean it up. As she wiped, she went on, "You keep speaking about this as if the whole of it was designed to be inconvenient to you. You had nothing to do with what happened. I could almost be sorry you were involved in any way, but that your quick actions saved me from—"

"Not about me?" He burst out. "When I was going to marry you?"

Rowena went still. "What did you say?"

He glanced in her direction without actually looking at her. "Surely you realized that I could not continue our engagement after this. There is no way to salvage your name, and I cannot now mend it by giving you the protection of mine." He rubbed his chin. "I had not meant to tell you so . . . so—"

"Shabbily?" she suggested. "Callously?"

"Well, but, Rowena, you have been saying all along that you had no intention of marrying me," he reminded her, petulance tingeing the nobility of his statement. "You cannot claim to be offended."

"And so I have said, but not for your reason," she said, astonished at how calm she was. "You have decided that I am an unacceptable bride for you because I may be the subject of gossip. You have not believed me when I have told you, for years on end, that I do not intend to marry anyone. Of course I am offended. You are behaving as if you have been sullied by me." She paced to the windows and back to the table. "How dare you?" she demanded.

"How dare I?" His repetition was incredulous. "Have you lost all sense of propriety, that you cannot perceive what your situation has done to me?"

She folded her arms, her fingers digging into the fabric of her sleeves. "No, Rupert: I cannot. And nothing you say will persuade me." She went back to the window again. "From the first you have not cared a fig for me. You made up your mind what I was to be, and followed that assumption without regard to anything I did or said. You are doing the same thing now. I wish to God—"

"Rowena!" he admonished her. "Intemperate language will not—"

"—that I had no reason to be grateful to you, for it would make it easier to hate you." Her restless steps took her the length of the room, to the sideboard, and back to the windows. "So. I thank you for coming to Schloss Saint-Germain. I would probably be dead by now if you had not done so. And undoubtedly you would mourn me with the certainty that I had doomed myself to such an end. No." She rounded on him. "It is my turn to speak. You will say nothing."

"But Rowena, you will regret—" he protested.

"I regret only that I would be unjust if I did not acknowledge the debt I owe you. But I will not be bullied by you ever again." She resumed her pacing. "That wrong-headed rectitude of yours! It is as unbearable as the fantasy you have constructed about me. When you marry—and you will marry—I pity your wife, for she will be a stranger to you from first to last."

"You're overwrought," said Rupert, starting to get to his feet. "I should not have spoken so hastily."

"I am *not* overwrought," she declared. "I am precisely what I have been all along; that is what makes this so demeaning." She motioned to him to remain seated. "I can't talk to you any longer." With that, she left the dining room.

Rupert went slowly on with his meal, consoling himself with the thought that a man with his arm in a sling could not be expected to restrain a woman on the verge of hysterics. When he finished, he decided to return to his room; all the upheaval of the last hour had exhausted him.

An hour later Inspector Blau returned with more telegrams in hand. He asked Roger to have Miss Saxon and Ragoczy meet him in the study. "I think they will be interested in what I have learned this afternoon," he said, his eyes alight with the first good news in this case.

"What of Mister Bowen?" Roger inquired.

"I leave that up to you," said Blau. "I can always speak with him later." He paused, in order to choose his words carefully. "I had the notion at luncheon that all was not well between him and Miss Saxon."

"I take your point. In that case it would probably be wisest to inform Mister Bowen separately. Will ten minutes be satisfactory?" Roger saw the Inspector nod. "The study it will be." He went off to extend Blau's invitation.

Ragoczy had changed his hacking jacket for a heavy black cotton tunic for work in his laboratory and he had a pen clipped to his breast pocket. He sank down in his Turkish chair and crossed one leg over the other. "You look heartened, Inspector."

"I am," said Blau as Rowena came into the study; Ragoczy got to his feet, watching her more closely than she realized. "We have a report from Amsterdam, and one from Italy." If he had not been holding telegrams, he would have rubbed his hands together.

"Promising, are they?" Rowena asked. In the last twenty minutes she had at last restored her composure, although somewhat precariously.

If she had to endure more discouragement, she was certain she would behave in a most unseemly manner, and she had done enough of that for one day, she reminded herself inwardly.

"I think so," said Blau, and held up the longest one. "This is from the police in Amsterdam," he announced, then shifted his eyes to Rowena. "You did tell me, did you not, that you struck one of your assailants on the head with a heavy vase?"

"Actually, it was a porcelain umbrella stand," said Rowena, feeling her pulse jump at the question.

Blau nodded twice. "Yes. Yes. It would seem that your efforts were rewarded, Miss Saxon, for this report informs me that the man in question was found two days ago in a wrecked Humber automobile, with the body of your housekeeper I am sad to inform you—in the boot." He saw Rowena's hands go to her face, and hurried on. "It appears that the reason the automobile crashed into the end of a bridge was that the man, known as Bernard, was suffering from a fairly severe concussion."

"My Lord!" Rowena whispered. "How awful."

"It is the opinion of the examining physician that your housekeeper had been dead for several hours, possibly as many as five hours, when she was put in the boot of the Humber," Blau went on. "I am sorry for her death."

Rowena nodded, "So am I." She took a deep breath, relieved that it was almost steady. "Is that the whole account?"

"From Amsterdam, yes, except for a few technical matters." He decided she did not need to know the precise state of the bodies when they were recovered.

Ragoczy spoke directly to Rowena. "You could not have saved her."

"I know, but I cannot help but think if she had not been working for me, she might still be alive." Rowena felt tears in her eyes, and wished she had a handkerchief.

"Here," Ragoczy said, offering her a square of soft black linen.

She took it wordlessly and daubed at her eyes. "What of the other telegrams?"

"Oh," said Blau, smoothing one of them. "We have word from Udine that von Wolgast stayed at an inn near the city night before last. The identification has been confirmed by the Italian authorities. He said he was bound for Venice, which has led me to suppose we must look for him in Croatia. Why would he tell the innkeeper anything but to be misleading."

Ragoczy agreed. "Yes. And with the unrest in Croatia and Serbia, he will have more opportunities to hide."

"We will be concentrating our efforts in that region, as long as the Emperor permits us access," Blau said, and leaned toward Rowena. "It will not be much longer, Miss Saxon, and you may see von Wolgast answer for all he has done."

Rowena tried to speak but no sound came past the tightness in her throat; to her dismay, she began silently to weep, but whether in satisfaction or despair, even she did not know.

Text of a letter from Egmont von Rosenwiese to his wife, Wendelin.

April 20, 1911

My dearest Wendelin;

I cannot apologize sufficiently for the shame I have brought upon you in these last several days, and you cannot excoriate my name more than I do myself. It was never my intention to subject you to any of this; in many ways, it was my efforts to prevent discovery that made me the tool of von Wolgast, as you now know. I pray that with the healing touch of time, you will come to forgive me for what I have done and what I am about to do.

It is with profound guilt that I tell you all you have heard regarding Bishop Kalthaus and me is true, and I cannot excuse it beyond stating that the actual deeds were done before you and I married. That is not to absolve the wrong I did then, and those I have done since, but I do not want you to think that I have no affection for you. I have always been most sincerely attached to you. I have admired and respected you, and it is out of these genuine sensibilities that I have found the courage to put an end to a life that can only now be an exercise in humiliation for you as well as for me.

I have prepared a complete account of all I have done at von Wolgast's instigation, as well as recounting everything he has confided to me regarding his plans and activities, legal and illegal, in the hope that this will aid in bringing him to justice. It may not seem a courageous act, but it is the best I can do for now. Let me urge you, if you have any wish to preserve the honor of our family, to present the information to the police, so that they may undertake to verify all I have said.

It is never an easy thing to make amends, yet I hope my death will prove to be of some worth in your eyes. I have decided to do the deed in the bathroom, for I am sure it will need cleaning, and the tiles will scrub better than the walls of my bedroom. You may instruct the servants to tend to it as soon as the police will allow.

I cannot explain why God or the Devil chose to align my lusts to my own sex, but whatever the reason for it may be, I pray the taint will not remain on you once I am forgotten. And I can hope for nothing more now than oblivion, my own and the world's. I plead with you to remember me with kindness, if you can. My acts have been done with the intention of sparing you pain, and have succeeded only in making it much worse. There is no way for me to repent now; it has all gone too far for that. You cannot guess to what depths I have sunk, all in the name of respectability and duty. For this, and for so many other trespasses, I beg you to find it in your heart to pardon me, if you cannot forgive. I cannot express how contrite I am in any way but through ridding the world of my presence.

Farewell, my wife,
Egmont

9

Five weeks of eluding the police in three countries had taken their toll on von Wolgast; he had lost flesh, and now his brown wool suit with the long coat, bright buttons, and velvet collar was stained, the sleeves frayed, and it hung on him as if it belonged to someone else, someone more robust and well-fed. Without Schmidt and Malpass to tend to his needs, he had found himself harried and pursued, unable to keep his clothes neat or his buttons sewed on—he had lost two off his shirt in the last ten days. He could not think of the sums he had spent purchasing a modicum of safety without cringing. Since his arrival in Trieste three days ago, he had paid outrageous amounts for a room no larger than his clothes closet in Berlin.

"I cannot allow you to stay here longer than tonight," the landlord had warned him when he had brought his dinner in the early afternoon. "Tomorrow morning you leave." His tone was final.

"Yes, you told me," said von Wolgast brusquely; he had cut himself shaving that morning and a little thread of blood still marked his cheek.

"If your friends cannot help you, do not suppose that I will; I do not run my inn for your sort," the landlord had persisted; he was a squint-eyed widower of fifty-three, with gnarled fingers and the temperament of a badger. He stood in the door, one hand on his hip, his expression as uninviting as any von Wolgast had ever seen. "Tomorrow. Mind." Smells of sour beer, rotten vegetables, and urine wafted on the air he let into the room; if he noticed them they did not seem to bother him.

"Yes, yes, yes," said von Wolgast as he plunged his spoon into the thick soup; he knew better than to examine its contents too closely. He noticed the bread was dry and the cheese had a suggestion of mold at one corner; he did not complain.

"The police were around again this morning, you know." The landlord seemed to take delight in making his well-paying guest wretched. "They will be back again tomorrow, and the next day and the next."

"I'm sorry it has come to this," said von Wolgast. "If you need more money, I will arrange for it tonight."

"When your friend arrives," said the landlord, his tone implying that this event was a fiction.

"Yes. He will be here in good time," said von Wolgast, devoutly hoping it was so. He was still reeling inwardly from the shock of Vaclav Persuic's refusal to assist him in any way, claiming that as an officer of Emperor Franz Josef he had to avoid any hint of political intrigue. Von Wolgast had read the telegram several times, convinced that the words would change if he stared at them long enough. Colonel Persuic, Herzog Persuic, who had accepted hospitality and favors from him now refused to lift a finger on his behalf: von Wolgast had been outraged, and frightened.

"I will make no exceptions for you, Mein Herr," the landlord persisted, his German good enough in spite of his accent. "I am not one of those cringing peasants, who despise their neighbors and bow to the man with the biggest whip. I will not hesitate to summon the authorities if you refuse to leave."

At the mention of the authorities, von Wolgast flinched in spite of his determination not to; he straightened up. "I do not want to remain here one moment longer than necessary."

"Bravo." The landlord cast von Wolgast a look of scorn, then left him to his meal.

"Ingrate!" Von Wolgast shouted after him, then concentrated on his meager supper. He had intended to eat slowly, but hunger soon got the better of him and he wolfed down the thick soup, mopping up the last drops with bread and finishing off with the cheese. He would have liked something to drink, but after one taste of the wine the landlord served, he had thought it best to keep to the occasional cup of inky coffee and well-water. Sounds from the street echoed eerily in the little courtyard, blending into a wash of noise like the sea. He sat and stared at the empty bowl, his mind roaming restlessly: he had discovered from the newspapers that Reighert was in captivity and had given a full report of all he had done for von Wolgast over the years. The press had gobbled up these scandalous accounts and publicized them with the kind of relish that infuriated von Wolgast. He had disliked reading that there was now some question of von Wolgast being linked to the murders of Renfred Meyer and his mother: would the police try to implicate him in every unsolved crime in Berlin? His participation in those murders had been so tangential that they could hardly be thought of as his. There had been other news that held his attention as well: orders for his guns had gone up, but he could not reach the money; his one hope lay with the Kaiser, who had stated that he did not trust a defrocked priest to give honest testimony, and charged the police to verify every accusation. Von Wolgast had read the account of von Rosenwiese's suicide with disgust. The man had been a coward to the end, unable to face the truth.

For the next hour, von Wolgast fought off an uneasy mix of impatience and boredom. He had not seen a paper for two days, which made him nervous; being abreast of the news was his one link to his former life, and he did not want to break it. He did not like to admit it, but he took a perverse pleasure in seeing the various revelations about him, and thought there was so much more they had not yet discovered. The most recent story was on the confirmation of the police investigation regarding Nadezna's death. How that had come back to haunt him! Between that and Reighert's confession regarding the murder of Antonia, von Wolgast knew that it would take ingenuity to continue to maintain his business. Undoubtedly he would have to sacrifice a portion of his profits, but in time he should be quite comfortable again. He would have a good house, would entertain, would hunt, would attend the theatre and the ballet, would keep desirable mistresses, might even marry again, once he was established.

The sound of footsteps in the innyard recalled von Wolgast to his present predicament; he got up and went to the door, leaning against it while he listened, hardly daring to breathe.

"Baron?" The voice was low but von Wolgast recognized it.

With a sigh of relief, he opened the door to Tancred Sisak. "It's good to see you, old friend," he said in a rush of feeling that took him aback.

Sisak patted von Wolgast's shoulder as he stepped into the room, as much to calm him as to extend any sign of friendship. "Not what you're used to, by the look of it, but better than it might have been," he observed. Unlike von Wolgast, Sisak was dressed in fashionable, well-fitting clothes, his hair newly trimmed, his face shaved without mishap, and he smelled faintly of cologne. "But necessity is a stern goddess, isn't she?" He had the same continual, meaningless demeanor of bonhomie that had so pleased von Wolgast at their first meeting.

"As I need not tell you," said von Wolgast, gesturing apologetically to his surroundings. "I must thank you for meeting me here. Circumstances being what they are—"

"You dare not be seen on the streets," said Sisak. "It is not easy to be a fugitive." His teeth flashed in what might have been a smile. "I have some experience of it."

"You've told me," von Wolgast reminded him. "And I would not have sent word to you without your understanding of the risks I am running. It is all absurd of course, and no doubt it will be cleared up—" It was less than the truth, but he wanted to be sure Sisak would be persuaded to help him.

"My dear Baron, if you intend to lie to me, I will not be able to help you," said Sisak, cutting short the recitation von Wolgast had begun. "You killed your wife, or arranged to have her killed. You killed Nadezna or arranged to have her killed. You kidnapped that Englishwoman with the help of your hired agents. I am sure you had your reasons." His smile remained fixed in place. "Will you tell me the truth, or shall I leave?"

"My wife," said von Wolgast sullenly, "was entirely mad. She had been confined in the care of nuns for some years. Nadezna had tried to blackmail me. The Englishwoman was a gamble that failed." He shot a single look at Sisak. "You know how things can go wrong, no matter how well you plan."

"Better than you do, Baron," said Sisak with another show of teeth.

"No doubt, no doubt," said von Wolgast urgently, continuing with more confidence than he actually felt, "I knew I could rely on you to help me. Our dealings together have always been profitable, have they not? We have been useful to each other in many ways; you might even say we have a genial friendship. I've done a lot for you, haven't I?" He had not intended to beg, but he heard himself and felt appalled.

"Yes; our dealings have been profitable for us both," said Sisak, his eyes making a complete record of the horrible little room.

"And they can be again, if you and I can hit upon the means to retrieve my fortune," von Wolgast encouraged him. "In spite of all this, I am a wealthy man."

"Yes, I think so, too," Sisak told him. He was waiting for something, but had no intention of hurrying the thing he sought.

"Fine." Relief swept through von Wolgast, making him giddy. He had to bite his tongue to keep from babbling his thanks. He cleared his throat. "I cannot stay here after tomorrow morning, so if there is some way you could arrange for me to remain safe, I would make it worth your while."

"Yes, you will," Sisak concurred; from the way he went on, it was apparent he had been planning this from the first. "As soon as it is dark, I will come back for you. I have one of my ships in the harbor. I will make a room available to you, and we can do our business in better surroundings than these."

"That will not take much. A barn would be an improvement," said von Wolgast, making an attempt at wit.

"Yes, this is not the Kreuzfahrer Hof, is it? and you have no one so lovely as Nadezna with you, but—" His gesture indicated his acceptance of the state of affairs. "Something will be arranged, to our mutual benefit."

"Better days are coming," von Wolgast said, hoping devoutly this was true. "The worst is over."

Sisak chuckled. "For both of us, I trust," he said smoothly, then took a brisker pace. "I will not stay. This is not the most secure hiding place in Trieste, Baron. Expect me about two hours after sundown. I will take you to the ship, and we will make our arrangements there."

"I look forward to it," said von Wolgast, doing his best to rise to the occasion.

"I should think so." Sisak took a last glance around, then left.

To von Wolgast, the remaining hours in the day went by at a turtle's pace, lumbering from minute to minute at an ever-slowing rate. Never had the sun taken so long to drop below the horizon. Now that he had some reason to hope, von Wolgast spent much of the interminable afternoon making plans, refining them, discarding them, until he had arrived at two or three he was certain would return him to a place in the world where he could live as he was born to live. He had two other matters to attend to before that could happen: Reighert would have to be discredited and Ragoczy would have to die.

When Sisak returned he was dressed in a heavy sailor's jacket and carried a djalabah with him. "You'd better put this on," he recommended. "Leave your coat here."

"But that—" von Wolgast protested, hating the thought of donning Arabian robes as much as he wanted to save his suit.

"The police are looking for a hunted European—a man in a suit. They might expect a disguise, but not anything like this: the reports have suggested you may have grown a beard or dyed your hair. They will not pay as much attention to you if you are dressed like an Arab," Sisak explained, then waited while von Wolgast made up his mind.

"Very well," he said, tugging his coat off and flinging it away. "You're probably right; I would do well to be rid of the rest of my clothes."

"Not at night," Sisak said knowledgeably. "In daylight your shoes would give you away if nothing else did." He watched while von Wolgast wrestled himself into the enveloping cotton robe. "You'll find it as comfortable as a nightshirt."

"It is like wearing a tent," von Wolgast complained. "Should I have a turban, or is there a hood?"

"You don't know how to wrap a turban," said Sisak as if he thought this was a failing. "I've brought a hood for you," he went on, holding it out. "The tassel goes in the back." He snickered as von Wolgast pulled it on. "Keep your head down when you follow me, and say as little as possible."

"I will," von Wolgast said, too frightened to be excited; it was borne in on him that he was taking the greatest gamble he had since he fled his lodge in Austria. What became of him in the next hour would set the seal on his fate for years to come. He faltered when Sisak stepped back into the courtyard. "I am worried about the innkeeper. I've paid him a lot of money, but he might still say something, if he thought he would get a reward."

"Yes, so he might," said Sisak with a fine show of unconcern. "Which is why my man Mamoud will come back after midnight and burn the place to the ground."

This announcement did not so much shock von Wolgast as it vexed him. "Will that not mean questions? I don't want to make my presence known, even after the fact."

"Who will answer the questions? The landlord will be ashes with his inn," said Sisak, and motioned to von Wolgast to follow him. "Not too fast," he warned.

"No; we don't want anyone to think we are being chased," said von Wolgast with a show of caustic humor that was lost on Sisak.

"No, we don't," he said as he started down the courtyard, only glancing back once to be sure von Wolgast was behind him.

Along the narrow stone streets of Trieste they went, their route indirect and unobvious, but leading eventually to the waterfront. They reached the docks without incident; the Greek freighter *Alecto* was ready for loading, large crates stacked on the pier, a single watchman protecting the cargo. It was not a very prepossessing ship, well enough kept but ruthlessly utilitarian, but it looked like Valhalla itself to von

Wolgast. The smell of tar and seawater was very strong on the night air. At a sign from Sisak a crewman removed the gate from the gangplank, and Sisak led von Wolgast aboard, no questions asked, and scant attention paid. It was apparent Sisak knew the freighter well, and went down a maze of corridors to a row of spartan staterooms, indicating one to von Wolgast. "This is where you will stay, when we are done with our negotiations." It was the first words he had addressed to von Wolgast in the last half hour.

Two weeks ago von Wolgast would have been disappointed; now he sighed once, and said, "When does the ship sail?" He did not want to be within reach of the police any longer than absolutely necessary.

"The day after tomorrow," Sisak told him. "We will have plenty of time to conclude our arrangements."

"And where are we bound, when we leave port?" He had a moment's dread that he would be on his way to a destination where he could be detained, or some place so remote he would be unable to find a way to gain access to his money.

"South Africa," said Sisak. "I have recently established an office there. I am certain we can turn that office to our mutual advantage." His manner suggested that failure to do this would end the voyage for von Wolgast before the ship arrived.

"Among the blacks?" von Wolgast could not keep from asking. "Lazy, dangerous people, I've been told, without respect for Europeans. It might be better to consider South America."

"The blacks are kept well in hand," said Sisak. "You need not pay any attention to them unless you employ them as servants. And they are far less danger to you than any peasant in Europe. As for South America, you would soon be surrounded by half-breed Indians who are just as lazy and unreliable as blacks are."

The force of this statement shook von Wolgast to the marrow of his bones. "Mein Gott, this will take some getting used to," von Wolgast said, feeling sweat on his face.

Sisak ignored von Wolgast's exclamation, glancing around the stateroom. "I'm going in to have a cognac in the main cabin. Join me when you are ready. I think you will find everything in order."

"What do you mean?" von Wolgast demanded, anticipating the worst. "I brought nothing with me."

"All the more reason to inspect the stateroom. I mean that there are clothes—not as well-fitted as you are used to, but serviceable and unobvious—a razor, soap, a toothbrush, socks, shoes—I had to guess the size—a pad of paper, pencils, a pen—in short everything you will need on the voyage." He looked amused. "You did not suppose you were going to be tucked away in the hold, did you?"

Von Wolgast shrugged. "It never entered my mind that—"

"That you would be taken care of?" Sisak asked. "It isn't lavish, but it will suffice until we reach South Africa." He held up his hand. "There are books and magazines in the main cabin. Most of them are in Greek or Italian, but a few are in German, so you will have something to read."

"What about newspapers?" von Wolgast asked sharply.

"Do you mean you want to know more of how your exploits are being revealed?" Sisak inquired with false cordiality. "Be glad we do not have such things aboard, or some of the crew might become curious."

"I have wanted to find out what has been said about me, and by whom. It gives me some notion of what I am up against, so I will know how difficult it will be to get my hands on my money once I am settled away from Europe. How I will establish myself again will depend in part on what is written about me." He noticed the heavy latch on the stateroom door. "You expect trouble?"

"No, we expect there may be heavy seas, and you will want to secure everything you can, including the door." Sisak slapped his hand on his thigh. "Well, shall we say twenty minutes?"

"In the main cabin," agreed von Wolgast. "Where will I find it?"

"Go along this corridor until you must turn. Bear right and it will be the first door on your left." He backed out of the stateroom, adding, "Oh, and think about South Africa again. It is preferable to a prison cell, blacks and all," before leaving von Wolgast to take stock of his situation.

"Twenty minutes," said von Wolgast as the door closed. After a moment's consideration he set the latch, deciding it was the prudent thing to do. Satisfied he would be undisturbed, he pulled open the narrow closet and saw four thick sweaters, two shirts, two pairs of dark trousers and an oilcloth coat hanging there. Relieved, he pulled his hood and djalabah over his head, wadding them up and thrust them under the pillow on the single bunk. He chose the darkest of the sweaters and put it on, telling himself he would blend in better in such a garment. The small mirror on the inside of the closet door showed him an image that seemed alien to his eyes, and he told himself confidently that his own mother would not be able to recognize him. He regretted now that he had sold his pocketwatch in Gorizia; he would have to obtain another. With a sigh, he released the latch, opened the door, and went down the companionway to the main cabin.

This turned out to be a small salon paneled in oak, with half a dozen wooden chairs and two tables bolted to the floor. A leather-padded bench along the wall provided more seating and a bit more comfort than the chairs. Shelves with braces across them held a number of books, and periodicals were stacked in a brass container near the door. It was as close to luxury as anything on the *Alecto* was. Five portholes provided a glimpse of the harbor, their brass fittings not quite tarnished, but not polished either, and a small bar at the far end of the cabin, now unoccupied, added a sociable note.

Sisak was seated at one of the tables, a pony of cognac held lazily in his fingers. Beside him, a man with Turkish features in an Italian silk suit was quietly explaining something to Sisak. He fell abruptly silent when von Wolgast entered the cabin.

"Good evening, Herr Baron," said Sisak with an ironic inclination of his head. "You will find your name on the passenger list is Manfred Baron, from Berlin. You are traveling for your health." His laughter was short. "This is my . . . colleague, Mamoud. Mamoud, Herr Baron. You have no need to know his family name; it would mean nothing to you in any case."

The Turk rose and bowed Prussian style, with a clicking of his heels. "Herr Baron, an honor," he said in quite acceptable German.

"And to you," said von Wolgast; he glanced around the cabin. "Are we the only ones?"

"For tonight, yes. Tomorrow we will be joined by two retired schoolteachers who are trying to make their way around the world before they die," said Sisak. "They will pose no problem, two men, from Graz, both over sixty."

Von Wolgast was not so sanguine. "If they are schoolteachers, they may have kept up with the reports in the press. If they were to report anything . . . "

"If such a problem arises, Mamoud will attend to it." Sisak nodded in the Arab's direction. "And speaking of such things, I recall there is the matter of the innkeeper to deal with."

Mamoud rose and said something in a language von Wolgast did not recognize, bowed again and left.

"You may consider the problem solved," Sisak informed von Wolgast as they were left alone in the main cabin.

"You mean that . . . that fop is going to burn down the inn?" von Wolgast demanded. "That's absurd."

"We do not all employ debauched priests to do our work," said Sisak, indicating the chair Mamoud had just left. "Sit down, Herr Baron; we have much to do before we retire for the night." He set his cognac aside, reached behind his chair and pulled out a leather portfolio.

Reluctantly von Wolgast took the chair Mamoud had just vacated, his attitude fussy; if he had had a handkerchief, he would have used it to wipe the chair first. He settled himself, his eyes on the portfolio. "Here I am," he said.

"Yes," said Sisak. He patted the portfolio. "I have been thinking about your situation for some days, Manfred, and I think I may have hit upon the solution to your immediate predicament." It sounded like the rehearsed speech it was. "You have to consider your future now, so that you may contrive to retain as much of your wealth and your company as is practicable. Do not let me rush you into anything. Still, I want you to give me your undivided attention for the next half hour or so." He opened the portfolio and drew out what was obviously a contract. "I had my solicitor draw this up last week, in case you decided to turn to me in this arduous time."

"I see," said von Wolgast, fighting off a sudden sense of panic. "Tell me about the contract."

"You will want to read it over tonight," said Sisak at his most affable. "But its principle provision is the creation of a partnership between you and me for the purpose of running your arms manufacturing from a company in South Africa." He paid no heed to the shocked expression on von Wolgast's face. "This way, you will continue to realize a portion of the profits you have worked so hard to achieve, I will realize greater profits from dealing directly with a company in which I have part owner-ship, and the authorities will not be able to challenge our partnership, for it will be part of a much larger consortium of businesses held by South Africans and operated in many countries overseas." He beamed at von Wolgast. "As you see, I have considered everything."

The enormity of this proposal left von Wolgast stunned; he realized that he was in no position to refuse the terms offered him, that he had been neatly trapped by the arms dealer for whom he had had veiled contempt. He held out his hand. "Let me see the terms."

"Of course, Manfred," said Sisak, handing a copy of the contract to him. "You must be aware that since I am contributing the more signif-icant portion of protection, my share is sixty-five percent. You may not think that is entirely fair, but without me, it would not be possible for you to reclaim any of your money, so you will see my portion is not un-reasonable. Call it a service fee, if it will make the matter easier for you."

"Sixty-five percent, leaving me thirty-five," von Wolgast echoed hol-lowly. "I suppose you're right. I am in no position to dicker." He thought that he should make some greater protestation for the unequal division, but the words would not come. He wished he had schnapps or cognac to drink, so he could blunt the pain of this agreement, but none had been offered, not even for a fraudulent toast to their venture.

"No, you are not," said Sisak with immense gratification. He was silent for a short while, giving von Wolgast a chance to look over the first few pages. "As you can see, this requires you establish yourself in South Africa and that you not leave there. I cannot have my partner apprehended on murder charges, can I? Your assets would be frozen in Germany, and that would not do either of us any good. You see, these terms make it necessary that I do my utmost to keep you out of the hands of the police. It is not as if you will be without any fortune. And when war comes, we will both prosper as never before."

Von Wolgast swallowed hard: he had no real alternative other than to accept the terms laid out for him, no matter how usurious. Sisak had imprisoned him as certainly as the police in Berlin wanted to. "I will agree to that with a single exception."

Sisak regarded him in some astonishment. "What would that be? You have just escaped the law by a slim margin, and you say you do not want to remain in safety? Do you have dreams of going to Tibet, or New Caledonia, or—"

"No," said von Wolgast with grim purpose, the result of weeks of rumination and plotting. "I want to find Franchot Ragoczy and kill him."

Now it was Sisak's turn to be alarmed. "Franchot Ragoczy? Surely you can't want to endanger yourself on his account?" He saw that von Wolgast was sincere, and did his best to persuade him to see the foolishness of his desire. "I should have thought you have had enough of him. Doesn't it make sense to leave him alone and save yourself?" He indicated the contract. "If it is so important to you to have him done away with, it must be possible to find someone, such as Mamoud, to do the task for you."

"I will not permit him to be free in the world while I am a fugitive. His mission was nothing more than an excuse to display his pride at the expense of the Czar, who was taken in by Ragoczy's display. I will not let a charlatan end all I have worked for. If I must accept so much loss, he cannot be allowed to exist." His small eyes glittered.

"Must you do it yourself?" Sisak asked, aware that von Wolgast was unwilling to consider giving up his revenge.

"Reighert is beyond my reach, at present," said von Wolgast sarcastically.

"But isn't there someone else?" Sisak asked. "Someone you have engaged this way before?"

"There is a fellow in Amsterdam, named Bernard. I have tried to reach him but without success; I think he may be hiding from the police, for there has been no news of his capture." He stared at the nearest porthole. "It would not be the same, having someone else kill him. I have to do it myself."

Sisak shrugged. "If you must, you must." He pretended to think a bit more. "But I have one condition I would like you to weigh in regard to locating Ragoczy: let me have the task of finding him for you, through my agents, so you will not have to be in Europe one hour longer than you must. I will have an investment to protect, and you will have your neck." It was a concession he was willing to make in order to convince von Wolgast to accept his other, more important terms; it would also provide him the opportunity of keeping von Wolgast in his sights.

"I have told you that I have no wish to stand trial or be sent to prison," said von Wolgast with the air of one suffering an injustice.

"No, nor should you have to, if we arrange this wisely. I will accept that one change in this partnership." He touched the contract again. "Read this carefully and think it over. You may have some questions, which I suppose you will ask me in the morning." He did his best to look sympathetic. "You will not like some of the clauses, but if you give them due thought, you will see that they are not only necessary, they will make it possible for you to continue without constant anxiety in regard to the German authorities. I think you will conclude that the contract is a reasonable one, benefitting us both and ensuring our continuing affluence, if not on the scale you have known before, it will be opulent enough for South Africa." He all but shoved von Wolgast's fingers more tightly around the document. "You are an experienced businessman, Manfred, and you will not let your pique stop you from doing what is best for your company. Will you?"

Von Wolgast made himself say, "I want my business to flourish." Never had the truth had such a bitter taste.

"And this contract will guarantee it will. You will be in a position to contribute to key decisions, and you will stand to profit from the enterprise." Sisak put the portfolio back under his chair. "You will live at ease in South Africa while your company continues to produce arms, and to sell them to a range of buyers you would not be able to reach without a great deal of—"

"Yes, yes," von Wolgast cut through Sisak's recitation. "You do not need to hammer in it. I do know what you intend. I cannot make changes in what you propose without putting more than my fortune at risk, which I do not wish to do. So I will read over what you have set forth, and I will not object to any of the particulars, if you will promise me you will help me to rid the world of Franchot Ragoczy."

"If you insist," Sisak told him. "I hope you will reconsider."

"Doing it myself?" von Wolgast asked, "Or having it done at all?"

"Both, actually," said Sisak in a measured tone. "You must understand that Ragoczy has become something of a hero in important eyes. His welfare is considered worth looking after by police from Amsterdam to Moscow. If you could wait, a year, two, three, he might more easily be reached, and his death would cause less sensation than it would in the next several months."

"So he has become famous, and at my expense," said von Wolgast resentfully. "I would appear to have done him a favor."

"I think not," Sisak corrected him. "The Count shuns attention; he has declared he prefers his privacy to the glare of public notoriety." He leaned forward, looking von Wolgast directly in the eyes. "Use a little sense, Manfred. Put it off for a year at least."

"When Ragoczy will be back in Russia, no doubt guarded by a dozen Cossacks. No, thank you. I would rather reach him while I can, and while his death will provide vindication for me."

"Vindication?" Sisak made a gesture of exasperation. "It would be more likely to make your situation more . . . let us say, constrained than it already is. You have enough hanging over you, and yet you wish to increase the burden."

"I have to know Ragoczy is dead. I trust no one else to do it." He gave a laugh that was not good to hear. "I have earned the right to do this, Tancred. I do not want to have to rely on assassins and such men, who can be paid to change their alliances." He shook his head. "No. I want to see his blood."

Now Sisak was aggravated, and he put his hand on von Wolgast's knee. "If you must do away with him yourself, at least choose something less messy than blood. There are poisons that cannot be stopped and take a long time to kill." To press his argument, he said, "Think. You could administer the poison and leave him to weeks of agony."

"I would not see it," von Wolgast protested. "He would die and I would not be there."

"Ah, but he would suffer, and you would see the start of it, and you would know there would be no cure." Sisak rubbed his hands together. "A little pitchblende in his food and there is nothing that can be done. The radiation in the mineral will eat away his guts, and no physician in the world can save him." He smiled encouragement.

"How can you be so certain?" von Wolgast asked warily; the notion of prolonged suffering made him listen with interest.

"I learned it from a man who spent many years learning how to kill. He said he was taught this by the sorcerers who lived near diamond mines, where pitchblende is often found. The mineral has something in it that glows very faintly. The sorcerers told the man I knew that the reason for it was the demon that killed was present." He leaned back. "Tell me you will consider it. I will obtain some for you, if you decide it will do as well as a shot to the head with a pistol."

"Poison," said von Wolgast as if tasting the word. "All right, I will consider it. But"—he held up his hands to make his stipulation—"I will have to administer it. And see what it does. I must see him suffer; if it takes a long time, so much the better."

"Yes; very well. I will procure the pitchblende." Sisak picked up the pony and tossed off the cognac, then he looked narrowly at von Wolgast. "You'd like some, too?"

It was degrading to have to ask; von Wolgast kept himself from saying what he thought about the position he was in. "I'd welcome it, thank you."

"And we can toast our contract," said Sisak as if the idea had not occurred to him until this instant. "An excellent notion," he enthused. "What a good omen." He got out of the chair and went to the untended bar, reaching behind it for a regular glass. He poured a small amount of cognac into it from his own flask and brought it back to von Wolgast, holding it out in a way that made von Wolgast have to reach for it. "Here." He refilled his pony and lifted it. "To our partnership, Manfred. To success."

"To success," von Wolgast repeated dutifully, then added, "And revenge." With that he drank the cognac in a single swallow.

Text of a letter from Horace Saxon in Chicago to Rowena Saxon in Amsterdam.

Chicago, Illinois
May 10, 1911

Dear Rowena;
I'm pleased as a colt in a carrot patch that you're going to come and stay with me in San Francisco. We'll have a wonderful time. You can stay as long as you want, whether I'm here or not. I know you'll like

the city. I've been about the world a bit and I haven't found anything
to match it, not for setting and not for style. You'll see that for yourself when you're here. It means the world to me that you'd come to
bring some joy to the twilight of my life. Not that I mean to keep you
tethered to me to be a nursemaid or that I am in my dotage; that's not
the case at all. If I learned nothing else about you, Rowena, I've learned
you're a bird who will not have her wings clipped, and I won't be party
to anything that hampers you. You got my word that I'm not going to
try anything of the sort. With all that goes on in San Francisco, you'll
be able to have all the excitement you want without having to stay at
my side, unless you want to, and if you do, you can stay as long as you
like. Whatever you decide, I'll be glad to know you're just a telephone
call away. I'm going to see to it you have a telephone, and no argument, not so I can check on you, but so you can keep in touch with
the friends you're going to make without having to leave your studio
to do it.

As you can tell, I'm on my way to Baltimore to meet your boat. You'll
come back to California with me in my private car, so we can have a
little time to get face-to-face acquainted, and you'll have a chance to look
at the country. This letter is being sent via my solicitors there with instructions from me on booking your voyage. All you have to do is choose
the ship and the port you like, and end up in Baltimore. Don't you worry
about a thing. I'm taking care of the cost so all you have to do is put
your trunks aboard and put a quarter out for the waiter if you like the
service.

For once your mother approves of what I'm doing for you. She's written to me twice, the first time beside herself because she was sure you
were ruined, the next time to tell me how I should handle presenting
you to all those grand ladies of San Francisco she used to turn her nose
up at. She is determined to make the best of what she calls the "unhappy
events." I've written back telling her I know a thing or two about society, and that we'll do fine. I didn't mention that I found you a great studio with north light, the way you described in your letter. It's out on
Clay Street, and I can't say for sure, but I think you'll like it. I know
your mother is worried about earthquakes, and has been ever since '06,
but I told her we got the worst out of the way for a while. My house
stood up fine through the shaking and the fire, which did the most damage, stopped three blocks away from my house.

I'm a little worried about this Rupert; he sounds like a real fly in the
ointment, talking out of turn. Your mother says he's been going around
saying it wasn't his fault you fell into the hands of kidnappers, and that

*he tried to make sure you weren't in their hands a second longer than
you had to be, but that they had you for three days, and everyone
knows what that means. She says he is telling anyone who will listen
that he was forced to end your engagement because your honor has been
smirched, that he didn't have any choice about it. Your mother calls him
paltry, and acts as if this is something new in him that she is shocked
to see, as if he went bad suddenly, like butter. I don't see it that way. He
sounds like a scallywag to me, all airs and graces so long as everything
goes his way, and then sulky as a wet cat when it doesn't. Your mother
says she thinks that you ought to question what that Ragoczy fellow did,
but I take a different tack on it than she does. From what you told me,
he came and got you and has kept his eye on you since then, which is
what any real gentleman ought to do. You make sure and tell him I'm
in his debt for what he did for you. It might not mean much to him, but
what he did for you means the world to me.*

*I'm looking forward to seeing your paintings and displaying some of
them in my house, if you'll let me. Don't you fret about coming here,
you'll like it fine. I know no one can make up for what happened to you,
but I'd like to think you can get over it better here with me than in England, with your mother fretting over you, or in Europe, with all the
reminders around you. Whatever you decide eventually, I'm honored
you're giving me the chance to help out. And Rowena, you know I don't
mean the money.*

Until Baltimore,
Your loving grand-father,
Horace Saxon

10

Around them the fields of tulips were sultry as a tropical sunset; not far
away a windmill turned its sails in the brisk spring breeze. The weather
had turned pleasant at mid-May and now, in the second week of June,
with the promise of summer burgeoning everywhere, Holland was
showing itself at its most picturesque.

"I'm so glad you could come," Rowena told Ragoczy as the strolled
along the narrow path beside the little canal, the only people within a

kilometer of the place. She was wearing a handsome spring suit of caramel-colored linen, a lilac-silk blouse with a high collar of matching lace, and neat shoes with Louis heels; she had left her straw motoring hat at home, preferring to let the wind muss her short-cropped strawberry-blonde hair. Her smile was almost relaxed, although the strain of the last few months lingered in her golden eyes, as she stopped and put her hands on his shoulders. "Why is it I always think of you as taller than you are?" she asked before she kissed him. "You never seem short to me."

"A matter of perspective? With those shoes on, you and I are very nearly the same height," he suggested when he could speak. His dark eyes rested on her face, his hands at her waist, holding her, content to memorize her features and to take in the whole of her. "I thank you for your telegram; I did not want you to leave for America without saying good-bye."

"And I did not want to go without seeing you. When the letter arrived last week from my grand-father, I had to let you know what I had decided to do. Mister Sunbury made finding you quite easy." She took his hand as she resumed walking, looking at nothing in particular, content to wander wherever the path led. "Have you ever been there? America?"

"Not to where you are going. I've been in South America, and up into Mexico, but not to San Francisco; that city did not yet exist when I was in Mexico." He paused, his memories stirring. "It is no longer the place I remember, not Peru, not Mexico. The Spanish have seen to that."

"You told me about Peru, about Cuzco and the Incas, and the Dona Azul. But I won't find any of those, will I? It was more than two hundred years ago that you were there," she said, proud of remembering this. "I didn't know about San Francisco, but I was sure it wasn't built yet, if you had been there."

His eyes grew distant. "One of my blood was there, in San Francisco, more than fifty years ago. She said it was quite beautiful." As always, the thought of Madelaine de Montalia brought a pang of special loneliness to him.

Rowena caught something of this from his demeanor. "What is it? What's the matter?"

He was about to dismiss the question when he decided she deserved an answer. "It is something that comes to those of my blood, in my life. It is one of the things that make our circumstances as . . . intricate as they are." His voice was soft but penetrating. "Because vampires must seek life, we can no longer be lovers together when both of us have changed; life is the one thing vampires do not have to give one another."

She tried to make sense of what he was saying, although she did not want to believe what he was telling her. "You mean, those who become like you are no longer . . . you do not, or cannot—"

"Cannot," he said as gently as he could. "The love remains, but not the loving."

"You cease to be lovers when both are vampires?" she asked, very nearly repeating his explanation, as if by saying it aloud it would be more real; she was doing her best to mask her incredulity.

He answered her with compassion in his dark eyes. "Yes."

"So when life is over, so is love." She shook her head several times.

"No, loving goes on, as you well know," Ragoczy said, his compelling gaze on her. "It is our nature to seek the essence of life; and blood alone is strict . . . fare. With the life that comes with the blood there is also the bond."

She tried to keep her voice level, maintaining her composure. "And this woman, the one who was in San Francisco fifty years ago, she is a vampire," asked Rowena. She waited for the answer, pausing in the shade of an elm tree, so that Ragoczy would not have to stand in direct sunlight; the leaves above her did not quiver as much as she did.

"Yes. Since 1744. Her name is Madelaine. You have no reason to be jealous of her." He reached out with his free hand and touched her cheek with the back of his fingers. "She has an estate in Savoy and a house northeast of Paris. When I am near where she is the blood bond is . . . heightened."

"The blood bond," she repeated. "The way you knew where to find me?"

His voice was low and warm. "Yes."

"And you miss her? Don't you? You miss this Madelaine who has been a vampire since 1744." Rowena knew the answer, but wanted to hear what he would say; her hand grew tight in his.

"Yes: I miss all those who are lost to me, no matter how they are lost, or when, by coming to my life, or dying the true death," he said quietly. "Madelaine is part of my . . . life, as you are, Rowena. As you are: as you will always be." His lips were tantalizing on hers; she endured it for a moment, then wrapped her arms around him and clung to him with passion, her body pressed as close to him as her clothes would permit, as if to fix an impression of her reality upon him. When at last she drew back, he said, "You need not fear I will forget you: I will not."

He had identified her worry so clearly that she blinked. "I . . . I didn't really think you would," she admitted, still holding him.

"Ah." He kissed her again, slowly and deeply, taking all the time she longed for; he felt her need as keenly as he felt the nearness of running water, though her desire was much more pleasant. He could sense the desolation of spirit that had possessed her since von Wolgast had had her kidnapped; he did his best to assuage it, all the while knowing that she would need time and distance to put it behind her.

"You'll stay with me, tonight?" she asked when she broke away from him. "I'd like you to stay with me."

"Then I will be honored to," he said to her.

She managed to laugh, her voice sounding only a little tense. "Will I come to your life when I die?"

He held her gaze steadily. "We have shared loving more than six times, and each time you have known what was happening to you; you've known me for what I am. You were not lulled into sleep and then dreamed something very pleasant but without form: if my life is what you wish to have, it will be possible, within limits." He saw her look of eagerness mixed with doubt. "It is not necessarily certain. There are things you must avoid: if your body is burned, or your spine is destroyed, or you are embalmed, you will not become vampiric."

"So few precautions," she marveled. "No stake through the heart? No silver bullets? No Host in the coffin?" She made these accusations teasingly, without apprehension or malice, but they stung anyway.

"A stake through the heart shatters the spine," he said seriously. "Severing the head does, as well. A bullet, of whatever metal, in the spine or the head is as deadly to us as to anyone alive, and bullet wounds, no matter where, are never . . . pleasant." He felt her hand go to the place on his side where the buckshot had ripped into him. "If you decide to come to my life, you will need to remember these things, for your own safety. The Host in the coffin is nothing but theatrics, and Christian chauvinism. And garlic," he added, one brow lifting in sardonic amusement, "fortifies the blood and keeps away mosquitos and other insects carrying disease; it has no effect on vampires."

The amusement had faded from her features. "I . . . I didn't intend to . . . to make your life sound trivial. I'm sorry."

He caught her hands in his. "There is no need to be; only keep these precautions in mind when you choose whether you will come to my life or not. A vampire gains many things in this life, but it is not without cost."

She looked away, out over the fields of brilliant reds and oranges. "I have thought about it, Count." For all he had told her since they met, she was not fully convinced.

"Do you wish to tell me?" he asked gently. "I will know your decision, eventually."

"I think now that I would prefer to live and die as most of humanity must." She found the courage to look back at him. "I may change my mind as I grow older, but now, I think I do not want to face all the things you have had to face."

Ragoczy nodded his head once. "It would be useless to tell you that you would not have to endure a great deal. Any reading of history will tell you otherwise."

"And you have lived it: the Pharaohs, Nero, Charlemagne, Jenghiz Khan, the Black Plague, the Italian Renaissance, the French Revolution—" said Rowena, her attempt at levity forgotten. "I do not think I could—" She stopped, staring at him. "Do you ever regret your life?"

"Not the way you mean," he answered, with such tenderness that she felt tears well in her eyes. "There are many things I would have changed if they had been in my power for me to change them; that is not the same as regret." Memories of many of these things ran through his thoughts: the madness that had consumed Czar Ivan, Laurenzo dying of a disease Ragoczy now knew had been leukemia, the hideous death Jenfra had suffered, the hopeless stand T'en Chi-Yu had made. . . . He made himself look at Rowena, and put his whole concentration on her. "I will never regret the time I have been with you; I will treasure it. If I could change anything in what has been between us, it would be what you endured at von Wolgast's hands."

The tears spilled over. "Oh, Count," she cried, and once again took refuge in his arms, letting him hold her while she repeated, "I don't know why I'm doing this," over and over in disjointed phrases. Finally she straightened up. "It's time we were getting back. Tomorrow the packers are coming, and I want as much time alone with you as I can have."

He smiled quickly. "You are alone with me right now," he pointed out, as she dried her eyes with great determination.

"Not *this* alone. You know the alone I mean; the alone when we are all there is in the world." She managed a defiant laugh.

"You want to say good-bye through making love," he said, remembering how often intimacy had been the only way to express all that parting would mean.

"Yes." She was aware that many would chide him for his blunt reply, but she welcomed his direct answer. "Yes. We will be back in Amsterdam in a little more than an hour, and then there will be the rest of the afternoon, the evening, and night for us." She moved away from the elm tree, going toward where his new automobile—an Opel 6/16—was parked, a short distance away.

He followed after her, saying as he went, "Would you like to drive?" "Yes," she responded promptly. "But the Dutch farmers are not always best pleased to see woman behind the wheel. I will look at the scenery while you drive; I will not be seeing Holland again for a while." She turned around to face him, continuing to walk, backward, toward the Opel. "Besides, I trust you to drive well. I saw how you drove the Darracq through all that snow." The mention of that drive put a shadow over her face; she shook it off as quickly as she could. "Roads along dikes and canals are nothing compared to the Alps in winter."

He kissed his fingers to her. "Brava, carina mia," he approved.

"You're flattering me," she said, unable to sound displeased; she turned and faced the way she was walking.

"Never," he told her, doing his best to keep from wincing at the vivid sunlight. His native earth in the thick soles of his shoes provided some relief, but not quite enough to ward off the full impact of sunlight and water; he would have to ask Roger to change the lining before they left for London at the end of the week. "You wouldn't like being flattered," he added.

"No, I would not," she agreed after giving the notion a little thought. "I had more than enough of that from Rupert—or his version of it, in any case."

"I'm sorry he has made your situation so awkward with your family," Ragoczy said with genuine concern.

"So was I, at first. I still think he has been ungentlemanly in his complaints. But at least it has shaken my mother's desire to see me married to the man, and I am . . . well, not quite grateful, but appreciative of what he has done." She was almost at the automobile now, and she turned around to look at him again. "I'm sorry there won't be time to finish your portrait before I leave."

"Another time, then," he said as he reached her side and helped her to don her canvas driving coat, and then to climb into the passenger's seat. "I'm sure we will find time when you return."

"Yes. I told my grand-father I would stay five years, whether he is alive or not, and I will abide by my word. I think it will take that long to make the most of the opportunity he is offering me." She accepted his offer of goggles as he went to crank the Opel's starter.

"From what you have told me of him, you will have a champion in him; your family will have to approve his support of you," said Ragoczy, drawing on his duster before bending to work the starting crank.

"I have a champion already," she said quietly, rallying herself with a mental reminder that she was the one who had decided to leave. She raised her voice to be certain he heard her. "So, shall we say sometime in May of 1916? We can work out the specifics later."

"Certainly; I will look forward to it," he replied as the engine caught and idled. He got into the driver's seat and eased the motor car into gear. "I have nothing yet scheduled for 1916."

"How fortuitous," she exclaimed as they rolled along the road between fields of gorgeously smoldering tulips. "We shall consider the appointment made, then? Would you like to decide the rest—where and on what day, or shall we leave it until I have booked my return?"

"You will have to decide those things when you have made your plans to return; what month and day you choose, and the place. I will do all that I can to meet you at the time and place you select." He kept his attention on the road, using his voice to maintain the closeness between them. "If you are willing to give me your grand-father's address, I would like to have it, although it is not necessary: you may send any letter to me through my London solicitor if you prefer. Sunbury will always know where to find me. With his son in the firm, it will not matter if the elder leaves, there will still be someone handling my affairs."

"What about your address in Russia?" asked Rowena, puzzled by his suggestion. "Will you not be receiving mail through Mister Golovin?"

"I may be," said Ragoczy carefully as he paused at the main road to let a horse-drawn wagon laden with cabbages go by before he turned in the direction of Amsterdam. "I may not." He was aware of the questions that coursed through her. "Matters in Russia are uncertain. I have greater confidence in Britain than I do in Russia. Britain has the habit of stability that Russia has yet to achieve." He slowed down as a matronly woman in a widow's cap hurried her gaggle of geese off the side of the road.

Rowena looked worried. "You do not think that there will be . . . more trouble in Russia, do you? The papers give accounts of unrest, but surely that is on the wane. I thought the reforms put in place would make for better government, and bring about greater participation by the people. The reports have said that there have been improvements. The Duma is supposed to keep the country operating fairly. As long as that is being done, what trouble can there be?"

"If I knew, I would not be apprehensive about the future of the country," said Ragoczy with a stern smile. "So, if you will, use my solicitor in England to reach me. Let him know when you will be coming back, and where you would like me to meet you, and I give you my

word that if it is . . . humanly possible I will be there." He waved to a
farmer on a cob who was crossing one of the small bridges over the
canal, letting him and his mount cross the road in front of the Opel. "If
you want to reach me at any time, I hope you will write to me. I will
want to know what you are doing, how life in San Francisco is for you."

"I will," she said, so quickly that Ragoczy knew she had been worried about how complete their separation would be.

"Good; I will look forward to your letters." They were almost at the
fork in the road, one of which led to Antwerp, the other of which went
to Amsterdam; Ragoczy steered his way onto the Amsterdam road, and
fell in behind a lorry.

"Can you overtake him?" asked Rowena after a few minutes.

"Yes, but the traffic is getting slower." He kept to his position, and
was rewarded for his patience at the next large intersection, where the
lorry turned away toward Rotterdam.

They continued on into Amsterdam, and were nearly at Rowena's
house when she said with false nonchalance, "Did you learn anything
more in Berlin? About the case?" There could only be one case she
would ask about.

"Reighert has made a full statement in the hope of securing mercy
from the court," said Ragoczy. "He gave a full account of Nadezna's
murder and your abduction, as well as the death of von Wolgast's wife.
Blau says it is horrific reading, and that if even half of it is true, von Wolgast will be condemned to death in absentia."

"And von Wolgast himself? Do they know how he has achieved his
absent state?" asked Rowena, her voice tightening as she spoke the
name. "What has become of him? Have you heard anything?"

"Nothing reliable. Inspector Blau told me that most of the profits of
von Wolgast's company are being funneled to a managing company in
South Africa, which may or may not mean anything."

"South Africa," she said dully. "Do you think he will ever be caught?
Really?"

"I think that will depend on von Wolgast," said Ragoczy with conviction. "He is the sort of man who may yet prove to be his own worst
enemy."

Again she fell silent; as the Opel turned along the canal fronting her
house, she said, "It has not been easy staying here."

"But you did not want him to win," said Ragoczy, certain of her emotions on this issue. "You remained so he would not have the satisfaction
of driving you out."

She smiled, her eyes wistful. "Yes; that's it. I also had to prove to myself that he had not driven me off."

"So that you can go to America with a clear conscience," said Ragoczy as he pulled into the narrow parking slot near the steps to the front door.

This time her face softened as she turned to him. "It will be good to have my last recollections of this house be of you and me together."

He set the brake and got out of the Opel, then went around to open her door for her, taking the goggles she gave back to him and stuffing them into his pocket. As he offered his arm, he said, "You said the removers come to pack tomorrow. When are they supposed to arrive?"

"I told them no earlier than ten," she said, a little of her old mischief flaring in her golden eyes. "You have nothing to worry about."

"I was not worried, Rowena," said Ragoczy, not quite truthfully; it was not the hour that troubled him but Rowena's unstated need for his annealing presence. Much as he longed to see her wholly recovered from all she endured, he was aware it would not happen from intention alone; time and experience would provide the anodyne she sought, far more than any fulfillment he could provide. Her desire for their shared passion concealed a more complicated craving, and he was unsure that he could address that yearning for restoration that held her as surely as her blood bound him to her: it would take more than a long night together to provide her with the inner strength she had for so long taken for granted.

She turned the key in the lock and went into her house, stepping aside for Ragoczy and locking the door behind him. "It seems wisest," she explained.

He made no comment for none was required. He took off his driving duster of black canvas and hung it on one of the hooks by the door. "You said there were some more studies of the canals you had done? May I see them?"

"We might as well get this behind us—so we can concentrate on other things," she said, a trifle too urgently; her fear of the house had not abated as much as she liked to think it had. She shrugged out of the wrapper she had worn in the Opel.

"I will follow you up," he said, taking her driving coat from her and putting it on the hook nearest the door.

"You are very good to me," she said suddenly as she started up the stairs to the floor above.

His smile was enough to make her breath catch. "I would say it was the other way around." He came to the bottom of the stairs and looked up at her. "Well, Miss Saxon?"

"Well, Count Saint-Germain?" she countered, and with a sudden laugh, she raced up the stairs, glancing back over her shoulder to be sure he was behind her. If her voice was slightly too high-pitched to indicate real pleasure, and if she ran more in flight than abandon, neither she nor Ragoczy mentioned it: she pounded up the second flight of stairs, and stumbled into the studio.

"Rowena?" Ragoczy asked from behind her, knowing that some abrupt change had come over her, for she stood, still and shaking, as if unable to move.

"Oh, God," she whispered, sagging against the railing beside the stairwell. "Oh, God, God, God."

Ragoczy went up the last four steps in a single, swift movement, and halted beside her, seeing for himself what had so transformed her.

The easel holding her portrait of him stood in the center of the room, angled to face the top of the stairs. The drape had been removed, revealing slashed tatters that obliterated the image in the painting.

"What?" Rowena whispered as she felt Ragoczy's arm around her shoulder. "Who?"

"Whoever it is, we are intended to be frightened," said Ragoczy with such calm that Rowena stared at him.

"Then he was successful. I *am* frightened." Admitting this restored her self-control; she went to the easel and lifted her hand as if to touch the ruined portrait. Then her hand dropped. "I am so sorry, Count. I had intended to finish it—"

"I am sorry, as well," he agreed, coming to her side again, trying to listen to every sound in the house, from the dripping of water in the bathroom on the floor below to the footfalls and voices rising from the street and the canal. "But you have no reason to apologize to me. You are not responsible for this."

She lowered her eyes, her anxiety growing stronger; her voice became a rough whisper. "He could still be in the house, couldn't he? You don't think—"

"That the person who did this is nearby?" He drew her closer, hoping to lend her some of his fortitude through his nearness as he admitted his foreboding. "Yes, I do. This is a message, meant to scare and anger us. Whoever did this would want to be certain he achieved his desired effect."

"And it has," she said, pulling back and turning away from the devastation of her work. "I can't—"

"Let me cover it with something. Where do you keep your drapes?"

Ragoczy asked, knowing that any activity was preferable to remaining paralyzed.

"In the cupboard, toward the rear of the room," she said absently, her gaze still fixed on the wreckage.

There was a sound at the foot of the upper flight of stairs: Ragoczy recognized it at once as a single crack of laughter. He felt Rowena stiffen beside him, and he reached out to touch her once more. "We will get through this," he told her very softly.

"How gallant," von Wolgast said derisively in German as he came up the stairs, a pistol in one hand, a long knife in the other. He was not the same affluent, arrogant personage Ragoczy and Rowena had seen in April: he was thinner, with the first telltale signs of self-indulgence softening his features; the flesh under his chin was sagging and the pouches beneath his eyes were more pronounced than they had been three months ago. His stance was subtly belligerent, no longer expressing hauteur, but something more menacing. His clothes were good quality but unremarkable, the sort of suit any traveler might wear on a sea voyage; there was a bulge in his waistcoat that Ragoczy assumed was another weapon. Only the shine of his eyes was harder than it had been, and his cupid's-bow mouth had become narrow and sullen. "Going to protect her, are you, you imposter? What makes you think you can?"

To her astonishment, Rowena spat at von Wolgast.

He laughed once more. "You will apologize for that before I leave—apologize and make amends to my specification," he promised her, his expression becoming implacable. He swung toward Ragoczy. "You should really instruct Erich Rotscheune to be more careful in what he tells persons asking for you. He has a high opinion of you, for reasons I cannot fathom, and it leads him to boast. He has more than once revealed things about you that you would prefer to have kept quiet. It took no more than one or two questions and my . . . associate learned all he needed to know."

"I suppose I should discuss the problem with him," said Ragoczy, his manner composed; he stood with every appearance of ease, as if he were not facing a knife and a pistol. "When I am next in Berlin, I will attend to it."

"When you are next in Berlin," von Wolgast repeated, mocking Ragoczy with everything from the tone of his voice to his posture. "You have given instructions to bury you there?"

Rowena heard herself gasp; she moved a few steps closer to Ragoczy, near enough to touch him. She understood enough German to know that von Wolgast intended more than harm.

"Actually, I would prefer to lie in my native earth, which is in the Carpathians, as you are no doubt aware." Ragoczy's urbanity was not what von Wolgast was expecting; the Count took advantage of this. "Was it your personal animosity toward me that made you ruin Miss Saxon's portrait, or was it something more?" He was well-aware that the destruction of the canvas had more than one purpose, but he would not say as much to von Wolgast. "If you despise me so profoundly, mightn't you have found a more direct way to express it? Why drag Miss Saxon into it again?"

"I am not the idiot you think me," von Wolgast proclaimed. "I will not let her escape me a second time."

This distressed Ragoczy but he maintained his outward aplomb. "You have nullified any claim to being a gentleman if you act against Miss Saxon. You have done more than enough to her already."

Von Wolgast shook his head, gesturing with his knife as if wagging an admonitory finger at Ragoczy. "Oh, no. You will not provoke me to anything hasty. I will not be robbed of my vengeance."

Ragoczy gave a little shrug. "In another century you would be telling me to name my seconds, Baron. If any would support you in so ignoble a challenge." His hand brushed Rowena's, a gesture so minor that it seemed unimportant, nothing more than a gesture intended to reassure her.

"Name your seconds? I would not sully my reputation with meeting you. You deserve only to be horsewhipped," declared von Wolgast, forgetting his resolve of a moment ago.

"You have come a long way for a task a lackey might do, and have exposed yourself to arrest as well: I must suppose you have gone to some effort to find me in order to exact your . . . revenge," Ragoczy pointed out, his outward demeanor remaining undisturbed. "I am still at a loss to understand why you detest me."

"You are right," von Wolgast said. "I have come a very long way, and with a single purpose." He stood more erect. "I have been dreaming of this moment for months."

"But why?" Ragoczy persisted reasonably. "What have I done that so offends you?"

"You are a charlatan! You are a deceiver! You cozened your way into the Czar's confidence, but you cannot work your hoax on me." This time his gesture with the knife was broader, more determined. "You took advantage of everyone, posing as something you are not, and doing your best to destroy my business! *My business!*"

Rowena stepped back, seeking to avoid any sudden thrust von Wolgast might make; she drifted to the right as the fleeting pressure of Ragoczy's fingers had urged her to do. She strove to fight off the nausea that threatened to overcome her, brought on by von Wolgast's presence; she had not realized until von Wolgast appeared how loathsome he was to her. As she attempted to position herself where Ragoczy wanted her to be, she stared with fascination as the Count continued his verbal fencing with von Wolgast.

"What convinces you I ever had the least interest in your business?" asked Ragoczy.

"You were in Germany to persuade the Kaiser to disarm, weren't you? You wanted to destroy all I have worked to achieve." He did not give any time for an answer. "You needn't deny it. Germany has friends in England, and word of what you tried with England's Edward reached me in time to thwart your aims. Your fraud was not perpetrated in Germany, and George of England knows better than to interfere with German aims in Europe."

"At another time, I might like to know what those aims might be," said Ragoczy. "At present I have more pressing things to attend to."

This continuing lack of fright that Ragoczy demonstrated made von Wolgast wild; his stance became more threatening. "You will have to hear them now, for you will never have the opportunity to do so again."

"And why is that?" Ragoczy made another slight movement of his fingers; Rowena slowly began to move behind him.

This was what von Wolgast was waiting for; he would have preferred to have Ragoczy cringing in dread, pleading with him for pity, but this would have to do. He was convinced what he told Ragoczy next would erase that maddening poise at last. "I have something with me." He tapped the bulge in his waistcoat with the point of his knife. "I have brought it especially for you. I have seen how it works." His tongue flicked over his lips. "I have pitchblende mixed with certain herbs."

Ragoczy heard this with trepidation, for he had seen for himself what pitchblende could do. "And what do you intend to do with it?" He folded his arms and waited.

"If you will drink it, in coffee or tea or wine—it doesn't matter which—I may spare Miss Saxon any further distress at my hands. If you will not, she will answer for your refusal in ways that neither she nor you would like." He rocked back on his heels. "I will not be able to stay to watch the whole of it, unfortunately. But I will have the chance to see the beginning, and take what pride I can in knowing nothing on earth can save you."

"Are you certain of that?" Ragoczy's one experience with pitchblende had been over two thousand years ago, and it had taken him more than a century to recover fully from the injuries the substance had caused. The only thing he had endured since his vampiric renewal from death that was worse than the ravages of pitchblende was crucifixion.

"I certainly am. I saw a man die of it last month, to be certain you would suffer enough for all you have done to me." He motioned Ragoczy to get back so there would be room to move about the studio while he talked. "It takes very little, and it can be inhaled as well as drunk, but if it is swallowed the death is more painful, although not quite so long. The pitchblende causes lesions at first, on the lips, very disfiguring. Poured into an open wound, it is worse than gangrene. Once in the body it begins to eat away at the vitals, slowly consuming them. I am told it can take up to ten days to kill. I understand some go mad from agony. I am sorry I will not have the opportunity to see if you are stalwart enough to endure it to the end. You may have to take von Rosenwiese's way out, and kill yourself like the coward you are." Again he used the knife to tap the bulge. "Pernicious stuff, you'll agree. I was warned that it must be carried in lead crystal, or it might cause me some minor discomfort. I have a considerable amount of it here: four grams."

Rowena listened to this hideous recitation with increasing dread. She wanted to tell Ragoczy to refuse to take the poison, but she could not make the words come. She never thought she could be so lacking in character, but she knew she could not tolerate having von Wolgast touch her, let alone anything more than he had had done already. She felt Ragoczy's hand on hers. "Count . . . "

"You have nothing to fear," he said to her in English.

Von Wolgast's amusement was triumphant, for although he did not know English well, he recognized the intent of Ragoczy's words. "Ach, ja. Console the little lady, Ragoczy. Tell her she will enjoy what she and I will do together."

Ragoczy discovered he could abhor von Wolgast far more than he already did. "It will not matter what I do, will it, Baron?" He made von Wolgast's title an obscenity. "You are not going to let her go, are you?"

"And have her accuse me again?" von Wolgast asked, savoring the little cry Rowena gave almost as much as the hatred he saw in Ragoczy's penetrating eyes.

"You will have the opportunity to find out," von Wolgast said, smugness turning his face to a travesty of good humor. "You will see it all. Your anguish will be beyond description."

Had he confronted von Wolgast alone, Ragoczy might well have cringed, giving the man what he sought until he made the fatal error of assuming Ragoczy was cowed. But Rowena was depending on him to sustain her; he felt this with staggering intensity; he would not have the chance to indulge von Wolgast's wishes to distract him. Whatever action Ragoczy took against von Wolgast, he would have to do it swiftly. He gathered himself for a single attack. "You have no reason to hurt Miss Saxon," Ragoczy said, knowing von Wolgast was expecting some endeavor on his part to hold off what von Wolgast believed was the inevitable.

"I have reason to hurt *you*, for all you have done to me." Von Wolgast's glare was severe. "If you had not tried to ruin me, if you had not supported Nadezna, I would have endured your existence. But you had to—" He stopped, visibly striving to master himself.

With Ragoczy serving as a shield, Rowena reached out to the cabinet where her store of painting supplies were kept and eased the door open, forcing herself not to hurry; speed could only bring about disaster. She knew where everything in the little cupboard was, and found the large cylindrical tin of turpentine by touch. As she closed her hand around it, she had to overcome the rush of fear that went through her; she concentrated on removing the cap, hoping that the odor would not alert von Wolgast to what she was doing. With more will than she realized she possessed, she seized the tin of turpentine and pressed it against the back of Ragoczy's thigh. She saw him nod slightly as his hand moved to take it.

"Well, I haven't got much time," said von Wolgast with amicable malice. "We might as well get started. Ragoczy, you will lead the way. Miss Saxon, you will go next, just in front of me, so that your supposed Count will not be tempted to do anything reckless." He wiggled the pistol, urging them to comply.

Rowena stayed close behind Ragoczy, concealing the turpentine tin and finding solace in Ragoczy's nearness. She looked down and noticed a large drop of turpentine had got onto the caramel-colored linen of her skirt, darkening it. Flinching at this, she hoped von Wolgast would not notice it, or realize its implication.

"Down the stairs," said von Wolgast victoriously. "Stop at the bottom of the flight before going down to the ground floor. Miss Saxon will be directly in front of me. I will use the knife on her, not the pistol. Keep that in mind."

Very carefully Ragoczy began his descent, appearing to hesitate with each step. He dared not say anything to Rowena, certain that his one desperate chance would fail if he alerted her; he would have to depend on her trust in him, and her good sense. When he was one step from the bottom, he seemed to stumble and to grab out for balance. His hand missed the railing and shoved Rowena aside as he spun around and flung the turpentine from its tin up into von Wolgast's face, at the same time pulling Rowena the rest of the way down the stairs and dragging her out of reach before turning to face von Wolgast.

The stink and the pain struck von Wolgast at the same time as the turpentine splashed into his eyes and down his face. He dropped his knife as he tried to wipe the liquid away, and in the next instant lost his footing and began a stumbling fall down the stairs. His pistol went off twice and he screamed out his odium for Ragoczy. He crashed to the floor prone, howling in pain.

In a breath, Ragoczy was standing over him, his foot on the back of his neck as he reached for von Wolgast's arm, intending to twist it behind him. Only when his wrist was in Ragoczy's steely grip did he remove his foot from the Baron's neck.

Von Wolgast screamed. "NO!" His face went ashen and he ceased to struggle with his captor, although his body was stiff with pain. "Mein Gott, no," he whispered.

"Get up, von Wolgast," Ragoczy ordered, without a trace of fear. "On your feet."

At the first pull on his arm, von Wolgast shrieked. As the pressure eased, he whimpered. "I can't."

"Then I will help you," said Ragoczy, and with a strength that was lost on von Wolgast, lifted the man upright in one fluid movement.

Then they all saw the blood. It spread across von Wolgast's waistcoat, staining his shirt and the lapel of his coat. As he took two steps away from Ragoczy, small shards of glass glittered in the center of the bright red aureole. "It . . . broke," von Wolgast said softly in the aghast silence. He put his hand to his waistcoat, and drew it back, pinpricks of blood on his fingers. "It *broke!*" he repeated as the full importance of the wound struck him. He stared down at himself. "The pitchblende . . . " His words trailed away.

Suddenly Rowena rushed at von Wolgast, her hands ready to gouge and tear. She yelled with frustration as Ragoczy caught and held her. "I will!" she shouted; she wanted to hurt him.

"It isn't safe, Rowena," Ragoczy said somberly, continuing to restrain her until she ceased to struggle. "You do not want the pitchblende on you. You do not want to cut yourself on the glass."

The quiet authority of his words finally reached her. "You mean what he said was true? There is such a poison?"

The enigmatic expression in Ragoczy's dark eyes held more visions of remembered wretchedness than she could imagine. "Yes. And he is unfortunate enough to know how he will die."

Von Wolgast began to wail, the sound like that of a lost child. He made an attempt to pluck out the splinters of glass, then gave it up with a groan. With an abrupt lunge, he dove for his pistol, now lying near the top of the other flight of stairs; Ragoczy was too quick, and kicked the pistol down to the ground floor before von Wolgast could reach it. This time he lay, his knees drawn up, mewing sobs.

"What is going to happen to him?" Rowena asked as she stared down at von Wolgast.

"He described it quite well," Ragoczy said, and went down on one knee beside the Baron. "Miss Saxon is going to send for an ambulance," he said kindly.

"Oh, no, I am not," said Rowena as her detestation of von Wolgast resurged.

"Oh, yes, you are," Ragoczy said quietly. "He will need all the care he can be given. And it will all be in vain." The desolation in Ragoczy's face was beyond anything Rowena had ever seen, and she was shaken.

"All right," she said, taking care to walk well out of von Wolgast's reach as she started for the stairs.

"If we leave him alone," Ragoczy added, his words colder than arctic midnight, "he might find a way to take his own life, and he cannot be allowed such a cowardly death, when he has condemned himself." He stared down at von Wolgast. "In another time I would have offered you syrup of poppies, to ease your torments. Remember as your last hours pass that you were prepared to let me endure what you will now endure."

The ragged cry of "You must not! Gott in Himmel, you must not!" that von Wolgast gave sped Rowena on her way; she could not bear to remain with her stricken enemy, afraid that she might begin to understand the relentless, stern compassion Ragoczy had shown, and what it had cost him to attain it.

Text of a dispatch from Sidney Reilly to "C", sent in code using Key 17, from Berlin, Germany, to London, England by English embassy communique, delivered October 2, 1911.

So you are putting me back on my tether. Very well, I will do your bidding once again. Your courier handed your instructions to me at the Flying Competition, in which, as you must have been informed, I placed second, in the person of Karl Hahn. I am delighted to be flying once again; it has been too long. Incidentally, this courier was an improvement on the so-called Angebot, but surely you could have found a more original name for him to use than Jones. I will be leaving for Prague in the morning, where Oertel Morgenstern will vanish once again, and Sidney Reilly will return, as per your orders, to Saint Petersburg, there to resume my usual style of life. If you intend this as a reprimand, you have not achieved your goal. If you intend to learn more about Franchot Ragoczy's activities, I will be well-situated to observe him, along with the others you have stipulated. I am curious about young Alexendr Kerensky as well as some of the others you have assigned; I am inclined to surveil him in addition to the rest. You may think he is nothing more than an intellectual firebrand, impressed with his own rhetoric, but I am not so sure that he will be gone from the public eye once his education is over.

The report from the Amsterdam hospital on von Wolgast's death makes grim reading. One day you must tell me how you contrived to get a copy of those records. To linger for nine days in such hideous agony. If I were a more soft-hearted chap, I could almost feel sorry for that corrupt, murdering swine. Is there any truth to the rumor that the company that now owns von Wolgast's arms factory is controlled by Tancred Sisak? For the sake of the world, I hope not: that is precisely the kind of gossip one expects when a new ownership takes over a crucial business. It is bad enough having Sisak dealing with every lunatic group with money enough for his purposes; if he had the capacity to manufacture guns as well as sell them, the peace of the world would be far more precarious than it already is.

While I have not been as diligent in my observation of Ragoczy, I have learned that he has assisted the police in trying to discover what has become of von Wolgast's fortune; whatever he was able to tell the authorities, I have not yet determined, but it must have been sufficient for their purposes. I had it from Erich Rotscheune that Ragoczy has wound up his affairs in Germany for the time being, which would tend to indicate he will not be returning here for some time. Rotscheune said he has no reason to expect him again until 1913, and for that reason has signed the title to the house over to Rotscheune, with the provision that it can only be let to Ragoczy himself. From what I was told, the offer was so generous that Rotscheune took it at once.

I continue to be absolutely convinced that the trouble in the Balkans is dangerous to the peace of all Europe. It may look like nothing more than one of those periodic escalations of hostilites that occur from time to time, but I believe what is happening now is substantially different than what we have seen before. With the Turks out of the way, all the old hatred are flaring. You may call me an alarmist, but I know you share my concerns. If you do not see them as the threat I do, it is only because you have not recently seen what I have. The peace in Serbia is a sham, and I tell you now it will not last. Now that I am back in harness, I will do what I can to persuade you to view the Balkans as dangerous to more than Austro-Hungary. Expect that next week's dispatch will come from Saint Petersburg, unless you countermand your orders in the next two days. I am only sorry to have to give up flying until spring, but an open cockpit over Russia in the winter? No, thank you.

Sidney Reilly (Capt.)

11

Franchot Ragoczy arrived at Countess Amalija Romanovna Kormanskaya's mansion as the first heavy snow was falling on Saint Petersburg, filling the night with a ghostly whiteness that made the whole city appear to be a gossamer image in a dream. He was pleased when Gennady opened the door promptly, and he murmured a few words of appreciation as he handed over his heavy coat and Astrakhan lamb hat. "They are in the dining room, I suppose?"

"Yes. They have eaten supper and they are expecting you. I trust you enjoyed the concert?" He indicated the stair leading up to the salons and dining room.

"Yes, thank you. I like Borodin and Grieg." Ragoczy nodded his understanding of the instructions he had been given as he twitched the sleeve of his faultless evening clothes; on the sash over his claw-tailed coat the Order of Saint Stephen of Hungary blazed, a starburst of diamonds. Satisfied he was in order, he made his way up the stairs and along the gallery to the dining room door, pausing to knock once before entering.

The long rosewood table was made to accommodate twenty; tonight there were places laid only at the far end, for an elegant, private party

of three: Countess Amalija, her nephew Duke Leonid Ohchenov, and
Nikolai Alexandreivich Romanov, Czar of all the Russias. Had they not
been in court regalia they might have looked like any mother dining with
grown sons; no servants lingered to wait on the small party, and the ease
of a casual evening belied the diners' formal evening wear. The remains
of a goose lay on a platter between them looking like the beams of a
long-wrecked ship, and other serving dishes attested to a lavish five-
course meal, accompanied by select French wines. At the moment two
bowls of chocolates were being passed among the three, and a bottle
of cognac stood open beside Leonid's elbow.

"Ah, Count," said Countess Amalija, rising to greet this new arrival.
She went toward him, her satin gown whispering, the jewels at her
throat, hanging from her ears, and standing in her hair twinkling in the
soft gaslight glow. She offered her hand to kiss, and smiled as he bowed
to her; the scent of violets, roses, and sandalwood was on her wrist. "I
was certain you would arrive before midnight."

"And here I am with twenty minutes to spare," he said, going to bow
to Nikolai, and then to shake hands with Leonid. "I know you have had
a wonderful evening; I need only look around to—"

"Not quite wonderful," said Nikolai, his expression somber. "I had a
telegram yesterday from Buda-Pest. My Ambassador there informs me
that the unrest in the Balkans is growing worse. The Serbs are an ob-
streperous lot."

"I am sorry to hear it," said Ragoczy, who was not surprised. "If I may
ask, how specific was the news?"

"You have the right to know more than anyone I could think of. It
is specific enough," said Nikolai, sighing. He made an attempt at levity. "Better in the Balkans than in the streets of Saint Petersburg, I suppose." The hesitant smiles that greeted this provided little relief for
him. "I have spent a good portion of the evening trying to think of anything more I can do; I fear I have not been the best company. You need
not claim otherwise; I know how I have been behaving. I apologize
for my preoccupation, but there is so much to consider. Sunny tells
me that Otyets Grigori will have the answer, but I am not convinced
it is so. Not that I question her devotion to Grigori Efimovich, or his
wisdom. I know our son would not be alive without him." He cleared
his throat. "We—that is the family—are leaving for Moskva tomorrow. There are matter of state that must be dealt with there, and
Stolypin has recommended it. Had the family been against it, I might
have refused to go, but . . . It will be dreary travel, but Sunny is certain that Moskva is better for Alexei in winter than is Saint Petersburg.

So—" He lifted his hand in acquiescence, his face sad.

"You have done all anyone could expect of you, Little Father," said Ragoczy, using the old honorific for the Czar with all the kindness he could offer; he shared some of Nikolai's distress, but not so acutely as the Czar felt it.

Leonid poured more cognac for Nikolai and then for his aunt, refilling his glass last of all. "I cannot help but worry about my children. If war comes, they will bear the brunt of the suffering, if they survive. War is worse than plagues for most children, for they are spared nothing. I am worried for my youngest brother, too. You've met him, Count. Konstantine. He is proud to be a Guard cadet, but in battle, he would be nothing but a green boy."

"Green boys do not often—" Nikolai began, halting before he said too much. "And my daughters are all honorary officers in my best regiments, not that there is the least chance they would ever have to face enemy bullets, but when I see them in uniform, I cannot hide my anxiety for their well-being. Of course, they would want to do their part: attend the wounded in hospital, and visit the men at the front to cheer them. I could never want any of my children to be hurt. It would be agony to see Alexei prepare to fight, he is so young, though the troops expect the Czareivich to be with them, to lead them. Alexei cannot be allowed to expose himself to danger, not while he is—" He silenced himself.

"And your heir is not a strong child, is he?" Ragoczy asked with such gentleness that he did not offend Nikolai.

"I would not like to see any of them come to grief," said the Czar stiffly, aware that it was not suitable for him to admit any failing in Alexei.

"Nor would any other parent," said Leonid, his regular features darkening with the thoughts crowding his mind. "I cannot bear to think of any child of mine having to suffer, no matter what the cause—bee sting or war, it is only a question of scale. To have a child die is unbearable, but to see one suffer is the torment of hell."

"For heaven's sake, not again," said Countess Amalija, her voice brisk and her eyes shining, "Must we end our meal shrouded in gloom? When we were doing so well? Can't we have a bit of amusement? Count," she plowed on, "tell us about the concert. Unless it was filled with dirges, or Mahler."

"It was Borodin," said Ragoczy, prepared to do as she wished. "All strings. Actually very nice. They ended with a little Grieg: the *Holberg Suite*. I think it must have been a concession to the Europeans in the audience."

"Grieg is Norwegian, isn't he?" asked the Countess, doing her best to bring about the participation of the others by enthusiasm alone.

"Yes, but that is closer to Europe than Russia," Ragoczy pointed out, smiling easily as he escorted Countess Amalija back to her place at the head of the table, then took a seat next to Leonid, his chair angled slightly away from the table.

"And better than some of the moderns. How anyone can listen to Richard Strauss, I cannot imagine," said Leonid. "I've tried to sit through some of his works, and I always end up itching all over before the music is half-finished." He, too, realized that it was not appropriate to speak about the Czareivich as they had done.

"The only Strauss I like," said the Countess as she selected another chocolate, "is Johann. Now there was a composer." She began to hum the *Village Swallows*, letting herself get caught up in the tantalizing three-quarter time. "When I was twenty years younger, I would waltz the night away, and think nothing of it. But that was twenty years ago." She shook her head once. "Now it is an effort to dance for more than an hour, and for the rest of the ball, I am content to relinquish the floor to those younger than I. Well, it is the way of all flesh, the burden of our years." She glanced at Ragoczy. "Or almost all."

Ragoczy held up his hands in protest, as if he misunderstood her remark. "I must apologize, my dear; I am no dancer. No, even in my younger days, I did not bow to Terpsichore's altar." Much as he loved music, he had never discovered any desire within himself to dance, no matter how much he appreciated watching it done.

"I've wondered about that," Nikolai said, doing his best to participate in the new direction their conversation had taken. "I thought at first you had had no opportunity to learn; then I realized you fence well and move gracefully, and I became more puzzled."

"Unfortunately, Czar, it takes more than grace and a good feint to dance. When it comes to dancing I often play the music, which, you will agree, is important." Ragoczy made a game of sighing, his thoughts going back more than two millennia, recalling the many times he had used his ability to play well to his advantage, and the many times it had provided him solace when nothing else could. "So while I play, I merely watch all those lovely women whirl around the floor in their partners' arms."

"And dream about them?" Leonid suggested with a wink.

"Perhaps." Ragoczy stared into the middle distance. "And perhaps, one of them might dream of me." For the last five months he had been able to spend time with Countess Amalija, but that would not continue indefinitely no matter how willing she continued to be. Eventually he would have to return to his more usual but less satisfactory source of sustenance—visiting women while they dreamed and providing their fulfillment without their knowledge of him; it was how he had survived as long as he had. The necessity of it saddened him.

"Who would have suspected you had such a romantic streak, Count?" Leonid said lightly.

"And in a man my age, too; shocking, isn't it." Ragoczy made a motion, declining the offer of cognac.

"I wouldn't say so," remarked Countess Amalija, her brows lifting significantly. "In fact, I am grateful that the Count is willing to say what he thinks; so many men become mealy-mouthed after thirty, as if they never had an improper thought in their lives."

"I've noticed that, too," said Nikolai. "The women often are that way from the start," he added, not quite disapproving. "Not that it would be fitting for women to swear like troopers, or laugh at lascivious jokes."

"I should think not," said Leonid with spirit. "There are women, of course, who bring out the . . . beast in men, but it isn't wise to marry one who does." He reached out for another chocolate. "Wives are meant to be our comrades in life, not our adventures," He glanced in the direction of his aunt, and added in chastened tones, "Not that I do not adore Irina, for I do. And you know I do not keep a mistress."

"You might, if you could afford her," said Countess Amalija, practicality taking the acid out of her remark. "You might want to have a mistress as capricious as Irina is loyal." She tossed her head and the diamonds in her tiara flashed. "I know the ways of men, and I have learned it is folly to try to hold them to the same standards of conduct that women are. You men are so worried about heirs and lineage, and their fear of comparison with others. Not that I am unmindful of family bonds, for blood calls to blood. Wouldn't you agree, Count?"

"Most certainly," said Ragoczy promptly, knowing that Countess Amalija was having a marvelous time tweaking him this way; he hoped she would discontinue her sport soon, for he wanted no awkward questions to arise in the minds of Nikolai or Leonid. "The bond of blood is undeniable."

"And it endures as nothing else can," said Nikolai, mistaking Ragoczy's meaning. "There are times I worry that my line will end with Alexei." He shook his head once, as if trying to sort out how he came to make such an admission. "Of course, my brother is alive and well, Gospodi pomilyiu."

"Your daughters, too, will no doubt marry suitably," said Leonid, and not simply to curry favor with the Czar. "They are all such beauties, most charming, and truly accomplished, not like some of the noblewomen one sees trotted about the world. Remember that Spanish Duquessa who was here four years ago? She was small as a dwarf and ignorant as a Crimean peasant. I do not wonder that her father was hard-pressed to find her a husband." He made no excuse for his sharp tongue, a sign that the cognac was getting to him.

"Leonid," his aunt reprimanded him. "The poor woman could not help those things."

"But her family had perpetuated them, marrying cousins to cousins for generation upon generation." He stopped and glanced at the Czar, whose background had its share of cousins, and whose Czarina was more closely related to him than was entirely wise. He stared down into the nearest bowl of chocolates. "Not that these things were understood in the past."

"The royalty of ancient Egypt usually married brother to sister," Ragoczy remarked. "Eventually the dynasty would not be able to sustain the rulers, and a new House would rise." In his centuries at the Temple of Imhotep, he had had many opportunities to see the results of this practice, and to realize that it was not a wholesome way to protect the royal blood from contamination. "In my view—which is admittedly that of an exile who has been about the world more than he intended—blood strengthens with diversity, as any good farmer knows."

"But what of race?" Nikolai asked, scandalized. He had more cognac. "Cross-breeding sheep is one thing, but men?"

Ragoczy shrugged. "Czar, all men's blood is red, no matter what color their skin."

"True enough; and as you say, a man in your position cannot permit himself to be too finicky," said Nikolai, helping himself to more chocolate. "Sunny would be furious if she saw how many of these I am gobbling." He looked directly at Countess Amalija. "You have done me a world of good tonight, including the chocolates."

"But a royal House isn't a merchant bank, after all, and it cannot be treated like a stable of horses; it must be kept uncompromised. Well, you know what I mean, Aunt Amalija," Leonid protested, and glanced in the direction of Nikolai. "I do not mean to say anything against your House, Czar. But you know, I do not think it is fitting for nobles to marry their children to persons who have nothing to recommend them but noble blood."

"Sadly, I must agree," said Nikolai, so heavily that Leonid stammered an apology for voicing his thoughts so bluntly. "No," he told Leonid, cutting off the claims of remorse. "You are quite right. We see evidence of it everywhere. There has been too much intermarriage; I am with you in that regard, as well. I worry about the futures of my grand-children for just that reason. The match must be suitable without so much consanguinity that . . . risks are taken."

"There are royal families who have not intermarried with the Romanovs," said Countess Amalija, her eyes alight with mischief. "You could guarantee there would be no more troubles with Japan, for example, arranging a marriage with the Emperor's son for Olga." She laughed aloud to show she thought the whole notion ridiculous.

"The Russian people would never stand for that," said Nikolai seriously.

"Nor would the Japanese," Ragoczy added for him. "They are as closed as any people in the world. You would find it difficult to persuade them otherwise."

"The Ottoman Empire is at an end, or you might find a match there." Leonid chuckled, grateful that Ragoczy had steered them away from such dangerous conversational shoals. "If you could convince the Metropolitan to countenance a non-Christian marriage."

"Between the Bourbons, the Hohenzollerns and the Hapsburgs, every royal house in Europe is connected by blood," Nikolai said, shrugging to show his helplessness in the situation. "The Greeks may be a possibility, and they are Orthodox, not Roman, which would sit well with the Metropolitan." He sipped at his cognac. "The Swedes have the French line in their royals, through Napoleon's General."

"But there are connections in that line, as well," Countless Amalija said, and glanced at Ragoczy. "What have you to say, Count?"

"Nothing," Ragoczy replied. "I am an exile, after all, and anything I may tell you is not applicable." He rocked his chair back on its two hind legs. "But if it were my decision, I would go as far afield as I could, and think of the success of my House, not the quibbles of the Duma or the Metropolitan; neither the government nor the Church should dictate my choice. And I should allow my child the opportunity to approve or refuse any offer made."

"But why?" Nikolai demanded, more shocked by this observation than any other.

"Think, Czar," said Ragoczy, his chair back on all four legs. "You have been uncommonly fortunate in your Czarina. You must be aware that this is not often the case. Consider Franz Josef and Elizabeth, before she was assassinated. You could not describe that union as . . . happy, no matter how much he cared for her. They may have been devoted after their fashion, but they were never truly close. Think of how often she was away from his side, and how ardently she took the side of the Magyars over the Austrians. You know what isolation royalty imposes. Would you want your children to have the burden of their heritage and be unable to find some relief from it with their partners, as you and your Alexandra have done?" He saw the look in Nikolai's eyes soften. "You know what it is to love your wife and children. Wouldn't it be kinder to provide them the same instead of chaining them to the dictates of custom and diplomacy." He knew that Leonid was trying not to stare at him, but he swung around in his chair to continue. "You have children. Do you wish to see them well-established or do you wish them to be happy."

"Must it be one or the other?" Leonid asked, as he put down his glass of cognac. "Cannot both be possible?"

"Well, the Czar has found both," Ragoczy said reasonably. "But he is one of the rare few."

"Yes," Nikolai said with a thoughtful nod. "I must agree with Ragoczy. And I know that the consolation of a loving wife can make everything easier to bear." He looked away. "Except the anguish of your children; that is something that may unite parents, but only in worry and grief." There was such sorrow in his voice that the other three were silent out of respect for his heartache.

"If you are going to become dismal again, I am going to take us into the salon," Countless Amalija declared roundly. "We were going along so well, and there you are, back at the same dismal point. I think we should not dwell on misery any longer. Come." She rose, and the men rose with her out of courtesy. "Count, give me your arm. Leonid, escort the Czar, if you will. It is time we left this room for the servants to clean up; they want to get to bed." She swept up to Ragoczy, who did as she commanded and offered her his arm. "Thank goodness we do not have to stand on ceremony, or we would all be stuck here until Nikolai decided to have mercy on us, and move."

"I hear you, Countess, and obey, as you intend I should," said the Czar from behind her. "I know I have a habit of worrying a subject to tatters; my Ministers often remark upon it. If you had grown up with my uncles, you would do the same thing." He had picked up his cognac and one of the bowls of chocolate, and fell in beside Leonid.

The parlor was ready for them, a fire in the enameled iron stove, the gaslights burning, the square Chickering grand piano open. Countess Amalija went over to the instrument and sat down on the piano bench, saying, "If you will permit me to prevail upon you, Count." Her laughter made it plain that she did not have anything against such talk, only that she felt it was not appropriate for the evening.

"You must tell me what you want to hear," he said, taking his place beside her on the bench and flexing his hands.

"You do have beautiful hands, Count," she told him, with a great deal of secondary meaning in her compliment.

"Yes," he agreed. "I think so, too."

She grinned at him, and for a moment she looked twenty again. "Male vanity! Well, at least you are not enamored of your face, as so many are."

"I can see my hands," he reminded her, and prepared to play.

"Nothing morose; we need invigoration, not moping," she warned him as she went to sit next to her nephew.

"As you wish; something rousing," said Ragoczy, and launched into Liszt's *Hungarian Rhapsody,* playing with more verve than artistry, knowing that it was what Countess Amalija sought. When he had concluded that flashy display, he began on his own piano transcription of Handel's *Music for the Royal Fireworks,* his style less flamboyant but expressed with greater musicality than before.

An hour later, when Ragoczy had finished playing, and the last of the cognac was gone, Nikolai rose and said, "It is getting late, and I must be going." He bowed to Countess Amalija, his eyes a little bleary, but that might have been the result of fatigue rather than cognac. "I thank you for a most pleasant and helpful evening, Amalija Romanovna. I have not had so . . . unencumbered an entertainment in . . . many months." He turned to Ragoczy, favoring him with a weary clap on the shoulder. "And I must thank you as well, Count, and not simply for your exquisite impromptu concert. There is another issue, one in which I have been inexcusably lax. You have done me a great service and have had no reward for it."

"I did not undertake your mission for a reward, Czar," Ragoczy said, his voice solemn.

"I know," Nikolai acknowledged, continuing with less exhilaration, "But I would like to express my gratitude in some way. That could prove onerous to do at present, with so many dealings in a state of flux. I would like to make it known how much effort you extended upon my behalf. Unfortunately, as you must be aware, it would not be wise to make such a controversial demonstration just now, and so I must ask you to wait."

"You need do nothing, Czar," said Ragoczy, wanting to avoid the issue if he could. "I am—"

"I will think of something to recognize; not your work in Europe and

England, but something. Perhaps those schools you are establishing for the children of the men working in your businesses. I could use your recognition as the means to encourage others to emulate you, and establish schools of their own. The Duma would approve of that. They are always debating about education for the common people. You thought I knew nothing about that," he went on with a trace of self-congratulations in his posture. "Yes, I could say I think you set a good example. Your status as an exile might make your work more laudable, and honoring it could bring about discussion on education in general. My father did not think it was wise to provide too much education beyond the Church; he thought it led to civil unrest and a disruption of order. So do most of my uncles. But my father did not have the Duma to contend with, and the people had not rioted . . . " His words faded, and then he continued briskly, "None of my Ministers could object to that, and neither could the diplomatic corps. Yes," he said as much to himself as to Ragoczy, "Your admirable work in educating the people of Russia must be shown the esteem it deserves. In a year or so, I will present you with some sign of—"

"Nikolai Alexandreivich, I prefer you would not," Ragoczy interrupted, taking the chance of offending the Czar by not allowing him to continue.

"What are you saying?" Nikolai looked at him, his eyes narrowing. "You disdain my honors?"

"No; no, nothing of the sort," Ragoczy said, soothing the Czar, knowing from long experience of rulers that he was now treading on very slippery ground. "I would be more pleased than you know to receive any credit for the work I have done in your service, whatever that work may be. I can aspire to no higher prominence in Russia than one bestowed by you. But I know you have many others to consider, and I think it may be possible that if you recognize me, an exile, before you show distinction to some of your more . . . forward-thinking Russians, your plan may well backfire, creating resentment where you can afford it least." He saw Nikolai's expression change, his face becoming less impassive, a sign that he was listening. "It might be more to your point to select a number of your own court, men whose innovations have gained approval, and see that they are acknowledged. The court will be more inclined to model themselves on one of their own number than risk copying a foreigner, whose radical notions may not be in tune with those of Russians." He chuckled once, his manner self-deprecating. "If you want to thank me for playing the piano well, or for sponsoring the ballet or symphony, I will accept it gladly, and count myself happy for it."

He would count himself relieved, as well; he kept this last to himself. Nikolai's mouth was tight and petulant, but he could not find fault with Ragoczy's argument. "If you are certain you want no other tribute?" he said, not entirely convinced of Ragoczy's sincerity. "If there is something, tell me now. I will not look with approbation on a later petition."

Ragoczy's penetrating gaze fixed on the Czar's eyes. "I will not ask anything of you, Czar. You have my Word."

"Yes," said Nikolai in a measuring way. "I understand you."

Knowing that Countess Amalija wanted him to keep their talk away from the somber, Ragoczy gestured to the glittering Order of Saint Stephen on his sash. "One of these is enough; two would be intolerably gaudy."

Nikolai was willing to laugh at this very minor witticism. "As you wish, Count," he conceded. "I will confer a distinction upon you for patronizing the ballet. No one will protest that, not even Otyets Grigori Efimovich. You and I will know the full meaning of the recognition, and that must suffice."

"I am grateful to you, Czar, and I thank you," said Ragoczy, his words simple and direct.

"No, it is I who am grateful to you," Nikolai reminded Ragoczy. "Including for your patronage of the ballet."

Because it was expected, Ragoczy laughed. "As you wish, Czar."

"If it was as I wish, Europe and Britain would be disarming, and we could do so safely, as well. At least you tried to make it happen, and at a higher cost than I imagined." For an instant the distress was back in him, then he made himself smile, and bow to his hostess one last time. "My chauffeur will be getting cold. I thank you once more for this splendid evening, Countess. You and your nephew make most engaging dinner companions." He looked at Ragoczy. "I am in your debt, Count."

"Nothing of the sort, Czar," said Ragoczy, punctuating his disclaimer with a single, formal bow.

Leonid bowed as well, and did not straighten up until he heard the Czar's footfalls descending the stairs. "I think I should let you two have some time alone together," he said when he was certain the Czar was out of earshot. "It was a wonderful evening, Aunt Amalija. I have enjoyed myself tremendously. So much, that I am glad Jurgi is the one driving, and not I. With all this snow, I would not like to wager on my chances of getting home without mishap." He bent and kissed his aunt's cheeks, then held out his hand to Ragoczy. "I will admit that I had doubts of you at first, and thought about warning you off, but . . . "

"I do not have to seek your approval," said Countess Amalija, taking umbrage with her nephew's tone. "It is not for you to select my friends."

"Certainly not," said Leonid, wholly unaware of the implied contradiction in his last two statements. "But I would be remiss if I did not look after your well-being, now wouldn't I?" With that, he gave a flourishing bow, then turned on his heel, calling for his coat and hat as he descended the stairs.

"He's a bit self-important, but he is an oldest child, and he has been in charge ever since his father died. He does not mean to take over, it is just a habit with him," said the Countess fondly as she watched Leonid prepare to leave the house. When she turned to Ragoczy, she said, "I am surprised that you declined the Czar's offer of advancement so summarily."

Ragoczy listened to the door slam as Leonid departed. "Those who patronize the ballet are not of any interest to anyone but ballet directors. Those who are given the Czar's confidence are of interest to everyone; they acquire enemies, sought or unsought. Their life is scrutinized, and those near them are subjected . . . " His words dwindled as he stared into the distance.

"As your English artist was subjected?" Countess Amalija suggested kindly.

"Yes. As she was. As many others have been." Something in his eyes kept her from asking any more. He kissed her gently, as if to banish any apprehension she may have felt. He went on more conversationally. "And speaking of scrutiny, there is something I must do tonight. I hope you will forgive me if I leave you for an hour or so?"

"Is your mission dangerous?" she asked, trying not to sound too serious.

"I doubt it," he answered. "An unfinished matter; nothing drastic." He stepped away from her and started down the wide stairs. "I will not be long."

"Then I will wait up for you, in the salon. I think," she said with a slight smile, "I will practice my scales. I am growing very sloppy about fingering." Lifting her hand to wave, she added, "When you come back, we will play duets. Some by Schubert, some of our own composition."

Ragoczy showed her his engaging smile before he went down to the ground floor and summoned Roger from the servants' hall, asking him to ready the Dupressoir. "It should not take long, this errand."

"At once," said Roger in mild incredulity; he had not expected Ragoczy to leave until just before dawn. "It is after two."

"So it is," Ragoczy said affably. "But Kuba's will not be closed quite yet. There is someone I must speak with, and tonight; I was told I could find him there."

Over the centuries, Roger had become accustomed to Ragoczy's deliberate obliqueness, and did not challenge it now. "I will be ready shortly," he said, and went to get the automobile out of the end of the stable.

Kuba's Restaurant on the Morskaya could exist only in Saint Petersburg: all the decor and chefs were French; all the waiters were Tartars, and vodka was served as often and as extravagantly as champagne. When Ragoczy arrived, two parties were still lingering over the midnight buffet in the side dining room, too tired or too drunk to be rowdy, but most of the restaurant was quiet.

The heavy-eyed waiter pointed Ragoczy to the rear of the restaurant, an out-of-the-way alcove lit by a single branch of guttering candles; a lone figure was seated there, hunched over a small, leather-bound book.

"Spasiba," said Ragoczy, handing the waiter two silver coins before threading his way between the empty tables, making no sound as he moved.

"Grammatikoff?" asked the man with the book as Ragoczy drew near. He turned slowly in his chair, not yet alarmed, looking into the darkness beyond the pool of candlelight.

"No," Ragoczy said in English.

At that, Reilly's face sharpened, his deep-set eyes grew brighter and he sat straighter. "How did you find me?" he asked in the same language, his wariness concealed with what seemed idle curiosity.

"Like you, Captain, I have my ways." He came into the spill of the candlelight and looked down at Sidney Reilly; he considered a moment before he held out his hand. "After all this time, don't you think we should—"

Reilly cocked his head, his edginess fading. "You were aware, then," he said, not as startled as he thought he would be. The two shook hands briefly.

"Of you, and of others, yes; in Berlin, in Amsterdam, in London, here," said Ragoczy, nodding to the vacant chair opposite Reilly. "Do you mind?"

"Go right ahead," Reilly said, beginning to welcome the chance to observe Ragoczy without having to conceal himself.

As Ragoczy sat down, he opened his coat, for the restaurant was still quite warm; the starburst Order glimmered; if he saw Reilly's brow twitch, he ignored it. "I am sorry it has taken me so long to attend to you, Captain." He paused, then went on, "First, I must thank you for saving me from . . . a great deal of trouble."

"I? In what context?" Reilly asked carefully.

"In the context of Oertel Morgenstern's statement to the Berlin police; is there anything else I should thank you for?" Ragoczy answered without preamble. "And pray do not demean us both by pretending you do not know what I mean."

Reilly considered his answer. "Very well. Then I will say you're welcome, as the Americans do."

Ragoczy accepted this with a nod, his dark eyes fixed on a spot somewhere beyond Reilly's right shoulder. "I appreciate the risk you took; what I would like to know is why you were watching me, and for whom."

At this, Reilly chuckled. "You don't seriously expect me to tell you, do you?"

"No," Ragoczy conceded. "But I trust you will tell me who it was *not* for."

A few bars of *Dark Eyes* strummed badly on a balalaika drifted in from the other room, and someone yelled for the player to shut up.

"I think I can do that. Within limits," Reilly said, fascinated by Ragoczy's composure. Most men in this situation would show some indication of unease.

"That is encouraging," Ragoczy told him, meeting his eyes at last. "May I assume you were not working for von Wolgast, in any capacity, directly or indirectly?"

Reilly's response was succinct. "That piece of shit had one of my best sources killed: Paul Reighert confessed to murdering Renfred Meyer and his mother, on von Wolgast's order." He reached for his cigarette case. "No, I was not working for him in any capacity whatsoever. Next question."

Ragoczy was ready for him. "Were you gathering information on me for more than one agency?"

"Occasionally; however I told both agencies the same thing." He tapped his selected cigarette on his thumbnail and put it between his lips, then took out a matchbox and lit his cigarette; each motion was precise, careful, and economical.

"Is that welcome news?" Ragoczy inquired.

Reilly shrugged. "Is there anything more?"

"As a matter of fact, there is," said Ragoczy. "I want to know if you are planning to watch me in future. And if you are," he went on without giving Reilly a chance to answer, "I must warn you that I will not treat your investigation with the same . . . sangfroid that I have thus far. Until a month ago, I might still have been engaged in tasks for the Czar, and, as such, I expected that surveillance was an unappealing but traditional part of the process."

"Would that others were so understanding," said Reilly sardonically.

"But I am no longer engaged by Nicholas in any way, as your sources will tell you, if you bother to ask them," Ragoczy went on, "and I would consider any further probing into my affairs as a deliberate invasion; I would not hesitate to respond accordingly." He leaned forward, his words clipped and level. "Captain Reilly, you are very good at what you do, but I would find you out."

Reilly was glad that his cigarette bought him a few seconds to think. "Go on." It was the safest response he could make.

Ragoczy sat back in his chair; the tone of his voice was suitable for drawing room small talk. Only the shine in his eyes was dangerous. "I advise you to stay well away from me. You have done me a service and I would not want to have to forget it. You would not like the consequences of interfering with me: believe this."

Threats rarely impressed Reilly, but this one, so unconventionally delivered, gave him qualms. "Why should I watch you, if, as you say, you are no longer in the Czar's service?"

"Come, Captain Reilly," Ragoczy chided him. "You are a capable and curious man. Do you tell me you have never watched anyone out of nothing more than speculation?"

Reilly nodded. "Once or twice."

"Be content with what you know, Captain; it will gain you nothing but grief to look further," Ragoczy said, rising. "I do not think we will see each other again, so I will bid you farewell." He held out his hand again. "If I did not have the greatest admiration for your talents, we would not have had this conversation."

This time Reilly did not release Ragoczy's hand from his powerful grip. "Fair's fair, Count. I answered you, and now I have a few questions that I would like to have answered." He put his cigarette aside, balancing it on the rim of an empty vodka glass. "You are a very puzzling man, you know."

Ragoczy withdrew his hand without struggle or effort. "Life is full of puzzles, Captain Reilly," he said. Then he turned and left Kuba's, going out into the blowing, bitter snow, where Roger waited in the Dupressoir to take him back to the affectionate warmth of Countess Amalija's bed.

❊   ❊   ❊

Text of a letter from Rowena Saxon in San Francisco to Franchot Ragoczy, via his London solicitor, Carlisle Sunbury.

San Francisco, California
August 16, 1912

My dear Count;
I am relying on Sir Carlisle to get this to you, wherever you are, and to do so without reading the contents. Let me apologize for taking so long to write to you, but after that hideous confrontation with von Wolgast, I fear I was unable to think of you without thinking of him. Poor payment for all the kindness you showed me that night, and all the other times we have spent together. My explanation must stand: I am learning how to forget von Wolgast without trying to blot the whole out of my mind. You told me it would take time, and I begin to perceive that you were right. I should have trusted you, but I thought, that with all your centuries, you had become inured to all the demands life makes, and no longer understood what impositions we all endure over the years. I now find I can go four or five nights without having von Wolgast intrude into my dreams, destroying my rest and my peace of mind with a single stroke.

As you can see, I am still in California. I have taken a house on Russian Hill—if you are still in Saint Petersburg, you may find this as amusing as I do. It is not a large house: seven rooms and a small apartment for my housekeeper over the stable-cum-garage. Aside from an eight-year-old gelding, I have bought a motor car, a Hudson, which is proving to be an excellent investment. Grand-father was willing to import a British or European one for me, but I decided I would do better with an American automobile in America. It took me a while to learn to drive on these astonishing streets; I am told that some of the hills are too steep for proper carriages and can only be got up on foot or riding a horse; a number of automobiles have come to grief on them. I haven't found one of those yet, but I no longer think it is completely implausible.

Do not think I have spent every waking hour gadding about the hills, seeing which of them is undrivable. Quite the contrary. I have been painting with a fervor I have not know before. I recently did a series of sketches of the Chinese one sees everywhere in this city, and I will eventually work them into a series of paintings, but I have not done enough work yet. My first group of studies of ships is being shown, not at a gallery, but in the lobby of the Saint Francis Hotel. They are well enough, but nothing remarkable, although the public seem to like them.

My time in Amsterdam has stood me in good stead for those works, for it made me familiar with the interplay of direct and reflected light.

You might find all the water here uncomfortable, but I think you would agree that it is a spectacular place. The mountains—which everyone here calls hills—are very handsome, and the bay presents so many visions of itself that I cannot begin to describe the variety of views I have contemplated since I arrived here almost a year ago. Whether the sun is shining, or it is storming, or the fog has drifted in through the gaps in the hills, I am struck anew with the opportunities San Francisco presents to me as an artist. I am starting to think it will take more than five years to exhaust the sources of inspiration I have found. I may remain here beyond 1916. If I do, we will have to reschedule our meeting.

My grand-father continues to amaze me. He keeps up a routine of work men half his age would do well to manage. He has kept his word, and has made no attempt to run my life, or to try to line me up with any personable man. He tells me I am old enough to live the way I want to, and he is not about to tell me what that is. I have made it a point to dine with him twice a week. He tells me I do not have to, but I know it pleases him. He may have lived a long and good life, but I know that he, unlike you, will not always be here, and so I intend to make the most of the time he and I may have together. I have you to thank for this, too, for you have shown me that a life is more than the sum of its days, and that we must value what we have while we have it. A strange lesson to learn from one who is conditionally immortal, but there it is.

I have attempted to do a second portrait of you, working from memory, but so far I am not satisfied with the results. There is something about your eyes that I have not captured, a depth that is unlike any I have ever seen. If I am able to complete it, I will ship it to Sir Carlisle, and hope that you are pleased with the results, when and if you see it.

Tonight there is a party I must attend, so you will not mind if I get on with dressing. I will be wearing your frogs. I am forever being complimented on them, so I will thank you again for them, and for so much more that I will never have words to express. I hope the paintings may, in part, suffice.

With all my heart.
Rowena Saxon

EPILOGUE

KING GEORGE V

Excerpt from the journal of King George V of England

June 30, 1914

What a terrible shock for the dear old Emperor, having his second heir carried off. One dead at his own hand, the other at the hand of an assassin in Sarajevo. Can't help but wonder if Nicky's mad priest wasn't on to something when he warned him not to make war; Russia might be ripe for trouble, but I wouldn't reckon that it would touch the Czar. Shouldn't think we have anything to worry about. No doubt the Austrians will put it all to rights. They say the stockmarket in Berlin hardly quivered when the news of Franz Ferdinand's assassination was announced, and there were no noticeable repercussions here. What can events in Serbia have to do with Britain?